An Arthurian Fantasy

Lavinia Collins

First published in Great Britain and the US in three volumes
on Kindle by The Book Folks, 2015.
This paperback edition published in 2015 by The Book Folks.

Typeset in Garamond
Design by Steve French
Printed by CreateSpace

Available from Amazon.com and other retail outlets

Published by
The Book Folks
106 Huxley Rd
London E10 5QY
thebookfolks.com

For Kay again,
because without Kay there is nothing

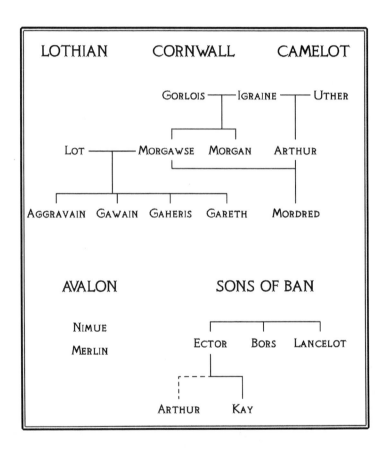

LOTHIAN   CORNWALL   CAMELOT

GORLOIS —— IGRAINE —— UTHER

LOT —— MORGAWSE   MORGAN   ARTHUR

AGGRAVAIN GAWAIN GAHERIS GARETH   MORDRED

AVALON   SONS OF BAN

NIMUE

MERLIN   ECTOR   BORS   LANCELOT

ARTHUR   KAY

Part I
The Witches of Avalon

And the third sister, Morgan le Fay was put to school in a nunnery, and there she learned so much that she became a great scholar of black magic.

Malory, *Le Morte d'Arthur*

Chapter One

In the fading light, I leant closer to the book, pulling it into my lap. The words were familiar, but unfamiliar. I knew the Latin, but the things it said – strange, and unbelievable. The smell of the vellum – old, dusty, animal – was comforting, and safe, and the feel of the ridges of ink on the parchment under my finger somehow magical, as though my touch were writing the words onto my own skin. Outside, through the open window, it smelled sweetly of the beginning of summer, of fresh-cut hay and sweet apples and firewood burning in the distance. I could hear the nuns calling me from the cloisters, but I did not want to leave the quiet haven of my cell. I did not want to leave the book. I dared to delay a little longer. The nuns would be looking for me, but they had never scolded me badly yet. I wondered if they were afraid to because my mother's husband was the king of the land, but they should not have been. He hated me, because I reminded him that my mother had had a husband before him.

When I folded the book closed at last, the sun was dipping against the horizon, bleeding out orange and red at the edge, far away. It made me think of the places in the distance; Camelot, where my mother and stepfather lived, the far, cold North that was my sister's home, and the lake on the edge of the forest, and across it Avalon, the place where I would go when my education at the abbey was complete. I longed for it already, and the sweet, dark secrets it promised, though I was sure I would miss Amesbury Abbey once I had gone. Amesbury was simple, and it was dull, but it was home.

As I came down from my cell, I saw two horses tethered in the stables. Horses I recognised. Suddenly filled with excitement, I rushed at a run into the cloister, and there they were, Sir Ector whose lands were next-door to the abbey, and his two sons, one dark, one fair, like two boys from a fairytale. I hung back at the entrance to the cloister garden, a pretty green patch filled with soft grass and winding vines around the stone arches that bordered it. I liked Sir Ector, and if I had been bold I would have run over to embrace him, but my shyness held me back. I did not know if Ector liked me. I knew that I made some people uncomfortable, though I did not know why. But, to my relief, the dark son, Kay, the elder of the two, saw me and his face –

which I was just becoming old enough to realise was handsome – broke into a wide smile.

"Morgan!" he cried, running over and scooping me into his arms, to spin me around. I giggled, despite my nerves. I knew Kay and I were getting too old for these games, for embracing one another like children, but I was always pleased to see Kay, and besides if I had asked him not to, in his excitement he would not have heard me.

"Don't hug the nuns, Kay!" Sir Ector scolded, but his tone was indulgent. "They don't always like it."

"She's not a nun," Kay protested, stopping still, but not releasing me from his embrace. He was right. I was not a nun, nor even a novice, but I lived and schooled in the abbey, a painful mercy of my mother's to keep me from my hateful stepfather's path. "It's Morgan."

"No, Kay," his father said, more firmly, "it is the *Lady Princess* Morgan."

I blushed at that. I was not a real princess, nor did I want to be called one. If I was a princess they might send me off to marry someone like they had my older sister, and I knew all too well how little that had pleased her.

Kay and I had splashed about at the edge of Avalon's great lake together naked as children, and Kay pouted against the new formality that, as we all grew older, his father grew more and more insistent upon. An impish smile grew across his face, and as his father turned away he snatched me up again and I squealed with laughter. Behind me, I heard Ector sigh, though it was a fond sigh. Kay's wonderful smile was his mother's smile. She had been a beautiful lady, with the same sparkling brown eyes as her son, the same charming, irrepressible smile. She had died when I was just a girl, but I remembered her well. She was the reason Ector came with his sons to the abbey so often; the nuns here had nursed her in her final illness, and Ector came often to pray for the wife he had loved.

I had, too, felt from Kay and his mother the feeling of the Otherworld. I did not know what it was until Kay told me, in whispers, late one night as we lay in the cloister garden side by side staring up at the stars. It was a secret, given in exchange for the names of Cassiopea and Orion, the Plough and the Great Bear. I supposed my knowledge must have seemed great to him, but to me his secret was far more precious. He had told me that we three, his mother and he and I, had the blood of the Otherworld in us, and we could sense it in others like us. He told me that she had taken him, once, to Avalon where the druids lived. Where I would go. Where the

Otherworld touched the world everyone else knew. I had not known, until then, what the feeling was at the pit of my stomach when I looked out at Avalon, and from that day, it had had a name. *Otherworld.*

When Kay released me from his embrace, I walked over demurely to kiss Ector's other son on the cheek. Arthur, the fair son, was a few years younger than Kay and me, and still a boy at twelve years old. Where Kay was tall and wiry, with the shadow of a man's beard, I had noticed, against his chin, Arthur was short and broad with their mother's golden hair and a boy's look still, and an open, friendly smile. I liked Arthur, but not as much as I liked Kay.

By the time we sat down to dinner with the nuns, it was clear why Sir Ector had come with his sons. I had thought it was just to pray for his wife, or perhaps also to see me, to check for my mother's sake that I was well, or to bring a letter from her as he did from time to time, but I could see from the concern on his kind face as we gathered around the long table, and the Abbess said grace, that Ector had come with sad news. When the prayers of the nuns fell silent, and they picked up their hunks of bread to dunk them in the vegetable stew we always ate, Ector cleared his throat, and I turned to look at him. Kay, beside me, looked at his father too, as did Arthur. I got the feeling that they were both reluctant to meet my eye.

"My Lady Morgan," Ector began slowly, turning his eyes on me in a fatherly look. "I come, I am afraid, with sad news. Your stepfather, King Uther, is dying. He is in the care of his witch, Merlin, but it will not be long. The chill he took in the winter has not left him. There are men at court saying Merlin has poisoned him, but the truth is Uther is old and weak and death will come for him soon."

I did not care about Uther, but I was old enough to understand the danger that the realm would fall into since Uther and my mother had made no heir together. Uther, a hardened warrior, had had no wife before my mother, and no child meant war among the lesser kings of Britain. Besides, I was more concerned about the danger that would befall a widowed queen when her husband was no longer alive to protect her. There would be men thinking already that a marriage to Queen Igraine would secure their claim to the throne. Or her murder.

"We must move soon to protect my lady mother," I told Ector, with quiet determination. Ector sighed and nodded.

"You are young, Morgan, to have such concerns on your shoulders," he replied sadly.

I knew he was right, but I did not feel so very young. I had seen wars before; I was a small child indeed when the war that killed my father came, but I still remembered it. The smell of fire and blood, and the sound of horses screaming as they died. I knew what war meant. I also knew what this would mean for me. People would start wanting to marry me, to try take Uther's place as king of Logrys. However, the obvious candidate was my sister's husband, Lot, who was already king in Lothian, and who had already three sons, two of whom must have been almost of age.

So Uther was dying. There would be a new king. But what did that mean for me?

"I will go with my lady mother back to Tintagel," I told Ector, mustering up all the sternness that I could. "In my father's castle she and I will be safe. War is coming, is it not, once Uther is dead?"

"I fear it is, Morgan," Ector answered darkly, "but for now you should remain here, at Amesbury. No one will try to harm you in the care of the nuns here, and I will be at court with my eye on Queen Igraine."

I nodded, but only because I did not feel brave enough to insist on my point.

That night I did not feel like playing with Kay and Arthur as they chased each other round the empty cloister, smacking at one another with sticks. Kay was old enough to train as a knight already, and yet it seemed to me the younger brother had the more natural skill at fighting. Kay was faster, more lithe, and yet his little brother seemed to land more blows with his stick, laughing with glee every time that he did. And yet when the time came, Kay would be the knight and Arthur the squire, age rather than ability dictating what role each boy was to take. I only watched for a little while, and then retreated to my room, to the lovely welcoming stack of books at my desk, to read.

Among the books in the abbey, old and smelling like ash and dust, blood and bone from the vellum they were made of, deep in the library, I had found these books, books that described strange things. Wonderful things. Impossible things. I understood little enough of what they said, at first, but the more I read the more it seemed to me that in them was an ancient recipe of words that would allow a person to change their shape. I wondered what the nuns wanted with books like these, but when I asked them, they told me that no such thing was possible, except when the bread and wine of mass became the body and blood of Christ. I stood before the books that night, and imagined myself turning into Kay. A boy, young and strong and free, without a stepfather King or a woman's place in a marriage-bed or abbey. I could have a life running free, if I were Kay. But, when I turned to look at myself in the window, reflected against the dark of the night beyond, I just saw my own dull, pale oval face, in its plain setting of long brown hair, staring back, and I was still tall and skinny, and weak as any girl.

Ector left the abbey the next day to return to court, but with no mother at home to watch over them, his boys stayed and I was glad of it. I supposed they had nowhere else to go. I grew bored quickly alone with the nuns, and I was glad of any company my own age. We walked out, the three of us, to the lake at Avalon, to swim. It was a hot day and on the walk there I felt myself sweat uncomfortably in the black wool dress, the sun beating down heating the thick hair on my head, burningly hot against my skin. The boys, in their thin shirts and light breeches, bounded ahead of me, laughing and running, and I struggled to keep up, holding the heavy skirts of my dress in a bunch around my knees. When we reached the water's edge, Arthur and Kay threw off their clothes and dived in. I stood at the shore, holding a hand up to my eyes against the dazzling light of the sun on the lake, and suddenly I felt self-conscious. Last summer, when we had done this, we had all been children, and suddenly Uther was dying and I had small but unmistakable breasts and I was noticing Kay in a way that I had not before and I did not want to be naked in front of him. Kay stopped to stand waist-deep in the water and turned back to me. I could see a shade of dark hair across his chest that, too, had not been there last year.

"Morgan!" he shouted. "Come in!"

Arthur, following Kay's shout, turned around in the water, gazing at me on the edge.

"She's afraid of the cold," Arthur laughed. Even on him, as well, I could see the beginnings of the shape of a man; powerful shoulders, a broad chest. I was suddenly no longer sure it was right for me to throw off my clothes and swim naked with them. I was sure if the nuns had known that was what we had set off to do, they would have stopped us.

"I'm not afraid of the cold," I said, quiet and defensive. Arthur splashed the water at me with his foot, and laughed as I squealed.

"Morgan, it's boiling hot in the sun. Stop being silly and get in," Kay called, as he turned to swim away from me and Arthur, sensing the potential for competition, swam off to catch his brother up. He would want to try to race to the other side, as he always did. They never made it to Avalon.

They might forget me if I snuck away, caught up in their games, but it *was* hot, and last year we had all swum together all summer long in a blissful timeless innocence. While their backs were turned I pulled off the wool dress, and then the undershift and dived in with a splash, feeling the delicious cold of the water rush through my hair, against my face, across the hot limbs of my body, and I opened my eyes against the cool, clear water of the lake. I always felt, as I swam in the lake, that I was being made new.

I swam under the water for as long as I could, until I spotted Kay's feet, pink and kicking under the water, and grabbed him by the ankle to pull him under playfully as I rushed up to the surface. By the time Kay caught his breath and bobbed back up beside me, we were both laughing, coughing and spluttering. We looked around for Arthur, but it was apparent where he had gone when Kay disappeared under the surface again and they both came up laughing hard. Kay shoved Arthur more forcefully, still laughing, and Arthur disappeared under the water again, just for a moment, and came up to spit a jet of water in Kay's face. Kay splashed him back, but it was clear from the wicked look on Kay's face that a different kind of game had sprung to his mind.

"Arthur kissed a girl," he told me, with an arch of his eyebrow. Arthur, blushed and pushed Kay angrily.

"I didn't," Arthur protested, but he was obviously lying. I wasn't sure why Kay was telling me. It was probably just to tease Arthur in revenge for Arthur spitting water in his face.

"It was just a servant girl, but I saw it. I'm going to tell the nuns that Arthur has been kissing girls."

Arthur shoved Kay again, harder than was playful, and Kay's grin flickered slightly on his face.

"At least I haven't been kissing boys," Arthur snapped, his face bright red. I was not sure if that was directed at me. I didn't see how it could be, since I had been only with the nuns, but before I could say anything, Kay had pushed Arthur under the water again with so much force that they bobbed down under the surface together. When they came back up, they were both laughing hard again, and the argument seemed to have been forgotten.

Then, loud and scolding and awful, I heard my name called from across the lake. I saw the Abbess standing there, her wrinkled old face knotted in anger, and my crumpled underdress clenched in her hand. I felt my heart thud suddenly in my chest as though I had been caught at something awful. *But last year this was not forbidden*; the words came to my mind, but I knew they would be useless in appeal against the Abbess. Beside her stood the Lady of Avalon, and behind her, her ward, the orphan boy Lancelot. From far away, I could not see him clearly, but I knew it must be him from his dark hair. It had been a year since I had seen him, too, and he was obviously grown taller, taller now than the Lady of Avalon herself. I was not sure how I liked him; he was always quiet and thoughtful, and when I saw him and Arthur and Kay in the summer I used to trail around after him, trying to get him to read with me, or walk with me while Arthur and Kay played at fighting, because he was quieter than them, calmer, and seemed to like books. He had never wanted to read with me, though.

"You're in trouble," Kay whispered by my ear, with wicked glee. Kay seemed always to enjoy it when someone else was being scolded. Perhaps it made a change for him. After all, it was not often that neat, quiet Morgan was reprimanded while the impish Kay stood by in innocence. I think I was Kay's favourite person of all to see scolded.

I swam slowly to the edge of the lake, reluctant to stand or get out of the water naked before the Abbess, and the Lady of Avalon, and her boy. As I swam closer I could see that Lancelot had grown not just taller, but out of childhood. Like Kay, he was tall and wiry, but where Kay's face was bright and smiling, Lancelot had grown quietly, darkly handsome. He looked far more serious than I had remembered him, with his steady blue eyes and high cheekbones, and I felt myself blush already, to feel nervous and strange before him in a way that I had not felt before with anyone else.

As I reached the edge and I felt the bed of the lake under my feet, grainy, muddy, disgustingly soft, I crossed my arms over my little chest and stood up in the water, where it reached up to my shoulders.

"Lady Abbess?" I said, in my most beseeching, obedient voice.

"Morgan." Her voice was stern, and the angry look on her face tightened even more. "You are a princess, and this is not seemly behaviour. Besides, you are far too old to be swimming with boys. Come on, get out."

I stood my ground. I wasn't going to walk naked out of the lake with the three of them standing there staring and watching me. The Lady of Avalon's eyes fell on me, soft light green against the blue-green woad that tattooed her face in swirls and whorls like the patterns of the movements of the stars, but she did not speak to spare me the Abbess' scolding.

"Come along Morgan. If you weren't embarrassed to get in like that, you shouldn't be embarrassed to get out."

I squinted up at her with what I hoped was an air of innocent supplication. Surely she was not going to make me walk naked from the lake when there was a boy my own age beside her.

"Please, Abbess," I pleaded.

Lancelot, beside his lady guardian, shifted on his feet and looked down at the ground before him, avoiding looking at me, although the water covered me almost to my neck. It wasn't just me the Abbess was upsetting, then. I felt my chest tighten with frustrated tears. It didn't seem fair. No one was here to punish Arthur, or Kay. They were still swimming far out on the lake behind me. The Abbess, however, did not relent, only held out my underdress in her fist towards me. Slowly, I moved from the water, my arms still crossed over my chest, until I was out, and dripping and shivering as the cold water evaporated from my skin in the fading sun. I snatched the underdress from her hand and pulled it over me fast, but the water on my skin made it go see-through and if anything I felt worse. My plaited hair, too, still soaking wet, left a trail of water down the back of my underdress, and as I pulled the black wool dress over the top, I felt it cold and clammy against my back as I felt my cheeks burn.

"Now Morgan," the Abbess said firmly, pointing her finger at me. I was taller than her already. She was a withered little woman, and I was tall and thin as a sapling, but I still felt tiny before her. "Remember how ashamed you feel now, and that will stop you behaving in such a disgraceful manner again."

I felt sick with shame and injustice as they led me back to the abbey, and worst of all behind me I could still hear Kay and Arthur splashing in the lake, and laughing. They were boys, and this was not their concern.

Chapter Two

Back at the abbey, I rushed to my room, wrapped myself in a rough wool blanket, sat on my bed and pulled one of the old books onto my lap. I didn't want to talk to anyone. Not the Abbess, not the other nuns, and *especially* not Arthur and Kay. I just wanted to be left alone, to feel the angry burn of unfairness, and nurse it inside me. But it was not long enough I was alone with the book, not long enough that I had to close my eyes and imagine myself as a dark-haired boy, that the bell sounded for the evening meal and I had to leave again. It had gone less well this time, too, for when I had tried to picture myself becoming Kay, I had instead been unable to shift from my mind the image of Kay waist-deep in the water, his bare chest, the shape of the muscles forming beneath, his hair damp against his brow from the water.

I wondered if I was still in trouble, but the Abbess seemed to have forgotten. She was displeased, I could see, by the presence of the Lady of Avalon. The Lady of Avalon did not bend her head to pray, though I noticed that Lancelot, the boy from Avalon, bent his head most dutifully and seemed to know all the words of the prayers better than I did. Across the table from me, I caught Kay's eye and he gave me a sympathetic shrug and a semi-apologetic look. I thought he was going to say something, but then Arthur elbowed him under the table and they began whispering to one another about something else, it seemed, because they were both laughing silently. Arthur hid it better than Kay, so it was Kay who earned the tut from the Abbess that stilled them both. I was aware, suddenly, that though Kay was as old as I was, they were still children. The world was not yet dangerous for them as it was for me. Nothing was at stake. Perhaps Ector would scold them, or the Abbess, or someone, but I was a woman, and old enough now that my body was dangerous, and my place as the stepdaughter of a dying king only made it more so. I was having to become, all of a sudden, some kind of *lady*, some kind of *princess*, and it burned all the more with unfairness that they did not have to do the same.

When the food was finally brought, the Lady of Avalon cleared her throat and turned to me, as I was raising a spoon of the vegetable stew to my lips.

"Morgan, have you bled yet?" she asked, loudly. Blushing hard, I dropped the spoon, and hot stew splattered back up across my face and the front of my dress. I heard the nuns around us gasp and tut with disapproval.

"I have, my Lady," I mumbled, looking down at my stew.

"That is well, Morgan. Then I shall take you to Avalon when the summer is out."

I felt too hot and sick with embarrassment to feel hungry for the stew any more, but I forced myself to eat it, not wanting to attract more attention from anyone as the talk continued quietly around me. I did not look up at Kay and Arthur. That would have been unbearable. I was not sure, now that the moment was upon me, how I felt about going to Avalon. I knew it was where I was meant to be, where I belonged, but my life with the nuns was all I knew, almost all that I could remember.

When the meal was finished and I slipped away quickly to my bedroom, as I passed the cloister I overheard Sir Ector talking to the Lady of Avalon in its little garden.

"I thought I would ask Morgan if she would like to spend the summer with us. This is the last summer of her childhood. Is that well with you?" he asked.

"That seems well to me, Ector," she replied gently. "It might be for the best that Morgan is not at the abbey, where there may be this king or that coming to look for her when her stepfather dies. That seems a wise course to me, until the time comes for me to take her to Avalon." My heart jumped within me. I hoped that I could take my books with me.

The next day, I packed up the few things I possessed – I was not a princess of jewels and silk dresses – and ran out early and eager. Ector and his sons were there already, and Lancelot with them. I supposed he must be staying with us, too. He often used to when we were all much younger. He had not got less shy, I noticed, and did not greet me as I came, though Kay and Arthur shouted greetings with joy. Kay bounded a step forward, but then seemed to remember his father's admonition that I was a princess and held back.

There were only three horses, and Kay leapt up behind Lancelot on his, wrapping his arms around Lancelot's chest to hold on, and I had to jump up behind Arthur with my bag of things. Arthur was less fun on a horse than Kay. Something about Kay put the horses at ease, and Kay and Lancelot's horse pranced ahead of the rest of us, while I plodded on behind Arthur, who was chattering away about becoming Kay's squire, and all the jousting and fighting they would do together, as though he had not been paying attention when Ector had said that King Uther was ill and dying. That meant real war and real fighting, not jousting and games.

The sun was dipping and the shadows becoming long when we arrived at Ector's house, a humble stone building unlike the castles of other knights, set in lovely lush farmland. I never saw that house without feeling a rush of affection, or gladness. But, also, sorrow, for I knew that Ector's wife would not be stepping from the door to greet us, wafting out with her the smell of fresh bread. Ector's heart had gone to the grave with his wife, and though he was not yet old we all knew that he would never take another.

When we stopped the horses outside the house, to my surprise Arthur leapt down from behind me to wait until Lancelot had slipped from Kay's horse, to grab Kay by the ankle and yank him from the saddle. Kay crashed into Arthur and they fell in a heap on the ground, laughing and shoving at each other. They were laughing hard, and it was just a game, but I saw the concern cross Ector's face, not that they would be hurt, for they were not, but that real war was coming, pale and deadly across the horizon, and Kay and Arthur still played at hurting one another like boys. Lancelot, too, stood back from it, regarding the brothers with a sort of melancholy that I could not place. Perhaps Lancelot wished that he had a brother to play rough with. He must have missed the company of other boys growing up in Avalon, with the druid women.

Inside the long narrow house there were plenty of clean, cosy rooms and it was busy with servants, and Ector's wife's sister, who was a strange wet-eyed women who jabbered to herself and whom the kind Ector had taken care of as long as we could remember. I felt much more at home in Ector's house than I had ever done with the nuns. I wondered if Avalon would feel like home. Kay had told me that everything in Avalon felt like the Otherworld, though I was half-sure he was making it up, and he had never really been.

We ate a meal of beef and vegetables that I knew was simple but was still finer than anything I would have had with the nuns. It was the lovely juiciness of meat that I longed for at the abbey, although because the nuns did not have it I had been unable to stop myself from equating the deliciousness of meat with sin, and I could not eat it without a heavy feeling settling around my stomach. It felt like greed to enjoy what was forbidden by the nuns, but somehow it also made it taste all the more delicious.

I slept fast in the bed that was half-familiar to me from previous summers with Ector, but I woke in the night thirsty from the meat. When I left my room, silent as I could to avoid waking Ector's wife's mad sister – for I was sure she was mad although that was the word that none dared say – to tiptoe to the kitchen to get some water, I heard low voices coming from Kay's room, a few doors down the corridor. The door was just ajar, as though someone had slipped inside, although it was dark. I thought it was strange that Kay was still awake without lighting a candle, and although I knew it was wrong to spy, my curiosity got the better of me and I crept to the door and peered in the crack.

Outlined in the faint, pale moonlight that filtered through Kay's window, I could make out two figures on Kay's bed, one on top of the other. The one on top seemed to be Kay, and the two of them seemed to be playfighting, as I had seen Kay and Arthur do many times before, but strangely slow and quiet. I could hear their ragged breathing, but something about it seemed very, very strange. I saw Kay sit up, as though he had been pushed back and away, his profile lighting white against the moonlight, and his glossy black hair shining.

"Kay, stop." I had expected it to be Arthur, but from the rich, low French tones of the voice I realised that it was Lancelot. I was surprised that Lancelot was yielding the fight so soon, especially since it did not seem to be that rough. "We shouldn't be doing this."

"Why not?" Kay whispered back, his voice daring.

"If your father catches us again he will be angry. He will send me away for good. And not just to Avalon; back to France."

I did not see why Ector would be angry, though I remembered his look at Kay and Arthur fighting when we arrived. I supposed that was why Kay and Lancelot were doing it in the dark, because they did not want Ector to see. Still, I thought it seemed a little unfair to send Lancelot away for it. I did not think that Ector would really do such a thing.

Kay didn't reply, but fell down on top of Lancelot again, and I could see the vague shapes of bodies squirming together on the bed, and a flash of pale skin as Kay's shirt rode up at the back. Low, and wicked I heard Kay say,

"Tell me to stop again, now."

And I heard Lancelot groan low in defeat and whisper in reply, "Shut up, Kay."

Behind me, I heard a noise and spun around, blushing in the dark, suddenly guilty for being caught spying. It was Arthur, standing opposite me in the hall, in just his nightshirt with his legs bare and his arms crossed over his chest. In the dark, he looked older, and I realised it was his boy's face that betrayed his age, for he was as big, as broad at least, as Kay and Lancelot, and his body as grown and strong.

"Kay's with Lancelot again isn't he?" Arthur hissed, low and annoyed. When I nodded he sighed in frustration. "I wish they wouldn't do that." He thought for a second, and then took a step towards me, "And *you* shouldn't be watching."

I drew myself up to my full height and crossed my arms over my chest. I wasn't going to be scolded by a boy three years younger than me.

"I've seen it before, a hundred times," I told him, imperiously. I had seen him fight with Kay, and hundreds of boys fighting. I didn't see why I shouldn't look.

Arthur wrinkled up his face in disgust, shook his head at me, and turned back into his own room, shutting the door with a deliberately loud bang. I heard scuffling and low, panicked voices in the room behind me. I didn't know why Arthur and Ector didn't want Kay and Lancelot to playfight like Kay did with Arthur. Perhaps it was something you were only supposed to do with a brother, or with your squire if you were becoming a knight. It didn't make any sense to me.

The next day, the atmosphere at breakfast was tense. Kay slept until past prime, or was hiding in his bedroom, and only came out when Ector sent Arthur in to shake him from his bed. I sat at the rough wooden table, staring down at the grain of it, past the quickly cooling porridge before me, aware that something was about to break around me, like a thunderstorm. Lancelot, beside me, was quiet, too. Kay came to his seat beside me and sat down hard, grabbing his spoon in his fist, his face dark and unreadable. Ector, opposite me, cleared his throat nervously, rubbing his brow. When he spoke his voice was weary.

"I heard some… moving about last night," he said, slowly. Kay, beside me, looked up to meet his father's eye, fierce and defiant, the spoon clutched in his hand like a weapon.

"It was me. I got up to get a drink of water," I said, softly. It was the truth, and besides I felt an instinct in me to defend Kay. Arthur, beside Ector, was looking down at his knees under the table. He looked sick with the awkwardness of it. Ector did not seem to hear me.

"Kay… we have spoken about this before. If there are any more… disturbances… I will be forced to send all of our guests home."

Kay, his eyes blazing, slammed his spoon down onto the table with a bang, standing so forcefully his chair behind him fell back with a clatter against the stone floor of the kitchen, and stormed out of the door. As he left, his father shouted after him, "Kay. *Kay!* You'll understand when you're older that this is *for your own good.*" Ector sighed back against his seat, and rubbed his face in his hands. Then, awfully soft, and as though to himself he said, "I should have married again. God knows that boy needs a mother."

Ector groaned and leaned his elbows on the table, not lifting his head from his hands. I peeped beside me at Lancelot, who looked pale and distant, staring into his porridge, but clearly seeing nothing. I did not understand why Kay was so angry, or Ector so upset, or the fighting so forbidden. Arthur was the only one eating. He was always, *always* hungry.

I felt sick and tense, confused. I wanted to run out after Kay and ask him what was so wrong. There had been nothing like this all the summers past I had spent days with Ector and his sons, but it seemed as though we were all on the edge of something, on the edge of our adulthood, and that made everything we did loaded and dangerous. I could not swim with the boys any more, and they could not play with one another as they had done before.

After a long, long pause, Ector took his face from his hands and turned to Lancelot.

"I think it's best, Lancelot, if you go back to Avalon."

Lancelot, beside me, nodded mutely.

The Lady of Avalon came to take Lancelot back with her in the afternoon, before Kay had returned from wherever he had stormed off to. Arthur and I lingered around the house, nervous and watchful, but neither speaking of what we had seen, or heard. To distract us from the tension of waiting, I tried to show Arthur one of my books, but he didn't know how to read properly, nor recognise any of the Latin words, so I quickly gave up. Instead, we lay side by side on his bed staring up at the ceiling, watching the little spiders make their webs. We left the door wide open, and when Ector walked past he said nothing, so I was sure, at least, that this, too, was not another newly forbidden pastime.

It was almost dusk by the time Kay came back, demanding to see Lancelot, and Arthur and I hid behind the door to the kitchen to listen to what Ector would say. Arthur was stocky and pushy, and stood closer to the door than I did. I had to lean around him to press my ear to the door and only managed it because I was so much taller. I could see the flush of danger about his cheeks; he knew we were doing something forbidden now, too. I was afraid, as well as eager, to listen. I wanted to know what was so awful about what Kay and Lancelot had done, but it seemed like it might be dark and dangerous even to know about it.

"You sent him away, didn't you?" Kay was shouting.

I heard Ector pace in the kitchen, his boots tapping against the stone floor.

"Kay." His voice was tired, full of the forbearance and the suffering of a parent. "You have to try to understand. I tolerated this when you were younger, but you're a man now and it has to stop."

"Why?" Kay's voice was thick with frustration and, to my surprise, upset. I did not think I had heard Kay distressed before. "We weren't hurting anyone. I don't see why it's wrong."

I heard Ector sigh.

"It is wrong because people think it is wrong, Kay. Perhaps it doesn't seem fair to you now – but think of our family. *Please*, Kay, try to understand. If people hear of this, it will ruin this family. You will understand when you're older. Kay," Ector sighed again, and I heard slow steps, as though he was walking over to his son, and his voice dropped softer, more gentle, "we can't change other people's ideas of right and wrong. We can't change the world around us." Ector paused again, and I leaned closer to the door, trying to catch every word. "We can't always have the life we want, Kay. We have to learn to be happy with the life we have."

"You married my mother. She wasn't meant for you," Kay replied, still stubborn, still petulant, but sad now instead of angry, and growing resigned.

"And I paid the price for it, Kay. I paid the price. There will be no great castle for you when I am gone. Besides, a man cannot marry another man."

Suddenly, in an overwhelming rush, I understood it had *not* been fighting that I had seen when I peeped through the door last night. Arthur's disgusted face when I said I had seen it many times before, Ector's anger, Kay's defiance, it all at last made sense. I had heard the nuns before talk with disgust of things like that, and name them as a sin. I did not know yet what I thought of it.

"Kay, you will meet a girl, and marry her and be happy. This is not the end of the world. You must accept that these boys' games are over. You are men now, you and Lancelot both, and you bear the responsibility of your family's name and honour. You will understand, when you are older, that I did this for the good of you both."

Arthur and I scurried away when we heard footsteps come towards the door, and I hid the rest of the evening in my room with my books. I heard Kay slam his door as he went into his room down the corridor from me, and I was grateful that Ector did not call us to dine together. I was glad that I, too, had not been sent away. Still, it filled me with uneasiness, all Ector's talk of family honour, his talk of how we were grown. I felt my childhood evaporating around me, slipping through my fingers like sand, and I was afraid.

Chapter Three

Kay was quiet for a week or so after that, and when he practised at fighting against Arthur with wooden swords, he hit at his younger brother with a deliberate cruelty, trying to strike him at the head, or trip him. I thought he might have blamed Arthur for Ector sending Lancelot away, thinking that Arthur told their father that Lancelot had been in his bedroom, rather than Ector hearing it. But the fighting seemed to slowly tire out Kay's anger. Arthur matched him blow-for-blow anyway, and though younger, he was Kay's equal in size and strength, so slowly Kay's wicked, flashing smile returned, and his ready, melodious laugh and his playfulness. I think Kay knew, too, deep down that his father was right, because they did not shout at each other again.

I sat reading and half-watching Kay and Arthur as they trained together, first with wooden swords, then with wooden swords and leather armour, then with real swords and real platemail. Kay had this wonderfully light set of dark-coloured mail that seemed to sit weightlessly on him, and when I tried to pick it up when he took it off, it felt weightless in my hand, but when Ector or Arthur carried it they needed both hands. Kay told me that it was because it was forged in the Otherworld, and his mother had had it made for him before she died.

By the time we were deep into summer and the days grew long and heavy, the sun low and orange in the sky making us all sleepy and lazy, Kay was fully his old self again. We ran together through the woodlands near his house to find wild strawberries and raspberries, and climb trees, though Kay was much better. He was fast and fearless, and in breeches his clothes did not tangle in the branches like the skirts of my dress did. Arthur liked to practise fighting, and besides he had discovered a new game of his own that he liked much better, where he would try to kiss the girls that came from the village carrying pails of milk as they walked down the little path to Ector's house. I was surprised how often they were willing, though Kay said that all the girls liked Arthur's golden hair and broad, open smile. He told me girls were afraid of him, and said his mother was a witch and he an imp from the Otherworld, so they ran away from him. I was not sure if he was teasing me, because I had never seen him try.

24

One day, as we sat in a tree, Kay with his back against a thick branch and his feet braced above him against the trunk, and I on an opposite branch, dangling my legs down into the empty air, Kay throwing little unripe apples at me playfully across the space between us, I heard him give a strange little noise of thoughtfulness, and looked over to him.

He was looking at me, an unfamiliar look in his eye, and a strange, handsome half-smile on his face.

"Do you think you're pretty, Morgan?" he asked me, teasingly.

I shrugged. "No."

I wished I could have said more, but I felt nervous, suddenly, and I could feel myself blushing. I wished I had said *No, but I'm clever. Far cleverer than you.* It would have been true. I could read in Latin and French, and Kay could barely read in English. He squinted at the words on the page and knew half of them, but that was the best he could do. And he couldn't write. And he didn't know the names of the stars. I didn't need to be pretty. I was clever.

Then, to my absolute surprise, Kay threw another hard little unripe apple at me, and said, "*I* think you're pretty."

I gripped the branch I was sat on hard, afraid suddenly that I would fall.

Kay didn't mention it again, when we climbed down the tree and walked back to his house. He was just the same as he always was. He pushed a blackberry against my face, and when the purple juice smeared over me laughed and told me that was how I would look when the ladies of Avalon had woaded me into one of them, and I laughed and shoved him back; but he was quicker than me and got away before I could rub a berry on *his* face. Still, I felt that something had changed between us, and I felt a new fluttering excitement, and there seemed to be something new in the smiles Kay gave me, but I could not be sure.

Our days continued the same, and Kay did not say he thought I was pretty again, but I *did* feel that something was different. Kay seemed ever happier and more playful, and sometimes would hold out the berries we picked together between his fingers and offer them right to my mouth. I felt a little daring rush inside me to take them, and feel his fingers against my lips. I didn't like it the few times that Arthur came with us. Kay was no different with me, but the nervousness inside my stomach made me different with him, quieter. As hard as I tried I could never put away my natural shyness, and something about Arthur's loud, simple way made it worse, made the thought of giving anything of myself away around Kay all the more unbearable. Arthur just charged over everything, barely noticing, stuffing his food into his face with barely time to taste it, and grabbing the milkmaids in his arms all the same as though he could not tell one from the other.

One night, Kay knocked on my door when I was asleep, and dragged me from my bed so that we could lie side by side in the garden and demanded that I teach him more of the names of the stars. Besides, he had forgotten already those ones I had taught him. At first he joked and pretended to give them all crude names instead, just to make me wriggle with embarrassment, but soon he was serious and intent, and he learned the names fast. We pointed up together at the pole star above, and our hands brushed, and I felt the little spark of excitement glow within me, and Kay turned beside me to look at me, a strange seriousness on his face, and our arms still dangled upwards into the air. I thought he might try to kiss me, but he did not. I found I was disappointed, and when the moment passed, Kay sitting up suddenly and declaring himself too tired to continue, I found I could not get to sleep for a long time. I would have liked him to, I realised.

It was late in the summer when the Lady of Avalon came back with the news that she intended to take me with her to Avalon in the next few days. Ector welcomed her, but both Kay and Arthur looked downcast that I was going away from them. I was sad, too. I would miss Arthur, but I knew that I would miss Kay far more.

I packed up my things, feeling nervous and a little sad. After the dark arguments of the beginning of summer had passed like a rainstorm, it had been blissful. I realised, too, that I had seen Kay and his brother grow from boys to men over only a matter of months, for before they had played at fighting but now they trained in their armour – or Kay in his armour, Arthur in a leather jerkin – like real men. I wished that my life was not set out for me, as the daughter of the queen, but that I could be a boy and stay with them. I felt, too, that the summer had passed me and Kay by with a painful almostness that I could not quite put into words, though I longed to say *something* to him.

The next morning, Kay knocked on my door before prime and told me he wanted to go climbing in the woods one last time. We went up a few trees, me after him, our hands growing sticky with sap, and green moss from the trees gathering on my dress, and found a patch of small, sweet wild strawberries that we sat beside and ate until they were gone. Kay held out the last one for me, and as I leaned forward to take it from his fingers, I felt them linger against my lips, and a jump of excitement went inside me, but the moment did not come and Kay stood up, offering me his hand to help me stand, and led the way on.

We came, just as the sun was passing midday and beating down in the fullness of its strength, to a lovely clearing. We had run through it before, almost without seeing it, and I recognised it. It was filled with soft grass, and lilac trees gathered at one side of it, filling the space with their smell. It was beautiful. Kay stretched his arms over his head, leaning his face up into the sun with a broad, contented smile, and sank down where he stood to lie half in the shade of a tree on the edge of the clearing. Tired from our morning's climbing, I sat down beside him, propping myself up on my elbows, and gazing up above at the patch of clear blue sky over us.

The lovely late summer sun filtered green through the leaves above, and butterflies floated by on the lilac tree beside us. I closed my eyes and breathed it in. I would be in Avalon soon, which would be different and strange, and there would be only women. I thought, for the most part, that I would like that, though I would miss Kay. Kay stretched out his long legs beside me, and sighed, propping himself up on his elbows, gazing across the little clearing, his hair ruffled up from running and climbing, a light flush high on his cheeks. If I were not the king's stepdaughter, perhaps I could have married Kay. If I were not meant for Avalon. For a different life.

Kay turned to me, suddenly, as though he could hear my thoughts.

"Morgan, have you ever kissed anyone?" he asked, flat out, like it was nothing. I felt myself blush. I shook my head. I wasn't sure what the right answer was – the answer that would make him kiss me – so I only told the truth.

"Have you?" I asked him.

"Not a girl," he answered, with a wicked smile. "Do you want to know what it's like?"

Implicit in what he said was the phrase *before you go*. So, he had come here with me with the same thoughts and hopes and fears that I had. That the summer had passed us by while we both wanted but dared not to take this step towards one another. I didn't think I should want to, but I did. I wanted Kay to kiss me, but I felt the shyness close me up again, and I dared not say anything in case this was just another one of Kay's teases, in case I had misunderstood all along, and if I said so, he would laugh at me.

But I did not have to say anything. Quick as a cat, Kay pounced around on to me, and I felt his lips against mine, and I was surprised at his gentleness. I had seen men and women kiss before, and I had seen Arthur grab girls and kiss them. They had seemed to enjoy it, wriggling with delight, but it had always looked rough and unpleasant. This was not. Kay's lips were light and soft against mine, and I gave a little, unconscious, sigh of delight. The grass tickled lightly at the nape of my neck, under the thick plait of my dark hair, and through my closed eyelids I could see orange from the light beyond. Kay, encouraged by my enjoyment, moved slowly on to me, so he was lying on top of me. I was surprised to find I liked the feel of his body against mine. I knew — I had read — about men getting on top of women and I had thought it would be heavy and uncomfortable, but Kay's body on mine felt tinglingly close and present rather than heavy and pressing. I wrapped my arms around his neck, feeling the thrill of nerves within me heighten and spread through my whole body. Gently, I felt Kay's tongue brush against mine, and a spark of something new light deep within me. I supposed that was desire, that I had read about in books also, that I had seen press men and women to one another. I could smell Kay's scent all around me; fresh grass and the wild of the woods, the sap of the trees. I could taste the strawberries sweet on his lips. He was bold and daring where I was shy and quiet and not only did I want him, I wanted to become more like him, to feel more pleasantly wicked. So, when I felt Kay's hands run up my body and across my breasts, though I knew I ought to push him away, instead I pressed against him, and I heard him give a low laugh of contentment. I didn't, in that moment, see why I should care about keeping myself perfect for marriage. Not while it was bright with the end of my summer of freedom all around me, and I could smell the fresh grass, and enjoy the feeling of Kay's lips on mine, his hands exploring my body.

My lips tingled softly with Kay's kisses, and I began to feel hot, and something else with it a little like dizziness, and I knew my body wanted something, but I did not know what it was, only that I hoped Kay would give it to me. The nuns had taught me well, but not well enough, what a man did with a woman, when alone, and there was only so much I could learn from what was written in books. I hoped that Kay would know. Filled with a new daring, I slid my hands up the back of Kay's shirt, against his warm, soft skin, and felt beneath it the muscles of a man rippling with strength. I was at once acutely aware that though we had been children together a long time, Kay and I were now grown, and what we were playing at now was not a child's game, but I did not hold back at the thought. If we had to live in a world of adult dangers, I would not hold myself back from adult pleasures. My stepfather was dying and there was no one left to punish me for not keeping myself from a man's touch before I was wed. Besides, this might mean I would never have to marry, or I might be even allowed to marry Kay.

I felt Kay's hand slide up my leg under my dress, and I kissed him harder. He made a low sound of surprise, and appreciation, in response to my eagerness for him, and I gasped as I felt his hand brush between my legs, and he slid his finger inside me, into a secret place I did not know I had. Somewhere that had the thrill of the forbidden. I felt hotter, and wilder, as though Kay's touch inside me was leading me somewhere even more daring, and I took his lip lightly in my teeth, with a hungry little tug, and I reached down to touch him where I knew I should not, under his breeches. It was warm and soft with secret hair, and hard and promising beneath. Kay groaned low at my touch and suddenly, throwing the skirts of my dress up around my waist, Kay turned me roughly over and pulled me against him. I gave a little cry as I felt him go inside me, but after the first small shock of pain, I felt the warmth of pleasure, of closeness with Kay spread through me, and I felt his tender kisses against the back of my neck where he pulled back the heavy plait of dark hair to kiss me, and his hands against my hips moving me against him. It felt as though Kay and I were not just connected with one another, but with the deepness and wholeness of the world, and the ancientness of the Otherworld, and we belonged together, and to everything else all around us. I felt the heat of my enjoyment light my cheeks, and the breath came fast and ragged for me. All too soon, while I still felt the glow of Kay's touch through my limbs, and at the centre of me, I heard Kay groan again, and it was over. He slid away from me, and gently smoothed the skirt of my dress back down over me, and drew me around and into his arms as he lay back down, with a satisfied smile, kissing me gently again. Kay was sleepy already; I could see his eyelids hanging heavily, and feel his arm fall away from around me, limp, as he began to doze in the sun, but I still felt full of a tingling energy that had been wakened with nowhere to go.

That night, after Kay had walked back hand in hand with me to his house in a happy silence, I reached my hand down to where Kay had touched me, and I had felt the spark within me, and there with the memory of Kay on top of me, and the smell of the grass and the warm light of the sun, I felt at last under the touch of my own hand what Kay must have felt with me to make him groan and sigh away with contentment, and it was good indeed.

Chapter Four

It was hard to say goodbye to Ector, Kay and Arthur. I hugged them all tight while the Lady of Avalon stood loading my things on to her horse. Kay kissed me softly on the cheek and whispered "I will miss you," and Arthur said loudly and proudly,

"Kay will be a great knight when we see you again, and maybe so will I."

I turned around to wave at them getting smaller and smaller as we rode away, until I saw Ector turn and lead them inside. I felt the nerves tighten in my stomach, and my shyness close my throat. I wanted to ask the Lady what Avalon would be like, and if there would be others my age there, but I said nothing. I wondered how the world outside would change while I was in Avalon, and what would happen when King Uther died. Uther had no sons, no children at all of his own. Perhaps some of the kings of Britain would try to marry me, though I did not think I would be enough to win anyone the throne on my own. Perhaps my sister Morgawse's husband would try to take it. They had three – or was it four? – sons already, the eldest a pair of strong twins Arthur's age, and men always wanted to follow a king with lots of sons. Sons meant peace, and security for the kingdom into the next generation. I wondered about my sister, whom I had not seen in so long. She had come to see me a few times, once huge with one of her sons, and I missed her. When my time at Avalon was finished, I thought I might try to go all the way north to Lothian to see her, and my nephews.

The journey was short enough, and we reached the shores of Avalon's glassy lake at just past midday. The air was beginning to smell of autumn, of falling leaves and damp earth and fragrant apples. The changing of the year, and the changing of my life.

There was a little barge tethered at the edge of the lake, and I got in after the Lady of Avalon, curling my arms around my knees. There was a chilly wind that seemed to blow through my dress. The Lady, the long rope of pale gold and white-grey hair snaking in a plait down over her shoulder as far as her waist, leaned back against the prow of the barge, stretching her legs out. The woad patterns on her face were old, and seemed to have faded into her skin, become a part of it, so I could not imagine what she would have looked like without them, if she would have been beautiful. She was certainly beautiful with them. As she pushed the barge lazily on, we moved through a mist. It smelled of strange, cloying herbs, and I coughed, and felt my stomach turn. There was something sickening about it, and if I were not afraid of looking weak I would have stuck my head out over the edge of the barge, in case I threw up. The Lady gave a little encouraging smile.

"You'll get used to it, Morgan," she told me, softly.

Avalon looked much larger as we approached it than it ever had done from the shores of its great lake. It towered over us, a craggy tor of bare granite rock, and carved into the side of it were a few buildings like the abbey; grand stone made with arches and little windows. When we arrived and stepped off the barge, I could not see back to Logrys when I turned around. I felt all over me, through my blood and my bones, the feel of the Otherworld.

The Lady led me inside one of the big stone buildings, to a little room that was not so different from my cell in the abbey, with a plain narrow bed, and a desk for reading and a couple of candles. She left me to myself, and I was glad of it. Glad to sit on my new bed and unpack my books and gather myself. I wondered when I would see Kay again. I wondered if he was thinking of me, too.

The first few days on Avalon were hard, and I felt miserable and lonely, my shyness holding me back from speaking to the women all around me I did not know. The cold stone, and bare halls and quietness of the place was miserable, too, after Ector's bustling house and the boisterous playfighting of Arthur and Kay. But, slowly, I grew used to the quiet, and realised that I liked it, as I had liked the quiet to sit alone and read in the abbey. I liked, too, to sit on the shore on the big, grey rocks and look out through the mists across the lake. The Lady had been right, too, that I would get used to their smell. By the time winter came and the frost settled on the dark, scrubby grass on the tor of Avalon, it already felt like home, and often a small girl, white-blonde haired and serious-faced, called Nimue would come and sit with me, or read with me at night, and though she was quiet and we barely spoke I felt that I was slowly gaining a friend.

I still did not know exactly what I was in Avalon to learn, and none of the other women or girls seemed to speak about it, though I knew that I would get the lovely patterns of woad that the Lady and some of the other women on the island had once I did know. The library was full of wonderful books, and I spent a long time in there, by the fire, leafing through them. A lot of them were full of healing magic, some powerful, that could bring a man back to life, but I was disappointed with how much seemed trivial and silly, things like spells for a sunny day, or charms for a broken heart. I tried to make the potion described in the book I had read in the abbey, but the instructions were vague, and though I found all the ingredients in Avalon, I must have mixed them incorrectly, because what I mixed myself made me sick when I drank it. I did not manage to find a book that matched or explained the one I had found in the abbey about changing one's shape, and when I asked the woman who watched the library she gave me a blank, aggressive stare as though she did not know and I ought not to ask.

I got a letter in the winter, from Kay. The Lady brought it to my room and left it there. She must have still been visiting Ector.

My dearest Lady Princess Morgan, I hope this letter finds you in good health, and not too blue in the face already. I am now an excellent knight, but Arthur is not a very good squire. He always loses my equipment and never pays proper attention. He is too busy pretending he too is a knight, or pulling strange faces at the girls he thinks are pretty. Last week I went to a tournament and Arthur forgot my helm. This big knight from Lothian almost had my head off. Perhaps he was one of your nephews. Father was quite angry. To teach Arthur a lesson I have started hiding the important bits of equipment. Yesterday it took him two hours to find my saddle. He is not very good at hiding games, either. Plus, he is not nearly so good at climbing trees as you or I, and since up a tree was where I had put it, it took him a while to retrieve it once he had found it. Everyone says Uther will die soon and I am afraid war is coming, which will go very ill for me if Arthur keeps losing my equipment. I have been thinking of you. I hope Avalon is not too boring without me. Ever your own good knight, Sir Kay.

So, at least, Kay had not changed even a little though months had passed since I had seen him. I had not seen Lancelot all the time I was in Avalon, and I wondered if he had, after all, been taken back to France. I did not want to ask about him because I did not really want him back. If Kay was still thinking of me, and writing to me, I did not want Lancelot to come back and remind him of whom he had been kissing before he was kissing me.

The next time I saw Nimue I was sitting out on the rocks wrapped in a cloak of furs that had once belonged to my mother, and I was surprised to see that she had earned her woad and was covered in lovely delicate little patterns of blue-green over her face, and hands, and in fact all of the skin that I could see. I felt a stab of jealousy. I was sixteen years old that winter, and Nimue looked to me to be only eleven or twelve. I did not think it was fair that someone younger than me should be able to earn it before me, but I kept my silence. I thought maybe, since she and I had spent a long time side by side, that she might tell me Avalon's secret ritual, but she did not.

When I asked her about it, she said vaguely,

"I was born in Avalon."

I wished I had found that helpful, even in a small way, but I did not. But then, after a pause staring off across her lake, her little pointy nose newly traced with blue leading off towards Logrys, she said.

"I found my gift quickly, because I have been here all along."

So that was it. That was how you earned your woad. I knew already what I *wanted* mine to be, but I was not sure it could be so, because I had only the one book and I had not yet managed to do it. I knew the Lady of Avalon had her gifts in the healing arts, and I had even heard it said that she could bring a dead man back to life with only the touch of her hands, but I knew they were not for me. It has to come from within you, and I did not think I had a gift within me for nurturing or healing. But I did know, and had always known, how to change my shape, to hide and disappear where I knew I was not wanted, to play a silent role. I had hidden from my stepfather Uther right beside my mother, and half the time when I imagined that I was as invisible as a stick of wood to him, his eyes had glossed over me and passed me by, but that gift had had no magic and often he had seen me, and shouted and raised his hand against me until I scurried away. It was not a bold woman's gift, it was a shy woman's and it was the one that I wanted. The ability to become someone else.

I gathered the fur more tightly around myself as the breeze came harder across the lake, and Nimue's long plait of white-blonde hair stirred its free wisps all the way down. It was a cold wind and, I felt, one of ill omen. I would have to find the rest of the secret of shape-changing soon. I wanted to be strong with secrets when Uther died. I would need them all to escape being married away. But Nimue had her secret now, and suddenly the idea sparked within me that she might help me.

"What was it, Nimue?"

She turned to me, her pale blue eyes fixing me vaguely, as though I had stirred her from a dream. She was like a creature from a dream, really. So pale, so delicate. Her eyes never seemed to focus on the world around her. It worried some of the other women, I knew, but I liked it. It did not make me feel, as some others did, that I was being scrutinized under a critical gaze, or being measured or judged. Nimue was just looking at me with hazy interest, as though I were nothing more than part of the landscape of her dreams.

She reached out and offered me her hand.

"Come with me."

I took it, standing awkwardly, my limbs stiff from the cold of sitting on the rock, and let Nimue lead me up over the scrubby grass at the foot of the tor, past the low dark stone buildings of the houses of Avalon, and round the other side. Though it was cold, by the time we arrived at the forge where it stood under the head of the tor on the other side of the small island, I was red in the face and puffing out steam.

It was not something I had ever paid that much attention to before, since I had no interest in armour or weapons, and I had never seen any of the women in Avalon wear them or bear them so I was not even sure why it was there, but then I remembered Kay's Otherworld armour that had felt light in my hand. Perhaps his own mother had been from Avalon, and it had been forged here. I remembered I had not yet written back to him. I was not sure what I wanted to say. I did not have Kay's easy, casual way with words, and I was afraid that anything I wrote him would betray too much of what I felt, of what had happened between us. I didn't want Arthur reading it, and I was sure he would. He was nosy and brash and I could not imagine him letting Kay have any secrets to himself. I didn't have Kay's skill in saying all the right things, but making it seem so effortless. I was afraid that anything I wrote back would be painfully honest, or painfully inadequate.

I followed Nimue slowly into the forge; perched as it was against the steep sloping side of the tor, I was afraid that I would slip, but I made it in. It was swelteringly hot and the fire at the centre of it filled the whole room with an orange light. Though it was frosty outside, Nimue stripped immediately to a sleeveless underdress in the heat of the forge, and I copied her, folding up my furs and then placing my dark wool dress on top. I also coiled the plait of my hair around and tucked it into a bun, afraid that its long ends would catch fire.

It was small and cramped and hot in the little forge and I did not see how it could have anything to do with Nimue's gift, but she was busying around already, blackened leather gloves on her hands, pulling together blocks to cast a sword. I had not seen a sword the whole time I had been in Avalon.

Nimue picked up a lump of iron as though it was nothing, and threw it to me across the forge. I was surprised when I caught it to find that I caught it as lightly as she had thrown it.

"Iron mined in the Otherworld," Nimue told me, a sudden focus in her pale eyes, and the slightness of a smile around her face.

I lifted it a little in my hands, feeling its strange weightlessness. To test it, I dropped it against the dirt floor, and when I picked it up again, I saw that it had left a deep and heavy dent. Nimue took it back from me and set it to melt in the forge.

I sat back against the little table in the corner to watch her work. She was slow and methodical, mixing the iron to make steel. It was as though she had forgotten I was there, she was so absorbed and careful. I got lost watching her, moving away from my body, already prickling with sweat in the intense heat of the forge, my skin already darkening with ash and dust. Nimue was mesmerising, her eyes growing wild, her tiny limbs, orange in the light of the fire, moving with a hypnotic grace, and I could not tear my gaze away as she seemed to half-dance through the forge, pouring the steel into the sword-mould, setting the hilt there, which she had made plated with gold and set with old jewels. She must have got them from some ancient sword, or some lost king's crown. By the time the sword was set in the mould, I had not realised that it had got dark outside, and when she pulled it out, still glowing with heat, to run down to the icy cold lake and temper it in those enchanted waters. When she brought it back up to me, I could see the blade shining smooth, and so sharp its edges seemed to disappear into nothingness. She offered it to me, and I took it. It felt weightless and wonderfully graceful in my hand. I swung it a little, as I had seen Kay and Arthur do before, and it seemed to move with me, as though it were a part of my limbs itself. Nimue disappeared into the forge, and I was suddenly aware that it was a winter's night and I was out in my underdress, my skin turned to goosebumps from the cold. I followed her inside, where she was holding in her hands a jewelled scabbard.

"I made this, too," she told me, her voice soft as a whisper. "Whoever carries this scabbard will never spill a drop of blood."

She handed that to me, as well, and I slid the sword inside. I made to hand it back to her, but she held up a hand in protest and shook her head.

"I made them for you. I think you will need them, Morgan. There are dangers coming for you."

Tentatively, not knowing how to thank her enough, I pulled on my dress and furs, and buckled the scabbard around my waist. She gave a rare, gentle smile to see it on me. I had never received so fine a gift, but it made me uneasy. It seemed like a gift for a woman of the world, a warrior queen, rather than what I wanted to be, a wise woman in Avalon. It seemed like a gift for the beginning of a life at war after King Uther's death, not the life of peaceful study that I coveted.

I thanked her quietly nonetheless, and as I turned to go, she said to me,

"Oh, Morgan. The sword has a name. It is called Excalibur. That means 'cutter of steel'."

A sword for war, then.

Chapter Five

I hid the sword and the scabbard under my bed, dimly aware that I ought not to have such things. I was not sure yet why Nimue had made me such a sword, or given me such a fine magical scabbard, though I always had the feeling that Nimue knew far more than she would ever say. So, her gift had been to forge Otherworld arms. Perhaps Kay and Arthur's mother had been such a woman on Avalon. She had not been much like Nimue, though. She had been always laughing, always smiling and telling stories. Dark-eyed and bright witted. I had heard people say that she was a fairy-woman and had enchanted Ector into loving her, but even if she had been a fairy-woman, she would have had no need for magic. She had been wonderfully pretty and clever and kind and everyone who had met her had loved her. Worse even than her death had been seeing how weak and silent she had grown when she was ill, the life and the colour fading out of her slowly. At least her elder son had had all the qualities that she had possessed, and the world had not had to carry on without them after she was gone.

I asked Nimue the next day why she had given me a sword, and rather enigmatically she told me,

"That is the finest sword ever made, and you will be a great queen one day, and you will need it."

That did not sound like a happy prediction to me. I did not want to be a great queen or possess a great sword. I wanted to live in peace minding my own business. I would not have minded one bit living in Ector's simple house with Kay eating whatever grew in the land until I was old and wrinkled. I supposed it was not to be, though. Kay was already a knight, and war was coming.

Winter deepened around Avalon, and Christmas drew near. I had not expected Avalon to observe its festivities, though, and it did not. Christmas at Camelot had been a thing of wonder, for sure, though I had only watched it from the edges, called back into the heart of nasty, brutish Uther's kingdom to show my face as the obedient step-daughter. I had only gone to get a chance to see my sister, and half in the thought that my presence there would protect her a little from Uther. We never sat at the high table, nor did we join the Christmas games. My mother Queen Igraine had thought it best if Uther, drunk on Christmas wine, did not have sight of his stepdaughters if it could be helped, and would not be made angry by the memory of the husband my mother had had before. I hated that brute of a man, and I hoped that he would die soon.

When I was alone in my room, I would often draw my sword and look at the smoothness and sharpness of the blade. Sometimes I imagined driving it into Uther's war-hardened flesh and imagining in the surprise on his face that the little girl he had mocked and struck had still retained enough strength in her to hate him.

I was sorry, then, when a few weeks before Christmas news came that Uther had died of his illness and I would have no chance for my own revenge. It came in a strange form, the news. I sat out on the rocks, staring through the mist, when I saw the barge come. I expected the Lady of Avalon, but instead I saw a young man, brown-skinned with thick glossy brown curls falling to his chin. He looked about my age, young and lithe, and he was dressed in simple woollen clothes under a rich and heavy cloak of dark furs. About his neck, too, he bore a strange chain of gold set at its centre with a huge sapphire that glinted like the eye of a dragon. I stood slowly to my feet, mesmerised, and I was shocked when, as the barge docked and the man tied it to Avalon's tiny wooden pier, he came over to me, took me by the hand and gave a little bow.

"My Lady Morgan." I was yet more shocked that he knew who I was. "I bring news from your lady mother, the Queen Igraine. King Uther is dead."

The shock of it went through me, and I felt my hand tremble against his. War would begin soon, then. And my mother had not come. Perhaps she had fled back to Tintagel, my father's castle, to hide from Uther's enemies. I hoped that was what she had done, for Camelot was right in the centre of Logrys and could be attacked from all sides, and my stepfather King Uther had had many enemies.

The man reached out and brushed my cheek lightly with his hand. Were I not so stunned from the news I had both longed for and dreaded I might have been surprised at this, but it reached me as though through a dream.

Thoughtfully, he said, "You look so like your mother at that age, you know."

It seemed impossible to me that he would have known my mother at sixteen. He looked no older than twenty to me, and more like my own age. I did not think, besides, that I could look like my mother. Everyone said that my mother was a great beauty, and that I was not. Too tall, too skinny, too serious about the eyes. This strange man was just being kind, or worse, just being polite.

As though waking from his own daydream, he shook his head, and the brown curls bounced lightly in time with it.

"Morgan, can you take me to the Lady?"

I nodded mutely, and led the way. I couldn't make sense of anything other than the relief and panic of Uther's death. He was gone, he could not hurt me now, but my mother and Arthur and Ector and – most of all – Kay, were out there alone in a realm that was soon going to be eaten up by war. Even if my sister's husband, King Lot, made a play to seize the southern realm of Logrys, it would not be easy. Men would die. Men I cared about. Women, too, and children. And they would not die with swords in their hands riding to battle. They would be slaughtered. Avalon suddenly did not seem so safe or so far from Logrys. It would, of course, remain untouched by war, but I could not forget those who were beyond the lake.

The Lady was in Avalon's great hall, which was called thus, but was no bigger really than the abbey's cloister garden. There were a few of the others with her, among whom I recognised Nimue. The Lady smiled when she saw the man with me, and came over to kiss him on the cheek.

"Merlin! What news from Camelot?" she asked. I had not seen her so pleased to see anybody before, except perhaps Nimue. The Lady of Avalon only liked those who were strong in their gifts, and I was not yet one of those, though I felt always the potential of my strength coiled within me.

Merlin. How could this young man be Uther's witch? He was not even painted with woad, so he had not earned his title on Avalon.

A chair was brought for him, though he did not sit, and the Lady sat in the great stone seat in the hall, and I and the others gathered behind. Nimue, who had come to my side, slipped her hand into mine. I was surprised, but glad, at the gesture. Nimue had not seemed the affectionate type to me before, nor, I had thought, I to her, but she must have sensed my need and I felt the strength of her presence beside me, and I felt more steady.

Merlin gave a little bow before the Lady of Avalon once she was seated. I felt it then, the strength of the power coming off him. It was of the Otherworld, but it was strange and unfamiliar to me in its quality. I remembered then that I had overheard one of the other women once say that Merlin's father had been an incubus and though he mainly practised the magic of Avalon, he had knowledge of the Black Arts, and had used them to put Uther on the throne. I could not believe those things, looking at the handsome young man standing before us now.

"My Lady, and ladies of Avalon. King Uther is dead." There was a flurry of noise, of muttering and of half-panic among the women gathered behind the Lady, and she raised her hand for silence. "It is said throughout the land that Uther died without an heir. However, I am come to Avalon with news that this is not so. Uther had a son, whom I gave into fosterage on Avalon." I did not think that could be Lancelot, though I knew of no other man who had been raised in Avalon. Besides, Lancelot knew who his father was – his father had been old King Ban of the southern lands of France. Surely, it could not be him. "However, it seems that the boy has been lost," he paused a moment, and a hard look I had not expected passed between him and the Lady, even though moments ago they had greeted each other as old friends, "and I do not know where to find him. I have set a test in the great Cathedral, and when the time is right the boy will identify himself by being the only one able to pull Uther's sword from the block of stone I have set it in. It will be soon. We must prepare ourselves for a new king. I have seen him in my dreams. He will not be like his father; he will love Avalon and protect your order. Greatness will come to Britain, and I am pleased to be the man who will raise up this new king."

A lost child? Uther's lost son? I never remembered another child, nor heard talk of it. It did not seem that this child could have grown into a man, though, so Uther's son must be younger than I was, which meant he must have had this son with another woman while he was married to my mother. Of course he had. Uther was that kind of nasty brute.

"I will take the Princess Morgan back with me when I return to Camelot," he added.

"No!" I heard myself shout, shocked by my own boldness, my own loud voice where I was usually quiet. Blushing, I gathered myself to add more calmly, "I cannot go. I have not finished my studies here."

This was not the whole truth of it. I did not want to go back to Logrys only half a witch, unable to defend myself, but I would have rather gone to Cornwall to be with my mother, or to Lothian to stay with my sister than to go alone to Uther's warlike capital.

"Morgan." He turned to me, and when his dark eyes fixed me I felt rooted to the spot. "Do not worry. It will not be right away. And the Lady tells me you are near to finishing."

When had she told him? The Lady must have *written* to him about me. I felt hot with anger. I was not near finished. I had learned a lot, but achieved nothing. I suppose I might have finished already if I had wanted to learn the arts of healing, since I had seen other women my age earn their woad quickly doing that, and though I did not want the gift, I found it came to me a little by nature, in the touch of my hands; but I was nowhere close to learning what *I* had come to learn. I had not even found all the books that I needed.

I went back to my room as quickly as I could when the Lady had dismissed us to talk to Merlin alone. I tried to sit at my books, desperate to learn as much as I could in the little time I had left, but when I picked up the book that was open at my desk, Kay's letter fell out from underneath it, hitting the stone floor with a papery whisper. I picked it up and held it in my hands, trying to imagine him sitting in his house making the charmingly clumsy letters that skittered across it. It was an old scrap, and on the back were a list of numbers, the accounts of Ector's housekeeper or something, but I could tell that he had written it with great effort. I had to write back to him, though I was not sure where I would find him now that the King was dead. I wished it were summer again and we were running through the woodlands, kissing under the trees. I wondered, obliquely, if Kay had yet killed a man. I thought that was when boys finally lost their innocence. I knew for us, for women, it was different, and that I already had, but the day would come for Kay and Arthur when they would have to kill, and that was, I was sure, when it would end for them. Kay still wrote like he was playing boys' games of fighting, but I could not really imagine Kay writing anything else.

I folded the letter tenderly and tucked it into my bag, between two of my dresses. I did not want to have any chance of accidentally leaving such a precious item behind in Avalon. Then, kneeling on the floor by my bag, I caught the glint of the jewelled scabbard of my sword under the bed, and feeling the need for comfort, I reached under and pulled it out. I stood up, holding it against me, closing my eyes and feeling the power of the Otherworld, and the companionship of Nimue, and what I realised now was the deep kindness and thoughtfulness of her gift, all around me. She had known this day was coming. Nimue, who saw things in her dreams, had seen my need for a sword. At least now this meant that if I was wed to a man I did not like I could kill him. That seemed to me an awfully likely outcome, and I was more glad of the sword that I had ever been of anything in my life.

Suddenly, the door opened and Merlin stepped in. I stepped back, afraid, and held the sword behind me, but it was too late. He had already seen it.

"That is a fine sword you have there, my Lady Morgan," he said, with a gentle smile. He was handsome enough that I felt uncomfortable in my room alone with him. His smile was not so unlike Kay's, impish and charming, and I felt myself blush to acknowledge my own attraction. "Let me see it."

He reached out for it. I would not have given it to him if I had been braver, or if I had thought more quickly. But, in the moment it seemed like denying it to him would have only made him take it from me violently, and I did not want it to seem as precious as it was. I was afraid he would take it from me, but if he thought it was of little worth then he would not – though I did not know how I intended to convince him that the jewels on the hilt and scabbard were worthless. Anyone of any degree would want such a lovely sword, even those who could not guess at its Otherworld strength, as I was sure that Merlin could.

He drew it slowly from the scabbard and whistled through his teeth to look at it, impressed. The low winter light from the window glinted of it. I held back my desperate urge to snatch it from him.

"I have seen this sword in my dreams," he murmured under his breath, his voice full of wonder. "*Excalibur.*"

I did not know how he knew the name of my sword, but I knew then that he coveted it. I wanted to ask what dreams they were, but I dared not know. After all, he said he had dreamed of this king,

Uther's bastard son. A king would want so fine a sword. Well, he would not have it. Not from me. Lingering for a moment, Merlin slid it back in the scabbard and handed it back to me. As he handed it back his hand brushed mine and he let it, for longer, I thought, than was accidental.

"Many thanks, Lady Morgan. A fine sword indeed."

I took it back, gathering it against myself protectively, wrapping my arms around it. I should have taken it casually as though I did not guard it jealously, but I was desperate not to lose it. It was my last safety. It would be all that I had when I left Avalon.

As though he had suddenly remembered why he had come to me, he jumped a little on his feet. "Ah," he began. "Yes, I will take you to Camelot when the King has revealed himself. Now, I understand that you have had some trouble locating a certain book."

I nodded. I wanted to slide the sword back under my bed, but then he would know where I kept it. I hugged it closer against myself.

"Macrobius' book on the changing of shapes, the *Formae Mutandum*," I told him, quiet with my shyness, and railing against it.

Merlin laughed, but he seemed pleased. "I know the book. I am surprised that *you* know it. Morgan, you must know that such things are considered by some as part of the Black Arts."

I had not known that. I had thought the Black Arts were spells of death, or spells that destroyed the minds of others. Such things that blackened the land, or blighted out the sun. I supposed that this explained why I had found no such book in the abbey or in Avalon, but I thought the Lady of Avalon might have warned me that I was wandering into darkness. It was too late, now, to turn back. I would not leave Avalon without such magic, and if it was magic from the borders of the Black Arts, then I would take it.

"I am not afraid," I told him softly. I was not. I felt shyness, always, hesitancy, but I was not easily made afraid. Not for my own safety. I had heard Black Arts could eat up the mind and soul of those who practised them, but I knew that I was strong in mind if not in body. I was glad, suddenly, that Merlin had come, despite the threat he came with, for he would complete my education, and make me strong.

"No, I see that," he said evenly. I could see that he was intrigued by me, and he raised his eyebrow and gave me a knowing smile. "I see that you are not easily made afraid, my Lady Morgan. Not easily at all."

Chapter Six

The next few days, I did not see much of Merlin. I saw him about Avalon, mainly with the Lady, but I did not see him when I passed through the library. I kept to my room, reading as much as I could, but feeling I was learning little. I sat with Nimue out on the rocks, looking out. She said she wished she would go to Camelot, and that she had dreamed of the King, too, and not just of the King but of a red-haired barbarian woman dressed in armour and riding into battle at his side. That sounded more like a fever dream to me than a vision of the future, but I held my tongue for the sake of the affection I had for Nimue.

I asked her if she had dreamed of a dark-haired man, hoping in vain that she might have had some vision of Kay, but she shrugged and said that she dreamed of many dark-haired men and I would have to be more specific, but I could not bear to, so I could not know.

The Lady called me to her the next day, not in her hall but in her private room. It was the same as all the rest of ours, only slightly larger and with a pair of chairs set out for us at the window. I sat neatly in the chair, gazing off out at the mist, heavy with the winter, and low over the lake.

"Morgan," the Lady began slowly, folding her hands in her lap. The woad on them was old and faded, the skin of her hands slack with age and papery. She was wise, and I longed to be as old and wise as she. I was afraid a different fate awaited me. One of marriage and politics. She sighed deeply. "This is not an easy thing for me to say." She fixed me with a look of intense sincerity and I felt myself drawn into her gaze. "It has come to my attention that you have requested a certain book from Merlin."

I felt my heart quicken within me, and felt nervous. I didn't know what Merlin had said, or why I had the sense that I had done something wrong when I knew I had not.

"It was one I needed to finish my studies. Macrobius' book on the changing of shapes. I could not find it in the library," I answered.

The Lady sighed again and reached out to take my hand in hers. It felt like the parchment of the books; dry and soft and old.

"There is a reason that Avalon does not have that book. If I had known this was the path your studies had taken, I would have stopped you long ago. Morgan, I'm afraid to say that I cannot allow it. Macrobius' *Formae Mutandum* is dangerous."

"But we have his other book." I felt the desperation fire within me. I would not be sent from Avalon having completed nothing, having no new power and no new strength. I felt the injustice of it burn within me. "We have his book on the theory of dreams. What is so forbidden about the changing of shapes?"

The Lady sighed again and shook her head. "The theory of dreams is a philosophical work. The changing of shapes is the Black Arts, Morgan."

"Why? Whom does the changing of shapes harm?" My desperation had made me bold, made me desperate to plead for myself. The weary look in the Lady's eye was the same as the one I had seen Ector give Kay the day he had told Kay that he must give up Lancelot for good. I felt the stab of its absolute parental concern. She would not let me argue her objection away.

"Morgan..." she began slowly, her voice careful, "dark things have been done with that book. Merlin, he has knowledge of it, and he used that knowledge to help Uther conceive this son of his. Uther..." She drew in a breath, as though she was steeling herself. "Uther desired a lady who had a husband, and Merlin changed Uther's shape so that he could lie one night with her disguised as this husband. This boy Merlin intends to put on the throne – now, he doesn't know it and it's not his fault – but he is a child of rape. This is evil magic, and it has done harm to that poor woman. It will harm others. Now, I cannot ban Merlin from Avalon, but I can ban his Black Arts. No such thing will be practised in Avalon, Morgan."

I felt the despair clench cold inside me. I held back the tears I wanted to cry, aware that they would betray my frustration and my youth. I did not want to go powerless back to Logrys. I had worked hard. I was so close, I was *sure* I was so close to changing my shape. *I* would not have harmed anyone.

"But... I cannot go back with no magic," I pleaded.

The Lady nodded and put a gentle hand on my shoulder.

"I know, Morgan. Nor would I send you unless you had earned your woad. But you are very well-learned in the arts of herbs. You know almost as much as many whom I have sent from here with woad for the art of healing. There are few who come from abbey schools who made such good use of their time there. You do not know, truly, how much you know. How much you learned in your time there. I will take you in to my personal instruction on this, and you will soon be ready. Before the Christians celebrate epiphany you will have your woad, and go from here a great healer. You must give up these thoughts of changing your shape."

I nodded mutely. It would not all be for nothing, then. It would just be for less than I had hoped. I had wanted the strength to protect myself from anyone. I was not sure I was suited for it, but I dared not contradict the Lady.

At least I still had the sword. When the Lady dismissed me, I went and got it out from under my bed, and held it tight against me. Excalibur would protect me. Still, I wished it were not so forbidden to change my shape.

I found that I did like my lessons with the Lady. She was strict and brisk, but in just a short week she had taught me enough of the arts of healing that I could make all of the potions in her book. She told me, besides, that I had a natural talent for it, that I had as much healing magic in my touch as she did, though I half-suspected that it was mainly said to dissuade me from any thoughts of shape-changing. But still, I was glad that I would go from that place a proper witch, with all the skills I needed to be recognised as one.

When the Lady told me that I was ready for the woad I felt excited nonetheless, and Nimue was excited with me. The day was set for a few days before Christmas, and Nimue came to eat her evening meal with me in my room and told me that it felt strange but that it would not hurt. I was glad of her company, of her quiet voice, but I knew that getting my woad would be the beginning of my journey away from Avalon, and a journey to Camelot, where I did not want to go. I did not want to go to Uther's capital. News had come that day, too, that a boy had passed Merlin's king-test and pulled Uther's sword from the stone. So, it was only just in time. I would have to go with Merlin to see this boy, to see if he was truly Uther's son. A new King so fast. I ought to have been hopeful, but I felt heavy with dread.

It was late at night and I was already dressed for bed, my hair loose, when I heard a soft knock on my door. It was deep dark outside, with just a few pale stars showing in the cloudy night, but I had my window open because I was still reading by the light of the candles, and I didn't want their smoke to make me cough and give me away for reading late into the night.

I thought it would be Nimue, so I did not bother to throw a cloak over my nightdress, but when I opened the door, I lifted my candle to see that it was Merlin.

"I brought you that book you wanted, Morgan," he said softly, and there it was in his hands. I handed him the candle and took the book from him in both hands, feeling the pleasant warm, smooth feeling of the old much-handled leather, turning away from him, too absorbed to remember to thank him, and walking into the room. I felt my heart thudding. Once more I had what I had desired in my hands. I ought to have turned him and the book of black magic away, but I did not. I could not. In that book was the hope that I could go into Logrys full of the power to defend myself. I would not turn that away. Not when I had almost given it up, and it had come to me. Behind me, I was half aware of him stepping in after me and shutting the door.

Merlin came behind me, close, and held the candle over my shoulder as I opened the book and traced the lettering, feeling the slight bump of the ink on the vellum, on the first page. The book was smaller than I had expected, but that was all to the good. It would be easier to hide. Despite the fact that I knew my Latin, I only half-recognised the words on the page, both familiar and alien in their ancientness.

"We should read it now," he said, and I turned to him and saw he had a skin of wine. I did not much like the taste of wine, nor did I really want to stay up all night reading with Merlin, but this might be the only chance I got to read Macrobius' book, and besides Merlin had poured two cups out already and handed one to me, saying, "It is best to read a book such as this in this way."

He sounded so authoritative, and everyone knew him to be wise, so I set the book down on my desk, and the candle beside it, and took the wine from him. I turned back to the book. I had the strength for the darkness within it. The wine was strong, and filled with delicious heady spices. After a few drinks from my cup, when I looked down again at the words they *did* seem to make more sense. I felt Merlin come close behind me, and follow the words on the page with his eyes as I read them. He reached around me every so often to point at words on the page, to explain their meaning softly, or where they had come from, or where I could find a certain herb. I was aware of his closeness increasingly, though I only realised how long we must have been reading when Merlin poured the end of the skin of wine in to my cup and I saw the last few little drops fall out. It was delicious, after all, and the more I drank the more I seemed to want, and the less the lateness of the night worried me, and the fact that I knew I would be woken early on little sleep. I just wanted to taste more of the wine, and read more of the book.

It was when I reached the page about transforming back that I felt Merlin lift my long, loose hair gently away from the nape of my neck, and felt his lips against my skin as he wound an arm around my waist and drew me back towards him.

"Merlin, no," I whispered. I was thinking of Kay, and the woodland, suddenly, and how good it had felt to have Kay touch me, and to be close with him. I didn't want anyone else. With the wine swimming in my blood the memory of it came back to me strong, overwhelming. I half-thought I could smell the lilac tree above me, and taste the sweet juice of strawberries in my mouth. This changed in me with the warmth of the wine from wanting no one but Kay to wanting *someone*. I tried to push the thought, push the desire away.

"Morgan," Merlin whispered in my ear, as he pressed his lips there, too, "You still have much to learn."

I wanted to say that I already knew it, that Merlin did not know all about me like he knew all about everything else, but my head was reeling and when he moved his hands around to my breasts… Merlin was wise and powerful, and I admired that. I didn't want him to leave. So, this was to be the exchange. Me for the forbidden book. I was not unwilling – I thought Merlin handsome enough – and I knew the price better than Merlin thought I did. If I did not throw myself into this chance for the book, then I might never get to finish it. Besides, I wanted it now, with his hands on my body and the wine strong in my blood.

I turned over my shoulder to meet Merlin's eye, and, sliding his hands into my hair, he drew me into a kiss. He was eager, slightly forceful, different entirely from how Kay had been, but I could not have said that in that moment I did not like it. I felt his hands untie the lacing at the front of my nightdress and slide inside. The sensation of a man's hands against my bare skin made me give an unconscious shudder of delight and anticipation, and the warmth of his touch spread through my body with the wine and I was filled with a glow of desire. He turned me around roughly to face him, and pushing the book out of the way, lifted me on to the desk. I heard the book fall to the floor, and dimly hoped both that it was not damaged and that he would forget it when he left. I felt his hand light between my legs until I gasped, then harder until the breath came ragged from me and I felt the heat rise up within me, mixing with the wine, drowning out the thoughts in my head of the lateness of the night, the book, even of Kay. No, it was not that I forgot my thoughts of Kay, but that they merged with the feel of Merlin, the hardness of his lips on mine, the insistence of his passion, and perhaps I foolishly imagined a tenderness that was not there, because that was all I had known with Kay. In that moment, I did not care. In the guttering light of the dying candles, full of secret knowledge and dreaming of power, I wanted Merlin, and I cried out when he went hard inside me, holding me tight against him, his mouth hot against mine. The feel of him against me, inside me, filled me with a bright heat that spread slowly through me, and deepened, and I swam with it, with the feel of his lips on mine, his hands on me, my memories of Kay. I held tight to him, my hands tangling through Merlin's thick curls, until he grasped me by the wrists and groaned with desperate relief.

I slid from the desk into his arms, as the heat and desire drained out of us both. Though he lay down on the narrow bed with me for a little while, he was gone before I had fully sunk into sleep.

It was only in the morning, when I heard the bells for prime – so Merlin's wine had made me sleep too late – and looked around the room, scattered with the disarray of the night before, that I realised what the real reason was that he had come to me last night, what I had really exchanged for that forbidden book.

Excalibur was gone.

Chapter Seven

I went to have my woad, burning with rage and resentment at Merlin for having tricked me. Still, I had his dark book wrapped in my mother's old fur cloak at the bottom of my bag. I looked for him in the halls of Avalon, ready to demand my sword back, but he was not there.

The ritual of the woad took place in a building high on the tor which was like a chapel, except empty of any decoration and open to the air that whipped through it, cold, from four huge open windows, and gaping rooflessly open to the sky. Inside stood the Lady of Avalon, and Nimue at her side – whom I was pleased to see, and who seemed to be swiftly earning herself a powerful position on the isle despite her youth – and a man I had not seen before with eyes dark black as coal, shaven-headed in a black cowl and tattooed all over his bald head, and the hands that peeped from his long, wide sleeves, with the blue-green woad. I could not guess his age from his strange looks, his grim too-pale skin beneath the woad, his teeth that peeped skull-like from his grin. I felt a quiver of fear within me at the sight of the strange man, but I supposed he must be some ancient practitioner of the ritual.

I had been prepared for this moment, at least, by the description Nimue had given me of it, and I was not alarmed when the Lady

48

instructed me gently to remove my dress. I stood naked before the three of them, the cold wind of winter whistling through the empty building raising the fine dark hairs on my skin, and giving me goosebumps. I thought those women that came in summer had by far the better deal. Still, I would not have put off this moment for anything in the world. I unwound the plait of my hair and felt the long, thick glossy rope of it fall loose around me, all down my back. The Lady stepped forward with a cup of something that she pressed in to my hands. I drank it in a single gulp. I knew from Nimue that it would taste thick and acrid, and I knew from the Lady's book what was in it. The same foul herbs that gave the mists of Avalon their smell, and those who breathed the mists their vivid dreams of the future.

I felt it cloud my mind, fast, and I felt myself slip away just as gentle hands lay me down on the ice-cold stone, and the far-off prickings of the tattooing needles, and smelled the earthy scent of the woad, but I was moving away from it already.

I saw myself first, though I barely recognised myself. I was a woman deep into adulthood, the woad faded on my face like the Lady's, but still visible in swirls and whorls of blue-green against my pale skin. I *did* look like my mother, though where age had made her grey eyes soft and kind, mine looked intelligent, yet harsh. I was not displeased with that, though I was alarmed to see a crown of dark gold on my head, twisted into points like a thick rope of thorns, and set with blood red rubies. I did not know that crown, but obviously I had been married to a king. I stood at the top of a spiral staircase in a dark stone castle, unfamiliar, but there was one thing familiar, and that was the sword drawn in my hand. So, I would get Excalibur back. As the vision of myself stepped towards me, it faded, and I saw myself with Excalibur in my hand again, standing on the shores of Avalon. I was older still, middle-aged, my hair striped through with grey at the temples, and my head was bare, my hair loose, and I was dressed in the black of mourning. Beside me was the red-haired woman I had dreamed of before. Her face was smeared with dirt, and through the dirt ran the tracks of tears. She was dressed in some strange dress that looked to be half rich green samite, half armour, with greaves up to the elbow and an armoured bodice. That vision faded fast, before I even had time to work out what I was seeing, who the red-haired woman whom I had seen with Kay, and with me, was, and I saw myself again, standing before a knight I did not know with Excalibur in my hand. I was younger there than I had been in the other visions, but before I could work out what was going on, that too faded and more and more images of myself rushed past me again and again. I saw myself with my sister, her hands wrapped around a huge pregnant belly, the two of us lying side by side on a bed I did not recognise, and tears running down her cheeks. I had never seen my sister Morgawse cry before. We looked young, in that vision. So, that would be soon. I saw the strange skull-faced grinning man beside Arthur, grown to a man and dressed in splendid armour. I saw Kay ride up to me on his horse and pull off his helm only for me to see it was the red-haired woman dressed in his armour, and all of these faces – Kay, Arthur, Morgawse, the skull-faced man, the red-haired woman, Nimue, myself, the Lady of Avalon, Kay again, Lancelot – all rushed past my mind in a sickening swirl. The last thing I saw before I plunged into darkness was Lancelot standing over Arthur, whose helm had rolled away and whose head was bare, his sword raised and ready to strike.

I had no idea what any of it could mean.

When I eventually woke again, I was back in my own room. I felt gloriously rested, and through the lovely fog of sleep it took me a while to remember all of the disturbing visions of the future I had seen. I supposed I had seen the futures of the men I knew; I did not see otherwise why so much of Arthur and Lancelot would have come to me in my dreams. Or Kay, though I was not surprised that I had dreamed of him, since I thought of him often. I wondered again who the woman had been, fierce-eyed and red-haired. And the shaven-headed man who had been there when I was woaded. Nimue had told me it was best to put them away, to think nothing of them, and wait until they made sense. I had to decide to do that. But I had seen much of Kay, and I thought with guilt about what I had done with Merlin. I was not sure if I should tell Kay, if I should confess to him. Kay might have found another woman by now. He had not written to me again, though I had not written to him.

I touched my face lightly. It was still slightly hot, slightly sore. I peered at myself as well as I could in the glass of my window-pane. I liked it, the blue of the woad. I looked frightening and mysterious, as a witch should.

I checked under the bed again with little hope. Merlin had not returned Excalibur. However, when I felt in my bag as I dressed and packed the last of my things into it, Macrobius' book on the changing of shapes was still unmoved. It was not a fair exchange, I thought, but it seemed to be considered a done deal by Merlin nonetheless.

I was not looking forward to seeing him when he took me to Camelot. He had tricked me and I was both furious and powerless to have any kind of revenge.

When I walked out with my bag and wrapped in a wool cloak to say goodbye to the Lady and Nimue at the little dock, I noticed that Merlin was still not there. Instead, the bald woaded man stood beside them. And in his hands he had my sword. Though I knew it was not likely to be so, I hoped that he had come to return it to me.

I thanked the Lady, and kissed her on the cheek, feeling the hot of my newly tattooed skin brush her cheek, cool from the winter breeze, and wrapped Nimue in to an embrace. Neither of us had expected me to do it, since it was neither of our manner, but after an autumn and winter of growing close, I would not have felt right leaving without it.

I looked around. Still no sign of Merlin.

"Where is Merlin?" I asked the Lady, keeping half an eye on my sword in the bald man's hands.

The bald-headed man grinned broad.

"I am Merlin," he said. I felt sick. Where was the handsome young man? The Lady's words rang in my ears, *dark things have been done with that book*. How had I not suspected that Merlin the shape-changer would have changed his ugly form to get what he wanted from me? This man was middle-aged, slightly bent in the back. His lips were blackened from taking some herb or another. He was repulsive. Of course I would never have touched him, or let him alone in my bedroom to read with me. I felt the resentment burn deeper within me. I had been tricked, too, into thinking I ought to be honoured by it. That he was a young man, a handsome man, a great man of wisdom and power. He was powerful, of course, but I hardly thought his nasty deceptiveness could co-exist with wisdom, and I was certainly not *grateful*. I suppressed a shudder. I felt suddenly cold, and clammy, and disgusted with myself.

The Lady met my eye, and I saw in there her understanding, and her sympathy, but also the warning that this was the danger, the darkness of the changing of shapes.

If I could have, I would have run from Merlin then. But it was too late.

My feet followed him into the barge, while my breath was frozen in my lungs. I wanted to cry out against it all, to scream to Nimue for help, or for revenge, but I went, obedient as a lamb, because I could think of nothing else to do. So I would go with the man who had tricked me to the castle of the stepfather who had threatened me and sent me away, to kneel before his bastard rape-child. I felt the disgust all over me. Still, I had tucked in my bag both the Lady's book of medicines and potions, and Macrobius' book on the changing of shapes. I was not vulnerable any more. Besides, I had seen that I would get back my sword.

Beside Merlin in the barge, I tucked my legs up and wrapped my arms around them, trying to make myself as small and as far from him as possible. He grinned at me. I felt sick.

"So, is this your real shape?" I demanded, resentfully.

"They are all my real shape," Merlin replied archly. "When I want something from a pretty young girl, I go as you saw me before, and when I want something from a warlike old king I come as a white-haired old man, and when I want something of an eager young king, I come like this. You will learn, little Morgan, that it is as well to frighten people as to seduce them to get what you want."

"Give me back my sword," I demanded again, though I had no room to bargain with.

"Give me back my book," Merlin countered, with a deepening grin. I did not assent. I had seen myself with the sword in the future, and I had not yet finished with the book. Defeated for the moment, I slumped back against the edge of the barge. Merlin clicked his tongue. "That sword is not meant for you. Its destiny is with the new King, and the new King's destiny is with it."

He was a fool. The sword was made for me. It did not belong to anyone else. We passed the rest of the journey in a resentful silence. I felt sick at the sight of Merlin. I was sure this ugly shape *was* his real shape. It was the woad. He had not had the woad when he had been the young man. The thought of his hands on me made me shudder, and I wished that I was brave or strong enough to shove him from the boat to drown in the water, but who knew the depths of the Black Arts that he knew? Besides, he might have taken the sword in with him, and then I would never get it back.

I wished that I had never left Ector's house. All those visions I had had of Kay had only made me miss him more. I decided I would not tell him, though, about Merlin. I was sure I could not explain how I had done what I had done for the sake of a book of black magic without making him hate me. I would keep that to myself, and only hope that he had not found a different girl. I did not know, though, how long it would be until I saw him. The thought suddenly struck me that Kay might have been killed. I pushed that thought from my mind, quick as it came.

The journey with Merlin was slow, because the snows had come. We did not get far each day, and had to stop often, so it was almost a month before we reached Camelot, and when we arrived, Camelot was almost empty. Everyone, they told us, was in the great Cathedral in London, watching Uther's boy prove his right to be king by pulling the sword from Merlin's magic stone.

So, we rode on. We reached London as spring did, and I was glad that we would finally be somewhere. Merlin and I travelled together in an inimical silence all the way from Avalon, only speaking when we needed to, and each jealously guarding the sword and the book.

Pavilions had been set up around the great Cathedral, huge with thick swathes of silk flapping in the spring breeze. I could hear sounds echoing inside, too, of shouting and cheering. This son of Uther's must have spent all winter putting the sword in and out of the stone to prove himself. Now at last Merlin had come to claim him. I wondered what Merlin would do to the boy. It seemed to me more Merlin's lust for power than his desire to see the right man on the throne that had brought him here. He had made Uther King, after all. Was that because he had wanted to control him? But once Uther was King, he had all but disappeared, until Uther was on his deathbed. What did Merlin want with Uther's bastard son? I was not sure I wanted Uther's son to be my king, not if he was anything like his father.

Men moved out of the way at the sight of me and Merlin, with our woaded faces, and he with his huge chain of gold and the huge sapphire set in it. They knew that we were witches, and they were reluctant to brush against us. Merlin pushed the heavy doors of the Cathedral open and inside I heard the roar of cheering again as a small figure at the far end, before the altar draped in red and gold, drew the rusting old sword from the block of stone and held it above his head. All I could see from where I stood was a glint of gold hair, and beneath it a red and gold surcoat that I knew as one of Uther's. So the son was wearing his father's clothes already. People were accepting him as their king. The boy's raised hands hid his face from me, but as Merlin and I walked closer and the cheering rose around us, the light streaming red and gold through the huge stained-glass window behind the boy, he turned, the sword held over his head to smile at the crowd, and I saw his face and my heart stopped. It was Arthur. *Arthur.*

"That's not Uther's son," I cried out, unable to stop myself, and a murmur of disapproval grew up around me. Arthur was the younger brother. Arthur was the *younger*. If Arthur was going to be made king, did that mean Kay was dead? I could not see Kay, nor their father, anywhere in the Cathedral.

Arthur saw me when he heard my voice and, dropping the sword, ran down to throw his arms around me in a rough, good-natured embrace. After a moment of this, which I barely noticed through how stunned I was, he held me away, at arm's length. His mouth hung open, stunned, and his eyes were wide and excited. Over the months of winter, when he had turned only thirteen, he had grown even more, though he was still not quite as tall as I was.

I could see the rapturous disbelief on his kind, honest face. Arthur had come to this moment by mistake. But all I wanted to ask was *where is Kay?*

Behind us, I could see other men lining up to pull the sword from the stone, but once it was in the stone again none of them could budge it, even though there were men twice Arthur's size there. Merlin's stone had truly chosen him king. Suddenly, awfully, the voice of the Lady of Avalon came back to me; *he does not know it, and it is not his fault, but he is a child of rape.* I did not know why I had not seen the likeness he bore to Uther before, how Arthur bore his father's fair, Germanic look, the look of the folk from the flat middle of Logrys. Kay and I were old Celtic blood, tall and slight, where Arthur was fair and stocky like Uther had been. I wondered what kind of woman his mother had been. She must have been kind-faced, for Arthur had not got that from his father. With an awful sinking feeling in my stomach I realised that I knew who Arthur's mother was. That Uther must have taken kind old Ector's shape to rape the mother Kay and Arthur shared. Perhaps he had wanted her magic blood for his own child, or perhaps it was just that he was a beast of lust, for Ector's wife had been beautiful. I wondered if Arthur had even begun to think about such things, such awful possibilities.

"Morgan…" Arthur began, his voice stunned. "Morgan… I'm the King."

I gave a slow nod, still taking it in. Arthur, though he had been performing this trick with the sword and the stone since Christmas, which was when Merlin had said he had done it first, still seemed as though he had not fully taken it in. I opened my mouth to try to answer, but Merlin stepped in front of me. I saw Arthur flinch back from the sight of him, and I did not blame him.

"Arthur, I was your lord father's chief advisor and counsellor, and I have come to offer myself in the same role to you. Also, it is I who put Uther's sword in the stone. Do you accept?"

Arthur nodded, as though he were hypnotised. I wanted to say *this man helped your father rape your mother*, but I said nothing. I would bide my time with Merlin, though I did not trust him.

"You're a witch?" Arthur asked him, with all the clumsy bluntness of a child. Merlin nodded, and Arthur looked warily pleased. "You, too, now Morgan," he said to me, with a smile.

"Me, too," I replied. I felt the warmth of my fondness for Arthur about me; the fondness of a sister for a brother, after all our years together as children. His sweet, youthful face beamed out at the men cheering his name, and to please them he ran back to draw the sword from the stone again, and the roar of cheering got louder. He was just a boy, but he was popular already. Merlin's little trick had made sure of that.

As dusk was beginning to fall, Arthur invited me and Merlin back to his pavilion, the grandest one in dark blue-green outside the Cathedral. Inside it was draped with silks, rich but faded. Uther's old things, inherited riches. Newly acquired, and Arthur, too, seemed not quite used to them. I saw no sign, still, of Ector and Kay. Arthur could, surely, not have forgotten his father and brother as soon as he was found to be king?

"We shall set the day for the official coronation, my Lord Arthur," Merlin began, in his rasping voice – it had been so different, I noted, while he had borne the shape of a young man – full of dark persuasion. He was going to try to control Arthur already. "And you shall take your father's seat at Camelot." Stunned and tired, Arthur nodded, shrugging off the red and gold surcoat and sinking into a chair in his shirt and breeches. "And, my Lord Arthur, I bring you a gift."

From deep within his cloak, Merlin drew my sword in its scabbard. I felt the rage within me. I was ready to open my mouth and say it was my sword, for I was sure that Arthur would have what was rightfully mine returned to me, when Merlin spoke again.

"This sword is Excalibur, cutter of steel, and it was made for you in Avalon. Its destiny is with you, Arthur, and you will become a great king with it at your side." Arthur, mesmerised at the sight of the gold and the jewels, and the silky, wheedling promise in Merlin's words, reached out, took it by the pommel and drew it. It weighed heavy in his hands, and it took both of them around its hilt for him to hold it point-upwards. There was no Otherworld in Arthur.

"Which do you like better, my Lord Arthur?" Merlin asked, softly, his eyes flashing with a dangerous amusement that I did not like at all. "The sword, or the scabbard?"

Arthur did not look down at the scabbard at all. His eyes were fixed on the blade of the sword, the gentle ripples in the smooth steel where the icy waters of Avalon's lake had tempered it, its paleness, its cool hard perfection.

"The sword, of course," Arthur replied, breathless with wonder at the weapon in his hands.

"Then you are foolish, sire. For, whoever wears the scabbard can spill not a drop of blood."

Arthur reddened, glancing down at Merlin and the scabbard. He looked like a scolded child. I could tell that he did not like being called foolish. He snatched the scabbard from Merlin and buckled it about himself, sliding my sword into it.

"Guard the sword and the scabbard well, Arthur," Merlin warned.

I did not want Arthur guarding the sword and the scabbard well. He had no magic blood; an ordinary sword and scabbard would be just as good to him. It was ridiculous. Excalibur and its scabbard belonged with me. I eyed him slyly, standing in his shirt and breeches with the jewelled scabbard slung low around his hips, his hand against the pommel of my sword, imagining himself a grown man and the king he must be, and in that moment, though I loved Arthur as a brother, I was resolved that whatever it took, I would get my sword back from him, and the scabbard too, even if it meant his life.

Chapter Eight

We rode for Camelot the next day, and I was glad of it. I thought I would get bored watching Arthur perform the trick with the stone again and again and again, and besides it made me uneasy to see Excalibur casually resting against Arthur's hip, and he half-ignoring it. I knew I could not snatch it back, and I would have to wait, so I welcomed the distraction.

The ride was short, though Arthur chattered eagerly all the way. I was anxious, and I longed to ask him about Kay, but I dared not with Merlin beside me. I was afraid his greedy listening ears would guess too much. It was just the three of us on the road. If it were just a young boy, and old man and a girl of sixteen, we would have been easy prey in the uneasy interregnum, but Arthur dressed in Uther's surcoat and Merlin and I with our woad faces kept any attackers at bay. I supposed my blue-painted face was a better protection from attack than any armour. No man would risk his life against a witch. Little would they know that at that moment my arts exceeded no more than mending wounds and curing chills, but soon I would have strength enough to be as Merlin was, a creature of any shape. As soon as I could be alone with the book I would learn what I could of its secrets, and properly this time.

Camelot was as I had remembered it in Uther's day when we arrived this time. A vast fortress with four tall round towers, encircled in a thick wall. News had reached Uther's old capital properly of his son's emergence, and silk banners flew from the battlements, and inside the great courtyard I could see knights gathered to train. These men had come to Arthur, not yet knowing who he was. I wondered if they would be disappointed by his youth. They would not be disappointed at his size or strength, but sometimes men only saw another man's age or station. For, besides, Arthur had been raised like a common boy, though his foster-father was a knight. It had been no castle for him, no lessons with a clerk or priest, no master-at-arms to teach him to fight with miniature swords. It had been wooden sticks in the fields with Kay that had made Arthur the king he suddenly was now.

"Arthur," Merlin announced grandly, as we rode in the main gates of Camelot, thrown open to receive their King, "this is Camelot, your father's capital and his fortress. It is your seat now."

Arthur nodded dumbly, gazing around. I glanced around, too, in the crowd for Kay, but I did not see him. I did, however, see his father at the back of the crowd, a kind smile crinkling his face. He raised a hand in greeting when he saw me, and I waved back in return. I wondered how strange we must have looked to him, the two children who not long ago were splashing around together in Avalon's great lake, one now painted with woad, the other now wearing the clothes of a king. It had not been so long ago that we had played together as children. Now, Arthur wore my sword, and I carried with me a book of forbidden knowledge, and I dreaded that both of these were at once our darkest dangers and our only protection. I wondered if he had even thought what Arthur's parentage meant for him. I wondered if he had known. After all, there had been no talk of how Arthur had been fathered, and I only knew from what the Lady of Avalon had said to me. I hoped that Ector had been spared the truth.

We slid from our horses and the crowd gathered around Arthur, cheering. I felt glad that the people liked him already, but it was all overwhelming, and besides I longed to be away from Merlin, so I carefully took my things, checking for the books at the bottom of my back and comforted by the feel of the leather, and snuck away, through the crowd, up to the room that had been mine as a child.

I was pleased to find it little changed, and unoccupied, and I thought to claim it as my own. Since I was the daughter of the Queen, I did not think anyone would challenge me. I wished, once I was there, that I had searched for Ector in the crowd and asked him where I could find his older – I supposed only – son, but I had missed him in my hurry to be alone.

I had not been long at Camelot before. Our mother had brought me when she had married Uther, but his displeasure at my presence had quickly showed, and after a few short months I had been sent to the abbey. She had sent Morgawse to be married after only a few weeks at Camelot. While I looked like our mother, Morgawse was the picture of our father. No man wants to stare in to the face of a dead rival, even if that face is worn by an innocent child. Not a man as small and greedy and jealous as Uther Pendragon had been. I hated him. I even hated the sound of his name. Despite myself, I even found myself liking Arthur less because I knew now that he was somehow Uther's son, though Arthur had done me no wrong.

I slowly unpacked my things, hiding the book of Macrobius among my dresses. Having lost my sword from under my bed, I was reluctant to hide anything else there. I did not think that anyone who was looking among my dresses would know what Macrobius' book on the changing of shapes was, let alone that it was forbidden. Actually, I doubted if anyone who would rootle in my dresses would even be able to read the Latin. Even Arthur, if I had thrown the book down in front of him, would not have had a clue what it was about. It was only Merlin, really, that I had to hide it from. He spoke as though we had made an exchange, but I did not think he was above stealing the book from me again. Especially if he thought he might get something from me in return if he offered to give it back.

When I had organised my things, I decided I would go out to the courtyard again, and walk around Camelot, getting my bearings once more. I ran lightly down the stairs and out in to the fading evening light, turning my face up to the pale spring sunset, breathing in the fresh smells of Camelot, the hay of the horses, the clean grass of the fields all around. As much as I hated Uther, I had loved this castle.

"Hey, blue-face." I heard a familiar voice behind me and turned around with a smile to see Kay lounging against the doorway to the tower with a sly grin on his face. I felt myself blush, suddenly self-conscious of the new tattoos, my new face, and unconsciously I raised a hand to my cheek.

"Oh, Kay… Oh, yes, I suppose I look quite different now."

I was suddenly, painfully aware of how much I had changed in so little time, and Kay had hardly changed at all, but Kay's smile deepened and I saw the wonderful wicked glint in his eye.

"I like it," he said, beckoning me closer. I came, casting a wary look around me. There was no one watching so I came close enough for him to whisper in my ear, and felt with a thrill the slightest brush of his lips at my ear. "Are you like that… all over?"

Kay, wonderful Kay, had not changed at all. I didn't answer, and I felt him slide his arm around my waist. If Arthur saw I was sure he would be angry. He would be angry that we had a secret – for I was sure from Arthur's anger about Kay and Lancelot that he hated secrets – and his advisors would tell him to punish Kay because I was a powerful political tool for him now he was King, and he would not want Kay involved with me. I was a stepsister princess ready to be married to secure Arthur's rule. Well, I was not willing to be so. I had not gone to Avalon, nor lost my sword for black magic to be bought and sold like a horse. I would do as I pleased. Especially once I had mastered that book, and won back my sword. Kay, too, never seemed to me to be one that cared for prudence, and I was glad of it. He would not have been afraid of Arthur's reprimands; Kay would have laughed at them. Kay leaned closer and whispered again,

"Will you let me see?"

I didn't answer, but I felt my heart quicken with the anticipation of it, and when I wordlessly walked around him and into the tower, I was pleased that he followed me up. My room was on the first floor, and I was glad it was not far because I felt the keen anticipation tingle all over me, and the memories of Kay against me in the sunlight rush around me. Besides, Kay was fully a man now, and I a woman, and we were not saying goodbye.

I had meant for us to talk. I had wanted to tell Kay everything about Avalon, about my dreams, about the book. But the moment we stepped through the door his hands were in my hair and he was kissing me in that way of his that was somehow gentle and reckless at the same time, and any resolve I had had to tell the truth melted completely away. I didn't know how much I had missed him until I felt his hands on me, until he slipped me out of my dress and whispered, "You *are* like that all over," with such great delight that I knew that I had come home to somewhere I belonged. We belonged to each other. I should have said, *not here, not now.* I should have said, *haven't you thought about what this means, now that Arthur is King?* But I didn't. I wanted him and I wanted comfort and closeness. I wanted something to undo being used by Merlin. Our coming together felt like that, and besides I was bolder now, and I knew what I wanted. And he was happy to give it to me.

So we didn't talk until afterwards, until it was growing late and we lay tangled together among the sheets that we had barely had time to pull back from the bed, and it was already too late to consider any of those things I knew we should have done. In the end, it was Kay who spoke first.

"I have missed you, Morgan," he said quietly. I moved closer against him, resting my hand on his chest. It looked strange, painted with blue, against the untouched paleness of his own skin.

"Why are you sad?" I whispered.

Kay sighed, and gathered me closer against him.

"Everything has changed, Morgan. Everything." He shook his head in disbelief, as though he were trying to work it all out. "I... Arthur and I went to this tournament, at Christmastime, and Arthur had been such a bad squire I thought I would teach him a lesson and hide my sword. Well, what does Arthur do, because he is too lazy to go all the way back to our tent? He ducks into the nearest building to look for one. It's a church, and he brings out that damned sword of Uther's stuck in the stone. Well, he can't read so he didn't know what it said on the stone, and he hands the thing to me and everyone's shouting, asking where I got the sword, and I turn to him and he said he got it from some stone, so I say I got it from the stone and everyone's shouting at me, demanding I go back and put it in and take it out again. Father is white as a sheet by now, and I can see him trembling and I'm trying to explain that *I* didn't take it from the stone, but no one is listening and it's only when they push me to the church to do it they finally listen when I say it's Arthur. Arthur is the one who got it from the stone. He can't read the damn stone, but I can. 'Rightwise King of Britain'. So, Arthur puts it in and pulls it out, and everyone around us falls to their knees, and father beside me pulls me down with him because I'm standing there staring like an idiot, and Arthur, poor Arthur, he stares at us with his eyes all huge and he looks like he's about to cry, and he says "So… you are not my father… and Kay is not my brother?" in this awful, tiny voice, and people are rushing all around us, and my father beside me is shaking his head, trying to explain to Arthur – and to me – why he brought us up as brothers when Merlin brought Arthur to him to be fostered, and Arthur looks all the time like he's going to cry but he doesn't because he's realising that he's the King now. It was awful. It was *awful*, Morgan."

The words tumbled out of Kay in a strange, jumbled present tense as though he was experiencing the whole disorientating rush of it around himself again. I could imagine that moment, when the world that had once made sense made sense no longer, and Kay had looked at his brother and seen someone else entirely. But I was relieved, just a little, that it had not been Kay's mother who had been Uther's victim. But then, who could Arthur's mother have been?

Kay sighed again, wrapping me more tightly in his arms. I rested my head against his chest, listening to the quick beat of his heart, feeling the softness of his skin against my cheek.

"I remember him, as a baby," Kay said, softly. "And before that, dimly, I remember my mother being pregnant. I suppose she must have lost that child, and that's why Merlin brought Arthur to her. But I remember him as a baby, his little gold head and – god, he used to cry. Now he is the King. The King of all of Britain." Kay sighed again, pressing a kiss against the top of my head. "I suppose that means we ought not to be doing this. I don't want to get you in trouble when it's time for you to get married. Though, I suppose, we spilt that milk a while ago now, before it seemed like it mattered, eh?" I turned my face up to Kay, and he kissed me gently again. "I suppose we won't do any extra harm, if no one finds out."

Kay sank back against the pillow, staring up above him. I saw him sigh with the realisation that we would not get the innocence of our summer days back. I wished I could have honestly told him that we would, but I could not. Kay was not, then, without the thoughts of politics and consequences that he had ignored just a little less than a year ago. He had seen his younger brother turn into the King of Britain. I supposed that made a man wonder about his place in the world, but I wished it had not made him wonder. Quietly, thoughtfully, he said, "Still, I'm afraid this cannot last."

"Why not?" I sat up, suddenly fired with a thought. "We could marry. I am a princess, and Ector is the son of a king in France. Why not?"

Kay shook his head, and an awful, dark, hopeless look came across his face.

"My father is a prince, but my mother was just a girl he met on the shores of Avalon. He lost his place among his brothers marrying her. You are Igraine's daughter. You are Cornwall. You'll get a king, not a half-commoner knight like me."

I lay back down beside him, disturbed by what I knew was the truth of his words. It would not be long before someone told Arthur to have me married off to someone. It was not a wise political move to leave a princess floating around on her own without tying down an allegiance with her. I did not want to get married, though. Not if it was not to Kay.

"Maybe no one will want to marry me," I said, quietly. "First I was plain, now I'm painted like this. Maybe no men will want me."

Kay said nothing, just gently stroked my hair. When I gazed at him, he was staring up, directly above him at the ceiling. We both knew that it would not matter. The world had changed when Arthur had pulled the sword from the stone, and we would all have to swiftly become political adults, thinking of the realm rather than ourselves. I was the daughter of a queen, and marriage would come for me, no matter how unwilling I was.

Chapter Nine

When I woke up Kay was gone, but he had left a little note scrawled on the back of a scrap of paper on my desk. When I saw it, I realised how slowly and carefully he must have written the letter he had sent me, for this was far scruffier and I had to struggle to read it. It just said,

"I had to go, very important knightly duties. I like the blue – K."

I folded it up tight and slipped it between my dresses, along with the book. When my hand brushed the book I felt another stab of guilt about Merlin, but I pushed it away. It had been a mistake. I did not have to carry all my guilty mistakes around with me.

I would wait a while before I read the book, I thought. I wanted to wait until Merlin had gone, but I did not know when that would be. I had the uncomfortable feeling that he would sense that I was reading it, and come back, and while Kay was in Camelot I wanted to keep Merlin as far away from me as possible. I pulled on my plain black wool dress and tied my hair into a plait. The dull, automatic actions of readying myself soothed me, just a little, and I walked down to the courtyard, to see what was happening. There was a crowd of knights gathered, fighting together in training. They all looked awfully young to me. At the edge of the crowd, I could see Kay standing beside Lancelot. They were leaning against the courtyard wall, and Kay was leaning down to whisper something in his ear. I felt the little flutter of jealousy within me, but I decided to ignore it. After all, Ector stood there with them, and I did not think that Kay would stand there with Lancelot and his father if whatever had been happening between them was still going on. He had seemed, after all, to heed his father's words. They seemed to have stuck with him, for there had been something of them in his worried words to me – that we ought to be thinking about our duties and our families rather than one another.

Kay saw me and gave a little nod, and a half smile, and when Lancelot followed his gaze and recognised me he gave a reserved wave. I was not sure what Kay had seen in him. He was dull and quiet and serious. Though, I supposed, to Lancelot I too must appear dull and quiet and serious. Perhaps it was people like us who were attracted to Kay, because he was bright and loud and fun.

I could see, too, on the other side of the crowd, Arthur, a stunned look still on his face, standing beside Merlin who was talking in his ear. That made me uneasy. The sun glinted on Excalibur's hilt at Arthur's side and I felt the little burn of anger in my stomach. I was still furious that Merlin had stolen my sword.

Trying to distract myself from them, I watched the knights training together. They were young, but many of them were good. I was surprised at how good they were. Lancelot, whom I had always thought of as small and slight, had grown even taller over the winter, and more wiry, and I was surprised to see him knock the swords from the hands of men almost twice his size. It was clear from the way he moved that he had a talent for it, for fighting. He would be a great warrior soon. He was among the strongest already, and he moved with a quick, catlike grace that made it hard for any of his opponents to land a blow on him. I could see Arthur's excitement as he watched him fight, and it was only when Arthur stepped forward with his practice sword that Lancelot seemed to be in any danger of losing at all. Arthur, the kind-hearted clumsy boy I had known as a child, had a warrior's blood in him, and was growing huge already about the shoulders and the chest. He was not as fast as Lancelot, but the power he put behind every blow was easy to see, and he appeared to do it with so little effort. I remembered, suddenly, the dream I had had while I was painted, of the two of them in battle, it had seemed, with one another, and Lancelot poised to kill Arthur. It had looked to me more than twenty years away, but even with that knowledge, I could not see what would turn those two men against one another. Their fight in the yard was good-natured, companionable, and they clapped each other on the back afterwards, when they had agreed a draw, laughing and flushed from the pleasure of fighting. They were like brothers. It was clear, too, that fighting had brought them closer together, as each recognised the other's skill. I could not imagine anything turning them against one another, no more than I could imagine Kay turning against Arthur.

It was Kay who stepped forward next to fight with Lancelot. Kay was a little slower, but sharper, more devious. Lancelot, with all the deadpan honour of a man who had been raised as a king's son, fighting fair, did not expect it when Kay darted a foot out to trip him. He stumbled back, but he didn't fall, and a noise that was half approval of Lancelot's skill, half disapproval of Kay's tricks rose from the crowd. But that was what battle was like. I hoped that sharp wit and clever tricks would be enough to keep Kay alive. But he was strong, too, and lasted a long time before Lancelot knocked the sword from his hand, and at the end they, too, were both laughing. But these were games, the swords short and blunted. What would it be like when blood was spilled, and the fallen friend could not be picked back up to his feet unharmed?

There would be those who did not accept a boy-king, especially since there had been no real proof of Arthur's parentage other than his golden hair and Merlin's trick with the stone. No mother had stepped forward to claim him as her child.

After the training was over, I saw Kay slip off to the stables as the others dispersed. Merlin and Arthur, too, I saw walk off to the tower that had been Uther's. Merlin had all of Arthur's attention, it seemed, and all of his trust.

It wasn't long before I saw Kay come out of the stables again, dressed in his black Otherworld armour, on a huge armoured horse and holding a shield that bore the great grey keys of the Seneschal's office. When he saw I was still out in the yard, and looking over at him, he smiled and waved. I walked over slowly. The horse was still and calm with Kay on it, and let me put out a hand to stroke its velvety nose. I peered up at Kay, against the brightness of the spring sunshine, and saw him smiling down at me.

"You're the Seneschal, are you?" I asked him.

He grinned. "Not bad for a shabby small town knight like me, eh? I suppose it pays if the King thinks you're his brother for almost fourteen years." He leaned down a little closer to me. "Morgan, Arthur's sending some of us to Cornwall, to fetch your mother. He thinks she will be safer here."

I nodded. I wanted to go. I wanted him to take me with him, and to see my mother and to see Tintagel, my childhood home, again, but I did not ask. I did not think Kay would be dressed to depart like that if it was going to be a safe journey. There was not peace and acceptance throughout Britain of Arthur's new rule, of course, but I was sorry to see that it was so in Cornwall.

"Shouldn't the Seneschal stay at court?" I asked. I thought it was his duty to keep the capital safe and in running order, to make sure the law courts were working properly, to keep track of the lands.

Kay sighed in his saddle. "If I don't go, there might not be a court. There's no one else Arthur trusts to fetch Queen Igraine. He thinks other men will be out to steal her and marry her and try to take the throne for themselves." Kay gave a wicked grin, then. "Who knows, maybe Arthur's not so clever to send me."

He was teasing me, pretending he would marry my mother. I gave him a playful shove, and he laughed.

"Oh Morgan, you know I would far rather steal *you*." It was a joke, or it had begun as one, but as he finished I saw the sadness creep across his face. We knew it could not be. I opened my mouth to say something, some kind of painful, inadequate goodbye, but as I did I heard a voice, familiar with its deep tones of southern French, call Kay's name from the gates. So, Lancelot was riding to Cornwall, too. Kay sighed and turned back to me. "I have to go, Morgan. I hope I will not be long."

He reached down his hand to clasp mine as I offered it up to him, and for a moment I saw him close his eyes as though he was making a wish, and then he let go of my hand, and waved, and flashed me his wicked smile, and left.

One late autumn evening when the sun was low and red in the sky, streaming through the window, I went to my bedroom, hoping to be alone. When I opened the door to my bedroom, I felt a shock go through me as I thought I saw Kay sitting in the chair at my window, but as I blinked in disbelief, he changed before my eyes in to Merlin as I had seen him as a young man. I felt the burn of rage within me. So, Merlin thought himself very clever. The young Merlin gave me a handsome half-smile, but I was no longer susceptible to him and crossed my arms in the doorway, refusing to shut the door.

"Oh yes, Morgan. I know all about you and the Seneschal. I have known everything about you. How did you think I knew that you liked dark, skinny boys?" Merlin stood, walking over to me. I hung back. I was not going to step in to the room with him. If he would not leave, then I would. "But not so skinny now, our Sir Kay. He's becoming a man made for war, and men made for war don't last long."

"What do you want, Merlin?" I demanded sharply.

"Nothing yet," he replied archly, coming closer. I stepped back into the corridor, and he laughed. "Have you finished with my book?"

"No. Have you finished with my sword?"

He laughed again.

"It's not your sword any more, Morgan. It's Arthur's sword."

"It is *mine*," I hissed at him, feeling the anger burn through my veins.

Merlin wrapped an arm around me and pulled me against him, into the room, slamming the door behind us with his other hand. He was stronger and faster than I would have thought, and he caught me by surprise, pressing his mouth against mine in a violent attempt at a kiss. I pushed him off me, hard, and he stepped back. I could feel that I was flushed with anger, full of its strength, breathing hard with it already. I did not have any weapon, nor even one tenth of his black magic strength, but I had my anger. If Merlin thought he could have me again because he had had me once then he was wrong.

"Merlin, *leave*," I demanded.

He gave a facetious little bow. "If that is what you desire, my Lady," he said, his voice returning to its rasping wheedle, his form to the ugly shaven-headed man. When he left, I bolted the door.

When he was gone, I wrote to Nimue, asking her what news had reached Avalon, and if she was planning to come to Camelot. With Kay gone, and Arthur utterly absorbed by Merlin and his newfound role as king, I felt as though I needed an ally.

When it was spring again, Kay returned with news that none of them could convince Queen Igraine to leave Tintagel. She would come, he said, when her daughter Morgawse was at Camelot with her. Morgawse, my sister, was Queen of Lothian and I supposed that our mother wanted the protection of a fellow queen at the court of this new king, whom she as yet had no reason to trust. I felt slighted, still, that she had not written to me, and did not seem to care that I was at Camelot.

Letters were sent to my sister and her husband, inviting them to come and pledge their fealty to their new High King. I did not think, from the little I knew of King Lot, that he would be happy to pledge himself into the service of a boy. But Arthur looked less and less like a boy every day, and more and more like a king. While Kay had been gone, though Kay was almost a head taller than his old father Ector, Arthur had almost caught him up in height, and was twice as broad. They were a pair of giants together, those two.

Camelot had grown as well, as more and more lords put themselves in Arthur's power. Those who did not faced the growing band of knights, whom Arthur rode out with, against Merlin's counsel. But it was for the best. Arthur was fearsome in battle, and the men liked to have a king who rode at their side. Soon all the lands of Logrys were securely in his power, and the King of Gore in North Wales had come briefly to pledge as well. We only needed to wait for King Lot, and Cornwall, and Britain would be Arthur's.

I didn't care about that, though, as much as I cared about the fact that Kay had returned. There was a feast for the return of the knights from Cornwall, so that Arthur could reward them and hear their stories. I caught Kay's eye as he sat beside Arthur, and he grinned at me. I smiled back, more reserved. Merlin was there, and I could feel him watching me. I felt too nervous, too sick with being so close yet far from Kay, and so unbearably close to Merlin, to enjoy the food. It was simple enough, I supposed, to the knights who came from rich families – just a beef stew with vegetables – but it was far richer than anything I had eaten in the abbey, or in Avalon.

I was glad of the wine to settle my nerves, and glad when Kay and Arthur had exchanged their stories, and I could slip away.

I had only just got to my room and begun to unwind the plait of my hair, when the door opened and Kay, flushed with wine and excitement, and the knowledge of what was forbidden, rushed in to the room, and shut the door behind, drawing the bolt. I rushed forward and took his face in my hands.

"Kay, is it really you?" I whispered, thinking of Merlin sitting there in Kay's form, suddenly worried. Kay looked confused.

"It's me." An amused half-smile crept across his face. No, I could not mistake the real Kay. "Was I away that long?"

I kissed him, hard, full of relief, relief to have him back and alive, and for a moment alone with him. I kissed him so I didn't have to tell him why I was afraid he was Merlin. So that I didn't have to talk about Merlin at all. And because it was easy, and familiar, and I had been so lonely without him.

Chapter Ten

The days after that passed quickly, and spring turned to summer, and to autumn fast. Kay was busy, and our need to be secretive kept us apart, but whenever he could he would sneak to my room, and we would come together with all the forbidden passion of secret lovers. I could see, though, that he was growing more and more wary. Arthur wanted him more and more at his side as Logrys became stronger, because as Logrys became stronger, and Arthur more established as a king, he became more of a threat to the other kings of Britain, and the time would come soon when they would either have to pledge to him in fealty, or fight against him for their independence from him. Arthur grew fast into his role as King, and as the end of summer brought his fifteenth birthday, I would have been sure that he was fully a man if I had not known it. He looked, certainly, of an age with Kay and myself, who were three years older than him, or even Lancelot who was a year older than us. I had found a kind of precarious happiness in Camelot, seeing Kay when I could, offering my services as a healer to the wounded knights. They were afraid of my woaded face, of course, but soon saw that I was not a danger to them, and only brought them health and wholeness. I had almost forgotten Macrobius' book, and certainly had forgotten my desire to know its secrets, but I still checked every day it was there. I would have, then, exchanged it for my sword, and I knew well enough what it was worth not to want to risk losing it.

But then, down from the far, cold north, my sister Morgawse came. I was stood with Kay in the courtyard – a decorous distance apart since Arthur was there – and Merlin and Ector, to watch the men training. Kay, still, leaned down to whisper in my ear every so often, letting me feel the little thrill of our secrecy, and the delicious potential of his closeness.

It was Kay who noticed her first, straightening up and focussing his dark eyes on the distance. She came with a large retinue of knights and servingwomen, but she was unmistakable at the head of them. My sister, the beauty. Her long, copper-gold hair hung in glossy waves down to her waist, drawn back at the front in little twists to reveal a broad, handsome face, fair and flecked with pale freckles that were so pale as to be almost golden, and bright, sparkling blue eyes. She had a cloak of white furs around her shoulders, clasped with a white gold pin set with diamonds, shaped like a little bird, and around her head was the dark gold crown of Lothian, wrought in warlike spikes. Beneath the cloak peeped an orange and cloth-of-gold samite gown, and at the low neck of the gown, the curve of her large breasts. Kay, seeing her, whistled through his teeth.

"This looks like trouble," he said under his breath. I thought, with a little flash of anger, that the whistle was for her, but when I turned to Kay he was not looking at her any more. He was looking at Arthur. Arthur, in the middle of the courtyard, had stopped his fight with Lancelot and stood frozen, his practice sword fallen with a clatter from his open hand.

Morgawse jumped lightly from her horse. She moved, always, as though she were about to dance. She still had the easy, pretty grace of her movements that I had envied when we were children. I was tall and gangly, and I knocked things down. Morgawse whispered past everything charmingly, her feet barely brushing the floor. She rushed over to me in a whirl of firs, and kissed me on each cheek.

"Little Morgan," she cried. "All grown. You look *just* like mother. Except the woad, of course." She laughed, and her laugh tinkled like a little bell. Arthur, I could see over her shoulder, was staring already.

"Morgawse," I replied, feeling the shyness that I had almost lost return to me with the memories of how charming and graceful and beautiful my sister was. "It's so good to see you. Are you well?"

Morgawse laughed again, her blue eyes sparkling bright. "I am now I am away from that wretched old husband!"

"How are your three sons?" I asked, unable to get the awkward politeness from my voice. We were *sisters*. I ought to have been able to chatter with her as I had done the few times I had visited her when I was younger. Out there, before everyone else, I felt awkward and inferior.

Morgawse wrinkled her face in annoyance. "*Four* now. I swear that old cretin will never be satisfied. And the more we have the more enthusiastically he wants to try to make another."

I was blushing, hearing her talk openly about it like that, but Morgawse had always been exactly like that. Unable to keep anything that ought to be private private. She was utterly, utterly unembarrassable. Had always been. Also, she was being rude. She was supposed to have found out who the King was by now, and greeted him appropriately, instead of standing in the courtyard with her sister complaining about her husband.

Morgawse's eyes lit, instead, on Kay, and I saw the little glint of intrigue in them. She had noticed that there was a man beside me who was young and handsome. *Go away, Morgawse*, I thought, *You have a husband*. Morgawse liked to see the effect her looks had on men, and push it as far as it would go. I did not think she had had a lover, for she had been always with her husband, under his mean and watchful eye, but she had loved to torment her husband's knights with flirting, and her husband by letting him watch her do it. Kay, however, seemed simply amused by her, and when he had taken her hand and kissed it, greeting her courteously as Queen of Lothian, he gave me a comforting little wink.

By now, Arthur had noticed the slight and coughed indignantly.

"My Lady, Queen Morgawse," Kay stepped forward tactfully, for I supposed that Morgawse could not be expected to guess that the empty-handed, bare-headed man staring at her was King of Logrys, "might I introduce to you my Lord King Arthur?"

Morgawse stepped forward towards him, and took the hand he offered her, and curtsied. Arthur, to my surprise, had gathered himself, and kissed her hand and gave her a charming smile, the kind I had not seen him give before. I suppose it was the one he had used on the milkmaids outside Ector's house. I had thought he would be flustered and overwhelmed, but he seemed in control. Perhaps he was growing used to his role as King, or perhaps it was his comfort in front of women, his trust in his own ability, that gave him confidence.

"It is an honour to have so fair a queen in Camelot, my Lady," Arthur said to her, his voice smooth and flattering. I saw Morgawse's face light up with a mischievous smile, a smile of interest. Why on *earth* had her husband sent her here on her own? "May I show you around the castle?"

Morgawse gave her tinkling laugh, and I thought I saw her *blush* slightly.

"Of course, my Lord," she answered, and he led her away before her retinue had fully dismounted from their horses.

When I turned back to Kay, he was staring off where they had gone, open-mouthed. He shook his head slowly, as though he was shaking his thoughts back in to place. He turned to me.

"She... is your *sister*?" I nodded. Kay shook his head again in disbelief. "She's not much like you, is she?"

"No," I agreed, feeling sad, and small, and inadequate. "Not really."

Even Kay seemed to see it. Morgawse's magnetic personality, her sparkling looks. But this was what Morgawse did. Turn up somewhere and absorb everyone around her. Morgawse needed attention. All the time. From all the men. I felt the stab of sisterly resentment deep inside me. Always compared to Morgawse. Kay put an arm around me and hugged me slightly to him, as much as he could in the public space of the yard. He had seen my look of sisterly jealousy, then. I appreciated the comfort of it.

Kay sighed. "I hope that Arthur doesn't get too... carried away. He doesn't want to go starting any wars. He has always been good with girls... I don't understand it. They all just... want him. It's worse now he's King, you know. I think I would be afraid of it, if I were him. Girls chasing me. I prefer the mysterious types, you know." Kay looked down and gave me a little wink. I felt better, a little warmer inside from the sight of his smile. There was one man, at least, looking at me, rather than at my sister.

Kay had to go to organise rooms for Morgawse's huge retinue, and I went up to my room. I thought I might try to read the changing of shapes book again. The sight of Morgawse had made me feel less happy with my natural shape, reminded me of all the reasons I had wanted to change it. But I had just settled down at my desk when the door burst open. I hurried to hide the book again, but I didn't need to, because it was Morgawse, her eyes flashing with wicked delight. She would not have cared what it was even if she had been able to read the Latin. She had no attention for books. She never had. She was smiling to herself, lightly flushed. She shut the door behind herself and leaned against it.

"Morgan," she gushed, "isn't Camelot *exciting* now it has a new King?"

I nodded.

"And isn't the King handsome?"

"He's ten years younger than you, you know," I told her sharply. Morgawse's smile twisted deeper on her face and she gave a flick of one coppery perfectly arched eyebrow.

"Well, when they said he was a boy-king, that was *not* what I was expecting." Morgawse bit her lip lightly, and laughed. "He looks like a *man* to me."

I felt myself becoming more tense, more uptight around Morgawse as she became increasingly carefree and reckless. She made me feel boring and serious, and it made me become scolding and righteous around her. Something about seeing my sister always forced us back into these roles.

"Well, be careful not to do anything that will get you in trouble with Lot."

I heard the lecturing tone in my own voice, and I bristled against it, but around my sister, I could not help myself.

Morgawse pulled a face of mock innocence. "But I am only doing as my husband bids me. Oh yes," she jumped towards me like a cat across the room, crouching down beside me as I sat at the desk, "he sent me on my own so I could *spy* on the boy-king Arthur. And that is what I have been doing. I have inspected the battlements, taken note of the defences. I let Arthur show me his *sword*." She laughed as I wrinkled my face at her. I hoped that she meant Excalibur, though that was bad enough. She leaned closer to whisper conspiratorially, "I think tomorrow I will ask to inspect the *royal bedroom*."

I pushed her away, crying out in disgust. Morgawse laughed. She had always loved to tease me like this, to get a response of shock or disapproval from me. I don't know why I always obliged. I was not even sure that I cared. Morgawse, still laughing, took my face in her hands and kissed me on the forehead.

"Sweet little Morgan," she piped, her voice tinkling with excitement. "I'll be careful. Don't you worry about me."

Arthur held a feast that night for Morgawse's arrival, ostensibly with the intention of honouring her lord husband as a loyal vassal king to Camelot. She sat at his side, and neither of them paid anyone else any attention all evening. I sat beside Kay, both of us quiet and darkly watching as Morgawse took the little cakes Arthur offered her between her lips, and giggled, and Arthur leaned back in his seat to cast an appreciative eye on her.

I noticed that Ector was not at the feast. Perhaps Arthur would have been more careful if his foster-father were there. As Arthur was refilling my sister's cup with wine, Kay leaned down to me and whispered, "I have written to your mother that Morgawse is here. I hope that she will come soon."

I nodded. It would be for the best. Morgawse was not really cowed by anyone, but if she would listen to anyone at all, it would be our mother.

I noticed, too, that Merlin was gone. He had developed this habit of coming and going silently now that Arthur had established himself properly, and it made me uneasy. I wanted to be sure that if a man burst in to my bedroom it was *definitely* Kay. It seemed to bode ill to have a missing shape-changer. Still, when I was close I could always tell it was him. I had learned the particular feel of Merlin's dark power well by now, and I was sure he was not at the feast.

Morgawse had her bedroom above mine for her stay, and walked back with me when it was over. In that moment, I would have rather she had gone off with Arthur. It would have kept him occupied, and I could have snuck away with Kay. As it was, Kay had bid me goodnight with a kiss on the cheek, lingering close for a moment, which was almost worse. Now I was alone with my sister with the feel of his lips burning against my cheek, and the longing woken within me.

Morgawse was sighing with contentment as we walked through the courtyard, turning her face up to the stars that peeped through the clear spring night. I supposed she was relishing her freedom from her husband. I had not liked Lot much the few times I had met him. He was a strange, wolfish man with mean eyes and a sharp tongue, and almost thirty years older than my sister. Morgawse's marriage to him had not been much of an escape from Uther.

Morgawse did not want to sleep on her own, and asked if she could stay in my room with me. Despite everything she said, I knew that Morgawse did not wholly like being back in Camelot. Not now it was dark, and it looked as it had done when we were children. I dimly remembered Uther shouting at her, and shaking her by her hair. She had been a bold-mouthed girl at eleven, and had made no secret of not liking her new stepfather, but she had not deserved the treatment he had given her. Though I would rather have been alone, I could not turn her away, and we lay side by side to sleep, as we had when we had first come to Camelot, and she had been eleven, and I had been three years old. My memories of it were clearer than those of my first few years in the abbey, because many of them had been tinged with fear.

When I was half asleep, I heard a little noise at the window, and saw Kay's head peeping in, but sadly I shook my head and pointed to Morgawse sleeping beside me. Kay nodded and gave a wry smile, and disappeared away again. As I fell asleep, I wondered what Morgawse would make of the things that I had done. I doubt she would believe it. I would always be to her the quiet, bookish sister, who was half-nun, half-witch, but nothing of the world of real men and women. Still, I loved Morgawse as much as I hated her, and I would have given anything to have been able to protect her, from our stepfather, or from Lot. I was more resolved in that moment than ever before that I would not give up the book. I snuggled closer to my sister and closed my eyes. I wished I could have magicked her away with me to Avalon when I had been three. I wished that I could magic away her bad dreams now. I would need to be strong, and brave, and ruthless if I were to be able to defend us both from this cruel, hard world of men.

Chapter Eleven

A week passed, and autumn shaded into winter, and Morgawse and Arthur continued to spend their days flirting together. I would come down from my bedroom and see them standing in the courtyard, Morgawse's back against the wall, Arthur leaning over her, one hand resting at the wall beside her, talking low and close, both smiling. Nothing had happened yet, though. Morgawse still spent every night at my side.

Then, one day, as I was on my way back up from the food stores, where I had been looking for herbs to make more of the potion that restored blood – Arthur's knights seemed to have need of it all too often – I saw them kissing. But it was not just kissing, not really. I came up the stairs to see them standing in the corridor, him moving towards her, she giggling, and then he grasped hold of her around the waist, and she pressed herself against him. He pushed them both back against the wall, his mouth rough and passionate against hers, and I heard her small sigh of pleasure. I saw his hands push back her cloak, and then against her breasts, and hers on his hips, pulling him against her. I felt my cheeks flush hot red to have seen it, and I scurried back down the stairs I had come up. I could not walk past them. What was I supposed to do if they wanted one another? Morgawse was sick of her husband, and Arthur was a young, free man and a king. It just made me disgusted to see the lust of others, and besides, I knew that Morgawse would want to tell me about it.

I waited until I heard silence fall, and crept back up to my room. To my surprise, Morgawse, when she came to my room, said nothing about it, although she pranced about the room with an ill-contained excitement. So it had not *happened* yet, and she was still skittering around in a haze of anticipation. I decided to say nothing about it. I did not think I could dissuade her.

I wished that she would just go and do it, and then I might get a night alone with Kay. I barely got to speak to him alone with her always with me, and Arthur always hanging around her. I just wanted to be alone with Kay, to hold him in my arms, and lay my head on his chest, and close my eyes and feel the Otherworld and his kindness and his love.

I did not have to wait long. Neither of them seemed like they could bear the waiting. The next day, we all went out hunting together, and Arthur and Morgawse rode ahead, talking and laughing together. It filled me with uneasiness to see it, but it let Kay hang back with me.

As soon as we were in the woods, and the others – for a small party of Arthur's and Morgawse's knights had come with us – were occupied with the hunting, Kay pulled his horse close to mine and leaned over to speak softly to me.

"I have warned him *again and again* that it will mean war if he does this. Lot will not stand for it." His voice was full of worry, of dread. They had fought, but none of them had faced real war yet, and Lothian's army was huge. Lot, too, was known for his brutality.

"He may not find out," I offered, but I did not really believe it. Arthur and Morgawse were not exactly subtle. Any one of the knights that had come down with my sister, who had seen them talking, and laughing and flirting, could have sent word back to her husband. Perhaps others, also, had seen them kissing.

Kay shrugged. He, too, did not think that avoiding war was likely. Then, he noticed that we were alone, and he leaned over, almost falling from his saddle, to grab my face and kiss me. I felt a sigh of delighted surprise go through me and, holding him by his shoulders to keep my balance on my horse, kissed him back fiercely. He moved away, just about regaining his balance in his saddle, with a smile.

"I have been longing to do that for a long time." He grinned, and I smiled in return.

"Me too, Kay," I said, softly.

Then, I heard the hunting horns close, and one of Arthur's knights burst through the trees across our path, chasing something. Kay whistled through his teeth. We had had a near escape.

We went on, rejoining the others, but my heart was not really in the hunt. I was worrying about my sister, about what would happen when her husband found out. He would be within his rights by law to have her killed. Perhaps I should not have let it go on for so long, should have warned her against it. But, if Arthur would not listen to Kay, I did not see why Morgawse should listen to me. Half the time these days she hardly seemed to hear me anyway.

It was getting rather cold by the time we returned, and I felt sick and tired. Tired of worrying, tired of watching my sister, tired of being far away from Kay, tired of it being Kay and I who were secret and careful where Arthur and my sister – for whom the consequences were even worse – laughed and held to one another right in front of everyone. Morgawse had always been wild and irresponsible, and always made fun of me for being sensible and well-behaved. It didn't seem fair that after everything she was having a wonderful time, and I was tense and anxious, and sick of it all.

As soon as we got back to Camelot, I waved a quick goodbye to Kay and slipped up to my room, bolting the door behind me. Morgawse would not be coming back tonight, I did not think. My stomach was churning and I felt weak and dizzy. I lay down, but I could still feel my empty stomach churning. It had come so suddenly upon me. I realised, too, that I had not eaten anything all day. I ought to have been hungry but I felt so very sick. A horrible thought came to me, all of a sudden. I should have bled a week ago, but in the disturbance of Morgawse's arrival, I had forgotten. Or rather, I had forgotten to worry about it. I had been glad not to have the inconvenience. How could this be happening *now*? When I needed my strength to go and tear my sister away from Arthur so her husband would not try to kill them both. It was so stupid. I should have thought of it. I remembered Kay saying *I suppose we won't do any extra harm*. How had neither of us thought about this? I supposed that Kay had thought because I was a witch I would have ways of stopping it, but I had not thought of it. I couldn't have a child. Not if Arthur would not let us marry, and he would not. Especially if there would be war with Lot now. I could not be wasted on an allegiance that was already held. No, the child would be taken from me, and I would be married off as a widow, excuses made for me, and I would not see the child again. Or, worse, I would be allowed to take it with me, to a stepfather that hated it as much as mine had hated us. The anger burned inside me that Arthur could do what he wanted, and we could not. He could start a war to please himself, and the rest of us had to bear the consequences.

Well, that was the way it was, and I could not have the child. Slowly, painfully, I pushed myself up from the bed, feeling the wave of nausea move through me, and found my book of medicines. The recipe was there, and I had made it before, though not for myself. I wanted it done before Kay came looking for me, which I was sure he would once he knew Arthur was occupied. I did not want him talking me out of it. I also did not want him to feel that he was complicit in the awful thing I was about to do. I did not think it was wrong to be rid of those that were unwanted, the children of rape, or unhappy unions, but something in me was repulsed by the idea that I was about to destroy a child of love.

I had what I needed in my room, the herbs, and a small jug of wine. The smell of the mixture made me retch, and even at the smell of it I felt a stab of pain at my stomach. It would be easier now, right at the very beginning, than if I waited. I was beginning to feel faint, but I forced myself to stay standing, to follow the instructions. When it was done, I drank the drink down in one long gulp. I didn't want to turn back.

The effect it had was sudden, and overwhelming. My head span, and I stumbled back, towards the bed, to lie down before I fell. I retched against the potion, but I held it down as I felt a feeling like the pricking of hundreds of needles deep inside my stomach, and an awful squirming feeling that was tinged with the power of the Otherworld. Oh, of course; this was a child of the Otherworld and it would not go easy. Still, I felt the blood began to trickle, hot and sickly between my legs as my head spun faster, and I swallowed down the awful bile I felt rising in my throat. Dimly, through this, I heard a knocking at my door, but I did not have the strength to stand, or to answer it.

When I came around, it was to the feel of the cold night air on my face, and a gentle hand at my brow. I forced my heavy eyes open to see that the window was open, and Kay was beside me. He must have climbed in when he felt the door was locked. I tried to look at his face, to see how he was, but my eyes were too heavy, and my head too full of the sickening swirl of the drink, and I drifted away again. Dimly, I thought *we should not be here, we should be trying harder to stop Arthur*, but the pain in my stomach was blocking everything else out, and the darkness was edging in all around me.

When I woke again, it was bright daylight, and Kay was still beside me, in the clothes he had been wearing the night before. His eyes bore the weary look of one who has sat up and watched all night, and across his face was a faint shadow of dark stubble. I was in a clean nightdress. Kay must have washed away the blood and made sure that I was well. I felt well, but sore, and hollow with loss.

Kay didn't say anything, but he leant down and kissed me on the forehead when he saw that I was awake. He slid down to lie beside me on the bed and gathered me in to his arms. I lay against him, expecting the tears to come then, but they did not. I had done the only thing that I could have done. It was better to have done with it right away.

We did not talk about it, and Kay left before prime to wash and change. He had duties, still, to do, even if Arthur had forgotten all the duties he had to his friends and people when he had laid eyes on my sister. I regretted not telling Kay first. He might have wanted it, he might have insisted we run away together, like his father had done with his mother, but I had not been sure enough to ask him to. I think he felt a desperate need to be near Arthur, to protect the boy who had been his brother from his new, dangerous role of King. It seemed that Arthur needed it, but it did not leave much room for me, or what I needed. Perhaps Kay's father's talk to him on family duty had worked *too* effectively. I would have preferred it if Kay cared less about that. If he had asked, I would have gone with him. Anywhere.

I dressed slowly and carefully, still a little sick, still a little sore, in one of my many plain wool dresses. I wished I had something finer like the clothes my sister had. That would have made me feel a little more protected, a little more distant from the world around me. They were another way of hiding, her fine clothes. Still, the black wool dresses were all I had. I plaited my hair up, and washed my face in the basin of cold water, and settled in to the seat at the window, to watch the men in the courtyard below.

Kay was down there already, checking the equipment of the horses. Today he did it with a kind of intense attention that betrayed that he was trying not to think of anything else at all. Beyond him, in the yard, Lancelot was teaching some squire the basics of swordfighting. I leaned my head back against the alcove of the window, and sighed in the cold new-winter air. I hated, intensely, this life that I had found myself in, where I could not do as I wanted, as was right by my heart, but had to do what was political. I had wasted not only a rare opportunity to be alone with Kay, but a precious Otherworld life that we could have had together. Maybe I would ask him to run somewhere with me. To disappear. I was not sure that he would say no. We were young, and I had not damaged myself with the potion. I could have another child. One day.

My thoughts were interrupted by Morgawse crashing in to my room. She was flushed and giggling and I knew for sure now that it had happened between them at last. I gave her a narrow look from my seat at the window, but she didn't notice.

"I know what you've been doing," I said sharply, "and I don't want to hear about it."

Morgawse laughed softly, her pretty blue eyes flashing with wickedness. She loved to do whatever she shouldn't, I knew that. Perhaps it had been a mistake to ask her not to tell me. A vain hope that she would ever listen to anything that I said.

"Oh Morgan, you prude, you've been too long around those nuns, you know." She wanted my attention even more now I had said I didn't want to know. She moved slowly closer, across the room, teasing. "You might like it, Morgan, if you were less uptight. You know he does this thing –"

When Morgawse touched the tip of her tongue with the tip of her finger to illustrate her point, I reached out to bat her hand away.

"That's a sin you know," I told her, curtly. I was in no mood to propitiate her.

"So is adultery," Morgawse replied with a wicked grin. She was enjoying this even more, I could tell, because I was resistant, and visibly horrified. "And they both feel *so good.*"

I shoved her away from me.

"Besides," Morgawse continued, as though I had asked for more, "he has a great big cock. Lot only has this little nub; he's worn it almost away to nothing with his whoring."

I shoved her again. "You're disgusting, Morgawse, you know that? The North has made you crude and wicked."

Suddenly, Morgawse's eyes flashed spiteful, and I felt an argument beginning in earnest between us. I tensed for it. Morgawse, when angry, was brutal. I wanted it. I wanted a fight. A little anger was making me feel better. Less sad.

"You sad little nun. You're just a miserable little virgin who doesn't understand the way the world works."

"I'm not a virgin," I said, quiet, defensive and resentful. I wrapped my arms around my knees in the window seat.

"Yes you are." I could see Morgawse was angry with me now, but she was the one who was doing wrong. She had a husband, and Arthur was ten years younger than she was. She *was* being disgusting. Besides, she was selfish and stupid, and she could not even see me before her. She had no idea that I, too, had a lover, and that I suffered because she had one. She could not see the cold lump of anger gathering inside me against her and Arthur, and the whole lot of them at Camelot. Even a little bit at Kay, with his infuriating dutifulness. Why was Kay watching out for Arthur, more than he was watching out for me?

Morgawse reached out and pinched me hard at the ear. I winced, and I was going to protest, but she spoke again and her words were sharp and angry. "It was all well enough for you, wasn't it, to go off to the abbey and have a sweet childhood with the nuns. You think you're so pure don't you, Morgan? Well, it's easy to be pure when you weren't given away to an old, disgusting man at *twelve years old*. And I had to let him kiss me, and touch me, and get on top of me, and put his cock inside me." Morgawse leaned close to my ear to say this last part and I squirmed with discomfort to hear her say the words. "And it's because of women like me who suffer disgusting old kings to get on top of them that women like you are safe to hide in your abbeys reading books and talking on and on about how pure you all are." Morgawse pushed me away then. I met her harsh look with a defiant stare of my own. "Don't you *dare* judge me, Morgan, if I want to enjoy myself a little, now that I am free. There's no dishonour in it. Arthur is a king, we are his vassal kingdom. That's how it *works*, Morgan, and don't you judge me if I want to just have a little bit of pleasure in my life. My marriage has kept us all safe. When Lot is dead, Arthur will keep us safe, for my sake. There's not just power in spells and potions, and hidden in the dusty books in the abbey. Just think about that."

Coldly, I gathered myself up in my seat. I had given up a child so that Arthur's kingdom might have peace. I was in love with a man who I knew would never marry me, not because he did not want me, but because he wanted what was best for his brother and king, and she was standing there before me pleased with herself for putting us all in danger. Selfish Morgawse, as she had always been.

"You'll bring war on all of us," I told her, making no effort to keep the icy resentment from my voice.

Morgawse flicked up her eyebrows in a gesture of chillingly reckless daring, and, leaning back and crossing her arms over her chest, replied, "Let it come."

Chapter Twelve

What Morgawse had said to me had dimmed my anger against her a little. She must have suffered in her life. Though I still wished that she could have thought of others, thought of me, just a little more. As time went on her words about her marriage reached me more deeply. I knew she had been lonely, from the times I had seen her, at Christmas, at Easter, and I knew that she missed the home that by now no longer existed. It had stopped existing when Uther had killed our father, whom she had known well, though I did not remember him. By her account, a gentle man with a low, soft voice, who used to sing to her and my mother in the evenings. I was sure that she imagined him more perfect than he was, but he was a different man entirely, certainly, from our stepfather Uther. No, besides, it was not only Morgawse who forgot her duty in this. It was Arthur who had a responsibility to his people and – in a fog of lust – had forgotten it.

I knew that war was certain when Morgawse came to me at last. As soon as I saw the panic on her face, I forgave her. She was sick and pale, and having felt it so recently myself, I recognised it well. So did she. She had had four children before. I offered her the drink that I had taken, but she shook her head.

"If there is war, and Lot loses, this child will be my protection against his enemies."

Morgawse was not as stupid as she seemed. Still, I felt the little burn of resentment within me. It felt as though she had stolen something from me, though I knew that she had not.

By the time that Christmas came, Morgawse had told Arthur. He looked sickeningly pleased with himself, as though he did not understand the seriousness of it all. Kay, when I told him, had crinkled up his brow and groaned in despair. I told him I had offered Morgawse the drink I had taken and she had refused, and he had nodded in quiet thoughtfulness, and I wished I had not told him, because it made him sad.

There was a huge Christmas feast, with all kinds of game birds and huge platters of vegetables, and fruit, and little cakes and many jugs of rich wines. I drank as much as I could. I wanted to have a little fun. I wanted to forget that war would come, and that I might soon be parted forever from Kay. It would happen as soon as Arthur was capable of tearing himself away from my sister for long enough. I hoped it would not be soon, for he seemed more absorbed in her than ever now that she was carrying his child. She even sat beside him at the table every night, as though she were his wife.

I drank more than I ate, and I was pleased with the effects. I felt less worried, and the thoughts of the child I might have had with Kay sank back in my mind under the heavy fog of alcohol. Kay seemed to be doing the same. He sat beside his father and Lancelot, flushed and laughing, as they told the story again to some other knight beside them of Arthur pulling Uther's sword out of Merlin's stone. Merlin was still, ominously, absent. If he had been here, he might have advised Arthur against an affair with my sister, and war might have been averted. But it was Christmas, and I would not think about that.

By the time the plates were being cleared away, I felt almost cheerful. Kay jumped from his seat to declare it was time for the Christmas games. Kay was a little unsteady on his feet, but on him it came across in little dancing motions, and he carried it well in his impish way. I wished that there might have been dancing instead of games. Kay was a good dancer, and I was very bad at the games.

This year, the Christmas game mainly, it seemed, consisted of Kay and Arthur throwing an orange stuck with cloves at one another, though I thought that was not meant to be the point of it. More and more of the knights joined in, and it seemed that it was the aim to catch the orange in one's mouth, but everyone was too drunk to manage it. I noticed that Ector and Lancelot, ever more reserved than most of the other knights, did not join in. Morgawse, too, sat back in her seat, more beautiful than ever, flushed with wine and with a wreath of Christmas ivy in her copper-gold hair, smiling at the games. Had she forgotten what would be waiting for her, now, when she finally went back to Lothian? Did she think she would never have to go back to her old husband? I didn't know what was going on in her head, what she was thinking. Maybe she didn't even have a plan. It didn't seem fair that she seemed to have forgotten about it all and even through the wine I could not quite. I could not quite forget.

With the thought of war, and Morgawse, I felt my feel for the festivities evaporate around me, and I had no more taste for it. I drained the last of my cup of wine, and left. I hoped that I would fall asleep as soon as I got to my bed, but it didn't seem likely with all the thoughts whirring around in my mind. When I stepped out in the courtyard, it was icy cold, the floor already slick with frost. It would be snowing up in Lothian, thick and deep, keeping Lot from marching down with his knights to see what was keeping his wife in Camelot. If she did not go back with spring, I felt sure that he would come to fetch her.

It was bitingly cold, so I hurried across to the tower than held my room. I was too distracted by hurrying from the cold that I did not notice Kay, close behind me, until I got to the door of my room, and I heard him call my name softly. I turned, and there he was at the foot of the stairs, his colour high from the wine, his black hair ruffled from the games. He was wearing this black and gold brocade surcoat that must have been made new, for I had not seen it before, sewn with twisting patterns like the patterns on his black armour. It must have been a gift for Christmas from Arthur. No one else could have had the money to give Kay anything so fine. Except Lancelot. I pushed the thought away. In the low torchlight of the stairway, the gold threads winked and glinted, and the light caught in his glossy hair, and against the darkness of his sparkling eyes. My breath caught in my throat, and I felt my heart hammer suddenly in my chest.

Kay was up the stairs in a few short leaps, pulling me into his arms. Our faces were cold from the air outside, our mouths warm as they came together, and I felt the powerful softness, the tenderness of his lips against mine, and I felt myself melt into his arms.

"We shouldn't," he said, but he was already following me as I pulled him into the room with me. I wanted to taste a moment of recklessness; to be like Morgawse, just for a moment. We tumbled in, both drunk, both clumsy, but it didn't matter. I stumbled, losing my balance in the darkness, and as Kay stepped forward to catch me we both fell, still holding each other tight. I was wild, desperate for the erasure that only passion could bring, and Kay seemed to respond in kind. He was impatient with the wine, though, and couldn't make his fingers work on the lacing of my underdress. After one particularly violent pull, it tore down to my waist.

"Sorry," he murmured.

"I don't care," I breathed, pulling him back down towards me. And in that moment, I did not.

Kay was still asleep when I woke, before it was quite light outside, but when I brushed a gentle kiss against his sleeping lips his dark eyes fluttered open and he smiled, drawing me closer towards him. I felt anxious, now. I already regretted my brief attempt at recklessness. I just didn't seem to be made for it.

"Mmm," he mumbled, through his sleep. "I don't want to go."

But he did go. He shouldn't even have stayed. We had forgotten Morgawse last night, though she had forgotten us. She had forgotten everything apart from Arthur.

I heard a soft knock at my door, and I thought it would be Kay, but it was Lancelot. I resented being disturbed from my daydream memories by anyone other than Kay, and I stood back in the doorway defensively, not letting go of the open door, but ready to shut it again. Lancelot stood tensely in the doorway, crossing his arms over his chest.

"Morgan." Lancelot shifted awkwardly on his feet, and he did not meet my eye. I suspected already what this was about, and I was unwilling to discuss it *at all* with him. "Can I come in?"

I couldn't think of a good excuse not to let him in, and anyway he was already striding through the open doorway. He ran a hand thoughtfully through his dark, gently curling hair, which was cut to his chin, the way the French men wore it. He had spent his life in Britain, in Avalon, and yet he was still unmistakably French, unmistakably *foreign*. I supposed as an outsider too, myself, I ought to have felt we were allies, but he was not here now to help me. As he turned back to me I shut the door and turned to him, crossing my arms over my chest defensively.

"Morgan," Lancelot sighed, rubbing his brow with his hand as though he was trying to find the right words. I hung back. He had interrupted my little moment of pleasant remembrance and I did not want to listen to him. "This is difficult. Ah…" I was not sure if he was searching for the English word, or if he was trying to formulate his words in the most appropriate manner possible. I thought I had heard the Lady of Avalon was French, originally, and though she was wholly a woman of Avalon now, and I could not hear it in her voice, she must have spent his childhood speaking to him in French. But this time, he had not lost his words. "Morgan, Kay is…" Yes, I knew this would be about Kay. "Kay is kind and gentle, and where Kay puts his heart he does so entirely. This isn't a game for him, Morgan. I don't think you should be doing this. It isn't fair, and it isn't kind."

How *dare* he come here and say these things to me? He had no idea. What did he think I was doing? What kind of nasty knowingness had he imagined in me, in his madness for Kay? I felt hot with anger, and also something else. A kind of nervous embarrassment, and I couldn't help thinking of the new, unfamiliar embarrassment I had felt when the Abbess had made me climb from the lake naked before him. That had not been so long ago. And we were alone, and I could not help noticing that he was growing in to his angular, thoughtful looks. I felt, as well as the heat of anger in my stomach, a flutter of nerves I was unwilling to feel, unwilling to acknowledge. Up close, like this, I could see, even through his black shirt, the lightly muscular shape of his body, the easy grace of his movements. I didn't want to notice. I did not want to be flustered by his closeness, I didn't want to be feeling any kind of attraction to him when he was only being rude to me, and that made me all the angrier with him.

"You are just jealous because Kay gave you up, and now he wants me."

"He didn't give me up," Lancelot scowled. So, I had hit a nerve. Good. That meant that Kay truly had not been with Lancelot since his father had told him it must end. That meant that Kay was all mine.

"Yes he did. I don't see how this is any concern of yours, Lancelot," I told him, haughtily.

"Because there is no future in it, Morgan. You will be married to some prince somewhere, and Kay will have to give *you* up as well." Hah, so he admitted now that he had been given up. "I don't think you know how much he suffered... before. It's not right, Morgan. You shouldn't hold on to him when you know this isn't going to bring either of you happiness. I know it isn't really my business, I know that. But I know that Kay would do the same for me, if he thought I was getting myself in danger like this. Isn't it bad enough what your sister is doing, without all this as well? Let him go. Let him be free to have someone he *can* have. This isn't fair."

I crossed my arms more tightly around myself. He was a hypocrite, really. He wished that Kay *hadn't* given him up for duty's sake, and yet he was asking me to do the same thing. I wasn't going to. I wouldn't be taken away from Kay until I was torn away from him. The new danger, the temptation I felt a spark of alone with Lancelot only made me more resolved that he would not separate me from Kay. I didn't want his words or his presence to have any control over me. I would not be weak to attraction, petty little thing that it was. I was strong, and clever, and I knew what I was doing. Lancelot would not sway me.

"You can't just give up love," I told him, harshly. "It's too precious. It's not my fault if you let it slip away from you before."

Lancelot reddened, and I could see the anger flash in his eyes, and the frustration. He knew that I was not going to listen to him. I didn't have to do anything that he suggested. I had put Kay in far less danger than he had. I did not know how he had known, but then I supposed that he would have been the only person looking out for it. Perhaps he had followed Kay last night. That was an unsettling thought.

"I have to get back to training," he said sharply, and before I could stop him he sprang past me, out of the door, and left. It was the same quickness that I had seen in the courtyard as he trained for battle.

I would wait for the time when Lancelot would regret the things that he had said to me. Kay was not *his*. Kay was mine.

Chapter Thirteen

I had not had time to grow calm before I heard the loud horns that heralded the arrival of a king or queen sounding in Camelot's great courtyard. My heart skittered with panic. *Lot.* I threw my cloak around myself, and rushed down from my room, running out into the courtyard. But it was not King Lot.

Riding in through the great gates with just a few knights behind her, a rich cloak of russet furs around her narrow shoulders and the white gold crown of Cornwall on her head, my mother, Queen Igraine. My breath caught in my chest, and a rush of joy and affection went through me. Years had passed, and I could see the threads of grey at my mother's temples where her hair, soft dark brown like my own, was drawn back into a long plait, and the crinkles in the corner of her eyes where she had often smiled. My mother often smiled. I had seen myself in my middle age, and I had borne no such lines around my eyes. But then, already, I did not often smile. She jumped lightly from her horse. In that she and I were different, too; my sister had inherited her dance-like movements from my mother, and somehow I had never quite grown in to my body, slightly clumsy, slightly too tall and slender to move with the easy grace of my mother and sister. Still, when my mother saw me, she rushed to me, and I let her gather me into her arms like a child, and I rested my head on her chest. I smelled her familiar smell; lavender and the dust of her thick brocade clothes, and the salty smell of Cornwall, and Tintagel where the waves beat hard against the rocks at the foot of our castle.

"Morgan," she laughed, her laugh soft and tinkling like Morgawse's. She gently held me away from her, looking over me with motherly approval. "A proper woman of Avalon now. I am so proud. Your father, too, would have been proud." She kissed me on the forehead, and suddenly I felt embarrassed, too old for her motherly kindnesses. "I hoped I would reach you before Christmas, but the snows near Wales were bad. Morgan, you are all grown." Fondly, she tucked a strand of my hair behind my ear, but then she sighed, looking sad. I wondered if it were a sigh for the lost past, for with all that had happened in Uther's last sickness, it had been three years since I had seen my mother. "Your sister is here, too?" I nodded. "I must speak with you both, right away."

I nodded. Someone behind us shouted an order to send for Morgawse. My mother turned to the men behind her, her voice changed entirely from motherly affection to the orders of a queen.

"Take my bags to my room in the east tower. Send word to King Arthur that Igraine of Cornwall is here, and that I request an audience with him this afternoon."

I thought it was strange that she did not want to present herself to Arthur first. There must be something very important that she had to speak to me and Morgawse about. Perhaps it was something secret to do with Uther's death. I would not have been surprised, now, if Merlin had had something to do with it.

My mother led me up to the rooms that had been hers not so long ago. I suspected that her bedroom was still filled with her dresses and books. She led me into her audience room, a small wood-panelled room with a long, broad table of dark oak and a few heavy chairs. In the middle stood a silver candlestick, a half-burned candle still in it, and the wax left where it had dripped. I wondered if my mother had fled Camelot for Cornwall in a hurry, and why she had refused to come back to Camelot when Arthur was crowned King unless Morgawse was here. She must have thought she was in danger from someone, though clearly she had been hoping that Morgawse would have brought Lot and his knights with her, because that was what she asked me as soon as we were alone. I shook my head. She sighed. She did not know yet quite how ill-advised Lot's failure to accompany his wife had truly been.

She shrugged off her cloak of furs to reveal a dress underneath made of lovely pale grey, sewn with silver thread. She was slender, like I was, and delicately boned. She was still a beauty, though she was no longer young, with gentle grey eyes and soft features. It was her gentleness and grace that made her so beautiful, and though I bore the same shape and features, that was what I lacked, and I knew it. Still, this was why I was so pleased with the woad. It gave me something else, an arcane gravitas, I thought. People saw me and saw all the greatness and mystery of Avalon.

When Morgawse came, she burst through the door with a cry of joy, jumping into my mother's arms so that she stumbled a step back. My mother smiled indulgently, but wearily, and Morgawse stepped away, pulling off her own cloak of white fur and laying it casually on the table beside our mother's. Beneath Morgawse was dressed in a stunning dress of green and gold samite, cut low at the neck and tight around the waist, and sewn around the neck with little emeralds. Beside the two of them I felt my shabbiness, and plainness. But then again, they both knew the price of being a queen, and I did not.

My mother touched Morgawse's cheek gently, and smiled at her, and turned to look at me with a smile as well. She also, thoughtfully, rested her hand on the already obvious swell of Morgawse's pregnant stomach, but absently as though it were something so mundane that it required no comment. She must have seen her eldest daughter pregnant many times before, and thought nothing different about this time.

"You girls might want to sit down," she told us, her face creasing a little in concern. I felt a flutter of panic within me. Was she ill? Was she dying? Neither of us moved. Morgawse crossed her arms over her swelling belly, and I gripped the back of the chair in front of me.

"What is it?" I asked.

"There is something I have kept from you both. It was partly because of my own shame about the matter, partly because it was a dangerous time, and I wanted to protect you both from the knowledge of it. Just after your father died, a man came to me who I thought was your father. I didn't know he was dead, and I was sure it was he and, well – there was a child. A boy." I already felt cold inside, but I could see it had not yet dawned on Morgawse. I heard the voice of the Lady of Avalon ringing in my head; *Uther desired a lady who had a husband, and Merlin changed Uther's shape so that he could lie one night with her disguised as this husband. This boy Merlin intends to put on the throne – now, he doesn't know it and it's not his fault – but he is a child of rape.* It explained so much. Why Uther had married my mother right away, why she had sent us both so fast away, just months after we came to Camelot. It was not just Uther's cruelty. She must have been beginning to show. Our mother sighed deeply again, and she seemed to be gathering her strength once more. "The boy was taken from me, as soon as he was born, by the witch Merlin, and send to Avalon to be fostered." She looked up at me then, and our eyes met, and she knew that I knew, but awfully, awfully, she did not know how bad it truly was. I glanced at Morgawse. She was silent, her face white. She was realising before she knew she was. I could see it. "That boy, that boy was Uther's son. Uther told me it had been him who had come to me in the shape of my husband. So, it is I. I am Arthur's mother."

Morgawse stumbled back under the blow of the revelation, and held her hand against her brow, her mouth falling open into a desperate 'O' of denial that she knew was useless. The blood had drained all out of her face, and she was trembling.

"No," she breathed, "*no, no, no.* Mother, *no.*"

Igraine sighed in frustration, a tone of annoyance and scolding creeping in to her voice. "It's not *that* bad, Morgawse. I'm sorry I didn't tell you, but there's no need for this display of histrionics."

I remembered then, despite myself, why I had such a deep affection for my mother. She was one of the few people that preferred my quiet reservation to Morgawse's demonstrative ways. But she did not realise how misplaced this scolding was now.

"Actually, Mother…" I began quietly, but I did not need to finish. Our mother's eyes had lit again on Morgawse's stomach. She knew how long her daughter had been in Camelot, after all. We had written to her when Morgawse arrived. Her eyes grew wide, and her usually gentle eyes flashed with anger.

"*Morgawse*," she shouted. "What have you done? *Morgawse*."

She stepped forward towards her, and my sister jumped away. She was shaking, gasping for her breath, shaking her head and muttering *no, no, no* over and over to herself under her breath. Suddenly, she rounded back on our mother, shouting.

"You should have said something before. *You should have said.*"

"Morgawse," the scolding tone had returned to our mother's voice, "I didn't raise you to be a harlot, letting any man who asks you nicely into your bed. How was I supposed to expect this would happen? If you had been able to keep your legs together –"

Morgawse had lost it; she was screaming already, and I could see the tears in her eyes. "You married me to an *awful* old man, who was cruel to me, and rough with me, and who still forced himself on me when I had only just had his children and I was bleeding and begging him to stop. And you expect me to turn away one chance I get of kindness, of even a little bit of gentleness? Arthur is a king, too, so I did not think there was any dishonour in it. *You did not tell me.*"

I had not thought it looked *gentle* between them, but I bit my tongue and said nothing. Mother drew herself up, steely, and I saw the hard glint in her eye of someone who had suffered through the same thing, not with Morgawse's wild resentful rebellion, but with dutiful quiet.

"This is the duty of all wives, Morgawse. This is the way of things. How dare you speak to me as if I treated you ill in sending you to Lot. I *saved your life* when I sent you to him. He has been a good husband to you, given you many children and his protection to you and your family. I had hoped that he might keep us all safe now, but I see that that cannot be hoped for, because of *your* foolishness. Many others have suffered as you have without thinking they deserve to indulge themselves with sin as their reward. And you have not just sinned in adultery, but *with your own brother*. You are disgusting, Morgawse." She turned to me then, her face set. "Morgan, is this too late to be undone?"

"*No*," Morgawse screamed. "No, don't ask her that. I won't do it. This is *my child*."

I did not know what to say. Both my mother and my sister looked on me, my sister in desperate appeal, my mother in steely determination.

"It could be done," I said very quietly, "but not without great danger to Morgawse."

"I won't do it," Morgawse said, stubbornly. I could see that my mother's words had shaken her through to the core, but it had not broken her as it might have broken me, such cruel words. *You are disgusting.* Yes, I thought I would have broken down and cried, agreed to give up anything to earn my mother's forgiveness, but perhaps Lot's long years of cruelty had galvanized Morgawse and made her stronger than I had given her credit for, because she bore it well now. She looked, as she squared up to my mother, her face defiant, every bit the queen.

Our mother shook her head.

"Get out of my sight, Morgawse," she snapped. Morgawse, with a haughty scoff, snatching up her cloak again, swept from the room, slamming the door behind her. I was glad that I had not released my hold on the back of the chair. It was the only thing keeping me standing.

When we were alone, mother sank down into a chair, and rested her head in her hands. Sadly, softly she said, "Perhaps I was too harsh with her, but she was always difficult. She could never just do what she was supposed to do. The things she used to say to Uther, Morgan. You would be too young to remember, but she used to scream and scream at him that he had murdered her father. I had to send her to marry the first man who would take her before Uther killed her." She shook her head. "Too stubborn. Like her father." She sighed again. "Perhaps too brave like him, as well. It's the brave ones, Morgan." She looked up at me then and I felt a chill go through me at the cynicism and long suffering I saw in her eyes. "It's the brave ones who die. We are all either brave or wise. Better to be wise. You and I are wise. Perhaps we cannot understand those ones like Morgawse who are brave. But they put us in danger. They put us in danger every day."

I knew it would be awful, when the time came to tell Arthur. I would have hidden away, but somehow I could not. I had not been able to eat anything at midday, my stomach too much in turmoil, too unsettled, and by the time Arthur had his audience with Igraine, I felt weak.

I walked in to the room with her, and Morgawse came behind us, her face impassive and set. I saw Arthur try to catch her eye as we came in. Behind him, Kay leaned against the wall of Arthur's audience chamber casually. When I caught his eye he gave a slight smile, playful, but when he saw my look it fell away, and he looked confused. I noticed that Lancelot was right beside him, and when he saw our look he leaned over to whisper something in Kay's ear. I thought that was more for me than for Kay. Lancelot was marking territory. Beside Arthur sat Merlin, newly returned from whatever dark, unpleasant journey he had last been on, whatever rape and deception he had of late been practising. When I felt his eyes on me, my skin crawled. He had done this, not just to my mother, but to Arthur and Morgawse and the child as well. He had known all along. Some awful fate awaited that child, I was sure. It was not good, the life of a bastard, and it would be worse still for a bastard born of incest. Merlin, bald-headed and in the shape I was sure was his real one, grinned at me. I looked away. On Arthur's other side sat Ector, who also did not know. It was Merlin who had brought him the child, after all, and Ector had only known that he was Uther's son. Behind them, along with Kay and Lancelot who were both lightly armed, stood a few more knights, among them one of Ector's brothers, Bors, and a serious-faced young man whose name I knew was Percival. Every day I saw him enter and leave the chapel several times. By all accounts a deeply pious man. I wondered what he made of his King's dalliance with another man's wife, and what he would make of it when he found out that that woman was his King's own sister.

Once the bows had been performed, and the greetings given, my mother stood up to give her announcement.

I watched Arthur's face fall, his skin go white. I saw his hand go to the hilt of his sword – my sword – for all the good it would do him. No, the black magic that threatened him had been performed long, long ago. Kay stood behind, his hand over his mouth, his eyes wide. I remembered, too, the night we could have stopped them. But I had been bleeding away a child, and Kay had been holding me in his arms. It was not up to us to think always of other people's duty. Not when we were suffering for our own.

Bors, not quite piecing together what this meant on a personal level, his mind full of politics and honour, stamped forward.

"You were dishonourable to keep this a secret! The suffering and peril this has caused my Lord King Arthur as he fought to establish his kingdom. It is treason! Besides, how do we even know it is true."

"I," Merlin stood up, his voice rasping and slimy, and I hated him more then than I had ever done before, "can vouch for the truth of this. It is I who brought the infant Arthur to Ector and his lady wife, and I who instructed Queen Igraine to keep her silence."

Bors, unwillingly, accepted this and stepped back. No man dared argue with Merlin.

When we filed out, all quiet, unsettled, slowly trying to take it in, I noticed Morgawse hang back with Arthur, and I lingered outside the door, wanting to know what he would say. I felt, too, a protective impulse towards my sister. After all, my mother had shown her no kindness in it, and someone had to. If it would not be Arthur, then it would have to fall to me.

"Arthur…" she began gently.

"No, don't touch me. I think you should go, Morgawse. Go." His voice was quivering with anger, or distress. I could not tell.

"Arthur, I can't go. You've made sure of that."

"I don't want you here. I don't want to look at you. You'll *have* to go." I could hear how tense he was, how upset. He had been foolish, of course. But he was young. He was fifteen years old and suddenly King. This was the boy that only a few short years before I had seen chasing rabbits around Ector's field with a toy sword, or climbing up Kay's back to get the blackberries from the top of the brambles, or standing with his arms crossed in his nightshirt, upset that Lancelot was in Kay's bedroom again, sulking like a child. This would age him fast. He would know, then, that all his actions had deep and awful consequences now he was King, and now he had put his trust in Merlin.

"Arthur, it's the middle of winter. I can't. Look, it was a mistake. We didn't know. It seems awful now, but –"

"Leave. *Get out.*" I would have heard his shout if I had been standing at the bottom of the stairs. As it was, it rang in my ears, and through me. He might have shown her some kindness. She had known no better than he.

That night, I lay in bed beside Morgawse and let her rest her head on my shoulder and cry silently into my nightgown. I thought, *I have seen this in my dreams.* Yet it had still caught me by surprise. What good was all the magic of Avalon if I could not understand it? If I could not stop things like this? What good was all my wisdom and my knowledge and my power if I could do *nothing*?

After a while, the still, silent tears stopped. In the darkness, she whispered,

"Come back with me to Lothian?"

What choice did I have? Lot would try to kill her when he saw, or at least to kill the child, and Morgawse had against all reason developed even more of a desperate need to have it now that others wanted to take it from her. If I were her, I would have wanted to be rid of it. The only thing that would keep her safe from Lot was me. He would not fear another man's sword, no. But he was the kind of man who would be deeply afraid of a witch. It didn't matter that my powers were as yet small and slight and benign. Lot would take one look at my woaded face and leave my sister be. At least, that was what I hoped.

"Of course," I whispered back in the dark.

Chapter Fourteen

I did not have time to say goodbye to Kay alone before we left for Lothian. Arthur was raging and upset, still, and did not come down from his rooms. My mother and Merlin were with him, I heard. My mother did not come down to say goodbye to me, or Morgawse. I packed up my things in the morning, tucking the book of potions and the book of Macrobius and the precious letter from Kay into the bottom of my bag, and dressing in the warmest clothes I had. It would only get colder as we rode up further and further north to Lothian.

Kay came out into the courtyard as I was saddling my horse. There were a few people around; Bors and another knight sharpening their swords in the corner, serving women carrying water and milk. He came and took the bridle of the horse, and stroked its nose. It whinnied in appreciation. All the horses liked Kay. Sadly, without looking up, he said, "You're going to Lothian."

I nodded. He was quiet, and I did not think that he had seen. I was about to speak, when he spoke again.

"I suppose there's no other way." He looked up at me then, and gave a slight, resigned smile. I felt the deep rush of love for him then. "I'll write," he added.

"I won't be long," I assured him, though I was not sure that I believed my own words.

"Come back before the war begins," Kay said grimly. "We should not be on different sides."

I nodded. Perhaps it was not safe for me to go up there with Morgawse. What if Lot realised that, as Arthur's sister, I would make a good hostage in the war? Though Lot did not yet know that Arthur was Morgawse's and my brother, and I doubted that Morgawse planned to tell him. That would, at least, give me a little bit of safety. I had to go.

Kay glanced around quickly, and when he saw that no one was looking, darted forward to kiss me, quick and light. I felt his lips on mine after they had moved away, and smiled, despite everything. But it wasn't enough; what I had with Kay belonged to an earlier time that was evaporating around me. I was afraid that I couldn't hold on to it forever.

"I'll wait for you. I'm very patient." Kay grinned as he offered me a hand to help me in to my saddle.

"You're not," I told him, smiling back.

"I am when it matters," Kay said, suddenly serious, and our eyes met. I felt the little jump of joy to have his love within me, and I knew I would return as soon as I could. I realised that I had not told Kay that I loved him, but now did not seem like the time. It would just have sounded like *goodbye*.

I did not look back as I rode away beside Morgawse at the head of her large retinue of knights and ladies. I didn't think she would notice, but I didn't want to give myself away nonetheless.

The journey was long and dull. Several days of travelling through hard, winter weather. The ground was frozen solid, and when the rain fell it was stingingly cold, and sharp with sleet. Morgawse gave me one of her fur cloaks, which I was grateful for, and I wore it over my own old woollen one. The landscape seemed bleaker and bleaker, more grey and stony, as we got closer and closer to Lothian.

We arrived at Lot's great castle as dusk was falling. It stood tall and thin and black-grey against the fading light, densely packed with tall, sharp-looking towers. It nestled in the rocky side of a mountain that rose high and close around it, and it appeared to be made of the same rock. It was beautiful, but harsh and forbidding, like the rocky landscape all around it.

The gates opened to reveal a small courtyard paved in stone, and waiting in it, King Lot himself, surrounded by his four young sons.

Gawain and Aggravain, the twins, flanked their father, already half a head taller than him and looking like warriors, though they could have been no more than sixteen years old. Both stood fully armed, though their father between them was dressed in his shirt and breeches, a thick white fur cloak around his shoulders, clasped in gold, and the crown of Lothian, made in dark gold and spiked like the turrets of his castle, on his head. Beside them, a few years younger, the third son Gaheris, who was the picture of his father, but with his mother's ready smile and bright blue eyes, loitered, and standing right before Lot, with a bright plume of orange-red hair, a young boy stood, still a child, of seven or eight. The youngest, the one I had not known of. I did not know his name. He cried out when he saw his mother, and ran forward. She slipped from her horse to gather him up in her arms and spin him around, laughing. Lot watched, impassive. There were women who would have thought him handsome, and been pleased to have him as a husband. He had a black beard, flecked heavily with grey now, cropped close to his face, and short dark hair striped with grey like a badger. His face was sly and shrewd, wolfish, and his pale blue eyes had a mean look about them. I think if I had been sent here at eleven years old to be his wife, I would have been unwilling, too.

Morgawse stepped forward to her husband and sons as I slipped from my horse, standing warily close behind. Morgawse went forward with her youngest son before her, and as she held him by the shoulders there he obscured the pregnant swell of her stomach. She could not, however, hide it forever.

Lot took her hand and kissed it, and she gave him a tense, unwilling smile.

"My Lady," Lot said with a little bow. "What kept you in Camelot so long, and what brings you back so suddenly now? You did not send word until you were on the road."

I edged closer, so that the woad of my face would be visible in the light of the torches held by the men around us. Gaheris, seeing the blue of the woad, shrank back. Good. Superstitious men were easy to frighten, and I would need to frighten these men to protect Morgawse. Merlin's voice echoed in my head, *it is as well to frighten people as to seduce them to get what you want.* I resented it, and I pushed it away.

"Oh, my business there was done, my Lord," she told him. Even now, when perhaps she should have come to him as a supplicant, she was defiant.

Lot's eyes fell on me, then, and I saw the flicker of casual lust there, and was disgusted. So now I was old enough for him to notice me, I was old enough to notice that he was one of *those* kind of men, to whom every woman is a possession waiting to be owned. I would have to make a special effort to frighten him.

"Ah, and this is your sister, the Princess Morgan." He stepped forward to take my hand, and press it with a kiss. Were all kings philanderers? He gave me his wolfish smile. I could see, now, why Morgawse had thought little of betraying him. He was doing this right in front of her. "One of the holy virgins of Avalon now, I see. I have heard much of you, from your sister."

He did not remember me, then, from the few times as a child I had come with my mother to visit Morgawse.

"We are not holy virgins, my Lord. We are witches."

I thought this would put him off, but he simply raised an eyebrow and smiled more deeply. Suddenly the thought came upon me that once he discovered Morgawse was pregnant by another man it would not be safe for me to write to Kay. He would consider me a spy for Camelot, and he would destroy my letters. I felt very isolated there, all of a sudden. Unsure whether I had put myself in a greater danger than I could have imagined by coming. It would have been immeasurably worse, though, to be alone. No wonder Morgawse had wanted me with her.

"Shall we go inside?" Morgawse suggested, with an attempt at breeziness. The little boy in front of her ran forward in excitement, but turned when his father stepped forward to grab Morgawse by the wrist, twisting her arm up and away and wrenching off the cloak of white fur to stare in horror at her shape beneath. The cloak of white fell into the dirt at her feet. Morgawse turned her face up to her husband, proud and defiant.

"Morgawse," he hissed, low and threatening. "What is *this*?"

Morgawse did not flinch; not a look stirred across her face. Mother was right. She was brave.

"A child," she answered.

"I know it is a child, Morgawse, but where did it come from?" he roared.

"Where all children come from." She was baiting him; it seemed that she could not resist.

He turned to his sons. "*Go!*" he bellowed. They scattered, Gawain scooping up the little boy in to his arms, scurrying off for the towers. So, his sons were afraid of him, too. He dragged Morgawse by the arm through the courtyard up to the central tower, and I followed close behind. If Merlin had not taken my sword I would have been far surer that I would not have let him hurt her. *Merlin, Merlin, Merlin; this was all the fault of Merlin.*

Lot dragged her up the stairs, and threw her into what looked like a small council room. It was dark and bare with the stone of the castle, and a dark wooden table surrounded by a few chairs stood in the centre. A torch burned low in a bracket on the wall, but the place had obviously not been prepared for use and there was only one that had not burned out, and this gave the room an ominous, glowering aspect. I rushed in before Lot could close the door on me.

Morgawse gathered herself back into a corner, the table between her and her husband, her arms wrapped around her belly, glaring at Lot from across the room. Of all the women in the land, my bold, irreverent sister had probably been the worst match possible for him.

Lot reached out a hand and beckoned Morgawse over to him, slow and threatening.

'Come *here*,' he ordered, his voice low. Morgawse did not move. Lot was in his fifties, but he had aged strong and wiry. He was still a fearsome warrior, though he had lost the powerful shape of his youth. If I were Morgawse, I, too, would not have moved.

'Come here,' he shouted. She crossed her arms over her chest and shook her head.

"What, so you can beat the child out of me? How do you know it isn't yours, Lot? Are you going to beat me to death in front of my sister? In front of your sons? What are you going to do?"

"Mine?" Lot laughed, and it was a harsh, scoffing laugh of disbelief. "Now Morgawse, I grow old but I do not yet forget how to count out my months. I sent you to Camelot while I was north in Orkney checking my borders. I had been there a month or more. I sent you to Camelot, where you stayed – what? Four more months? Five? No, Morgawse I'm no old fool."

Morgawse shrugged with dangerous nonchalance.

"It could be. It could be a small child, for once. Or little twins again. Are you going to risk killing your own child? Are you that sure?" I remembered the letter that she had sent me when Gawain and Aggravain had been born. Little twins, almost two months before their time. What giants those boys were now, and strong. Everyone had expected them to die. There had been more twins after that, two little girls, and they had died.

Her eyes were narrow on him, daring.

"You are lying to me, Morgawse." He took a step towards the table, the threat in his voice deepening. "So, the child may be mine, but do you think no rumours ever reach as far as Lothian? There is a man in my dungeons who tells me that you have had the boy-king in your bed."

Morgawse shrugged again.

"I would ask him to produce his proof."

"You may yet produce the proof in time, Morgawse," he said, wryly. And then his eyes fell on me and I felt a quickening of fear. I took a small step back towards the door. He glanced back to her. "I suppose family honour means nothing to you, does it, Morgawse? Otherwise you would have thought twice of shaming me like this. We shall see how you like the honour of your own family."

Morgawse said nothing, her eyes still narrow on him, hanging back. I sensed the danger shift to me, but I did not sense it soon enough. Lot seized hold of me as I leapt back away from him towards the door, and dragged me over to the table. I shouted and struggled, but he was far too strong for me to wriggle free of him. He forced me down face-first, pinning my arms behind my back. I could hear Morgawse screaming at him, "Lot, *stop*." I felt the wood of the table cool and rough at my cheek, felt the edge of the table dig uncomfortably in to my stomach. Through the almost dark, I could see at my eye level the gold thread glinting in Morgawse's dress over her swollen stomach as she rushed towards us, but already I felt Lot throw up the skirt of my dress at the back. He was shouting, too, shouting at her about honour. He was pushing hard against my arms where he had pinned them and it squashed the breath out of me. I heard the metallic click of Lot opening the buckle of his belt and the panic shot through me and I screamed for him to stop.

"Don't you *dare* touch her, Lot," Morgawse shouted.

"I will do just as I please," he bellowed back. I had no weapon, and I had been denied any Black Arts, any real ability to protect myself.

"She's a witch, Lot." Morgawse, beside me, tried to push him away from me, and he released one hand from me to strike her across the face, knocking her back. She shouted, desperation in her voice, "She'll curse you for this."

Lot laughed, unafraid. As I felt him release one hand from my arms again and the fear deepened through me, I was struck by a sudden idea, from what Morgawse had said. Lot knew nothing of the magic arts. I began to mutter in a scramble of Latin and ancient words, meaningless, cobbled together from half-remembered poems that I had read in the abbey, books from Avalon, the offices I had learned from the nuns, but it worked. Lot jumped back from me. *It is as well to frighten people as to seduce them.*

"*Stop!*" he shouted. I turned, pushing my dress down again, stepping back to stand beside my sister, still muttering and he shouted again. "Stop. *Stop.*"

I stopped, and let a wicked smile form across my face, forcing myself to play the part my sister had suggested for me. I could not appear afraid of him.

"You will not touch us again," I told him, mustering all the cold threat I could to my voice. I did not need to have any dangerous powers, as long as Lot thought I did. He turned to Morgawse, his face twisted in anger, his belt still hanging open.

"And you bring a *witch* into my house." He spat at her, and left, slamming the door.

Morgawse let out a breath that shook right through her. I could see she was trembling. So was I. We had both only just escaped. Morgawse shook her head. She wrapped her arms around me and held me close to her. I hugged her tight against me. Her hair, brushing soft against my cheek, smelled of woodsmoke and spices, familiar and comforting. Up here in Lothian, we only had each other. I wondered what her sons would make of this, if they would stand with their mother, or with their father.

Chapter Fifteen

Morgawse, when she had stopped shaking, led us to her room. I was glad that she had assumed that we would sleep side by side. Neither of us wanted to be alone in separate rooms. When we were at last safe and alone, a fire roaring in the room with us, Morgawse turned to me and took me by both hands, her bright eyes fired with something new, a steely desperation.

"Morgan, now is the time for your book of black magic," she told me.

I felt a flash of rage, and of panic.

"You went through my things!" I cried.

Morgawse shrugged. "Of course. I wanted to see if you had anything useful."

I thought with a jolt of fear of what else she might have found. My letter from Kay. She did not say anything about it, though, and it had seemed to me that she would have been more interested in that than in my book of Macrobius.

Casting her a look of censure, I nonetheless went over to my bag and got it out, laying it on her table at the window. Morgawse's rooms were richly furnished, in thick brocade and everything sewn with gold thread. In the glowing firelight, her room was a little haven of cosiness and safety. Still, I was more comforted by the heavy bolt that she had drawn across the door.

Morgawse came over and eyed it with interest. I was surprised. I had not even been sure that my sister could read in Latin. In fact, I was not sure she had *read* the title of the book. She had probably just guessed from the fact that I had this book of magic and had kept it secret that it was a dangerous book.

I had not been sure that I was ready to cross this line, but now I did not think I had any choice. I opened the book carefully. It was old and the vellum smelled pungent. The old inks it was written with had cracked on some of the pages, and the spine creaked a little as it opened. The first step was to make the drink. The list of things I needed was long. Wine, that would be easy enough to find, but there were many herbs, not all of which I was sure could be found in Lothian, and other more occultish things; items acquired at a certain phase of the moon, or time of night. I thought about writing to Merlin to ask him for help, but I knew what the price of that would be, and I was not that desperate yet. I could write to Nimue, but if it reached her on Avalon, the Lady would know that I had begun with the Black Arts despite her words to me.

I read off the list to Morgawse and she nodded along with it. She seemed to think that she could bring me all of the items. As she nodded, she absent-mindedly held the back of her hand against her bleeding lip, where Lot's blow had split it, as though it were nothing at all. I supposed that to her it was. I supposed that she had done so many times before. I wished, then, that I could always escape marriage.

I felt horribly nervous. It had gone wrong before, and I had thought I had everything. I was not sure that Morgawse would know what she was doing, would recognise the right things. Merlin had *not* taught me as well as he pretended that he had when he had robbed me. The only thing he had taught me properly was not to trust him.

I sighed. "It says we also need a drop of virgin's blood. I don't know where we will get that."

Morgawse laughed for a moment, as though she thought I was joking. "Morgan, you're not going to pretend you're not to get out of giving a little drop of blood."

I turned around to face her, annoyed.

"Morgawse," I said, my tone exasperated, "I *told* you."

"Alright then. If you're not, then *who was it?*"

"Merlin," I told her. It was half a truth, and that was all I was willing to give her.

Morgawse wrinkled up her face in disgust, and for the first time I noticed her slight family resemblance to Arthur, and it made me feel uneasy.

"Morgan, *why*?" she gasped.

I turned back to the book, angry and embarrassed and defensive.

"Why do you think, Morgawse? To get this book. Anyway... he didn't look like *that*."

"Hmm," Morgawse was incredulous, "really? I suppose your love was so wild that it made all his hair fall out, and aged him thirty years."

I wheeled back round to her. I wasn't going to be made fun of by her, or to be called disgusting. She had had her brother. I didn't know why, after the first little spasm of distress, she remained so stunningly unbothered by what she had done.

"Morgawse, do you want my help, or not?"

"Fine, fine," Morgawse shrugged, "I'm sorry." She sighed again, and then, thoughtful, asked, "Does it say it has to be a woman?"

I looked again at the recipe. It didn't seem to specify. I hadn't even thought of that, since it was only women that everyone else seemed to care about.

"It doesn't," I told her.

"Good. Well, I'll fetch Gareth. He's only eight, so I think we're safe there." She paused thoughtfully again, wrapping her arms around herself, fixing me with a strange look, her head on one side. "No one ever asks men about these things, do they? No one ever bothers with what they might have been doing. I don't expect anyone is shouting at Arthur and calling him disgusting, or striking him in the face, or threatening to rape that odd, sodomite foster-brother of his." Morgawse saw my look of surprise and interpreted it as disbelief. "Oh yes, Arthur's Seneschal foster-brother, you know, the funny impy man." I nodded. Morgawse had, then, already forgotten eyeing him up when she had met him. "Well, he, ah, he used to sleep in the same bed as that other strange dark-haired one, the French one who never says anything."

I shrugged like I didn't care, but it made me uneasy for Kay's sake that everyone seemed to know. I was sure that it did not go well for him that people did. I could not forget what Ector had said about shame, or the way that Lot had shouted about family honour. It was life and death to them, the men.

"Anyway," Morgawse sighed more deeply, "I'm sure this is going to go much worse for me than it does for Arthur." A note of anger and frustration crept in to her voice. "It's all very well for him deciding he won't talk about it, or deal with it with me, but I can hardly get away from it, can I?" She pointed to her swelling stomach. I nodded in agreement. It *was* unfair. Arthur was absolving himself of responsibility for it by sending her away. Maybe he was just too young to deal with something like this, but I was not sure that I forgave him for it on that count. Whatever he had not known, he had begun it all knowing that she had an angry and vengeful husband. He hadn't thought like a king. He had thought like a selfish boy who finds he can suddenly have whatever he wants.

Morgawse left to fetch the things for the potion. I thought it was brave of her, since Lot was still about, but she did not seem to think that he would be up late at night, nor be where she was going. She seemed to think herself safe enough. I supposed she knew the castle, and its ways.

While she was gone, I leafed through the rest of the book, to the place where I had stopped reading with Merlin. I skimmed through the section on turning one's shape back, for it was just a description of the sensation, and realised then why Merlin had stopped before reading the final pages. They were Macrobius' warning to the witch.

To whomever practises such arts, the art of the changing of shapes, be warned that after the first act of changement, the body is forever altered to be in a state of flux. From thence a person might become another at will, or change from place to place on a wish. While this is not necessarily a disadvantage, the prudent witch must exercise caution. If one transmutes their body to that of a person who is dead, or who does not truly exist, one acquires also their state. Similarly, if one wishes to travel to somewhere that does not truly exist, the same fate befalls. Similarly, if one wishes for a place that is long-gone, one can achieve it, but then must live one's life out at that point in time, as well as in that locus. Many have been lost through the art of the changing of shapes, and I, Macrobius, counsel you to exercise them with the extremity of caution. It is easy, in another's shape, to lose oneself.

Though I stood before the fire, I felt cold. My hands trembled slightly, and I felt myself to be on the precarious edge of something. Becoming someone else. Losing oneself. But maybe I did want to lose myself a little. As I was, I was powerless. If I could lose shy little Morgan and become something fearsome, I and my sister and those I cared about would be safer.

Morgawse came back fast, with her smallest son with her, sleepy-eyed and in his bedclothes. I don't know why she had brought him when she could have just taken a little of the blood. She had everything else with her. I was impressed. I supposed Lothian must have had a witch once, perhaps long before Lot who seemed not to like our kind, and there was somewhere in the castle – somewhere Morgawse knew about – that held the witches' store.

Morgawse fussed at the sleepy boy as I poured out a full cup of wine, and reading slowly under my breath the Latin of Macrobius' instructions, added the ingredients carefully. The smell in the room grew more acrid from the bitter herbs, more foreboding. As I nodded to Morgawse that it was time, she drew out a little knife she must have brought with her for the occasion and lightly pricked her son's finger. He pouted and screwed up his face in sleepy displeasure, but he said nothing, and I caught the drop of bright red in the cup. Morgawse gathered him up into her arms, although he was too old for that, and large besides, and she pregnant, and carried him back to his room.

By the time she returned, I was sure the drink was ready. From Macrobius' description of the finished potion, this was it. It smelled like the bitter herbs that were in it, but beyond that something heady which was not quite a smell, but a feeling, like the moment before one falls asleep, or the half-sleep of waking in the morning. I wondered how much we would forget when we became someone else.

"So," Morgawse said with an eager smile, "what will it do?"

So, she hadn't read the Latin. She had just guessed the book was Black Arts from the look of it.

"Well, we drink the potion and we can change our shape."

Morgawse's face fell.

"Is that all?"

I shrugged at her, annoyed. "Morgawse, what did you think it would do?"

"I don't know! I don't know what it says in that book. Is that the *only* thing that that book tells you how to do?" She gave a little cry of frustration. "I thought we were going to kill Lot! I thought that was what we were doing. I thought you were going to make a shadow man to go and stab him in his sleep."

I shook my head in disbelief and frustration at her. "Morgawse, those aren't real. Witchcraft is an art, a skill. You don't just wish for what you want and get it. You have to learn each piece. This piece is the only piece I have. This piece will keep us safe. We drink the potion, then whenever Lot is around we can change our shape so that we look like one of your sons, and he will leave us alone. Besides, if we wanted to kill Lot there are easier, far less risky ways than black magic. This is dangerous stuff, Morgawse. I don't know what might happen when we drink it."

Morgawse's face darkened from frustration into furious disbelief. "You don't know – you mean *you have never done this before?*"

"Of course I have never done this before!" I shouted back. "Morgawse, this is the *Black Arts*. I wouldn't be doing this if we had any other choice. Do you know what this means for me? Do you? Do you have any idea how *forbidden* this stuff is? This isn't a love-potion, or a sleep-potion, or a potion for seeing the future, this is *dangerous*. There is no going back once we take this." Unspoken behind those words, I thought, *I cannot go back to Avalon.* I snatched up the cup. Too late to think about that.

Morgawse stepped back warily, but I was fired with fear and anger, spurred by her disbelief that I could not do it if I had not before, and I drained half the cup. It felt like liquid fire down my throat, and I could not suppress a cry of pain. *Had I made it wrong?* There was no description of *pain* in Macrobius' book. I felt it burn down my throat, through my stomach, and spread, seep out through my body, through my limbs up to my head. My whole body felt like it was burning away, being seared through with the drink. The pain was intense, but it gradually began to pass. I felt a strangeness settle over me, like the shadow of a feeling. It was a feeling of power, of dark, pressing power close to me. It was like the feel of the Otherworld in its feel of ancientness, immediacy, but utterly unlike it in its quality. It was richer, blacker. It felt wonderful. I felt strength coursing through my blood, I felt potentiality run through me as, recovering from the pain, I gasped.

I glanced up at Morgawse, who stood back against the wall, horrified. I held out the cup to her, and warily, she came forward to take it.

"It hurts?" she asked.

I nodded. "It hurts."

Morgawse, to her credit, was not afraid. She drained the rest of the cup, but instead of pain across her face, I saw the colour drain out of her. She groaned with nausea, and ran to the window. I heard her retching and retching until all the precious potion was gone. Perhaps it was only made for witches, but King Uther had had not a drop of witches' blood in him, and Merlin had changed him into my father's shape. There must be more. More forbidden books, more forbidden spells. A witch must be able to change someone else's shape for them. It would not work for my sister, Macrobius' changing of shapes. I was annoyed with Merlin. How little he had given me in return for what I had ceded to him.

Morgawse turned back to me, her eyes wide with fear, her hands clamped over her stomach.

"He's wriggling around like I've hurt him, Morgan. Was it the drink? Was it? Have we killed him?"

I ran over and pressed my hand on her stomach. Beneath the skin, deep in her womb, I felt something writhe and kick. The child wasn't dead, but it had felt the potion. I did not know what that would mean.

I shook my head. "I think he will be fine. I... I don't know. There's nothing in the book about... children."

"What about you?" Morgawse whispered. "Did it work for you?"

I closed my eyes and pictured myself as Kay. Perhaps I was giving too much of myself away, but I thought it was safest to try first to become one whom I knew so well, whom I could picture so clearly. I felt a tingling through my limbs, as though I were becoming numb, and a rushing in my head as though I were spinning around, but soon these settled, and when I opened my eyes and looked down, I saw Kay's hands peeping from the sleeves of my wool dress, felt it stretch taught across the muscular shoulders I had acquired. I could feel strength all through the body whose form I had taken. Morgawse's mouth fell open when she saw me, and then she laughed until she slid to the ground. I reached up and ran my hand through the short, velvety dark hair that I knew would be there. I had done it. I had become someone else.

At last, I thought. At last.

Chapter Sixteen

When I slept that night beside Morgawse, I dreamed strange dreams where I stood at the mirror, and every time I blinked saw someone new before me. *Me. Kay. Morgawse. Arthur. Lancelot. Mother. Gawain. Lot. Morgawse. Me. Kay. Ector.* It was not a bad dream, but it made me feel uneasy. *Lose oneself.* But I was resolved. I would not lose control. So, the potion would not protect both me and Morgawse as I had thought, but it had made me feel strong, and though she could not change to keep herself safe, I could do my best to protect her.

105

The next day I wrote to Kay, trying as hard as I could to pass the message that we, and Arthur, were in danger from Lot, without saying it in so many words. I wanted it to seem like a mundane note, not worth intercepting. I wrote:

K – remember that boy that used to squire for you who lost all your equipment? Same silly boy has caused awful trouble with what he has left behind with us. Hope he is prepared to fight with things in this state of disarray. Not sure when we will return to the south, might not be until lost equipment is found. Hope all well. M

Morgawse did not speak about the potion again, though I was sure she was glad that it had worked for me, for she stuck close to me as we went around the castle together. Her sons were pleased to see her, and spoke kindly to her. For a while they seemed to choose to believe that it was a full brother of theirs inside her belly. Though, as spring came and the snows around Lothian thawed the possibility that it would be her husband's evaporated, and an atmosphere of anger and resentment returned to Lothian castle. I stayed close by her, and whenever our path crossed with Lot's, I would meet his look of violent rage to her with a cold stare, and he would edge away. I did not want to change my shape unless I had to, and Lot seemed afraid enough of my woaded face to leave us be, for now.

Late in spring, though I did not feel it up in the northern cold of Lothian, Morgawse's time grew near, and the strain began to show between the brothers. I sat with Morgawse in the public room below her bedroom, reading to her from my book of potions, one on the easing of pain in childbirth, while she told me what she thought they did and did not have in the stores, when Gawain burst in to the room. I could see that he was angry; his face was flushed and his lip trembled slightly. He was a huge man already, and had to duck his head a little to fit under the doorway. Since it had become clear that the child in his mother's belly was not his father's, I had seen Gawain sink into resentment slowly, and I had feared this confrontation would come. The talk had intensified around the castle over the last few months, and I could see that the whisperings about his mother had hit Gawain harder than the other brothers. He had inherited his father's fanaticism for family honour.

Morgawse stood to greet him, a motherly smile on her face, but she had not seen what I had seen and I moved close behind her, wary. Gawain towered over his mother, his hand raised as though he was going to strike her. She stood her ground firmly, but I could see in her eyes she was afraid.

"You *whore*," he spat. She crossed her arms over her chest and jutted out her chin defiantly. Under her crossed arms her pregnant belly swelled, huge. "You have shamed my father. I do not know how you dared to come back here like this."

Morgawse shrugged, as though the huge man leaning over her was nothing more than the little boy she raised having a tantrum. So she *had* been prepared for this.

"Your father shamed us all by being a snivelling coward. I have had two kings in my bed. There is twice the honour in that, and no shame. Your father, afraid of open war, sent me to spy on Arthur." She gave a cruel laugh. "That's a coward's work to be sure. The King of Logrys is brave and strong, and your father is pathetic and weak."

Gawain's open palm smacked hard into his mother's face. She stumbled but she did not cry out, simply lifted one hand to the patch already reddening on her face. Gawain's chest rose and fell hard in his anger, but it did not seem to have touched Morgawse. She was bearing it well, the talk around her. I supposed she was glad that talk had not yet reached Lothian that Arthur was her brother, and gossip calling her a whore seemed nothing in comparison to that awful revelation.

"Gawain, you should not strike your mother," I scolded, quietly from the corner.

"Come forward, witch, and say that," Gawain shouted at me, but suddenly I saw why Morgawse was not afraid. This was the anger of a boy. I could see tears in his eyes. He was *upset* that his mother had betrayed his father. The anger was a mask. "I have a hand for you, as well."

"Gawain, you will not speak to your aunt that way," Morgawse reprimanded him, stern again, drawn up to her full height, both her hands on her huge belly. Gawain opened his mouth to speak, but then flushed red and rushed from the room. Morgawse did not see it, but I was sure he had run away to cry.

Morgawse shook her head. "It's his father. He didn't mind so much before, but Lot whispers in his ear telling him that I have shamed him. That *all* women are whores. It's ridiculous."

Morgawse, more and more resigned, more and more hardened to the anger against her, shrugged it off lightly.

One evening, when Morgawse was huge and her time must have been dangerously near, Lot summoned us to a feast in the great hall. I was wary, but Morgawse was eager to go.

"I'm not going to show that disgusting old coward any fear," she told me, her eyes set and determined.

Morgawse sat at her husband's side, and I beside her. Opposite us on the high table, her sons sat. Gawain and Aggravain at the centre of the table, and the younger brothers either side of them. Aggravain, of all the brothers, seemed the least concerned. Gareth was worried and confused, Gaheris embarrassed and Gawain upset, but Aggravain took it all in, his gaze impassive. When the meat was brought and the breads and vegetables, Lot cleared his throat to speak. I felt the pang of hate go through me. Lot, too, was someone I would like to punish.

"Now, I called you here today because we must discuss what is to be done with this bastard child when it is born." Lot announced, not looking up from the piece of meat he was hacking at.

"Lot, you have no say about this child," Morgawse said. Lot ignored her, but I saw Gawain redden with anger.

Lot laughed cruelly. "You misunderstand me, Morgawse. I care nothing about the whelp. I mean, what are *we* to do, to redress this? Well…" He cast his wolfish eyes over us then, grinning with the savour of what he planned to do. "I will march on Camelot to punish this boy-king for shaming us. I have the knights of Lothian, and the armies of Orkney. Four other kings have pledged their forces to the battle, and besides them the armies of Carhais are coming from Brittany, with its queen. We will wipe out this King Arthur, who calls himself King of Britain. The message must be clear; Lothian will *not* be shamed. You may keep the child as it pleases you, Morgawse, but it shall not have honour or acknowledgement from me. It can be a servant in the castle, or if it is a fair girl child, I think it is only right that I should have her for myself. That seems an adequate reparation for the shame you have done me."

Morgawse wrapped her arms around her huge belly, and glowered at him, but said nothing. Lot stood, though the feast had only just begun, and dabbed the meat grease from his lips.

"I am an honourable man, so I have sent word to this King Arthur to tell him to prepare for war. We will march when I hear word that the knights of Carhais have landed at Dover. Between us, he will be easy to crush."

Lot, with a nod to his sons, left. I had not heard anything from Kay. I was afraid, now, that my letter had been lost. I hoped it had not and that they had had time, there, to gather some power for themselves.

"We must ride to war," Gawain cried, banging his fist on the table. Beside him, his twin brother Aggravain shook his head, laying a hand gently on his brother's arm.

"No, Gawain. Consider; Father is strong, his armies do not need us. What honour would there be in riding out to war and leaving no one to defend Lothian castle? Some of Lot's sons must stay here to defend our home, and you and I are the only two who are of age. Besides, someone must guard our lady mother. Now, I am sure that our lord father will be victorious, but of course," here Aggravain paused, to cast his eyes over all his brothers – *we are all either wise or brave*, I thought – "if he were not, it is that child in our lady mother's womb that will be our only protection against King Arthur's anger if he is defeated. If his own child is our brother, we are his kin, and we shall be spared. No war is certain, and no man's life is safe. We must be prudent, Gawain."

I wondered how two brothers born from one womb at one time, who looked so similar, could be so different. Gawain was fierce and hot-tempered like his mother, Aggravain cold and sly like the father. Gaheris, beside Aggravain, murmured in agreement with him. Gareth, beside Gawain, looked as though he was about to cry.

"No," Gawain shouted, jumping to his feet. "I will ride to war."

Aggravain shrugged. "Well, I shall stay here and guard Lothian while you and Father are gone."

Aggravain's eyes fell on his mother, narrow and calculating, though devoid of the open anger she faced from Gawain. He looked as though he was about to say something, but he did not.

The child came a few days after that, on Mayday. It was bright full sun by the time he came, Morgawse half-swooned on her back from the drink I had given her to ease the pain, me up to my elbows in blood pulling out the child. It was a little boy, golden haired and unmistakably Arthur's child. Morgawse cried out in joy to see him, as though she did not remember at all the trouble that his making had caused throughout the land. I wrapped him in a clean cloth of linen and handed him to her. Exhausted, half-drugged, her hair plastered to her face with sweat she smiled in the utmost joy down at the little boy she cradled in her arms as he screamed with new life. She looked on him with such deep love, such peace and contentment. I supposed her children must have been the only reason that she had survived in

Lothian with her cruel husband. I felt as though I should not be there, so great was the rawness of love I saw on my sister's face.

The little boy opened his eyes slowly, and I felt a stab of fear as I looked in to them. They were so dark that they appeared black. I was not sure if they would lighten to grey like my own, or if he were just a strange-looking baby, but something deep in me feared that it was the work of my black-magic potion, and that there might be some of that darkness born into this child. His mother, in her rapture, did not notice.

I sent another letter to Kay. It just read,

K – item has been retrieved. Cannot stay here longer, please send escort back to south. M

I hoped that it would reach him, and someone would come.

When she had rested a little, and she was holding the baby at her breast, I asked my sister what she would call her baby son.

"Mordred," she told me.

I felt uneasy at the sound of it.

"That's an ill luck name, Morgawse."

Without looking up from her baby, she shrugged.

"He is a child of ill luck," she said.

Chapter Seventeen

A knight came for me just a week after that, but it was not what I had expected. I had dared to hope that Kay might come himself, though I knew as Seneschal he ought not to leave Camelot, but I had not expected this. It was Lancelot, come alone. I supposed that a large band of knights would be too warlike, but still I both did not feel entirely safe nor entirely comfortable returning to Camelot with only Lancelot to escort me.

I was reluctant to leave, too, before I was sure that Morgawse was safe, though Aggravain came to me and assured me in private that he would make sure no harm came to his mother. He was not quite like his father, either, I supposed. More politic. He did not have a strong sense of family honour, only a strong sense of survival. I wondered if, in that, he was like the father I had not known. No, he could not have been, for that father had been killed by Uther, fighting, now I realised at last, to protect my mother. No, Aggravain's pragmatism must have been born from necessity rather than being in his blood. He knew that if the war was lost, the survival of his mother and half brother would keep them safe.

Morgawse, I was surprised to find, seemed untroubled by my departure. She was utterly absorbed in her new child, and seemed suddenly to fear no death or danger to herself. Perhaps Aggravain had assured her, too, that she would be safe. Nonetheless, I left her with some potions I had made up that I hoped she could use to defend herself. They were little things. Against lost blood, or ones that would put Lot to sleep, but I hoped they would give her a little help. Lot, already, seemed too engrossed with his approaching war to bother with his anger for her anymore. I hoped that it would be enough, and that my sister would be safe. If I was honest with myself I was glad of the chance to go back to Camelot. I would miss my sister, but I had developed no affection for Lothian castle, and I was eager to return to the south.

I packed my few belongings into my bag, and kissed my sister on the cheek, and walked down into the courtyard. Lancelot was standing, holding his horse, dressed only in light armour and a thick wool cloak. He had his sword, but I was not sure we would be safe riding across the country together in a land where war was coming. Lancelot bore his father's rather than Arthur's colour on his horse, but it was well known that all the sons of King Ban had pledged with Arthur, not Lot. I thought it would be better to either go heavily armed or like peasants through Lothian, but Lancelot seemed to have struck entirely the wrong balance, somewhere in-between.

He nodded slightly as I came towards him.

"Morgan, I am glad to see you well."

So formal. As though we had not splashed around naked together in Avalon's lake, or sat side-by-side watching Kay and Arthur chase each other with pretend swords made of sticks when we were children. I nodded at him, saying nothing. He took my bag and tied it to the back of the saddle. After he had gone around to get on his horse, I gave it a little tug to test it. I was sure he thought it was just clothes, but after all I had given for it I was *not* going to lose my book of Macrobius.

I looked around the courtyard. Of course, Lot had not provided a horse for me. Aggravain, alone, lounged in the corner of the courtyard, leaning against the wall, watching. He grinned at me and gave me a wave, which I returned. Lot was not the kind of man to spare a horse for courtesy's sake when war was coming, so I supposed I was not going to be offered one, though I had come with one. That meant the journey was going to be slower and more uncomfortable than the journey up here.

I jumped up behind Lancelot and wrapped my arms around his chest as he kicked his heels into the horse and it sprang into motion. We had never been this close, and it felt suddenly intimate. I felt the muscles of his chest move under my hands as we rode. I tried not to think about it, but I could not entirely block it out. He smelled like pine, like the depths of the forest, and leather. I wished that we had not be forced into such sudden closeness by the need to have me fast back to Camelot from Lothian.

We rode in silence until the light began to fade. I was not sure if it was because Lancelot was watching carefully, or if he did not know what to say to me. I was glad to be left alone with my thoughts. I was not sure how angry with him I still was.

We stopped at an inn just outside Lothian's borders, and Lancelot handed me my bag and put the horse to the stables. It was only when we were sitting in the corner of the smoky room, lit only with the low light of the fire that Lancelot spoke at last, over his bowl of steaming stew. He did not seem to notice his food, but I was starving hungry.

"I am sorry, Morgan, about your sister," he said, quietly. "I hope that she is well."

"She is. She had the baby," I told him, between spooning the stew into my mouth. I was so hungry that I did not care it was too hot and burning the roof of my mouth. Lancelot thoughtfully picked up a piece of bread and dipped it in his.

"I suppose we had better tell Arthur that, though I do not think he will be pleased to hear it."

I nodded. I didn't want to talk about Arthur. I was still angry with Arthur. He seemed to blame Morgawse entirely, though it was just as much his doing and neither of them had known. I had thought it was more his doing than hers, anyway.

"It is a boy child," I said, hopefully, though I knew this would not really make any difference to Arthur. The child probably would have been safer if it were a girl. The thought suddenly hit me that Arthur might see his little son as a threat.

Lancelot didn't say anything for a while after that. It wasn't until we had finished eating that he spoke again, rubbing his face in his hands.

"None of us have ever gone to war before, not really. Only Ector, and that was a long time ago. We are strong, all of us, and good fighters, but I fear that will not be enough. God, I fear, is not on Arthur's side in this."

God is not on Arthur's side. I had no idea that Lancelot was so pious. I had never heard Kay or Arthur speak of God in that special tone used only by those who truly, fervently believed, and they had spent half their childhoods together, and Lancelot the other half of his in Avalon, where no one mentioned God. God had been in Amesbury, in every waking moment of my life, but it had not stuck with me, the innocent fervour of the nuns, and it was strange to hear a knight speak of it.

"You truly think so?" I asked him.

Lancelot sighed, and shrugged.

"No – I don't know," was all he said.

He stood up then, and I followed as he led us up to two rooms side by side. He lingered a moment at the door of his, and alone in the almost darkness I felt a strange pull towards him, one I did not want to feel, but I did. I did not know what he was thinking or feeling; he was silent, his look distant. I felt myself lean towards him.

"If you fear any danger," he whispered, the formality of his voice pushing me gently back, "wake me."

I nodded, and stepped into my room, shutting the door tight behind. It smelled stale, but the bed was clean enough. I lay down in my clothes, unwilling to undress in an unfamiliar place, and sank into a fitful sleep.

The next day, I woke sore, and tired still. Clammy from sleeping in my clothes in the room that had grown a little chilly overnight. When I had checked I still had all my things, I went down to look for Lancelot and found that he was waiting outside with the horse already saddled and prepared. He was talking to one of the stableboys whom I could hear, in his broad northern accent, warning him that war was brewing around the land. The boy did not seem to fully understand the reason why, for he told Lancelot that it was because Lot did not want to pay Arthur the due tribute. I was glad that was what people thought. That seemed a well enough reason in politics for people to go to war. And it meant word had not spread that Arthur was Morgawse's brother, of which I was glad.

When Lancelot saw me, he bid goodbye to the boy, and gave him a coin from his purse. I handed him my bag and he tied it on the saddle and we climbed back on the horse. It was an unpleasant spring day, by turns a little rainy, and with a chill breeze, but I hoped it would be kinder weather as we moved south. The landscape I could see softening already from bare, dark stone crags to smooth hills and thick forests soft with trees.

I wished that we had got something to eat at the inn before we left, for as midday came Lancelot did not seem to have food on his mind, and we continued on. My stomach was rumbling. It was not even autumn so there was no fruit on the trees to grab as we went past. I supposed I would have to wait until we stopped.

We came over a low hill, through a small copse of trees on the top of it, and emerged to suddenly find a band of knights, fully armoured, and bearing Lot's insignia, the two-headed gryphon, on their shields. Lancelot did not have his shield. They were on foot, their horses put to grazing, but I still felt the threat when they saw us. I counted quickly five of them. The one at the front of them drew his sword, and stepped forward. Lancelot's hand rested on the hilt of his own, but he did not move.

"Well," the knight coming towards us said with a grin, "look who it is. The famous Lancelot. You are younger than I thought you would be, from the tales that have reached Lothian of your deeds of arms for your boy-king. I must say, also, that you are smaller than I thought you would be, too, for such a fearsome fighter."

Lancelot famous? Well, then he was more the fool putting us both in danger by not going disguised.

"Knights, stand aside. As you can see I am escorting a lady," Lancelot declared. It made me wince inside, not only his painful formality, but his crashing naivety that these men would even care for such things. He had clearly never lived in the North.

"I can see you are escorting a *witch*," the knight said, with a laugh. Behind him, the other knights picked up their swords and gathered.

"All the more reason to let us pass, sirs," I told him, coldly. *It is as well to frighten people*, I thought.

"Well," the knight said, laughing again, "I hear a witch dies as well as any other woman without her head."

Lancelot dropped from the horse, drawing his sword. I pulled the horse back a little. I didn't want it to be killed, and I didn't want to lose my bag with my books. He was far more lightly armoured than the knights, but I saw them draw back a little as he stood before them. He appeared slighter, less bulky than them only because he was unarmoured. He stood taller than the knight before him, on his long legs, and I could see already on the man's face that he feared he had misjudged Arthur's great champion when he had seen him only astride a horse. Lancelot struck forward fast and for a moment, it seemed that nothing had happened, and the man gave a little cough, and then I saw the line of red across his throat, and suddenly the blood bubbled forth and he was choking on it, grasping at the open cut as though he was trying to hold it together. His fellow knights stood transfixed, as did Lancelot, as the knight fell to his knees and slowly to the ground.

There was a moment of awful pause in which I saw Lancelot tense for the fighting to begin again. It did. The other four threw themselves on him all at once.

"Morgan, run!" I heard him shout to me, but I did not. I was sure they were going to kill him. I jumped from the horse, pulling free my bag, and stepped back into the cover of the trees. The four left alive did not seem concerned with me. Perhaps they were more afraid than their leader had been. I felt the burn of rage once more that Merlin had taken my sword from me. I could have helped. I wished I could change into someone strong, but my heart was racing and my mind was fogged with panic and I was not sure I could right now. I had only done it once before. But then I saw I might not have need. The other knights were slower in their heavy platemail, and though they all struck at Lancelot he seemed to dance out of the way of their blows. One of them had already fallen to their knees, their head leaning forward. I thought I saw a stream of blood down under the helm, running down the platemailed chest. But still it was three of them against a man alone. I heard the horse whinny, and I hoped it was running away to safety.

When the third man went down under Lancelot's sword, he saw his opportunity to turn and dart into the woods. He would have a great advantage there, being less armoured, and faster. The two surviving knights lumbered after him, and I shrank back among the trees. I heard swords clashing, and shouting, but I couldn't see anything. I heard a man scream in agony, and I feared it was Lancelot slain, but when the clash of fighting continued I realised it must have been one of the others. So there was only one man left. I ran through the trees, looking for them while trying to hide myself. I could hear them close by, but the trees were thick and close and I could not see.

All of a sudden, I turned to see the ugly leering face of a man, his helm knocked from his head, his face spattered with blood, close by me, towering over me. I screamed. He lifted his sword over his head with an awful grin and I jumped back. But there was no need. With his arms over his head holding his sword he froze, and his eyes bulged. Then I saw the point of a sword peeping out from under the breastplate of his mail. I heard the sound of steel drawing out of flesh, and blood bubbling from his mouth, the man sank to his knees before me, and Lancelot was behind him, his sword bloody to the

115

hilt, his face pale, his chest heaving with the exertion. I was shaking, too, the nearness of my death close about me.

Dropping his sword, he leapt over the body of the dead knight and took my face in his hands.

"Morgan, are you hurt?" he asked softly. I shook my head. We were both breathing hard, both trembling a little, and I put a hand lightly against his chest, a little to steady myself, a little for him; but then our eyes met and suddenly we were kissing, desperate with the relief. I threw my arms around his neck, and he pulled me closer. We stumbled back, until I felt the tree behind me at my back, and he fell against me. My head swam with surprise, and his wild intensity. His lips were light on mine, his mouth hot, but it was passionate and sensual and I felt it overwhelming me. Through the rushing adrenaline from running from the men trying to kill me, I felt the familiar thrill of desire, and the two mixing together as I slid my hands into his hair, thick and velvety against my hands, and I felt his body pressing hard against mine. His tongue fluttered lightly against mine in response, and I felt his hands at the small of my back, between me and the rough bark of the tree, but when I grasped the buckle that held his breastplate at the back, he gently pushed me away.

"Morgan, stop," he said softly. I felt my cheeks burn red, and the potent mix of desire frustrated and anger and embarrassment filled me. He stood back. His chest was still rising and falling hard, he was still gasping for his breaths. He shook his head slowly, running a hand through his hair. "Morgan, I – it was the fighting, and – we should not."

I crossed my arms over my chest, trying to hold my breath steady, to fight against the feelings of hungry desire that were crowding out my anger. What did he think I wanted from him? I was not asking for marriage.

"I did not mean to make you... confused," Lancelot said, softly. Right then I felt a stab of hate for his low, French tones. There seemed to be something superior in that voice.

"I am not confused," I replied, coldly. He rubbed his face. I could feel my lips burning where his had been on them, and the heat of my body woken for nothing. And, dimly beyond that, the awareness that I had betrayed Kay a second time, and once again for nothing.

Lancelot found his horse grazing where he had jumped from outside the little clump of trees, and we climbed back on. We rode on for the rest of the day in silence, but it was a different kind of silence. Embarrassed on his part, resentful on mine.

We had meant to reach Camelot that day, but the fight had slowed us down, and night was falling so we stopped at another inn. We ate our meal in silence, Lancelot avoiding meeting my eye. I was not going to make it easier for him. He was not going to do something like that and then leave me to feel uncomfortable. *I* had not done anything wrong. I was a free woman. Besides, I was not convinced that Kay would even care if he knew. I could not work out how he felt about things like that.

I went to bed early, keen to get away from Lancelot, but for a long time I could not get to sleep because my mind was playing the kiss again and again in my head, and I felt the hot frustration gather unbearably around me. I knew that I wanted him, but I also knew I was furious with him. Did he think Kay was the only person with emotions? What about mine? But then Lancelot's problem seemed to be that he had too many emotions and all those he had were either shame or regret. Certainly, he was troubled still by his history with Kay, and felt an odd kind of responsibility to him. Perhaps I ought to have done as well, but right then, with the frustrated desire pounding in my veins, I didn't feel it.

When I finally did fall asleep, I dreamed of Lancelot, too. It was a strange dream, strangely clear in its focus, detailed; more like a memory than a dream. I dreamed of him standing in a pavilion, at the entrance, waiting for me, and when I came, he pulled me inside, and kissed me furiously, and we fell on to the silk cushions lining the pavilion floor. The dream was so vivid, I could feel them against my skin; I could feel his lips on my neck, his voice whispering in French at my ear. I could smell the spring night all around us, hear the trees whispering in the wind above the pavilion. It was dark, but there was a low orange glow from a brazier filling the pavilion with a dim, atmospheric light. I could feel the fresh spring chill against my face. I felt the silk of the cushions we lay among against my bare skin at my back, and the delicious feel of his bare skin on mine, his hands on my body. He held me firm but gentle, by the hips, as he kissed me slow, and passionate, and I wrapped my legs around him. I felt his hands run down my thighs, gently parting them, and his mouth open under the passion of my kisses. I could taste sweet wine and spices on his lips, and felt my head reel pleasantly with it. I reached up to touch his chest and felt it as though it was really there, smooth and warm, hard underneath with the muscles of a warrior. Our eyes met, and I felt a shock through me at the look he gave me in the dream. It was a look of utter desire, and of love. I did not think I had been looked at like that before. There was no other word for it. My breath caught in me, and, our eyes still locked, he ran a hand lightly down my body. I noticed that, in the dream, I did not see myself woaded with blue, but it did not seem strange somehow. In the dream, I was not surprised to see myself that way. I reached up and wound a hand into his hair, pulling him down towards me, and as we came together in a hungry kiss, he went inside me, and I felt the heat of pleasure gathering through me. His love was slow and passionate, sensual and intense. He was powerfully responsive to my touch, and moaned in pleasure with me as we moved together. He looked into my eyes as I felt the heat rising, tightening around me, and at last, I felt the bright hot shot of bliss spark through me. I cried out with ecstasy, and woke myself suddenly, sitting up in bed, flushed hot and even more angry than before. As soon as I woke, the dream faded, its sensations and details receding away, but I felt as though Lancelot had got inside my head in a way that made me feel strangely vulnerable. I did not want to want something I could not have, because that would make me weaker, and I needed to be strong. War was coming, and I had left my sister behind in danger, and lost my sword, and given myself to black magic. I could not be longing for a man who did not want me, as well.

By the time I heard Lancelot knock on my door softly at dawn, I was exhausted, frustrated and desperate to get to Camelot and away from him as soon as possible. I had only slept a few hours, and those restlessly. When I dressed and opened the door, the sight of him made me blush with the fresh memories of my dream. It had not really happened, but it felt as though it had. It felt as though we had been together last night. It had been so vivid, it had felt so real. I had tasted his lips, and felt his naked body under my hands and had him *inside* me. It had felt so *real*. I wondered, then, if it was a dream from Avalon, but in that case I did not know why I had dreamed of myself as I had used to be, without the woad on my body.

I had been ready to be angry and haughty, but I found that, that morning, it was I who could not meet his eye. The journey back to Camelot was mercifully short from there. I wondered how I would feel, now, when I saw Kay. Nothing and everything had happened between me and Lancelot. Nothing, for him, I was sure, but I felt raw and soft and vulnerable around him now, because I had, in my dreams, known him so intimately. It made me wonder how they had been with one another. It must have been something neither of them wanted to give up, if they had been with one another as they had been with me.

Chapter Eighteen

As we came through the great gate of Camelot, I saw the courtyard was full of men equipping themselves for war. They would ride off soon, then. I spotted Kay easily among the men in the yard. He was dressed in his dark armour, all except the helm, and was helping a squire buckle a saddle properly onto a horse. The horse was quiet and pliant when he felt Kay's touch, but as soon as the young lad tried to do anything, the horse became restless and walked away from him. I heard Kay's laugh across the courtyard and felt a twinge of yearning in my stomach for his smile, his touch, the gentle, innocent love we had together. It was nothing like the sudden intensity I had felt with Lancelot, and that had made me afraid that what Kay and I had was the love of children. It was too simple, too innocent. Already it was slipping away from me, becoming the substance of memories, and dreams.

He saw us as we came in, and ran over, impossibly light on his feet in the armour. He held the horse by the bridle as Lancelot jumped down, and clapped him on the back with a smile. I saw that the smile Lancelot gave him in return was slightly tense. Kay noticed, of course. Kay noticed everything.

Lancelot stepped aside so Kay could offer me a hand down. I slid down before him, and felt the reassuring warmth of love flood through me as he smiled at me. It had only been a dream, with Lancelot. It was just a dream. I had not given up or betrayed or forgotten Kay. It was *that* – the moment dreamed with Lancelot, not the real love with Kay – that was the dream.

"Ah, my Lady the Princess Morgan. I trust the escort I sent to fetch you treated you chivalrously?" Kay asked with a wicked smile.

I could not help but smile in return. "For the most part."

I flashed Lancelot a narrow look, but Kay just laughed.

"For the most part," he repeated, laughing and giving Lancelot a playful shove. "Well, you're here safe." I wondered if either Lancelot or I would confess our kiss to Kay. He smiled, and for the first time I noticed that his smile seemed unsure, a little unsettled. "Listen." He glanced at Lancelot, and I saw suddenly that there was something that they knew about that I didn't, and I felt afraid. "Things have happened quickly here while you were gone. War is coming fast and

Arthur – well..." Kay sighed and smiled again. "You don't have to hear this now. Go and rest. I'll..." Under Lancelot's glance, Kay paused. So, Lancelot had had some kind of talk with him as he had had with me. "I'll see you when I can."

Kay gave a little bow, and as he turned from me, a wink. Kay had not changed.

I went up to my room, and unpacked my bag, hiding away the book of Macrobius among my dresses again. I pulled off the clothes I had travelled in and dressed myself again, and lay back on my bed. I felt a pang of guilt that Kay had obviously sent Lancelot to get me because he could not go himself and Lancelot was the only other person he trusted to bring me back safely. Lancelot was already well-known as the best of Arthur's knights; he would not have been spared to fetch me, princess though I was, unless Kay had asked for him specifically. But it had been nothing more than a kiss. I had nothing to confess, nothing for which to feel guilty. Kay would have laughed at me heartily indeed if I had come to him, guilty of a dream.

I heard a soft knock at the door, and I jumped up, hoping it was Kay, but it was not. It was Ector. His kindly eyes looked worried, and the smile he gave me was uneasy.

"Morgan, my dear, Arthur would like to see you in his council chamber."

I took the hand Ector offered with the gentlest smile I could muster. Ector had been more of a father to me than anyone else. This must have all been as hard on Ector as it was on any of the rest of us.

But he led me through the castle in an uneasy quiet. I supposed that Camelot was still reeling from new-declared war, and Arthur from finding out that Morgawse was his sister, but it made me feel unsettled. I would have liked some gentle words of comfort from Ector.

The first thing I saw when I came into Arthur's council chamber was Kay, both his hands braced so tight against the back of the chair he was leaning on that his knuckles showed white, his eyes as they lit on me dark with dread and his usually twinkling face pale and set. I felt the trepidation hit me, and I looked around at the others there. Kay knew what this was about. That was why he had been uneasy when I arrived. All that slightly forced jollity, all those tense looks between him and Lancelot. And I had thought it was because of something so small and petty as childhood jealousies. Arthur stood beside him, dressed in the king's clothes that he still did not look used to, the rich red and gold surcoat embroidered with Uther's dragon, and the crown on his head. He smiled when he saw me, but I already knew what it was that had brought the awful look to Kay's face, because opposite Arthur and Kay and Ector stood a stocky man in battered armour, his sandy hair lightly threaded through with grey at the temples. He looked to me to be about fifty years old. I was still not yet twenty. The man had a rough, unpleasant-looking face, tanned and wrinkled and scarred. He had small pale-blue eyes that squinted angrily out of his wrinkled face and the look about him of a hardened warrior.

I had known this day would come, but I wished that any one of them had prepared me. Kay and Lancelot had known. Ector had known. Lancelot could have told me on the way. Could have prepared me. Kay could have written. No one had warned me. They had plotted this for me while I was away with Morgawse and now they had brought me back to sell me off like cattle. I should have know. *I should have known.*

"Morgan," Arthur began cheerfully, and I lingered in the doorway. I looked at Kay, but he was looking down at his feet, a slight flush high on his cheeks. *Why won't you look at me?* "This is King Uriens, from the Kingdom of Gore, in the north of Wales, one of the vassal kings to Logrys."

"It is a pleasure to meet you, sir," I said softly, as a reflex. It was not a pleasure to meet him.

Uriens gave a low grunt of assent, looking me up and down. He did not look pleased to see the blue on my face, or the skinniness of my body or the plainness of my clothes, that were still those I had worn in the abbey. Yet the man who liked those things about me stayed silent. *Say something, Kay,* I thought. *If you say something I won't have to marry him.* Because I knew that was what this was about. Arthur would be angry, but only for a while. I did not think Arthur would deny Kay anything that he truly wanted.

"Uriens, this is my sister, Morgan. Do you assent to the marriage?"

Uriens gave another grunt, and a nod. *I don't assent.* Then I thought, he has not spoken because he does not really want to marry me, he just does not want to offend Arthur, and begin a war, or be forced onto what he thinks will be the losing side. Or he wants Cornwall and the rich castles there, my father's fortune, which he does not know does not exist because Uther took it all away.

"Then the date is set, as we agreed, for the end of the week," Arthur said, businesslike. With a curt bow of his head, Uriens left. So, it was that swiftly that I was bought and sold. No, I would not have it. If Kay would not step forward to claim me then I would claim myself.

"Arthur, I will not marry him."

Arthur, collecting the papers from his table – the maps of Britain, the letters from foreign kings – did not look up to answer.

"Morgan, Lot is poised to squash me like a fly. I *need* Uriens. Lot has almost all the North, and Carhais and Brittany have gone with him. I have Ban's sons in France, and I have Cornwall but I need Uriens and I need Gore, and I need North Wales." He looked up, and suddenly I did not see the eyes of the playful boy I had spent half my childhood with, but the hard grey eyes of a king. Perhaps Arthur *was* born for this. His voice was different, more commanding, more firm. He had, while I was gone, grown fully into a man. He seemed so much older than Morgawse's eldest sons, who were of the same age. I supposed when he became King he became the man that he was always destined to be, but I could not say I liked it. "You marry Uriens, or we all die," he said, in a tone that invited no argument.

He turned back to Kay, who hardly seemed to be listening, and Ector – who had moved around to stand behind his son – then rubbed his face in his hands.

"So, we have Logrys, obviously, and Cornwall and Ireland and North Wales with Uriens. We have France. But Lothian and Orkney are against us, and they are strong, and besides, the knights of Carhais will ride against us from Brittany. Is there any way we can get Carhais on our side? Isn't there a princess in Carhais? Doesn't Leodegrance have a daughter? Kay could marry her; wouldn't that get Brittany on our side?"

Ector sighed thoughtfully and tapped his foot, shaking his head.

"Arthur, Leodegrance's wife's sister is married to Lot's brother. Besides, King Leodegrance can trace back ten generations of Celtic royalty in his blood, including Queen Maev of Cruachan, and the Bretons are proud people."

"Kay is the brother of a king – isn't that enough?" Arthur asked, irritated.

"Kay is not your brother by blood. The girl is betrothed to one of her own people, and even if she were not I have heard it said besides that Lot plans to offer marriage with his son Gawain to have her. If you were going to compete in marriage to get Carhais the only offer you could match that with would be yourself."

"No." Arthur shook his head, pacing around the table, pushing aside papers until he came again to the map. "A king should not marry until his lands are safe. If Leodegrance will not have Kay for the girl, then we must do without Carhais. What about his sons?"

"Arthur, you are out of sisters. Nothing else will do. You can hardly offer his young sons your lady mother." Ector's tone was weary, and I could see that this was a discussion they had had before. Arthur did not have enough female relatives to ensure all the allegiances he wanted. I could see why he was worried; the knights of Carhais were almost as famous as the armies of Lothian, and he was a beardless boy-king with nothing but the prophecy of a sword and a witch by his side. Still, I resented being given for North Wales. Why could *I* not marry into Carhais? Someone my own age? But it would not be enough. Not if the king there was brother-in-law to Lot himself.

"One of Ban's sons could marry her."

"Arthur, we have been through this; we are many and the land my father ruled has been split into little pieces between his sons. Carhais will not bargain away its only princess for less than a realm or less than royal blood."

Arthur gave a violent sigh of frustration.

"Very well, we fight Carhais as well. Send for Merlin. I want Merlin here before the war begins." I did not think Arthur would have much success in *sending for* Merlin. He would come when he was ready. Or perhaps he was already here.

I resented it, I resented being given away, and then them talking marriage and war around me as though I were not there. I resented Kay for refusing to look at me.

"Shall I leave, then?" I demanded, loudly. Arthur looked up at me, confused. He had forgotten I was still there. A thought crossed his face, the thought I knew would come.

"Morgan..." He stepped towards me around the table. Though we were among friends, all of whom knew, he spoke quietly, as though it were too much to say in full voice. "The child, Morgan?"

I nodded. "Safe, healthy. A boy."

Arthur winced, which I had not expected. Despite its ill-fated conception, the boy was still his. I had thought, in the moment, he would be happy. He was happy enough before he knew that Morgawse was his sister. He rubbed his face. "What day was he born?"

"Mayday," I replied, confused as to why it would matter, until Arthur spoke again, and his voice chilled me to the bone.

"Ector, send some knights to Lothian in secret, unmarked for this court. All the boys born on Mayday in Lothian. I want it done fast, and in secret."

"Arthur –" Ector began, his tone both entreating and fearful. I understood this fear. I would never have expected that of Arthur. Arthur held up an authoritative hand.

"*See it done*, Ector." He turned to me then. "You may leave now, Morgan."

I walked back to my room, my head reeling; Kay's silence, my swift betrothal, Arthur's quest to murder his little son. When I got back to my room, I wrote two letters. One to my sister, warning her in the clearest terms I dared of what Arthur wanted for their son, and one to Nimue, begging her to come to Camelot before I was married.

The next few days passed in a blur. Arrangements were made around me for a wedding I did not want to happen. It was going to be a showy celebration, Camelot demonstrating that even as war loomed over it, its king could give a rich wedding for his sister and one of his vassal kings. One night at dinner Arthur even ostentatiously declared that he would provide a rich wedding dower, as though his father had not robbed it from mine in the first place. Kay seemed to be largely absent, or very busy with his duties as Seneschal, all of which helped him to avoid me. I felt the hot bristle of anger. He had left me to this fate, and now he was ignoring me. Just a little time alone with him would have been enough to make me feel less trapped, less alone. Lancelot, too, had gone with a band of knights to his castle to prepare for the war. I was glad, however, that he was gone.

Nimue came, two days before my wedding was set. I could have cried with joy to see her ride through the great gates of Camelot. She was dressed in a wonderful dress of sky-blue that was covered from its high neck to its waist in tiny sapphires that sparkled in the early summer sunlight, making her seem iridescent, sparkling in the sun like Avalon's lake itself. She slipped from her horse when she saw me, and ran into my open arms. I hugged her to me. She was small as a child, and tiny and hard against me, but so comforting.

She came up to my room with me, with her small parcel of things. So, she did not plan to stay long. At least I would have a friendly face at the wedding. She told me that the Lady of Avalon had died and she had taken her place, and her title as Lady. I felt a spasm of jealousy. I was being sold into marriage, Nimue had earned freedom and honour on Avalon. No one had asked me, and I was many years older than she. Still, I forced myself to be happy for her.

"I have a gift for you," she whispered, her pretty, childlike face still with seriousness. She pulled from her bag a dress like her own, but black and sewn from its low V-neck to the waist with black jewels, and all down its long sleeves. It was a perfect fit. I thanked her warmly, embracing her again. Nimue climbed on to my bed and sat with her legs crossed and pulled up to her chest, her arms wrapped around them and her chin on her knees. "Marriage, Morgan."

"Marriage," I nodded in grim agreement. "He's an old man."

Nimue nodded in thoughtful sympathy.

"I suppose all the black magic in the world can't save you from who you are, Princess Morgan," Nimue said, after a pause. I felt my heart race a few beats in panic. Nimue was the Lady now. Perhaps it was her task to ban Black Arts. There was no point in denying it in front of Nimue.

"How did you know?" I asked her, in a whisper, still standing, leaning back against my desk.

"I worked it out. Why you were upset that Merlin's real shape is ugly, what you had been reading in the library, and now you *feel* different." She lowered her voice, and leaned towards me, a fierce intensity gathering in her pale eyes, "I want it too, Morgan. Between us we can make Merlin give up his secrets. Give me the book of Macrobius, and I will get the rest from him."

I was shocked. I had expected her to demand I give it up, or to punish me. But she wanted it. So Avalon would be different now.

I had traded the sword for the book. How would I ever get Excalibur back if I traded the book away? She could see I was hesitating to trust her. I thought I had a right to, considering that my short life had proved to me already that no one could be fully trusted.

"How do I know I can trust you to not take the book?" I asked, tentatively.

Nimue shrugged. "You don't. I don't know that that book isn't full of rubbish, and that you and Merlin aren't trying to trick me together. All I have is you, and all you have is me. And we have a common enemy. Merlin. Give me the book, and I will make us both so powerful that we can have whatever we want. Remember, it was I who gave you the sword that Merlin stole from you. I am the only person who can protect you."

Her face was a hard little mask of ambition, but I could not help but admire her. Who would have known that sweet, demure little Nimue had a hunger in her for power? She was honest, and she was, as she said, the only person who had helped me yet. I got the book from the cupboard and pressed it into her hands. I, too, wanted more.

Chapter Nineteen

The night before my wedding, I wanted to be alone. I did not even want to be with Nimue. I locked my door and sat with my books, looking over everything from the book of potions without reading them. I could not escape this with magic. It would do me no good to change my shape, because they would only look for me. I supposed I could kill Uriens, but he had not yet actually done me any wrong. I could drug myself so that I would want him, but I did not want to use my magic on myself, and live a half-deluded life.

I had seen myself as Queen in my dream at Avalon, so I supposed it had to be. I would go, and be his wife, and bide my time. He might be killed in the war, and then I would be free of him. It was a good life, the life of a widow. I wished, as I had done many times before, that Morgawse would make it safely through the war. Then we might be together again, two happy widows in a house full of my nephews. I thought I would like that.

I heard a soft knock at the door. I thought it might be Nimue, so I ignored it, pretending to be asleep. The knock came firmer, and I heard Kay's voice call my name. I stood from my seat at the window, and walked over to the door. I lay my hand on the bolt, but I paused there. Kay had not warned me. He had not fought for me. But, tomorrow I would be married to an old man who seemed to find the look of me distasteful. I thought I deserved a last night of proper happiness with a man. As long as that was what Kay had come for.

I slid back the bolt slowly and opened the door. Kay stood there in his black and gold surcoat in the half dark. When he saw me open the door, he jumped through, taking my face in his hands, and kissing me hard. Any resistance, any anger I had in me, drained out in that blissful kiss. He pushed the door shut behind him with his foot, and I felt the excitement spark through me. We were alone together again at last. Kay murmured my name as he kissed me, hard and passionate, as though there was something he was desperate to say, that he could only say with his kisses. I scrabbled for the bolt, drawing it without breaking away from him. His hands ran through my long hair, pulling it loose from the plait, and I felt myself getting lost in his passion. I wanted to forget.

Suddenly, he stopped, still holding my face in his hands. I looked into his lovely brown eyes, full of resignation. My life was not going to end when I got married. I would not let it. I reached forward, to lay a hand against his chest. It rose and fell lightly under my hand. I had so much to say as well, but I could not. Too much of it was too painful, and if I said it, we would have no last lovely night of freedom.

Slowly, I flicked open the buttons of his surcoat with my fingers, and when it fell open, pushed it from his shoulders. He paused for a moment, gazing into my eyes, and I saw the excitement, the desire flash through him, and he pulled me hard against him, kissing me urgently, pulling me towards the bed with him. We fell back on it, me on top of him, and I tore the shirt from him. I knew, since it was the last time, I ought to have savoured it, ought to have been slow and careful to hold on to each moment, but it had been so long, and now he was there alone with me, it was overwhelming, the strength of his desire, and more so when I laid my hands, and then my lips, against his bare chest, smelled the familiar skin, brushed my fingers through the fine hair of his chest, then down his stomach, following the dark, tantalising line of hair down from his navel. Kay groaned softly and closed his eyes as I slid my hand down into his breeches. I felt his hands brush up my thighs under the skirts of my dress. As I pulled my hand away with a teasing smile, Kay sat up beneath me, pulling my dress over my head. He unlaced the underdress carefully, wary, still, I noticed, from when he had torn my underdress in half, and kissed lightly across my breasts as he opened the dress, following the opening down as his fingers pulled the laces free. I felt hot and light-headed, breathing fast already, feeling deliciously hungry for him. I felt his lips, then his tongue, lightly brush against my nipples, and I gasped. With a low murmur of desire, Kay pulled the underdress away and I felt the wonderful freedom of my bare skin against his hands, under his mouth. I heard him kick away his boots. I pushed him back down on to the bed and tore away his breeches. A wonderful smile of contentment and desire spread over his face as he took me firmly by the hips and moved me on to him. When I took him inside me, I felt my body flood with pleasure and relief to be back thus with Kay, to be close with him, to feel the joining of our love, and our bodies and the powers of the Otherworld. I laid my hands against Kay's chest feeling the heat of his skin, the beating of his heart. I saw the pleasure rise in him, flush the pale skin of his face and his chest, and it brought the hot spark of excitement fast to the centre of me. I did not want it to be over quickly, but my blood was high and my longing strong and

I felt the sweet spark of it growing fast at my centre. Kay, seeing me close, grasped hold of me, and turned us over with one powerful movement. He twined his fingers with mine, holding my arms over my head, kissing me dark and deep, as he moved hard and slow within me. But I was already there, and the wave broke over me, filling me with bright heat, and I gasped for Kay, through my desperate breaths. He sighed, too, low and long, and sank down on to me, his grip on my hands falling limp. Neither of us, much as we wanted to, could have held on to it any longer. I slid my arms away to wrap them around him. He nuzzled his face into my neck and kissed me softly there.

"I love you, Morgan," he whispered.

I said nothing. I did not want to say it too, not like he said it. He said it like *goodbye*.

Kay stayed until I fell asleep, holding me in his arms in a silence that was half contentment, half dread, and I laid my head on his chest and closed my eyes. I wanted the moment to last, I wanted to stay awake in Kay's arms as long as I could, and for the morning and my wedding not to come, but somehow with Kay's comforting presence beside me, I fell asleep quickly, and when I woke in the morning, he was gone.

Some serving maids came in the morning with a bath for me. I had rarely had baths before. I had always washed in the river, or in Avalon's great lake. The bath came for me steaming and smelling of rose and lavender oils. So, I was to be a show of Arthur's fine taste and sophistication as well.

Resentfully, I got into the hot water, sending the women away first. I had not grown up with servants as my sister had, and they made me uncomfortable. The nuns and the ladies of Avalon had done everything for themselves, and having women around helping me felt intrusive. I sank down into the hot water, and rubbed my limbs clean. Through the water, the patterns on my skin looked distorted, as though I was mottled all over in blue like a fish or a lizard. I liked it, though I was sure that my new husband would not. Not all men were like Kay. Most men were not like Kay. I was not sure, actually, if any other man was like Kay. Would every other man be afraid of my blue skin? My knowledge? Because that was really it – no man wanted a wife who knew secrets that he could not even guess at.

I ran my hands through my hair, feeling the clean hotness of the water against my scalp, and while the water cooled around me, wove it into a long four stranded plait, which was the most elaborate way I knew how to dress my hair, and not much better than the usual plait, but I supposed I ought to look different the day I got married.

I stepped from the bath and rubbed myself dry with a clean sheet, then dressed as slowly as I could in the dress Nimue had brought for me. It would make me feel a little stronger, a little safer, to have something from Avalon with me. Nimue came in as I was dressing, and helped me tie it tightly at the back. I ran my hand over the bodice, feeling the smooth bumps of the gemstones, gleaming like the scales of a dragon. It was a magnificent dress. Not beautiful, like Nimue's, but better. Fearsome.

Nimue looked me up and down in it.

"You look wonderful, Morgan," she told me, sincere and earnest. "Beautiful."

She leaned up and kissed me on the cheek, and I gave her a shaky smile.

There was another knock at the door, and without waiting for a response, my mother stepped through. I was shocked to see her, having forgotten that she was at Camelot. She had not been there when they were talking about having me married, though I supposed she would have had to agree to it. She looked beautiful as always, more beautiful than me, I thought, though she was twenty five years older. The thought struck me hard that at my age, my mother had already had my sister. I had had a few more years of freedom than she. She was dressed in a grey and silver silk dress, her hair wound into an elegant bun at the nape of her neck and secured with a silver net. She smiled when she saw me, and kissed me on both cheeks.

"Today you become a woman, little Morgan," she told me kindly, stroking my cheek as though I were a child. She cupped my cheeks in her hand. "You will make a wonderful queen. Just remember that men are rough and simple, and as women we must be wise, but also obedient." She kissed me on my forehead. "You are prepared... for tonight?" she asked, fixing me with a look of concern. "You know what to expect?"

I nodded. She smiled again and took my hand and squeezed it.

"Good. I hope you will be a happy wife, Morgan."

I wondered if she had been a happy wife with my father. Or with Uther. I could not imagine that she had been with Uther. Uther had killed her husband and tricked her to have her. Morgawse always told me that our mother and father had been happy together, had loved each other, but I was not sure if that was really true, if that was not the dream Morgawse had of her childhood before Uther.

She drew me in to a tender, motherly embrace, and I held her tight. I was not sure if I would get one of these again. Uriens would take me away to his lands, and war might tear me and my mother apart. She took my hand and tucked it in to the crook of her arm, to lead me from my room. I wanted to turn and look at it one last time, to have a final savour of my life before marriage, but I only caught a glimpse before the door was shut fast behind me. I closed my eyes and steeled myself. It would be over soon.

Mother led us down, Nimue following behind, and across the courtyard into the chapel. It was already full of people. I felt my heart beating hard and nervous inside me. I felt small and nervous, childlike with fear and anticipation. I glanced through the crowd as Mother led me down the centre aisle. Kay hung at the back, not in the pews, but leaning against the back wall, his arms crossed over his chest, one foot braced against the stone. He was staring straight ahead of him. I did not think he was ignoring me. He seemed lost in thought. In the pews, I saw familiar faces from around Camelot, but then my eyes caught on a head of glossy chestnut-brown curls. As though sensing my look, the man turned and I saw with a stab of anger and fear that I was right; it was the young man Merlin. Of course he had come like that to see me married. He gave me a cruel little grin. I looked away.

Arthur stood at the back of the chapel, near the altar, with Uriens. Arthur was dressed in red and gold and with his crown. He did look every bit the king. I supposed he was dressed like that to remind my new husband what a fine prize he was getting. He took my hand from my mother's, and led me up to Uriens. I saw a look of distaste pass across Uriens' face as my hand was placed in his, and I felt myself harden inside with resentment. Did he think I was pleased with him? I was only woaded blue; other than that I was young and desirable enough. I was the daughter of a king, the sister of a king. He ought to have been glad to have me.

The ceremony passed in a blur, and Uriens' kiss at the end was a dry, perfunctory brush. He still had not spoken a word to me. I was relieved when I heard the people in the chapel cheer, and Uriens led me away to the feast. At least there I could drink enough wine that I might not notice him on top of me later, or slip into a hazy, drunken half-sleep where it might not be so bad.

I sat beside Arthur, with Uriens the other side of me, at the high table. I suppose the places had been set as a subtle reminder to Uriens that I was still closer to the king that he was, but I would have preferred not to be sat next to Arthur. I was still angry with him. On the other side of Arthur sat our mother. When I caught her eye, she gave me an encouraging smile. I must have looked as full of discomfort as I felt.

Kay sat opposite Arthur, moved further from his usual place by me and my husband. I could see that he was drunk already. His cheeks were flushed from the wine, and when he drank, he tipped his cup back clumsily, spilling a little against his lips. Usually cheerful, and usually guiding the conversation with his charm, Kay's sudden silence at the feasting table made conversation awkward. I didn't want to talk pleasantries with Arthur, and my new husband was no conversationalist, so it was mainly composed of our mother asking polite questions about the homes of various lords and ladies around us.

I knew the food was rich and opulent, but I could not really taste it through my nerves. I felt better when I had drained a few cups of wine. The fuzzy feeling than ran through my limbs made me feel further from my body, more disconnected from my limbs. I would endure Uriens better like this. When the food had been cleared, the music for the dancing began and Kay jumped up with a sudden cheer. Arthur, flushed, too, with wine, laughed with joy and relief to see Kay suddenly back to his usual self. Kay sprang away to join the dancing. I glanced at my husband. I was pleased, at least, that he had as little taste for dancing as I did. He was picking a piece of meat, or something, from his teeth. He looked bored. I did not know how a man as stolid and boring as he could be bored by anything.

There was a group of people dancing already. Among them, I saw Kay twirling around with a girl with glossy brown ringlets, whom I did not think I knew, but who looked oddly familiar. His hands were at her waist, and he seemed to be dancing pressed unnecessarily close to her. I felt a burn of jealousy. I knew that I was going to bed with another man, but it did not seem fair for Kay to be drunkenly dancing like *that* with other women right in front of me, even if it would make him feel better that I was getting married. I caught sight of the girl's face as Kay spun her around again, and realised with a little jump of fear that the girl looked familiar because she looked in the face like the handsome young Merlin. I glanced around the room. I could not see him there. *Surely* Merlin would not be doing this? What would he have to gain? Only upsetting me.

Arthur, beside me, got up from his seat with a happy laugh and went to join the dancing. His mistake with Morgawse had not served to make him more shy or more careful around women, I noticed. Uriens, beside me, gave a little cough and I turned to see that he had stood from his chair and was offering me his hand. I supposed that meant it was time to go.

"My Lady Morgan," he said, politely. I took his hand. As I turned to go, I saw the girl dancing with Kay suddenly grab him by the face and kiss him. He stumbled back a step, stunned, or perhaps just drunk, but then, slowly, put his arms around her. I hoped that I was wrong, and that she was *not* Merlin.

Uriens led me away, up to a room in the King's tower of Camelot. It had obviously been specially prepared for the event. Candles were already burning. It was summer, so there was no fire, but in the low candlelight the bedsheets gleamed with gold and silver threads. They were obviously fine silk, the finest that could be found. Arthur would want Uriens to believe that every room in Camelot was as fine as this.

I noticed for the first time how richly dressed Uriens, too, was. I had barely noticed him beside me all evening. He was dressed in a brocade surcoat sewn in pale gold and silver on grey, and he had huge gold rings on his fingers. Now we were alone, he undid his surcoat and shrugged it off, folding it carefully and placing it on the chair in the corner of the room. He stood back for a moment, looking me over. I stood uneasily, feeling the door at my back, the desire to run away. I had nowhere to go. Not really.

"So, you're witch," he said flatly. It wasn't really a question. He did not seemed pleased.

"I was schooled in Avalon. I know some of the healing arts. That's all," I told him softly. Best to play obedient, to play innocent, for now. There was no point in my having got married if I could not keep him long enough to make sure that we won the war against Lot. Morgawse would be safer if Lot was dead. I had to keep him happy for now, for her sake.

He made a small grunt of half-acceptance. He pulled his shirt over his head, and folded it, and put it with the surcoat. The hair on his chest was grey, and wispy. Beneath he was corded with lean, ageing muscle and tanned and lightly speckled with freckles from the sun. He looked at me expectantly. I did not know what I was supposed to do. I was glad that he was not going to try to kiss me, but I was not sure what I was meant to do on my own. I wished that I had drunk more wine.

"Did no one explain this to you?" he asked, annoyed. I didn't know what the other women that he had been with must have done. *I* knew what I was doing. It seemed to me that he did not know himself.

"I need help with my dress," I told him, already feeling myself withdrawing, resolving to hate him. It was unkind and unfair of him to be angry with his bride for not knowing or doing what he wanted. For all he knew, I was a virgin raised in an abbey. I could have been terrified, as my sister had been. As it was, I was just reluctant.

He walked over and turned me roughly around as I held my plait out of the way so that he could unlace the dress and pull it over my head. I turned back to him, and saw the distaste deepen on his face as he saw that I was tattooed in blue all over. He ought to have been grateful to have one of the wise women of Avalon as his wife. If he were more open-minded, I might have offered to change myself into a form that he would have found more appealing, but he did not seem like the kind of man to be interested in that. He felt as though he had compromised for politics on his bride, and he was resentful. He ought to imagine how I felt. I supposed he thought himself attractive. He had a rough, plain, square face and a sullen look on it. I would never have described him so.

Still, in the spirit of duty, I went to unlace my underdress, but he put a hand over mine to stop me.

"Don't take that off," he said, gruffly. *He doesn't want to look at me.* Not the blue skin, not the skinny body. I felt the burn of embarrassment on my cheeks. He could have been just a little kind to me, and we might have made the best of it, but he was determined for me to know that he did not want me. "Get in the bed," he said, turning away from me to unlace his breeches and pull them off.

In my underdress, I slipped beneath the covers. I felt the wine swim a little in my head, but I had not drunk enough. I thought of Kay, kissing the brown-haired girl. Maybe he had gone to bed with her by now. What if she was Merlin? What if Merlin did something to Kay, to hurt me? Perhaps he had found out that I had given Nimue the book, and he was angry. What if he hurt Kay? I felt an urge to run from the room, around the castle, looking for Kay, to warn him. I felt more and more sure that it *was* Merlin.

My thoughts were interrupted by Uriens climbing in to bed on top of me. He had blown out all the candles, obviously not wanting to look at me, and the suddenness of his weight on top of me surprised me. I gave a little involuntary jump, and he made a shushing noise that was half-comforting, half-patronising. Not comforting enough for me to forgive him for it. I felt his hands pulling up the underdress to my waist, and then moving my legs apart. No. I couldn't do this. I didn't want to be married, he didn't want to marry me either, we could stop now and the marriage could be undone. *Stop*, I wanted to say, but my voice had left me. I felt my body tense against him, but it was too late. He thrust himself hard into me and I bit back a small cry of pain. I would not give away any weakness. I screwed my eyes tight shut and tried to picture something else, but all I could picture was Kay with the girl who looked like Merlin, or suddenly and awfully, Arthur with Morgawse, kissing her against the wall of the corridor.

It was thankfully over soon and Uriens rolled away. I felt more naked, more dirty than I had ever felt with Kay, or even with Merlin. I felt sore, too, and my skin cold and clammy with unwanted touch. Uriens was soon snoring beside me, but it was growing light outside before I could finally fall asleep. I wanted to cry, but I dared not. I didn't want to wake Uriens, or to give in to weakness of any kind. I would need all my strength to survive being his wife.

Chapter Twenty

Through the half-sleep of my morning I felt Uriens leave the bed and get up to dress. I was glad that he was not waiting for me, and that he was leaving. I turned my pillow over and pressed my face into the cool side, slipping back off into sleep. But, as I felt myself drifting away, Uriens tore back the covers from the bed. I groaned, tired and annoyed, but he was searching through the bed desperately, as though he were looking for some lost object on which his life depended. He pushed me roughly out the way, as though he were looking under me for something, but I was awake now, and angry. I had put up with his coldness last night, but I wasn't going to be shaken from my bed by his strange behaviour. I sat up to protest, and he grabbed me and turned me over, looking over me as well. I tried to wriggle away from him, but with a low grunt of anger, he grasped me hard by the arm and dragged me from the bed. I struggled against him, but I couldn't get my arm free of him. Despite his age he was strong, with many years of fighting behind him, and I was small and skinny, the only strength I had hiding deep inside me for when the time came I could use it.

"What is wrong with you?" I shouted at him, as he dragged me from the room, but he did not seem to hear me. He pulled me with him through the corridor and up the flight of stairs to Arthur's bedroom.

"What are you doing?" I asked again, angry and embarrassed. My hair hung loose and long around my shoulders, down to my waist, and I stood in only my underclothes, my feet bare against the cold stone. I didn't want anyone to see me like this, nor did I think my new husband ought to be dragging me through Camelot like this.

He didn't seem to hear me, but banged hard on Arthur's door. Before waiting for a response, he turned the handle and strode in, dragging me behind him.

Arthur stood before his fireplace in his shirt and breeches, the shirt hanging loose and his hair still tousled with sleep. Behind him, I noticed Kay. He didn't look up when he heard the door.

"Uriens, what is the meaning of this?" Arthur asked.

Uriens, his face red with rage, not releasing the tight grip on my arm, shook me slightly, and through his anger, sputtered, "She isn't a virgin."

Arthur's eyes glanced over to me, but just for a second. He drew himself up, giving Uriens a look of disdain.

"Uriens, I am not sure what you want from me. Do you want me to congratulate you for taking your wife to bed? If so, dragging my sister to me like this in her underclothes is no suitable way to encourage me to do so." Behind him, Kay had turned to look, but resting his head still in one hand. I didn't meet his eye, but I was glad, at least, that he seemed to be safe and well. I didn't want to give anything away.

"No, Arthur –"

"*My Lord King* Arthur," Arthur corrected sharply. I saw Uriens bristle. He had come in his anger, thinking himself clearly in the right, and he was fast losing ground, losing ground to the king that he had possibly – as many others had – dismissed as a boy.

"No, my Lord Arthur. I mean she was not a virgin *when we married.*"

Arthur squared up to him then, turned fully to face him. He rubbed a thoughtful hand across his mouth.

"You have proof of this?" he asked, looking steadily at Uriens.

"There was no blood."

Arthur shrugged. "There is not always blood. Morgan has not been a princess locked in a tower, she has spent her youth riding horses, which has made her strong, but many girls lose their first blood that way and have never known a man." Arthur turned from him, and began to pace for a moment. Uriens' hand was so tight around my arm, I was beginning to lose the feeling in my fingers. Kay was watching Arthur, wary. Arthur stopped and turned back to

135

Uriens, his tone thoughtful, but his eyes cold, and hard. "Here is my problem, Uriens. The morning after I honour you by giving you my own dear sister as your wife, you dishonour me by dragging her through my castle in her underclothes accusing her of having known another man. Do you think me an honourable man, Uriens?"

I glanced at him beside me. His nostrils flared and a vein showed in his forehead, but I could see from his face, from his eyes, that he was the man in the weaker position.

"Yes, my Lord Arthur."

"Well, then you see the difficulty I am in. I tell you she has known no one else, and you dishonour her and me by questioning it. Not to mention this rough treatment you have given her, my own dear sister. I have knights to spare, and power yet that I could easily crush a few small castles in North Wales on my way up to Lothian." I knew this was not true, but Uriens seemed to believe it, and Arthur spoke it like he believed it. "How can I let this insult pass?"

Uriens said nothing, flustered, overwhelmed. He had lost control of the situation. I supposed he thought he could drag me before Arthur and have Arthur's sympathy. I was pleased that Arthur seemed to be defending me, but not pleased enough that I forgot it was he who had sold me into this in the first place, for his own political gain.

"Well, Uriens. You are fortunate, for as I am an honourable man, I am also a merciful one. If you make the appropriate apologies to my sister then I will let this pass as nothing more than... a small misunderstanding."

Slowly, reluctantly, Uriens turned to me. I could see he was not at all sorry, and I feared I would pay for this later. Nothing would happen while we were still in Camelot, but once we were in his kingdom, I feared that his anger would come out. I had before me in my mind my sister with the back of her hand pressed against her lip, as though she had done it a thousand times before. He drew in a breath as though it pained him.

"My apologies, my Lady," he said, stiffly.

Arthur nodded, as though satisfied, and gave a wave of his hand, as though to dismiss us, but when Uriens went to lead with me with him to the door, Arthur spoke again.

"I think you had better leave my sister with me for now, Uriens. It won't do to drag her through my castle in her shift once more. But you might send for some women to come here with her clothes."

Uriens dropped my arm and nodded. I felt the blood rushing back down to my hand, and my skin throbbing where his fingers had been. I felt myself beginning to shake, just slightly, as he slammed the door when he left. I did not want to ever have to go back to him. I wrapped my arms around myself defensively, and stood back for whatever anger I was sure I would have to face from Arthur now. Behind him, Kay was pressing his forehead into the heels of his hands, still barely moved from where he was.

Arthur, however, gave a huge sigh as though he had been holding in his breath and shook his head, turning to Kay.

"Well, I really thought he was just going to hit me, or demand a pitched fight or something. Maybe that would have been easier; I would have won. But..." Arthur shook his head, rubbing his face. Kay looked up at him blearily, his face unreadable. Then Arthur turned back to me, and I was surprised to see he did not look angry, just weary. "Morgan, whoever this man was —"

I opened my mouth, with a vague intention to protest my innocence, but Arthur carried on speaking.

"No, I don't want to hear about it, or hear some excuse. I'm not stupid, Morgan. Whoever it was, or whoever they were..." I thought this was unnecessary from him, as was his tone of censure. Arthur did not seem to be restraining his lust for women at all, and he was scolding me for less than he had done. "Morgan, don't see him again, don't speak to him again, don't write, not even to explain. The laws of this land still allow a king to put his wife to the fire for having another man. It's barbaric, I know, but it's the law, and don't think Uriens isn't the kind of man to uphold a law like that. Does this other man know you are married now?"

"Yes," I answered, sharply. Kay was rubbing his face again, and didn't look up.

Arthur nodded. He seemed to consider the matter dealt with. He turned away from me, rubbing his face. Then he looked at Kay, who was rubbing the heels of his hands in to his forehead again, and he laughed. Kay squinted up at him.

"Kay, what did that girl *do* to you last night?"

Kay blinked painfully, as though the light stung his eyes.

"What girl?"

Arthur laughed again, louder. Suddenly he was like the boy who just a few years ago had played like a child in the fields around Ector's house, and thrown off his clothes to jump in the lake.

Kay, sitting up and leaning back in the chair he was in, groaned.

"Where is Lancelot?" he asked, holding a hand over his eyes.

"Still at Joyous Guard," Arthur answered, sounding a little annoyed. I thought he seemed far more comfortable talking to Kay about some nameless girl than he did about Lancelot. He must worry about them still. "Why?"

Kay groaned deeper, sinking further back in to the chair. "How much did I drink last night? I could have sworn he was... here."

I felt suddenly cold. *Merlin.*

"Arthur," I asked, "have you seen Merlin?"

Arthur threw up his arms in a gesture of frustration. "I might be King here, but I don't know where *everyone* in my kingdom is at any given time. No, I don't know where Merlin is. I sent for him, but he hasn't come, and no one can find him. I'm sure he'll turn up when he's good and ready." Then he paused, his eyes fixing on me, widening as the thought struck him. He wrinkled his face together in the same expression of distaste I had seen my sister give me, but though he made the assumption, he did not say anything. He may have been right, but he was wrong about why I was asking for Merlin.

Arthur pulled on his surcoat and left, dragging Kay with him, as women came in with my dress. I was glad they brought the lovely jewelled dress that Nimue had made for me. At least I felt a little stronger, a little more powerful with it on. I would have to face Uriens again, soon, and I was unwilling to go without any protection.

When I came down to my room, I hoped to see Nimue, but instead when I opened the door I saw, lounging in my window-seat, one leg dangling, the other drawn up, Merlin the young man. He flashed me a smug smile. He was pleased with himself about something, and I thought I knew what. I shut the door behind me and slid the bolt across. I crossed my arms in front of my chest.

"What do you want, Merlin?" I asked, sharply.

"I have a bride gift for you," he replied with a grin, slipping from the seat and walking over to me. I turned my face up to him, bold and defiant.

"I don't want it, Merlin. You know Arthur is looking for you."

He ignored me, and reached out to take my hand. I pulled it away. I knew what he had come for. He had come for the book. Well, he didn't know I had already given it away. Nimue had it somewhere safe, and she was going to get the rest from him. He wasn't going to get anything else from me. I didn't have to trade away anything else for his magic.

He took another step towards me, and I moved back. He shook his head and tutted.

"Morgan, we could have got more from one another with kindness," he said, with a tone of mocking sadness. "I don't like having to resort to threats. I need my book back, and I *do* come with a gift of my own in return. Do I need to make you understand how powerful I am? What I could do to you, to those you care about?"

I didn't say anything, just hung back, my arms still crossed over my chest. He gave a low noise, like a growl, that was both anger and enjoyment. Of course, Merlin would enjoy the prospect of fighting dirty. He didn't know I had an ally. He jumped forward again, and this time he caught me by surprise, and he had me in his grip. He was stronger than I remembered, stronger than I expected and turned me around roughly, holding one arm hard around my waist, and he clapped his other hand over my eyes. I opened my mouth to shout, for Nimue, for Kay, for anyone, but the voice froze in my throat, and through the darkness of his hand over my eyes I saw an empty room, as though in a dream.

My body felt suddenly as it would in a dream, weightless, spaceless, fuzzy. My tongue, too, thick and filling my mouth, blocking out my voice. I fought to wake from this dream Merlin had plunged me in to, but I could not. The room was a small, plain bedroom with a simple bed laid out in the corner, a plain wood table and a chair, and on the chair in a messy pile, unmistakable, Kay's black Otherworld armour. A fire burned low in the fireplace, filling the room with low red light, and a little smoke. I walked over to the table. The two letters I had written Kay were there, weighed down with a smooth stone. It looked to me like the kind of stone that lay around the shores of Avalon. I reached out and laid my fingers against the smooth surface, but through the hazy dream-feeling, I felt nothing of its smoothness or coolness.

Suddenly the door flew open with a clatter, and Kay and the brown-haired girl stumbled through together, her pushing him back into the room, kissing him hard. He stumbled back, clumsy, drunk. He seemed a little confused, a little resistant. She kicked the door shut behind her, pushing him towards the bed.

"Wait, wait," I heard Kay slur, gently pushing her off him, prising her lips off his own. As he did, in his hands the brown-haired girl turned into the young handsome Merlin, the clothes changing with him to men's clothes. I had not managed that when I had changed. I needed to learn. Kay squinted, surprised at the person he was holding, but he seemed to consider his confusion a function of his own drunkenness, and didn't question it. Merlin took Kay's face in his hands and kissed him hard, and I saw Kay step back against the forcefulness of it, and relent for a second, drunkenness and desire getting the better of him, but as Merlin pushed them again towards the bed, Kay pulled away from him again. "I can't," he protested, looking down at his feet, his hands on Merlin's shoulders, as though he were steadying himself.

Then, while Kay was looking away, I saw Merlin change again and it was as though Lancelot truly stood there before me. It was all the same. The dark, glossy curls, the tall, lightly muscular body. My breath caught, and I clamped a hand over my mouth to hide my gasp, but I didn't need to.

"Kay," he said softly, and it was Lancelot's voice, low, smooth, tinged with French. He laid a hand against Kay's cheek, and Kay looked up. The look in his eye changed from surprise, to something far more complex that I had never seen before, a kind of desperate relief, as though some deep wish within him had been suddenly granted, but he ought not to have it. "Kay, it's alright. It's me."

Kay gave a gasp, taking Lancelot's – Merlin's – face in his hands as though to check he was real, and then Kay kissed him fiercely, pulling him close, winding his hands into Lancelot's – or the man he thought was Lancelot's – hair. Lancelot pushed him down on to the bed, and Kay fell back obediently, staring up at Lancelot, propped up on his elbows, in rapturous disbelief. Lancelot pulled off his shirt, and the low firelight threw shadows against the curve of his muscles, the lean frame, packed with strength. I had to tell myself it was really Merlin, for I felt the desire rising in me to look at him, and unconsciously I stepped closer. I could see Kay's chest rising and falling hard with eager anticipation, his eyes locked on Lancelot. He suddenly did not seem so very drunk anymore. I felt a stab of jealousy that I did not think Kay had ever looked at me that way. Lancelot climbed on to Kay, and Kay lay back, running his hands through Lancelot's hair again, pulling him close in a passionate kiss. I knew I ought to look away, ought to remind myself that it was Merlin, really, and that this was meant to frighten me, but the sight of their mouths locked together in passion, their two bodies pressed close filled me with a wonderful forbidden thrill. Kay's hands ran slowly down Lancelot's chest, and when Kay had him by the hips he suddenly threw them both over in a rush of passion, and their kisses became harder, hungrier. Lancelot's hands rushed at the buttons on Kay's surcoat, and pushed it off his shoulders. Kay threw it off him, and away. It landed inches from the fire. With the tip of my foot, I pushed it slightly away, out of reach of the sparks. Just like in a dream, it did not move. I looked back, and Lancelot pulled off Kay's shirt. His hands ran down Kay's back, then around to the front of Kay's breeches. Kay gave a low groan, his face creasing with pleasure and desire. Clumsy with wine and urgency, Kay pulled away Lancelot's breeches, and I heard the fabric tear. Lancelot pushed Kay's down, and Kay kicked them away. They fell together again, their kisses wild and passionate, and looking at them I saw a tangle of muscular bodies, dark hair, and felt the heat of desire stir deeper in me. *That is not really Lancelot, that is Merlin,* I reminded myself. But it *could* be Lancelot, and it had been before.

That was when Merlin drew his hand away sharply, and I was back in my bedroom with him, my head spinning, disorientated, trying to catch my breath. I could not work out why Merlin had wanted that, and why he had shown it to me. Was it just to prove that he would find a way to take anything or everything from me? Was it to show me how vulnerable Kay was? Did he think that I had never known what had passed, long ago, between the two of them? He could, after all, have killed him then.

I wheeled around to face him. He was grinning, pleased with himself.

"You should be grateful, Morgan, that I did not kill him. He has a weak and gentle heart, your Sir Kay. He is a vulnerable man. Next time you think that you do not need me, just remember, last night your lover held me close and told me that he loved me." Merlin grabbed me by the back of the neck, and around the waist, and pulled me against him. I felt his breath against me, and beneath his physical strength, the dark power of his magic. My hands against his shoulders, I tried to push him off, but he did not budge. He tightened his grip on me, holding me against him. "I will have whatever I desire, Morgan. Your life will be easier if you comply. Now *give me the book.*"

He was so close that his lips almost brushed mine as he hissed at me. I pushed at him again. I was sure that he had not been this strong before.

"I don't have it," I hissed back.

He kissed me hard, and for a moment, still hot with excitement from the sight of Kay and Lancelot together, my lips parted under his in a reflex of desire, and he pulled me tighter against him. I seized the moment to push him off more forcefully, shaking myself out of it, forcing myself to picture Merlin how he really was, bald with his skull-like grin, stooped under his hunching back. It was harder, too, to remember and be resistant when I would have liked an opportunity to spite my husband after how he had treated me. But the one man I hated more than my new husband was Merlin.

Merlin drew back from me, a cruel smile on his face.

"What do you mean *you don't have it?*"

I shrugged. "When I was in Lothian, Lot took it. He burned it. He didn't want magic books in his kingdom."

I could see that Merlin did not believe me, but that he was not sure enough to force the matter. I suspected that he had already checked and found that it was not in the room. He gave me a narrow look, trying to work out how much truth there was in what I said. He moved towards me again, as though he would try to kiss me, but when I moved back he gave a low, cruel laugh and left, disappearing into nothingness before me. I hoped Nimue's destruction of him would be swift. I hated him, then, more than ever.

Chapter Twenty-One

I packed my things carefully, hiding my book of healing arts among my clothes. I wondered if I would ever wear the plain wool dresses again. My mother had left in my bedroom some old silk dresses of her own, and some of her jewels. I supposed these were gifts for me now that I was a wife. I remembered her wishing that I would be a happy wife. Too late for that already.

The silk dresses that she had left were beautiful, well-chosen for me. Midnight blue, one, sewn with silver thread to look like stars. Another a deep blood red, plain, but made from silk that almost shimmered and felt liquid under my touch. Beautiful dresses, dresses for a queen. I was a queen now. A queen under my brother's vassalage, but a queen nonetheless.

There was a knock at my door, and before I could answer, Nimue slipped through. I was pleased to see her. She did not ask me how it had been, but she ran into my arms for a tight, desperate embrace.

"Nimue, come and see me in Gore." Uriens' kingdom, from where he commanded the north of Wales. Not my home. No sweet name like 'Avalon' that promised beauty, belonging and rest. It was an ugly-sounding place, and I did not look forward to seeing it. Nimue nodded against me. I remembered Merlin. "Nimue, Merlin knows I don't have his book anymore." She nodded again, and I leaned closer to her ear to whisper, "Get his secrets as soon as you can."

She kissed me on the cheek, her kiss dry and papery, like the kiss of a child. She squeezed my hand as she left, telling me she had to go back to Avalon. There was more for her to do.

I felt exhausted, suddenly, when she left, and I lay on my bed, wrapping my arms around my head to block out the light, and let myself sink into sleep. When I slept, I dreamed of Kay, his mouth against mine, his hands on me, as passionate and intense as I had seen him with Lancelot.

I woke to a gentle hand on my shoulder, and looked up to my mother, full of gentle concern. I sat up to embrace her, and told her what she wanted to hear. That I thought I would be a happy wife, and I hoped to see her soon. She kissed me on the cheek and left. I felt as though everyone was saying goodbye to me, one by one. But Kay did not come.

The time came at last, just after midday, when I was called to depart with Uriens for his kingdom. I looked all around my room before I left. I hoped that I would be back soon. I had been torn from three homes already, Amesbury, Avalon, and now Camelot.

I picked up my bag, and I called for a servant girl to take my mother's dresses and pack them in one of the bags. When I walked down to the courtyard, I hoped I would see Kay among the horses, where he often was, but he was not there. I felt the cold clutch of betrayal at my stomach. He was not even going to say goodbye. I could forgive him for spending last night with one he thought was Lancelot, for their love was older than his and mine, but I could not bear that he had not come to say goodbye to me. He had led me like a lamb to the slaughter into this marriage, and now he had melted away, so that he did not have to face his guilt. Perhaps he was guilty because he loved Lancelot more than he loved me, but really I thought it was because he loved Arthur more. Arthur, the little brother for whom he would sacrifice anyone. First Lancelot, so that he would not be sent from his brother's side, and now me, so that Arthur could win the war he caused with his foolishness. Yes, that was it.

When I walked down, Uriens was already mounted on his horse, dressed in his battered armour, but without his helm, his sword at his side. Arthur stood at the side of the courtyard with Ector, dressed in his red and gold coat, his crown on his head, to say goodbye to his *dear sister* whom he had sold for some knights for his war.

Uriens nodded brusquely when he saw me. I went over to Ector and kissed him goodbye on both cheeks, letting him pull me into a fatherly embrace. I would miss Ector. He held me gently by the arms and smiled at me.

"My Lady, Queen Morgan, I hope I shall see you again soon," he said, kindly. I gave him the steadiest smile I could in return.

"Me too, Ector."

Arthur stepped forward and kissed me goodbye on both cheeks, too, but as he did, he whispered in my ear, "Make an *effort* with him, Morgan. I need you to help me in this."

I gave him a cold look as we parted. As I climbed onto my horse, I looked around for Kay again, but the only other familiar face I saw was Merlin, still in his young form, loitering at the edge of the courtyard. *Kay is not coming to say goodbye.*

Uriens gave the shout to leave, gave a deferential nod to Arthur, and our small party departed. I wondered as we left if any of my letters had reached Morgawse. I hoped that they had. I would write to her again from Gore, so that she would know where I was. I would have liked to have seen her. I hoped that this war would not part us forever. I hoped that Aggravain was serious about protecting his mother. I hoped that he was old enough, and strong enough, to resist his father, and keep the promise that he had made to me.

As we rode away, Uriens moved beside me on his horse. I glanced sideways at him. He seemed as though he wanted to talk to me, but I was not going to make it easy for him. Not after what he had done to me this morning. But I did not need to speak first. He began, his voice tense with thwarted rage.

"That brother of yours thinks he's so clever. So powerful. He's just a boy. Without me, Lot would crush him in his bare hands. He thinks he's a great king, he's just a boy."

I let a moment of silence pass between us, staring ahead of me as we rode.

"A boy of whom you are afraid," I replied, pointedly. I didn't look at him, but I was sure he was bristling with anger. Perhaps there would be parts of this marriage I would enjoy. Uriens was easy to bait, and flashed with anger fast.

"I am not afraid of Arthur," he growled tersely.

"*King* Arthur," I corrected, unable to keep a wicked smile of enjoyment from my lips. I felt him turn to look at me, burning with frustration, but I gazed off into the distance, enjoying myself at last.

The ride to Gore was not far, and we reached Uriens' castle as night was falling. I was pleased to not have to spend a night on the road with Uriens. Perhaps he would be tired from the ride, and want to go right to sleep. I hoped so. Uriens' castle was built like Lothian castle, tall and narrow with sharp spires, densely packed. It looked unwelcoming. Like Lothian castle, it did not have a great courtyard like Camelot with a welcoming wooden gate, but we entered through a barbican gate with two unfriendly rust-toothed portcullises. Inside, a small band of knights waited for their king and their new queen. At their head stood a knight with a torch to welcome us. In the light of the torch he held, I could see he was youngish, roughly of an age with me, not more than five years older, I thought, and handsome. Fair hair swept back from his face, dark gold stubble across his chin, and a thoughtful, angular face, just a little rugged. But I had had enough of handsome men for the moment. The young Merlin, threatening me, Lancelot kissing me then turning me away, and worst of all Kay, telling me he loved me then abandoning me at the final moment of my need.

He appeared to be Uriens' steward, and he greeted him first, taking the reins of his horse so that he could jump down. Making a show of courtesy in front of his men, Uriens walked around to me and offered me his hand to help me down. I took it and slipped from my horse. I landed on my feet right before his steward, who greeted me with a confident, charming smile. He gave a small bow.

"My Lady Queen Morgan. Welcome to Rheged castle." He kissed my hand and I gave a nod of my head in response, resistant. I was not going to give anything of myself away again. I had suffered from it too much.

Servants came out to take our belongings into the castle, and Uriens excused us, saying he was tired from the ride. He led me in silence through the courtyard to the castle's central tower. When we walked through the door, a jolt of recognition went through me at the sight of the staircase. I had seen myself at the top of it, in my dress of black gems, wearing the crown of Gore. This was my future, then. I wondered how long it would be before I saw the red-haired woman, before she and I stood on the shores of Avalon, Excalibur drawn between us. I could not remember who had been holding the sword when I had seen it in my dream of the future. It had to be me. I *would* have my sword back.

Uriens led me to a bedroom where someone had lit a few candles in preparation for our arrival. I wondered if I would have a chamber of my own here. I hoped that I would. It would be well enough to have somewhere of my own, far from Uriens. But this seemed to be his chamber, for once I followed him in and he shut the door, he began to undress, unbuckling and pulling off his armour, and setting it down. He pulled off his shirt, too, and went to a basin set on the table, and splashed his face with the water, then rubbed it dry with the cloth beside the basin. I stood back, watching, dreading. Perhaps he would just go to sleep. He did not. He strode over to me, and grasped me by the shoulders, pulling me against him in a rough kiss.

145

I would have been glad of it if, though I hated him, I could have at least enjoyed myself in this. I knew I was capable of it, but he was *too* rough, his lips brusque and coarse against mine, his grip violent rather than passionate in its roughness, and I felt my body stiffen instinctively against him. He turned me around roughly and unlaced the overdress, and pulled it over my head. I thought about refusing, about protesting. He had been rude to me. He had done dishonour to me, so I did not know why he thought I would go willingly with him now.

I stepped away from him, crossing my arms over my chest. A cruel smile played around his lips. Part of me wondered if he was hoping that I would refuse him. If he had been testing my wifely obedience, how far *I* was guilty. How far *I* was sorry. He was spoiling for a fight after losing his argument with Arthur. He wanted to feel he could get *someone* to obey him. It would not be me.

"Uriens, you have apologised for your treatment of me in public, but not yet to me in private. I will not go to bed with you as your wife until you apologise."

He gave a low, mean laugh. "I don't have to apologise to you. I have to pretend I believe Arthur, but," he shook his head, "between us, I know you're nothing more than a whore."

I slapped him, hard across his face, feeling the anger fire through me, heat my blood. I wished, then, that I knew more, darker magic. Little good it would do me now to change my shape. I wished I could have wrapped my hand around his eyes and made him watch something he did not want to see.

It took him a moment to register that I had struck him, then his face darkened and twisted with anger. He went red, then white, and I saw the vein bulge in his forehead. I felt a flutter of fear in my stomach. I could see the hunger in his eyes, the desire for revenge, to assert his power. He had been shamed by me, and by one he considered to be a boy. Now he was alone with me, he was going to prove the one way he was stronger.

I jumped back as he lunged forward for me, but there was nowhere for me to go. He caught me by the wrist, and dragged me over to the bed. I pushed at him with my free hand, but I didn't have the strength in my body to get him off me. Vivid and awful, the memory of Lot holding me face-down on his table flashed back through me and I struggled hard against Uriens, but he did not loosen his grip on me. He pushed me down on the bed and climbed on top of me, pinning me down with an arm across my chest. I screamed out, screamed for him to stop, but he clamped a hand over my mouth, leaning close to hiss in my ear.

"I am your lord husband, Morgan, and you *will* be obedient to me."

I kicked at him, but I could not push him off, and I screwed my eyes tight shut, against the tears, against the room around me, this awful place I had been brought to. I wished that I could move outside my body, leave it behind me. When he thrust inside me, grunting over me, and puffing out his breaths, I lay limp and hopeless, closing my eyes, trying to imagine I was at Avalon, swimming in the lake, or lying with Kay under the trees. But when I thought of Kay I felt angry and hopeless again. There was blood on the sheets this time, but I did not think he would be satisfied now. I tried to drift as far from my body as I could, and all the while I thought, *I will kill Uriens. I will kill him.*

And after a while it became, *and I will kill Arthur.*

Part II
The Curse of Excalibur

And Queen Morgan said, "Tell Arthur that I will not fear him while I can change me and mine into the likeness of stones, and let him know that I will do much more, when I see my time."

Malory, *Le Morte d'Arthur*

Chapter Twenty-Two

That was how I found myself. Alone. Betrayed by everyone; those I had trusted most, and those I had not trusted at all. Sold by Arthur into this marriage for the sake of an army for the war he had started out of selfishness. Forgotten by Kay. Alone in Rheged Castle with the husband who despised me almost as much as I hated him. Already they had all forgotten me. Even Nimue. Merlin had tricked me, and stolen my sword. Old friends and old lovers alike had left me behind. Only my sister, my careless, thoughtless sister, with no one else to protect her, kept me where I was. If I stayed, at least I had some power to protect her. To protect her child. The child Arthur had wanted so badly to kill.

The others could wait, but I was determined to have some revenge on Uriens as soon as possible, and to remove myself from the danger I found myself in now that I, as wife, was prisoner in his castle. I waited in the morning until I heard him get up, dress and leave, and I slipped from the bed. I went over to my bag and pulled out my book of healing arts. I thought I remembered something useful in it, and it was there, at the back, in the section of potions useful for women. It was called, 'potion to take a man's power'. I hoped it meant what I thought it did. I hoped it would humiliate him. He deserved it after what he had done to me.

I glanced down the list of ingredients. Simple enough. I thought I could find them all, as long as Rheged Castle had a proper herb store. Otherwise I would have to go out looking for them, and it would be more difficult getting Uriens to let me leave the castle on my own. I dressed in my black jewelled dress, and a clean underdress. I felt fragile, weak, and I hated it. I plaited my hair slowly, hoping that the habitual movements of my hands would soothe me. It did, but only a little. Before I left the room, I scribbled a quick letter to Morgawse.

"Marriage as you described. War soon. Hope you & M safe. Morgan."

I hoped that Morgawse had managed to protect her little son from Arthur's assassins. I was not really sure it was such a good idea for the boy to survive, but it seemed cowardly and immoral to send knights to kill a helpless baby. I pressed the letter into the hand of a servant, with instructions for it to be sent as quickly as possible. I hoped that it would reach her before the war began.

151

I walked down, through the castle, out to the courtyard. I was pleased that Uriens was not there. Autumn was drawing near, and the air smelled of it. Of hay, and sweet apples. The smell reminded me, painfully, of my summer with Kay. There were a few knights preparing their horses, checking their equipment. Uriens would be gathering his army at his borders, preparing to march north to meet Lothian's attack. They would be caught between the Lothians coming from the North and Lot's Breton allies landing at Dover. Arthur was in the weaker position, having to fight outwards towards his borders. He was not an experienced general, he was young. All he had was his men's faith in him. I hoped that it would be enough. I hoped, too, that Uriens' men would be strong and loyal, and that I would not have been given into this suffering for nothing.

I noticed the steward I had seen the night before at the edge of the courtyard, and walked over to him. He would know if Rheged had a store of herbs. He stood in his armour, plate on the chest, chainmail underneath, his dark gold hair swept back off his face. I had not imagined, before, that he was handsome. Well, I was not going to be betrayed by another man. All I wanted from him was his knowledge of the castle.

He saw me coming towards him, and turned to me with a smile.

"My Lady Morgan, how do you find the castle?" he asked with a little bow.

"Well enough," I replied. "I wondered if you could tell me if this castle has a store of dried herbs."

He gave a small, amused smile.

"You are one of the ladies of Avalon."

"I schooled there," I replied evasively. He shook his head.

"I had a sister *schooled* in Avalon, but she had no skill and they would not give her the woad." I could see in his eyes that he was intrigued by me, by the blue of my skin. It was a shame that he knew too much. I hoped he would not tell Uriens that I really was a witch. "I know enough about Avalon to know that the woad is truly an honour, and given only to those who show especial talent for the magic arts." He took a step closer to me, as though carried forward by the power of his own words, his own curiosity. "My sister told me, besides, that the woaded women of Avalon are painted in blue, not just on their hands and faces, but *all over*."

I saw his eyes flicker down, over the bodice of my dress, and he ill hid what I knew he pictured as he looked at me. I drew myself up to my full height, and regarded him coldly.

"You are bold, aren't you? For a steward." He leaned back a little, but the smile still played around his lips. "Just tell me where the herbs are kept."

He led me down a passageway, down the steps to the underground stores. I felt my heart racing in me, already nervous. If I could not find what I needed, I did not know how I was going to protect myself from Uriens. The steward lit a torch as we went down the steps. It was dark, and slightly damp in the stores below. That was not good for the herbs.

I followed him through the room, lined with barrels of food, prepared for a siege. Some were dusty, but many looked new, as though Uriens had made recent preparations for being stuck inside his castle. I could not imagine anything worse than being held to siege with Uriens. The steward stopped suddenly, and I almost walked into his back. He turned to the side, and lifted up his torch. In an alcove in a wall at the back, bunches and bunches of dried herbs hung from a series of wooden poles that looked as though they had been set up for the purpose. *Everything* was there. My heart skipped with joy. There must have been a witch at Rheged castle before me.

I squeezed in front of him to reach them. He did not move aside, so I had to brush past him. I ignored him when I felt him watching me as I gathered what I needed. When I turned back around, I saw he had not moved back, but stood close to me, the torch held over us, and he was smiling his curious smile.

"What are you making, my Lady?" he asked.

"A casserole," I replied.

He reached out to touch one of the herbs clutched in my hand, and as his hand brushed against mine, I felt myself startle, just a little, in a mix of fear, and the thrill I had not expected to feel at his touch. I was not ready. What kind of steward was he, anyway, already making eyes and flirting with his Lord's new wife? For all he knew, I was still giddy with the fresh joys of marriage.

"I do not think I have ever tasted *this* in a casserole," he said, raising an eyebrow at me, but he moved his hand away, and he didn't question me again.

As I followed him out, I tucked the herbs up the sleeve of my dress.

That night, I slipped the mixture I had prepared into Uriens' drink. He did not seem to notice. Not until he decided it was time for us to go to bed. I followed him up the stairs, quiet and compliant as a little lamb, and he seemed inordinately pleased with himself. I supposed he thought he had broken me. I lay back and tried to keep the smile from my face as he grunted with frustration over me, finding that his ability had suddenly left him. He gave me a narrow look of suspicion as he rolled off me, but he was too embarrassed to make any kind of open accusation, and besides, he had drunk a lot of wine that night.

When this happened to him again and again, he began to grant my requests. My request to have my own chamber, far from his, and to send letters to Nimue in Avalon. Before he had only allowed me to write to my sister, or to Arthur. I wrote to Nimue, asking her if she had got anything more from Merlin, and asking her to send me any news, and to come if she could. I thought about writing to Kay. But I was still angry that he had not come to say goodbye to me.

I started to feel my freedom a little, and to enjoy wandering about the castle battlements, gazing at the wild country that surrounded it. It was all thick forests and dark craggy stone, beautiful in its own way. Almost like Avalon. I ran into the steward, who told me his name was Accolon, sometimes. He was always polite, but friendly, though he did not touch me again, nor wonder aloud what I looked like under my clothes. I think he sensed that I was wary, or that Uriens was angrier and angrier, more frustrated, every day. But I had guessed right that Uriens would not make any kind of open attack against me now that he knew it was his power as a man that I held hostage.

The morning that Uriens came to tell me that they were departing that day, I felt sick. He came in while I was sitting at the window, wide open to the mid-autumn chill, trying to settle my stomach by breathing in the cold air. It wasn't working, and I knew the cause.

I only knew he was there when he spoke.

"What is wrong with *you*, then?" he asked, gruffly.

I turned around to see him standing in the door, dressed in his platemail with his helm under his arm. I was glad that he was leaving. The potion I had mixed to keep him from me was running out, and I was almost out of the herbs I needed to make it again. I didn't know where I could find more, and I knew that if it was while he was here that he ran out, he would want to take all of his humiliation, his frustration and his anger out on me.

I didn't answer him.

"So, you're leaving today," I said, flatly, leaning my head against my hand. I didn't feel strong enough to sit up straight.

He nodded. "I'm leaving the castle in the care of my steward. He is going to write to me, so don't think that while I am gone you can do as you please."

"I am ever your obedient wife, sir," I said.

He threw me a dirty look, and left.

I felt a rush of joy in my heart when, from my bed, I heard the hooves of the horses galloping away to war. *Perhaps someone will kill Uriens*, I thought. One of Morgawse's sons. The angry one, Gawain. I imagined Gawain slicing off his head in battle. That gave me some comfort.

By the time that winter reached its depths, and Uriens' men had been at war a few months, I could not have mistaken the cause of my sickness, even if I had been the innocent little maid I was supposed to have been. I had thought of getting rid of it, as I had before, but the thought had struck me that it was likely enough to be Kay's, rather than Uriens'. Besides, I was alone here, and I had seen how happy Morgawse's children made her, and I hoped to have my own happiness that way, if I could.

I did not want to tell anyone until it was necessary, but people had noticed. The serving women whom I largely ignored, preferring to take care of myself, noticed that I had not bled for a long time. Someone must have written to inform Uriens, because I got a letter from him telling me that he had sent for some sister of his to come and attend the birth. He didn't trust me. I wondered if his mistrust would be well-placed. But I was dark-haired myself. I thought if it were Kay's, it would be a while before it was evident. Someone must have written to Arthur, too, for I also got a message from him, though it was not a letter. It came in the form of a distant cousin of ours, a dull girl called Elaine, whom he had sent to keep me company, take care of me, and possibly to spy on me, until the baby came.

She came through the thick snows of midwinter, though she was only small and weak-looking. Doe-eyed and olive skinned. As a child she had looked strange, her eyes too large and peeping like some night-time creature, but since I had seen her last, she had grown into it, and I had to admit she was very beautiful. She slid lithely from her horse and came over to wrap me in a gentle embrace. Her hair was soft, glossy, a lovely chestnut brown, and her frame was small as a child's. She annoyed me, though I knew she was trying to be kind. She tried to read to me from a book of romances that she had brought with her, but I liked neither her soft, slightly babyish voice, nor the pointless, vacuous stories. She looked a little hurt when I told her curtly that I did not like them.

I did not mind, however, having some company at night. I let her sleep in the bed beside me. It was warmer that way, and at night I would forget it was her as I fell asleep, and think it was Morgawse beside me, and that made me feel less lonely.

One night, when the winter was just beginning to recede, and the swell of my stomach was just beginning to show beneath my clothes, I woke in the middle of the night from strange dreams of Kay and Lancelot, of them riding into battle side by side. I could not say what it was about it, but the dream filled me with panic. I sat up in bed, and gazed out of the window. Through the cloudy glass, I could see the points of stars. I thought it might calm me to go out, to get some air. No one else would be about. It was the middle of the night. I wrapped my woollen cloak around my nightdress and slipped on a pair of shoes, and snuck as quietly as possible out the door. If I woke Elaine, I would have to face her insipid concern, and then I would be too annoyed to go back to sleep.

The castle was quiet and cold outside my room, where the low fire still burned in the grate. I was glad of it. It felt as though it was clearing my head. I walked out into the small courtyard. It was empty, and quiet. I turned my face up to the stars above me, taking in a deep breath of the winter night air. As I stretched out under the cold, crisp night, preparing to go back to bed, I noticed a light coming from the stables. I didn't particularly want to talk to anyone, but I thought I might like to see the horses. Horses reminded me of Kay, and the gentle way he had with them.

When I walked into the stables, I saw Accolon at the back, fiddling at something on one of the horses' saddles. I got the feeling from him that he would rather be riding out to war than left at Rheged to oversee Uriens' household while he was away. He looked like a man built for fighting.

I said nothing as I went in, going over to the nearest horse, and stroking down its long, sleek nose. The horse gave a little whicker of appreciation, and Accolon looked up. Dropping what he was doing, he rushed over.

"My Lady, what are you doing here? It's the middle of the night."

In the suddenness of his concern he had rushed close. It was cold outside, but it was warm in the stable from the heat of a fire and the horses, so he was dressed only in his shirt and breeches. His shirt fell open at the neck and I could glimpse dark hair and a muscular chest through the opening. I forced myself to look up at his face.

"Oh, I couldn't sleep," I answered absently.

He nodded, but he did not look away, or move back from me. I felt a dangerous flutter of excitement in my heart. Chance had brought me here, alone with him in the middle of the night. I was not sure what I wanted.

"And... you are well?" he asked, carefully. I saw him glance down at my stomach. The shape of me showed, just a little, through the nightdress. Unconsciously, I pulled my cloak tighter around myself.

"Well," I answered.

He leaned away a little, looking at me, his eyes narrowing with thought.

"Are you happy?"

It seemed a strange question. Women were not allowed to say they were unhappy about children, especially if they were married. I thought I would be happy enough if it were not Uriens'.

"Oh, yes."

His face crinkled more deeply, as though he were trying to puzzle something out. Something he had been wondering about for a long time.

"So, your marriage was a love-match?" he asked, unable to keep the confusion from his voice.

"No, no. Of course not. No."

Accolon shifted on his feet, and still looked troubled.

"I would not have thought that a witch from Avalon would have to marry a man she did not love."

"I did it for my sister's sake." As the words came out of me, I realised that they were true. I felt raw, too honest, around him. Part of me wanted to leave, but I was deep in the middle-of-the-night honesty, and it was too late for me to walk away from it. "I did it in the hope that Uriens, or my brother, would kill her husband. Then her husband won't kill her. She has... she gets herself into trouble. Morgawse has always needed my rescuing."

He looked shocked.

"Your sister is Morgawse of Lothian?" I nodded. "I would have thought a woman with four sons would have had a happy marriage."

"You don't understand much about marriage," I replied, more sharply than I meant to. He looked at me, as though he suddenly saw me properly. He opened his mouth slightly as though there was something that he was going to say, but he did not. He reached out and, lightly, put a hand against my cheek. I felt my heart race, my

157

blood rush in my veins. The look in his eyes was sudden understanding and, awfully, pity. I did not want anyone to feel sorry for me, but it drew me towards him, the real care I saw for me. If it had not been the middle of the night, if I had not felt vulnerable and raw, perhaps I would have questioned it, but I did not. I leaned towards him, and he leaned down towards me. I smelled the lovely warm scent of the horses nearby, and the fresh hay, and the smoke from the fire. I felt the anticipation tighten through me. I looked up to meet his gaze, his eyes, the dark green of the woods, and he was close enough that I could see the light covering of dark-gold stubble across his lip, his chin, and I let my eyes flutter shut. When I felt his lips against mine, I gave an unconscious sigh of pleasure. His lips were soft and gentle on mine at first, then quickly rough and urgent as, holding my face in his hands, he drew me towards him. It had been so long since a man I had wanted had touched me. I had not felt the loneliness of my body until that moment.

"Morgan," he murmured, as he moved his lips down, against my neck. I was breathing fast, and I felt the flush spread up through my body. I was hot with it already. I leaned my head back, closing my eyes, letting the feel of his lips, his hands sliding down my back pulling me closer, wash over me. It was overwhelming.

Was I going to give in to it? I still felt bruised and vulnerable from all the betrayals I had felt at the hands of men. I wanted him, but I did not want that again.

Accolon's lips met mine again, and I met his kiss with an urgent passion of my own, losing my thoughts as I felt the brush of his tongue against mine, and a shock of desire went through me. I ran my hands through his hair, coarse and rough, and pressed my body against his. Through the thin material of my nightdress and his shirt, I felt the heat of his skin. He gave a low murmur of desire in response, and I felt his hand at the lace at the top of my nightdress, pulling it undone. He slid his hand gently inside, and the feel of his hand on me as he pressed to my bare breast underneath made me sigh again. My mind was becoming clouded with it, with his closeness.

No, I didn't want to. The horrible thought struck me that, like Merlin, he had only been kind to me to get something from me. My body, a magic sword; it was all the same. It was all so soon, so sudden. He was too eager to betray his King – a part of me wondered fleetingly if this might have been something Uriens had arranged so that he could prove to everyone that I was the whore he thought I was. I was not going to fall like a fool again.

I put a hand against Accolon's chest, prepared that I might have to shove him forcefully off me, but when he felt my resistance, he moved back immediately. I was surprised. I gathered my cloak defensively around myself. My body was still hot, still full of desire. But when I saw him step forward, as though to begin again, I held out my hand for him to stop.

"I have had enough of men," was all I managed to articulate, but miraculously, he seemed to understand.

"I can wait," he said, evenly, and he stepped back towards me, putting a gentle hand at the back of my neck. I looked up to meet his eye. "Just know that not all men are like Uriens."

Chapter Twenty-Three

Whenever I saw Accolon after that, he was kind and polite as before, but now he was also watchful, waiting for the signal from me that I was ready. I bided my time. A letter reached me from Morgawse, but she had tried rather too hard to be cryptic, and it did not make much sense. Still, I gathered from it that she was safe, and so was her youngest son. I did not think she would be afraid to tell me if he were dead.

It was as spring was turning to summer, and my stomach grown large and heavy before me, that news came, but not in the form of a letter. It came in the form of Arthur, and Uriens and a small band of knights, and worst of all Merlin, arriving at the castle gates. I was standing with Accolon and Elaine as he was talking me through what we had in our stores. He leaned a little closer than he needed to, let his hand brush mine as he pointed to items on the list, but I did not mind. I had been enjoying it more and more, the pleasant tension of expectation growing between us.

We heard the horns that announced the arrival of the castle's Lord, and looked up. Arthur and Uriens rode at the head of the party. I glanced through the others, but did not see Kay. It was only Merlin, in his real form, wearing a cowled robe of rough black wool, that I recognised in the party. They had a prisoner with them, bound and led on a horse between Arthur and Uriens. At first, I thought it was a small, scrawny man, but as they came closer, I realised that it was a woman. She sat tall and proud on her horse, her hands bound before her, dressed in light leather armour set with battered plates of steel. She was covered in dirt, and dried blood, but she carried herself with haughty dignity. She must have been some great woman for them to have brought her as a prisoner, rather than slain her in the field, or worse.

I stepped forward to greet Arthur. I noticed Uriens hang back. Good, he had learned his place. Arthur kissed me on both cheeks. He grinned, pleased to see me. Had he forgotten how he had treated me? There was no hint in his open, honest face that he knew that I hated him now, for what he had done to me. Uriens was not the only man who had wronged me. But I played the part of the loving sister, and gave Arthur a courteous smile.

"It is a joy to see you, brother," I told him.

He smiled, holding me by the shoulders and looking down at the hugeness of my belly between us.

"I, too, am glad to see you, and to see you so happy."

I put my hand on the top of my stomach and gave the easiest smile that I could. Why did all men think a woman with a child must be happy with her husband? I had read a book of Galenic medicine in Avalon that had been full of such rubbish, and had suggested that a woman had to enjoy to conceive. I had thrown it away. It seemed the men of Logrys still foolishly believed such tales.

Arthur moved past me, giving the orders to Uriens' men to take his horses to the stable. His small band of knights dismounted and followed him. Uriens came over to me, his face a mix of pleasure to see the promise of a child he dared to hope was his, and displeasure to see me.

"Morgan," he greeted me tersely. I gave him a slight nod.

"Uriens. I am pleased to see my husband safe."

"Morgan, I would be a very foolish man to believe a single thing you ever said to me," he said sharply. "Can I trust you to guard our prisoner until we decide what to do with her? Actually…" He looked past me, and saw Accolon. "Steward, come here. I need you to put this prisoner somewhere."

"No," I interrupted. "I will take care of it."

I did not want the woman put in some awful dungeon. Nor somewhere that Uriens could get his hands on her. No one deserved that. Uriens walked back and pulled her roughly from her horse, dragging her by the arm across the courtyard to me. Elaine behind me gave a demure little gasp. I wasn't sure if she was gasping at the sight of the warlike woman, dressed in armour like a man, or at Uriens' treatment of her. The woman had an empty scabbard at her side. So she had once been armed like a man, too. She already had the marks on her of a man's rough treatment. A dark bruise showed against the pale skin of her cheek, high on the bone, and her lip was split. Those were not the wounds of the battlefield. When she was dragged up to me, I saw the animal fear in her fierce blue eyes.

I reached out, and took her from Uriens. He let go of her arm reluctantly. I turned to her.

"Come with me. No one will try to hurt you. You will be safe, as long as you do not try to run."

Her eyes looked back at me, uncomprehending, and wide with panic.

"She doesn't speak English," Uriens told me, with a cruel grin.

"What does she speak?" I asked. He shrugged. I was sure that he knew. "Who is she, Uriens?"

He said nothing, just gave me a mean smirk, walking off. I turned round to Elaine.

"Elaine, what languages do you speak?"

She shook her head, overwhelmed.

"Just English."

I glanced at Accolon. He shook his head. I knew some French, but not much. I could hardly speak to her in Latin.

In my slow, childish French, I asked her, "Do you understand what I am saying to you?" She nodded, but she did not speak. "I will keep you safe. Just don't try to run." She nodded again. There was resistance in her eyes. She did not seem as though she would make a willing prisoner.

Elaine and I led her up to my room. I sent Elaine to fetch a bath. The woman watched me warily. She was measuring me up. She was tied, but I was heavily pregnant, and I could see she was strong. Her arms were bare – caked in blood and dirt, but bare – and I could see that she was leanly muscled. She was a woman who had grown up fighting. I suspected that she was Breton, perhaps even the queen that had come from Brittany with Leodegrance's army, but I had no way of telling for sure. She didn't have a crown, or a circlet, or any other mark of royalty on her.

Elaine came back with another serving girl, and Accolon and another of Uriens' knights. Obviously, she had not felt safe leaving me alone with the woman, but I was not so sure. I could see that after she had noticed my pregnant belly, she had noticed my woaded face.

Elaine set the bath down before her. I waved my hand in the direction of the woman.

"Someone cut her bonds, then you men wait outside."

Accolon stepped forward and cut the rope that bound her hands with his dagger. I noticed that he was gentle, careful not to cut her, or pull roughly on the bonds. There were men that would have relished a little chance of violence against an enemy woman. He glanced at me over his shoulder as he left, his look one of concern. Before I could scold her, Elaine slipped out with them. I rolled my eyes. The girl was insipid.

I crossed my arms over my chest, and leaned back against my table.

"You can get in the bath, if you like," I told her, in my slow French. She did not move, but she did rub her wrists, bringing the blood back down to her hands. "Are you Breton?" I asked her.

She said nothing, just regarded me with a wary look. I sighed hard, shaking my head.

"I'm not going to hurt you. I'm trying to help you."

She pulled her armour off over her head. Underneath she had a thin, stained vest marked with sweat and dirt and blood. She was wounded. When she moved, I saw the cut, deep into the flesh of her upper arm. She showed no pain, but I was sure she felt it. She pulled off her chainmail leggings and stood before me defiantly in her stained vest and woollen leggings, crossing her arms over her chest.

"You are a witch," she said, her own French as clumsy as mine. I nodded.

"I can give you something for your wound. For the pain. To stop sickness." I pointed to her arm. She glanced down at it and shrugged, as though she barely felt it. But then, after a moment, she nodded. As I turned from her to go to my book, and my small collection of herbs, she pulled off her underclothes and stepped into the bath. I could hear the water splashing as she rubbed herself clean. When I had made the poultice for her wound – a simple enough mixture – and turned back, I saw she was gently washing the cut with the water from the bath, and wincing as she did. Her wrists were burned from the rope, and I could see the dark marks of bruises all over her arms. She had pulled her hair loose and soaked it in the bathwater. It glistened a dark auburn-red. She must have been a beautiful woman in her youth. As it was, she was a striking woman now in her middle age, her face angular and proud. She was tanned from the sun, and freckled lightly across the forehead, nose and shoulders.

I knelt down awkwardly beside her, slow with my huge belly. She let me pat her arm dry with the hem of my skirt, and then apply the poultice and wrap the bandage around it. She could not hide the pain of its stinging on her face.

"I am sorry. The sting is healing," I told her, not sure if my French made sense. She nodded, though, as though she already knew.

I went to my cupboards and brought out for her a clean underdress and one of my old black woollen dresses. I laid them on the table, where she could see them, and left her alone.

When I came out of the door, Accolon and the other knight were still waiting there, and Arthur, Uriens, and Merlin were with them.

"Did she tell you anything?" Arthur asked, as soon as I was out of the door. I shook my head.

Arthur gestured that we should walk together. I glanced at Accolon as I followed them. Arthur led us in to the room beside mine. It was an empty bedroom, set with a simple bed, long unused and dusty. I sat down heavily on the edge of the bed, exhausted already and uncomfortable from moving around with the child huge and near its time inside me. I sighed heavily as I sat down leaning back on my hands.

Arthur rubbed his face. "What are we going to do with her?"

Uriens shrugged. "Kill her. Unless you have another use for her." The look he gave Arthur was narrow and accusatory, but Arthur wasn't looking at him. He was shaking his head.

"No, no. That isn't right. Can't we bargain for peace with her?"

Merlin remained silent, watching the two men.

"Bargain for peace?" Uriens scoffed. "When we're winning?"

"Peace is better than ever more war, Uriens," Arthur snapped.

"Who is she?" I asked again.

Arthur shrugged, turning to me. I could see that he was trying to think of a way that meant he did not have to harm her. So eager to protect this woman he did not know, yet so eager to throw his own sister into suffering.

"We do not know," Merlin cut in, his rasping, unpleasant voice slimy in its tone, "but we suspect that she is the Queen of Carhais, Melita of the Bretons." I nodded. Merlin gave his skull-like grin, and I felt my stomach turn. I pressed a hand against my belly as I felt the child within move, as though in fear of Merlin. "We cannot learn her identity, for none of us speaks a language that she understands. Or, rather, none of us *seems* to speak a language that she understands. I might remind you all that since she was with Lot's army, who receive their orders from Lot *in English* it is highly unlikely that her understanding is as limited as she pretends."

Arthur shook his head again. "But this doesn't help us decide what to do with her. Can we keep her here?" He turned to Uriens. Uriens shook his head.

"When there is hardly enough food for my own people? Feed one of the enemy? Leave her with my wife, when she is like that?" He gestured carelessly at me. "Imagine the harm she could do here unguarded, and I cannot spare the men to guard her."

Arthur nodded reluctantly.

"Where is Kay?" I asked, suddenly. The words escaped me. To my surprise, Arthur turned to me, eager to answer my question, a bright smile spreading across his face.

"Kay was *magnificent*. He slew two of Lot's ally kings in battle. That only leaves three of them against us, so we match them now. You should have seen him in the field. He is at Camelot now, holding it against the enemy."

I was glad that Kay lived, but he was not forgiven.

"We have not solved our problem," Uriens pointed out, impatiently.

They continued to argue back and forth, but I had stopped listening. Arthur wanted to keep her somewhere safe, Uriens wanted to execute her in front of the men. He thought it would be good for morale. I was only concerned with not letting either of them lay their hands on her before she met either fate. She was a brave, proud woman, and she did not deserve that kind of dishonour.

Slowly, I pushed myself back to my feet and excused myself to go back to my room, ignoring Merlin's nasty, beady black eyes on me.

When I got back to my room, the woman had dressed in my underdress, but had torn the skirt off to wear it like her vest, and had put her woollen leggings back on, dirty though they were, and was buckling her armour back on. I did not blame her.

I sat slowly down into my chair. I felt safe enough with Accolon and the other knight outside. She only eyed my pregnant belly as though she might try to run from me, anyway. Not as though she would try to hurt me. She was of the age that if she had children, they would be almost grown by now. I thought any woman who had known pregnancy and childbirth would never try to take another at the advantage in such a situation.

"Truly," I asked her "you do not speak English? It would be easier for me."

She shook her head.

"How did you understand messages from Lot?" I persisted.

"My sons. They knew English." *Knew*. She looked up at me then, her eyes steady and cold. "I had three sons. Your King Arthur killed them all. The youngest was no older than you. He had a wife your age. When we left Carhais, she too was with a child inside."

So, she was indeed Leodegrance's Queen. Or at any rate, an important woman at his court. So, she looked at me and thought of the son she had lost, the grandchild she would probably never see. I remember Arthur's talk of marrying Kay to the Princess of Carhais.

"You have a daughter?" I asked. She nodded. "Does she fight?"

The woman laughed then. I had not expected that. I sat back in my chair, and wrapped my hands around my belly. I could not help smiling in return.

"She wishes. She thinks she is a warrior. She is still a little girl. Already they all talk about marrying her to some prince or another. That nasty boy of Lot's who rapes the girls who go with the camp. No, that is not for her." The woman shook her head. "She will marry a boy from her home, and be happy. I have made sure."

I felt a sudden rush of warmth for this woman. My mother loved me, I knew that, but as much as my mother saw me as her daughter she saw me as a princess with a duty, and with sacrifices to be made. This woman didn't care about that. She just wanted her daughter to live happily. It seemed to me that there would be little chance of that. If all the girl's brothers were dead, then whoever won this war would marry their son to her to get hold of Carhais. It was not rich, it had no treasures and its lands were small, but it had the Hundred Knights of Carhais, and that was enough for any king to covet. If I kept this woman alive, she might protect her daughter, might hide her from the men trying to snatch her up. I wondered if the girl would like Gawain, if it came to it. I wondered if Gawain would even survive.

I was not afraid to go to sleep with the woman in the room. I found her proud, quiet presence more calming than the fluttering Elaine. I heard her looking through my things. Perhaps she was looking for a weapon, but there was nothing for her to find.

Chapter Twenty-Four

The next day they took her away from me. I think it made Uriens uneasy to leave me alone with her. I think he suspected that we plotted against him. I barely knew enough French to ask her if she was alright, to ask her to show me her wound again. I might have tried to conspire with her against him if I had known enough, if communication had been easy.

They came to take her away when I was wrapping a new bandage around her arm. Uriens with two of his knights, and Arthur lingering behind, looking uneasy. I suspected that Uriens and Merlin had talked him into it. Uriens stood before the woman as she turned her proud face up to stare him in the eye. Uriens took hold of her chin roughly.

I could see her skin go white under the force of his grip. She showed no pain, no fear.

"It is death for you, my Lady," he said in loud, slow English. She gazed back evenly. It seemed a painfully small gesture of kindness, in light of this, that I had tried to heal the wound in her arm.

"May your wife curse you," she replied coldly, in her uneven French. It was for my benefit, for Uriens looked at her without understanding. However, I thought I saw Arthur's attention catch. He must have learned some French, enough to understand what she said, in his short time as King. "A man without mercy deserves no mercy from the gods."

Uriens, further angered by the language he did not understand, dragged her from the room. She did not look back at me, and I felt as though I had let her down, though I did not know what else I could have done. Arthur lingered behind as all the others left. I wished that he would leave as well. I wanted to be alone. He pushed the door gently shut.

"Morgan..." he began uneasily. I thought he was going to ask me to absolve him of that woman's murder, but he would not have that from me. To my utter astonishment, he unbuckled Excalibur in its scabbard from around his waist, and held it out to me. "I must ask something of you. I need you to guard my sword in your safekeeping until I return for it. I am always afraid someone will steal it while I sleep, and the jewelled scabbard attracts too much attention on the battlefield. We're sleeping in ditches, in the mud, in caves – I can't have a sword like this with me. Even if one of the enemy did not try to steal it, we would have bandits on us in the wild lands around here. I will take an ordinary sword from Uriens' armoury, but will you look after it for me? I know I can trust you with it."

My heart raced, and I stepped forward for it. Was this really happening? Was Arthur really doing this? Was he testing me? Tricking me? I reached out a hand and laid it against the scabbard. A wonderful, overwhelming sense of belonging, the strength of the Otherworld, the deep connection between me and my sword, rushed through me and I could not contain a smile.

"I would be glad to, Arthur," I breathed.

Was it to be so easy? Had the sword come back to me of its own will? Arthur pressed it into my hands, and I held it close to me, feeling its Otherworld strength fill me, feeling the lightness of its steel as I held it. I would have pressed the hilt to my lips if Arthur had not been there.

166

"Thank you, Morgan." He leaned forward to kiss me on the forehead. "I will be back for it when we have finally defeated Lot. We depart again today. I am sorry that guarding this prisoner has kept you from your husband the little time he has been back, but I shall return him to you soon."

How little Arthur understood about marriage, and about me. He left, and I hid Excalibur, not beneath my bed where I had left it in Avalon, but at the back of my cupboard under my dresses. That had been safe enough before, with the book. Now all I had to do with the time I had was figure out a way to keep it for myself when he came to claim it back.

I lay in bed, my eyes closed, to listen to the crowd in the courtyard baying for blood as they executed the Breton Queen. I heard them roar with delight when they cut off her head, for I knew that was what they would have done. She was an enemy captured in battle. At least it was a warrior's honourable death for her. I thought of her daughter, far away, who did not know she had lost her protector. That girl would be sold now, to whoever was the highest bidder.

When the noises of the crowd had died down I listened to the horses' hooves as Arthur and Uriens and Merlin rode away again. I was glad that they were gone, and more glad than I could say that Arthur had left Excalibur behind with me. *I know I can trust you with it.* How little Arthur truly knew.

It was high summer when the child came. Uriens' sister arrived to attend the birth, and only just in time. She was a squat, ugly woman, with the same craggy ill-tempered face as her brother, almost the very image of him, only shorter and fatter. Elaine stood hovering around the room, worrying out loud about anything and everything. I had drunk deeply of the potion for pain I had given Morgawse, and I lay back in its haze, letting them fuss over my body as I moved away from it.

Though I had prayed and prayed the child would be Kay's, the boy came out sandy-haired and dull-eyed like his father. Unmistakable. I didn't want to hold him. I remembered Morgawse's rapturous joy at the sight of her son, and I looked at mine and felt nothing. I didn't want to hold him and feel my own hollowness. I told myself it was the drink for the pain, but Morgawse had smiled still, and held her baby to her breast. I waved mine away, and groggily ordered them to send for a nurse for him, before I sank into a heavy sleep.

167

I didn't leave my bed for a long time. I did not feel like getting up, and I did not want to see my son. Uriens, when the news reached him, came back from the battlefield. They must have been winning easily, then. He was obviously happy for the boy to be nursed by someone else, for no one brought him to me, and I was glad of it. It felt like a betrayal by my own body, that it had chosen Uriens over Kay. My breasts grew heavy with milk, and sore, but it quickly passed as my body realised that I was not going to nurse my child. When a week or so had passed, and I felt like getting out of my bed, I made a drink from my book of medicines to make sure the milk stopped. I was sick of being sore, sick of being bored and powerless.

I sat at my desk and wrote to my sister, and Nimue. I asked Nimue to come as soon as possible with more of Merlin's Black Arts knowledge. I called for a bath, and washed, and dressed in my black dress of gems. I plaited my hair carefully. Elaine fluttered around me, constantly trying to help, but I didn't like being fussed. I wanted to just take care of myself.

When I was properly dressed, I went to find Uriens. I did not really want to speak to him, but I did want news of Arthur's war. I wanted to know how long I had to work out how I could keep Excalibur for myself.

When I found him, he was in his bedroom, holding his son. *Our* son. No, when I looked at the boy, I could not picture him as my child. Though he had lived in my body, in his father's arms he seemed unbearably distant. How had I been denied the comfort that Morgawse had found from her child? I supposed that Morgawse had *wanted* Arthur, before she knew he was her brother. But she loved her sons by Lot as well. Why was everything that was effortless for Morgawse denied to me?

Uriens looked up at me as I came in. He was dressed in his shirt and breeches, his arms around the little baby, whose small pink fist grasped one of his father's fingers. His look was one of gentleness that I had not seen before, but he sat up and back a little in his chair as he took in how I was dressed, how I had come not to hold our child in my arms, but as his Queen.

"Morgan," he began tentatively, "I am glad to see you up and well."

I nodded, hanging back in the doorway. I did not want him to hand me the child. I didn't want to look down at my son and feel how much I lacked, how the comfort I had hoped for left me cold.

168

"What news from the battlefield?" I asked coldly. The baby gurgled in his arms, and he bounced him a little. He shrugged.

"It's over. Well, not over, but the end is decided. On midsummer's day, Arthur and his knights met with Lot's forces. Pellinore killed Lot, and his army scattered, but not before Arthur and his knights had cut most of them down. And those that ran, we met them as they tried to cross through the mountains on our borders, and we cut them down. Lothian had many knights, but most of them were mercenaries, and when word spread that their king was dead, they scattered. Lot's son, Gawain, pledged himself to Arthur."

"*Gawain* pledged to Arthur?" I asked in disbelief. I could have imagined Aggravain would have done it, but not Gawain. I would have thought Gawain would have rather faced death.

Uriens gave a grim nod. "He was impressed, I think, by Arthur's strength on the battlefield. And besides, after his father's death news managed to reach him that Arthur was not just the father of his youngest brother, but also his mother's brother. With his father dead, the clever young prince of Lothian decided that his blood ran as thick on his mother's as his father's side, and pledged to Arthur. The other brother will pledge his faith, too, when the two remaining kings fall. That will not be long. Between Lothian and Logrys, they will be easily crushed, and Arthur will be King of all Britain."

I nodded, trying to take it all in. This was what I wanted. Morgawse was safe. War would come to an end. I could not stop thinking about the Breton woman, executed in the courtyard. That was what war made men into. Arthur should have stopped it. I felt my head spinning, and leaned against the doorway. In the corner of my vision, I saw Uriens stand, as though he would come over to help me, but I held up a hand, gesturing him away. I was fine. But I had to decide what my next move was going to be. My next move would have to ensure that I kept Excalibur.

"Morgan," he said quietly. I looked up. He had come closer than I had thought. He still held the child, cradled close to his chest with one strong arm, and he leaned back against the wall beside the door, regarding me with a strange detachment. "You dislike me, but your womb likes me well enough, and we should have another child. You cannot – you should not – keep me from your bed forever."

I shook my head, stepping back, but I was still dizzy and I had to rest back against the other side of the doorway. I had not thought he would come back. I had not prepared any more of the potion I had given him before. I was weak from bearing the child; I could not hold him off me. The only weapon I had left was fear. I was not even sure that I could hold him back with Excalibur.

"Don't you want another child?" he demanded.

I shook my head. I felt nauseous, and faint. I could feel my stomach turn within me, my vision blur. I thought I had survived having the child, but I must have lost a lot of blood. I knew the signs from the books I had read. I needed to make the medicine for the blood from the book. I went slowly, leaning against the wall, from the room, following the way I knew down to the herb stores. I was pleased that Uriens did not follow me. I heard him call for Elaine. I wondered what he thought she could possibly do to aid the situation.

When I stumbled out into the courtyard, I saw Accolon notice me, and come over. He glanced around himself before he walked over. He must have been checking for Uriens. He came, and slid an arm around me, holding me around the waist, steadying me.

"I don't need your help," I said, irritably.

"No, my Lady, you may not need it, but you might benefit from it," he said, close and quiet. I glanced up at him. There was real concern in his eyes. "Where do you want to go?"

"I need to go back to the stores."

He nodded, and went with me. I resented my own weakness, but I was glad to have someone to lean on, and for him to hold the torch as I picked out what I needed. It smelled pleasant down there, of apples and old wood, of dried herbs and cool stone. When I had collected what I needed and tucked it into the sleeve of my dress, I turned around to leave, and found Accolon closer behind me than I had thought. I felt my heart give an unconscious flutter of excitement. He leaned forward, sliding an arm around my waist, resting his hand at the small of my back, stepping tentatively closer. I tilted my face up towards his, placing my hand against his cheek. I heard him give a low groan of anticipation as our noses brushed together, and I felt his hot breath against my lips.

"Accolon," I whispered, "do you know how to forge a sword?"

He gave a low laugh. "I can forge a sword for you, Morgan."

Our lips met, and I sank against him with a slight tremble of desire. It could not be here, it could not be now, but it would be soon. I felt sure enough of Accolon now to have him as my lover, and perhaps even more than that. I would wait for that, though, until I was sure.

I pulled away from his kiss slowly. I could see the hunger in his eyes, the desire, and I was pleased. It was too long since a man had looked at me that way.

"Soon," I whispered to him. He gave me a gentle smile, and helped me out, and back to my room. Conscious of Uriens close by, and the danger that he might happen upon us if we lost ourselves in a kiss, I only brushed my fingers lightly against his lips as I said goodbye. I felt their softness against my fingertips long after he had left. It would be soon.

Chapter Twenty-Five

Autumn came, and I felt my strength return to me fully. Elaine chirruped about how I looked my old self again. But it was not enough. Nimue had not answered my letters, and I needed to know if she had learned Merlin's secrets from him. Uriens' ominous promise that I could not keep him from my bed hung around me, and though he had not tried to come to me, now I was recovered from my childbed weakness I was afraid he would try again soon. I had prepared the mixture for him as I had done before, but I had precious little of the herbs I needed for it left, and I warily kept them for when I might have urgent need of them.

As the leaves were turning red and beginning to fall, I called Accolon to my chamber in secret to show him Excalibur, when I knew that Uriens had ridden out to hunt. When he came through the door, he shut it behind himself, and I saw the excitement on his face; but I had a different kind of excitement in mind. I was holding Excalibur in its scabbard behind my back, and when he stepped forward to take me in his arms, I held it out before him. I saw his eyes widen, and a gasp escaped his lips. I drew the sword, and held it out in front of him, feeling its Otherworld lightness, as I held it aloft in a single hand. He gasped again.

"You do not need me to make you a sword if you have a sword like *that*," he murmured.

I rested the blade against his upturned palms, and he ran a hand down the flat of it, whistling through his teeth. My hand was still around the hilt, and he let his hand brush over mine as he stroked it down the sword. He looked up at me, and our eyes met. When he saw the look of sly ambition on my face, a smile of intrigue curled across his face.

"This is Excalibur, isn't it?" he asked, quietly.

So, he had heard of it. I nodded.

"I want you to make one the same. When Arthur comes to collect Excalibur from me, I will give him the false one. He will not know the difference. He has not a drop of Otherworld blood in him. Excalibur was meant for me."

Accolon threw Excalibur from my hands, and I heard it clatter across the floor, but I did not care, for he had grasped me against him, one hand winding through my hair, pulling loose the plait, the other around my waist, holding me against him, pulling me into a hungry, demanding kiss. I was fired with it, too. Fired with the daring of my plan, the sense of my own power, the power we might have together, I ran my hands down his chest, feeling the huge, dangerous muscle beneath. I wanted him, and I wanted him now. I slid my hands up under his shirt, feeling the bare skin of his chest underneath, lightly covered in coarse hair. He groaned low under my touch, lifting me lightly against my little table beside us. I felt my hair fall loose around me as he moved his lips to my neck, and I felt the pleasant weakness spread from the base of my spine, as the breath came to me fast and I leaned into it. I let a hand trail down to his breeches and found him hard already, as excited as I was, both by our sudden closeness, and my daring ambition. I saw the pleasure and desire pass across his face as I slipped my hand inside. His hands went fast to the lacing at the back of my dress, pulling it open, his lips following down as he slid the dress down, off my shoulders, and, hot with desire, I sighed out his name.

Then, suddenly, I heard Uriens in the corridor outside calling my name. He had come back sooner than I'd thought. I pushed Accolon back.

"Hide," I hissed at him, as Uriens called my name again.

"Where?" Accolon mouthed. I pointed under the bed. I would have to get rid of Uriens quickly. I pulled my dress up over my shoulder and pulled the lacing tight as best as I could. Uriens stepped through the door as I jumped from the table, smoothing down my dress. He looked irritated.

"Oh, Morgan. You *are* in here." Then he seemed to notice my hair, loose all around me, and the expression on his face changed. I realised that, though we had been married more than a year, he had never seen my hair loose. Well, that was his own fault. He took an unconscious step towards me, and his hand reached forward to touch it. I supposed it must have looked inviting to him; long and thick, and glossy dark brown, the only part of my looks that could have been called typical feminine beauty. But he had missed his chance to appreciate my looks. He had seen only the blue, and my secret knowledge with it, and been cruel to me. I stepped away from him.

"What do you want, Uriens?" I demanded. I suddenly remembered the sword lying on the floor. I did not want him to notice it. I felt flushed still, frustrated, angry to have been interrupted at a longed-for chance to be alone with Accolon.

"Morgan, we have a child together. Don't you even want to try to get used to me? We ought to have more children."

"*Get used to you?*" I shouted.

"You will like it if you get used to it," he objected, flatly.

"*I will not,*" I shouted. Uriens stepped forward and grabbed hold of me by the shoulders, and pressed his mouth against mine. I pushed against him, but he did not loosen his grip on me, and when he released me, he threw me towards the bed.

"I am doing this for your own good, Morgan. You must just become used to it, and you must resume your duties as my wife. No more witchcraft against me, no more hiding." He climbed on top of me as he spoke, while I tried to wriggle away from him, but he was far stronger than I, and he held me fast by the wrists.

"No, Uriens. *No,*" I hissed, as quiet as I could. I didn't want Accolon to jump out from under the bed to defend me and get himself killed. He had come unarmed, and Uriens had a sword at his side. Perhaps we would have a chance enough if Uriens threw it off, but then we would have to explain to Uriens' knights why his steward had killed him in my bedchamber.

Uriens was pushing up the skirts of my dress, and while one of his hands was off me I kicked him hard away, and he stumbled back, released his grip just long enough for me to wrench away, jump from the bed and pick up Excalibur. When he saw the point of a sword before his face, he seemed to understand that I was serious about refusing him. He stepped back from the bed, his hand on the hilt of his own sword. I was not afraid. I had all of the strength of the Otherworld in me with Excalibur in my hands.

"Where did you get a sword?" He growled.

"This is *my* sword. A dear friend returned it to me. You will not touch me again. Do you understand?"

Uriens threw me a dirty look, and moved towards the door. He hesitated in the doorway, and turned back to me.

"You are truly the foulest of witches, Morgan. I don't know how you managed to get someone to fuck you before I did. I don't know how any man could stand you."

He slammed the door when he left, and I gasped, collapsing back in relief and victory. I did not care what he said to me, or what he thought of me. I was safe. While I had Excalibur, I was safe. I leaned against the wall, closing my eyes, catching my breath.

I heard Accolon climb out from under the bed and I opened my eyes as he came over to me and took my face in his hands. I looked up at him, fierce and proud. He leaned down to kiss me, and I laid my fingers against his lips.

"Come to me again when you have the sword," I said.

I did not offer him Excalibur to make the copy from, nor did he ask for it. We both knew that I needed it with me.

The next day, a letter came to me from Nimue.

"My most dear Lady Morgan, I hope queenship suits you well. I dreamed of you as a queen. I have gained nothing from Merlin, and he pesters me daily to have him in my bed. The war is drawing to its final close, and talk in Camelot is beginning to turn to whom Arthur should take as a wife. Thanks to his long war, there are many fine princesses in the lands about whose betrothed will not return to them, so he has plenty of choice. By the end, it was nothing less than total destruction. Once the sons of Lot joined with Arthur, victory was assured. He rides with the eldest, Gawain – or is the other twin the eldest, I don't know – and assures me that he will return to Camelot soon to settle the matter of his marriage. I hope that means I shall see you soon for the grand occasion. Nimue."

The letter made me feel anxious. It meant that Arthur would come soon for his sword, and I was not ready for him to take it from me.

But I did not have to wait long. It was late at night, and I lay in my bed, with its curtains drawn against the early winter chill. I strained to read in the low light of the fire that only just filled the room. I could barely make out the words on the page, but I got comfort from looking over, again and again, the sleep-medicine that I would use – as soon as the time was right – to kill Uriens.

I heard the scrape of metal on wood as I saw a hand push through the bed curtains and tear them back. I sat up sharply in bed, prepared to run for Excalibur, but I felt bright relief surge through me as I saw, silhouetted against the low fire in the gap of the curtains, a new-forged sword gleaming in his hand, Accolon. His eyes were wild with triumph, and I could see the breath coming to him hard and fast. He threw the sword down on the bed beside me, and I turned to glance at it. It was the very picture of Excalibur. I was sure I would only be able to tell the difference if I took it in my hand. I turned back to him. His mouth opened slightly, as though he were about to say something, but before he could speak, I leapt forward and grasped him by the front of his shirt, pulling him into the bed. The curtains fell shut behind him, and we fell back beside the sword. He kissed me, hot and hard with urgency, and I felt his hands rough and fast, pulling the nightdress up over my head. He smiled gently to himself as he looked my body over.

"It is true, then," he murmured, tracing one swirling line of blue across my stomach.

I suddenly heard Kay's voice in my head, *You* are *like that all over.* But Kay had forsaken me, and at last I had found another man who was not afraid of a woaded woman.

"It is true," I whispered back, and he kissed me again. This would bind us together. He could be my partner in this; the others had all been afraid. Kay, Lancelot, Uriens. Not quite brave enough. I pulled him to me, and I felt him tremble in surrender. I pushed him beneath me and tore him free of his clothes; he was just as fine beneath as I had hoped. All broad muscle and dark gold hair. All big, rough hands that tugged in my hair, just enough, and eyes that ran over me with the desire and wonder I had long deserved. So it was swift and wild, all the more so because I had been lonely so long, and it left us both gasping and tangled together in the pleasant exhaustion of lovers who at last have had what they have long waited for.

It was a while after, when the light from the fire was almost dead, and we lay side by side in the sweet haze of pleasure that he spoke.

"So you are pleased, then," he asked, "with the sword?"

I laughed softly. "Quite pleased. It is a perfect copy. You had it made very fast."

I felt his hand slide into my hair, and I rolled into his arms once more in the darkness.

"I knew that it would be worth my haste," he replied.

I covered his mouth with mine before he could speak again, growing lost already in the knowledge of him as mine, and the raw rush of power from my coming revenge, and the sword sleeping beside us.

Chapter Twenty-Six

Accolon's haste had been wise, for Arthur came for the sword a week before Christmas, just days later. I heard the horns that announced his arrival from my room where I was standing with my book of medicines, checking one last time the mixture I would make for Uriens.

175

It would have been Accolon who sounded the horn, and the noise of it made me smile to think of him. I had found some joy in my life here, at least, even if it had not been with the child. And I might yet have a child that would give me joy, for I felt sure I could love a child, if it were one by a man of my own choosing.

Arthur had come from Lothian, where the winter snows were deep already, and he rode in on his armoured horse dressed in rich, heavy furs of a dark grey-brown. He rode without his crown and with just a small company of knights. Among them I recognised Gawain. Every time I saw Arthur he looked more like a king; not in his clothes, but the way he talked, the way he held himself. The war had made him a strong leader and an experienced warrior; I could see that from the way he moved, the easy way he had with the men that rode with him. The boy I had known was almost entirely gone.

He jumped down from his horse as I walked out into the courtyard, and I saw Uriens kneel before him. I wasn't going to kneel, so I hung back. Uriens got to his feet and Arthur clapped him on the shoulder with a friendly laugh. Behind Arthur, I caught Gawain's eye. His look was unfriendly, glowering. This could not have been easy for him.

After the formalities of the greetings, Arthur made an excuse to leave with me. He told Uriens he wanted me to show him his new nephew. When he had shut the door behind him in my room, I saw him breathe a sigh of relief. He unbuckled the sword around his waist and laid it on the table.

"It will be good to have my sword back again," he told me, with his open, trusting smile. "Morgan, I am so grateful that you took care of it for me."

I gave him my sweetest smile. He would not know how I hated him for selling me to Uriens, and for failing to protect Morgawse. I went to where I had hidden the copy that Accolon had made. I was sure it was not the real sword, for it felt heavy in my hands, and I needed both to lift it. Arthur did not notice that the sword I had carried easily in a single hand before I now lifted with difficulty in both. They would weigh the same to him, anyway. Arthur looked it over with a smile when I handed it to him.

"You have cared for it well. Thank you." He leaned forward and kissed me on the cheek. Oddly, it reminded me strongly of when we had been children. We had greeted each other always like that, the three of us, when we had been young. It was strange that he still did it, when so much had changed. Arthur turned as if to go, and then turned back to me. "Oh, Morgan. The scabbard."

The scabbard. Accolon had not copied the scabbard. The scabbard was the more powerful part. I was prepared to lie, to refuse to give it up, but Arthur had already seen it, the glint of its jewels peeping out from between my dresses, giving it away. He reached for it and buckled it around his waist before I could even speak. At least, I thought, I had not put the real sword in the true scabbard. Then I would have lost them both.

"Morgan, many thanks for your safekeeping." Arthur kissed me on the cheek again and, picking up the scabbard, buckling it on and sliding the fake Excalibur inside, led the way out. He did, after all, want to see his little nephew, and I stood, leaning against the doorway, as he picked up the little boy from his nurse's lap and threw him playfully in the air until he giggled. Arthur had a son of his own whom he had tried to murder. He would be married soon, and have more children. I wondered if Mordred would have been safer if he had been born a girl. An older son would be a dangerous rival to the children Arthur would have with whoever he was about to take as his wife.

"What is his name?" Arthur asked, interrupting my thoughts.

"Ywain," I told him. "Uriens named him; it's some old family name of his."

Arthur nodded, and seemed pleased. I was relieved when the little boy began to cry and had to be handed back to his nurse, and we could leave. I was relieved, too, that Arthur had not noticed that I did not hold my own child.

Because Arthur and his knights were staying overnight to avoid travelling the cold winter evenings, we all ate in the castle's great hall. There was far more food than was necessary, and the sight of it all around us, all the roasted game, the apples, the bread, the vegetables from the stores, was sickening when I thought of Uriens' excuse for killing the Breton woman. Clearly, we had plenty of food. I had to sit through their eating and drinking and tedious stories of the war. Every single man was the greatest fighter, the bravest knight, and all of their victories had been glorious. None of them mentioned how one of the sovereigns they had defeated had been a woman prisoner, bound and executed. No, they would not want that for their honour. I let my attention drift away. Accolon sat with Uriens' men at the trestle tables in the main hall below the high table on the dais. When I caught his eye, he gave me the slightest of smiles, and I felt the warmth of secret knowledge at my centre, and I held it tight.

Then talk turned to Arthur's marriage. He said that he had received offers from the fathers of a few princesses, but he wanted to consult with Merlin before he sent for a wife. I thought he seemed reluctant. I supposed he was rather young, but he was the King, and he had a responsibility to secure peace. Besides, he had married me off to Uriens only a couple of years older than he was now, and he had had almost six more years of freedom than Morgawse when she had been sent away to be married.

"Well, my Lord, they say Princess Isolde in Ireland is the most beautiful woman in Britain," one of the knights with Arthur suggested, jovially.

Arthur laughed. "So I have heard, but she is twelve years old. I don't want to marry a girl; I want a woman my own age who will be useful as a queen as well as... desirable. I want someone wise, and brave, not just someone beautiful. Besides, Kay has met Isolde, and he says that she is... simple."

Another of Arthur's knights, a softly-spoken man with short mousey hair and a reserved manner, who was, I think, Percival, cleared his throat softly to speak. "She ought to be the daughter of one of your old enemies, to keep the peace more strongly."

Arthur nodded. I grew quickly tired of the conversation as more and more names of princesses were raised and then dismissed. I got the feeling that the discussion wasn't serious, and this was just dinnertime sport. They were men; they did not understand what a serious matter marriage was.

I saw Accolon leave early, with duties to attend to, but with Arthur here Uriens would notice if I slipped away. As it was, bold with drink, Uriens tried to follow me to me bed when an end was called to the feast. I only noticed him when I was at my door, and he seized me from behind, holding me tight against him in a manner that I could only imagine in his drunken state he thought to be seductive. He had not desired me at all before I had produced a son for him, but now it was as though I was as lovely as Isolde of Ireland herself. I pushed him off. *I* was not drunk.

"Leave me alone," I snapped, pulling the door open and stepping through. After I had frightened him with the sword, I did not expect him to try to follow me, but he did. He was drunk enough that I could push him back, and I drew the bolt on the door once I had shut it, and leaned back against it, closing my eyes, pushing away the awful memories that crowded around me: Lot holding me down on the table, Uriens with his hand over my mouth, whispering at my ear, *you will be obedient to me*. I would kill him soon.

The days in the depths of winter passed slowly, until the nights came. Uriens did not try to come to my room again; when he was sober he remembered well my sword. Reassured that we were safe, Accolon would come to me and we would love passionately together. He was rough, often, and I liked it. I wanted it. I pressed myself into the touch of his hands. I liked the rough rub of his stubble against the smoothness of my own skin. He was far more masculine than the men I had known before. Kay and Merlin had been smoothed-skinned, smooth-faced, and where Kay had been gentle and tender, and Merlin quick and demanding, Accolon was raw and hungry in his passion. I wanted him the more for needing my touch so badly, and I was the more hungry for his kisses for their insistent heat against my mouth. I began to hope more and more strongly that I would have another child. I did not even care that Uriens would know that it was not his.

It was early in spring that I came back to my bedroom to check back through my books, and found Kay there. Well, I knew it was not really Kay. He sat lounging in the chair beside my table, flicking through my book of medicines.

"What do you want, Merlin?" I demanded.

He gave Kay's sparkling grin, but then turned back into the form he bore as the young man. It was cold outside and I had come in wearing furs, but I was reluctant to take anything off while he was there. When he changed back into himself I noticed that he was wearing the big, ugly sapphire around his neck again. I wondered what it did, if there was some Black Arts secret to that ugly necklace.

"So unkind, Morgan, when I come with an offering of news." He threw the book down casually on the table. He would not have taken it. There were others like it. It was not like his book of Macrobius. He got lithely to his feet and stepped towards me. I did not move into the room, or shut the door behind me. He came closer, and I noticed that he had made himself taller, so that he looked down on me, as he felt he needed to intimidate me. Perhaps it was the sight of the dress Nimue had made me. I was sure there was some magic in it, a little protection. He slid an arm around my waist, pulling me against him. I pushed back, but he did not release his grip. He leaned down close to me, hissing close and threatening. "But before that, I need you to tell me something. The sword that Arthur brought back with him from here *is not Excalibur*. Where is the true sword, Morgan?"

I stared back at him, unmoving. I did not have to give in to him. Nimue would have his knowledge from him and I would never have to negotiate with him ever again.

"I don't know what you're taking about, Merlin," I replied.

He pressed his body against mine, as though he thought he was being persuasive, and I pushed him away. He moved back this time, and he changed back into the shape I knew as his own, the grinning skull-faced man.

"Either tell me your news or leave, Merlin. There will be no more transactions between us," I told him, turning away, walking over to the table to pick up the book.

Softly, behind me, I heard a voice that I was surprised to find sent a flicker of nervous pleasure through me, and in its low and lovely French tones it said, "Morgan, I can give you what you want."

I wheeled around, and it was truly as if Lancelot stood there before me. I hated the betrayal of my body; I could not stop it. I felt my cheeks flush hot, the breath catch. Merlin had seen it. Merlin knew my weakness. Suddenly I saw myself again, fifteen years old, climbing naked out of the lake, feeling the strange new embarrassment to be naked before Lancelot. There had been something different about it from that long ago, even. I knew I had loved Kay, and I thought that perhaps I was growing to love Accolon, but the overwhelming power Lancelot's presence alone had over me made me wonder if there was another kind of love, somewhere beyond that, that I would feel, that I *could* feel, if I could only be alone with him, and away from the rest of the world. I had dreamed it, in a dream as clear as day, that we would be together. I closed my eyes for a moment, sinking in to it, and I could almost feel his lips on mine again, in the forest, and in the dream.

I opened my eyes to find that Lancelot had stepped towards me again, and he reached out to brush his fingertips against my cheek. I felt the blood in me grow hotter. *It's Merlin*, I told myself, but I was frozen to the spot. I knew I should push him back and run, but the shock of it held me still. Slowly, gently, he took my face in his hands and, as my breath fluttered fast from me, he leaned down and our lips brushed. I sighed with longing, and in response, I felt his lips open on mine, his kiss become deep and passionate, and the wave of sweet excitement run through my body. I could feel my heart racing, and my spine weaken as I felt his tongue against mine, and his kiss grow more powerful and hungry with my need for it.

But when I felt the forceful grip of his hands on the skirts of my dress, pushing it up, I thought again *this is Merlin*, and this time the feeling that flooded through me was raw disgust. I pushed him back and slapped him hard across the face. Grinning, he changed back into himself. I would have killed him if I had had Excalibur in my hands.

"Well, it is well enough that Arthur does not have Excalibur. He can pose no mortal danger to me without it. Still, I shall have the sword for myself, Morgan."

"It's a pity that you cannot get a woman to touch you in your real form, isn't it, Merlin?"

I felt that I had some ground to win back from him. He had surprised me, and found me vulnerable. I wanted him to feel weak as well. "You think you are the only one who knows other people's secret desires?"

I closed my eyes and pictured Nimue; the small-boned frame, the white-blonde hair, the pretty, attentive face. When I opened my eyes, it was the first time I had seen Merlin in his real form with anything other than a grin on his face. His ugly face had fallen, drooping low around the mouth, his eyes wide and staring.

"But, Merlin, *I* am not here to give you what you want," I said, and the voice that came from me was Nimue's whispery soprano, not the voice I knew as my own. "Why so surprised, Merlin? Did you think I would not study the book that I exchanged for my sword? Or did you think I did not know that you desire Nimue, and she has denied you?"

Merlin was struggling to regain his control again, and I was beginning to feel stronger and bolder. He tried to gather his expression into one of superiority, and he gave a cruel laugh.

"You have so much to learn, Morgan." He leaned closer, to whisper it at me one more time in his rasping voice, "*You have so much to learn.*"

As I reached out to slap him again, he disintegrated into mist under my hand, and he was gone. Gone without my ever knowing his news.

Chapter Twenty-Seven

The news came nonetheless. Arthur was getting married. Uriens and I would have to ride to Camelot. I told him I did not want to take Elaine. She avoided me now that she knew she irritated me. I wished I could have liked her. It would have been nice to have some female company in Rheged Castle. I missed the communities of women that I had known at the abbey and in Avalon. I missed the conversation of women. I missed Morgawse. I was sorry, too, that now I was married we would not sleep side by side as sisters. I knew I would worry for her, afraid and alone, and unable to sleep in Camelot.

It was decided that Uriens and I would travel with only two of his knights, leaving the household and our son behind in the cares of Accolon and Elaine. I was sorry to leave Accolon behind, but I thought it would be hard to be secretive with Camelot full of people. We did not talk about parting, the night before I left for Camelot. I would be back soon, and when I was back the mixture I had made for Uriens would be ready. I had not told Accolon yet, but when I returned from Camelot I would.

We left before light was fully up, to reach Camelot before it was too dark to ride anymore. Uriens did not like the thought of spending a night on the road with me any more than I did with him. It was cold, still. The air was fresh with the coming spring, but it was not yet warm, and I wore my light furs, thin and glossy-black over the gleaming black dress Nimue had made me. I was pleased with how I looked. A little fearsome, I thought, and that was how I wanted it. Uriens wore his crown. I had seen myself wearing it in my dreams of the future, and the sight of it heartened me. He would soon be gone, and his lands would be mine.

When Camelot came in sight, a huge black silhouette against the fading sunset, Uriens drew his horse up to mine and leaned close to me.

"You will not embarrass me when we are in Camelot. You will be a proper wife to me. Do you understand, Morgan?"

I said nothing.

I heard the horn sound for our arrival, and the gates opened wide. Camelot's great courtyard was filled with people holding torches. At the head of the group Arthur stood, dressed in his crown and his red and gold surcoat. Merlin stood beside him, his nasty black eyes shining from within his hood, his face a mass of bluish darkness in the shadow the torches threw. Just behind them stood Ector. My mother – our mother – stood at Arthur's side. It was what was proper, but I thought Arthur would probably have preferred to have Ector beside him. Beside his father, in his black and gold surcoat, stood Kay. He was even more handsome than I had remembered, his dark eyes intense and thoughtful where they were usually bright with laughter. He did not look at me, but I knew he was thinking about me. In the light of the torches, the soft thickness of his black hair shone. I looked for Morgawse in the crowd, but I did not see her.

I jumped from my horse before Arthur and accepted his kisses on my cheeks, then kissed my mother.

"You did not bring your son," she said softly, with disappointment.

"He is still very young," I protested gently. She nodded indulgently, thinking me the doting mother. Whenever I thought about the child, it made me feel hollow and sick.

As I made my excuses that I was tired, Kay slipped through the crowd to meet me on my way to my bedchamber.

"Morgan, you," he gave a weak smile, "you look well." I returned his smile. "Arthur tells me you have a son. Ah..." Kay shifted a little on his feet. "How is he? Is he...?"

I sighed with annoyance, both at how the boy had turned out, and with Kay's inability to ask the brave question. "He is the image of his father, which pleases the old man tremendously."

Kay nodded thoughtfully. He looked a little disappointed, and I was sorry for my sharpness. I wished that we were in a place where I could touch him, could kiss him, could talk honestly with him.

"Well, I am so happy to see that you are well. Goodnight, my Lady Queen Morgan." He took my hand and kissed it softly. I knew how those lips felt all over my body, and I felt their impression on the back of my hand after he had slipped back away into the crowd.

I undressed and climbed right into bed when I got to my chamber. It was dark and no one had prepared a fire, but I didn't care. I was exhausted from the ride, and I wanted to be asleep before Uriens came. I hoped that he would leave me alone if I were asleep.

I fell asleep fast, and I dreamed a sweet dream. The dream began with me and Kay lying side by side in the woodland clearing by Ector's house. It happened as it had before, and Kay turned to me and kissed me, and we melted together with it, with all the exploratory delight of young love. I felt the sensations again as I had felt them before, the quiver of excitement when Kay found the secret place within me I did not know I had, and the heat of his breath against my neck, and most of all, the gentle power of the first kiss which was full of the smell of the lilacs and the lazy feeling of the end of summer. Then, in the dream, before it was over, Kay turned me over again beneath him, and I was lying on my back in the grass looking up at not Kay, but Lancelot, and the kiss I felt against me was the intense sensual kiss I had felt in the forest, only this time I was not denied, for he was there, at the centre of me, and all around me, our lips and bodies pressed tight together in the ecstasy of passion. In the lovely haze of the dream I felt myself growing hot and eager with it, I felt it gather tight in the low centre of me, deep in my stomach.

But I was forced from my dream by the feel of Uriens' rough hands on me. Still slow with sleep, with the dream, still hot and full of longing, I tried to push him off me, but my mind was hazy still, and my limbs heavy. He did not move. I felt him force his hand up between my legs. He felt my desire there and could not believe that it was not for him. I kicked at him, and I opened my mouth to shout, but he clamped his hand over it before I could get the noise out, covering my nose as well so that the strength left me with my breath. He rolled on to me and, pushing up my nightdress, went hard inside me. I screamed against his hand, but it ate up the sound, and I had already lost the fight. It did not hurt the same as it had before, but I hated the feeling of his heavy body squashing down on top of me, his unkind grip over my mouth, and the other hand wrapped around my wrist. I would see the marks of his fingers against the white and blue of my skin tomorrow. The woad would hide them, but I doubted I would get any sympathy from anyone anyway. A wife's duty. I felt sick. Thankfully, it was over fast, and he rolled away into the darkness. I felt the hot tears of my powerlessness prick at the back of my eyes, and I held them back.

When I was sure that Uriens was asleep, I slipped from the bed, smoothing my nightdress down and wrapping a cloak around my shoulders. I had not been wrong to hope that Morgawse would be in her old room. I could see a light from under the door, and I opened the door without knocking. Morgawse was sat, fully dressed still, even wearing her crown, cross-legged on her bed. She had the little boy Mordred on her knee and was fussing his fine strands of golden hair while he giggled and kicked his feet in delight, but when she saw me come through the door in my nightdress she slipped from the bed and set him in a wooden crib. She walked over to me, took my hand, led me into the room just enough to shut the door and bolt it behind us. She gently pushed the loose hair back from around my face and kissed me on the forehead.

"Marriage as you described," I whispered, and as I said the words, and acknowledged the depths of my unhappiness to my sister, it broke in me, and I could not hold the tears back. Morgawse held me against her, and hushed me gently. I wrapped my arms around her neck and buried my face in her hair, which smelled of wood-smoke and spices as somehow it always had. When I felt calmer, I pushed gently back up off her shoulder. "I thought he would not try to… hurt me in Camelot. I thought he would be ashamed to in a castle full of people." I shook my head, fighting back the tears again. Morgawse took off her crown, shushed me again and, taking both of my hands, led me towards the bed where we lay down together side by side. I closed my eyes. We could have been girls again.

Morgawse did not put out the candles, but they guttered out as we fell asleep. When I woke in the morning I did not remember where I was for a moment, but I did know that I had slept beside Morgawse, and I woke feeling safe. It was only when I was fully awake that my mind flashed back to Uriens with his hand over my mouth.

I did not have to wonder long why Morgawse had not come out to greet me the night before. She woke before me, when she heard the first little murmurings of wakefulness from Mordred. She was already dressed in a different dress, as rich as the one she had worn before, a deep plum purple and edged with fine white fur around the neck and sleeves. She looked beautiful, still, after everything; far more beautiful than I would ever be, despite the fact that she was seven years older than I.

She smiled when she saw me awake.

"Morgan, you're awake. When I woke up this morning and saw you there, it made me think of when we were girls." She shook her head with a gentle smile of disbelief, shifting the weight of the little child in her arms. "So much has changed, eh?"

I climbed out of the bed and wrapped my cloak around myself. I would have to go back downstairs, to Uriens, to get my dress. Morgawse set the child down on the bed when I got out, and turned to me, crossing her arms in a gesture of anger and frustration.

"Do you know Arthur is refusing to see me?" she said. I shook my head.

"I don't know why *he* is angry with *me*," Morgawse raged. "*I* ought to be angry. My sons were born princes, and now they're just his knights; he won't acknowledge his son, and he refuses to talk about it, like he thinks *I* did it to him!"

She seemed to have, strangely, forgotten the worst; that Arthur had tried to have their son killed. The little boy sat on the bed staring at his mother, quiet and still, but his eyes following her attentively. Under the bright lick of fine gold hair on his head, he had a curiously serious face for a child that did not seem to come from either of his parents. Absently, Morgawse walked over to the bed and picked him up in her arms again. He grabbed hold of her long, thick hair and rested his head against her breast, closing his eyes. She stroked his head gently. I saw the look of love she gave him, and the deep happiness she got from even this cursed, ill-fated child, and I felt the raw stab of jealousy.

"He is a strong boy. Any other father would have been proud."

"Do you tell him," I asked warily, "who his father is?"

Morgawse looked up at me, in disbelief. "Of course! Well, it hardly did his father any good not knowing who his parents were, did it?" I supposed that she was right.

"Should you have him here? Isn't it dangerous?" I asked.

Morgawse spoke gently, still gazing down at her child, but her words were harsh. "It is safe enough. I wrote to Arthur before we came saying that I was bringing him. I told him, if he ever tried to harm any of my sons again, I would let it be known throughout the whole land that it was he, not Merlin the witch, who played Herod to all the little boys in Lothian, and then he would have war on his hands again."

I was glad that she had found a way to be safe.

There was a knock at the door. I gathered the cloak more tightly around myself as Morgawse walked over and opened it with one hand. But I didn't need to; it was our mother. She kissed Morgawse on the cheek brusquely, casting her a look of disapproval as she came into the room and Morgawse closed the door behind her.

"You brought the child with you, I see," she said, her tone thick with distaste.

"Yes, mother, I brought my child with me. I had to, because I was afraid that his father would try to have him killed again."

Mother ignored her, and came over to kiss me on both cheeks and take my face in her hands.

"Little Morgan." Her kind eyes crinkled into a smile. "Not little Morgan any more, but a wife and a mother." She kissed me on the forehead. "It suits you well."

I did not think it suited me at all. Then my mother's face turned to confusion as she looked at me properly.

"Morgan, why are you here so early? Why are you in your bedclothes?" She asked, her tone halfway between concern and reprimand.

I opened my mouth, unsure of whether to tell her the truth or not. Morgawse stepped in for me.

"She slept here last night," Morgawse told her, firmly, striding over to stand beside us, Mordred still in her arms. He seemed to be sleeping.

"Why?" Mother asked softly. I glanced at Morgawse. She was as unsure as I was. I did not think I could bear a speech about duty.

"Uriens has been hurting her. Look." Morgawse grabbed my wrist with her free hand, holding it up in front of our mother's face. I had not thought she had noticed the blue-black marks of his fingers through the woad, but she had, and I was grateful. I did not know why I was surprised; she had felt them herself.

My mother sighed heavily and gently took my wrist from Morgawse. She laid her fingertips against the marks lightly, as though trying to soothe it better.

"Men can be rough. Perhaps I was wrong to send you to the abbey. Marriage must have been a shock for you. Just," she sighed again and drew me into an embrace, pressing a kiss to the top of my head as though I were a child, "Try to do what he wants. Marriage *does* take some getting used to. And don't listen to your sister too much. She frightened you about it, didn't she?"

"I told her the *truth*," Morgawse shouted. Mordred woke in her arms, and began to scream.

"Oh!" My mother said, suddenly moving me back from her, holding me by the shoulders. It was as though she thought the matter entirely dealt with. "I forgot – I came to tell you that Arthur and his knights are meeting the new Queen at Dover today, and the wedding will be tomorrow."

I nodded. I didn't care.

"At Dover?" Morgawse asked as she shushed Mordred quiet again, seemingly utterly distracted by this news as my mother was. "So it's a foreign princess. Isolde?"

My mother shook her head.

"He didn't want Isolde. She seemed like a lovely girl to me, but Arthur didn't take to her. She was Merlin's choice." My mother made a little noise of disapproval in her throat. I was not sure if she disapproved of Merlin, or of Arthur ignoring his advice. "Anyway, we should make ourselves ready to welcome this new Queen. Now," she turned to me and took my hand, "you had better go back to your own room, Morgan. To your husband."

I cast a plaintive look at Morgawse, but I went willingly with Mother. When I reached my room, I was relieved to find that Uriens was gone.

Chapter Twenty-Eight

There were serving women waiting there for me, and though I did not like being fussed by them, I was grateful for the warm bath they brought, and grateful to close my eyes and feel my hair being brushed. I dressed in one of my mother's old dresses that she had given me at my wedding, a simple grey and silver brocade dress, and pulled my woollen cloak on top.

I found Merlin where I sought him. He had a room in the same tower as Arthur's bedroom. It was dark and smoky, and I was sure he kept it stuffed with bizarre herbs and animal parts in jars in order to scare people. Nothing he had in that room looked particularly useful or felt particularly powerful to me. On my way up the stairs, when I was sure no one was around, I closed my eyes and imagined myself as Nimue. I had done it once before, so it came easily, and I felt my limbs change, grow smaller and lighter, and my shape become hers. I wondered if Merlin would be fooled.

I pushed the door open, and for a moment he was, but then a smug smile gathered on his face.

"Ah, Morgan. Have you come to reconsider my offer?"

I strode into the room and jumped up to sit on the table, resting my feet on the chair beneath me. I did not bother to allow my shape to change back.

"Why didn't Arthur marry the woman you suggested?" I asked. My boldness sounded strange in Nimue's soft voice. I wanted to distract him so that I could look at the spines of his books, see if there was anything I knew I could not get anywhere else.

Merlin scoffed and shook his head. "Your Seneschal lover told him that Isolde is a simpleton. It is the truth, but simpletons make good wives. The woman he has chosen instead is Leodegrance's daughter. Many of the Bretons are still pagans, and the princess grew up without a mother's guidance. The girl is half-wild." He shook his head again. "He has insisted upon her because I told him that she has the blood of the witch-queen Maev of Cruachan in her veins. That was meant to *dissuade* him. Queen Maev cursed two of her husbands with her blood, and with one of them she took as her lover his finest knight. He seemed to think I was *recommending* the girl because of it. His god has cursed him for that bastard child he got on his sister. I have seen it. I warned him of his bad destiny. I warned him that the child would bring his death, but he has got this idea in his head that this princess of Leodegrance's will give him an Otherworld child that will protect him from his god. It's ridiculous. Destiny cannot be escaped. But he has set his heart on her, and where a man sets his heart he will not be dissuaded." Merlin said this last sentence in a funny little voice, as though he were trying to imitate Arthur.

I saw something on the bookshelf that caught my eye. A thin leather book with MACROBIUS printed along the spine. It was too thin to be either of the volumes I knew about. It must be the third volume, where Macrobius described how to change things other than oneself.

I pointed to it.

"Is that the *Theory of Dreams*?" I asked. Merlin gave his skull-like grin.

"I hoped you would notice that. I am open to an offer of a fair exchange, Morgan."

"I did not think that was the *Theory of Dreams*." I climbed down from the table, still in Nimue's shape. I crossed my arms. "You will not have the sword."

"Ah, Morgan." He pressed his lips together in disappointment. "Then you shall not have the book."

I leaned closer to hiss at him, "That is what you said to me last time."

And then I left. When I was on the empty stairs, I allowed Nimue's shape to slip from me and became myself again. I had got information from Merlin, and I had seen his books. I knew what he had, and I had nothing with me in Camelot that he could steal in return that was worth anything near as much to me as that book.

I spent the night before Arthur's wedding in Morgawse's bedroom again. I did not think our mother would come back. Like Arthur, she spent her time pretending that Mordred did not exist, and so avoided seeing him at all costs. The day of Arthur's marriage, Morgawse and I got ready together, as though we were girls again. I sent the serving women to get my jewelled dress from my room, and Morgawse plaited my hair. She still wore hers as my mother did, according to the Cornish fashion, drawn back simply at the front, and loose at the back. I would not have been allowed loose hair in the abbey, and I had grown used to the fashions of Logrys now, so much so that I felt naked when my hair was not neatly plaited away.

I made an excuse not to go down to the wedding in the chapel. I wanted a moment on my own, in my own room, without being afraid that Uriens would come in. I had not actually seen him since I had left in the night. I was sure he would be angry. I waited in Morgawse's room until I heard the noise in the courtyard fall quiet. I wondered what the Breton princess was like. I thought of the Breton queen that I had failed to save at Rheged. She must be this girl's mother, but she had talked about her like she was a child, and the princess Arthur had chosen was of roughly his own age. Did mothers always see their daughters as little children? I supposed Morgawse still saw her huge sons as children. My mother still called me *little Morgan*. Did this princess even know that Arthur had killed her brothers and had her mother executed? Oh, I doubted that anyone would tell her. I wondered if she was afraid. What if she had come over without a word of English to be given into the hands of the man who had killed almost all of her family? If she was like her mother, she would be proud and defiant. I wondered if it was better to be that way, or to be simple and compliant. *Simpletons make good wives.*

When I got down to my room, I at first thought I was alone, and was relieved. I walked in and shut the door, but as I went to sit in the window seat, Uriens stepped out from behind the bed where the bed curtains had hidden him.

"Been hiding from me, Morgan?" he accused, striding over to me. I ran a few steps back from him.

"Don't touch me," I half-shouted.

"Morgan," he sighed, rubbing his face. "I don't do anything to you that I... shouldn't. I have been a good husband to you. I do not beat you. I have not told anyone that you were not a virgin when we married, or tried to shame you. I do not keep other women indiscriminately, or take whores. I have let you have your freedom, to write to whom you please, to move about the castle, to control some of the gold at my disposal, to organise your part of household. I have been good to you. You have to *try*. Do you think this is what I want? That I find it easy? I haven't made a secret of the fact that I don't like your pagan woad, and we do not have any real affection for one another, but I have made efforts in my duty, and you have made none. We would both be a lot happier if you accepted that this is what marriage *is*. This is what married men and women do."

I could not even speak. I was too angry. The way he was with me was awful. I could feel his disgust, his stolid duty, and I didn't want it. I thought we would have both been happier if we agreed instead to live separate lives.

"Uriens, you *force* me. You put your hand over my mouth. That isn't kind." I gave one, desperate attempt to explain to him that what he was doing was *not* reasonable for a husband to do. I was as much his property as a dog might be, but people still spoke with disapproval of men who kicked their dogs, or beat them. He should not have been violent with me.

"I have to. Do you think I want other people to hear your screaming? It is not my fault that you do not enjoy it."

"*Yes it is,*" I shouted.

"All of the other women I have had have enjoyed it," Uriens said, crossing his arms in front of him.

And all of the other men I have had, I have enjoyed, I thought. I did not say it. I did not want him to hit me or call me a whore again. I drew myself back, against the door.

"I hate you," I said, very softly. Uriens shrugged.

"How you feel is of no importance in the matter," he answered.

I ran back up to Morgawse's room and locked the door. I lay on the bed and closed my eyes. The room seemed oddly quiet without the little burbling of the infant Mordred, but I was grateful for the peace. Uriens did not come looking for me, or if he did, he could not find me. No one tried the door until Morgawse came back from the chapel. When she rattled the handle and found it did not move, she knew it was me, and called out for me to let her in. I opened the door to see that she had all her sons with her, and the whole lot of them rushed into the room. They were all dressed alike in Lothian's dark blue, and on the surcoats of Gawain and Aggravain were sewn Lot's two-headed gryphon in gold thread. Morgawse herself was gorgeous as usual in a dress of dark orange embroidered in lovely patterns with gold that shone like her red-gold hair, and she had a necklace of amber beads around her neck, resting against her pale breasts where they swelled at the neck of her dress. She put Mordred tenderly in his crib and, placing a kiss on his head, came over to take me by the hand. There was a slightly sad look in her eyes as she squeezed my hand.

"Arthur has a wife now," she said.

I nodded. I supposed that he was the only man who had treated her kindly, at least for a time.

"Is she beautiful?" I asked, idly.

Morgawse shrugged. "It's hard to tell. She's covered in jewels. Mother's old jewels. He must have sent them to her."

"I think she is quite beautiful," Gaheris, who was just coming of an age where he might notice such things, said. "Her hair is very lovely. Red."

"You didn't *see* it." Gawain beside him groaned, clearly overcome at the memory of his sight of the Queen. "When we met her at Dover, she had it loose. She looked like a savage, like a barbarian, but I couldn't stop staring at that *hair*. There is so much of it. I wanted to just grab a handful and —"

Morgawse gave a little scolding cough, and Gawain gave her a sharp look, but he did change his tack.

"Well, she is a fitting Queen for Arthur, who is the finest King this land will ever know," Gawain said.

It seemed a strange statement for a seventeen year old boy to make, but no one disagreed with him. I was not sure I agreed, but then I could not think of any kings I knew of who I thought had been particularly fine. From the sound of it, they were all brutes.

Aggravain made a low, derisive noise. "It's a mistake for a king to have a wife that other men covet. But she is not so beautiful. She looks somewhat ordinary to me."

"Aggravain, you did not see her *hair*," Gawain insisted.

It seemed as though no one but Gawain was sure of quite what to make of her.

They milled around me, getting ready for the feast. Morgawse took Gareth and Mordred off to the bedroom that Gareth and Gaheris slept in, and I heard her instructing Gareth to watch his little brother carefully while she and the eldest three were gone. I had heard that Gaheris had just pledged into Arthur's knights as well. Morgawse was running low on sons to keep her company now that she was a widow in Lothian Castle.

When Morgawse returned, she checked the clothing of her three eldest sons and kissed them all on the cheek. We were ready to go. Even though Gawain and Aggravain towered over her, she still treated them like boys. Morgawse would never tell anyone who was the older of Gawain and Aggravain. She had told me that she feared the younger one would feel cheated of his birthright, and by refusing to tell she had made it so the twins shared Lothian Castle and its armies between them. I followed them out, through the courtyard, and to the great hall, where I could hear that the feast had begun already.

Chapter Twenty-Nine

When I saw the girl that Arthur had married, I felt a shock go through me. She was the woman in my dream. The same deep red hair and white face; the same small, angry red mouth twisted into a little tense knot that was still, somehow, unbearably beautiful. I did not think she would have looked so beautiful were she not so angry. It gave what might otherwise have been a placid face a kind of power. I could not tear my eyes from her. It seemed, as I had hoped, that she was angry and defiant as her mother had been. It did not, however, bode well for Arthur. I wondered why he had set his heart so firmly on her, until, when I came up to the table after my mother to greet Arthur with a kiss on the cheek, I felt the unmistakable feel of the Otherworld all about her. It was not how I had felt it before, though – not with the ladies of Avalon, or Kay. This was an Otherworld foreign in its quality to me. Something about it felt ancient, and portentous. I remembered, suddenly, what Merlin had said to Arthur about the witch-queen Maev. I didn't entirely believe it, but there was some powerful destiny hanging about this strange, angry girl. She was in my dream. I would one day stand with her on the shores of Avalon, with Excalibur between us. We were all tangled together, all of us, around her, around Arthur, around the sword Excalibur. This was the beginning of it all.

Uriens was already sitting in the seat beside the one meant for me, and I ignored him as I sat down. Morgawse was right behind me, and Arthur greeted her awkwardly. He did not want her there. He would not kiss her on the cheek. When she came to sit by my side, she leaned down and hissed in my ear.

"I don't fancy Arthur's luck tonight." Her eyes were on the new Queen. No, I did not either.

I kept my eyes on her, and on Arthur. I could hear her speaking to my mother. She was definitely Breton; I could hear it in the rich tones of her accent when she spoke – thick, though her English was good. So, it was as I had suspected, and this girl, who had been meant for a simple life of happy marriage in her home country, in the wishes of her mother, had been summoned by Arthur across the sea to be his wife and protect him from his bad destiny. I wondered if she even knew how it was Arthur himself who had slain her brothers in battle.

Her Breton accent was pretty enough; the English words sounded richer and crisper on her tongue than they did on native speakers'. Her English was *very* good, and she seemed very comfortable speaking it. I supposed that was a mercy since I knew that Arthur did not speak a word of Breton. She looked uncomfortable, still, though I could see my mother was trying to be kind. I noticed, too, that she drank *a lot* of wine, until a red flush came high on her cheeks. Perhaps Arthur would be luckier than Morgawse thought. As the evening wore on, and she became flushed and bright with anger and wine, she was all the more enrapturing. Half the men's eyes around the table were on her.

My gaze fell on Arthur. I had seen him look with desire before, as I had seen him look on our own sister, but the look he cast on his new bride was something else entirely. He looked at her as though there were nothing else in the room. Surely a dangerous way for a king to look on any woman, I thought. Especially one who was yet, it seemed to me, to look on him at all.

Arthur left the feast early with his new wife, to the cheering of his men, especially Gawain. Gawain's eyes followed Arthur and the Queen out of the room. He was the least able of the men around that table to hide the fact that they were all picturing themselves leading the new Queen to their own bedroom. I thought uncomfortably of Gawain's wish for a fistful of her hair.

"To Arthur the conqueror," Gawain cheered, raising his cup. The men cheered lewdly and smashed their cups together, except Kay, whose eyes I felt on me. He had not been sat far from her. He must have felt the Otherworld, too. When I caught his eye, he stood from his seat to come and stand behind Morgawse and me. He gave a sly smile.

"What do you think of our new Queen?" he asked, archly. He had obviously drunk enough that he had forgotten to be nervous and awkward around me.

Morgawse, beside me, shrugged, and the wine that filled her cup sloshed out the side a little. With my eyes on the Queen's cup, I had not noticed that my own sister's cup had been filled and emptied many times, too. I supposed that this could not have been easy for her.

"She seems angry," Morgawse said, slurring slightly.

I turned over my shoulder to look up at Kay. He was gazing off where Arthur had gone. I had hoped to find him sharp and alert as always, but either he was drunk or even he as well was picturing himself with his brother's new wife.

"And well she might be," Kay answered, thoughtfully. "When we picked her up at Dover yesterday, Arthur was with us, but he didn't reveal himself to her. He told me it was because he wanted to be sure she had Queen Maev's Otherworld blood in her. I think he just wanted to check she wasn't ugly. Well... I think she's even more lovely than Arthur hoped. Beautiful." Kay's tone was odd, worried. Morgawse, beside me, hiccupped. Kay put a gentle hand on the top of her head, a gesture of comfort.

"Poor Gawse," he said, softly, and she turned to give him a bleary smile.

Uriens beside me, whom I had been doing my best to ignore all evening, leaned over to join the conversation. He stank of ale and I could see from the lack of focus in his ugly, dull old eyes that he was drunk as the rest of them. I hoped he would continue drinking, and be too drunk to stop me slipping away to sleep side by side with Morgawse.

"You know, they say that red-headed women like her," he jabbed his finger clumsily off after where Arthur had gone, "and your sister Morgawse here…" He jabbed his finger in her direction, narrowly missing catching me in the face. "They say that red-headed women love to be fucked by a man."

"*Be quiet*, Uriens," I hissed at him. People were looking already, but he carried on, droning with all the loud, drunk crassness he could muster.

"I bet that Breton girl squirms like an eel when Arthur fucks her tonight. Oh, of course she looks angry, but it's the angry ones that want it, really. Except Morgan, of course. You're always angry, aren't you? And you never want to be fucked. Funny, isn't it, how the King fucks all the best women, and leaves me with *you*? You're hard and dry as an old twig, aren't you Morgan?" I refused to look at him, gazing off across the table at my mother whose face was turned away, and who was making polite conversation with Ector beside her, but who I could tell was listening. She should have come over and silenced Uriens. She was still a queen. Uriens had leaned across me to leer at Morgawse now. "All you red women love the feel of a man, don't you?"

Beside his mother, Gawain banged his fist on the table and made to stand; the only thing stilling him was his brother Aggravain's hand on his arm. I was sorry for it. I had hoped that Gawain would strike Uriens. Gawain was strong enough to kill him, I thought, with a well-judged single blow to the head. I would have been grateful for that.

Aggravain spoke, low and threatening, not lifting his hand from his brother's arm, and the harsh, cold sound of his voice seemed to sober Uriens a little. "Be careful what you say, Uriens. Our mother is your sister by marriage now, so any shame you say to her is shame upon yourself. Besides, do not think because our father is dead that Lothian has lost its strength, and will not crush those who dishonour Lot's blood. You are drunk, sir, and have been foolish. But remember this: the next time you insult the sons of Lot or our lady mother – who is Queen of a realm ten times the strength of yours in arms – will be the last time."

Uriens reeled back in his seat, flushed with ale and impotent rage. I supposed that he had barely noticed Aggravain until then. Morgawse, happily, was too drunk to have paid the whole argument any attention, and simply sat leaning back in her chair, her eyes closed and a slack smile on her face as she rested her head against Kay's hand. He lightly rubbed her hair, as though he were scratching a little cat. She murmured happily against it.

"Still," Uriens began again, bracing himself against the edge of the table and blinking hard as though trying to steady himself, "I know what women like *her*..." It was unclear which of the several women he had been variously insulting he was talking about, "I know what women like *her* like. What they all want."

I glanced up at Kay, and saw the annoyance tightening across his face, dragging him away from whatever thoughts had held him distant and staring off after his foster-brother.

"You don't know what women like as well as you *think* you know, Uriens," he snapped, and there was a new note of deliberate cruelty in his voice that I had not heard before. "Just go to bed."

Uriens stood to his feet, pushing his chair back and squaring up to Kay. Neither of them had spoken to each other, or even, it seemed, acknowledged one another before, and Uriens was a little thrown off balance by Kay's sudden familiarity, and insult. I hoped *someone* was going to hit Uriens tonight. As he stepped forward, Kay lifted up his hands, showing his palms in a gesture of peace-making. "Uriens, *just go to bed*," he said.

Uriens grabbed Kay by the front of his surcoat. "What would *you* know about what women like, eh? Don't pretend you know *anything* about women. I know what people say about you. I've heard. So don't pretend that you know what women like when every man and woman in this room knows that you're a sodomite."

Uriens did not see it coming. His eyes were on Kay's right hand, over his own hand on Kay's surcoat, prising his fingers away. But Kay was mirror-handed, another gift – he had told me once – from his Otherworld mother. Kay's fist struck him out of nowhere, hard on the jaw, and he collapsed to the ground. Kay stared down at him, wincing and shaking out his hand.

"I probably should not have done that," he said.

Aggravain shrugged. "I saw nothing," he said, drinking from his cup again.

I turned around in my chair to peer down at Uriens, sprawled on the floor behind me.

"Is he dead?" I asked softly.

Kay prodded him with the toe of his boot, and shook his head. "He's breathing. I didn't hit him very hard." Morgawse moaned and rubbed her face beside me. She was beginning to move from the pleasant oblivion of wine to suffering with it. Kay noticed, and sighed. "Can you get someone to take Uriens to his bed? I'll take Morgawse."

I nodded. Kay leaned down and wrapped his arm around Morgawse's waist, pulling her up with him. She slumped against him, but looked happy again. If I could have done, I would have left Uriens lying on the floor. As it was, after he had finished his cup of wine, Aggravain offered to take him, and threw him over his shoulder. I was pleased that he would not be handled gently. He did not deserve it.

I lingered a while, thinking Kay might come back. I had had enough wine to feel daring, and for my anger at Kay to feel fuzzy and distant. I remembered the feel of his hands on my body, of his thick, soft hair between my fingers, and his mouth on mine, and I wanted to feel it again. It would be just a moment's escape back into our childhood innocence. I supposed it was taking him a long time to drag Morgawse to her bed.

I didn't want to go back to my room to lie down beside Uriens' unconscious body. I walked to Morgawse's room. I hoped that she would not be too sick from the wine for me to sleep beside her. I really, *really* did not want to have to sleep in my own bed with Uriens.

When I reached her room, I hung back, for Kay was still with her. Kay was trying to open the door with one hand while holding her up with the other. He must have been a little drunk, too, because he fumbled against the latch for a long time before the door swung open, and when it did he gave his low, soft laugh.

"Goodnight, Gawse," he said, kissing her clumsily on the forehead.

"Come in with me," Morgawse, who seemed a little recovered from the walk to her room, but not greatly, replied in tones of teasing pleading. She took hold of the front of Kay's surcoat in both hands and pulled him towards her, and the open door.

"Morgawse," Kay replied gently, trying to release her grip on his surcoat. "I don't think that's such a good —"

But Kay did not finish, for Morgawse leaned forward suddenly, and kissed him. I saw him reel back under it for a moment, as though he was going to pull away, but then he seemed to yield beneath it, wrapping his arms tight around her waist, and responding to her kiss. I wanted to shout out to stop them, but it was too late. Morgawse pulled Kay through the open doorway with her, and he reached out a hand behind himself to slam the door as they stumbled through. The sound of it seemed to resonate through me, sending an awful shock through my bones. Though I had a different lover now, it still felt like

197

an awful betrayal. I was not sure which of them I was the more angry with. Kay. It was Kay. Morgawse did not know. But Morgawse knew why I did not want to sleep in my own bedroom. Now she was in there with Kay, I had nowhere to go.

I supposed there was one other woman in the castle who, that night, would have nowhere to hide from her husband. The Breton princess was far from her home, and tonight she would have to go to bed with her conqueror. The thought didn't comfort me very much.

Chapter Thirty

I wandered down into the courtyard, cold without the cloak I had left in Morgawse's room before the feast. It was a pleasant, clear night and, though I was feeling very tired, it was soothing to stand under the open sky and look up at the stars.

Across the courtyard, I saw Ector striding towards me.

"My Lady Morgan," he called to me, and ran over the last few steps. I could see that he was worried. "Morgan, have you seen Kay?" he asked, breathless.

Unsure of whether to lie for him – whether I needed to, or whether I wanted to – I decided on the safest truth.

"Last time I saw him he was taking Morgawse to her bedroom."

Ector nodded, with understanding. He had been at the feast too, after all.

"He is supposed to be taking the first watch outside Arthur's chamber. Just in case." Were they afraid that the new Queen would try to kill Arthur? "He will have to take the second one, for I have set Percival at it now." He shook his head. "Kay manages to disappear whenever I am looking for him. Oh." His brow crinkled with concern. "Morgan, I am sorry about your husband," he whispered very low. It was the first time anyone had said it, anyone but Morgawse had acknowledged that he was not a good husband and not a good man. I could have wept with relief, and with love for Ector, but I did not. I just wrapped my arms around him in a tight embrace.

I decided that I was not going to go and try to get Kay to his watch. I didn't want to see him, and I wasn't sure if I cared if Arthur's new wife murdered him in his sleep. In the end I went to my mother's room and crawled into bed beside her. I expected her to shoo me away and send me back to Uriens, but she did not. Nor did she ask me why I was not with Morgawse.

In the morning I went back to Morgawse's room. I was glad that I did not run into Kay. I knew he had been drunk, but I did not think I could have kept myself from slapping him. When I got to Morgawse's room, it was still before prime, and she still lay in bed, in her nightdress. Her hair, loose and wild, spread around her across the pillows and over her shoulders. She was smiling and there was a light flush on her pale cheeks. I had thought she would be sick from all the wine, but she just looked pleased with herself. Kay had left, but his surcoat lay forgotten in a heap beside Morgawse's bed. He must have gone in a hurry.

"Oh Morgan," Morgawse sighed when she saw it was me stepping through the door. "I'm so sorry. You didn't have to sleep in *your* room did you?"

I shook my head, climbing onto the bed beside her. I was angry with her as well, but she had suffered last night, and I didn't blame her, really. She had only wanted a little human comfort. Just like I had.

"I stayed with mother," I said softly, lying beside her and resting my head against her stomach. She stroked my hair like she had done when we were children.

Morgawse gave a happy sigh. "It is good to be a widow. To be a *rich* widow. With plenty of sons. A lady in my situation may do what she pleases. I will pray for you, Morgan, that you might be a widow soon."

She laughed her bright, tinkling laugh. Once again, Morgawse had got her way. Well, soon I would as well. I would be a widow sooner than my sister thought.

Morgawse gave another sigh of contentment, and I felt her stretch out a little under me. I knew what was coming, and I did not want to hear it. She spoke as if to herself, but I knew it was for my benefit.

"I did not expect love like that from a man everyone says likes to have boys in his bed. Well, Morgan, I must tell you those rumours are not true. He knew what he was doing with a woman." She puffed out a little breath as though to illustrate how impressed she had been. I held tight to the anger and jealousy twisting tight within me. "I have not been loved like that by a man since –" Morgawse stopped dead, and with a cold clench at the base of my spine I realised that she had been about to say *since Arthur*. She gave a little cough, and continued. "For a long time. Oh, Morgan." She rolled over to face me in the bed, and laid a gentle hand against my cheek. "Little Morgan, you should find yourself a lover. A young man. Then you will know what it's really like, between a man and a woman."

The chapel bell was ringing for mass. Morgawse flopped back onto her back and sank further against the pillows with a little pout.

"I'm not going to mass today. Morgan, stay with me." I was happy to nod my agreement and lie down next to her. "I have had my own unholy communion with a man from Otherworld last night. I think I might give up mass in favour of that in the future." She turned to me with a playful grin, and when she saw I was not laughing, she gave me a playful prod. "Oh *come on* Morgan. Don't always be such a nun. You must have something to say about it. You let that ugly old Merlin put his —"

"Morgawse, *shut up*," I shouted. I had so much more to say, but nothing else would come. I felt my angry tears close to the surface. Morgawse reached out and squeezed my hand.

I thought she was going to say something, but she didn't. After a long, long pause she said, softly, "Uriens is truly a disgusting man, isn't he?" I nodded. So Morgawse remembered the things that he had been saying about her, and me, and Arthur's Queen.

Morgawse called for some breakfast and the serving women brought us some fresh bread and honey, and we lay in the bed and ate it, putting off dressing and leaving the sanctuary of the bedroom. Morgawse ate with a clumsy enthusiasm, spreading crumbs around herself, tangling a little honey into her hair. Even if I had wanted to relish everything in life with Morgawse's wildness, I did not think I could have done. I stayed neat and immaculate, as always.

Aggravain and Gareth came by just before the mass must have been about to begin to give Mordred back to their mother, and then we lazed there with the little child between us, stumbling through the folds of the sheets, and trying to pick the gold pattern off the brocade bed curtains. He had an intelligent, attentive look about him as he moved about, and I could see that Morgawse doted on her youngest son.

When it was eventually time to dress, Morgawse called for baths and we soaked in the water, our iron tubs side by side. Then we both dressed – me in my black jewelled dress, Morgawse in a dress of light blue silk that was beautiful with the soft, warm gold of her skin and hair, and richly embroidered in gold. She looked lovely, as always. She picked Mordred up in her arms.

"Morgan, I am going to take him out to the meadows. I think it is best if I stay out of the way of Arthur's new wife. And Arthur. Just... in case." I did not think Arthur would have mentioned it, but I did think this was the safest option. "Morgan, could you take Kay's coat back to him? I just – I don't want Arthur to find out. It would only make him more upset about my being here."

I nodded. I kissed Morgawse and little Mordred on the cheek, and scooped up the fallen surcoat from the floor, folding it in my hands, and left to find Kay.

I found him in Arthur's bedchamber, one of the first places I checked for him. He was there with Arthur and Gawain. I could not think of a worse combination of people. I expected Gawain would be quite upset indeed if he knew. Arthur sat in the frame of his window, his feet on the chair beneath the window, and he was grinning. Kay sat against the table that the chair belonged to. He had a small wicked smile on his face as well. Gawain stood, leaning against one of the bedposts. The curtains were pulled back, and the sheets on the bed were still tangled and thrown back. The sight of them made me feel uneasy. I did not want to think of Arthur holding the Breton girl down, his hand over her mouth, the sheets crumpling beneath them. Had Arthur searched through the sheets in the morning, looking for a drop of blood?

"Morgan!" Arthur greeted me excitedly as he saw me. I saw Kay's eyes catch on his surcoat where I held it behind me, and I saw a slight blush redden his cheeks. I was glad that he was ashamed. "Morgan, did you enjoy the wedding?"

I caught Kay's eye again, and he quickly looked away. He was guilty.

"Yes, Arthur." He was grinning like a boy. I forced myself to ask the polite question, unsure of how detailed an answer I would get. "I trust you also enjoyed your wedding?"

Arthur laughed, and gave a shrug. "It began badly. When I got my wife alone at last, she told me that she would kill me if I touched her. But I managed to convince her otherwise."

I felt suddenly cold. That sounded a lot to me like Uriens telling me I would *get used to it*. Arthur had not been unkind to Morgawse, but she had *wanted* him. I did not put it past Arthur to force an unwilling woman. Perhaps the Arthur I had known three years ago would not have done. I was less sure of him now. He was a king, not the boy I had known, and a king had his honour.

Gawain was laughing and shaking his head. "Arthur, she is lovely. *Lovely.*"

Arthur laughed in agreement. They were all laughing and smiling. Where *was* this girl?

"Morgan, I'm sorry. Did you come to see me for anything in particular?"

I was saved, as Uriens burst through the door behind me. I had not expected him, but for once he was welcome. I did not want to hand Kay back his surcoat from Morgawse's bedroom in front of Gawain. Uriens' jaw was bruised dark purple, but it did not seem to have been broken, unfortunately, for he was able to speak.

"Arthur —" He gave a cough of frustration at Arthur's hostile look. "*My Lord* Arthur, last night your Seneschal struck me-"

Uriens had not noticed Gawain in the room. When Gawain stood forward, squaring up to him, Uriens stepped back. Uriens was not a small man, but beside Gawain he was nothing. Gawain was bigger still than when I had seen him in Lothian, bulked out by the long war. He was muscled like a bull, and he was scarred from battle already.

"Uriens, do you remember the things you said last night?" Gawain growled, and Uriens stepped back from him.

Arthur, annoyed that his moment of basking in the conquest of his wife had been shattered, demanded, "What happened?"

Kay cleared his throat softly, and I saw Uriens reel around to look at him with undisguised hate.

"Uriens was insulting to Gawain's Lady Mother, and to your beloved sister Morgan, and," he added quietly "to me."

Arthur stepped forward, his expression darkening. I thought he might strike Uriens right there, but he did not. He turned to me.

"Morgan, is this true?"

I nodded. Kay had neglected to mention Uriens' comment about Arthur's new wife, but I thought that had been wise. That might have sent Arthur into a rage that would have led him to kill Uriens where he stood. I would have liked that, but it would have caused more war, and war had only just ended. Besides, it would deprive me of the pleasure of doing it myself.

Uriens was unrepentant. His eyes locked on Kay's, he growled, "It is not an insult, Sir Kay, *if it is the truth.*"

Kay jumped to his feet and forward. Arthur put out a hand to hold him back, and if he had not been there, then Kay would have been on him again.

"Uriens," Arthur began, his voice low with threat, "I do not tolerate slander against my kin, and I count Kay as my foster-brother among them. Do you understand me?"

I could see Uriens bridle against it, and I could see him burn with the repeated humiliation, but he nodded in agreement. He threw a dirty look at Kay, and then at me, and left, slamming the door shut behind him.

Arthur turned away from us towards the window with a groan, pressing the heel of his hand against his forehead. "Kay," he murmured in frustration, "*tell me* it has stopped."

Arthur knew what the insult would have been.

Kay, still on his feet and poised to strike Uriens, reeled around to Arthur. I could see the angry disbelief on his face. "*Yes*, Arthur. Long ago. How can you even ask me?"

Between them, Gawain stood awkwardly, only half-understanding. I took the opportunity to excuse myself, and as I expected, Kay slipped out soon after me. He pulled me into Merlin's room which was thankfully empty.

"Morgan –" he began, his tone imploring, but I was not listening. I threw the surcoat hard at him, and he caught it in both hands.

I was too angry for words. I left.

Chapter Thirty-One

Nimue came to court the next day, but she went straight to Arthur, not to me. I felt the little burn of resentment. She had not seen me at all since I was married, and though she had promised me Merlin's secrets in return for the book, she had given me nothing.

A hunt was called, and I went down to watch them set off. Nimue had brought it as a gift – the hunt for the White Hart. I had read about it, the white beast of the quest, and the spell that called it. It was a simple thing, an innocent thing, but I was sure in Nimue's hands it would not be the only purpose of her wedding-gift to Arthur. Uriens was going on the hunt, and I was glad that he would be gone. I stood beside Morgawse and watched the knights come down from the towers in their light hunting armour, and climb on their horses. The horses were as eager as the men, whickering and stamping their hooves.

A sudden murmur went through the crowd, and I could see people pushing forward to look at something. Beneath the murmur of interest was a low mutter of disapproval, and when I pushed up onto my tiptoes to look, I could see why. Arthur's new Queen had come to join him. But she was dressed in what must have been the clothes of her own people. She was wearing light hunting leathers, but the kind I had seen only on young boys before. She wore boots and breeches like a man that showed the lightly muscular shape of her legs, and a leather hunting vest. It was a beautiful thing, lightly made and engraved through the leather in swirling patterns, and held together with shining bosses of brass; but it left her arms bare, and a flash of pale flesh showed at her back, beneath the vest, and above it the soft white skin of the back of her bare shoulders. I could hear the women close to me whispering. Her hair was tied back still, but more simply than before, in a rough bunch tied with a leather thread, and I could see bright, wild coils escaping from the knot already, shining bright red in the spring sunshine.

Beside me, Morgawse clicked her tongue. "She is *so obviously* not from around here."

Arthur did not seem to mind the mutterings of his people. When he saw her, he strode over to her and pulled her approvingly against him. He was saying something to her − I could not see what, but it did not appear to be *cover yourself*. His hands were against her bare skin where it peeped between the breeches at the vest just above her hips. Even from across the courtyard I could see the hunger in his grip. I saw him hesitate, as though his desire to go hunting had been replaced with something else entirely. He leaned down to kiss her, and she turned up her face to meet his. It was the kiss of a moment, before he moved away to climb on his horse, but the rawness of Arthur's desire that I saw in it, that he showed in front of everyone, made me feel uneasy.

When the men and the Queen had ridden away, I saw Nimue standing at the open gates, staring out through them. I walked up beside her and stood next to her, staring off after them as well.

"So, what is this magic hunt?" I asked her. I glanced at her, and saw a little smile curl across her face.

"I have filled the forest with those dreams of the future we have in Avalon."

I felt a chill down my spine. I had never read of such things in Avalon, which meant that Nimue had got hold of some of Merlin's knowledge and not shared it with me.

"Black Arts?" I asked her, softly. She shook her head.

"Not really. But it is knowledge I stole from Merlin. But Morgan…" She turned to me then, her pale blue eyes suddenly fierce. She was so much smaller than me, so frail-looking I found it hard to fear her. She still looked like a child, but I knew she was serious, and I could feel the strength of her Otherworld power all around me. She was stronger than me. "I hear that you have been stealing something from me. *My shape.*"

"I did it to frighten Merlin. To show him that I am capable of the same kind of magic as he is." It was half true. I did it to punish Merlin for taking Lancelot's shape.

"Morgan, I don't want you to take my shape again," she said, sharply. "I will share with you what I know, but only if you promise you shall not."

I gave her the promise, though I did not see why.

I wondered what she meant by this magic hunt. We spoke a little; less than I had hoped, only half-honest with one another. She mainly spoke of Arthur. There was something in the way she said his name that made me think she might have an interest in him beyond protecting his kingship. I wondered how she felt about the new Queen, if she too would have preferred that Arthur had married the halfwit Isolde. Once, we might have told each other the truth. I remembered when we had sat side by side on the rock, staring out across the lake of Avalon. A long time ago.

I was disappointed when the knights began to return. Arthur was first, just an hour or so after they had set out, and he looked pale and shaken. He was alone. He nodded brusquely to Nimue as he rode through the gates, and jumped from his horse. He barely saw me. I glanced at Nimue. She had a look on her face as though she knew what he had seen. I felt pretty sure that in the woods Arthur had seen the image of his son. Well, it was no more than he deserved for abandoning the boy, for denying him. He came to stand beside us, and stare back, looking for the others. I saw him cast a wary, suspicious eye on Nimue, and then gaze back out at the woods.

"Arthur," I asked softly, "where are the others?"

He did not answer. His face was dark with concern, and I wondered then how he had managed to lose the Queen so quickly in the forest.

Others came back slowly. Uriens came next, with the mousey-haired serious youth whose name was Percival, and after that Ector, who was the only one who did not bear a dark look back from the forest. I supposed that Ector was older than the rest, and had suffered much already. The visions of the wood would not have frightened him as they had the others. We all stood tensely, waiting and watching for when the rest would return. I had a very uneasy feeling about it all, as though Nimue was involved in something dark that I could not understand. The Queen, Kay, Gawain and Pellinore – who was a northern vassal-king who I had heard had been the one to kill Lot in battle – were still in the woods. I glanced at Nimue. She was still watching with rapt attention. I wondered what else she saw when she looked. It was as though she could see right into the woods.

At last, as the sun was beginning to sink down in the sky, out of the woods came Gawain, and Kay and the Queen riding on the same horse. Kay sat behind her, and I could not tear my eyes away from his hand, pressed against the stomach of her vest. I was surprised that Arthur did not notice, but he and Nimue ran forward to meet them, and I saw the Queen slip from the horse into Arthur's arms. They were talking to each other, but I could not hear, and I turned away. The whole thing had given me a deeply unsettled feeling.

I walked up to Morgawse's room, but I stopped before going in, because I could hear, through the open door, her sons inside. Gawain, more favoured by Arthur than the others for his part in the war, had been the only one on the hunt, and he was telling his brothers about it. I could hear, as I crept closer, that he was talking about the Queen.

"Well, I just found her wandering around on her horse all on her own. I don't know why Arthur had left her. But," Gawain made a low noise of frustration, half like a growl, "what she was wearing – is that what Bretons wear? I don't remember seeing any young girls dressed like that in the war. It's like she doesn't know what men see when they look at her. And she was just there, on her own. Well, I got hold of her horse, and she was right there in front of me and – if she had been any man's wife other than Arthur's I would have just pulled her from the horse and –"

"Gawain." I heard Aggravain's voice cut sharply through his brother's, and Gawain fell silent. "Think such things if you must, but you should not say them. Not even to us. Not about any man's wife, and *especially* not about Arthur's. For my part, I think it's ridiculous. She's just an ordinary woman."

"She was supposed to be *my* wife, do you remember that?"

"Yes, Gawain." Aggravain answered his brother more sharply still. "And then you lost the war, and you surrendered to Arthur, so everything that was once yours and mine is now his. I, for one, am pleased enough with things as they are. Arthur is a good King, and a brave warrior. I was growing tired of Lothian. Besides, you would not have had her as your wife for sure. I heard the mother hated you."

"She was a bitch," Gawain said, but he sounded sulky and defeated.

I could hear Gaheris talking, but I could not make out his words. His voice was lighter than his brothers', his tone more careful. He was the handsome one of the brothers, and I supposed that Lot must have been handsome in his youth, before his cruelty came out in his looks. I did not find my affection came as easily for Gaheris as it did for my other nephews, and it was because of his resemblance to his father.

I decided that I had to see the new Queen for myself. Properly, and up close. She seemed to have three women who were with her every day, two Breton, one English. There was no way that I could turn myself to the shape of the Breton women, for then I would be stuck if anyone spoke to me, or if I was expected to speak, in the Queen's own language. After a couple of days, I got used to their patterns of movement, their comings and goings, and I thought I could take the English girl's place to have a better look at the Queen. I avoided Uriens, spending the nights with Morgawse, dreading the time – which would be soon – when I would be sent back to Gore with him. I could not hide from him so easily there. I avoided Kay as well. He did not come back for Morgawse again, nor did she seem to expect it. She never mentioned him again.

I stopped the English girl at the bottom of the stairs that led up to the Queen's rooms. She seemed afraid of me, flustered by the sight of my woaded face and strange clothes. She was a simpleton. I sent her to the village market to buy some things. She would be gone all day. I waited until I was sure that Uriens was out of my room, and I snuck away from there one of my plain woollen dresses. I found an empty room, and changed into it, and then closed my eyes and imagined myself as the dull-witted English maid: the mousey hair, the soft, pretty features. When I opened my eyes and peered into the window pane to look for my reflection, I seemed to have done it successfully.

The girl had been fetching water when I had sent her on my errand, and had been too flustered to finish the job. I picked up the heavy bucket, walking slowly with it and sloshing it all over my feet and legs, looking through all the open doors until I came to the very top of the stairs. My mother's old room. The Queen's chamber. I tried the door, and it opened. I felt a flutter of excitement. I would finally see this woman up close for myself, see what she was really like. I might hear, too, what she truly thought of Arthur.

When I stepped through the door, I could hear the two other women chattering in Breton with the Queen. The room was filled with the bright light of the spring morning, and the sound of laugher not just from the Breton maids, but the Queen herself. Her laugh was low and soft; reserved, shy almost, though I did not think from her striding through the courtyard in her hunting clothes that she could be shy. The curtains on her bed were pulled right back, and she was sat up in bed, holding the sheet against her front; but her back was bare, and I could see her pale skin, white as milk against the dark red of the hair that spilled free and wild down her back. I could see now why it had captured Gawain's attention. I should have liked to grab a handful of it, too, though I was sure not for the same purpose as Gawain.

Her eyes still a little foggy with sleep, though it was past prime, she was talking with her women in Breton. I could not understand what she was saying, but I recognised among her words Arthur's name. The elder Breton woman appeared to be asking her something, and in response, she stuck out her bottom lip and puffed out a breath that made the coils of hair resting on her forehead rise and fall in a little dance. She was annoyed.

"What is wrong?" I asked, suddenly. I expected the older Breton woman to scold me, but she did not.

"Oh, Margery, I did not see you there. Is that water for the bath? Come and put it in the tub." I stepped forward with it. I dipped my hand into it tentatively. It was not as hot as it had been when I had taken it off the other girl, but I thought on the warm spring day it was hot enough. There was already some water in the tub that was steaming, so I thought it would do. I poured it in, and as I did, to my surprise the younger Breton woman, who was little as a bird with bright, pretty eyes and a sweet, girlish face, answered my question with a wicked little giggle.

"Guinevere is complaining that she has not had enough sleep." I realised that until now I had not known the Queen's name. It was a strange, foreign-sounding name, but I thought it pretty.

The elder woman clicked her tongue at the girl, but her look was indulgent. These women all seemed very close; I would not have spoken to any serving women I had known like that, nor let them giggle about me in front of them, but Guinevere was smiling slightly to herself. She yawned and stretched her arms up over her head, and I was shocked to see that she let go of the sheet, and let it fall down around her waist. It was as though she was unaware of her own nakedness. Her hair fell over her breasts, which were small but full, and a soft, pale pink at the nipple, which I saw when she scooped her hair back with one hand as she stepped from the bed to get in the bath.

She slipped into the bath water, splashing a little as she got in, letting her hair trail out the back of the bath and sinking back into it with a murmur of pleasure, closing her eyes.

The young maid said something to her in Breton, and a slight smile played about Guinevere's lips in response, though she did not open her eyes. The elder women clicked her tongue.

"*English*, Marie," the older woman scolded. "It is not fair for Margery."

I sat beside the young woman, Marie, next to the bath. No one seemed to mind. The older woman sat at its foot in a chair, sewing carefully at something. She was attractive still, about of an age with Morgawse, I thought, or a little older. Dark, dark, black hair and pale skin, with sharp blue eyes.

The young girl, Marie, looked a little flustered at being scolded.

"Sorry Margery. I was just saying that I am amazed that Guinevere can spend so long in bed, and get so little sleep."

She looked embarrassed to say it to me, as though Margery were a prude, or that she was only used to teasing the Queen in Breton. Without opening her eyes, Guinevere lifted a hand in the bath to splash Marie with some of the water. Marie squealed.

The older woman made a shushing noise.

"Margery doesn't want to hear your crude jokes, Marie."

Suddenly, without warning, Guinevere slipped down in the bath, sloshing water out of the sides, to dunk her hair through the water. When she came back up from the water, she pushed the hair back off her face, and flashed her slight, reserved little smile at me and Marie, pulling her knees up close and wrapping her arms around them. The water dripped from her thick hair onto the wooden floorboards with a soft tapping noise.

There was still something childlike about her, though she had obviously grown to womanhood. Marie had begun to comb through her wet hair, and Guinevere wrinkled her small, pointed nose with discomfort every time Marie tugged at a knot.

"Marie, you will tear out all my hair," she said, half-laughing. I realised that this was the first thing that she had said. Her voice was soft and low, reserved without being shy, like her manner, and rich with her Breton accent.

"*I* am not the one who tangles it up," Marie quipped with a smile. Guinevere splashed her again.

"*Marie*," the older woman scolded, glancing warily at me. Were they afraid that I would tell someone how they talked? Or was Margery truly as shy and prudish as they acted as though she was? I had heard my sister talk far more candidly. But they were talking about it as though it were something happy, and Guinevere still wore her half-smile of secret amusement.

It suddenly felt painfully unfair that I was so unhappily married, and yet Arthur had summoned a woman whose family he had slaughtered to be his wife, and they had found some kind of tentative new-married happiness. I could not believe that she would have wanted Arthur as much as he wanted her, and yet there was no hint in anything anyone said that he had been forceful with her. Had I misunderstood so much? Had my own experience of marriage made me believe that everyone was unhappy?

"Where did you say Arthur has gone?" Guinevere asked, standing suddenly in the bath now that Marie had untangled her hair and wound it, still wet, into a tight plait and then a bun at the nape of her neck. She stepped naked from it, the water running off her on to the floor. The two other women barely seemed to notice. Guinevere picked up a sheet from the table beside the older woman, and wrapped it around herself to dry.

"To speak with the woman from Avalon."

Guinevere made a small noise of assent, as though she barely cared, or as though she was thinking something that she would not say. I hardly thought that Arthur would desire Nimue in return. She looked like a child still, and the woman who was newly his wife had the strong, full body of a woman. Suddenly, looking at her made me feel my own inadequacy, my thinness, my plainness. But perhaps it was better. No man would ever talk about me in the awful way I had heard Gawain and my own husband talk about Guinevere.

When she waved me and Marie away to fetch her clothes, I heard her speaking to the older woman in Breton, faster and bolder than her English. I thought about what Arthur had said, that she had threatened to kill him. I could not make any sense of it.

I made an excuse to slip away, and when I was alone, I returned to my own form. That night, sleeping beside Morgawse, I dreamed a strange dream about Guinevere, the Queen. I dreamed of a man like and yet unlike Arthur, holding her down on the floor in her bedclothes while she struggled and kicked, and then the same man, who might or might not have been Arthur, in the same place, still on top of her, but she kissing him, wrapping her arms around him, and pressing her body against his in hungry desire. The dream was sharp and clear, like the dreams from Avalon, but it did not make any sense. If it had truly happened, it would have already taken place. I did not think the dreams could show me the past. But it left me nervous and unsettled, and the dream stayed with me long after I had woken.

Chapter Thirty-Two

The next day was the day I had to return to Gore with Uriens. I had not spoken to him, really, the whole time we had been in Camelot, and once we were back at his castle, I would not be able to hide from him with my sister. I asked her to come with me, but she had to return to Lothian with her two youngest sons. She was afraid to leave it too long, in case one of her barons tried to seize it from them. With Gawain and Aggravain in Camelot, there was less of an incentive for them to hold back from trying to seize power from her, and she did not like leaving her kingdom long.

When I had kissed her goodbye, and her two youngest sons, and they left, I sat down on the edge of her bed, the bed we had shared like children for the past few weeks, and let out a sigh. I should have brought some kind of protection with me, some weapon, some magic, but all I had was my power to change my shape, and I could not hide from Uriens forever.

There was a soft knock at the door, and I was afraid it was him, but it was not. It was Kay. Nervous and awkward, he stepped through the door and shut it softly behind himself. I had never seen him look so uncomfortable, but I was not about to ease his discomfort. He stepped towards me, and I stood to meet him. I wanted to look him in the eye.

"Morgan, I hoped I would find you here, before you left," he said gently.

"So you were not looking for my sister, then?" I demanded.

"No, Morgan, listen." He stepped forward again and tried to take my hand, but I pulled it away. "Morgan, that was a mistake; I was drunk, I —"

I crossed my arms over my chest, against his pleading look. I could see that he was sorry, but I was not ready to forgive.

"Morgan —" He began to speak again, but the words seemed to freeze in him, as though they were not enough. I reached out to slap him, but, quick as a cat, he caught me by the wrist. I tried to pull away, to strike at him again, but he held me fast, and as I stepped back away, I felt the bedpost at my back. He stepped towards me, and I felt the fire of anger in me turn suddenly to the heat of desire as he, fired with the same potent memory of our past passion, pulled me against him and kissed me hard. When I felt his lips against mine, all of the wonderful memories seemed to rush fast around me; lying together in the sunlight, the first time, Kay falling to the floor with me and tearing through my dress in a haze of passion, the night before I was married, when he had told me he loved me. I was drowning in the memories and I ran my hands through his hair, pulling him tighter against me.

I was about to slide my hand up under his shirt, when I heard the door open suddenly behind us. We jumped apart, both still hot and breathing hard. It was Uriens, and I saw the dark rage flash across his face. He had seen. Good. He stood warily back from Kay. The shadow of the bruise still lingered green-yellow against his jaw, and he remembered all too well which man had given it to him. I saw him notice, too, that Kay's sword hung around his hips, his hand resting on the hilt.

"That's my wife, you know? Not a boy, though I know she looks like one," Uriens sneered at Kay. Kay turned around to face him, but said nothing. Uriens' eyes fell on me. "Come, you nasty little whore. It's time for you to go home."

Kay drew his sword as Uriens made to stride across the room to seize me. Uriens stopped where he stood, but I could see in his eyes that he would make me suffer for this when he could. Kay could not stand there between us forever.

Uriens held out a hand towards me, and Kay stepped suddenly towards him, and Uriens jumped back.

"What's the matter, Uriens?" Kay demanded, his voice edged with cruelty. I was glad, at least, that he seemed to hate my husband as much as I did. "Are you jealous? Do you want me to fuck you as well? You might enjoy it. *I know what men like.*"

Uriens looked terrified for a second, as though he really thought Kay meant it. He did not seem to follow the point that Kay was trying to make. Flustered and afraid, Uriens turned back to me.

"We are leaving. Now," he spat, and turned and fled from the room. Kay put his sword back in his sheath, letting the breath sigh out of him. He ran a hand through his hair thoughtfully, before turning back to me. He looked sad. I missed the bright laughter of his eyes. I would have thought he would enjoy frightening Uriens more than he seemed to. He walked back over to me and, taking my face gently in his hands, kissed me softly, deeply. I hated it, because it was so wonderful, and because I knew it was a kiss goodbye.

It was only when I was on my horse, riding away from Camelot, that I remembered how angry I had been with Kay. He had been with my sister; he had kissed her like he had kissed me, he had touched her like he had touched me. And he had kissed me as though that made it all go away. It did *not* make it all go away. I knew I had no right to be angry since I too had another lover, but the thought of Kay and Morgawse was unbearable. Morgawse got *everything* that she wanted. But I could not hate her.

Uriens and I rode a long way in silence, side by side. It was only when the sun began to sink in the sky and I knew that we were near to Rheged that he spoke.

"I suppose you did that to spite me, Morgan," he growled.

"What?" I snapped.

"Your little play at being lovers with the Seneschal. Only because you know how much I dislike perverse little men like him. I do not know why you make it your life's aim to cause me humiliation and suffering."

"*I* cause *you* humiliation and suffering?" I cried. He had not experienced true humiliation. He had been embarrassed in front of Arthur a couple of times. That was all. He had never felt his own awful weakness underneath the hands of man.

"You know, Morgan, it makes me very angry the way you treat me. You are no good wife to me, and no good mother to our child. If I could, I would take another wife, and send you back to the abbey. That you continue to refuse me when I have been a good husband to you despite your shortcomings as a wife makes me very *very* angry, Morgan."

I turned to look at him. He was red in the face, slightly spitting his words. I could see the vein bulge angry with blood on his forehead. I shrugged my shoulders and turned away again, gazing off into the distance.

"Well, Uriens," I said, "how you feel is of no importance in the matter."

I did not need to look at him to know that his anger was great enough to choke him into silence, and I was glad.

I thought he would try to punish me when we reached the castle. I expected him to grab me by the hair in front of his men, and drag me off with him, but he did not. He was too angry even for that, and he jumped from his horse and stormed off as soon as we arrived. It was late in the night, but still mild with late spring warmth. I was happy to linger in the courtyard once I had slipped from my horse, tired and sore from the ride. There were a few knights milling around in the courtyard, but I could not see Accolon. Surely he had not left?

I had not thought of him much while I was in Camelot – that felt like a different life entirely – but now that I was back in Rheged, I knew I had to see him.

I took hold of my horse's bridle and led it to the stable. When I stepped inside, I saw him there, as though he had come at my wish. I froze in the doorway with the bridle in my hand, and as though he sensed me there he turned around. I had forgotten how much I liked his rough, handsome looks.

"Morgan," he breathed, stepping towards me as though in a dream.

He took another step forward to take the horse from me, and our hands brushed on the bridle. I felt the touch of it go through me, strong and delicious. I saw it flash through his eyes, too, and I knew that he wanted what I wanted. I let go of the bridle and grasped hold of the front of his shirt with both hands, pulling him against me, pressing my forehead against his. I felt every beat of my heart rushing the hot desire through me.

"I have been too long away from you," I whispered. He gave a low groan of lust and kissed me, hard and eager. I felt the relief at his touch flood through me. Still, I pulled away for a moment.

"What if someone comes?" I whispered. He kissed me again, his hands running through my hair, unwinding the plait.

"No one comes here at night but me," he whispered, reaching out to slam the door shut. My horse, only just through the door, whickered in alarm and walked deeper into the stable, into the place that it remembered as its own. Accolon pushed me up hard against the stable wall, and once again I felt the dangerous thrill of his strength. He tasted of honey, and spices, and wine. He had never betrayed me. I still had the heat in me from Kay's kiss, and from my own anger, and I had a man in my grip who was all mine. I could feel the heat of his skin against mine already, in anticipation. I took his face in my hands.

"I want you now," I whispered to him. "*Now*."

He lifted me and braced me hard against the stable wall, and had me as I had commanded him. I wound my fingers tight into his hair and held his gaze to mine. I had longed for him, and he had given himself to me. The force of our coming together burned through me, leaving me deliciously clean, and making me strong. Things were simpler here than at Camelot. I knew whom I wanted, and I knew whom I hated, and there was no one in between.

214

I woke the next day to the sound of Uriens banging on the door and shouting for me. So, the punishment I had anticipated was coming for me. Elaine – who it seemed had been sleeping in my room all the time I was away – was already awake, her big doe eyes wide with fear, and cowering in the corner of the room. I rolled my eyes at her and grabbed her by the arm, dragging her towards the door.

"You had better go, Elaine. Oh don't look so afraid. This isn't for you."

I did not think having her here would stop him, and besides, I wanted to draw Excalibur on him again and see the fear in his eyes, and I did not want her to know about it. I opened the door and pushed her out. I heard him greet her, suddenly gentle and kind, before she scampered away. He pushed the door open and strode in. I already had Excalibur in my hands.

He sighed in frustration at the sight of me, in my nightdress, my hair loose, the sword bare in my hands.

"Morgan, why am I cursed with you as my wife?" he groaned.

I wanted to step forward, to kill him, but I held myself back. I wouldn't risk it like this, when he might be strong enough to get the sword off me. The mixture was ready; I just had to get him to drink it.

"Uriens, *leave me be.*"

He shook his head in frustration. "I will go, for now. But you cannot continue this forever. The more you do to vex me, the more unkind I will be when I can get my hands on you away from your witches' tricks."

I had to kill him soon. But not just him. No. It was Arthur who had brought me to this. Arthur who had chosen for himself the wife that he desired.

The days passed, and I kept Uriens from my bed with my threats of witchcraft, and Accolon within it. I spent those days and nights kindling the flame of anger that burned deep within me. I found I was angry with Arthur in particular. He had followed his own desires, turning down the advice of his counsellors, and pleased himself with the Breton girl, and yet despite my protests he had sold me to this brute who forced himself on me. I had given up everything for the sake of my sister, and of the kingdom, and he had cared about neither. And he had taken a woman as his wife who had the blood of Maev in her veins. That was a dangerous choice. Maev, warrior and adulteress. *Half-wild*, Merlin had called her. And every man that laid eyes on her seemed to desire her. That seemed an ill combination to me, and yet Arthur had taken her as his wife anyway, because he always did as he pleased. I suffered, and Morgawse suffered, and Arthur lived careless and happy. I hated him. I hated him for changing, too, from the kind boy I had known as a child into this selfish king. They were all liars. Arthur, Merlin, Kay. I would punish them all. I would have Merlin's secrets from him, and I would use them to destroy all of those who had made me suffer.

One night, at the hottest peak of summer, Accolon tore back the curtains of my bed, where I had been lying in the depths of my rage, and I saw him there and I felt the rage mingle hot with my desire. I was glad that Accolon had come. I wanted his hungry roughness, I wanted the power of my rage to move through our coming together. I threw him down on the bed beneath me and tore his clothes from him. I gave myself to the feel of his hands gripping me at the hips, and his eyes running over me with awe and desire as I slipped my nightdress up over my head. I took him deep inside me, and I saw how my wildness excited him, and it made my own desire hotter. I could hear him sighing my name, and my body filling with the power of my own pleasure. I held back a little, from the edge, but only until I could be sure that he had had his fill, and then I let it wash over me. I was not sure if it was all the more filled with trembling ecstasy because I knew how he loved me, or because I knew that my revenge was near.

I sank down beside him, and we lay a long time in a pleasant silence. I did not hurry to ask him. I knew he would not deny me. Only when the candles were low and the night at its blackest depths did I speak. I lifted a hand to stroke through his hair, and he murmured with appreciation.

"Do you love me?" I asked, softly. He pushed himself up to sit facing me.

"Of course, Morgan. Of course I love you," he said, pleased. Pleased that I had asked. I saw a smile spread across his face. He was anticipating sweet, meaningless lovers' talk, but that was not what I had in mind.

Fixing him with a serious stare, I asked him softly again, "Would you do anything for me?"

He leaned over and kissed me, slow and tender, and then whispered, "*Anything*."

I put a hand against his cheek, and looked him deep in the eyes once more. He looked yet more pleased, slightly excited even. *He thinks I am going to ask him to kill Uriens.*

"Kill Arthur," I said.

I saw the surprise pass across his face. He drew back a little. "*King* Arthur?" he asked. "Your *brother* King Arthur?"

I leaned away, letting my hand fall away from his cheek.

"Every man swears his love easily before he hears the price," I said. I did not want a coward.

"No, Morgan, no." He laid a hand on my bare shoulder. "Just... you are sure this is what you want?"

"I am sure," I told him.

He thought for a moment, and then, drawing in his breath deep, he nodded.

"I will do it," he declared. He did not sound so absolute, so entirely certain as he had done before.

I took hold of him by the chin, turning his face up to mine and looking deep into his eyes. I could see that he would do it. I could see that he was entirely mine.

"As you love me," I told him softly, "you will show no mercy."

"No mercy," he whispered in agreement, and I kissed him with a wild passion, and he pulled me into his arms once again.

Chapter Thirty-Three

I sent Accolon away from me early in the morning. The time was not yet right to strike against Arthur. When the time came, I would press Excalibur into Accolon's hands, and he would not fail. First, I would go to Camelot and retrieve the scabbard. I wanted to make sure that my lover would be safe.

Arthur could wait, but I would deal with Uriens now. I had to wait until the evening, but that was not long at all. He kept away from me, and he would not drink from my hand, but that was no matter to me. When the sun had at last dipped below the horizon and the summer stars were bright in the sky, I closed my eyes and pictured Elaine's sweet, doe-eyed face, her little, girlish frame. I felt myself change easily into the form I knew so well. I had sent her on a long errand, to the next town, and I knew she would not be back. I took the drink I had prepared for Uriens in my hand and I went to Uriens' room. Her movements were slick and graceful, and I felt my

217

borrowed body skip light through the hallways and up the stairs to his bedroom.

I knocked lightly, and he called me in. He smiled when he saw it was Elaine. He had been sitting at his window in his shirt and breeches, trying to get some of the cool summer breeze. He gestured me over, and I came, holding the cup of wine out before me.

"My Lord," I said, hearing her demure little voice come from my lips, "I brought you some wine. To help you sleep."

"Thank you, Elaine. That is kind," he replied, gently, taking the wine from me and placing it on the table beside him. "I wish my wife were as kind as you." To my surprise, he reached out and took me by both hands, pulling me onto his lap. So, he had not been pestering me to get into my bed because he had been with Elaine. I wondered if she liked it. He behaved as though it was a mutual desire. He slid his arm around my waist, holding me close, and reached up to turn my face towards his. The kiss he gave her was entirely different from the dry, perfunctory way he had kissed me. It was complex, sensitive. He was gentle and deep. I wanted to shout, *Why did you never kiss me like that?* I would never have loved him, but I could have stood him, if he had shown me even the tiniest bit of kindness.

He murmured Elaine's name under his breath, and his kisses became more urgent as I felt his hand at my breast. I wanted to push him off, angry and disgusted. I was hurt, too. He had not ever tried with me. It was *him*; he was the one who should have been making an effort to get used to *me*. I did not want him to touch me anymore. I laid a hand on top of his, and to my surprise, he responded, stilling his hand and letting it fall away. So, he could be refused. Just not by me. He pulled away gently, taking his arm from my waist, and letting me stand.

"Of course, Elaine. Of course," he said kindly, as though in response to a question. Perhaps there was somewhere Elaine had to be this time of night. But then he reached for the wine, and drank deep from it. I felt a jolt of excitement go through me. The time of my revenge was near. As the wine hit him, I saw his forehead crease. He could feel its strength, but it would not hold him back. He reached for it again, and drained the cup. I could see it run through him, making his limbs heavy, making his mind fog. It would rob the strength from his limbs and leave him at my mercy. But he had shown me no mercy.

I reached out a hand for him, and he took it. I could feel from the way he pulled on it, it was difficult for him to stand already. I led him towards the bed, and he went willingly, a look of sleepy excitement on

218

his face. He thought Elaine had changed her mind. I pushed him down on the bed, and he fell back with a smile spreading on his face. I climbed to sit over him, pressing my hands down against his chest and looking down into his eyes. He put his hands around my back, and murmured Elaine's name again. I leaned over him, looking right into his eyes. I could see him struggling through the sleepy haze to focus on me.

Very close, I whispered, "I have to do this. *I don't want people to hear you scream.*"

His mouth formed the word, *what?* But I had let myself turn back to my real form over him, a grin spreading across my face. Revenge was sweet. As I saw his eyes widen in fear, I grasped the pillow beside him and forced it down over his face. He tried to push me off, but there was no strength in his limbs and his hands fell heavy and powerless against me. I pushed harder and harder, feeling the joy of relief break deeper and deeper over me with each breath I drew, and each breath that came weaker and weaker to him. How many times had I felt weak under his hands? How many times had I lain underneath him, vulnerable and afraid? I hoped in his last moments he was repenting his cruelty to me. I hoped that he was understanding how it felt to be powerless under another's strength. I would never feel that again. I would never be vulnerable again. I would never be afraid again. I would destroy everyone who had ever made me feel afraid.

I waited until I could no longer see his chest moving before I took the pillow away. I leaned down to feel for his breath against my cheek, and felt nothing. His eyes looked glassy and vacant. I gently pushed his eyelids closed. I wanted people to believe that he had died in his sleep. I supposed that if I had to do that, I would have to undress him, too. With distaste, I pulled off his shirt and breeches. I tried to look away as best I could, until I could throw the covers over him.

I folded the clothes and set them on the chair. The vivid memory of our wedding night came back to me, when he had folded his clothes so carefully as he had taken them off. I had been an innocent then, really. I would never have thought of killing a man. Well, I had tried to be kind, and people had been cruel to me, and I had tried to be trusting, and people had tricked me, and I had tried to be loyal, and people had betrayed me. Instead of all those things, I only needed to be strong. That was the only way to protect those I loved. My sister. Myself. Accolon.

That night, when Accolon came to me, I told him it was done, and he grasped me to him in the rough, desperate passion of relief. I felt the relief, too. I was free of Uriens, free of fear. I sent him from me in the middle of the night, as soon as our passion was spent. I did not think it would look well for me to be found with a lover in my bed the morning my husband was found dead.

I woke in the morning to the sound of Elaine screaming. I slipped from my bed and into one of my mother's old dresses, a light dress for summer of pale moss-green. I did not think it would do to look too funereal.

I rushed to Uriens' room when I was called, and I cried with the rest of them to see him. They were real tears, but they were tears of relief. I would never feel him on top of me again, never feel his hand over my mouth, him forcing himself inside me. I closed my eyes and the tears shook harder through me. *I was free.*

The funeral arrangements were long and tiresome, but eventually dispensed with. I could not tear my eyes away as I watched his body burn. I demanded to be made Queen Regent until my son came of age, and since I had the support of Uriens' steward, the rest of the household gave in. I took the dark gold crown of Gore in my hands and set it on my head in front of Accolon in the great throne-room of Rheged. It was deep in the night, and in the autumn midnight dark torches burned low in the sconces on the wall, casting long shadows through the room. I wore my black jewelled dress, and the long shadows made me appear taller, grander, more powerful. I had seen myself as such a queen. I sat in the throne that I had never seen Uriens sit in during my whole time in Rheged, and beckoned Accolon to me with one slender finger. He came to me, and I stared into his eyes as I pulled open his breeches, and watched his need for me overpower him. He murmured my name and I pulled him down to me in a hungry kiss as I felt him grasp hold of me, throwing back my skirts and pulling me hard on to him. I wrapped my legs around him, and we came together, hard and fast, rough and eager, against my husband's throne, and I with his crown on my head.

I dealt, too, with Elaine. I knew that she was hiding from me, and I let her hide a little while longer before I dragged her from her room by the hair. I did not care about Uriens, but it had been an insult to me. I shouted at her until she cried, calling her a whore, shouting through the castle what she had been to my husband. I sent her back to her father, weeping and ashamed. I was not sorry to see her go.

"What now?" Accolon whispered to me, as we lay curled together naked in the darkness.

"Now," I whispered back, winding my hands through his hair, "I steal my scabbard back, and I bring it to you, and you will kill Arthur."

He gave an eager murmur of assent, and I rolled back on to him as our mouths met.

Chapter Thirty-Four

The task of stealing the scabbard meant that I had to go back to Camelot, and without Arthur knowing, but I knew how I would do it. I had given Nimue the book of Macrobius, but I still remembered its secrets. I practised a few times first, closing my eyes in my bedroom and imagining myself in the stables, feeling a light-headedness pass through me, before I opened my eyes and was where I had pictured myself. Accolon was there, and he smiled to see me, as excited as I was now about the prospect of Arthur's death. Beyond the initial satisfaction of revenge also glimmered the hope that I might have Logrys for myself; but that was dimmer, and more distant, and I was not sure how it could be done. All I knew was that the more power I felt in myself, the more I wanted, and the more I needed to be sure that no one could hurt me again.

When I was sure of myself, sure that I could go from place to place without losing or damaging myself in the thin mist of black magic I passed through to get there, I closed my eyes, and pictured my room in Camelot. When I opened my eyes, blinking away the delicate dizziness of my journey, I saw the familiar room with wonder. It had seemed easy enough to move through Rheged on a wish, but I had come far across the land.

Well, I could not move through Camelot as myself without alerting suspicion. Besides, I wanted to get into Arthur's bedroom to get a hold of the scabbard. I was sure he would keep it there. I thought the safest option was Merlin, but when I tried to become him I watched in the smudgy surface of my hammered mirror as my form flickered alarmingly between the young man, and the bald grinning man, and an old man with a long white beard, and a little child with shiny black eyes like a beetle. Did Merlin truly have no real form? Or had I never seen it? Or perhaps his black magic had eroded him so much at the centre there was nothing of him anymore for me to anchor to; inside he was just dust and darkness.

That left me with two options: Arthur, or Guinevere. I did not want to be mistakenly snatched up and manhandled into bed by Arthur, so I decided that it was his form that I should take rather than the Queen's. Safer, by far, to take the form of a strong man. When I remembered what Gawain had said about the Queen, I was even more sure of my choice. But, first I had to find some men's clothes. Morgawse's room above mine was empty, too, and some of her sons' clothes were folded away there. I dressed in a shirt and breeches of Gawain's – I imagined – and closed my eyes to imagine myself as Arthur. I was surprised how clearly I could picture him; the kind, open face, the broad frame, the gold hair, and my mother's – our mother's – grey eyes. My own, also. The clothes were a good fit, and when I peered at myself in the window, I was pleased with what I saw. I felt my heart flutter with excitement; my victory was close.

When I moved through the castle, wary of running into Arthur every time I turned a corner, or opened a door, I was not bothered by anyone. People simply inclined their heads respectfully as I passed, or smiled affectionately. Much as I hated him, I could not deny that he was liked by the people of Camelot.

I came into Arthur's bedroom to find, to my surprise, it was not empty. Guinevere was there, standing at the window, dressed as though she had just stepped in from the outside, a light flush from the cold on her cheeks, and a cloak of dark furs around her shoulders. From beneath, a dark green dress sewn in gold peeped, and in her hands she held a large square of parchment which seemed, from across the room, to be a map of Europe. She was looking at it attentively, and with her dark red hair gathered in a thick plaited knot at the nape of her neck, I could see the white skin of her long neck, soft and inviting as fresh snow, beneath. I had forgotten how enchanting she was.

When she heard me, heard Arthur's heavy footfalls at the door, she looked up, and smiled. I realised I had not seen her smile properly before; it broke across her face like dawn. *She loves him,* I thought. How could that be? Had everything I had dreamed about her been wrong? It was all so confusing, and all unfair.

"Arthur," she said. She ran the few steps across the room to meet me as I walked towards her. Her movements were lithe and light; she had the easy strength and grace of a woman who knew her own body well, and still the same impulsiveness with which I had seen her flick water from her bath. She held out the map before me and turned around so I could look over her shoulder as she held it out, pointing with a slender finger. "I've been looking at this map, and Arthur, look – here beside Carhais, it's not marked, there's some thick woodland. From here, if Lucius' forces come north, we would have cover to defend our own lands. We would avoid an open battle, you'd need fewer knights, fewer losses. You should send men to Carhais now, try to prevent open war."

She was not just beautiful, then; she was also clever. Or at least shrewd and careful in the workings of war. She was talking about the Emperor of Rome. Word had come to us as well that he was not pleased that there was a King of Britain, and that he was planning to invade Arthur's allies in France. I remembered what Arthur had said, about wanting a wife *who will be useful as a queen*. He had got everything that he wanted. It was so unfair.

As she spoke, I leaned over her shoulder a little to follow the trace of her finger, and felt her lean back into me just a little. It was a small movement of marital intimacy, of tenderness, but I noticed it. Her hair smelled of roses, and as I leaned nearer I noticed that she had tucked old dry rose petals from her garden into her plaited hair.

I felt her sink further back against me with a little murmur of content, almost too soft to hear. She let the map slip carelessly from her fingers, taking one of my hands and tucking it inside her cloak to rest against her stomach. She had been hiding herself under the layers of winter clothes, afraid of too many people knowing, I supposed, but I felt her secret. Under my hand I felt the small but unmistakable swell of a growing child. Not much, perhaps three months, but there. Suddenly, overwhelmingly, I saw before my eyes as clear as the dreams from Avalon, the image of a girl – tall, golden-haired and grey-eyed like Arthur, but with Guinevere's proud high-cheekboned features, mounted on a horse and clad in armour like I had seen the Breton queen wear. Her hair streamed down around her, shining in the sun, but she was dressed for war, with a sword at her side. I blinked the image away, but it stayed with me. Arthur would have been hoping for a son. That would have made sure his kingdom never went to Morgawse's child.

Guinevere slipped her hand on top of mine, and leaned back just a little more against me. I felt the body I had borrowed respond, and it shocked me. It was not like my own awakening to desire, and it did not touch me with it, but I felt it go through the body like a flash of lighting. It was not like my own slow heat, it was a flash of sudden fire. Was that what it was like to be a man? It was powerful enough to stun me for a second, but when my mind and the borrowed body did not accord, it passed away as quickly as it had come.

I reached up with my other hand and lightly brushed my fingers against Guinevere's neck. I could make Arthur suffer now, if I wanted. There was strength enough in his hands that I could have killed her right there. I could feel her pulse against my fingertips. But I could not bring myself to do it. I too had known what it was like to bear a child inside me, and Arthur's Queen had not harmed me.

She turned around in my arms and laid her hands against Arthur's chest.

"Did you decide not to go hunting in the end, then?" she asked gently, her brow crinkling slightly in confusion. *Good*, I thought, *Arthur is out hunting*.

"No," I replied, unsure of how he was used to speaking to her when they were alone. I had never really overheard them talk, or even heard them talk at all. I had often seen him touch her. "I had matters to attend to here. Guinevere, where is my sword?"

She gave her low, gentle laugh, moving away from me to beside the bed, the far side from the door. I would not have seen it coming in to the room.

"Arthur, it is right here where you always leave it."

She leant down to pick it up, one hand resting on her stomach still. She had to move it away to lift the false sword with both hands, and there it was, my lovely jewelled scabbard, just a few steps across the room from me, and coming closer and closer. I expected her to hand it to me, but she came right up close and reached around me to buckle the scabbard on to me. She let our bodies press together. I felt strangely about it, but I knew I could not move away without her suspecting that something was wrong. She turned her face up, her lips met mine in a soft, loving kiss. She moved away swiftly once the kiss was given. It was the casual, soft kiss of a loving wife, of one who was sure of another. How did Arthur have this already? They had not even been married a year. She was *supposed* to hate him. Everyone else hated their husbands.

She walked back over to the map to pick it up off the floor where she had dropped it. She turned back over her shoulder once she had it in her hand.

"Arthur, I will see you tonight?" she asked.

"Tonight," I agreed, giving her a nod, and rushing out the door.

As I went down the stairs, flushed with victory just a little, I noticed that the door to Merlin's room stood slightly ajar. I tentatively pushed the door further open. It seemed to be empty. I didn't trust Merlin not to be hiding in there, but I thought it would be worth taking the risk. I stepped boldly into the room, and there it was, just on the shelf, Macrobius' final book. I rushed over and was just reaching for it when I heard the voice I had been afraid I would hear, close behind me.

"I thought I would be seeing you again, Morgan," Merlin laughed behind me. I turned around and there he was, in the form of the young man. He had pushed the door shut behind him without my hearing it. It looked as though the door was bolted. That didn't matter now that I knew I could disappear back home in a moment. "So, you're prepared to renegotiate for Macrobius?"

He stepped forward, putting his hand around the scabbard at my waist. Under his touch I felt the borrowed form slip away from me, and I stood before him in men's clothes, hanging loose on my slender frame. I pushed his hand from the scabbard, but he did not let go. I drew the sword with both hands and he jumped back, but I did not intend to strike him. I placed the sword on the table beside us.

"Arthur can keep his sword, and he does not care for the scabbard. The scabbard stays with me. I leave Arthur his sword, you give me Macrobius."

Merlin grinned broader across his face, moving towards me again, backing me into the bookshelf until I felt it bump against the base of my back. I could smell the old leather of the books, and the dust. Merlin reached up over me, leaning closer, so close that I felt a glossy brown curl of his hair brush against my cheek and our noses touched, to pull Macrobius off the shelf. I reached to snatch it off him, but he lifted it up out of my reach. I reached up and wrapped my hand around his wrist, trying to pull his arm back down, and it was in that touch that I felt with a shock that passed right through my body, the full power of his dark magic strength. I gasped. It was not just the Black Arts, not just dark knowledge, but a natural power beyond that that had been turned to blackness through it. How had I not felt it before? We had been this close. Closer. He had been *hiding* it before, and now he wanted me to feel its fullness, to know how weak my negotiating position was.

While I was still reeling from it, he pressed his mouth against mine, dropping the book to the floor to grasp me with both wrists and hold my hands over my head against the bookcase, pinning me in his grip. I tried to pull away, but he only kissed me harder.

"What do I care whether Arthur has his sword or not? No, I want the same exchange as before. Excalibur for Macrobius," he whispered. I shook my head. I kept my face cold and aloof. He would not think he could intimidate me with this. I had killed Uriens. I had destroyed what had made me afraid, and I had the strength in me to do it again.

He did not move back. I felt one of his hands release my wrist and slide down my arm, and over my breast through the thin fabric of the man's shirt. He was distracted by his lust, I realised. The men's clothes showed my shape, and through the thin white shirt the patterns of the blue woad beneath. He threw himself at me again, his kisses wild and rough, his hands pushing the shirt up as I tried to push it back down. I felt his hands force themselves inside, and I was disgusted by his touch. I pushed him back hard, and, surprised and distracted, he stumbled back. I seized the moment as it was given to me and snatched up the book from the floor, closing my eyes and holding it tight against my chest, picturing bright and clear as I could in my mind the stables at Rheged, desperate to disappear before he got his hands on me again and I was under his power.

Mercifully, I felt the dizziness rush over me, and when I opened my eyes, I stood there before Accolon, the book clutched to my chest, and my enchanted scabbard at my side. When he saw me, wild-eyed with victory, he threw down the bridle he held in his hands and strode over to take me into his arms.

"Is it time?" he breathed, kissing me once, soft and tender, then suddenly rough with passion. I put a gentle hand on his chest and he stilled. I looked up at him.

"It is time," I told him.

He threw the book from my hands, and held me tight against him, and we fell into the straw together.

Chapter Thirty-Five

I stood in my bedroom, dressed in my black dress of gems, the crown of Gore on my head, buckling Accolon into his armour. It seemed right to prepare for this dressed as the queen I was. I had seen myself like this, with Excalibur in my hands. Now was the fated moment. I had never dreamed of Guinevere with Arthur, when I had dreamed of the future. This would be his end. He would not have to wait for his bad destiny.

Accolon was quiet, focussed. He stared off into the distance, as though he were running through in his head what he would do, what moves he would make. When I had buckled all his armour on to him,

I took up the scabbard and buckled it around him. I took Excalibur from its hiding-place and stood before him, holding it pointing straight up before me. *I have seen this moment.* Accolon wrapped his hands around mine on the hilt of the sword.

"No mercy," I told him.

"No mercy," he agreed, with a single nod. I let go of Excalibur, and he slid the sword into its scabbard. He turned back to me and, wrapping an arm around my waist, pulled me against him and into a deep, passionate kiss. I melted against him for a moment, then gently pushed him back, taking his face in my hands and looking him deep in the eyes.

"When you return," I promised, giving him one last, lingering kiss.

I climbed up to the battlements to watch him ride off into the distance. He would go to Camelot, and bide his time in secret nearby until Arthur rode out on his hunt, and he would kill him.

I was not concerned when a few days passed and the snows began to fall. I expected Accolon to have to wait, to be a little wary, before he struck. Besides, I was occupied with the final book of Macrobius which, as I had hoped, described the changing of other things at the touch, and the changing of the self into other objects. The book was as simple as it was slim. There was no new potion to be made. One simply had to be born with the gifts of the Otherworld and know *how*.

It was in the very depths of winter, when the Christmas festivities had passed me by unobserved in Rheged, that news came to me. I was sat in my room beside the fire, the book of Black Arts secrets open on my lap, when one of my knights knocked on my door to announce that a lady had arrived at the castle, and a knight had been seen on the horizon who seemed to be riding towards us. What kind of lady preceded her knight?

I should have known. It was Nimue. In the bright, cold winter sun, she had a stunning, brittle beauty about her. She had a cloak of thick pure-white furs thrown over her pale blue dress of gems, and her plaited hair shone almost white against it. She had a cold, tense look on her face. She strode up to me.

"Morgan," she began, and I could hear the cold fury in her voice, "I must speak with you."

I gestured her inside with me. I took her up to my bedroom, and slid the bolt on the door behind us.

"A knight from Rheged Castle has tried to murder Arthur," Nimue began, her voice sharp. "What would you know about that, Morgan?"

Tried, I thought.

I shrugged.

"How do you know it was a knight from Rheged?" I asked.

Nimue took a step closer, and I saw the anger in her eyes, and her voice lowered to a deadly whisper.

"Because, as he died, he was begging for forgiveness, and he told me that he was your lover, and he had done it for you."

It took a moment for her words to hit me, but when they did, I staggered back under them. I could hear an awful rushing in my ears, and the desperate beating of my own heart. I gasped for my breath. *As he died.* I had been so sure we would not fail. But he had died, and with his final breath he had betrayed me. Nimue watched me, impassive.

"Arthur killed him?" I choked out through my gasps, in disbelief. He had had Excalibur, and the scabbard. He should not have spilled a drop of blood. Arthur. Arthur again. All of my suffering came from Arthur.

"No, Morgan," Nimue answered, cold. "*You* killed him." Nimue stepped forward to me again, and her voice became low and threatening. "Let this be the last time you try to harm a man under my protection."

"*Under your protection?*" I cried out. "What about me? Am *I* not under your protection?"

"No, Morgan." Her eyes were fierce. "You are under your *own* protection."

And she wheeled around and left.

Accolon was gone. Was I to blame? Had I really killed him with my lust for revenge? I closed my eyes as the memory of him washed through me, of the first night we had been together, his hand tugging rough in my hair, his hunger, his need, his utter devotion to me.

Suddenly the door opened again. I could have screamed. I was desperate to be alone. Kay stepped through the door dressed in his black armour. One of my knights, behind him, stepped apologetically up behind Kay.

"I am sorry, my Lady; we could not stop him."

I waved an impatient, dismissive hand at my knight, and he scurried away. Kay slammed the door behind him. He rubbed his flushed face with his hands as he stood before me, his eyes wide as

228

they fell on me, but I did not care. Kay had told me he loved me, and then gone to my sister's bed. Kay had never forgotten Lancelot, but he had swiftly forgotten me. He had been weak. He had given in. He had not been brave enough to love me as he should. He had loved Arthur more.

"Morgan, what happened to you?" He stopped before me. "I don't even recognise you anymore. I mean – you tried to kill Arthur. *Arthur*. What is wrong with you?"

I drew myself up to my full height and crossed my arms.

"You abandoned me, Kay," I said.

"*Abandoned* you?" he shouted in disbelief.

"You let Arthur give me to Uriens and you forgot me."

"Morgan." Kay stepped forwards towards me, and I saw the flush of anger against his neck, and I felt the raw power of his rage, and the Otherworld beneath it. "I let you go *because I loved you*. Morgan, what do you think happened? I *begged* Arthur not to marry you to that man, but I couldn't change his mind. When you married him I *had* to let you go – how do you not see this? Did Uriens seem like a kind man to you? A forgiving one? What, do you think if he had known it was me when he dragged you in front of Arthur after your wedding he would have spared either you or me, or left Logrys without a war? We are not children anymore, Morgan. It is not just you and me. Arthur is the King and you are his sister and many *many* people's lives were at stake. I didn't want to follow you and put you in danger. How do you not understand, Morgan? If I had followed you here and Uriens had caught us together he would have killed you." The anger washed out of him in a sudden wave. I felt the steel within me weaken, and bend. I was weak with the loss of Accolon, and I had missed Kay. I was angry with him, so angry, but in him was everything sweet and innocent that I had lost. I could not deny that in that moment, I wanted it back, desperately. I wanted to step forward to him, to ask, *Can't we all go back to the beginning?* But what he said to me stilled me where I stood. "You thought I had *abandoned* you? You thought I had *forgotten* you? What, because I spent one night with another woman? Don't you know what it's like to be lonely? To make a mistake? Could you not have imagined what it was like for me, seeing you with *him*? I never cared for another woman. Do you think I don't know about everything else that you have done? Your lover you sent to kill Arthur? I knew about *him* before. And Lancelot. And *Merlin*." Kay paused, reeling under his anger. I was too drained to be shocked that Kay knew every little way I had betrayed him. Together we had destroyed the wonderful thing we had had. I did not know how, but it

229

was gone now. "But I didn't *care*. I never *knew* anyone else, I never *loved* anyone else. I *never* forgot you. I knew you. Or I thought I did. No, Morgan stop." I had stepped forward towards him. Turning his face down and away from me, Kay stepped back. "Whatever there was between us, it is over now. *Over*." He looked back up and I could see still the tears that were there, shining as he held them back. "You didn't trust me. You have become a creature without trust, without love, without kindness. I heard what your *lover* said – oh yes, because though I knew you had a lover, I still did not forget you – when he died." He paused, and I knew what was coming. He hissed it out, shaking with rage. "*As you love me you will show Arthur no mercy. No mercy.* Morgan, no mercy? Who are you? The Morgan I loved was a good woman. She loved Arthur as a brother. She loved me, too."

I had nothing to say to him. How could I defend myself against the rawness of Kay's truth? I had not trusted him. Every step I had taken to defend myself had been a step that had taken me further from the good love that had once made me whole, and now this last step had robbed me of the two men who had loved me, Kay and Accolon. I was finally alone. Alone, and once again robbed of my sword. I could not turn back. I could only go further into the darkness.

"I will do you *one last kindness*, Morgan," he said softly. "I will not tell Arthur it was you that took his sword." *It is my sword*, I thought, but I held my tongue. "But, Morgan, do not try to harm him again."

I fixed him with a sharp look, drawing into myself, drawing all the power I had about myself. I could see him feel it, though he tried to hide it.

"Tell Arthur what you please. You and Arthur and all the knights of Camelot could look for me all over God's earth and not find a trace of me if I did not wish it. I am not afraid of Arthur's vengeance; I will do much more than this, when I see my time."

Kay sighed deeply, and I saw it go through his whole body. He rubbed his face one last time.

"Morgan, *please*," he said.

I neither moved nor spoke, unwilling to assent. Kay might not have forgotten me as utterly as I thought he had, but Arthur had, and if Kay was with Arthur, then Kay too must be my enemy. Kay and I were finished, and he had declared his place at Arthur's side. The coldness and absoluteness of the end of it all cauterised me against any of the pain I felt, for Kay, and for Accolon, and I did not cry when he left.

Chapter Thirty-Six

They brought his body back to Rheged, but I could not look at it. Among the armour they stripped from him, I found the scabbard. It had not saved him. The belt was sliced through, as though Arthur had cut it from him in battle, but he must not have known it was his own scabbard because he had not taken it with him. It was caked in mud, and I only knew that it was truly Excalibur's scabbard from the feel of it in my hand. But I could not bear to keep it. I had no need of a magic scabbard. I had my own ways to protect myself, my own potions to stop myself spilling a drop of blood.

I stood on the battlements to watch the smoke rising from the pyre as they burned Accolon. Even he had abandoned me at the last. He had not even left me with a child.

When the smoke stopped rising, I called for my horse, and took the scabbard, and rode to the shores of Avalon. I would return the cursed thing to where it had come from. Night was falling as I arrived, but I did not care. A thick mist rose off the lake, and I hurled the scabbard out into it. I did not hear it fall into the water, but I knew it was gone. I climbed back on my horse and rode back to Rheged, fast. The ride was long, and I did not get back until the depths of the night, but it had cleared my head, and when I lay in my bed that night, I felt colder, calmer, more resolved than ever to make myself invulnerable.

I knew it was time to make a final, desperate effort to get Merlin's knowledge. I was afraid, now, that Nimue would not bring it to me, and I was determined to have it. I wrote to Camelot, asking him to come to me.

I did not have to wait long for Merlin after I sent for him. I thought that he would be intrigued. It was a bright evening, early spring, and I stepped into my room to find him leaning against the window-frame, in his young, handsome form. He had, then, come to negotiate. I closed the door behind me, and drew the bolt.

"Good, you came," I said, briskly, walking into the middle of the room to face him. He was only wearing a shirt and breeches, though the chill of winter still lingered in the air. He regarded me with an amused interest, leaning back against the window, his elbows resting on the sill.

"What do you want with me, Morgan?" he asked.

"I want the rest of your secrets. The rest of the Black Arts," I told him.

"That is interesting." He stepped forward, walking right up to me. I did not back down. I was not afraid of Merlin, and I knew the price. I was prepared. I would give anything in my possession for the rest of Merlin's dark knowledge. He reached out and laid his hand lightly against my throat. I could feel my pulse quicken under his hand. He had not left, so he was considering it. "And what do you possibly have of equal value?" He let his hand trail down, over my breast, down my stomach, and then around my waist, to pull me against him. He whispered close, his voice lower, more threatening, more unpleasant. Though he was still young and handsome in his form, I felt my skin crawl as it had when I had looked on his true shape. "You have lost the sword, you have lost the book, you have thrown away the scabbard." He leaned closer still to whisper in my ear, and I felt his lips brush against my neck. I did not push him away. I was prepared to get the knowledge from him by any means necessary. "If you were hoping you could get my secrets from me by offering me your body again, you should know that Nimue has matched your offer." I felt his teeth, lightly, at my ear, and he pulled me closer against him. "But," he continued, his hands reaching up my back to pull open the lacing at the back of my dress, "Nimue is a lovely young virgin, and you have had many men before. So, you will have to offer me something more convincing, like – the child."

I pushed him back then, suddenly enough that he stumbled away from me.

"What child?" I demanded. His smile spread slowly across his face, and I felt my blood grow chill.

"Morgawse's child with Arthur," he replied.

I thought for a moment. I had seen what joy the little boy gave my sister, what happiness. I had seen how much she loved him. But, if she could be convinced to give him away to be fostered, why not with Merlin? Then he could protect himself from his father's anger with secret knowledge. Merlin might agree to take the boy when he was fifteen years old and of the age to become a knight. It would be no different to her than what would happen anyway. Every boy must become a knight someday; if she had to let him go anyway why not to become a witch?

"He is not my child to give," I answered slowly. Merlin leaned away, and I could see that he was about to leave. "But," I added, swiftly, "I think I could persuade Morgawse to give him up, if she could be sure of his safety."

Merlin gave a harsh laugh, "Sure of his safety? Morgan, you misunderstand me. I do not want the boy alive. There is powerful

232

black magic to be done with his blood, and that is what I want. *All* of it."

I crossed my arms over my chest, disgusted, drawing back.

"Then you shall not have him." I was not going to give away my sister's beloved child to be murdered. There were still things I would not do; betray my sister, kill a child. Merlin shrugged.

"Then you shall not have my knowledge."

"How do I know that the rest of your knowledge isn't nothing more than some cheap small-town conjuror's tricks, learned to scare kings into listening to you?" I demanded, suddenly angry. I knew well enough how it was easy to convince someone you were all-powerful with but a small display of magic tricks.

Merlin grasped a handful of my hair, at the base of my neck, pulling me back towards him, turning my face up towards his. I could see the wildness of his anger in his eyes, and I felt once again all around me his dizzying strength.

"Do not play games with me, Morgan," he hissed, twisting his hand tighter in my hair. "I am stronger than you. I am cleverer than you. I know of things you could not even dream. You will not win." He leaned down, and brushed his lips against mine, and softly, he whispered. "*Surrender*, Morgan."

I was unwilling, not wanting to give without a promise of return, and I wanted to push him away, but under the force of his power all around me, I felt myself obey, and my mouth opened under his, responding to his kiss. *I have lost control of my body*, I thought, with terror.

"You see, Morgan? I could have you against your wishes any time I pleased, and yet I am kind. I offer you the choice. If you cross me, I may not continue to be kind. I am offering a fair exchange. You only need surrender to my wishes, and we shall both have what we desire," he whispered, and I felt his control slip from around me. He had only been showing me his power. It was only a taste. I could feel my heart thudding in my chest.

"Not the boy," I insisted, staring back into his soft brown eyes, that I had seen smile and look kind, that hid beneath them the black, cruel beetle-eyes of his real form.

"No boy, no secret knowledge," Merlin answered, tightening his grip on my hair.

"Why does it have to be him?" I asked.

"A king's blood."

A sudden, awful thought came to me, and before I could consider it fully, before I could hold it back, in my desperation to spare Morgawse, the words were out of my mouth.

"The Queen is with child."

I felt cold at the words even as I had said them. *What had I done?* Merlin released his grip on my hair, and he laughed, a bright, tinkling laugh that did not suit him at all. I wanted to unsay the words, but it seemed to me that the only other option was to offer my own sister's little child, and I would not do that.

"How do you intend to prove this, Morgan?" he asked, but I could see that he believed me.

"Go and see for yourself. She hides it well, but it is there."

"What a secret, Morgan. *What a secret.*" He pulled down my dress over my shoulder, still loose from where he had untied it, and traced a line of blue with his finger across my shoulder, swirling across the top of it. He pressed his lips lightly against my skin, and I felt myself shrink away inside with disgust. He looked up at me again. "So, this is the exchange you offer?"

"It is," I said, softly.

He gave a brusque nod. "Well, Morgan, the deal is done."

He moved away from me, to sit in the chair before me. I had hoped that he had gone to fetch something for me, some book he had hidden, but he had nothing. He just sat back in the chair, looking at me with a smile on his face.

"Now, Morgan, as a show of good faith in our agreement, I will have you. You can consider it a down payment on the secret knowledge you covet, until I get my hands on the child. Take off your dress."

I pulled my dress back up over my shoulder.

"Merlin, I am not your whore," I snapped, crossing my arms over my chest. Merlin stood back swiftly to his feet, stepping over to me, grasping hold of me at the hair again, his other arm wrapping around my waist so that I could not back away from him. I could not escape anyway, since the strength had left my body under the pressure of the dark Otherworld power coming off him.

"Are you not, Morgan?" he hissed, pressing his forehead against mine. "You have received payment from me in return for your body before. Don't you remember the first exchange we made, for my book of Macrobius?"

"You took my sword," I hissed back, only more angry in my powerlessness. "*That* was the exchange, unfair as it was."

Merlin laughed, low, touching his nose against mine, letting his lips brush against mine as he whispered.

"So it was. And yet you gave yourself to me anyway, didn't you? You wanted it, you wanted *me*." He made a little movement as though he were about to kiss me, and under his power I felt my mouth open slightly in response, in anticipation, but the kiss did not come. "I felt it from the moment I saw you. I could feel your hot little virgin body quivering with desire whenever you saw me. But you gave yourself away cheaply, didn't you? Even I was shocked how willing you were. A few cups of wine, and that book before you, and you melted into my hands. Ector's Otherworld boy was not much on your mind that night, was he? Did you tell him it was I who had you first? Did you tell your husband?" He kissed me then, and though my mind fought against it, my body responded. My breath quickened under his eager kiss, and I even felt a flush of heat run through me, though in my heart and mind I felt nothing at all. At last he released me.

"It was not much of a choice you gave me, Merlin," I said flatly, staring up at him. "I thought you had brought me that book out of kindness, or out of interest in my studies. I feared that if I refused you, you would take the book from me, or perhaps you would have forced me and taken the book away anyway. I see you are not above forcing a woman."

"Oh Morgan, you make me sound like such a monster." He moved away, releasing his grip on me, and slipping back into the ugly bald-headed form that I knew. His expression was strange. "Very well, I shall come to collect the rest of my payment when my work is complete. Then – *only then* – will I give you my knowledge."

Before I could object, he disappeared before me, into nothingness. *What have I done?* I thought again. *What have I done?*

I waited for news as spring began to break around me, and the snows around Rheged thawed. My heart still felt cold. I dreamed of Accolon at night; over and over again my mind played back the first night we had spent together when he had pulled back the curtains of my bed, and put his rough hands on me. In my sleep I felt them tangling through my hair, still, I felt his hot mouth against mine, I felt his stubble graze the skin of my neck, and then I would wake and pull back the bed curtains, and the room would be empty, and I would remember that he was dead.

I tried moving my room, to sleep in Uriens' bed, but that was worse. I dreamed there of Uriens on top of me, his hand over my mouth, or worse, of pushing him off, and him being be limp and dead, his dull eyes unfocussed. I went back to my own bed.

The only news that came to Rheged was that the Emperor Lucius had finally given in to his fear of Arthur and was beginning to invade the vassal territories in France. He had attacked Carhais and taken it. He had killed its King. News, too, came to me that my mother had died and that Cornwall had come not to me or my sister, as it should have, but to one of her cousins, Mark. I wrote to Arthur protesting this and received no reply. I hoped and did not hope that this meant that Merlin had succeeded.

I received, too, a letter from Morgawse which read:

"Dearest sister, sad news about mother. I hope you are well. Also, I heard that you are a widow, too, now. I am sure you mourn your husband just as much as I do. Lothian thriving. Gareth almost of age to become a knight. Wish he was a girl. Morgawse."

I certainly intended to mourn my husband as Morgawse mourned hers, but after the loss of Accolon I did not feel ready for another lover. Not right away. I thought of Morgawse and all her sons. But if she had had girls, they would have been sent away to be married at the same age or younger. Every child must leave its parent, and she still had Mordred. I did not even have the son I had, not really. He was always with his nurse, and he seemed happy and healthy enough. I wished that I had loved Ywain. I would have had something left, then.

Chapter Thirty-Seven

The next news that came to Rheged was from Nimue, but it was not a letter. I had been with the new steward of Rheged, who was a dull but efficient man of middle age, and some of the local Barons, giving my instructions for the spring. We needed to decide how many men we should prepare in case Arthur sent to Gore for men for his army to march against Lucius. These duties completed, I walked back to my room to find Nimue standing there when I opened the door.

She did not speak, but reached out and took both my hands in hers. Instantly, I felt the room quaver around me, and a light-headedness pass through me. The room dissolved, and instead a high windswept cliff came into focus above me, and on it, towering over the rocky bay below, was the castle that had been my childhood home, Tintagel. It was black against the bright white cloud of the spring day, rising sharply up over us. I had not lived there since I was three or four years old, but I recognised it well. Why had Nimue brought me back to my father's castle? It was Mark's castle now. I hoped for a moment that she had brought me back to return my castle to me, but when I glanced at her, she was not looking at me.

She was looking the other way, across the rocky bay, to the other side where a dark, deep cave led off into darkness. There was a big rock at the mouth of the cave, and I could see the figure of a man lying slumped on top of the rock. From where we were, I could not tell who it was. She turned to me, her pale blue eyes bright with a wild anger.

"You need to see this, Morgan. You need to see how I deal with those who cross me, and who harm those under my protection."

I could feel the power coming off Nimue already, and she was as dark as Merlin. She must be deep in the Black Arts by now. So, Merlin had taken up her offer rather than mine. But, when I followed her closer, I saw that the man slumped on the rock was the young Merlin. He was breathing quickly, as though he was in pain, his eyes open but unfocussed and looking up at the sky. Nimue climbed nimbly up onto the rock to stand beside him. I hung back, wary.

Nimue was talking to him, but I could not hear what she said. But, when she leant down over him, I saw him flash through his forms; the young man, the ugly bald man, an old man with a long grey beard, a child, the brown-haired girl, over and over again, as though he was trying to wriggle away from her magic by changing his shape. But there was nowhere for him to go. I felt a wave of dark power come from Nimue, and it turned my stomach. Then, fast after, came a blinding flash of light. When I opened my eyes, Merlin was gone, but from deep, deep under the rock, I could hear him, screaming and screaming and screaming. Nimue, seemingly unfazed, jumped down off the rock beside me, and without a word, took me by both hands and the landscape melted around us.

When my room rematerialized around me, I was on my own. I felt cold and sick and clammy. So Merlin had given all his secrets to Nimue, and now she meant to threaten me to protect Arthur. I supposed that meant that, at least, no child had died. But that night I dreamed dreams that were filled with blood.

I thought it was best at least to behave as though Arthur had my support, and I wrote to him asking what I could do to help with his war with Lucius. He meant to march out soon. I suggested that he might need my help as a healer, and suggested that I might leave Ywain in the care of his Queen. I thought that if she had an infant child, then it would be suitable enough. I did not say so, though. I offered the help of Gore's armies, and expressed all the sisterly affection I was able. It was easy to pretend.

Arthur wrote back quickly, though I suspected that it was actually Nimue who penned the letter, since it was neatly written in fine script and I had seen Arthur squint and struggle over his books as a boy. The letter thanked me for my offer of help, and accepted it, but said that I could not leave Ywain in Camelot since Guinevere was riding out to war with him. Did that mean she had lost the child anyway? Or that Merlin had taken it? Had he begun whatever he had been planning?

On the back of Arthur's letter, Kay had scrawled three words: "Go to Benwick."

Benwick was the dead King Ban's castle in the south of France. Lancelot would be there, and I was glad to go, but I suspected that Kay had suggested that because he wanted me far from Arthur. I ought not to have blamed him for his care for his foster-brother, but I did.

I made the arrangements for my armies in Gore to ride with Arthur's to Brittany, and left before them, alone, with only my books and the essentials I needed for my medicine and magic. The journey was long and tedious, and I hated travelling across the sea. It made me sick. I had never been to Benwick before, so I could not wish myself there, and I had forgotten how long and uncomfortable and tedious a ride across country could be. I was safe enough riding alone; my woaded face kept the robbers and rough men away.

I was glad when, after a week of travelling, Benwick Castle emerged over the horizon. It was different from the castles that I knew in Britain. Not tall and sharp like Lothian Castle, or Rheged, or huge and grand like Camelot, Benwick was small and squat, round-towered but encased in a square wall that looked dangerously low after the sheer towers of Rheged. It had, at least, a moat around it, but it did not seem to me as well-built for siege as Britain's castles were.

The drawbridge was lowered for me as I arrived, so there must have been someone in the castle who knew who I was.

It was Lancelot who had commanded I be let into the castle. I recognised him instantly, standing in the middle of the courtyard in his armour, his helm in his hand. If anything, he was yet more handsome than when I had seen him last. Warfare suited him, like it suited Arthur, though in a different way. It made Arthur hearty and bold where it made Lancelot watchful and thoughtful. He greeted me with a nod, and came forward to take my horse's reins as I rode into the courtyard and slipped from my saddle.

"Lady Morgan," he greeted me softly, "Kay wrote to say I should expect you. Are you well?"

"I'm well," I answered.

"Kay told me you lost your husband. I'm sorry." He shifted uncomfortably on his feet, looking down. Why was *he* uncomfortable? I wondered how much Kay still wrote to Lancelot, how close they still were. I did not know what to say. I was not sorry at all, nor did I really know why Kay had told me. Of course, this meant that Kay had also told him that I had tried to kill Arthur. I didn't care.

I made some noncommittal noise to accept his sympathy and he led me up to the room he had for me. He talked on the way of the plans they had for the war, and he seemed far more comfortable talking business with me.

"You have come at the right time, Morgan. In less than a week we will ride north to meet Arthur when he arrives at Calais."

I was glad when he left me alone in my room. It was small and plain, but I did not mind. It was a welcome change from a room seeped in memories. But nonetheless, when I slept I dreamed strange dreams. I dreamed that I lay in my bed in Rheged, and a hand drew back the bed curtains, but it was not Accolon, it was Lancelot, and he took me in his arms and we had the same desperately tender love we had had in my dream long ago, and I woke still warm with it, with the feel of his kiss against my lips tingling around me, like the kiss of a ghost.

I dressed in the black jewelled dress, and the crown of Gore. It was best to look as powerful as I was. Lancelot came in the morning to bring me to his counsel. When he came, the memory of the dream was still close about me, and I felt nervous. He seemed distracted with thoughts of war and he rushed ahead of me to the small room where he met with the others who commanded his army under him. The others were already there, and among them I recognised Ector's brother, Bors. He bore little resemblance to Ector, or to Lancelot with whom he shared only a father, being stocky and short with sandy-brown hair and an angry, square face. I wondered what he made of being under the command of his younger half-brother, but Lancelot had a quiet authority and I had never known a man question him. When Bors saw me, he started back.

"Lancelot, you are not bringing a witch to counsel, are you?" he asked.

Lancelot looked innocently between us, and his brow crinkled slightly in confusion.

"You're not afraid of her, are you Bors?" he asked.

Bors blustered back, shaking his head, upset at having been accused of being afraid of anything.

"Morgan is wise from her time in Avalon, and she has the knowledge of healing. She will be very helpful to us," Lancelot explained.

He turned and gave me an encouraging smile, and I felt my stomach flutter slightly. I felt angry with myself for being vulnerable to my desire for Lancelot. I was not a shy little virgin anymore, a simple country girl to be flustered by the attention of handsome men. I ought not to be pleased to have a smile from him. He had been rude to me. I was a grown woman, brave and powerful. I knew the Black Arts and I had killed a man. I would *not* be made weak but one knight who had kissed me in the forest.

It was only two days later when the army began its march north. It was a short march, and Arthur had not yet come, so Lancelot's army set up its pavilions to wait for him, on the borders of the land Lucius had taken. I stayed mostly with the camp, with the local women who followed behind either to heal with what limited magic and knowledge they had, or to give their comfort to the knights any other way they pleased. I knew what war was like, and I was not surprised to see men I knew as honourable knights take the peasant women that followed the camp as they chose, but I was pleased that Lancelot was not among those that did so. The camp grew as the men set up pavilions in preparation for Arthur's arrival – one in white and blue-green with Uther's woad-blue dragon flying from the top of it for Arthur, and one in Lothian's dark blue for the sons of Lot, and others, more and more besides to await the arrival of the rest of the army.

Injuries were few whilst we were waiting, and I had little work. I avoided Lancelot. I felt a little lonely, a little lost among all the men. At least people either respected me – the blue of my face, my knowledge of healing – or they were afraid.

When Arthur's army came, there was great celebration and feasting, though there were fewer of them than I had expected. I had dreaded their coming, for that was when the war would begin in earnest. They were young men, still, only tested in the small wars of Britain. Arthur and his men were about to throw themselves against Europe's mightiest force, Rome. I was not sure we would survive it, but it was either that or sit in our castles in Britain and wait for Lucius and the armies of Rome to come and crush us.

Arthur had, at least, brought healing women with him. There were a couple from Avalon, but they were before their woad and I only knew they were from Avalon from overhearing them talk. Among them, too, were the two Breton women who had come over with Guinevere. I wondered how much healing they truly knew. I joined the healing women, glad for female company. The two Breton women kept mostly to themselves, I noticed.

Then the first battle came. We stood in the centre of the camp, the other healing women and I, waiting for when the first injured man would come. I had put away my crown and my jewelled dress, and had returned instead to plain black wool. I did not want to speak to Kay, or Arthur, and I was happy to stay innocuous. A few of the women chattered, but most of us were quiet and tense. We could not see the battlefield from where we were, only the crowd of pavilions and the short, scrubby grass around them. There was something vulnerable about the pavilions made in rich silk. Beautiful, but strangely unwarlike. When Arthur had fought with Lot, the men had slept wild, in the dirt, in the forest, in caves. Already, Britain and France were powerful enough and rich enough to wage war in luxury. There was something perverse about it.

Only a few injured men came, and I was glad. Everyone returning seemed pleased, flushed with victory. I did not rush forward to any of the injured men, since there were plenty of us, and no one I recognised was injured. Instead, I wandered through the camp towards the dark blue tent that would house Lot's sons. It was right by Arthur's, and I did not want to run into him or Kay, but I wanted to see my nephews.

I was pleased to see Gawain, Aggravain and Gaheris standing outside their pavilion. They all greeted me warmly, but Gawain made a quick excuse to leave. It seemed that he was commanding a wing of Arthur's army. I imagined Aggravain would be jealous; his twin brother had won Arthur's favour fighting at his side in the war with the five kings, and he had been left behind.

When Gaheris greeted me with a kiss on the cheek, I took his face in my hands and gave him a fond smile. At sixteen years old, he looked fully a man at last. He would never be as big as his brothers, but he was tall and strong with his father's wily look about him and his mother's kind eyes.

"You are a man now, aren't you?" I said.

Gaheris laughed. "I like to think so. Our mother does not."

I could imagine that. I remembered how Morgawse had spoken to Gawain, though he had towered over her.

The tent of Lot's sons was right by Arthur's, and as we spoke, Arthur rode past with Guinevere. I almost did not recognise her, her red hair hidden under a mail cap, but her light leather and plate armour vest left her white arms bare, betraying that it was a woman that rode beneath the armour, and I did not think it could be any other woman than her. She held the reigns of her horse with a casual, practised power as though she had ridden to war all her life, and she sat easy in the saddle. Nonetheless, her bulky armour made her look small in comparison, like a boy riding to war amongst men. Arthur rode with his helm under one arm, and I could see the sweat and the dirt from the battlefield on his face. His eyes were wild still from the fighting, and glanced over us seeing nothing. Neither of them seemed to see us. He jumped from his horse, and lifted Guinevere from hers as though she were as light as a child, and they disappeared into his pavilion, leaving the horses standing around in front. Gaheris whistled through his teeth, but said nothing. There was obviously no child.

"It is strange to have a woman ride to war," Aggravain observed. "I cannot imagine our mother riding to war."

Gaheris did not seem to be listening. I walked forward to take the bridles of the horses. I did not think they should be left to wander around the camp.

When I held the bridles in my hand, I looked up, and I froze. From where I was standing, I could see through the cloth door of the pavilion as it stirred in the light breeze, a thin strip of what was inside. Down in a pile of silk cushions I could see Arthur's bare back, and the pale white legs of the Queen either side of it. I saw her clasp her hands suddenly at his shoulders and I thought I heard Arthur give a low groan. I quickly looked away, to see Gaheris and Aggravain laughing at me, and the blush I felt heat my cheeks. So they had deliberately left me to take hold of the horses. They had seen this before.

As I stood there, staring at my laughing nephews, Lancelot rode up and lightly jumped from his horse. He, too, had thrown off his helm and was still dirtied from the battle.

"Sir Lancelot." Aggravain stepped forward to greet him with an admiring nod. So, Lothian remembered well the tales of Lancelot and his deeds in Arthur's war. I had not seen Aggravain ever look impressed before.

Lancelot looked distracted, and gazed between the three of us for a moment before forming his words.

"I'm looking for a woman," he said, breathlessly. Aggravain laughed, soft and low.

"There are plenty of women," he said.

Lancelot shook his head. "The woman who was with Arthur's archers. Is she with the Bretons? Does anyone know who she is?"

I saw the look that passed between Aggravain and Gaheris. For a moment, both looked the picture of their father.

"She is not with the Bretons," Aggravain told him, unable to keep a smile from his face.

"Why are you looking for her?" Gaheris asked. Lancelot ignored him.

"She is not Breton? I did not know any other realm had fighting women any longer."

"Oh, she is Breton," Aggravain replied. He was enjoying teasing Lancelot. Lancelot did not respond well to being teased; he was slow on the uptake at games like this, I remembered that from when we had been children. "But she is not with the Bretons. Not anymore."

"Anymore?" Lancelot asked, lost.

Gaheris, kinder than his brother, put Lancelot out of his confusion. "She is with us. She is Arthur's wife."

Lancelot seemed to take it like a blow, stepping back against it, but he nodded slowly. I thought it strange that he would care so much. What would he care who Arthur's wife was?

"Ah, I missed his wedding," Lancelot sighed.

"Well that was because you spent two years in Benwick hiding from Kay the Seneschal," Gaheris teased, with his sly smile, but Lancelot understood *that* and did not share his joke. He stepped towards him, and Gaheris started back.

"You don't know what you're talking about," Lancelot said, firm and low and threatening.

Gaheris, to my surprise, gave an apologetic nod, and threw his brother beside him a dirty look.

"My apologies, sir. I must have been listening to the gossip of someone who is full of shit."

Lancelot stepped back. So, Aggravain had been gossiping about Lancelot and Kay. I thought that had died down long ago, but clearly it had not. So Morgawse had passed *one* of her qualities besides her red hair onto Aggravain.

Lancelot looked up, away from the brothers, and seemed to notice for the first time that he had come as far as Arthur's pavilion.

Half to himself, he said, "Since I have come so far, I ought to greet Arthur and his new wife."

He stepped forward, and Aggravain rushed around to stand in his way, holding out a wary hand to keep Lancelot back.

"I would not, sir, go in Arthur's tent."

Both of the brothers had become more formal with Lancelot, after seeing the flash of his anger. I did not blame them. Everyone knew of Lancelot's strength in battle, though he was shy and naïve in other ways.

"Why not?" Lancelot asked. He was so infuriatingly naïve sometimes.

Aggravain gave an awkward cough, and Lancelot still did not seem to follow. Gaheris stepped forward to help.

"Sir, Arthur has not changed in his... habits since the wars in Britain." Then, as though he had given up entirely on subtlety and decided that crudeness was his only option, he continued. I supposed that he too had more of Morgawse in him that I thought. "Arthur is straight off his horse and on to a woman. The only difference now from the war with the five kings, is that now it is always the same woman."

"I shall return... later, then," Lancelot said, looking down at the ground. Before any of us could speak, he had jumped back onto his horse and ridden away. It all seemed very strange. Why Lancelot should be so embarrassed, why he should be so desperate to find out Arthur's wife's identity? It made me uneasy.

Chapter Thirty-Eight

The war continued, and Arthur continued to win ground, but Lancelot did not go back, after all, to greet Arthur and his new wife. He was quiet, as he always was, but there was something new and unsettling about his quiet.

I worried for him on the battlefield, and I was proved right in my concerns when only a few days later, he rode into the centre of the camp where I was waiting with the other women, slumped on his horse. One of the women at the front of the group stepped forward, but when she saw me rush to him, and noticed the woad of my face, she moved away deferentially. *At least,* I though, *some people still respect the magic of Avalon.*

I jumped on the horse behind him and took the reins, letting him lean back against me, and riding back to his tent. Suddenly, my awkwardness around him had left me. There was no time for it now. I supposed I should have known before that this might be the way, that even the greatest warriors are made of flesh and bone.

He was badly injured, and delirious from it, and I had to wrap his arm around my shoulders to lead him into his pavilion. I tried to let him down gently on to his bed, but he fell heavily as soon as I let go of him, and gave a low groan of pain through his gritted teeth. I had not been inside his pavilion before, and I was shocked by how rich everything inside it was. Ban must have left many riches for his sons that Ector had never seen. The bed was a low makeshift structure of light planks, but it was laid with silk sheets in dark red and purple, sewn with gold thread, and everywhere around was gold and rich silk. Even the drinking cups were gold, or gold-plated. Everything was old, too. Treasures from another time.

I climbed on the bed with him and pulled off his helm. He groaned again, but I was pleased to see that he was not injured in the head. His hair was plastered to his head with the sweat of battle, but his skin was clammy and cold where I put the back of my hand against his brow. I pulled off his leather gauntlets, and then unbuckled his breastplate and pulled it away. It was hard, for I had to lift his weight to get it over his head and he was heavy with dense muscle, and he groaned with pain as I pulled him up to sitting to lift it off, but when I did I saw the wound. It was at his side, just below the ribs. I put my head against his chest. At least his breaths seemed to be coming in and out clean, so he seemed not to have been struck in the lungs. I pulled off the greaves from his legs, and his boots. I called out of the tent door for hot water, and, moving to sit over him, I pulled his shirt over his head. I could tell he was getting weaker, because he only murmured with pain.

I tried not to look at his bare chest, to be distracted by his naked skin close by me, and to focus on the wound at his side, but it was difficult. I had been long without a man, and Lancelot of all men made me weak enough to burn with anger at myself. He was only half-conscious, his eyelids fluttering open and shut, his lips gently parted with his breath, the dark glossy waves of his hair falling half across his face. Unconsciously, I reached forward and gently brushed the hair back from his face, and heard him give an appreciative murmur at my touch. I let my fingers brush against his lips, feel their softness, feel them tingle against my fingertips, and at the secret centre of me, but then the hot water came in.

I ordered it to be set beside me, and sent one of the girls who had brought it to bring my bag of medicines. I glanced back over him, his lightly muscled body, the fine line of hairs across his chest, and then sank down over the wound, focussing there. The girl came back fast, and I cleaned the wound and bound it up with linen. It was deep, but it seemed clean, and I thought he would heal well enough. When the girl was gone, I mixed him a drink that would restore his blood and knit his muscle and skin back together when he slept. It was powerful magic, but I was sure that I was up to it. There were other potions that would be slower, and safer, but I thought that he and I were strong enough for this one.

I climbed back onto the bed with him, and gently held him up to hold the cup to his lips. He drank obediently; I was not surprised. The drink was sweet and pleasant with the strength of life. Quickly after he had drunk, he seemed to fall from semi-consciousness into sleep. Last of all, I pressed my hand flat against the wound, and let all that I had in my natural healing touch rush out into him. I felt the warmth of his life, comfortingly close by me, and knew I was helping, just a little, to bring him back. It made me tired and shaky, and when it was done I settled beside him, still in my day clothes, and closed my eyes, and sleep came quickly for me, too.

I woke in the morning when I felt him stir beside me. I had slept a sweet and dreamless sleep, but in the cool morning air of the pavilion, and having slept in my clothes, I felt grubby and unpleasant. I turned to look at him beside me. He was still waking, still stirring. Caught with a sudden desire, a sudden impulse, and a relief that he had survived my potion and it seemed to have healed him, I sat up, and gently leaned over him, and tentatively pressed my lips softly against his. To my surprise and delight he responded with a happy murmur, his mouth opening under mine, and his hands running up my legs, up my thighs, drawing me on to him, coming to hold me gently around the waist. My mind began to fill with the memories of the dream I had had, the feel of his hands in my hair, and his lips against my neck, and the wonderful moment when we finally came together. The memory, too, of the look he had given me, the look of love. I realised, then, that despite how happy I had been with Accolon, how great our love together had been, it had lacked that raw, intense tenderness. It had been dominated by my ambition, by his devotion. But I would have that with Lancelot. It would happen. It could be now; I had dreamed of us in a pavilion, in the springtime. It was blissful, for a moment. But, then, he seemed to wake properly, and push me back. He looked up at me, his eyes suddenly wide open, and his look was angry, and tinged with fear.

"Morgan, *what are you doing?*" he half-shouted.

I felt the hurt hit me at the centre I thought I had strengthened beyond any such thing. That was the worst; to feel that after everything, I was still vulnerable before Lancelot. He took me by the shoulders and lightly lifted me off him, setting me beside him on the bed, jumping up and looking around for his shirt to pull over his head. I noticed that he had not bled through his bandage overnight, so my magic must have saved him.

"Lancelot, I have saved your life," I protested. He lifted his shirt to look down at his wound, but it did not seem to ease the expression on his face, or the resolution in his mind. "Lancelot, why are you being like this? You were pleased with me a moment ago. Besides, need I remind you that it was *you* who kissed *me* first, when you brought me back from Lothian." I almost added, *and we have, besides, spent the night together before*, but then I remembered that that had been a dream. It had felt so real. It still felt real.

Lancelot rubbed his face with his hands. "Morgan, *please*, that was a mistake. It was just one kiss. I do not want you," he said, gently. It still struck me at the heart. "Please, Morgan. Just stop this."

"Is this because of Kay?" I demanded.

Lancelot sighed in frustration. "This is not because of Kay," he insisted.

"Well, then, who did you think I was before you so rudely shoved me off you?" I stood from the bed and walked around to face him. He would not look right at me. If there was someone else, I would rather know that than it be simply that there was something wrong with me. But who else could there be if not Kay? He barely knew anyone else and he was too shy to make friends, and *I had saved his life*. Why would he not care even a little for me because of that?

"Morgan, I was just confused. Morgan…" He stepped forward and took me gently by the shoulders, looking at me. I did not want him to touch me, if he would not accept me properly, but I did not push him away. "I am fond of you, but I cannot – I will not – make all the pretences, do all the deeds, of love with anyone I do not love. It would not be fair on either of us."

I knew he was being reasonable, but it made me angry nonetheless. He might find he loved me afterwards, and besides, I had never asked for love from him. I had never asked him to tell me he loved me. I had never said I loved him. I only wanted to feel our bodies coming together, as I had dreamed of it. Then a thought struck me; it was the thought of Merlin with his hands over my eyes, and the secrets I had learned from the book I had stolen from him.

"Kay has fucked Morgawse," I told him. He flinched.

"That isn't true," Lancelot protested. He sounded suddenly as he had those years ago when he had turned up at my bedroom door, to lecture me about *love*. Well, he still had that annoyingly naïve idealism, and if anything I was helping him.

"It is true. Kay doesn't believe in *only for love* anymore. That's a child's silliness, Lancelot. If you had ever been married you would not talk about *only for love*," I said, stepping towards him, pushing my point. I was ready to make him understand.

"I don't believe you," he insisted.

I jumped towards him, wrapping my hand over his eyes, and to my surprise I felt myself lurch into my memory with him. So, Merlin had been there with me, too, when I had seen him with Kay.

Lancelot and I stood where I had stood at the top of the stairs, watching Kay, Morgawse slumped against his shoulder, fumbling at the latch on the door. It was faded, fuzzy, as though in a dream, but it was clear enough what was happening when Kay went to leave and Morgawse grabbed him by the front of his surcoat to pull him into a kiss. I glanced at Lancelot, whose face was set and eyes fixed on the pair of them as Kay went to pull back, and then weakened under her kiss, and followed her inside to slam the door.

I thought we would only see what I had seen, but suddenly, with a rushing movement I felt lurch in the pit of my stomach, we were inside the room. I felt suddenly afraid, afraid that I would not bear to see what I was making Lancelot watch. I didn't know how to make it stop. Morgawse pulled Kay down on top of her on the bed.

"This is a really big bed," I heard Kay mumble, in surprise, and Morgawse laughed. They were both drunk, and clumsy with it, and I was surprised to see that Morgawse was the one who seemed to be better in control of herself. She pulled open his surcoat, and I saw one of the buttons pop off, and heard it skitter across the floor. Neither of them seemed to notice as she pushed it off his shoulders and he threw it away into the corner of the room. I glanced back at Lancelot beside me. He looked pale, and nervous.

When I looked back to Kay and Morgawse, she was tearing off his shirt, and he kissed her, rough and passionate. I could see him grasp two fistfuls of her thick silk skirts and push them up. I heard him sigh with longing, and it was so raw, so painfully familiar. Morgawse turned her face to the side as Kay kissed her neck, and I saw her slide her hand down into his breeches. Kay gasped her name, in pleasure and surprise.

Lancelot turned to me and grabbed me by the shoulders.

"Morgan, *make it stop*," he cried.

In awful, desperate panic, I realised that I did not remember how. I knew that Merlin had taken his hand away from my eyes, but, like in a dream, what I did with my body here did not seem to match what I was doing in real life.

"I don't know how," I confessed.

Lancelot ran his hands through his hair, pressing the heels of his hands into his forehead in despair. He turned back, as though he could not help himself, to Kay and Morgawse. Kay had pulled off Morgawse's dress, and she lay in her shift, stretching her arms over her head while Kay, burying his face in her hair, his lips against her neck, ran a hand up the inside of her thigh. I looked away when I saw her gasp and her forehead crease in that almost-painful delight. Suddenly, now I too was desperate for it to stop, I felt aware enough of my real body to pull my hand away, and Lancelot and I stumbled apart, both shaken.

"That's a nasty trick, Morgan," Lancelot said.

I turned to him, shaken as he was, but strengthened by my anger. "It's the *truth*, Lancelot. Ask Kay if you don't believe me. He won't lie to you."

"Just *go*," Lancelot said, tense and angry, as he turned away from me. I had meant for him to understand that people did not need to love one another, that no one else was sleeping alone until they fell in love, and that he did not need to feel that he owed Kay some kind of misplaced fidelity. I had not meant to upset him. I had not meant to upset *myself*. It had been the way Kay said her *name*. Had he not loved me? He could not have possibly loved Morgawse. He had been different with Lancelot.

I left, wishing I had never tried my hand at the new Black Arts I had learned on Lancelot. I wondered, suddenly, if Merlin were still screaming under that rock, the sound of the waves drowning him out. Perhaps he would scream for the rest of time, and no one would ever hear him again.

Lancelot did not speak to me after that, if he could help it. I felt awkward too, nervous and uneasy. I spent most of the time I was not with the other healing women with my nephews. They were always laughing and joking, and it was relaxing to listen to their easy chatter. None of them seemed to be worried by the war. All three were strong and brave, and Gawain a seasoned fighter already, so I did not worry for them. I only worried a little when I saw Aggravain watch his twin brother called into war councils with Arthur without him, or honoured always for his deeds on the battlefield while Aggravain was ignored. The rumour was that Aggravain was the elder, and certainly he was the more shrewd. I kept my eye on him. Perhaps this was what Aggravain wanted. Perhaps he thought he could have Lothian all for himself if Gawain grew close enough with Arthur. If such a thing would happen, Aggravain would know about it. Aggravain heard – and repeated – every scrap of gossip that came through the court. It was from him I learned what had become of the awful bargain I had made with Merlin. He told me that everyone at Camelot said that Merlin had pulled the child from the Queen's womb as retribution for Arthur fathering a bastard child with his own sister. I knew that was not quite true, but I felt the cold clamp of guilt at my stomach that I had given away the life of the girl I had seen full grown for the sake of nothing at all. Well, Morgawse and her youngest son were safe. He told me, too, that it was only *after* that that Nimue had returned Excalibur to Arthur. I wondered if she had needed it for that awful magic that she had used to shut Merlin beneath the rock.

Chapter Thirty-Nine

The campaign against Lucius was going well. Arthur took Carhais back, and said that he would leave Kay and a small contingent of knights behind there to hold it while he turned his attention south to Lucius' forces that were still pressing upwards against him. Still, though there was already a sense of tentative victory around the camp, and though the knights now rode south from the camp rather than defensively back on themselves to the north, I sensed a change in Arthur. I did not see him often, since he was either on the battlefield or in his pavilion with his wife, but when I did he seemed tense and anxious. I noticed, too, that Guinevere no longer rode with the archers, who hung back from the battlefield, but right at Arthur's side.

My fears were proved correct one day when the spring was just shading in to summer. It was bright and warm, and I stood with the other women at the centre of the camp, waiting. Against the bright of the sun, I could see a knight riding from the glint off his armour, but it took me a long time to recognise him against the glare. It was only when I saw the sun catch on something bright red that, with a stab of fear, I realised there were two people on the horse riding towards us. A knight, and the Queen. I stepped forward first, and the two Breton women close behind me. I saw the older one cast me a suspicious look, but I ignored her. As the knight rode closer, I saw it was Lancelot from his red and white striped shield. The Queen was slumped back against him, her eyes shut, her face pale. He had one hand around her waist, awkwardly holding her tight against him. It looked, from where I was, as though his hand was up under her armoured vest. That meant a wound. Her hair fell all around her; she had lost her mail cap, and there was mud on one side of her face and down one arm, as though she had fallen from her horse. I was sure that Arthur could not be far behind.

The two Breton women stepped forward to catch her off the horse as Lancelot stopped before them. He jumped off, tearing off his helm and throwing it aside, and he lifted her from their arms as they awkwardly tried to carry her, and strode ahead of them, the Queen in his arms, into Arthur's tent. I ran in after the Breton women.

Lancelot laid her gently on the bed and pulled off his breastplate and his greaves. His hands were already bare. One of his hands was dark with blood. He did not seem to notice. The Breton women rushed to her side, the little one gasping and fussing, the older one clicking her tongue. I thought she might have expected Lancelot to move back, but he did not. I walked around the other side of the bed to get a better look. The Queen did not look conscious.

The older Breton woman cast Lancelot a sharp look, as though she expected him to leave, but when he either did not notice, or did not care, she sighed in frustration and began to unbuckle Guinevere's armoured vest. She and the young girl lifted it away. Beneath, Guinevere had a thin vest of silk that was soaked all down one side with blood. The older woman, who was the one, I understood, with the knowledge of healing skills, leaned over her and slowly pulled up the vest at the side until the wound showed. It was a deep cut a few inches long, down her ribs, but there was no bruise, so I thought with a wary hope that the bones there were not broken. I leaned forward, to offer my help, the healing that was in my touch – for there had been enough to heal Lancelot's wounds overnight – and the older woman – whom I had liked when I had come as the English maid to Guinevere's bedroom – slapped my hand away.

"Get your death hands away from her," she snapped. Then under her breath she muttered, "*Avalon*. That's no school of medicine I have ever heard of."

Lancelot said something to her in French, too fast and low for me to understand, and she turned and started shouting at him in French.

251

I imagined it was about me, and whether or not I should be allowed to touch the Queen. He had *felt* the power of my healing, so I was sure he was defending my right to be there. Lancelot was shaking his head and gesturing at the wound in her side, and the woman was shaking her head in return, her French too fast and heavily accented with Breton for me to follow. Then, suddenly, the younger woman, who had leaned over the Queen, gasped and the other two stopped. She had two fingers in the wound, and between them, covered in blood, I could see the dark grey of a shard of iron. She pulled, and a shard the size of her thumb came out, and with it, a gush of blood. The three of them froze, staring at it in disbelief. I walked around to pick up the armoured vest, and snatch the shard, and fit it into a broken plate of armour on it. Something had struck her to break her armour, and a shard of it had embedded in her side when she fell from her horse. I was pleased to see that the shard fitted exactly, so there was nothing left inside her.

The older woman was telling Lancelot to leave in French, but he was shaking his head, saying he wanted to stay until Arthur got there. The woman rolled her eyes, and pulled the blood-stained vest off Guinevere. Lancelot turned away. I saw him blush. He should have listened to her.

"You," the older woman said to me, sharply, "make yourself useful and get some hot water."

What would happen when Arthur came to find his wife unconscious, injured, and half-naked with one of his knights refusing to leave her side?

I came back quickly with the water. The woman quickly cleaned the wound, and wrapped it with linen and pulled a clean vest over Guinevere's head, casting another dirty look at Lancelot. He did not see, he was still looking away, but the young girl, Marie, kindly tapped him on the shoulder and he turned around. Marie moved so that he could see her properly, taking a cloth soaked in the hot water and placing it against her brow. Guinevere seemed to stir a little, and murmured.

Lancelot asked the girl something in Breton, and she replied. I was surprised. I had not known that he spoke Breton, though I supposed he had grown up in France.

I could hear Arthur shouting outside the tent, and I rushed outside. He was jumping from his horse, Kay close behind him. Neither of them saw me; they both rushed inside, as though I was not even there. Lancelot left as they came in, but he did not go far. He stood with me outside, listening. Kay had not gone in far, but hung back by the entrance to the pavilion. So, he was wary, too. That meant that Arthur was angry.

For a long time it was quiet; then I heard soft voices. The Queen must have woken up. However, the soft voices soon became shouting. I could hear Arthur shouting, and I could hear the raw anger in his voice, and I was surprised to hear her shouting back, her anger as powerful as his. So, she was not afraid of him. Was he angry because she had wanted to fight? But it was more than anger, really. I had seen him. He was afraid, and upset. Suddenly, Arthur strode angrily from the tent. As he passed us, I heard him shout, "Someone take her back to Britain."

Lancelot looked at me, his eyes wide with dread. Kay followed Arthur out, shaking his head and rubbing his face. He glanced at us, gave a defeated half-smile, and walked off after Arthur.

Before the night came, a small party of knights and the older Breton woman left the camp, north, for Britain. I heard from Aggravain that Lancelot had asked to go with them and Arthur had refused, saying that he needed Lancelot with him. I sent a letter to Morgawse back with them. It said,

"Your sons are doing well at war. Much better than the Queen, who has been sent back to Britain injured. Now might be a good time to send Gareth to Camelot. Hope all are thriving in Lothian. War is very dull, but we seem to be winning. Morgan."

And we were winning. I stayed with the medicine women, still wary around Lancelot. Now that Guinevere was in Britain, both Arthur and Lancelot seemed to fight harder on the battlefield. Arthur seemed relieved his Queen had gone home.

We marched south, all the way to the south of France when summer was at its height. We had left Kay and a small garrison of knights behind to hold the retaken Breton city of Carhais, and as the weeks wore on I grew jealous of those who had stayed in the cooler north. In the south, it was unbearably hot, and the men sweated hard in their armour, and I, too, under my black woollen dress. I thought we would turn back then for Britain, but we did not.

I was lonely, but none of the other women seemed to like talking to me that much. They were guarded, secretive, awkward when I tried to make conversation. Not that I often tried. Word had got around how quickly I had healed Lancelot, and how I had not been allowed to touch the Queen, and people whispered about me. I heard what they had begun to call me. *Morgan le Fay*. They began to say I could curse a man with a look, make a woman barren with my touch. But, in the depths of the night, a few of the women who followed the camp came to me, alone and afraid, asking me to give them the drink I had taken myself long ago, when I had been with Kay's child. I had been strong, and I had had magic in my blood, but some of the girls I gave it to were weak or sickly or somehow wrong-blooded, and when the bleeding began it did not stop, and they died. I warned them well enough when I gave it to them, but I was still blamed for their deaths. I did not ask, because I did not want to know, if those children I killed were fathered by my half-brother Arthur, or my old lover Kay, or my young nephews. I doubted some of the women would even have known the names of the men who had taken them up and then casually cast them away. I did not ask their names, nor did they often want to tell me. Those women were the casualties of war that men never spoke about.

By the autumn, the camp had moved south to Marseille. Arthur, no longer distracted by the presence of his wife, spent most of his time off the battlefield with Gawain and Lancelot, talking strategy. I was pleased that Lancelot was busy, still embarrassed to have once again been kissed and rejected by him, and to have shaken us both with that awful spell. But I had learned from it, and would be more careful next time.

The time came when Arthur had to decide whether to march south into Italy and turn the attack on Lucius or, his lands defended and re-garrisoned, return home. I was surprised when I was called to his counsel on this.

When I arrived, it had already begun. Gawain was dressed in his armour with his helm in his hand, but Lancelot and Arthur were in their shirts and breeches. It was the end of the day, and someone had lit a brazier in the tent that threw a warm light through it, and warmed against the new chill of autumn in the air. There was something cosy, something homely about it that seemed desperately at odds with war, and made me long for Britain and home. Aggravain and Ector were there, too, but hanging back, listening. Arthur was pacing up and down before the other two when I arrived.

"If we pull back, securing our borders on the way, then we will lose no more men. If we march on Rome, it is riskier, but then the threat from Lucius is gone forever," he was saying, almost to himself.

"We have to attack Rome," Gawain said. "Lucius dishonoured you by attacking the lands under your protection, by demanding tribute from Britain. This is a question of honour, Arthur. We can't turn back."

Arthur nodded. I noticed Lancelot cast a wary look back at Ector, who said nothing. It must have been strange for him, having to keep his thoughts quiet around the boy he had raised as his own.

"Arthur," Lancelot began gently, "peace is better than ever more war. Lucius has suffered heavy losses. I do not think he will attack again. Meet and make terms for peace. A marriage, or something like that. Lucius has a daughter, and you have many unmarried nephews."

Gawain gave a derisive snort, as though he did not like the idea of marriage much, but Arthur seemed swayed a little by what Lancelot had said. Still, after Britain, Arthur had got a taste for war, for conquering. I knew he would want it. He was young, and he was tired of men questioning him because of it, tired, I thought, too, of being known only as Uther Pendragon's son. He had won back his father's kingdoms against the five kings, and the chance was offering itself to him, now, to be so much more than his father had been.

"Arthur," I stepped forward, cautiously, "it might be best to sue for peace. Make a marriage to seal it. Go home."

Arthur turned to look at me as though he had forgotten he had sent for me, but he did nod in agreement.

"But, Morgan, a man must have his honour," he replied softly.

"Arthur, don't you want to go back home? Back to your wife?" Arthur sighed heavily and ran a hand through his hair.

"I cannot return to her without a proper victory." I did not think she would care.

"Arthur, my Lord Arthur!" A cry came from outside the tent, and a boy ran in, barely more than a child, his face flushed, his eyes wide with fear. He was gasping for his breath as though he had run or ridden hard all day to get to us. He was gasping too hard to speak as he handed Arthur a scrap of parchment. When Arthur read it, I saw his face turn dark.

"What is it?" Lancelot asked.

Arthur crumpled the paper in his hands.

"It is Kay."

"Kay?" Lancelot asked.

"Lucius' forces have crept back up around us and attacked Carhais again. Kay and the knights with him killed them all. Kay has been injured. They are sending him back to Britain. *Why?*" Arthur shouted suddenly. He turned to me. "Morgan, why would they not send him *here*? You are here. You have saved many men's lives with your hands. *Why have they sent Kay to Britain?*" Arthur tore the letter in his hands into pieces and threw it in the fire. He rubbed his face, hard. "Well, then we have no choice," he said. "I cannot leave Kay unavenged. Lucius will be punished for this. We will march on Rome."

I saw the apprehension cross Lancelot's face, both for Kay and for the war. And I sensed the victory on Gawain's mind. Gawain had a hunger in him for glory, I could see that. I did not blame him entirely. He had knelt before Arthur in submission. I somewhat believed that Gawain wanted someone else to know how that felt. I could not say that we were entirely different, in that regard.

Kay, I thought. I had forgotten that I still cared for Kay. Certainly, I did not wish him dead. The Breton medicine woman was in Britain, at least. I did not think much of her skills, more science than art, but perhaps it would be enough.

"I want to go back to Britain," I said, suddenly. Arthur turned to me in disbelief.

"You can't, Morgan. I need you here," he said sharply.

I could feel Lancelot looking at me. He would step in to agree with Arthur, I was sure, if I objected. He would want to keep me away from Kay.

So, I was kept there, and the decision was made to march on Rome. The opposing forces were depleted, and Arthur's army swift, and so it was only the tail end of autumn when we reached the city. Lucius had gathered back his forces to defend the heart-centre of his Empire, but Arthur's army outnumbered them three to one, and when they descended on Rome it was over fast.

From where I stood in the camp with the other women, we could hear the screaming and the clashing of steel. In the evening, when the late autumn sun was setting behind Lucius' huge palace, the men pushed the great gates open and we all walked in, through the smoking city, half in ruins, many of the houses still burning, right to its centre. Arthur's men had torn through it, hungry for destruction, and I could smell in the air that there had been slaughter, and it made me sick.

Arthur stood before his men on the steps of the ancient senate-house. They were all shouting and cheering. Gawain and Lancelot stood either side of him, too, Gawain grinning with victory, Lancelot still and pensive. They did not see me in the crowd. It was only after a moment that I saw, clasped by its grey beard in Arthur's hand, the head of the Emperor Lucius.

The knights pulled up the barrels of food and of wine from the cellars of the Emperor's palace, and pulled down the benches of the senate-house into its central floor for makeshift trestle tables. When Arthur saw me, he called me to his side at the high table he had set up, with Lancelot and Gawain at his side, and Ector and Gawain's brothers further from his special favour, and I sat with them and watched as Arthur's knights drank Rome's wine and shouted and cheered and sang. Over and over again they told and re-told the stories of the final conquest, the work of that day, and I looked out over the shouting, swearing, drinking men who had torn down the benches of the senate house to make themselves a mead hall, all dirty and sweaty and bloody from battle still, and I thought *what savages we are*.

I had read some histories of Rome in the abbey – Livy's *Ab Urbe Condita*, the great epics of Virgil and Statius – and I had read the work of Roman poets and philosophers – the wry humour of Catullus and Horace, and the harsh philosophies of Seneca and the Stoics. I knew what they would make of Arthur and his rabble, who shook the heads of their enemies in front of their baying army, who tore down the ancient civilisation around them for the sake of a night of drinking and feasting. The men were wild with victory, and drunkenly grabbed at the women among them. I was glad to be far from it, to be on the high table – if it could be called such a thing. Still, the talk here was hardly less crude. Gawain was laughing with his brothers about the Emperor's daughter. I had missed the beginning of his story, and I was glad of it. I did not want to listen to my nephews talk about such things. Arthur was drunk, flushed and grinning, talking to Lancelot, who was quiet and sober at his side. He should have been drinking like the rest of them.

"I will ride back to Britain," Arthur was saying, slightly too loud, slightly too slow, "and I will tell my wife that she is an Empress now, and then I will..." Arthur made an expressive gesture, and Lancelot blushed, "love her like an Emperor should."

"If she is not still angry with you," I said, before I realised I had spoken. Perhaps I had drunk more of the Roman wine than I thought I had.

Arthur turned to me. "What are you talking about, Morgan?" he demanded.

"It did not sound to me like she wanted to be sent back to Britain," I pointed out, haughtily. I did not like the way he talked about her. It made me think of the Breton queen, to whom I felt a strange sense of duty still, long after her death.

"You don't know what you are talking about, Morgan," he replied, with a shrug. He did not seem bothered. He did not seem worried. But Lancelot caught my eye, and I knew that he understood. I stayed quiet for the rest of the feast, and when the men began to disperse, I hung back, hoping that Lancelot might want to speak with me, but he left with Arthur once Gawain had dragged one of the women out with him, and I was left to walk back to the camp on my own. In the cold autumn night the stars seemed sharp and hostile.

Chapter Forty

The journey back to Britain was slow. The army was tired and winter was setting in, and got colder and colder as we moved north. But, we returned with victory.

When we came in the great gates of Camelot, I heard the shout go up and the horns sound. There was crying and shouting with joy; it was a city welcoming back its conquering King. The boy Kay had teased as a child was now truly a great man. He had defeated an Emperor, he had made Britain safe. A small party had ridden ahead to warn of Arthur's coming, Lancelot among them, and when I rode into the courtyard beside Arthur, I saw the Queen waiting there. She had a cloak of thick grey furs around her, but beneath, a dress of plain, rough wool. She was not wearing a crown, or any jewels, and she looked thin. Was this how things had been in Camelot? I glanced through the crowd for Kay. News had not come to us of his death, so I hoped that he had survived, but it felt ill not to see him.

Arthur did not seem to notice how thin his Queen looked, how hungry his people, after his long war, but he jumped from his horse to lift her into his arms, and pull her against him in a passionate kiss before she could even speak. I saw Lancelot walk out from the stables where he must have been setting his horse to feed, and his eyes followed Arthur as he took his wife by the hand and rushed her up the stairs of his tower with him.

I was not sure that Kay would want to see me, so I waited until I was alone in my room, and I took Lancelot's shape to go looking for him. The last book I had learned from allowed me to change the shape of my clothes, too, and it was easy for me to become the man I saw almost every time my eyes closed. He was easy, so easy for me to become. Too easy.

I knew where Kay's bedroom was, and I found him there. When I pushed the door open, Kay sat up on his bed, where he had been lying, and his familiar smile spread across his face.

"Lancelot, you look well. War suits you. It did not suit me so well, as I suppose you heard."

He pulled up his shirt, and at the side of his stomach, I could see the pale knot of a scar. It should not have looked so healed already. Someone with strength in healing as great as mine – or more – had done that. It made me feel wary, uneasy. Who could it have been? Not Nimue. Nimue was many things, but she was no healer.

"You are well healed," I said, hearing Lancelot's soft French tones come from my mouth.

To my surprise, Kay gestured him – me – further into the room. I stepped in and shut the door behind me. I was not sure that I was prepared enough for what was expected of me if Kay wanted to take Lancelot to bed, but he did not seem to want to. He stood up and rubbed his face, pacing before me.

"Lancelot, I am going to tell you something I should not," he said thickly.

"What is it, Kay?" I asked.

Kay ran his hands through his hair before turning to look at me. I could see that he was trying to work out what he wanted to say.

"So, you know that I was injured and I was brought back here? Well, when I was brought here, well, I don't remember the journey. I was feverish, had strange dreams, but through those dreams – awful dreams – I began hearing this voice. It was speaking to me... in *Breton*. I did not even know that I had arrived in Camelot, or that Guinevere was here, but it was her voice I heard over and over again, in Breton and in English, saying *wish for life, wish for life*. And I remember lying side by side with her on the Round Table. I was dying Lancelot, *dying*. I had disease in my wound, and she wished it away. I felt it. It was all her. Oh, I don't know – how can it have been? But there was only darkness, and her voice. Then, when the fever passed away, and I woke, I was in Arthur's bed and she was there, sitting in a chair on the other side of the room, asleep against her hand as though she had sat up with me all night, and it was like I was seeing her for the first time. I have heard the others talking about her – Gawain, his brothers, you know, the men, the others – but it was as though I had never truly seen her before that moment. She saved my life." Kay shook his head and ran his hands through his hair again. "You were gone a year. *A year*. It was a different world here – I – it is not as if anything was said, it is not as if anything was done – I do not even know if she —" Kay shook his head, as though he was trying to shake his troubled thoughts into order. "It was easy to forget the way things truly were. You were all long gone, we were here alone, struggling to feed everyone, to keep the castle in order — but I should not have — I have *thought* things — ah, I know that sounds like nothing — but I cannot pretend that I have not imagined what it would be like — and then you all returned, and I stood at the window, and I watched Arthur jump from his horse and pick her up in his arms, and I... The world as it was here while you were all gone was an illusion. It was easy to forget, but I should not have done. He is my *brother*, whatever anyone says about blood. Arthur is my *brother* and I... But things will go back to the way they were. Yes. I am sure. I do not suppose you like to hear this, though we ought to be long past jealousy now," Kay added wryly. Then he sighed, "I wish I could undo this."

I did not know what to say. I had no comfort to offer Kay, and I was angry and disgusted that now even he was besotted with the Queen. Why would he tell Lancelot? Why would he tell Lancelot about this, and not about Morgawse, who I was sure had been meaningless to him?

"Perhaps you will forget," I offered, knowing it was a useless suggestion.

Kay reached out, and laid a hand against my arm — Lancelot's arm — and fixed me with a look that he had never given me as myself before.

"I did not forget *you*," he said. I opened my mouth to speak, but I had nothing to say.

I felt oddly embarrassed by Kay, embarrassed on his behalf, by how weak he was. Unable to let go of Lancelot, but teetering on the brink of something worse. A new obsession. I was angry with him, too, for forgetting me entirely. But, it did give me an idea. An idea of how I might begin to punish Arthur for the suffering he had caused me. He had made me a miserable marriage, and I could take his happy marriage from him. There was clearly no child involved, and so I did not see how I would be harming innocents. The only problem was, how would I convince the Queen that she should take a lover? I hoped that she was still angry with Arthur for sending her back to Britain. I hoped that would be enough.

There was a great feast held, and I did not go. I did not want to hear more men's talk of women and fighting and glory. I lay alone in my bedroom and tried to sleep, but more and more and more I

260

thought of Lancelot, and the dream I had dreamed of him long ago. It *had* to come true. It had to.

The next day, I thought I would go disguised as the English maid to see the Queen. I wanted to see how easy it would be to push her from Arthur. I caught the girl, as I had before, on the way down the stairs, and sent her off on some fool's task. She went willingly. She was afraid of my woad as anyone else, and obeyed without question.

I found the other maids waiting outside, and when I approached, the older woman, whom I remembered my dislike of, but who seemed kind enough when she was among her own, put her finger to her lips. It was the middle of the morning, past prime already, so the only reason I could imagine for Guinevere's women waiting outside her door was that Arthur was in there. Supporting my assumption was the fact that the little maid, Marie, looked as though she was holding back giggles. I was glad that I did not stand so close to the door as her.

After a while, the door opened and Arthur stepped through in his shirt and breeches, with a friendly nod to the women, and disappeared down the stairs.

The older woman, whose name I had learned only after she had left the camp as Christine, led the way into the room. Guinevere was sat in the bed, which was spread with a rich fur over the covers for the winter, with her knees drawn up and her chin resting on them, and her arms around her legs. Her hair spread loose all around her, and she pushed out her bottom lip to blow it off her face, as I had seen her do before.

Marie was chattering to her in Breton and she was replying, shrugging her shoulders. She looked a little angry, a little petulant still.

Christine clicked her tongue. "*English*, Marie."

I noticed that she only scolded the maid, never Guinevere, though it was the pair of them talking in Breton.

"There will be a tournament tomorrow," Marie said, brightly. "A great great tournament, and all the brave knights from King Arthur's war will show their strength. I am very excited." She chirruped as she pulled out an undershift from the bundle of clothes in her arms and handed it to Guinevere.

"I am not," Guinevere replied, slipping it over her head from under the warmth of the covers.

Christine clicked her tongue again. Guinevere slipped from the bed in her underdress. I saw her shiver against the cold as she stretched up, wriggling her wakefulness into her fingers.

"Men need their games," Christine said, authoritatively. "We may not like it, but they need it."

The Bretons did not joust like the French. The whole tedious pageantry of it must have seemed very strange to Guinevere.

"Arthur has been away for almost a year fighting his war, and now he wants to come back and see more fighting?" Guinevere shook her head and made a little noise of frustration as Marie pulled a dress of thick plum-coloured wool over her head. It was simple and plain. I had seen her with fine dresses before. Alone here, she must have sold them to keep Camelot in meat and grain. Guinevere held her hair up and away so that Marie could lace her into the dress, and continued, her voice sharper than I had heard it before. "He has been away at war, and I have been here on my own, not knowing if he is dead or alive, when he was coming home." Then, after a pause, and a short sigh of annoyance that seemed to pass through her whole body, she muttered, "I am sure *Arthur* was not alone all year long."

I felt the spark of victory light within me. So, she was a jealous woman, and a jealous woman that was right to know her husband well. I, too, knew Arthur as a man with a lust for women, and I had heard his own men say the same.

Christine sighed, and clicked her tongue once more. "The wise woman does not ask her husband what he has done while at war. On the battlefield or otherwise."

Guinevere did not reply. She was proud, as she had a right to be. But her pride would be an easy weapon for me to use against Arthur. Would it be so easy? And were Breton customs so different? I had heard Morgawse joke about the other women Lot had had, but then she had not loved him. Why was Guinevere even surprised enough to be angry? But I was glad of it. If she was angry with Arthur, and Kay was besotted with her, my revenge on Arthur was ready-made.

On my way down from Guinevere's bedroom, intending to go back to my own room and slip back into my own form, a familiar voice caught my attention – Lancelot's voice – and another I was sure I recognised. When I stepped out of the door of the tower, there Lancelot was, standing at the edge of the courtyard leaning against the wall, and Gareth beside him. He looked much, much older than when I had seen him last. On the cusp of manhood. But he still had the open, trusting face of a child. He had not known war.

I crept closer to try to overhear what they were saying. I was sure that they would not notice one lowly, plain maid.

"Do you have a lady?" Gareth was asking Lancelot, his voice bright with innocence, with simplicity. How little he knew, I thought. To my surprise, Lancelot gave a soft laugh in response.

"Every knight needs a lady," he told him. I saw a knowing smile play about his lips, just a little. I had never seen him like that before.

Gareth nodded. He paused a moment, cast a shy look at Lancelot, and asked again, "Is she your paramour – I mean, your lady, do you... sleep in her bedroom?"

Lancelot looked a little shocked. "Gareth, who taught you to ask that kind of question?"

Gareth blushed, deep red. But Lancelot had a lady. I felt my heart quickening within me, but I pushed down the hope. It was silly. He had not wanted me. Besides, he had not said anything definite. It would be in his interest to pretend he had a lady. It would stop people gossiping about him and Kay.

Gareth shuffled his feet on the spot, and a little sulkily tried once again to find out what a knight ought to do with his lady.

"Does she let you kiss her?"

Lancelot gave Gareth a gentle, forgiving smile. "I have kissed her."

It's me, I thought, and I pushed the thought away as soon as it came. It could not be true. It could not be me. Surely, not.

Gareth made a thoughtful noise of approval. "She must be a very beautiful lady, for a knight like you to love her."

"I think she is beautiful, but every knight thinks his own lady the most beautiful," Lancelot replied. Gareth nodded, studiously, as though he was trying to remember everything Lancelot said.

"Does she love you?" Gareth asked.

Lancelot gave a strange sigh. "I am sure she does. I can feel it, when I am near her, like the heat coming off a fire." He sounded sad, and Gareth was as confused as I was. I, also, was embarrassed. Was it so obvious? I was not sure I knew it myself. I knew I wanted Lancelot, but he felt *love* coming from me, whenever we were close?

"Is that bad?" Gareth asked, confused. "Do you not love her the same?"

Lancelot turned to Gareth, and put a comforting hand on his shoulder. "I love her the same. I never stop thinking about her, and when I feel her eyes on me, it feels like the touch of the sunshine. But there are some things that cannot be. That should not be. When a boy becomes a man, he has to learn the difference between what he *wants* to do and what he *should* do. There are others who would suffer if my lady and I were to give in to the fullness of our love, and it is a man's duty to do what is right."

I saw Gareth's face fall under such seriousness, and felt my own heart sink in my chest. It *was* me, and Lancelot was keeping himself away for – for what? For Kay's sake? For Arthur's? Why were these brave men always so wary of offending one another? What about me? He ought to have cared what I wanted.

One kiss, and a love that we both felt, that loyalty to others held us back from. It was both joy and pain to hear him say it. But I had suffered waiting before; I had suffered holding back with Kay, because Kay was wary of Arthur. I would not again. I would be brave.

"Oh," Gareth said, and he sounded a little disappointed. "Well, I have a lady, too. But she will not kiss me, and I do not think she loves me. Not like a lady loves a knight, anyway."

"Who is she?" Lancelot asked.

"The Queen," Gareth said proudly, and he flushed deeply again when Lancelot laughed. "Everyone laughs at me. I'm serious. I told Kay the Seneschal and now all he does is make fun of me. But I think she is the most beautiful lady in all of Britain."

Lancelot's smile became softer, more thoughtful, but he turned to Gareth in comfort. "Don't worry about Kay the Seneschal. If he makes fun of you, that means he is fond of you."

Gareth nodded, but did not seem comforted. I had stopped listening, though, and bright with hope I rushed up to my bedroom. Lancelot *did* want me. Well, if he dared not act on it that did not matter, for I did. If he wanted something honourable, something that would not betray the trust that Arthur and Kay had in him, then that could be done. After all, I was a young widow, and he a single man. I was Queen of my lands, and he my equal – or thereabouts – in lands and wealth. I let myself slip back into my own shape, and pulled on my dress of black gems, and rushed down to the courtyard, hoping he was still there. Now was the moment, I was sure of it.

When I saw him, standing on his own now, watching Gareth play-fighting with Kay, with his words still fresh in my mind, and quickening in my heart, I walked over towards him. He turned when he saw me, and our eyes met. I felt the flutter of nervousness pass through me, but he gave me a gentle smile when he saw me.

"Are you well, Morgan?" he asked. I nodded, smiling tentatively back at him. He looked as though he was waiting to fight, dressed in the light armour that the men trained in. He looked good, with a light flush from the winter chill on his cheeks, and his hair blown through by the wind. He pulled off one of his gloves to take my hand in his. It was gentle, intimate.

"You look well," he told me. It was awful and wonderful to feel his bare skin against mine. I let my eyes blink shut for a long moment, and I could almost feel his lips against me. When I opened my eyes, he was leaning down towards me, and my heart jumped within me, for I thought he was going to kiss me, but it was only on the cheek, sweet and brotherly. But of course it was. We were in public, and I his King's sister. He wanted a wife, not a lover, and I was more than happy to give him what he wanted to get what I wanted.

"Come with me," I said, feeling excited already. He would not say no. He would be pleased, that what he had wished for, that he had thought he could not have would be suddenly his. He would be grateful that it was I of the two of us who had dared to be brave. We would be happy together. I would not be lonely in Rheged. We could have a child of our own. I had *seen* us together in love. Lancelot would not have wanted to betray Arthur by dishonouring his sister; he did not have to. I did not know why I had not thought of it before.

I found Arthur in his council chamber. The old table had been replaced by a big, round table that I thought must have been the Round Table that Kay had mentioned; Leodegrance's witches' table that had been part of Guinevere's dowry. I could feel its ancientness and its power. I could not believe that Arthur would be foolish enough to simply sit around it to see to the affairs of his lands. I expected that that, too, made Guinevere angry.

Arthur looked up in surprise to see us, me eager with excitement, Lancelot trailing behind me, confused but pliant. I thought he would be truly well pleased when he realised that I knew what he wanted.

"Arthur," I said, trying to keep the girlish excitement from my voice, "I have had a wonderful idea. Lancelot and I should be married."

I saw Arthur struggle to keep a smile from his face. Of course *he* thought it was funny. Lancelot was handsome, and I was thin and plain. I glanced to Lancelot. He was shocked.

"Think about it, Arthur," I continued. "Then your greatest knight would also be your brother."

Arthur was only pretending to think about it. I felt foolish already; I felt myself burn with humiliation. Arthur was trying not to laugh. Plain Morgan, thinking Lancelot, the great knight, the handsome hero of the wars would want her. He thought I was ridiculous for thinking a man might want me. But even if Lancelot did not love me as he had said he had, there was no reason for us *not* to be married. There was nothing *wrong* with me. I had produced a son. Together, we might have had as many sons as my sister. I felt myself blush. Why were they acting as though it were so ridiculous?

Arthur turned to Lancelot, and I could hear he was holding back laughter.

"Lancelot, what do you think about this?"

I saw Lancelot wince. He was not going to accept me. Why not? There was nothing wrong with me. He had *said* he loved me to Gareth. I had been brave.

Lancelot sighed, and I could tell that he was trying to be kind. "I never thought to be a wedded man. Marriage is well enough for kings, Arthur, but if I had a wife I would have to leave off tournaments and battles, and journeying, and that is not the life I want."

This is about Kay, I thought.

I rounded on Lancelot, and in the face of my burning anger, burning from the humiliation that went with it, I saw him reel back a little.

"You are refusing me, then?" I demanded. How could he be doing this, now? After everything that he had said?

I did not wait for the answer. I could see it in his eyes. Why was Lancelot such a coward? Of whom was he so afraid? It was just an excuse, his desire to continue fighting and journeying. No man wanted that when they could be with a woman they loved.

Well, I had ways of making him brave. I would have the truth from him. He would not refuse me again, just because he was afraid. Was he afraid that the others would laugh at him? *Morgan le Fay* — Lancelot was weak enough to fear the other knights making fun of him. Enamoured of his own wonderful reputation. A knight of great repute could not marry a plain, widowed witch. So it was not just about right and wrong, but about honour in the nastiest, meanest way.

I went to my book of medicines, and there it was. The drink that would make Lancelot give in to his heart, which would free the truth from him. I would have it. I was brave, even if he was not.

Chapter Forty-One

The morning of the tournament, I went to catch the dull girl again, to try to find out as much as I could of Guinevere's secrets, but when I met her on the stairs, she had a black lacquered box in her hands. I noticed her shy back from me. Perhaps she was less dull-witted than I had thought.

"Margery," I said sharply, "what is in that box?"

"It is a gift for the Queen, from the King, my Lady."

"Show it to me," I said, softly.

With blind obedience, Margery opened the box, and I recognised the crown instantly. Arthur had robbed it from the treasures of Rome. It was the crown of Queen Cleopatra. It was shaped like two snakes coiled together, with eyes of bright emerald. I reached out and laid a hand gently against the cool gold.

"I'll follow you up, Margery," I told her. "I want to see the Queen put it on."

"Let me give it to her first," Margery begged softly, and I agreed. I waited outside until she came back outside to bring me in with her. I supposed she didn't want the Queen to think that she was more my woman than hers. Little did either of them know.

She pushed the door open, and the first thing I saw was Guinevere standing framed in her window against the bright winter morning. She was dressed in a dress of rich green brocade embroidered in gold thread with crosses. It was tight enough to hide how thin she had grown while Arthur had been at war. Arthur must have brought the dress back with him, too, or at least bought it with gold taken from Rome, for Camelot's fine things had dwindled while we were gone. Her hair was plaited and twisted into a bun at the nape of her neck, held in place by a gold and emerald net, and she was leaning her head forward for Marie to clip a chain of gold that had hanging off it hundreds of little emeralds around her neck. It seemed that the treasures had returned all at once, with the victory.

"Morgan said she had to see it," Margery said, as I stepped into the room.

Guinevere turned to me, and a thoughtful look passed over her face, as though she were seeing me properly for the first time. She did not look surprised or afraid at my woaded face, but she did not look friendly either.

In her hands was Cleopatra's crown. I stepped forward and took it from her. She did not shy away from me as I took it, so our hands brushed. Hers were soft, and warm. I set Cleopatra's crown on her head, among the thick curls of her hair. It fitted perfectly.

"That crown," I said softly, fixing her with a serious look, "was taken by Arthur from the treasures of Rome. It belonged to the Queen Cleopatra, who was the lover of two Emperors, or... one and a half." I paused. Her gaze on me was steady, unreadable. I could not stop thinking of her mother, and her on the battlefield in her armour. Perhaps Arthur knew her better than I thought. This was not a gift for a queen who stayed in her castle looking pretty. This was the gift for a powerful warrior queen. Then I remembered Merlin's words again, *halfwits make good wives*. A clever, brave, jealous wife seemed to me not so likely to also be an obedient and faithful wife. "She was a fearsome queen, who rode with her people into war. He must have thought it an appropriate gift for you, my Lady."

The ghost of a smile flickered across Guinevere's face, but I did not think she would smile for me. She reached up and touched the crown on her head, her face thoughtful. She murmured some kind of thank you, and I left.

I sat for the jousting at the back of the raised platform that Arthur shared with those he favoured most. Guinevere sat at his side, the stolen crown on her head, and a thick fur of white flecked with black around her shoulders against the cold. I was wearing my dress of black gems, and wore one of my mother's old furs. Not as rich as the Queen's, nor as fine as the cloak of white fur Arthur had over his red and gold surcoat, but warm enough.

For the most part, the jousting was dull. Those expected to do well did well; Gawain, his brothers, Lancelot and Kay. When Lancelot rode into the field, I noticed that he had a cloth of gold tied to his helm, and I turned to the woman beside me – the wife of some knight or other who had found particular favour with Arthur during the war – and asked her whose token it was.

"Oh, don't you know?" the woman replied, with a smug smile to know more than the King's own sister. "Sir Lancelot rides for the Queen. He has been named her champion, since he saved her life on the battlefield."

I watched Lancelot ride, knocking man after man down, and I watched Guinevere's eyes follow her cloth of gold back and forth up and down the jousting field. When he was not there, she looked bored and restless. Arthur was gripped by it all, and by the way he sat forward in his chair, I could tell he longed to be out there in the lists.

At last, it was only Kay in his black Otherworld armour and Lancelot left. When they crashed together, both men fell from their horses, and a shout came from the crowd. Guinevere, too, got to her feet. I saw Arthur reach out and take her hand, saying something comforting, but she did not look away from Lancelot and Kay, fighting on foot now. I could not see properly from where I was, but I knew what the outcome would be, anyway. Lancelot would win. Far more interesting was the fact that Guinevere had jumped to her feet when they fell from their horses. She had been alone with Kay in Camelot all winter long, healing him of his wound, perhaps telling him her secrets. They both had Otherworld blood in their veins, and I knew that he had grown fond of her. More than fond. What had he said? *I cannot pretend that I have not imagined what it would be like.* What had he imagined? What it would be like to kiss her? To tell her how he felt about her? To hear her tell him she felt the same? To take her to bed? Things he should never have imagined of his foster-brother's wife. And she had jumped to her feet when she saw him fall. Could it be true? She was angry with Arthur, blamed him for leaving her alone in Camelot, suspected him of having other women while he was on campaign. Kay was handsome, charming and kind, and she had saved his life. It was not unreasonable to believe that a natural affection had grown between them. Would it be so easy?

After Lancelot had been declared the victor, Guinevere rushed away, though I knew we were all supposed to be going on to a great feast to celebrate – once more – Arthur's great victory.

I slipped away, too, and followed her up to her room. If she was going to crack, I would have to push her now, while she was flustered and vulnerable. I was slow through the crowd that she had evaded with her swift exit, and by the time I got to her chamber, she seemed to be about to leave for the feast. She had taken off her crown and set it on the table by her window, and thrown off her furs. I could see the flush against the pale skin of her chest still, though, and a promising wildness in her eyes. I shut the door behind me, and leaned back against it. I wondered if I could coax her into some kind of feminine confidence with me, as I had seen her share with her Breton maids.

"Morgan," she said, softly, "are you coming down to eat?"

She was polite, but distant.

I glanced at the crown on the table.

"You're not wearing the crown," I observed. I wondered if she had taken it off because of what I had said about Cleopatra being the lover of two different men.

"It's heavy," she answered, drawing back into herself. I saw I would not win her confidence. She was resistant, defensive.

"You should," I told her. She did not react. She gave a little impatient sigh as though she wanted me to move out of the way. I tried one last time. I could not appeal to her sympathy, but I could appeal to her pride.

"I took a lover," I told her. I had her attention. "Many men do it, some women. We should do as they do, our husbands. That is, just as we please."

"I do just as I please," she answered immediately, her voice cold and sharp. I had her. She had been easy to tempt. The proud always were.

"As does Arthur," I replied, slipping away through the door, leaving her with the thought.

I went to my own room then, to collect the drink I had mixed for Lancelot. Perhaps it was risky, distracting myself with this second quest of mine, but I wanted both. I wanted Arthur's wife *and* Lancelot to be free to express their own desires. His for me, hers for Kay. And why should I not encourage her? Would she not be better with a kind man like Kay, than one like Arthur who boasted to his men of the nights they spent together? I had been happier once I had had a lover. I was not entirely sure that I was ready to offer Kay up to another, but I did not think I would care once I had the truth from Lancelot. It would be worth the exchange.

I came early to the feast. Lancelot would take his place beside the Queen as her champion, so it was easy to fill his cup with what I had brought before anyone else arrived. I was pleased to see that Nimue was there, and to see her sit at my side. She had made her threats, and she was friendly enough now. She thought that I had submitted myself to her. I had helped Arthur. She seemed to have forgiven me. She even told me she had missed me.

Kay and Lancelot came in together, and Kay sat in the seat beside Lancelot. I saw him notice that Lancelot's cup was the only one that was already filled, and glance at me, but I looked away before he could catch my eye. The seats around us were filling, and the men were filling their cups with wine, so it stood out less. I was beginning to feel the little glow of victory about me when Lancelot seemed to be about to drink from his cup, but then I saw him notice something, a speck of dust or dirt on the cup waiting in the space beside his. Guinevere's cup. I noticed, too, that she had not yet arrived. Lancelot swapped the cups over, with that thoughtless deferential instinct that he should spare his Queen the dirty cup. Kay went to stop him, but it was too late, and Kay would not get the cups switched back, for at that moment, Guinevere entered the hall and took her place beside Arthur. As soon as she sat, she reached for her cup and took a deep drink from it. I saw Kay wince.

I was sorry that I would not have the truth from Lancelot, but perhaps this would be even better. Perhaps the Queen would finish her cup and then throw herself into Kay's arms. I could hope for that. Arthur, who seemed to have arrived at the feast from some other celebration of the tournament with Gawain – whose loud voice I could hear already garrulous with wine – leaned over and pressed a clumsy kiss against his wife's cheek. I thought I saw a look of distaste flicker across her face. Arthur's war was already fracturing them apart, and her jealousy, and Arthur's complete obliviousness.

As the feast went on and the hall filled with the heat of people drinking and celebrating, and the smell of the firewood, even I, whose head was clear of wine, was feeling a little hazy. Still, I kept my eyes on the Queen, and I knew Kay was watching her as well. I ate a little of the food; it was sweet and rich, and I had never lost my taste for plain, simple food that I had acquired in the abbey. The flush came quick to Guinevere's cheeks, and, for the first time in public, I saw her bright smile break across her face as she began to loosen up with the drink I had given her. She was talking to Lancelot beside her, but I could see Kay's eyes following her movements, following the cup as she lifted it again to her lips. She had finished it already, and someone had re-filled the cup with wine. I had mixed it for a full-grown man, and Lancelot was, I would have guessed, half her weight again.

Nimue beside me was, to my surprise, drinking heartily from her own cup, giggling with the knight Dinadan beside her, a small, quick-eyed man with a keen smile. I wondered if she was drinking because she did not like so well to look on Arthur and his wife. She met with him alone. Perhaps she liked to pretend that the wife did not exist.

Suddenly, it turned. Guinevere pressed the palms of her hands into the table as though she were steadying herself. I could see her flush darker for a moment, and then pale. It *had* been too much. Lancelot beside her was asking her if she was alright, but she did not seem to hear him. She pushed herself up to her feet, blowing her breath out slow, trying to get herself under control. I noticed, with annoyance, that even reeling and sick, there was some kind of fierce perfection to her, a kind of abandon all about her that I did not want to look away from.

Arthur beside her suddenly seemed to notice that she was standing. He reached out and took her hand, his gaze up at her tender, and loving, but bleary with wine.

"My love, where are you going?" he asked.

271

She shook her head, as though trying to shake away the dizziness. If only Kay had managed to stop Lancelot. "I don't feel well," she said, thickly, her Breton accent stronger with the wine.

"We're only beginning. Stay, come on." Arthur groaned in disappointment and pulled her into his lap. I saw the flash of anger go across her face, and the flush light once more in her cheeks. This time it was not my drink. He leaned closer to her, in a way I imagined he felt to be appealing, and continued. "I'm not finished with you for the night."

Guinevere jumped from his lap.

"If you are looking for a woman who will go to your bed whenever *you* desire it, *my Lord*, I suggest you send for a whore," she shouted. The chatter about the table went quiet.

She turned and stormed from the room. I could not have been more pleased with my mistake. This was almost as good as having the truth from Lancelot. Arthur stared after her, his mouth open. He did not see what he had done wrong. Of course he did not. I glanced around the table. Kay, too, stared after her in disbelief, Lancelot down at his plate, blushing. Gawain and Aggravain sat side by side, twin pictures of indignation to hear their King so spoken to by his own wife.

There was a moment of awful stillness before, as I knew he would, Kay made to stand. Lancelot put his hand over Kay's – for once Arthur was too distracted to object – and said, softly, "No – I will go."

And he slipped from his chair and followed her. Well, the drink had got the truth from someone. Kay cast a dark look at me, but I did not care. He would be grateful one day that my other desires would help him get his.

Chapter Forty-Two

I wanted to change into Guinevere's English maid and slip up to her room the next morning, but as soon as I was out of my bedroom door, Kay jumped out, as though he had been waiting for me, and grabbed me by the shoulders, pulling me back into the room with him and kicking the door shut.

"I don't know what new game you were playing last night, Morgan, but *it has to stop*," he hissed.

I pushed him off me.

"I don't know what you are talking about," I replied. He looked as though he had slept in his clothes overnight. He was just in his shirt and breeches, his hair ruffled still with sleep.

I could see Kay straining to find the words for his anger.

"Morgan," he whispered, tersely, "I don't know if you're trying to punish me, or if you have just got so deep into your black magic that it has eaten away your mind, but trying to *drug* Lancelot? What has he ever done to harm you?" When I did not answer, Kay stepped further into my room and I rushed to block his way. I had left my book of medicine recipes open on the desk. "What did you use? What was it?" Kay cried, jumping for the book. I grabbed it as he did, and we both pulled hard towards ourselves. There was an awful crack, and I thought the book would break in two, but it held. Kay was surprised enough by the sound of the binding cracking that he let go just enough for me to snatch it off him, and I hugged it to my chest.

"Morgan," Kay growled, "give me the book."

I shook my head, stepping back.

Kay lunged forward and grasped the book again. He was stronger than me by far, but my arms were wrapped tight around the book. I stumbled back, and we crashed back together against the wall, and for a moment we struggled still for hold of the book. But then as suddenly as we had begun fighting, we were kissing. Hard, angry kisses. I did not know who had begun first, if it was he or I, but I could not pretend that his body pressed up close against mine in anger had not brought to my mind vivid memories of us pressed together in that same room in the depths of passion. We were different people now, and that love was gone, but it was a long time since I had felt the love of a man. Kay pulled the book from my hands, and this time I let him, and he threw it away, down to the floor beside us, pushing me harder against the wall. For a moment, I didn't care that he probably wasn't thinking of me. I didn't care that he must have been imagining thick coils of red hair between his fingers rather than my own fine brown strands. I, too, was thinking of another. But then, all those imagined images of him with her crowded around me, and my memories, too, of him with Morgawse, and all at once his mouth hot against mine and his hands wrapping around my waist and pulling me against him repulsed me, and I shoved him back.

"You should go, Kay," I said, coldly.

His eyes were unfocussed, his mind lost in some far-off dream of another, and I seized the opportunity. I reached down and picked the book up from the floor where he had thrown it, and wrapped my arms around it once more. Kay's look hardened. He never smiled at me anymore. He never laughed. From across the courtyard, I had seen him laughing with Guinevere, favouring her with his charming smile. That was lost to me now.

"It is not too late to give up the Black Arts, Morgan," he said.

He reached out towards the book, and I stepped back from him, fast.

"Leave," I snapped.

He stepped through the door, and I slammed it shut behind him.

After that, I kept a wary eye on all that happened around me. I did not try to put anything in Lancelot's drink again, because I felt Kay's eyes always upon me, but I watched him. I watched as Lancelot and Guinevere began to ignore each other more and more concertedly in public. At first, I thought she was angry with him. I had seen her anger, tense and passionate as it was, and the more I saw, the more different I thought this was. As spring broke around us, I could not understand how everyone else around could find it bearable, the way they would never look at one another. Kay, too, was often around Guinevere, but her way with him was friendly, and easy, and he seemed the same with her, despite the feelings he had confessed to me, thinking I was Lancelot.

Something was going on. Had Lancelot warned her off Kay, as he had tried to do with me? Was that what made her angry? Nimue told me that news had come that Mark in Cornwall was being besieged by a giant and had sent to Arthur for help. She told me that Kay had named Lancelot to go. I thought this might be why Guinevere was angry, but why would she then not be angry with Kay? I was determined to find out what was spoiling my plan. Arthur called the knights to his council, for the decision to be made who would go to Cornwall. *Mark.* Mark had taken what was mine. I did not know why Arthur should help him. Mark had, too, married Isolde of Ireland, the people in Camelot were saying, who was almost as much younger than him as Morgawse had been younger than Lot when she had married. Just another thing a king was owed, I supposed – a young wife.

I was not called to the council, though Nimue was, so I would know what had happened there. I waited until I saw Kay walk across the courtyard, and stepped out into his path. He looked angry, upset.

"I'm sorry, Kay," I said, grasping his hand and pulling it across my eyes. The Otherworld was strong enough in his blood that I would get from him what I could have given to him through just my touch on his skin. I felt the little lurch, and then we stood there, he and I,

274

looking at him and Lancelot and Guinevere, sat around the Round Table. Kay lounged in his seat beside Guinevere, who was staring hard at Lancelot, who was looking shyly down, away from both of them. Kay was not practised in magic, so the image we saw before us was blurry, and I could not hear what any of them were saying, but I could see well enough what was going on. Guinevere wanted to talk to Lancelot, but Kay would not leave. Kay was teasing her, and made a playful grab towards her. I saw the name *Gareth* on Kay's lips, and I knew what he was teasing her about. She slapped his hand away and shouted at him. Somehow, wordless and silent, her anger was all the more powerful. Kay, visibly hurt even through the blur of his unpractised memory, pushed back his chair and walked angrily out. We did not follow his memory. I glanced beside me. Kay looked confused, and worried, his eyes fixed on the scene before us. I felt a flutter of nerves in my stomach, and I was not sure why. There was something about the way Lancelot and Guinevere sat across the table from one another in silence, him looking away from her gaze, which felt unbearably tense. I noticed, too, that Arthur was not there. *Where is Arthur?*

Lancelot stood to leave and Guinevere moved into his path, crossing her arms stubbornly across her chest. They were arguing. They must have been arguing about Cornwall. Or perhaps they were arguing about Kay. Lancelot turned away from her in frustration and she stepped towards him, putting a hand on his shoulder, though not in comfort. It was demanding. It was the hand of a queen commanding her champion to listen to her. He turned fast, grabbing her by the wrist. She jumped back, and he let her go. I glanced at Kay again. His eyes were fixed on the room in front of him. Lancelot turned away from her, closing his eyes and bracing himself against the back of one of the chairs, as though he was trying to get his anger under control. What was she saying to make him so angry? I did not think I had ever seen Lancelot angry. But then I realised, he was not angry. While she was still shouting at him, he turned in a flash and pulled her against him, into a kiss. I could not tear my eyes from their lips coming together. I had felt that kiss, I had felt its sensual passion, the intoxicating touch of Lancelot's lips, soft yet overwhelming. She melted in his arms, her anger, like his, becoming passion, and she wound her hands into his hair. He pushed her back against the table, his lips against her neck, and lifted her lightly on to it. She leaned her head back at his touch, her eyes fluttering closed, and her lips parted slightly in a sigh of longing. I felt the blush rise in me at the sight of it, but I could not look away. I had *never* seen Lancelot like that; never so bold, never so wild. I barely recognised him. Suddenly, they jumped apart, hearing something that was missing from what Kay and I could witness, Guinevere pushing her skirts back down to the ground, Lancelot turning away, and Arthur strode into the room.

That was when it faded, and Kay and I stood face to face in the courtyard, in the cool spring night, the stars bright above us, both shocked, shaken, betrayed. I could not take it in. When I had encouraged Guinevere to take a lover, I had not intended for her to take *mine*. *Oh no*, I thought. *Oh no, no, no*. The day he had come looking for her in Arthur's camp. That it had been he who caught her when she fell from her horse; he had been watching her. It was he, not Kay, for whom she had jumped to her feet as she watched them fight. Everything he had said: *I have a lady*, he had said. One whom he could not be with, for the sake of others. It was not me.

"Morgan," he breathed, "is what we saw... the truth?"

I nodded, and Kay rubbed his face with his hands.

"Well," Kay said, "then he must go to Cornwall, mustn't he?"

But it seemed that Kay did not need to push Arthur to send Lancelot, for Lancelot had volunteered himself. Arthur seemed to have no idea what he had walked into the night before, but was his usual cheery self, clapping Lancelot on the back and congratulating him on his bravery for volunteering. Guinevere was quiet and showed nothing.

I could hardly believe that it was true. I walked through the castle like a ghost. The day before I had been on the brink of a love-affair, and now I was rejected once more.

I had to see Guinevere again. I had to go and look at her, see what she had that I lacked. Why had I dreamed of us together, Lancelot and I, in the clear dreams of the future, if it was not to be? I set off towards Guinevere's room. I would not have to pretend to be someone else just to look at her. All I wanted to do was look. But I was caught on the way by the sound of her voice coming from the little walled garden that sat at the foot of her tower. As I crept closer, I heard that Lancelot was with her. Was she so bold? So reckless? They were arguing again, but their voices were soft and I could not hear the words until I came to the entrance to the garden and hid behind the stone archway that led inside.

"No. You don't have to come to me, I'll come to you. I have gone out hunting in the woods before; Arthur won't deny me. No one will suspect. Go up to my room, and take the book of Ovid. Send it to me, when you are ready, and I will find you." She paused for a moment. Perhaps he spoke, but his voice was too soft to hear. They made a strange pairing; him shy and quiet, her angry and demanding. But then, I would think myself the better match, would I not? "Tell me it's not what you want, that you don't love me, and I will not ask you again," I heard her say, softly. They were talking in English. I was sure that Lancelot understood at least a little Breton. It was foolish of them, reckless. What if I were Arthur?

There was a sudden quiet from the garden, and, my heart thudding, I peered through the archway. I could see them clasped together in a kiss, her hands in his hair, his around her waist, both lost in it. I could see the petals tucked into the plait of her hair, twisted up into a bun. I had seen that hair loose and wild, and he had not, and I had known him in my dreams in a way she had not yet known him, and neither of them knew the intimacy I had had with them both, and neither of them saw me. She not at all, he not really. She had taken a lover from her husband's knights, as I had, and yet hers would live. No man – not even Arthur – would kill Lancelot. He was *mine*, too, and she had taken him for her own. But she was bolder than I had ever been, wilder and far more lovely. What was left for me, for women like me, when there were women like her?

I forced myself away. Suddenly, awfully, I was filled with same feeling that I had had when I had stood before Accolon with Excalibur drawn in my hands. *This is a moment of destiny*, I thought. I had not seen this moment, but with a sudden cold dread I realised that I had seen the moments afterwards. Lancelot, the pavilion, the springtime. My skin, pale white and unmarked by woad. It was *her* skin. I was her in my own dream. Was that really something I would do? Something I *could* do? I thought, once again, of the Lady of Avalon, long dead now, and her words about Arthur's conception. *He does not know it, but he is a child of rape.* I was not sure I was capable of it, and yet I knew, I knew with a deep and empty dread, that I was, and that it had to be.

Chapter Forty-Three

I did not have to wait long. Every day, I waited in the shape of the clumsy English maid at the foot of the stairs until the book came back. It was less than a week. Lancelot was, then, more eager even than he had seemed.

On a bright spring morning, I stood at the bottom of the stairs when a grubby peasant boy, paid for the errand with a shiny silver coin I pressed into his hand, handed me the book of Ovid. I glanced down at it. I had seen it before among Guinevere's books. I could see why she was not hesitant to hazard it. It was a paltry thing – a small volume of Ovid's stories, translated into French and bastardised with clumsy morals tacked on the end. I took it back to my bedroom, and opened it. Inside the front cover, Lancelot had written something in French. It said, *Edge of the woods. Seven miles north.* I felt my heart flutter within me.

Whose will was I doing? My own? I was not sure I wanted it this way. I wanted Lancelot to want *me*, not to have him in the guise of someone else. But perhaps it would be good to prise him from his affection for the Queen. Better for everyone. Suddenly, as clear as the time I had seen it first, I saw once more the vision I had had in Avalon of Arthur, his head bare, fallen from his horse, and Lancelot standing over him with his sword drawn and lifted, ready to strike. Would this be my revenge on Arthur? And something for myself? What did destiny want from me? If I turned back from this moment, all that I had seen might not come to pass. I would never stand on the shores of Avalon with Excalibur in my hand. It had to be. It *all* had to be.

Once I was sure, I went back in the shape of the maid Margery again, and from the rumpled sheets of Guinevere's bed, I took her nightdress, and tucked it among my own belongings.

I took my leave of Arthur, saying I had to return to my own kingdom. Arthur seemed sorry that I wanted to depart, but my young son was enough of an excuse to sway him. I had not brought a retinue – no ladies, no knights – so it was easy for me to gather my belongings and leave. I did not know the place, so I had to ride north until I found it. I felt tense and sick inside, but sure that this was the only path that I could take. It was what destiny demanded.

When I came upon the pavilion it was empty. I had some of the mixture I had made before left, and I took the opportunity to pour it into the skin of wine I found among Lancelot's things. It would be for the better if he was hazy, and unquestioning.

When I had had a good sight of the place, I closed my eyes and pictured myself back in the stables of Rheged. They were not empty when I opened my eyes and found myself there, but that was all to the good. My own people knew I was a witch, and were afraid of me. No one questioned me anymore; no one suggested that a woman should not govern her dead husband's lands and castle. I did not mind that the quality of their respect was tinged with fear, only that I had it, and had it without question. I took my belongings back to my room, and locked the door. I pulled out Guinevere's nightdress. It was soft, thin silk, and the scent of it, oddly familiar. Had I spent so long around her, come so close, to know so well the delicate smell of rose petals in her hair, of the fresh grass? I shrugged away the strange, unsettling feeling of it, and pulled off my own dress, and the nightdress on, and stood before the mirror to watch myself become the woman who had everything. My hair, brightening from dark brown to deep, rich red, the patterns fading from my skin, the lines of my face softening, just a little, and my body shrinking, my long limbs moving more into lithe, feminine proportions. I smoothed down the dress over the body that was newly mine. I felt tense, but the sight of myself as her was oddly comforting. We were not so different. We were both angry. We both loved Lancelot. We would both stand on the shores of Avalon, with Excalibur. I knew so much of her, I had dreamed so much of her, I wondered if I was not, already, fading into her. *It is easy to lose oneself in another's shape.*

I closed my eyes, and pictured Lancelot's pavilion on the edge of the woods. I saw the light in the pavilion before anything else, glowing dark purple through the silk fabric of its walls. Then I saw the trees around it, as I had pictured them, and the low, soft grass around it in the little clearing. The night was dark, and clear. I could see the stars bright overhead, and a sliver of the growing moon. A good time for it. I began to feel the world more solidly around me, the grass beneath my bare feet, the light spring breeze on my cheeks, and through the thin silk of my stolen dress. It was strange to see my hands before me without the blue of the woad, to feel the different movements of another's body. She was a little stronger, a little more lean and muscular than I. But it was not really her body tonight. It was mine.

I walked over slowly, and stepped into the pavilion. For a moment, Lancelot did not notice, as he sat in a small wooden chair, staring into the low coals of the brazier. They lit his face orange, casting shadows against his high cheekbones, his thoughtful mouth. A gust of breeze flapped the tent door, and the noise of it made him look up. He saw me then, and as though unconsciously, as though moving in a dream, he stood to his feet. Taken with a sudden rush, he strode across the pavilion towards me. He gently took my face in his hands, and pressed his forehead lightly against mine. I could feel the fluttering of my heart within me, the heat already kindling deep within. I forced myself to push away the thought that it was not me that he saw. I turned my face up towards his, closer, and I felt his nose brush against mine as he leaned down to me.

"Guinevere," he whispered, but I did not care. He drew me into a kiss. On his lips I tasted the wine, and the heady spice of the herbs that I had given him in it. I felt the slightest tremble of desire run through me, like a spark of fire. I pushed him back gently towards the pile of silk cushions beside the brazier and the chair. I slid my hands up under his shirt, feeling the hardness of muscle beneath, the softness of his skin, and the brush of the soft, inviting hair that ran down from his navel. I should have held back, I should have been more cautious, but I had waited so long, and the desires of my body were clouding my mind. I had dreamed long ago of this, and I had waited and waited and this was the moment, and I could not hold myself back from it. I pulled the shirt up over his head, and threw it aside. He drew away then, holding my face gently in his hands.

"Guinevere," he whispered, his voice thick with anxiety that I had not expected, "I have to tell you, I... You are used to a man who has known many women. There has been – I have known no other woman. I... I am not sure that I know exactly –"

I rested my fingertips lightly against his lips, and shushed him gently. He closed his eyes for a second, and I felt his lips yield slightly under my touch. I took a step back from him, and unwound my hair. I was half-surprised to see it fall, thick and red, in curls around me. I was already forgetting that I had come in another's shape. Then I reached down and slowly pulled the fine silk dress up over my head, and stood naked before him. I saw his eyes mist over with desire, and a low sigh escaped his lips.

"I am sure nature will take its course," I replied softly. The voice when I spoke was her voice; low and sweet with its Breton tones.

Lancelot did not need any more prompting. I expected him, however, to rush at me all at once the way all the others had done, wild with desire. He no longer hesitated, but his touch was light and teasingly slow as he ran his hands over me. I had never been touched like that; not by a man whose eyes were full of wonder, not by one who wanted to know every inch, not by one who was not hasty to have his own pleasure. He let me wait until I was wild for him, my body aching, though no longer because he did not dare. I slipped him from his clothes and pulled him down among the silk cushions with me. And then it was all the cool silk of the cushions, and the fresh smell of the grass, and his hands sliding up my thighs, still making me wait; and though I had thought that I would have to lead him through this, I found there was greater delight in committing myself to this sensuality that I had not known before. And when I took him inside me at last, it was with all the rapturous relief that my dreams of him had promised. Everything else fell away, but the pleasure of the moment.

In the darkness afterwards, he whispered, "I love you."

He does not mean you, I told myself, but I could not stop myself from believing it.

I dreamed strange dreams that night. I dreamed of Guinevere, lying out in the grass of the clearing, asleep in the moonlight in the nightdress I had stolen. It was she, but her pale skin was traced with blue-green woad, and when I went over to her, and knelt beside her, she stirred and murmured my name. In her sleeping hands she held Excalibur, clasped tight in her grip, and when I reached for it, the dream faded away.

I woke suddenly in the morning, my heart racing, as though from a bad dream. I sat up sharply in the pile of cushions, and Lancelot murmured beside me and turned over in his sleep. It was cold. I felt the dewy spring morning against my bare skin and shivered. I should not have slept there. I still wore her shape, still saw pale white limbs free from the lines of woad before me, dark red hair falling in front of my face. *What was I going to do?* I could not just leave. He would speak to her about it, to Guinevere, and they would work out that it had been me. He knew my powers, and he would hate me. His memory would be hazy, his mind clouded with the drink I had given him, but he would not be so befuddled with it that he would think he could have confused a woman painted with woad with one who was not.

Then, I thought, *Elaine*. No one at Camelot had met her. No one knew who she was. She had been a comely girl, and Lancelot would have a hard time convincing anyone at Camelot that he had not desired her for her own sake. She was a cousin of mine. He could not put her away, nor me if I wore her shape. I could bear it.

I closed my eyes, and pictured her as I had last seen her. Big brown doe-eyes, long shiny chestnut-brown hair, small, delicate frame. When I opened my eyes, I saw that it had been accomplished.

Lancelot stirred again beside me, and I put a hand against his chest. He, still half-asleep, took it and pressed it to his lips.

"Good morning," I said, softly. I saw his brow wrinkle in confusion. He took his hand from mine and rubbed his face, and when he drew his hands away and opened his eyes to see a woman he did not recognise, he cried out, jumping up in surprise and snatching his sword into his hand.

"Who are *you*?" he shouted, grabbing his shirt from the ground and pulling it over his head, still keeping hold of his sword. I pulled my knees up and wrapped my arms around them, casting him a pitiful look.

"Sir, you do not remember?" I said. I could feel tears gathering at the back of my eyes, strange tears. I did not know why I should cry, but at once I felt sad and vulnerable. Perhaps it was the thought of the awful thing that I had done, or it was the knowledge that he would be even more dismayed if he knew it was truly I.

"What did you do to me?" Lancelot demanded. I could see the fear in his eyes, I could see that he was trembling. *What had I done?* I pushed it away. I had to. The tears came suddenly then, and at the sight of them I saw Lancelot weaken, and he dropped his sword and came back to kneel beside me, picking up the nightdress and handing it to me gently so that I could pull it on. He did not seem to notice that, while the woman had changed, the dress was the same.

"Who are you?" he asked, more gently, taking my face in his hands, turning it up towards his. "How did you come to be here... with me?"

I wiped the tears off my cheeks with the back of my hand. "It is a part of our destiny," I said, shakily. I could not think of any other explanation, and it seemed inadequate. The words seemed foreign, too. "My name is Elaine, sir. I am a cousin unto King Arthur."

Lancelot leaned away, and I saw the frustration and the despair pass across his face. He knew that whatever there might have been with him and Guinevere was over now, before it had begun.

He gave a slow nod.

"I know that you thought I was the Queen, sir," I said, putting my hand over his. He jumped slightly, and looked nervous.

"Elaine," he replied. "I am sorry. I will take care of you, I promise. I must go, for Cornwall, but I will give you any protection you need from me. May I... take you anywhere?"

I shook my head. I did not want him to take me to Elaine's father's castle only to find there were two of the same girl.

"I live close by," I lied. "I should like the walk."

He nodded.

"Come back for me," I told him, putting a hand against his cheek. I could see him soften, could see he was sorry.

He nodded again, and leaned down to kiss me, softly. There was no passion in it, no love, but there was kindness, and I felt that wrench within me. I had tricked a kind man, and I would be sorry for it, always.

I stepped from the tent, and pictured myself back in my bedroom in Rheged. When I opened my eyes, I was there, and I was myself. The days passed, and I wrote to Elaine's father. He accepted all of my requests, and committed himself to obedience to me. Elaine must have told him what a witch I was. I was glad.

I began to feel sick, and weary. I knew what this was. I thought of Morgawse, and her child, far away in the North. I had not written to her, had not heard from her or seen her, in a long while. I ought to, soon. But not now, not yet. I was too ashamed of what I had done.

Chapter Forty-Four

When news came that Lancelot had passed out of Cornwall, I took my place at Elaine's father's castle, in her shape. I chose dresses that showed well my swelling belly, and I waited for the moment to come. It was the very height of summer, and the sun was hot and low, and gorgeously warm when he came. Five months he had been away, from the very beginning of spring to the full ripeness of summer, and it showed on me well.

Lancelot rode through the gates of the small castle with a woman at his side. Mark's Queen by the look of her. This was the woman that Arthur had turned down in favour of Guinevere's magic blood and sharp wit, which – little did he know – was turned against him now. She was truly a beautiful creature; pale golden hair down to her waist, big, blue eyes and a soft, pink full-lipped mouth. She had a placid expression, and a dreamy look in her eyes. I had not yet heard her speak, but I would not have been surprised if Kay's estimation of her as *simple* were accurate. Still she was lovely, and dressed richly and beautifully. She wore a circlet of white gold, set with sapphires and pearls – which I recognised with annoyance as my mother's crown – and a dress of pale pink silk, sewn with pearls. I wondered what she was doing with Lancelot. Surely it was not just *any* queen that he wanted.

He jumped from his horse to greet me and Elaine's father, then helped her down and introduced her. She gave me a look of disdain. I wondered what she knew. Lancelot's eyes, when they saw the swell of my belly, did not register surprise, only resignation. I had at least thought he might be pleased. A child is a child. Everyone had expected *me* to feel joy at the conception of my son.

"Sir Lancelot," Elaine's father greeted him, brusquely, "I trust you intend to stand honourably by my daughter."

He played his part admirably. Lancelot nodded, flustered.

"A man cannot be constrained to love, nor to wed, but I expect you to take my daughter with you to Camelot, and acknowledge this as your child. She was a maiden, sir, when she came to you."

Lancelot nodded again, his face tense and set. He knew the anger that would be waiting for him when Guinevere heard.

The journey back to Camelot was short, and tense, and when the castle came in sight over the hills, Lancelot said we had to stop and make camp. I knew what he wanted to do. He wanted to sneak ahead and make his apologies to Guinevere. Well, it was too late. Elaine's father had written to Arthur before we left and I, and my child, would be expected.

The next morning, they were gathered in the courtyard to greet us as we came through the gates. I saw Arthur first, dressed to meet us in all the grandeur he had. I supposed he wanted Isolde to go back to Cornwall and tell her husband what a fearsome king Arthur was. Gawain stood beside him, dressed in his armour, as he always was. The other side of Arthur, Guinevere stood, squinting into the sun at us riding towards her. She did not look as angry as I had expected her to, and I was a little disappointed. In the summer heat she wore a dress of blue and white silk, sewn with silver thread that glinted in the sun, and a circlet of fine gold glinted, half-hidden in the thick curls of her hair. The delicate dress looked wrong along with the fierceness of her looks. I thought she had suited much better the hunting leathers that had made the women of Camelot whisper behind their hands.

Lancelot jumped from his horse first to greet Arthur. Arthur pulled him into a hearty embrace, clapping him on the back. Of course Arthur would be pleased that Lancelot had returned with a woman carrying his child. I was surprised to see that Kay was smiling, too. I would have thought he would be jealous. I couldn't hear what they were saying, but I was sure that it was about me, and I was glad.

Isolde beside me had tried to get down from her horse, but had tangled her foot in the stirrup, and the horse was whickering and stumbling away from her. I saw Kay step forward to take hold of the horse's bridle, as Lancelot came towards me to lift me gently down from the horse. Elaine's little body was small and light, and even with the child growing strong inside, he lifted me easily down. I was pleased. I wanted Guinevere to see him put his hands on me.

Arthur greeted me first, kissing me on the cheek and making some kind of meaningless compliment that I was not paying attention to. I could feel Guinevere's eyes against my skin.

I turned to Guinevere and she took my hand with all politeness, but then I felt in the pit of my stomach the feeling I had felt once before, when I had seen her on her wedding-day. Up close again, and my own dark power working within me, I was overwhelmingly aware of the ancient Otherworld blood in her, and it seemed to recognise the dark magic in me, and both bridled at one another. I could see her feel it, see it pass across her face. I saw her breath catch. But it passed, and she said nothing. She did not see through me, as I had feared for a moment she might. She kissed me on the cheek, and we gave each other the proper greetings, commending each other's beauty. I could see her eyes measuring my form, testing Lancelot's excuse.

Since Isolde was here, and Queen of a rich if no longer powerful realm vassal to Arthur, some court had to be paid, and Guinevere led the small group of women that we made into her walled garden. It was a lovely place, small and intimate, smelling of roses and honeysuckle. Someone had set out silk cushions and thick silk rugs over the grass, and we – Isolde, Guinevere, her three ladies, and I – sank down among them. I was glad to sit down after the long ride. I had forgotten, too, how tiring it was to have a child growing inside me. Guinevere lay back among the cushions and, closing her eyes, turned her face up to feel the hot summer sun against it. I could see Isolde beside her chattering away, her soft pale-pink lips moving strangely slow. I suspected that Guinevere was not listening.

There was a lute player there, and Isolde stopped talking to watch him, and I saw Guinevere put a hand over her eyes to shield them from the sun, and gaze up at Isolde. She was, certainly, avoiding looking at me.

Her maid Margery was sat beside me, the girl who did not know I had taken her shape many times to spy on her Queen and mistress. I turned to her and gave her the sweetest smile Elaine's pretty little face could manage, and she smiled back, at first warily and then, glancing towards Guinevere and seeing her engaged in some conversation with Isolde, leaned down close to me to whisper.

"You are lucky, lady, to have had Sir Lancelot as your lover. He is a very handsome man. I do not doubt that there are many women," she could not hide her eyes' unconscious sweep back towards Guinevere, "who envy you that."

I gave a gentle nod of agreement, and a smile of complicity.

"Tell me what it was like," she whispered, leaning even closer, encouraged. "I don't know what it is like to be with a man, and no one will tell me."

At the other end of the garden, I could hear Isolde beginning to sing.

"Well," I began coyly, "not all men are the same, or so I have been told. Some are rough and mean, but the man I have known, he was gentle and loving."

Margery giggled, as though I were telling her some great, forbidden secret.

Suddenly, Guinevere was standing over us, demanding to know what we were laughing about. She had lost that steely control I knew so well; her anger had overtaken her, and the opaque calm I had seen on her when we had ridden into Camelot had utterly evaporated. She grasped me hard by the arm and pulled me to my feet.

"What amuses you two ladies so?" she demanded, in her anger her Breton accent thick, her English words too formal.

I gathered my best politeness around myself. I only wanted her to appear more wild, more out of control than even she was. The more scandalous it seemed, the more the gossip would eat away at her, and I would have what I had waited for.

"Forgive me," I began, demurely, fixing her with the most innocent look I could muster. It was difficult, for I was enjoying myself. "I was telling Margery of the love of Sir Lancelot. I know I should not speak in public of such things, but he was so tender. So," I drew in an expressive breath, and saw the rage catch deeper in her, "*manful*, I –"

To my absolute pleasure and triumph, she slapped me hard across the face. I barely felt the pain, I had such a rush in my veins. I heard Margery gasp beside me. I had won. Perhaps I would even go to Lancelot, and cry, and say that she had been unkind, and then he would hate her for it.

With a sudden lurch of guilt, I wondered if it might not be about the child as much as it was about Lancelot. The child I had offered up in exchange for Mordred's life. Once the thought struck me the guilt did not leave easy. I had been happy to enjoy her suffering when I had thought it was a lover's jealousy, but for a lost child – I was not so sure. It had been a year – two? – since then, and there was no sign that she might have another. It struck me that only a woman who

286

knew she would never bear a child would demand her lover's compliance as boldly as I had heard Guinevere do. She had nothing to fear. It was too late for hesitancy now, though. Too late for doubt.

As I walked back to the room that had been set aside for me, I overheard two voices I knew almost as well as my own, arguing. It was Kay and Lancelot, and I thought to burst in, and throw out my tears so that they would know what a cruel and jealous woman the Queen was, but when I came closer and pressed my ear to the door, I held back.

"Well, you can't go," Kay was saying, angrily.

"Kay, *I don't know what to do.* If I don't, she's lost to me forever. I know, I know I should not, but Kay, I don't know what else I can do."

There was a short silence, and even through the door it felt tense.

"Why are you telling me this?" Kay snapped. "What do you expect? Is this just so that if Arthur ever finds out you can tell him you had my blessing? Because you don't, Lancelot. Not at all. Do you truly need me to tell you how foolish this is?"

I heard Lancelot sigh, so deep that the sound came to me through the thick wood of the door.

"I *know*, Kay. But I cannot stop it. I cannot."

There was a long silence, and I wondered if they were talking too quietly for me to hear. I leaned closer to the door. For a moment, there was more silence, and then I heard Kay speak, soft and low with anger.

"You know, Lancelot, if you were going to go and do something like *this* anyway, if you truly do not care about what people think is right and wrong, I don't know why you gave up so easily on me."

"Kay, I did not –" Lancelot began, but Kay interrupted him, forcefully.

"No, Lancelot. You ignored my letters, you refused to see me –"

"*Kay.*" I had not heard Lancelot shout before, and the sound of it shocked me. "I was sixteen years old. I was *afraid.* Your father sent me from his house in disgrace. What was I supposed to do? Besides," his voice sank, became the slightly sulky tone I had not heard fully since he was a boy of that age, "it was you first, who... knew another."

I heard Kay give a groan of frustration. "*Morgan?* Are you *still* angry about Morgan? You know, she wasn't anyone else's wife. She was kind, and she was *there.* You were gone. What, was I supposed to spend the rest of my life alone because you didn't want me anymore?"

"Not just Morgan," Lancelot answered, grimly, after a pause.

"No," Kay replied, "not just Morgan."

"Her sister, too."

Kay sighed, this time. "I suppose Morgan told you that."

"Well, is it true?" Lancelot demanded.

"Yes," Kay said, "it's true. We can't all live like you, waiting for the great power of true and perfect love before we have anyone. I am a man of flesh and blood, Lancelot. I will not live my life lonely, because I cannot have any of those whom I have loved. And I will not be made to feel ashamed of it by you. *You* should be ashamed. For God's sake, give up your thoughts of Guinevere. Marry this girl who has your child. Live an easy life, a happy life."

"Like you, Kay?"

There was the sound of some kind of scuffle, as though one of them had lunged at the other, and a fight was about to begin, but it stopped as quickly as it had begun.

I heard Kay reply, "Never, Lancelot, *never* come to me with this again. I do not want to hear it."

I slipped away, my heart cold within me. Lancelot was planning to go to Guinevere again, even though he had me, and I had his child. He was still involved with Kay. They might not share a bed anymore, but I had never known two people to argue like that who had totally forgotten one another. I thought, too, of the last time Kay and I had argued, and the scuffle I had heard. Had it been about to go the same way? Who had grasped hold of whom? It seemed it was over for Lancelot, if all he thought of was the Queen, and yet he was still angry that Kay had loved me, once he was gone. *Sixteen years old*, Lancelot had said. Had it been so long ago? Seven years? Despite how much had changed, how much I myself had changed, I could hardly believe that so much time had slipped past me. Too late to think back, too late to turn back. I had already become who I was.

Chapter Forty-Five

There was a feast that night, the food richer and finer than ever before. Arthur *was* trying to impress Isolde. I ate heartily, made hungry by my victory. I sat beside Lancelot, letting one hand rest on my pregnant belly, watching Guinevere. She barely ate the food before her. Arthur beside her did not seem to notice. He ate and drank freely, laughing and joking with Gawain at his other side, and as much as he could with Lancelot who, beside me, was tense and uncomfortable. I could feel Guinevere glance at me whenever I looked away. I was enjoying my new power, seeing another woman rejected and discomforted. I knew I should not, but I had had so little victory in my life. I wanted this. I *deserved* it.

I saw Kay drape an arm around the back of Guinevere's chair from where he sat beside her, and lean down to whisper something in her ear. She turned to him. Their faces were close; the way they spoke, intimate. No one around seemed to see anything unusual in it. I, surely, could have been forgiven for thinking before that it was Kay she wanted as her lover, rather than Lancelot.

Whatever Kay had said to her, Guinevere did not like it. I could imagine, from what he had said to Lancelot, that she would not. She gave him a sharp look, drained her cup of wine and, placing it a little too hard against the table, made her excuses to leave. This time, Arthur did not protest. As she left, she cast a look towards Lancelot that I think only he and I saw.

It would be tonight, then, that he would come to her. It would not happen. He would not so easily slip from me. The knights and Arthur were growing louder, drunker. I supposed Guinevere could be so bold because she knew Arthur well, and that once he had begun drinking with Gawain it would be late before he came to her, if he came at all.

Lancelot made an excuse to leave not long after. I was his excuse. Arthur was very approving when Lancelot said he wanted to escort his pregnant lady to her chamber. I was happy to go along with it. But I was not sure that he intended to go to Guinevere, for when he walked back with me to my room, which was only beside hers – I was sure that she had me there to keep watch on me – he kissed me goodnight on the cheek, and walked off, down the stairs. When I went into my own chamber, I could hear Guinevere moving around inside hers. He had known she was there, and walked away? Had he truly listened so closely to Kay?

But this ruined my plan. I had wanted him to come to me, thinking I was her, and for her to see, and for it to be over between them for good. Best of all, she might scream all through the castle about it, and then Arthur would know as well.

I dressed in one of my plain wool dresses, and let myself become Margery. When I felt the growing mound of the child disappear under my hand, I panicked a little, but when I slipped back to myself to check, it was still there. My own magic seemed to know what I wanted; for the child to be seen when I was Elaine, and not when I was another. I prepared a cup of wine for Lancelot, the same that I had made before, and bore it with me in my hand.

I slipped down the stairs, through the castle to where Lancelot's bedroom was, far from the Queen's chambers, among the rooms for the knights that were simple and plain.

I knocked on the door, and when there was no answer, I pushed it open and walked in.

Lancelot was lying on his bed, still in his shirt and breeches, staring up at the ceiling over him.

"Sir," I said, my tone scolding, and loud enough that he startled. "Surely you are not going to sleep? My Lady waits for you."

Lancelot sat up sharply in the bed, his eyes wild and unfocussed. I held out the cup of wine towards him.

"Do not be nervous, sir," I assured him. He sat up, took the cup and drained it fast. He *was* nervous. He thought he had succeeded with Guinevere before, and now he faced the task again. But I knew, as well as Guinevere did, what a difference there was between a man one desired, and one's husband.

Lancelot groaned and, setting the cup on the floor at his feet, rubbed his face with his hands.

"I should not be doing this," he mumbled, but it was only to himself. He got to his feet and followed me from the room, as obedient as a lamb. I rushed on ahead of him, back to my room, to change into the stolen nightdress, and Guinevere's shape. When I heard the sound of his boots coming up the stairs, my heart raced in thrilling anticipation. After tonight, I hoped two victories would be won; Lancelot would be mine, and Arthur would be destroyed. When I heard him reach the top, I opened the door and stepped out before him.

The sight of me – of her – in her nightclothes, hair loose about her shoulders, stopped him where he stood. If there had been any doubts in him before, they were gone. Once more I tasted my magic drink on his lips. Once more I led him with me to bed. Once more I found myself quickly lost in his sensual intensity. He did not try to speak this time, for he feared being heard. He did not, either, seem to think it strange that he had been lured to this room, and not the one that was her usual chamber. Tangled in the net of longing and disappointment that had ensnared us both, he was as weak for me – for who he thought I was – as I was for him. We wound together in a haze of desire and delight, as great as I had known with him before.

It was only after we had lain side by side in the exhausted silence of satisfaction a long time that Lancelot murmured, "I should go."

But the drink had done its work well, and he fell into a slumber. I closed my eyes, too, but it was not to sleep. It was to feel once more our lips come together, our bodies, the rapture of his love.

I heard sounds coming from the corridor, or the room beside me. I sat up, glancing down at Lancelot. He stirred, but did not wake. *Perhaps it is Arthur,* I thought. *I want him to see this.*

I pulled the stolen nightdress over my head and, still in Guinevere's shape, stepped out into the corridor. It was empty, but I could hear movements. I walked warily towards Guinevere's bedroom door, only to find it suddenly wrenched open, and in the doorway, Guinevere. She was still fully dressed, and she was white with rage. I stepped back away, but I was not fast enough. She grabbed hold of a handful of my hair – her own thick, red curls – and I could not get away. I let the figure in her hands change back to Elaine. If anyone came, it would be better if there were not *two* of Guinevere.

She dragged me down the steps, her grip tight in my hair. She dragged me through the castle, and up to the room with her Round Table in it, and slammed the door. I could feel the power from the table, as well as from her, and the two coming together. I should not have been surprised; it was her father's table, made, perhaps, by those of her blood. Then, as if from nowhere, she drew Excalibur. I had not seen it in so long, and I felt a tug of longing, of *belonging* at the sight of it. I *needed* it back. She held it easily in one hand. Of course she did; and one day she would try to snatch it from me on the shores of Avalon. Today it was in her hand, but it would one day be in mine.

I thought, then, that my one last option would be to try to make her believe that, in her jealous rage, she had imagined it. I could see she was still angry, still wild. I let Elaine's features crinkle into distress.

"Please," I begged, as pitifully as I could. "Please don't hurt me. I don't know what I have done wrong."

Guinevere stepped closer towards me, lowering the point of the sword towards my swollen belly. I saw she would not be fooled. No, nor would I if I had sensed the Otherworld on another. Then she would know how selfish she was. Could she not leave Lancelot for anyone else? Barren and married, she had nothing real to offer him. I could have given him everything.

"What kind of woman are you, good Queen? You have Arthur. Women all over this realm pray every night for a man such as him, and yet you long for another. But you do not love him enough to let him be happy with some other woman, but you must draw Lancelot ever back to you. You desire only to possess him," I said.

"Get on the table," she demanded, taking another step towards me. Excalibur's power, too, was making it harder and harder for me to hold on to the illusion that I was Elaine. I could feel my head growing dizzy, spinning, could feel myself struggling to keep a hold of it.

The door opened behind her and Lancelot stepped in, his hair tangled still, his clothes thrown roughly on him, and breathing fast as though he had run here. Guinevere did not turn around to see who was behind her. She knew who it was.

He darted forward and tried to take the sword off her, but she stepped aside, still giving me no ground. "Guinevere, what are you doing!?" he cried, "Guinevere, please, let her go – she hasn't done anything wrong – stop!"

He had not understood as quickly as she had, but then he stopped, confusion passing across his face at the sight of her, fully dressed with her hair still braided neatly away.

"Who was with you, just now?" she asked him.

He shook his head, lost and confused once again. "You," he answered.

It was making me feel nauseous, gripping on to the shape of Elaine, and I was feeling it slipping away from me.

"*Get on the table,*" Guinevere demanded again, and as she moved towards me, I stepped away, up on to it. I was not sure that she would not strike me with the sword and try to kill me. I had lost everything else. I would not lose the child.

As I got on the table, I felt the illusion slip fully from my grasp at last, and saw the deep shock on Lancelot's face. The moment before I closed my eyes to picture myself back in my bedroom at Rheged Castle, I saw them both there, side by side, both shocked, both shaken. I hoped, at least, that I had torn them apart.

Chapter Forty-Six

Back at Rheged I passed my days waiting for the child to come in a haze of bittersweet half-absence from myself. None of the men questioned why the lord of the castle's widow of two years was growing great with child, not even my own son Ywain, who, when I saw him infrequently, called me mother and kissed me on the cheek, ever quiet and obedient. He asked me once how his father had died, and I told him that the devil came for him. He did not ask again, after that. I had learned well enough from the abbey what words frighten quietness and obedience into little children. To think, I had once, too, been afraid of the devil.

I dreamed strange dreams with the black magic child inside me. I dreamed of Kay, with Guinevere, his hands in her hair, his mouth against hers in a kiss as gentle and powerful as that I had felt myself long ago, when Kay had still loved me. I dreamed of Kay with Lancelot, too, though not as boys. They were grown men, older, far older than now. The three of them, Kay, Lancelot, Guinevere; they were what filled my thoughts, what tangled me in. Arthur, for all the King he was, was strangely on the edge of it all.

It was in the depths of winter, just before Christmas came, that my second son was born. I sent to Avalon for Nimue, because there wasn't anyone else. I could not have survived it alone. I knew she was angry, I could see it all over her neat little face, but she said nothing. I drank the drink to kill the pain and lay back until it was done.

This time, when I sat up in the bed and reached out my arms for the boy, I felt what I had seen pass across my sister's face. A rush of joy from the centre of me out, and love. I held him close to my chest, and he opened his eyes, deep, dark blue like the eyes of his father. I could have cried for joy, but I would not with Nimue standing over me, silent and cold. When she was sure I had survived it, she left without a word.

I called the boy Galahad; this had once been Lancelot's name, long, long ago before he had been taken into the care of the Lady of Avalon as little more than an infant himself. It seemed right, somehow. Galahad was perfect in the way I thought no creature could be, from the slick of dark hair already thick on his head, to the tiny little fingers and toes on his hands and feet. Though he had been conceived in magic and darkness, I felt nothing of that when I held him, only a deep peace that settled through me. For the first time in a long, long time, I forgot my anger.

I was glad, strangely, that his father did not come to look for him. I loved him jealously, as a thing all mine. Ywain wanted to see him, and I let him look from across the room. He wrinkled his nose in displeasure at the sight of another child, a half-brother. He was as much of a coward as his father had been, afraid of what he did not know. Ywain had nothing to fear from Galahad. His father's castle would be his. I hoped that Galahad might go to Avalon, and school there, and have the woad as Merlin had. It was a rare man that had the gifts of the Otherworld, but I thought a son of mine like Galahad would have those talents in him.

In the joy of having at last a child that I had wanted, I forgot the world around me. I was lost waiting for his smiles, as they came, and his happy sounds, and cries. The fingers of his little hand grasping around mine. I forgot Arthur, and Lancelot, Guinevere and Kay, far off in Logrys. I did not write to Morgawse. I wanted to, but I was afraid she would be disgusted with me. I still remembered, though I pushed it back into the depths of my mind, the Lady of Avalon's words about Arthur's conception: *he does not know it, but he is a child of rape.* It was not the same. It was *not.* I had done only what I must, only what I had seen. Besides, Galahad was so perfect, I did not see how he could have come from anything but the greatest goodness.

A year passed, and then another. Galahad could say my name, could ask for me. His world was still complete; he was not yet old enough to ask where his father was. Ywain, too, had no father, and Galahad's sweet presence had brought Ywain closer to me, too. Once he was used to him, he seemed to like his little brother, and was happy to sit with him, play with him, listen to him try to form his words. Galahad was much brighter than Ywain, I could see that already, and he had a ready laugh that his brother had lacked even as an infant. Ywain was dour and serious, but Galahad was full of an endless joy that spread into me as well, whenever I had him in my arms. I wondered if this was how I would have been, had Uther not married my mother. This, too, I thought, was what Ywain would have been like, if he had been Kay's. Still, as I saw more of Ywain, I began to see a little of myself, though they were the parts I liked the least. He was shy, too, and reserved. He was prickly, and would not talk in more than two or three words at a time. Still, there was a gentle, happy domesticity in sitting with my sons around me, Galahad taking tottering, unsteady steps across the room while Ywain stood with his arms out to catch him. Galahad was strong already. I could see he would have his father's strength. Perhaps Ywain would be a great man, too, though he would be stolid like his father. It was in those days that I wished the world would tighten, close in, so that all that was left in it was Rheged Castle and Gore, and no one would come for me, or for my sons, and I could have lived my life in simple happiness. *Live an easy life, a happy life.* A simple life was where happiness was.

I knew Nimue would come. I knew that she was angry with me, and I knew that she would return, but I had feared it would be as soon as it was. I sat in my room, with Galahad playing on the fur rug beside the fire. Autumn was coming, and the air had turned chill, though the sun was still bright. I had had two and a half years – more – of perfect joy with Galahad, and that day I had felt close about me the threat of its ending, of its drawing to a close with the summer. I had pushed the fears away as silly or superstitious, but I was a witch with witches' blood in me, and I knew I did not fear for no reason.

Nimue appeared before me, in her dress of pale blue set from the neck to the waist with pale sapphires, her hair long and loose down to her waist, ghost-white against the faint blue-green patterns across her skin. At her side, hand clasped in hand, came the aged Abbess. I felt an old sting of anger, and revulsion, at the sight of the old nun. She had taught me to be afraid, taught me to be ashamed. If there was someone largely to blame for the anger in me, it was she.

"Morgan," Nimue began gently, and I did not like the tone of her voice. "It is time to give him up."

I reached out my arms for Galahad before me, and obediently he tottered into them.

"It is *not* time," I protested, quietly, smoothing down Galahad's hair, more to comfort myself than him. I was glad Ywain was not there today. As lacking as my motherly affection for him was, I did not want him to hear me beg to keep his little brother, when I had handed him carelessly to a nurse the moment after his birth. Galahad grasped hold of the plait of my hair, and rested his head against my chest, closing his eyes. He was falling asleep. If he were older, I could have told him to run.

"Morgan, do not make this harder than it has to be. You have a destiny, your son has a destiny. It must be. He does not belong here, he belongs in Amesbury."

I was not sure I had the strength in me to fight Nimue. I did not want to end like Merlin, shut under a rock, screaming until the end of time.

"He belongs with me," I resisted, stubbornly.

Nimue shook her head. She looked a little sad, but it did not make me forgive her. This was not hurting her like it was hurting me. If they took Galahad from me, it would take the last of my happiness, and I would be back in the place where I had been; dark, angry and alone.

"He belongs in Amesbury."

"He is *my* child," I protested, and though I struggled to be calm the words came from me like a shout. I wrapped my arms tighter around him. Nimue's face was set, and pale under her woad, and the Abbess beside her said nothing, but looked on, tight-lipped. Nimue sighed, and shook her head.

"Morgan, this is the way it has to be. Did I not warn you about the dangers of the Black Arts? Besides, Morgan, you already have a child. A natural son. This child, he was made in darkness, and the only good that can come through him is if we give him up to the Abbey, and they raise him for the Grail."

"*We?*" I cried, and Galahad woke in my arms, his little face crinkling as though he was about to cry, but I held him closer and he fell quiet. "He is nothing to do with you. Anyway, what about Arthur? He was made the same way, and he lives a natural life."

Nimue shook her head. "That was different. Merlin was not Arthur's father. Morgan, you *must* give him to us."

"No," I insisted. Nimue glanced at the Abbess, who was staring at me, narrowly. Of course she was. I was sure she hardly recognised me now, blue with woad, a queen in my castle, but I remembered her. She would not have my child.

Nimue held out her hand towards me, and I felt my arms obey, though I struggled and resisted.

"Nimue, *no*," I pleaded, but she did not look at me. I did not have the strength in me to resist her power, and when she stepped towards me for the child, my arms opened and she took him from me. In her arms his dark black hair began to change, and first I thought a light was glowing around him, as at the top it shone white-blonde like Nimue; but then it spread all through it, and my child was changed before my eyes, to look like her, all silver-white.

"I am sorry, truly, Morgan," she said, but still she took the Abbess' hand in hers and they, and my child, faded from sight before me.

It was a long time, a *long* time, before I began to feel alive again. I spent long hours with my books of magic, committing all I could to memory, and then I burned them all. It did not matter how strong I was, if someone else could be stronger. Merlin had hidden his secrets in his mind, and that was how he had been so strong for so long. It was only his weakness for Nimue that had led him to his death. I would not be weak like that again. Now, I would have only myself.

I wrote to Galahad in Amesbury, but I was sure Nimue burned my letters before they reached him. Everyone would say that Elaine was his mother. I would not exist. There was no one I could call on to help me. No one who would understand. Merlin was amoral enough that he might have helped me if I had had anything to offer in exchange, but when I went back to the rock Nimue had shut him beneath and put my ear to it, I could still hear him screaming and screaming and screaming, and though I screamed down to him, he could not hear me. I was glad, then, that I had burned my books. Nimue would not have them. I did not care for her apologies. They were only lies, to me. She had taken my joy from me. I would not forget. I would not forgive.

I longed to know the future, to know my fate. On the shortest night, when dreams were sharpest and clearest, almost two years from when Galahad was stolen from me, I mixed from memory the drink of knowing and seeing from Avalon. I had to know, if Galahad would come back to me.

The first thing I saw as the sudden sleep came over me, I thought at first was Galahad grown, but it was not. It was Lancelot. Dressed in his armour and soaked with rain, stepping into a pavilion where Guinevere, wearing only a thin nightgown, stood to greet him. In the dream, I could smell the heavy late summer rain. Against the white-blue light of the summer lightning, they rushed together, her jumping up into his arms, wrapping her legs around him, he running his hands through her hair, pulling her mouth against his in a kiss that was unbearably passionate to watch. The way they came together, it was as though they had been waiting all their lives. So, despite what I had done, it would happen after all.

Next, I saw my sister, riding through the gates of Camelot, with a man at her side who I would have thought was Arthur had my sister been twenty years younger. Arthur's son. She looked proud, and defiant, he dark and serious. Standing to greet them were Arthur, his face clouded with anger, and beside him, Guinevere. So, Mordred would return to his father. In a sudden flash, I saw again the dream I had had, where Arthur had forced Guinevere against the floor, just for a second. I wondered, then, if it were really Arthur I was seeing. But what would Arthur's son want with his father's ageing Queen?

As though summoned by my thoughts, I saw Guinevere again, standing before the altar in the chapel. I could not see what she was looking at, but whatever she saw as she gazed towards the chapel door had frozen her to the spot. With resentment, I had to recognise that if anything she had grown more beautiful with age. Gone was the prettiness of a girl, any softness, and with it she had the proud looks of a queen. She looked grand, and powerful, and yet whatever she looked on had robbed the strength from her, I could see that well enough. I wondered if I did not see what it was, because it was I.

The last thing I saw was Kay, standing beside his father, his arms crossed over his chest. There was a strange look in his eye, of resignation, of loss. He looked older, maybe even ten years older than I had last seen him, and tired. Beside him Ector looked grim, as I had never seen him before. I was there, I knew I was there.

So, this was what was to come. Mordred. That seemed the answer to everything. If I wanted to destroy Arthur, I only needed to bring his son to Camelot. I did not know how I would get Morgawse to part with him, but I knew that it had to be done, and I knew – because I had seen it – that it could be done. For the first time in a long *long* time, in too long, I wrote to Morgawse.

It was only after, when I lay awake in my bed, that I realised that I had not dreamed at all of Galahad.

Part III
The Fall of Camelot

And then Queen Morgan said, "Ah, my dear brother! Why have you tarried so long from me?"

Malory, *Le Morte d'Arthur*

Chapter Forty-Seven

I t was time for me to act. I felt strong. I felt ready to begin again on the path to vengeance that I had given up. I had lost everything that might make me vulnerable; Nimue had taken my beloved son, my lover was long dead. I had nothing to lose and everything to gain, and I coveted revenge against Arthur most of all. Lancelot and Guinevere had begun – or were about to begin – in earnest the love-affair I had almost thwarted. I wrote to Arthur, saying as much, though I did not expect he would believe me. Still, it was worth planting the little seed of jealousy, and letting it grow.

Morgawse answered my letter quickly, and I moved to join her in Lothian before the snows came. I knew that my revenge had to begin with Mordred, her son and Arthur's shame.

As I travelled back up towards Lothian, feeling the cold gather closer around me with every mile north, I could not help thinking of the journey I had made with Morgawse to Lothian all those years ago, when I had been not much more than a girl, and she pregnant with Mordred. I had left Kay behind, thinking that nothing would have changed when I saw him again, but he had brought me back only to offer me to Arthur, for him to sell. Lancelot, too, had begun what had ended with Galahad then, kissing me in the forest, only to deny anything he might have felt for me. That was so long ago. I had been a child. I had not even imagined that Lot, in his anger at Morgawse, would try to harm me as he had. I knew that men did such things, but men like that seemed distant, far away. The adult world of brutality had been something I had only heard of from others. I knew it well enough, now.

I rode into Lothian Castle with the crown of Gore on my head. I was dressed in thick grey furs and a pale grey and silver silk dress that had belonged to our mother – some of the clothes she had given me when I was married – and I felt pleased in the knowledge of how powerful I looked, how rich, how like a queen. Morgawse, running across the courtyard to greet me with her usual disregard for proper courtesies, laughed when she saw me.

"Morgan, I thought it was mother back from the dead to *scold* me, until I saw your woad."

I slipped from my horse and kissed her on both cheeks. I did not realise how much I had missed her until I saw her again. The years had treated her well, and she looked beautiful still.

"Morgan," she kissed me one more time on the cheek, her tone lightly scolding, "it has been too long since you came. I would have come to you, but you know I cannot leave my son."

"Where is he?" I asked. Morgawse wrinkled her nose in motherly annoyance.

"He's out with his knights."

"*His* knights?" Surely, they were *hers*, or at the very least Gawain and Aggravain's. How old was Mordred now? I thought he must, surely, have still been a child. Twelve years old, perhaps.

Morgawse sighed and shook her head. "You'll understand when you see him."

I supposed that I would.

"What's he like now?" I asked, out of idle, auntish interest as I followed Morgawse up.

She waved a hand in response. "He's... high-spirited," was all she would say. I remembered Arthur at that age, grown to the height of a man, though he had grown taller still, and strong. Boyish and playful. I supposed Arthur could have been called high-spirited. The Mordred I had seen in my dreams had not seemed that way at all.

She showed me into the room she had had prepared for me. I was pleased to see that she had done it carefully, with a space for me to read and – though richer than I liked – it was less full of silks, and gold and amber beads from the east than her own rooms.

Still, there was a pile of plump silk cushions in the corner, and she settled down among these, while I pulled up a wooden chair to sit beside her.

"Morgan," she sighed, settling down deeper into the cushions, "truly, it is a joy to see you. But you did not bring your son!"

That was the question I had dreaded her asking. I could not say, as I longed to, *my son was stolen from me.*

"Oh," I replied, with a forced air of casualness, "the lords of Gore will not let him leave without half of them accompanying him. Unlike you, I do not have enough grown sons to bully men into obeying me."

Morgawse made a little noise of acceptance. She did as she pleased in Lothian, and it was no secret how her sons were devoted to her. I wondered if that would change when Mordred was grown, or if any of her sons would turn against her. She had not married again –

302

though she was a great beauty, no man seemed to be in a rush to marry Britain's most notoriously unfaithful wife, though perhaps she had not wanted to, either. Still, without a husband, if the day came when her sons were against her, or gone, she would have no one else to protect her. I prayed that day would never come.

"Morgawse –" A man burst in, seemingly in a hurry, one I recognised as one of Arthur's knights, but when he saw me, he blushed and drew back, with a little bow. "Forgive me," he mumbled, blushing darker. "I shall return later."

After the door was shut and he had hurried away, Morgawse released a peal of bright laughter, fixing me with her wicked, flashing eyes. So, that explained what one of Arthur's knights, a man I recognised as Sir Lamerocke, was doing in Lothian.

"Oh dear," she giggled. "He is a shy boy sometimes."

She had not been far wrong calling him a boy; of course, he was a man grown, but in comparison with her, of tender years. He had been handsome, with dark golden hair and a masculine face. He had even reminded me a little of Accolon, the lover I had sacrificed to my first attempt to be revenged upon Arthur.

"He *is* young."

Morgawse laughed.

"Oh yes, he is young. And he is utterly devoted to me. He has a kind heart," she peeped out at me from under her eyelashes, the smile curling on her face as she drew us back into our girlhood games, her teasing, me scandalised, "and he is very *very* thorough in his duties. You would make a much merrier widow, Morgan, if you kept a knight like him in your service," she informed me, smoothing down the skirts of her dress.

"I am glad just to be a widow," I said, softly. Beneath the weight of the memory of lovers I had lost – Kay, Accolon, Lancelot – I barely remembered Uriens at all. All I knew was that I was painfully glad of his death.

Morgawse stretched out her legs, relaxing back among the cushions and flashed me her wicked smile.

"You want a young man, Morgan," she told me, with an authoritative grin. "Half your age, or thereabouts. A young man is eager to please. They'll do anything that you want. *Anything*, Morgan." She gave me a knowing look, but I didn't know what she meant. Morgawse stretched her arms over her head and gave a contented sigh. "No, a man your own age fucks you and expects you to say 'thank you, sir', whether it's any good or not. A *younger* man – they're all eager to please, Morgan."

It's easy for you to go on about the joys of younger men, I thought. Morgawse, though just past forty years old, was still an attractive woman. Like our mother, her looks had changed with age from fresh-faced loveliness to a more subtle and dignified beauty. Morgawse's hair was still thick and full, and age had faded it from copper to pale gold. Besides all of that she had the wicked spark of desire always in her eyes, and I knew that the men liked that. I, on the other hand, was tall and thin, and painted with woad. Men did not desire me often; mostly, they were afraid of me.

"You might be surprised," Morgawse told me, "what you like." She, seeing my confusion, sat up a little straighter among the cushions, her smile curling deeper across her face. "You don't *know* what you like, do you Morgan?" She laughed her pretty, tinkling laugh, but she was laughing at me, and in my ears it sounded cruel. "You've been married, you've had a child, but you're still a little virgin nun at heart, aren't you?"

She laughed again. I did not know why she was so proud of herself for having known so many men. Especially since one of them had been her own brother. If I had loved my sister any less than I did I would have pointed that out to her sharply. But I did not.

"I know what I like," I said. So, we were back in the same pattern again. I was sure we had had this same conversation – what, nine, ten years ago? No, longer – in Camelot, when she had scurried into my room, flushed and proud of herself from being with Arthur. She did not seem as though she was ashamed of it now. Arthur was the first younger man that she had had, and she did not seem now to consider it ill-advised, or bad luck. I wanted to shake her, to shout at her, to demand from her why she was not more ashamed. But why should she be ashamed? I was angry with her because I *was* ashamed, and I could not work out why.

"Most of them are just curious," Morgawse continued, as though with a different conversation, sinking back into the cushions, and her previous train of thought. "Curious about me. They want to know if there's anything different about a woman who's fucked her brother."

I felt myself blush.

"Oh Morgan," she complained, kicking me lightly with her bare foot. "Grow up, will you? That was fourteen years ago. More. Everyone talks like it was something awful, but for god's sake, *we didn't know.* Anyway, Arthur's not my brother. Not really. It's only a mother we share, and we did not grow up together. It was just an accident. I have a son from it, a good strong son, and a son conceived in love, even if his father forgot it – *denied* it – right afterwards. That's something to be grateful for." She sat up again, fixing me with an intense, slightly wild, look. "I'm not sorry for it, Morgan. No one will make me sorry for it. Not even him. Not even Arthur. He will *not* make me sorry for it."

She is still in love with him, I thought. If our mother had never told us the truth, if she had died and taken it to her grave with her, perhaps Arthur would have married Morgawse, and they would have been happy. I would not have had to marry Uriens; Arthur would have killed Lot, and there would have been no war, and Britain would have an heir, rather than a barren queen. And a queen with a lover, who the King refused to believe existed. What good had the truth done any of us?

"Were you never happy," I asked gently, tentatively, "with Lot?"

"Oh," Morgawse sighed, suddenly dropping in tone. "There was a time – after Gaheris was born – I suppose I was, what, eighteen, nineteen. I wasn't a child anymore, so it didn't hurt, and I was used to it, and him, and I loved my three sons. I suppose I found him handsome enough – he was not yet so very grey, and he was strong. I had not seen him be cruel, not really. I was happy. Fool that I was, I thought I loved him. But then, just when I thought contentment had finally reached me, I found him, in *our* bed, with some whore. A *whore*, Morgan. As if anything could have been more disrespectful to me. No, I knew my own worth even then, and I was so angry. Well, I shouted at him. I screamed and called him every name he deserved. I told him I would never have him in my bed again. I was young, and rash, and proud. But worse than that, I was embarrassed. I had believed, for that brief time, that he had felt the same for me as I had for him. I had been, for a brief moment of stupidity, in love.

Well, then Lot told me that it was his solemn duty as a husband to teach me that it was he who decided whom he *fucked* and when, and where, and not I. He told me I was a foolish girl if I believed I had the right to forbid him anything. He told me he was doing it *for me*, because it was better that I learned obedience. He dragged me down into the courtyard of the castle, and called his knights. *Gawain* was with them. Gawain. He was only eight years old. That was all I could think about the whole time: *Gawain should not see this*. Well, when they were all gathered, he told them what I had done, and he grabbed me by the hair and forced me down, in front of him. That was how he always liked it. He didn't like to think a woman might look him in the eye. He – well, he had just been with the whore, so it took a long time. A *long* time. I didn't scream or cry. I didn't want him to think that he had won, but more than that, I didn't want Gawain to know

305

that his father was hurting me. Then, nine months later Gareth was born, and he is the sweetest and kindest of all my sons. He won't be a great man, like Gawain, but he will be kind. I'm grateful for Gareth. He makes me think that there might be kindness, somewhere, in this blood that Lot and I have mixed between us. Though, it certainly doesn't come from him."

I did not say anything – I could not say anything – but I moved around to sit beside Morgawse, among the cushions, and rest my head against her shoulder. She reached her arm around me, and smoothed my hair. Morgawse was the one creature in this world who had never let me down, never abandoned me or lied to me, never betrayed me. I had given up the most for her, but I had given it willingly. Here we were, once again. But this was different. We were not hiding from Uther. We were both strong and powerful women ourselves. But still, *still* we were both afraid.

Morgawse sighed heavily, shaking her head. "It's *husbands*, that's the problem." I could see that she had held this all close, all deep inside her. It was rushing out of her now, wild and angry. "Husbands and high-born men. For all his faults later on, afterwards, Arthur was always kind. Of course he was. Before me he had been screwing milkmaids and peasant girls. He couldn't believe his luck, to have a queen in his bed. Well, he had grown up half a peasant, hadn't he? Those kinds of girls didn't owe him anything, he never grew up learning to expect anything, so he was kind, and he was grateful. So was I – no man had been kind to me like that before. Well, that's the problem, isn't it? As soon as you make a man someone's husband, he thinks that woman *owes* him something. He owns her, he's entitled to her. Lot owned me, body and soul. He liked to remind me, that without him I would be dead. When he felt cruel or I had defied him, he would whisper in my ear that my mother had begged him to have me, before Uther killed me. No, a man doesn't have to be kind to his wife. Do you think Arthur is kind to his wife? Arthur used to be kind. Well, it's honour and marriage that makes men cruel, Morgan. It's pride. I'll never let a man think he owns me again." She cast me a narrow look, and I felt the old spark of cruelty light within her. "Your woad didn't save you either, did it? Though you think it makes you better than me."

"I don't think that, Morgawse," I replied, quietly. It was so unpleasant, because staring at Morgawse, jaded and ageing, was like staring at myself. But Lot had been far crueller to my sister than Uriens had been to me. Lot had been stronger, shrewder. Morgawse had been a child with no magic, and nowhere to run.

Morgawse, however, seemed suddenly to shrug her anger off, reaching for an apple, and biting into it, settling back down among the cushions.

"I am only saying," she said, "that if one wants a considerate lover, one should choose young, and low-born. Plus," she flashed me her wicked grin, "men like that have strong hands."

Suddenly, the door flew open, and Mordred stepped through it. I recognised him instantly from my dreams, but more strongly from his resemblance to Arthur. He did not look fourteen years old. He could have been a man of eighteen. He came in wearing his hunting armour, and dirty and sweaty from the hunt. I could smell it on him.

"Mother!" Mordred cried, running over to pull her into an embrace as she stood to her feet, wrapping his arms around her neck and nuzzling his face into the top of her hair in the extremes of filial devotion. Morgawse hugged him back tight.

"Mordred, my love, this is your Lady Aunt, Morgan," she said, gently.

He turned to look at me. His eyes were still so dark as to be almost black. I felt the spasm of guilt within me that I had done that to him, with my dark magic drink. I had hoped that they would lighten to grey, like Arthur's, and mine, or even to Morgawse's bright blue, but they had not. He gave me a gentle bow, and cast his dark eyes over me curiously. It was not the curiosity of a child, though. He inclined his head in a gentle bow.

"Are you the one they call Morgan le Fay?" he asked, his gaze on me, steady. He was not so much like Arthur as he had looked at first glance. He had Arthur's boyish handsome looks, his large, muscular frame and his golden hair, but his look was sly, like his mother could be in her meaner moments, and his face broader, harsher somehow, with the same pale freckles Morgawse had across the bridge of his nose which did not fit the rest of his looks.

"Mordred," Morgawse scolded gently. "That isn't polite." She turned apologetically to me, but her tone was indulgent. "Mordred believes every bit of gossip he hears."

"I am," I told Mordred, evenly. I did not mind. I liked the nickname the common people had given me. He did not apologise, or move away, but kept his gaze on me.

"Here in Lothian, they call *me* Mordred, son of Arthur, Prince of Britain," he told me.

"Well, they shouldn't," Morgawse fussed, crossing her arms and rolling her eyes at me behind his back. I thought perhaps she ought to take his ambitions more seriously. He was still her youngest child to her, but to the rest of the world he must have looked like a man.

"Why shouldn't I?" He rounded on his mother, his anger still retaining a little of the childhood tantrum. "My father has no legitimate children, and I am royal blood on both sides. I am a worthy heir of Arthur's. He will recognise me. My time will come."

He seemed proud, rather than ashamed, of his incestuous heritage. He was sure of himself because he had never been tested. Morgawse looked weary, as though they had had this same argument before, as though Mordred in his "high spirits" had been charging around Lothian, declaring himself Arthur's heir.

"Mordred, my love," she said, gently, "go and wash, then you can dine with me and Morgan."

To my surprise, he nodded obediently. He went back to Morgawse and pressed a kiss against her lips. It was brief, a kiss of filial affection, but it made me uneasy. It was, I thought, a moment too long, a little too close. I supposed Galahad, the son whom I had loved, had not grown to adolescence with me, so I did not know what was proper, or natural. When the door shut behind him, I was left with an uncomfortable mix of unease and victory; he unsettled me, but he was an ambitious man, and fixated on his goal. He would be easy to control.

Chapter Forty-Eight

News came from Camelot as soon as the snows began to thaw around Lothian Castle. I sat in Morgawse's bedroom with her and Mordred while she read the letters. It was cold still, though the snows were thinner, and the rivers beginning to move again, and I sat cross-legged on a fur rug beside the fire, feeling its lovely warmth through me, while Morgawse reclined close by on a pile of velvet and brocade cushions. Mordred lay beside her, his head on her shoulder, one arm draped lazily across her waist. I found it strange, their constant closeness, but no one else seemed to. Not even the knight Morgawse had taken as her lover. I saw him sometimes cast wary looks at Mordred across the courtyard, but these were clearly wary of his knowledge.

Morgawse sighed with annoyance, reading the letter in her hands.

"Aggravain only sends me more gossip. Who is fucking whom. I don't care."

She went to crumple it and throw it in the fire but, with a sulky murmur of protest, Mordred took it from her hand and read it, with avid interest. There was nothing of interest to me in it. I already knew that Lancelot and Guinevere were lovers.

Morgawse picked up the next one, and sighed again. "Gaheris writes again, wanting to be married."

She seemed unduly irritated by this, and it piqued my curiosity.

"Why shouldn't he?"

Morgawse shook her head, her manner suddenly scolding, as though she were talking to Gaheris before her. "Oh, he can marry if he wishes, but not to this girl he writes about here. She's a lady-in-waiting to the Queen, Breton, a half-peasant no doubt, for those Bretons have funny ways. Oh, he thinks he can do as he pleases since he has two older brothers, but no, no. He is still a prince of Lothian, and he shall not marry beneath himself. If he wants to get married, he can marry the sister of Gareth's wife. She has a rich kingdom, and the match is suitable. She is supposed to be beautiful enough. Certainly, she'll have finer clothes than this servant girl he has set his heart on."

Morgawse crumpled the letter in her hand and threw it into the fire, where it turned black, and dissolved into ash before my eyes. I had not known Gareth was married. When I had seen him last, he had been a child. How my life had slipped past me.

"Gawain writes of a quest for the Holy Grail," Morgawse commented, raising an eyebrow at the letter in her hand. "The next letter I receive from Gawain will be about a hunt for unicorns, or the cyclops, I am sure."

She threw that letter into the fire, too, but I felt that one strike me at my core. Nimue had taken Galahad for the Grail quest, but he was just a child. It could not be time yet, surely.

"I want to go," Mordred declared, half sitting up beside his mother.

"No, love," she said. "You're too young, yet."

I was surprised how easily this angry, powerful young man was placated by his mother. In her arms, he was like a child, but I was sure he was not so in front of his men. At fourteen years old Mordred was too young to be made a knight, but it would not be long. When the end of spring came, and Mayday, he would turn fifteen, and Morgawse could not expect him to stay with her in Lothian, if he did not wish to.

Morgawse read through the rest of the letters, but I was no longer listening. I was thinking about Galahad, anxious to get back to my room and the letter I expected – and dreaded – to find there for me.

I made some excuse to leave after a while. Mordred stayed, unwilling to part, it seemed, from his mother's embrace.

When I came back to my room, the letter from Nimue was waiting for me. I knew it would be there. I had been away, and no one had come to check the fire, so it had died, and the room was half-dark and cold. I suspected that many of the servants in Lothian Castle were afraid of me, and my blue woad. This was not Rheged, or Camelot, where men were accustomed to seeing the woaded women of Avalon, and in Lothian the superstitious terror of the witch remained strong.

I did not send for the fire to be lit. I could not wait to open the letter, to see what Nimue had written, and if it was as bad as I had feared.

"My dear Morgan, I am sure you are still angry, but I assure you again that I did only what I must. One day you will understand. But I am not writing to you now to ask for your forgiveness. I am writing to tell you that we have sent Galahad to Camelot. The time of the Grail came faster than we expected, and I had to have him grow to meet it. Your son is a man grown, now. But, Morgan, you must not go to Camelot to see him. Do not try. Do not write to him, do not send a message to him, and most of all do not try to see him. He belongs to his destiny, and he will not know you. Save yourself the sorrow. I will explain in full when I see you, but Morgan – you must not try to see him. Nimue."

I wished, then, that I had a fire to cast her letter into.

Well, I would go. I would go and see my son. See what she had done to him. He was too young. He was still a child. I had wanted a childhood for him of innocence and peace, and Nimue had turned him into her *thing*, for the sake of this quest for the Grail. Her letter only made me more determined to see him, and to get in the way of whatever she was trying to do with him. And Arthur; it only made me more determined that it was he who should be punished, too. This was, after all, so much his fault. He had *laughed* at me, laughed, when I had gone to him asking to be married to Lancelot. As though I were such a plain and ugly thing that no man would want me. He had taken my sword. He had married me to Uriens. He lived his happy life of peace and ignorance, and all the while Lancelot – who had refused me – was making love to his Queen. And none of them suffered. Not Lancelot, not Arthur, not Guinevere. Not Kay. But I did, and my sister did, and her son. Far from Arthur's love, and his grace; and those who were truly betraying him he kept close, in his foolishness. I wanted Arthur to see his charmed life disintegrate in his hands. I would do it. I would, and Mordred would help me. *Mordred, Prince of*

Britain. A greedy man was easy to control. I would offer him what he desired, and he would be mine to command.

The next day, I went to see Mordred. I had to keep reminding myself that he was a teenage boy, despite his size. I had to be sure that Mordred would go through with it. I had to be sure that he wanted it *more* than I did.

When I knocked on his door, he called me in, but I opened it to see that he was in the bath. He grinned when he saw me, pleased to have embarrassed me, leaning back lazily in the tub, letting his arms rest down its side. He looked far beyond his years; his chest and shoulders already heavily muscled, and dark gold hair, light but discernible, already growing across his chest.

"It is not *urgent*, Mordred," I said, irritably. His casualness about it made me wonder if he was naked, still, in front of his mother, even though he was grown. Was this normal? I had never known what a grown boy was like with his mother.

Mordred laughed, low and soft, standing in the bath, the water sluicing off his body. I looked away. Out of the corner of my eye, I saw him wrap a sheet around his waist, but he did not move to get dressed.

"Mother told me that you were raised by nuns," he laughed. So, the pair of them laughed at me. Of course they did.

I turned back to him, and met his look of amusement with an even stare, ready to scold him for being rude to me, but he was talking again already.

"I've heard it said," he began, grinning, "that the wise women of Avalon are tattooed in woad all over their bodies."

His words hit me harder than I had expected. He was just teasing me, but they reminded me, unbearably, of the first time I had spoken to Accolon. He had said the same thing to me. My anger, my resentment at Arthur for his murder, had eclipsed my grief, but now the sight of my sister's lover – young, muscular and darkly golden – and Mordred's words brought my memories of him, and the pain of his loss, to the surface of my mind. Unconsciously, I put a hand to my brow, stepping back. I wished I had not already shown Mordred a sign of weakness, but I hoped that in his youth he would think it was only my nunnish modesty that he and his mother had laughed so heartily together about.

"Morgan," he said, quietly, and I looked up at him. "I did not mean to upset you."

He was a strange boy. The way he spoke was strange, too. Always direct, never respectful. He never called me *Lady* Morgan, nor Aunt. I wondered if that was a sign of his respect, or his disdain. I did not think he was particularly clever, but he was certainly shrewd, watchful. I suspected him of knowing enough about Avalon not to have disdain for me, or my skills.

"I am not upset," I told him. He crossed his arms over his bare chest, looking at me with his curious stare.

"They say that Merlin gave you his secrets before he died."

"Some of them," I answered, warily. "And there was a price."

"What?"

"He took a precious magic object from me." I forced myself to try to be calm, I forced myself to remember what I had come for. "What is your interest in the magic arts, Mordred?"

He shrugged. "Mother tends to exaggerate. I just wanted to know if you really were a powerful witch or not."

I could not help but smile then. Mordred knew his mother well. So, now I knew what would win him around to an alliance with me. A display of power. I closed my eyes and pictured myself as Guinevere, dressed in one of her fine dresses of green silk, her wild hair plaited into a bun, the picture of reserved, demure, queenly power. When I opened my eyes, Mordred's face wore an expression that betrayed both how impressed he was, and how useful he thought this would be to his own ambitions. I closed my eyes and let my shape shift through others; Kay, Lancelot, Arthur, Gawain, his mother, back to myself. When I opened my eyes, he was grinning.

"Very impressive, Morgan." His smile changed. "Morgan... who was that woman?"

Of course. Of course Mordred, like every other foolish man who had ever laid eyes on her, had conceived a desire for Guinevere. But this would not necessarily go ill for my designs.

"That," I told him, with a smile of my own, "was your father's wife."

Chapter Forty-Nine

My victory with Mordred was enough to put my thoughts of Accolon from my mind for the rest of the day, but it was not enough once I was asleep. In my dreams, I woke to the sound of the bed curtains being pulled back, and I opened my eyes to find myself back in my bed in Rheged, and him there, standing at the foot of the bed, his hand still on the bed-curtain, and in the other hand, the sword forged as Excalibur's double. He threw it down, and I leapt into his arms as he came towards me. Our mouths met in a desperate passion, and I felt it as though he was really there in my arms, the roughness of his stubble against my face, the hunger of his kiss, my own body's passionate response to it, the hot longing rising up in a wave of heat from the core of me. The dream was a haze of remembered sensations, and it only left me hot and frustrated. I woke with Morgawse's words, *You want a young man, Morgan*, echoing in my ears. But I didn't need a young man. I needed revenge. I needed payment for Accolon's death, and my betrayal. That was the only thing that would give me satisfaction.

Before I began in earnest, though, I had to know if Galahad was safe, and I had to see him if I could. Nimue had given her orders, but I was resolved to go to Camelot. I dressed in my fine dress of black with the black gems sewn into it from neck to waist, and I closed my eyes, and pictured myself back in my room at Camelot. I saw the wood of my table, the empty fireplace, the plain bed, but as the room appeared before me, so did Nimue, standing small and stern, her arms crossed in front of her chest, her childlike, pretty face, swirled through with blue, turned up in anger towards me as I appeared standing over her.

"I knew you would come anyway," she said, sharply.

So, she had learned great secrets from Merlin. I did not know how she had sensed my coming, and come to meet me. But she would not stop me. I went to step past her, and she held out a hand, and I felt my legs freeze still. I could feel the strength of her. She was stronger now than Merlin had ever been. The only difference between them was that Nimue considered herself noble, and Merlin had acknowledged his own selfishness. She was just as selfish as I was, or he had been. She only wanted to protect Arthur because he was the man she favoured – I wondered idly if she still desired him – and she only hoped to secure her own power as the Lady of Avalon. She never had shared Merlin's secrets with me, as she had promised that she would.

"Morgan, please, go back to Lothian."

"Why him? Why did you have to take my son? Was it just to punish me? Do you hate me so much that you would hurt me so deeply as to *take my son* and forbid me from seeing him?" I cried.

"No, Morgan," Nimue said, gently, and I saw the regret in her eyes, but I was not moved by it. "Morgan... it had to be him. I saw it, long ago. I am sorry that Lancelot did not... wish to stay with you.

But, Galahad, he was conceived in magic, he has magic in his blood from you, and from his father, he has all the greatness of a perfect knight. It is only he who can find the Grail."

"What is the Grail to you?" I snapped. I knew that Nimue was no Christian. "What do *you* want with the blood of Christ?"

Nimue shook her head. "The Grail is not the cup of Christ. It is the blood of the world, the blood of the Mother. Galahad will bring it to us, if anyone can. It was the last of Merlin's secrets, the blood of the world. With the blood of the world, anything can be done. Anything can be changed. Even a man's destiny."

Arthur's destiny.

"This is all for Arthur, then," I said.

"For him," Nimue admitted, with a small nod, "for Britain. For your sister's son. Maybe for you as well."

"What have you seen about *me*?" I demanded, suddenly alarmed. I had never thought of my own destiny. Destiny was something the men had, and I was on the edge, free to do as I pleased, now that I was free of men. I did not want some great hand of destiny hanging over me, deciding my fate. But Nimue did not answer, she reached out and took my hand in hers, and I saw my room in Lothian appear before me, and her dissolve away.

She had taken my son, she had kept me from him, and she was trying to use him to protect Arthur, because she loved him. Well, it would not be. I did not even believe the Grail – either Nimue's Grail, or the Cup of Christ – existed, and I would take destiny into my hands without the help of Merlin's secrets. I had the instrument of destiny within my grasp, and I would use Mordred as ruthlessly as Nimue had used my own son.

The end of April came, and with it, Mordred's entry to adulthood. It was time that he should become a knight. The question remained unanswered whether that would be in Lothian with his mother, or in Camelot with his father. Morgawse arranged a great feast for the day, and a tournament. The men of Lothian did not joust, considering it a game for French dandies, but instead fought all their tournaments on foot, with blunted but real swords, and dressed in full armour. Mordred was easily the victor of the day. I wondered, to watch him fight, how he would have fared against his brothers, or Lancelot. Or Arthur. He had all of Arthur's powerful strength and muscular bulk. I had seen Arthur on the battlefield, and he was graceful for his size, every move powerful and smooth. Mordred had all the same power, but behind it a kind of reckless wildness, a savagery almost. He never seemed to feel his own wounds, or the blows other men struck at him, though when he took off his helm at the end to be named the winner of the day, he had a line of dried blood thick against his scalp. As it was, no man in Lothian could stand long against him, but soon he would no longer be in Lothian, and the men of Camelot trained hard and grew huge from the fighting. It was easy to see him as a giant among men here, but I wondered how large and strong he would look at his father's court.

Morgawse was already drunk when the feast began, but pleasantly so. She was upset, I could tell, that her last son had become a man, but she wore it well. I had been half afraid that she would get drunk and cry, but the wine seemed to have put her in good spirits, and her love for her son to have won out over her desire to keep him to herself. Her lover, Sir Lamerocke, sat down among the other knights on the trestle tables, and she barely seemed to notice him there, though I often saw him glance towards her with an ill-disguised longing. I noticed Mordred see it, too.

I sat at Morgawse's left side, and Mordred sat at her right, in the place he always held. He ought to have, now he was a man and the last prince of Lothian left in the castle, have taken her seat, but it was clear he did not want to take that from her. Morgawse had ruled like a man in Lothian with the threat of her grown sons not far away, and it was clear to me that every single one would have given anything to protect their mother.

Mordred did not drink much, and neither did I. I had no taste for drunkenness, and nothing to erase like my sister had. Morgawse, a light flush on her cheeks, and against her neck, was laughing beside me, her blue eyes sparkling, her easy grace flowing out of her. She looked beautiful, as though the years had not touched her, her long, copper-gold hair flowing in waves over her shoulders, pulled back at the front and clasped with an ornament of gold and amber. Around her neck she had a string of amber beads, the colour rich and gorgeous against her pale skin and the pale gold freckles that covered it. She still had the full figure of her youth, and she wore a dress of dark orange and gold cut low and square at the neck that showed it well, and around her shoulders, rich red furs. She did not wear her crown, but it was clear to everyone what a queen she was. I wondered how thin, and hard, and dark I must have looked beside her in my dress of black gems, my woad, my long, dark brown plait of hair. Morgawse and I must have looked like creatures from different worlds. I always felt my plainness most acutely beside her, but she never seemed to notice either my plainness or her own beauty at all.

Sat around us at the table were the noblest lords from the lands surrounding Lothian, the Lord of Orkney, who was vassal to Morgawse and Mordred, and the Barons of the Highlands, all come to pay their respects to the youngest prince of Lothian to grow to manhood. I could see, from the looks some of them gave my sister, that they also had regards they would like to give to Lothian's Queen – and perhaps had, in the past – but would not tonight. Not under the watchful eye of her son.

He was proper, and courteous and polite with them, but I could see that he made them uneasy. Unless he was mocking someone, he was not ready to laugh or smile as his mother was, and they cast the same wary eye on me as they did on him. Some of them seemed genuinely afraid of him, even. But they poured their attention on Morgawse, flattering her with tales they had heard of men fighting for the sake of her beauty, or recounting the great deeds of her husband, in his youth. She seemed to especially like those stories, though she had not liked her husband. No one spoke directly to me. They were all afraid.

Towards the end of the evening, when the wine had turned Morgawse from giggly to sleepy and her eyelids drooped slightly, and the little sweet cakes had been brought out and eaten with great enthusiasm by the lords, and less enthusiasm by Morgawse, who I suspected was feeling a little sick, Mordred stood to thank his vassal lords for attending. A hush fell instantly.

"Thank you, good vassals to Lothian, for coming today. I am a man grown now, and I wish to announce my intention –" I saw his gaze, unconsciously, flicker to his mother. "My intention to gain my father, King Arthur's, recognition as his son. If he fails to acknowledge what, to every man in this room, I am sure is plain to see, then I ask you to honour your pledges to me today, and I will gather my armies and march on Camelot –"

"*No!*" Morgawse, as always discarding any code of politeness, got to her feet, shouting. She did not look so drunk anymore; the shock of her son's words had shaken it out of her. She turned to her lords, but they were already muttering among themselves. They liked the sound of Lothian and its vassal kingdoms taking their power back from Arthur. They remembered the early days of greatness and independence under Lot. In Mordred, they saw the potential for a Britain ruled by Lothian. "Sirs, I did not bring you here to talk of *war*," she cried, staring at her son.

The Lord of Orkney, an ageing warrior with a scarred face, a thick, brown beard down to his chest and a bald head, shifted in his seat. The look he gave Morgawse was one of intimacy, as though he had spoken to her alone before many times.

"Of course, my Lady. But," he glanced around to the men around him, "we would all be happy, I am sure, to pledge again our allegiance to your son, to *all* your sons, and to Lothian. In peace," he added, delicately, "of course."

Morgawse was not a fool. But she was also not so bold, not so wild that she would deny this. The lords wanted Mordred. They turned their greedy eyes to Britain, and they thought Mordred would bring it to them. They would get rid of him afterwards. A bastard child of incest – he would be easy to throw from his place, if he got it, as King of Britain.

"Thank you," she sighed, but I could see she was still angry. "Lothian is grateful for its noble allies."

She sat, slowly, back in her seat, and Mordred followed. The conversation after that was tense, and faltering. I was glad when the Lord of Orkney made an excuse to leave. He was the most powerful of all the lords there, and the others could not leave until he did. He walked around the table to bow before Mordred, and take Morgawse's hand in his, and press it to his lips. I watched Mordred's eyes follow his mother's hand, and rest on her face.

Once they had all left, Morgawse stood huffily from her chair and rushed from the room. I saw Mordred run after her, and I followed. Out in the courtyard it was growing dark.

"Mother," Mordred called out after her, running over and pulling her back round towards him, holding her by the shoulders. She pushed him back. He did not let go. It was clear that any time he had been obedient to her before had been out of his choice, for he was strong enough to do always as he wished. She tried to push him away again, and I could see as I came closer that she was fighting back angry tears. I was not the only one who had noticed them struggling, for across the courtyard came Lamerocke. I thought about shouting at him to leave, but it was too late, for Mordred had already seen him. He let go of his mother with one hand to turn on the knight, and all the softness he turned on his angry mother faded, and his eyes blazed.

"*You*," Mordred shouted at him, and his voice echoed in the courtyard. Lamerocke froze where he stood. He was older, a more experienced fighter, but I could see he was afraid of Mordred. "This is no concern of yours."

"Mordred," he tried. "See, she is upset. Let her go."

Mordred lunged forward, and Lamerocke jumped back, and Mordred laughed, low and cruel. "You think because you are fucking my mother that you have *any* say in what happens in Lothian Castle? Any control over me?"

So, Mordred did know. And he was jealous. Morgawse was too angry, too upset, and too drunk to protest their arguing over her in the middle of the courtyard. I wondered where the Lord of Orkney was, and if he was listening.

I stepped between them, giving Lamerocke a cold look. Mordred was right at least insofar as this was nothing to do with him.

"I will take my sister to her chamber, thank you, sirs," I said, sternly. I reached out for her hand, and she took it. She was trembling, though I suspected it was with rage. Mordred held on for a moment, a demonstration to me of his strength, that he was only letting go because he wanted to, and then released her. I rushed us both up to her chamber and shut and bolted the door. As soon as we were alone, Morgawse, carried by the strength of her rage – and the wine – paced into the middle of the room, pushing her hair back from her face and shaking her head.

"Morgan, *what am I to do with him?*" She turned to me, her face wild with exasperation. "He has said these things to me before, of course, but I never thought he would do something like this, in front of the lords. They will be behind *him* now, not me. They want it. They're all greedy for it. Especially Orkney. Ugh, *Orkney*. He has become a nasty, cowardly, greedy old man. Not so long ago, he was brave. But they will all go with Mordred if they think there is something for them. Then Orkney will be wanting to wed me again, though it's not like I am going to be having any more children at my age. But that's not what he wants. He wants Lothian Castle. Mordred would give it to him, as well, just to get some recognition from his father. *Arthur.*" She sighed in annoyance again. The way she said his name, it was as though he were just in the next room. There was a startling intimacy about it, a rawness I did not want to hear. "If Arthur could just – *ugh* – just show him the smallest amount of interest, proper to what any other father would show a strong, noble son of his. I am not some *peasant woman* he had at the side of the road, I'm a *queen*, and it is an insult to me as well that he does not, he *will not* acknowledge our son."

"You are also," I reminded her, tentatively, "his sister."

"Morgan," she cried, and I saw the tears gather in her eyes, "*you* are my sister. We share all the same blood, we grew up together. Arthur is *not* my brother. Not really."

"It is all the same to him, Morgawse," I told her, softly. Morgawse covered her face with her hands, and I felt the stab of pity at my heart for her. All of those men she had claimed to have enjoyed, and she was still thinking of Arthur. I wondered how easy it had been for Arthur to forget her.

That night we lay side by side, as we had done so long ago, and so many times now since we were girls, and she fell asleep fast, tired out with the wine, and the shouting, and the tears that she had kept inside herself; but I lay awake, thinking of Galahad, and his father, who probably hated me more than Arthur hated my sister, and I could not sleep all night.

Chapter Fifty

In the morning, Morgawse was weary and thoughtful. She had gone to sleep thinking of Arthur, and he was still on her mind. As the day had come, I had just drifted into an uneasy sleep, but I woke again when I felt her sit up in bed beside me. I looked up at her, blearily, the sheets gathered around her, her hair falling loose around her shoulders, her arms wrapped around her knees where she rested her chin. She could have been a girl of eleven years old again. I sat up beside her and put my head on her shoulder.

"I still remember the first time we kissed," she told me, softly, "like it was just yesterday. It was on the battlements, at Camelot, and we were looking out. He was nervous. I could tell. He was nervous right up until the moment that it happened, and then he did not seem nervous at all. I had never kissed a man, apart from Lot, then, and it was something different entirely. He loved me. I *know* he loved me. How could it disappear all in a moment like that? How do men's feelings change, so sudden? I know, I do, that it was wrong, but that didn't make any difference to how I felt. It didn't *feel* wrong. I don't suppose he ever thinks about it, now. It is as though Mordred and I don't exist for him, anymore."

I didn't know what to say. I knew she wanted me to say that Arthur had asked about her, but in truth I thought she was right.

"You should try to forget, too," I whispered.

She nodded, but she did not seem to mean it.

We did not talk about Arthur again. Spring shaded into summer, which was not warm in Lothian, and I felt myself longing for Camelot's long, sweet summers, its ripe apples and pears, the days spent lounging on the soft grass in the shade of the trees. Lothian's summer was short, and somehow bleak. Mordred said nothing more

319

about marching to Camelot, though I was sure he still thought of it; nor did he shout again at Lamerocke, though I noticed the knight took greater pains than before to avoid him. I felt as though the moment was beginning to slip away from me. I did not want Mordred to lose interest in his ambitions, but I was not yet sure enough to try to have him leave Lothian with me. I wondered how much of my black magic had reached his blood. I could not tell. I felt nothing from him that I recognised as such, but I had some deeper, unconscious sense of something powerful about him. Whether it was just the black destiny that hung over him, I was not sure. Nimue might have known for sure, but I was not in such a position that I would take her into my confidence.

As it happened, I did not have to force the matter at all. Mordred was keen as I had hoped to be at his father's side. It was a late summer day, and the sun was bright, though the air had not lost its northern chill. We three, Mordred, Morgawse and I, sat in her council chamber. I did not like it there; I had too vivid a memory of Lot holding me down against the table in that room to want to return there often, but news had come from Camelot that Gawain and Aggravain had returned from the Grail quest, and Morgawse had called us there to tell us. News reached Lothian slowly, it seemed, for the last I had heard there was only talk of the Grail. Had Galahad even still been in Camelot when I tried to see him and was stopped by Nimue, if men were already returning? Time was beginning to slip past me in fits and starts, fast then slow, then fast.

"You see, Mother," Mordred began, pointedly, "I have missed the quest for the Grail. It is time I became a knight. I want to go to Camelot. I need my father's recognition, otherwise it is dishonour on Lothian. A grown man cannot be without a father to name."

Morgawse shook her head. "Mordred, my love." She stepped forward and took his face in her hands. He put, I noticed, a hand against her waist in response. "He will not give it to you. I am sorry for it, too, but it is better to stay here. Besides, my love, really, you are too young."

"Mother," he was beginning to sound annoyed, "I am fifteen years old."

"His father was such an age, when he was made," I pointed out, gently.

"He was not," she snapped. "He was much older. Eighteen years old, at least."

She must have known that was not true. She turned back to Mordred.

"A few more years in Lothian will not do your honour harm, Mordred." She stroked his cheek lightly with her hand, and he leaned his forehead against hers, closing his eyes. "I will be lonely without you," she whispered.

"Mother," he sighed, drawing her tight against him, into an embrace. "I could take you with me," he said, softly, into the top of her hair. She rested her face against his chest wrapping her arms around his neck. They looked for all the world like two lovers. I was sure she had never been so intimate with any of her other sons. His resemblance to Arthur, her lingering affection, the possessive way in which they behaved towards one another all filled me with unease.

Morgawse shook her head, against his chest. "No, my love. Your father would refuse to see me. Just, forget Camelot. Stay. Stay with me. Morgan," she turned to look at me, her eyes imploring, "tell him he should stay."

Of course I wanted him to go, but I was weak as always in the face of Morgawse's pleas for help.

"Morgawse..." I began, warily, but she did not want to hear what I had to say.

She moved back from Mordred to take hold of his hands. "Don't think I don't know what you want there. Arthur won't stand for it, you turning up and demanding to be made his heir. He has a wife, who is still young, and may yet have a child, and if you go there demanding to be his heir you will get yourself into danger. We don't want another war, Mordred. You shouldn't be trying to start one."

Mordred was suddenly angry, too, but his anger was different in quality from his mother's. There was something beneath it, something darker. It wasn't the red-hot flash of rage I had seen in Morgawse and Gawain. No, it was the slow-burning anger of his father. "I only want what is rightfully mine," he shouted, towering over his mother who let go of his hands to cross her arms over her chest.

"It is better giving up on wanting something you can't have," she retorted, and I could hear the bitterness in her voice. It had hurt her, giving up on Arthur.

"*Men*," Mordred growled, "do not give up."

"Men are all stubborn fools," Morgawse shouted back.

Mordred opened his mouth as though he was going to say something else, and I knew it would not be kind, but Morgawse did not wait to hear it. She turned from him, and rushed past me from the room, slamming the door behind her. I did not know which was worse for her; the thought of her son leaving her, or the thought that it was to be with Arthur, who had abandoned her. But it would be now. I was sure of that; sure that the moment for me to take this into my hands was finally upon me. Mordred would do anything I said now, if it would get him what he wanted. I had shown him my power, and now it was time for me to show him that we wanted the same thing.

I waited until I heard Morgawse's footsteps fade to silence as she walked down the stairs. Mordred stood looking away from me, leaning back against the table, his hands braced against it beside him as though he were holding himself back from something. I could see his chest rising and falling. How long had he been angry like this? Every single day that he had heard his father was the King of Britain, and that he would get nothing for it. That his was a cursed life, and a cursed birth, and it was he who caused the mother he loved to suffer.

He did not seem to notice that I was still there, but he would. I stepped in front of him, crossing my arms over my chest, and he looked up.

"Mordred –"

"I do not need another lecture," he growled, not meeting my eye. I did not know if he would crack with the strength of his emotions if I took him to Camelot. *I* was ready. I had waited and waited for the opportunity, and now it was so close I thought I could feel the net tightening around Arthur, and just the thought of it quickened my heart a little.

"Actually, Mordred, I thought we might be able to help one another," I said, carefully. He looked up at me then. "You and I both have reason to hate Arthur, and you and I both want the same thing. Well, not the same thing, but they can be achieved through the same means. I want to punish Arthur, and you want what is rightfully yours by birth. Is that correct?"

Mordred did not answer, but stood up straight, suddenly attentive. I could see the quiver of dread excitement run through him. I could see the hunger for what he thought was justice, and perhaps for destruction as well, light in him.

"Good. I suggest we make an agreement between us. I will help you take the throne that is your birthright. I will put all my skills and power behind you, and we shall not fail. We will destroy Arthur. In return, *I* shall take the sword Excalibur."

A cunning smile spread over Mordred's face, and he nodded.

"Though, I should like the sword. What if I gave you Lothian once I was King?"

I shook my head. "There will be no negotiations, Mordred. If you want my help, the price is the sword."

He thought about it, but only for a moment, before he nodded in agreement. I felt a dark thrill go through me.

Mordred had begun to pace thoughtfully before me.

"But how is it to be *done*, Morgan?" In the thoughts of his own greatness, his anger had dissipated, dissolved as if it had never been, and was replaced with a manic fervour. When he had paused his pacing to glance to me for an answer, I gave him an arch smile of my own in return.

"Arthur is strong, and his knights are always with him. We cannot simply walk into Camelot and kill him. However, Arthur does have a weakness. His wife." Mordred, intrigued, stepped towards me, and I saw the light spark in his dark eyes. "Arthur loves his wife. Arthur's wife loves –"

Mordred nodded, as though the same thought was coming to him. "Sir Lancelot. I remember – Aggravain's letter – but I thought that was just gossip."

I shook my head. "I have tried several times to... draw Arthur's attention to the matter. He sees only what he wants to see. At present, Lancelot is far from court, on the quest for the Grail, if what Gawain writes is true. I will convince Morgawse that now is the right time for you to take your place among your brothers at Arthur's court. You will go, you will be obedient and loyal, and you will be made a knight. We watch, we wait, and when the time comes, we will bring the matter to Arthur's attention in a way he cannot ignore. It will break him to see the wife he loves with another man, and once he is broken, he will be easy to kill."

Mordred looked at me narrowly, as though he were seeing me properly for the first time.

"How did I never notice that you were this wise, Morgan?" he said. So, we had found what we needed in one another. He reached forward, and, putting an arm around my waist, tried to draw me in to a kiss. I pushed him back.

"Mordred, I am your *aunt*, and this is *not* that kind of arrangement." He simply shrugged, unembarrassed. I could not disguise the look of disgust in my eyes as I regarded him, nor did I mean to. I only wanted his assistance, for I could not do it alone; I did not want his friendship and I *certainly* did not intend to have him as my lover.

"You're a little pervert, aren't you Mordred?" I sneered.

He gave a rough laugh, turning from me to leave. "I get it from my father," he spat, as he left the room.

Chapter Fifty-One

If we were to have success, Mordred and I would have to bide our time. I knew that Morgawse could not be approached with it right away. She was still too upset. I, too, wanted more time to plant the thoughts in Arthur's head. I knew he would not believe me – he had ignored my letter saying as much – but if we were patient I thought he would give in to the truth eventually.

We waited, Mordred and I, and summer passed into autumn, and autumn into winter, and it was too thick with snow for him to go to Camelot. Once Morgawse felt assured she had her son with her for another year, she was her old self again. Mordred seemed desperately relieved about this, for he had missed his mother's affection. I had been more pleased when Morgawse had been wounded and sulky with him, for now I had to sit with them as the nights drew in while they cuddled together by the fire, she lying in her pile of cushions, he with his head on her shoulder, or – worse – on her stomach. I read to them – news from Camelot and Rheged (my son Ywain wrote often, assuring me that the castle was well, and of the loyalty of my lords; his letters were businesslike and without affection), or some preposterous stories from one of Morgawse's books of romance. She liked those, but I found them trivial and silly. I would have liked to have read some Latin, but Morgawse could not only not understand it, but claimed she could not abide the sound of the language, so it was either news or frivolous tales of nonsense that kept us entertained.

Mordred came to me one night, the week before the Christmas celebrations.

"Morgan," he said, striding into my room and taking hold of me by the shoulders, "we have made this pact, you and I, and nothing has yet been done. *Do* something."

I shook my head, firmly pushing his hands off my shoulders.

"*Patience*, Mordred. When the snows have thawed, I will talk to Morgawse. I will make her understand there is no other way. This will take time. We will have no success if you demand to act before the time is right."

Reluctantly trusting in my words, Mordred stepped back from me. A curious look passed over his face, and he regarded me half-sideways.

"Show me that woman again," he demanded.

"What woman?" I asked.

"The one who you appeared as to me before. My father's wife."

I shook my head. "I'm not some market-town trickster with a bag full of frogs, Mordred."

"Show me, Morgan," he insisted. "After all, am I not to see what we are dealing with, when we reach Camelot?"

I could see that he would not be dissuaded, and I did not see what harm it would do. I was reluctant to perform magic at his request, for I did not want him to think that I was his creature to command, but I wanted to keep him on my side. I closed my eyes and pictured Guinevere again. Her image was still as vivid in my mind as my own. I had taken her shape many times before.

When I opened my eyes, Mordred was staring at me. Was he *so* stunned by the look of her? He reached out a hand towards me, and before I could step back, his fingers brushed lightly against my neck, and suddenly the room disappeared around me, around both of us, and we stood in Arthur's chamber at Camelot. At first, I thought I was looking at Arthur, for the man before us both wore Arthur's red and gold surcoat, but as the room came into focus, I saw it must be Mordred. Guinevere was there with him. Mordred stood facing her. Their eyes were locked together, and his hand was pressed against the base of her ribs, his fingers spreading out across her chest, as though he was holding her against the wall. She did not, however, seem to be attempting to push him off. Still, there was a strange defiance on her face, and resignation. He, on the other hand, looked lost, consumed with some unspeakable desire, some fervour like the one I had seen him in when I had promised him the throne. He leaned down and kissed her, and she did not push him back, but seemed to respond with an equal passion.

I felt Mordred draw his hand back, and I saw the victory on his face. He, then, had not seen her strange, equivocal expression, had not wondered what his father's wife would want with him. I let myself slip back into my own form. I did not want to be faced with an over-excited Mordred. He was grinning, pacing with half-jumping steps.

"Morgan, was that from me, or you?" he asked. I did not know. There must have been some of my black magic strong in his blood for his touch to send us both there, into the same vision of the future.

He did not wait for me to respond. "Will that truly happen?" he demanded, his black eyes bright with grim excitement.

I hesitated. I knew the danger too well myself of the things I had seen.

"Mordred..." I began, tentatively, "you did not see, I think, quite what you thought you saw."

"I saw my father's wife giving herself to me. What a victory, Morgan. *What a victory.* You know what this means, of course?" He looked at me, eagerly. "A day will come when I will be recognised not only as greater than my father, but greater than the knight Lancelot, who all men say is the greatest living knight. When I have my father's wife in my possession, men will understand my greatness, and recognise me as the rightful king I am."

Possession. The word made me feel uneasy. It made me think of Lot, and Uriens, and Arthur. Of the men at Arthur's wedding shouting *Arthur the Conqueror*, of the feel of a hand clamped over my mouth.

Mordred took me by the shoulders and stared at me, wild and intense.

"Morgan. Talk to my mother. I *must* go to Camelot."

When spring came, I broached the subject with Morgawse. Lamerocke had gone back to Camelot, summoned by Arthur, and I had begun to spend my nights sleeping side by side with her once more.

It was on a bright morning in late spring and we sat side by side in the bed. Morgawse was eating an apple, and spilling little bits of its juice over the furs spread over the bedsheets against the cold. Morgawse had always been messy. The annoyance reminded me of our childhood, for I had always been shy and neat while Morgawse was bold and clumsy, and I felt the tug at my heart for what I was about to push her into. But I was doing it for her; Arthur deserved to be punished for her sake as much as for mine. I took a deep breath.

"Morgawse... I think it is time that Mordred went to Camelot."

To my surprise, she nodded. She did not look at me, but she stopped taking bites of the apple, and just stared at it in her hand. I could see a tear rolling down her cheek.

"I know," she said, softly. I put my hand on her shoulder, and she rested her cheek against it, closing her eyes. She added, "I just hoped for a little longer. I will not have any more children, and when he is gone, I will be alone."

I put a hand comfortingly on her hair.

326

"You could come," I suggested, doubtfully.

Morgawse gave a rough laugh.

"I'm sure Arthur would be pleased to see me," she said. I kissed the top of her head, and we were quiet again.

After that, we began to make the arrangements. I wrote to Ector. He was the one person at Camelot who I thought did not have a reason to mistrust me, and I was sure he would be kind. I told him that Morgawse wanted to present her son to Arthur. I thought it was best if we knew, even a little bit, what kind of reception we were likely to get there. By the time Mordred had turned sixteen, I had a long reply from Ector, detailing all the news from Camelot. All of the men had returned from the quest for the Grail apart from Lancelot, Bors, Galahad and Percival. I wondered how restless the Queen was becoming, with her lover away for so long. It was not ideal for drawing it to Arthur's attention, but I was sure that Lancelot would return alive, and after such a long time apart, I was sure that the time would be right for us. The letter was long and detailed, but lacked a direct answer to my questions about whether Arthur would receive his son. That in itself did, however, seem to imply that the reception would not be favourable.

I showed it to Morgawse and she shook her head and sighed. She wanted to use it as an excuse to keep Mordred with her. They shouted again, Morgawse raging and hysterical, Mordred determined. She cried, he yelled, but it would not be changed. She knew that he would have to go to his father eventually.

It was not until autumn was coming that Mordred set off for Camelot. To my surprise, Morgawse insisted on riding with him. We did not send word to Camelot to say that they were coming. I did not want to give Arthur the chance to refuse.

I did not ride with them. I was unsure how welcome I would be in Camelot in my own form. I did not know how many people Guinevere and Lancelot had told about the true identity of Elaine. I imagined that they would not have told anyone at all, for it would have been hard to explain the whole truth without giving themselves away, but they might have lied enough about it to Arthur to only tell the truth about me. Besides, I thought I would be better in secret. I could observe more carefully what was happening around me if I were unrecognised.

I closed my eyes and pictured myself back in Camelot, and in the form of a nondescript serving girl, one I had seen around Lothian

Castle. She was shortish, medium build, with mousey hair wound into a long plait, and then up around her head. She would not attract any attention, and since she was not one of Camelot's servants, no one would try to make me do anything, and I would pass unnoticed. Dressed in one of my plain black wool dresses, and wearing a plain face, I was confident of my ability to exist at the heart of it all, utterly undetected.

Chapter Fifty-Two

So I went, and I waited for Mordred's arrival. I was eager to see Arthur's reaction, and I was not disappointed. It was an early autumn day. While it was cold in Lothian already, Camelot was still mild and warm. The courtyard was almost empty when I heard the horn sound as someone spotted their approach. They would have looked like a royal party even from far off. Arthur was not, then, prepared for their coming. I had been afraid that Morgawse would write to him.

Arthur rushed down, Guinevere at his side, just as the gates opened and Morgawse rode through at the head of her party. He was not at all prepared; he was without his crown and gilt surcoat, wearing instead a plain doublet. He looked more of a warrior in his plain clothes. Somehow the grandeur of his king's clothes hid his powerful strength. Guinevere, at his side, looked just as I remembered her. She had that same strange sulky loveliness that I had seen when I had seen her married, the slightly pouting red mouth, the unreadable expression of her eyes as she watched her husband's bastard child ride through the gates of her castle.

I could see that Arthur was angry. But unlike Guinevere, he was not watching his son, he was watching Morgawse. I hoped he felt ashamed, to stand there beside his wife, with Morgawse riding towards him. She was as lovely as she had been all those years ago, in a rich robe of dark red, edged with white fur, her copper-gold hair all but loose around her shoulders, only drawn back at her temples, and on it the crown of Lothian, dark gold and studded with rubies.

Mordred jumped from his horse first to offer Morgawse his hand. She took it with a gracious smile to her beloved son, and slipped down. Arthur was bristling. They walked up to Arthur and Guinevere, and Morgawse curtsied low and Mordred bowed. Guinevere did not take her eyes off him.

"Why did you bring him here?" Arthur demanded. Morgawse bore it well, giving Arthur a casual, easy smile, as though they were two old acquaintances making conversation.

"It is fitting that he comes to fight for his King, Arthur. Lothian is still a vassal kingdom of Logrys, so it is only right that you accept my sons — all my sons — as your knights. You can't just take the ones that please you. Besides, Mordred will please you. He is strong already, and it is his wish to become one of your knights," Morgawse added.

Arthur did not say anything for a long time, and I noticed that Mordred had not spoken. His eyes flicked across the courtyard to me, and I felt them lock with mine, and I knew that he saw right through me. He should not have been able to. I felt my heart thud suddenly with fear. I had a lost a little ground from him.

Arthur made some angry gesture of acceptance and turned to leave, storming back up to his tower. Morgawse turned back to her son, and to her attendants to arrange where their things would be taken, and in the business of that, I saw Guinevere turn and slip up to her own room. I was surprised that she did not follow Arthur. Perhaps she was angry. I followed her, looking out for Margery on the way. If I could, I would send her off on some errand and take her place. I did not see her, and I was wary to take her shape if she had died or been sent from the castle. I did, however, run into the younger of the Breton women, Marie. When I told her that one of the women in the kitchen wanted her, she rolled her eyes as though she was above it, but she went nonetheless. I closed my eyes and took her shape, though it was an effort, for I had seen less of her and it came less readily to me, but I was convinced it was done well enough. The only problem now was that Guinevere would speak to me in Breton, and I would not know how to answer. I was curious enough to risk it.

When I pushed the door to her room open, she was sitting at her window, staring out, down at the walled garden beneath her tower. I could see her profile, the soft lines of her face. She looked different alone.

When I pushed the door shut behind me, she looked up, and a gentle, tired smile came to her face.

"Oh, Marie," she said. She had not said anything in Breton, and I sensed my chance to speak to her in English.

"You have seen Queen Morgawse's son, my Lady?" I asked, tentatively.

Guinevere gave an odd laugh, looking down at her knee, picking at a stitch in her dress. "Arthur's son, you mean?" She was so open with her women, so different.

"What do you... think about it?" I asked, not sure how much directness I could dare.

She shrugged without looking up, biting one side of her lower lip. "I don't know," she answered, honestly. She turned to look at me, her fierce green eyes soft for once with thought. She looked as though she were about to say something, but then she pressed the heel of her hand to her forehead.

"Marie..." she sighed, shaking her head, but not lifting away her hand or opening her eyes. She did not say anything else, as though it was too tight within her, the emotion. Suddenly, she seemed to close off, and pull herself together, rubbing her face lightly with her fingertips, patting her hair to check it was in place, standing up. "Marie," she continued, suddenly brisk, "I will be in Arthur's rooms tonight."

I nodded, not sure what to say in response. I was sure, from what I remembered, that the Marie she knew would have had some joke to make about that, but I had none. She walked swiftly past me, leaving the door open, careless. If she would not even tell her confidantes that she was not pleased that Arthur's bastard child was at court when she had no child of her own, she would not have spoken to them of Lancelot. She had such control, to hold her secrets within herself, and hold herself together behind that stern mask. She would be harder to break than Arthur, or Lancelot.

Morgawse knew what shape I would be in, and knew to look for me. I had let myself slip back into the plain servant girl from Lothian's shape. Morgawse found me in the courtyard as the sun was going down. She was flushed and annoyed. Arthur had shouted at her, demanded that she go back to Lothian, tonight. We talked in hushed tones at the side of the courtyard. I did not want anyone to guess who I was. One could never be sure in Camelot if someone was listening.

"Morgan," Morgawse took my hands in hers, imploringly, "stay here and make sure that Arthur is good to him."

I promised Morgawse that I would write to her, and she seemed deeply relieved. She kissed me on both cheeks, and reluctantly she mounted her horse and left. I was surprised how much it hurt to watch her go. The two years I had spent in Lothian with my sister had reminded me of how deeply I loved her, and how I would do anything for her. Especially this. For her, for me. For the Breton queen even, perhaps. As I turned to go up to my room – which I knew was unoccupied – I noticed Kay, in the corner of the courtyard. So, he was here, not hunting for the Grail.

Mordred was waiting for me, and I could see that he was agitated. He began talking almost before I had shut the door behind myself.

"Did you see how he looked at me? The disrespect he showed to me, and Mother?" He paced before me, tense with his anger. I sighed and shook my head.

"Calm down, Mordred. We must play this slowly, and carefully, if we are to succeed. You will have to win his trust, and that will take time."

He was not listening to me. "I thought when he saw I was strong and true, my likeness to him" – it was, truly, an uncanny likeness – "he would be pleased."

He would not stop pacing until I took hold of him by the shoulders, and then he turned to face me.

"*Patience*, Mordred," I told him. "Patience."

He nodded, and I could feel him beginning to calm down.

Almost to himself, he added. "At least I have the satisfaction of knowing I will have her, despite him. That, at least, is to come for me."

I knew what he was talking about, and I did not like the sound of it. But he left, and I pushed the unease from my mind. This would be hard, and I would have to be strong, if I was going to have my revenge.

Chapter Fifty-Three

Reluctantly, Arthur agreed to have Mordred made a knight, but he left the knighting to Gawain, and I saw Mordred bridle under the insult. Gawain, Aggravain and Gaheris seemed pleased to have Mordred there, but I saw Gareth shy back from him sometimes. Perhaps he sensed something, or perhaps it was the look that Mordred cast on Gareth's young wife that made him pull back. She was a pretty girl, golden-haired and sweet-faced. I wondered if Mordred had ever been with a woman. I had seen no sign of him with one the whole time at Lothian Castle. None but his mother.

After the knighting ceremony, Arthur called a feast. He referred to Mordred always as his *nephew*, though it was clear to everyone that Mordred was his son. This was the first time that I had observed a feast from the vantage-point of the low trestle tables. I had always been up there, on the high table, with Arthur and his knights, and the nobles. I could see so much more clearly from down here. The men were coarse, but I was plain enough in my borrowed shape that they ignored me, and the food here was worse, but the wine was the same, and the drunker those around me got, the more and more they were happy to pay me no attention and I could watch.

Kay sat at Guinevere's side. Gawain occupied the place of honour at Arthur's right, another insult to Mordred. With Lancelot gone, the place went to Arthur's second most beloved friend. Arthur did not want to sit beside his son. Mordred, instead, sat opposite his father and his stepmother. I saw Kay lean down beside Guinevere and whisper something in her ear. She turned to look at him, and they were so close that their noses almost touched. Lancelot was long gone, departed long ago looking for the Grail. Perhaps Guinevere resented Arthur. She would not have been the first wife to live with her anger. Perhaps it was not that she had wanted Lancelot so badly, but that he had wanted her and presented her with the opportunity. Now Kay was there, and though he was no Lancelot, he was handsome and attentive. Kay's arm was around the back of her chair, and he leaned towards her protectively – or was it intimately? But then, if there was anything between them, they would not have been talking so close in public. I remembered the blisteringly intense way Lancelot and Guinevere had ignored each other, before I had realised that it was they two who were in love, not he with me, and she with Kay.

They were talking about Mordred, I could tell. Though they were trying to hide it, I saw Kay whisper something else to her, and his eyes flicker over Mordred. Arthur, at her side, was quiet, his face dark with anger. Gawain was drunk already, and cheerful, glad of the sight of his half-brother. Aggravain, ever politic and quiet, was watchful and sober, but Gawain, Gaheris and the newly returned Lamerocke were carrying the celebrations between them, and anyone sitting down at the trestle tables would never have guessed, if they did not know what I knew, or were not watching as closely as I was, that anything was wrong.

Marie walked past the high table, as though to bring some jug of wine, but as she did I saw her place her hand on Gaheris' shoulder, and lean down to whisper something to him that made him smile. I remembered Aggravain's letter to Morgawse. I could not believe I had not pieced it together before. Perhaps she still hoped that they would be married. Maybe that was why she had rolled her eyes. If she were hoping to marry a prince, she would of course be finding it tiresome to carry out other people's errands.

The food seemed to be finished fast at the high table, as though everyone were too awkward to want to savour their meal, and someone was calling for the musicians and we at the trestle tables, our food not yet finished, were pushed aside for the dancing.

I saw Mordred stand at the high table, and I thought he was going to leave, but he did not. He walked around and offered his hand to Guinevere, as though he wanted to dance. I was surprised, but not unduly, that she took his hand. He was a knight at Camelot now, and it was up to her, as Queen, to foster good relations. I was sure that I would lose Mordred to Arthur if his father showed him even the smallest kindness. I wanted Mordred to try and try, and be refused. Then he would be mine, and I could turn him on his father. A stolen weapon.

Guinevere was dressed in a fine dress I had seen her in before, dark green sewn with gold crosses, and a fine circlet of gold made like ivy leaves. Those were, then, her finest clothes (though I noticed she did not wear the heavy, thick gold crown of Logrys) and she had come to make an effort on Mordred's behalf. That, truly, I had not expected of her. I glanced at Arthur, and I saw his eyes follow Mordred and his wife, down from the dais and into the dancing. Kay watched too. They were wary of Mordred already.

Mordred did not let go of Guinevere's hand. I could see that she was tense, and trying to hide it. Mordred was staring right at her, strange and intense. What was he doing? Hadn't I warned him about patience? I could see her growing uncomfortable. He was saying something to her, too close and quiet for me to hear, and I saw her shrink back from him. He did not move away. Worse, he put a hand at the small of her back, almost possessively. I could see him whisper something to her, his lips right by her ear. She turned her head down, away from him. She did not push him back. Of course she did not. She was nervous of causing trouble between Arthur and his son. He was young. She would put it down to *high spirits*. She slipped away as the song ended, and he did not protest. Mordred stood for a moment, watching her weave back through the crowd, and turned away to leave. Arthur looked tense, and worried. It was beginning. Arthur's perfect world was beginning to chip away.

Mordred did not try to find me after the feast, and I was glad. I thought he was probably with his brothers. Gawain and Aggravain seemed to like him, seemed even to enjoy his strange company. Alone in Camelot, I dreamed of Kay.

Kay was here, I was here. I did not have to sit, remembering. Perhaps a distraction would do me good. I pulled a cloak around myself. It was dark, but I still took the shape of the plain girl as I slipped through the castle. I knew the way to his room, but he was not in his room. He was out in the courtyard, sitting at the edge of it with a small nimble-looking knight I knew as Sir Dinadan. Kay was sitting beside him on a bench at the side of the courtyard, leaning his head back against the stone wall, looking up at the stars that were bright and clear in the autumn night. He was dressed just in his shirt and breeches, all in black, and with his dark hair, only his face shone, pale and white, in the moonlight, the same moonlight that caught Dinadan's white shirt beside him where it peeped from under his surcoat. I suspected that Kay was drunk, since he did not seem to be feeling the cold. Dinadan was looking down at his boots, tapping the toe of them idly with his sword. I noticed that Kay, too, had his sword at his side. I snuck around the edge of the courtyard in the shadows until I was close enough to hear what they were saying.

"Do you think he's dead?" Dinadan asked Kay, quietly. So, they were talking about Lancelot. Kay didn't look at him. He was still staring up at the stars. He shrugged.

"Your father thinks he's dead," Dinadan continued, tapping his foot still with the flat of his sword.

"Sometimes," Kay said, as though to himself, "I think that might be for the best."

I thought of all people, it would be Kay who longed most to have Lancelot back at Camelot. Dinadan didn't say anything. I remembered him as a chatty man, but he seemed to be responding in kind to Kay's uncharacteristic thoughtfulness. Kay knew about Lancelot and Guinevere. Did he care enough about Arthur to wish Lancelot dead? The sudden, awful thought came to me that Kay might want Lancelot dead if he wanted Guinevere for himself. The last I had heard between Kay and Lancelot had been that terrible fight where Kay had told Lancelot never to come to him again talking of the Queen.

Kay turned to look down at Dinadan, and Dinadan looked up at him. They were sitting, I noticed then, rather close to one another, so when Kay turned his face to Dinadan's, they appeared quite intimate. I shrank back further into the shadows, to come closer. As I did, I saw Kay lean down towards Dinadan, who pushed him sharply back.

"Kay, you're a mess," he said, gently.

Kay jumped to his feet, indignant. "I am *not* a mess," he snapped, slightly too loud. He *was* drunk, then. "You weren't so shy yesterday," Kay added.

Dinadan shook his head in exasperation.

"Kay –" He was still patient and gentle. "As if this weren't a bad enough idea already, I'm tired of listening to you talk about Lancelot, or about Guinevere. I'm not taking a risk like this for someone who doesn't know what they want. I'm sorry."

Kay crossed his arms over his chest, reeling slightly, casting a narrow look at Dinadan. He paused for a moment, then he shrugged.

"Your loss," he snapped, turning and striding from the courtyard. Dinadan sighed, leaning back against the wall. I rushed away back to my room. It had been foolish to think I would get anything from going to Kay. Kay, who seemed to have been spending his time trying to get into bed with anyone and everyone in Camelot. I could not believe I had forgotten how much Kay had changed. That had been Arthur's doing, too. Kay *was* a mess. Now I had seen how he was, I had less taste for my happy memory of him.

Chapter Fifty-Four

As winter began to set in, Mordred became more restless. He came to me often, and always with the same complaint. He would pace before me, complaining that Guinevere showed no signs of either having an affair with the absent Lancelot, or being interested in him. He, too, thought that if there was an affair, then it was with Kay, but I assured him it was not. He did not believe me. He was growing increasingly angry, less willing to heed my insistence on patience.

Christmas was tense and its festivities flat. There was a brief moment of jollity after Guinevere, who had been tense and silent the whole evening, had retired, and Arthur and Gawain had been drunk enough to start singing, though I saw Gawain notice that Kay slipped out close behind Guinevere. This was short-lived anyway; before long Arthur wanted to retire. As soon as Arthur left, the arguments began. They had the distinct flavour of arguments that had been had many times before. Aggravain wanted all the brothers together to press the matter of Guinevere's affair with Lancelot while Lancelot was still away. Gawain thought that was disloyal. Gaheris thought it was dishonourable, and slipped off as soon as he could with his Breton mistress. Gareth, openly upset at the accusations, objected loudly and refused to listen to another word. Mordred suggested that Arthur might not believe Aggravain, who was apparently something of a gossip, and almost got struck by his brother for saying so. That left the three of them who remained at the table, Gawain brooding, Aggravain insulted and frustrated, and Mordred scheming, at an impasse. I slipped from the high table down through the kitchens to see if I could learn anything further, but the talk was all the same. Of Lancelot and Guinevere and Arthur. I loitered behind two girls scrubbing at the big iron stew pots and heard the same suspicions, the same doubts.

"I heard," one said, "that Sir Lancelot is long dead. Or at Joyous Guard with Queen Isolde. All those rumours about him loving the Queen were all lies."

"They weren't," the other insisted, quiet and defensive, as though they had had this discussion before, and she had been told she was wrong then, too. "I saw them kissing in her garden."

"You're making it up. Besides, in France men kiss all the ladies to show how courteous they are."

"It wasn't like that. She had her hands all in his hair, and he was holding her right against him, you know. I'm not making it up. I think she misses him. I think King Arthur sent him away to look for the Grail because he was jealous." She looked up at the girl beside her. "I think she's sad. Don't you think the Queen looks sad?"

The other girl shrugged. "I think she looks angry. She always looks angry."

It was then that some busy kitchen-mistress hustled me away. Gossip and rumour was well enough, and that even now it was all anyone could talk about boded well for my plan to persuade Arthur, but it could only go so far. I needed Lancelot back in Camelot.

I slept late, and Mordred came to me while I was winding my hair into a plait, still in my own shape. He burst through the door, his hand held strangely against his nose. He slammed the door and bolted it behind him. Mordred, his eyes burning with anger, lifted his hand away from his nose and fixed me with a wild stare. A thick stream of blood ran from it. I crossed my arms over my chest.

"What happened to *you*?" I demanded.

"Guinevere," he said, thickly. I almost laughed, but I knew he was a proud man already, so I held it in. I reached out and wrapped my hand over his nose. He winced, but he did not back away, and there was enough healing in my touch alone to stop the bleeding. He would not need anything else. I wetted a cloth and wiped the blood from his face. The gesture struck me as oddly maternal, and I pushed those feelings aside. Mordred was no child of mine.

"So, what exactly happened?"

He did not answer, but put his hand over my eyes. I was surprised that he knew what to do. As with Kay, his lack of knowledge blurred the words away, but it was clear enough what I was seeing. First it was Guinevere alone in Arthur's chamber. She was dressed carefully, as though for some occasion, the little gold circlet in her hair, a gold necklace hung with emeralds around her neck, and she was pacing. I was not sure, for I could not see as clearly as if I had begun it myself, but I thought she was trembling slightly. She was nervous. The door opened, and she looked up sharply, but when she saw it was Mordred she unconsciously shrank back. I saw Mordred draw the bolt on the door. He stepped towards her, and I could see her making an effort to be kind and friendly. It was strange to see her so, when she was always so reserved around everyone else, and when it was clear to see how uneasy he made her. Suddenly, Mordred grabbed hold of her, pushing her up against the little table in the corner of the room, grasping her by her hair, and kissed her, hard. I saw her hand reach for something, anything, and close around a silver candlestick on the table beside her, and she brought it, hard, against the side of his head. Mordred drew his hand away from my eyes.

I was furious.

"Mordred, *what were you thinking?*" I shouted. "She will tell Arthur, and you will be sent away, and all will be for nothing."

"She will not tell Arthur," Mordred replied, sulkily, feeling his healed nose tentatively with his fingertips.

"How do you know that?" I snapped.

"I told her that if she did I would tell Arthur about her and Lancelot."

I gave a groan of exasperation. "He won't believe you, Mordred, and she knows it."

"She doesn't know that. In her position, she would be wise not to risk it. But, Morgan –" He stepped forward, suddenly aggressive, and, caught off guard, I warily stepped back. He reached out and grabbed me by the shoulders. "This was not the easy success your little vision promised me. Were you lying to me, to get me here, so that I could steal your precious sword for you?" He grabbed me by the hair, grasping the thick base of my plait, twisting my face up towards his and leaning down threateningly. "Aunt or no, I will not tolerate being lied to. If I find that you are trying to use me, I will destroy you."

I closed my eyes, and let myself take his shape, feeling his grip close on nothing as my long hair disappeared. When I opened my eyes, he looked shocked and I was pleased. I wanted him to know that I had more power than he could guess at, and if he thought he could frighten me with his strength, then he needed to know that his strength was something I could take for myself. I squared up to him, crossing my arms over my chest. His body was huge, and powerful, and I could feel the raw power in every muscle and limb, and it was good to feel such power.

"We want the same things," I told him, and the voice that came was his, low and darkly threatening. I wrapped my fingers around his wrist, which still hovered, stunned, where my hair had been, and pushed his arm back towards him, letting him feel how real the borrowed strength I had was. "And rest assured, Mordred, if your recklessness ruins my plans, then it shall be you, not I, who suffers for it. Patience. I warned you, and you have put us both in danger already because you will not wait. If you are finding yourself out of control, I would remind you that Camelot has *many* other women."

Angrily, he pushed me back by the shoulders, but I had the weight of his bulk on my side, and I did not move, but shoved him hard in return. Having tested my strength and found me no weak opponent, reluctantly he turned and left, slamming the door once more behind him. I let his shape slip away from me. It was only then that I realised that I was shaking, slightly, and that I had been holding my breath.

News came that Bors had returned, which left only Lancelot, Percival and Galahad looking for the Grail. I felt it in my heart that my son was dead. I blamed Nimue.

Spring came, and then summer. Guinevere seemed always restless. I sometimes took Marie's shape, when I knew the girl was with Gaheris. At first I was wary that Guinevere would try to speak to me in Breton, but it seemed she did not want to speak very much at all. She seemed to want to spend the hot, lazy summer days sitting in her walled garden with her two Breton women – where Margery had gone, I did not know, but she was nowhere to be found – listening to the older one read. Often, Kay was there, and he would sit beside Guinevere idly for an hour or so, before he wandered away to the rest of his duties, and sometimes Gareth and his wife Lynesse would come to sit with her, and she was cheerful around them, though I noticed they did not bring their little girl, and Guinevere never asked. She did not seem to be aware of anything around her, but lay back on the grass, her fingers playing idly through its soft, thick blades, staring up through the leaves over her with half-closed eyes, as though dreaming of something very far away.

Chapter Fifty-Five

By the time winter came, Mordred was once more restless. He came often to my room at night, demanding to know when the time would be to act. He told me that he was tormented by the dreams of victory I had showed him, and he would not be content until he had his father's throne. When I told him to wait, to be patient, he became increasingly angry. He was no longer sure, almost five years after his departure, that Lancelot would return alive, and he wanted to make some other plan.

One night Mordred came to me, and I thought he was drunk, though I had never seen him drink the wine or the ale that was offered to him. His eyes were bright and wild, and he took my hand with a manic insistence and led me through the castle in the depths of night and up the stairs of Guinevere's tower, and into Guinevere's bedroom.

I followed Mordred in to the room, though I was still not sure why he wanted me there. I was afraid that someone would wake and see us. It was a clear winter's night, freezing cold, and through the window the pale moonlight shone bright, lighting against his profile, against the gold of his hair, the white of his shirt. In the half-light, he could have been Arthur. I could hear my heart thudding in my ears, and I was afraid that it was loud enough for others to hear.

Mordred moved soundlessly across the wooden floor, and I followed carefully. It seemed dangerous, reckless to be sneaking in to people's bedrooms like this at night. For what?

I followed Mordred around the bed, his face disappearing into the darkness as he turned away from the window. He paused when I was by his side, staring at the thick bed curtains before him, black in the night-time, though the threads of gold through the fabric caught in the moonlight, bright. He appeared to be bracing himself for a moment, flexing his hands, and then he leaned forward slowly, slowly, and drew back the curtain. The metal rings holding the curtain up scraped along its pole. What was he going to do, stab Arthur in his sleep? Would it be that simple?

But Arthur was not in the bed. Lying before Mordred, her chest rising and falling slowly in the rhythm of sleep, was the Queen. Beside her, the heavy winter covers were thrown back as if Arthur had left in the night. Mordred did not seem to be surprised. So, he had not come looking for his father. Mordred's hand still rested on the curtain where he had pushed it back, and he stared down at her. The cold light of the moon fell across her white face, and against it, trailing in to the darkness, her thick red hair looked black in the night, everywhere except around her face where it shone, dark and glossy as blood.

I glanced at Mordred, and saw him step forward, and, grasping the edge of the heavy winter covers of furs and thick brocade sheets, pull them slowly back, and throw them aside on to the empty half of the bed.

"What are you doing?" I hissed. "She is going to wake up."

Mordred flashed me an angry look, and pressed his finger to his lips, turning back to the Queen. In her sleep she gave another murmur, her red lips parting slightly in her sleep, reaching for the covers that had been pulled away, but she soon seemed to forget when her hand did not find them, and to fall back in to a deep sleep. Though it was winter, she had only a thin nightdress on. In the brightness of the moonlight, through the thin white silk, the shape of her body was half-visible, and when I turned back to Mordred, he was just staring at her. He reached out, slowly, his hand hovering over her body for a moment. When I saw him brush his fingertips across her stomach, I grabbed him by the wrist and pulled his hand away. Guinevere, in her sleep, sighed and turned over, reaching out for Arthur beside her, and when she felt nothing, she sighed again, more deeply, and seemed to settle back to sleep.

"Mordred, *what are you doing*? What did you bring me here for?" I whispered angrily. He seemed to have gone mad. I did not want that. I did not want to have lost control of a madman.

Mordred shook his head.

"Morgan, this was *your idea*. You told me that Arthur's weakness was his wife, that she has had one of his knights as her lover. She refused me. Now she's going to learn that I am not a man to be refused, and you are here to go and fetch Arthur so that he can see. I will have my victory, and he will see it done."

I stood back, appalled.

"Mordred, that's *not* what I meant. I meant if we can get Arthur to see the truth, he and Lancelot will have to fight for their honour, and while they're fighting we can take back what belongs to us. I didn't come here to help you rape an innocent woman. She is nothing to do with our quarrel with Arthur."

Mordred turned fully to me then, his dark eyes cold. I stepped back again.

"What do you care what happens to her?" I felt my blood run cold. I thought of the Breton queen I had failed to save a long, long time ago. I wondered what she would say if she could see me now, failing to protect another woman again. Mordred took a threatening step towards me, and I stepped back again. "Our deal was for the sword, nothing more. Everything else is mine for the taking, including the Queen, if I desire it."

I was going to speak again, but I was mercifully spared from having to decide if I had the strength in me to stop Mordred, by the sound of boots on the stairs, and the door scraping open, making Guinevere stir. I pulled Mordred back with me in to the shadows, and let the image of us becoming like the stones in the wall fill through me. I prayed that it had worked. "You left," she said softly, slightly sad.

Arthur sighed and rubbed his face with his hands, moving into my field of vision as he climbed back into bed naked beside her.

"I couldn't sleep. I went for a walk. I keep dreaming that Lancelot has come back, and then I wake up and realise it's not true."

Guinevere shushed him gently, taking his face in her hands and kissing him softly. He responded at first slowly, but with an increasing passion, rolling on to her and pulling her around under him. I was surprised to see her respond with an equal passion, pressing her body against his with a low moan of anticipation. When Arthur ripped off her nightdress and threw it out of the bed where it landed in a crumpling heap at our feet, I was ready to leave. I turned to Mordred, who was transfixed. Tough. I was not staying. I grasped his hand and pictured the garden beneath us in the moonlight, the winding vines of the roses, the low, soft grass gathering frost as the dawn approached. I opened my eyes and we were there. Mordred looked annoyed with me, but I didn't care.

I couldn't believe it. That was not the married life I had expected to see. I had never felt passion like that, and yet she had Lancelot as well. It hardly seemed fair. No, I had felt passion like that. And Arthur had killed that man, and Nimue had helped him.

Resentfully, beside me, Mordred growled, "You see; she would have had me. In the dark, I don't need your black magic to take my father's shape. It would have been easy. You've wasted our chance." He turned as though he was about to leave, and then had another thought, turning back to me so fast and violently that I jumped back. "Besides, she's not an *innocent woman*, is she, Morgan? She has been offering herself to Lancelot, don't forget that. As far as I'm concerned, that makes her any man's who can win her."

And he stormed off into the night.

Chapter Fifty-Six

Mordred was angry with me for days after that, but this gave me some respite from him. I could not decide whether to write to Morgawse to say he was in danger. I was not sure if *I* was in danger.

Christmas came again, and at least this year it was less tense than the last. Even if Arthur had not recognised Mordred as his son, but still called him his "dear nephew", he was more used to him being there. With Bors' return, there was a little more merriment than the last year. Bors himself was not much fun, gruff and sensible, but Ector was glad to have his brother back, and the men were pleased to hear his tales of the Grail. Kay, too, was in good spirits and had arranged his usual Christmas games. Even Guinevere laughed a little. I saw her dance with Kay, and where she had been tense and unhappy with Mordred, I noticed that she danced with becomingly neat and bouncing steps. Arthur watched his wife dance with Kay with a deep smile on his face, fuelled, I suspected, by desire and wine. Mordred was watching her, too, his expression dark. I was afraid that he was waiting for a moment like this, when everyone was drunk and distracted.

Enflamed, it seemed, by the sight of her dancing, Arthur took his wife by the hand and excused them both from the Christmas feast, as soon as she was returned to the high table. It was late in the night by then, and most of the wine drunk, and all of the food that anyone could manage gone. The dancing was still going, though, and Gareth was still trying to catch a chicken than was running away from him as part of one of Kay's games. His wife was watching, her little girl on her lap, and laughing.

As Kay walked past Mordred, Mordred put out a hand to stop him. Kay turned to face him, resting a hand on the hilt of his sword. It had been a long time since I had seen Kay go about unarmed. In my borrowed, plain shape, a jug of wine in my hands, I shrank back into the shadows to watch.

"Do you, Kay, await the return of Sir Lancelot as eagerly as my father does? And my father's *wife* does?" I saw Dinadan a few places away at the table, unable to keep his eyes from flickering towards Kay.

Kay shrugged. "Every man awaits his friend's return eagerly." Kay's reply was even, and calm, but he did not move his hand from his sword.

"What manner of man *are* you, Kay?" Mordred asked, leaning back in his chair, pushing the sole of his boot against the table to tilt it back on its back two legs. "For I have heard *strange things*."

Kay gave an odd smile. I wondered, suddenly, if he were not looking forward to a fight.

"Well, Mordred." Kay leaned down close, teasing, putting one hand on the arm of Mordred's chair so that he was leaning over him. "Would you like to find out?"

Mordred pushed him back, and I was surprised to see that he looked suddenly embarrassed, and a little afraid. Kay laughed, and his laugh was harsh and unkind.

"No, I thought you were a coward. As it turns out, more men are afraid of fucking a man than fighting one." Kay slammed his hand against the back of Mordred's chair, and it fell back onto all four legs, pitching Mordred forward. Mordred's face grew dark with anger, but he was caught on the back foot and embarrassed. "Well, Mordred, I suggest you substantiate your rumours a little better before you try to embarrass anyone, because," he leaned down again, and Mordred leaned away from him, and he whispered, "*I am far braver than you for this, Mordred.*"

Kay laughed again, and skipped off. Gawain looked annoyed, but Aggravain – to my surprise – looked amused. Kay had been drunk enough not to bother denying it, and I had thought that it would go badly for him, but it seemed that Mordred was more cowed by that than any threat of violence. Still, I wished that he had not done it. I could not imagine Mordred letting an embarrassment like that go, and while Kay had won for now, it could not last, for Kay would forget, and Mordred would remember.

Mordred was distant with me still after that, but when spring came, he knew he had to return to me, and submit himself to obedience to me again, if he was going to have any success. He had failed without me, and he knew it.

News came to me that Lancelot was back after almost everyone else knew. It was Mordred who brought it, and I wished that he had not, for I knew that in front of him I had to hide everything I felt. I still thought of Lancelot, still treasured the strange memories of our love. I wanted him still, though I knew that he would never have me.

I was not sure that I wanted to see him, but the time had come suddenly upon me, and I knew that I could not shy back now.

News came, too, that Percival and Galahad were dead. Mordred did not know that Galahad was my son, and I did not offer him the truth, I just let it sink through me. I had known it before, and I endured it.

Some great feast was hastily arranged for Lancelot's return, but it was not in Camelot's great hall, but in Arthur's council chamber, the room with the Round Table. Everyone was merry and happy when I arrived, carrying some of the food, unnoticed in my servant's shape, and let myself hide at the back of the room, sliding into the shape of the stone wall. Guinevere came late, when the food was already there, and the men already laughing. This was the moment, when I would know what was to be, if success would be easy. Lancelot glanced up towards her as she came in, but she did not look at him. He sat at Arthur's right, his return earning him the place of honour, where he would usually have been beside her. She sat between Arthur and Kay, who watched her tentatively. I felt a rush of victory. I did not know how Arthur, sat between them, did not see it. It was unbearable, the way Guinevere ignored Lancelot. She would not even turn her face towards him. Five years had changed nothing between them. No woman would ever ignore a man that intensely if she did not truly love him.

The feast was uneventful, and Lancelot told his story of the Grail. I was sure it was all lies, for it was all dragons and glory and the transcendence of God, when I knew that all quests were blood and wounds, and pain and loss.

When the food was finished the men began to mill about, and Kay went to Lancelot. Arthur had gone to Gawain, and they were laughing and talking. He did not seem to notice how his wife was. She did not notice, too, Mordred creeping round to sit beside her. She did not notice at all, until he put his arm around the back of her chair, and leaned down towards her. I could not hear what he was saying, but when he spoke, she startled a little, suddenly sitting up straight in her chair. But he was not speaking to her, he was speaking to Lancelot, two seats away. Kay, who was sitting on the table talking to Lancelot, was half-turned towards him, and Lancelot's eyes were fixed on Mordred and the Queen. As he spoke, I saw him brush his hand down across Guinevere's neck, and I saw her hand close around her metal cup. But he was not there for long, and once he had made his point to Lancelot he moved away. I did not need to know what it was, for I knew what he was trying to do. Trying to provoke Lancelot into giving himself away. It had been quiet, and brief, and no one else seemed to have seen. Mordred was finally learning the patience to wait for the right moment.

Mordred came to me after that, and I could see he was excited.

"The time is now," he told me.

"The time for what?" I asked.

"Go to Arthur," he demanded. "Show him. I know you have your ways."

Now *was* the time. Lancelot was here, new-returned. If he was not with Guinevere now, he would be soon, and that did not matter, for they had been, and I would have Arthur see it. I closed my eyes where I stood, and pictured myself in the room with the Round Table. Its power, which I had felt through its ancient wood, would give what I was about to show him all the more strength. Luck was with me, and Arthur was there alone. Mordred seemed to be right indeed. All the time was coming together in this moment, for us.

Arthur smiled when he saw me, unsurprised that I had appeared before him out of thin air. He was pleased to see me. He did not even seem worried when I slid the bolt of the door shut behind me. He jumped forward to wrap his arms around me in a brotherly embrace.

"Morgan, dear sister, it has been too long since I have seen you. Are you well? What brings you here?"

"I'm sorry Arthur," I said, my voice cold. "The truth brings me here."

I wrapped my hand over his eyes, and the room melted away around us. I was not sure what encounter we would see, but I trusted my strength enough, and the magic all through my blood and all around me, that it would be enough.

The scene that emerged around us was of Guinevere's bedroom, in the night time. She sat at the window, the moonlight streaming over her face as she looked down at the garden below. Arthur beside me sighed gently at the sight of her. The door opened behind us, and Lancelot stepped through.

Guinevere stood to her feet when Lancelot came in, her face full of hopeful surprise. Lancelot drew the bolt on the door behind him, and rushed across the room to take her in his arms and kiss her. His lips against hers were soft and sensual, and I could see she was trying to draw away from him but could not force herself, for a moment, to give the feel of them up; but she did, gently pushing him back.

345

"Arthur might come," she warned, softly. I glanced at Arthur. I could not read his look, if he believed yet what he saw.

"He won't," Lancelot replied, moving his lips to her neck. She closed her eyes, and her lips parted slightly in a silent sigh of longing. He gathered her closer against him, and I could see her losing herself already.

"How do you know?" she whispered. Lancelot did not take his lips from her neck, and I saw his hands slide around her back, wrapping her tight against him. She was fighting against her whole body's urge to give in, to forget the danger.

"Nimue has just arrived," Lancelot said, absently, his mind already taken up by other things. He looked up at her for a moment, and their eyes met and both of them were still for a moment. He brushed his thumb lightly across her lips, and they parted gently under his touch, and she closed her eyes.

"I don't think it's safe with so many people around. We shouldn't," she breathed.

"We're alone now," he said, softly, and she leaned up towards him, as though she could not help herself. Their lips brushed, their mouths opening slightly in anticipation.

"Someone might come looking for me," she protested, weakly. She was lost to it now. Her eyes closed, as his hands wound into the hair at the nape of her neck, pulling it loose, letting it fall around her shoulders.

"Let them," he whispered back, kissing her, soft and teasing so that she leaned towards him for more. "It will not be Arthur, and this is no one else's concern." And he kissed her again, and she sighed in surrender.

I glanced at Arthur beside me, but he had forgotten that I was there. He had the look of a man having a bad dream. I was not enjoying myself all that much either, watching Lancelot slipping Guinevere out of her clothes, and her melting under his touch, the pair of them falling together into Guinevere's great bed. Not when I saw the dizzying rapture I had known under Lancelot's touch pass over Guinevere's face, and saw him be as passionate, as tender with her as I had known him to be when I wore her shape. Only when I was sure that Arthur had seen his wife's sigh of ecstasy with another's man's name on her lips, in the same bed where he himself had been with her time and again, did I draw my hand away. Surely, this was enough.

Back in the room with the Round Table, Arthur pushed me roughly away from him, his grey eyes flashing with anger. In that moment, his resemblance to his son was all the more striking.

"What evil magic was that, Morgan?" he shouted. His voice was loud and powerful enough that I felt it shake through me, but I was not afraid. I regarded him calmly.

"That was the truth, Arthur. I am only trying to help you."

"That was *lies*, Morgan," he raged. "Don't think Lancelot didn't warn me about your wicked tricks." So, with uncharacteristic shrewdness Lancelot had told Arthur what I was capable of, just to be sure that Arthur would never believe me. "And don't think I don't know what your interest in all of this is. I will *not* force Lancelot into marrying you, and I will *not* let you cause disharmony in my court because of your selfish jealousies. Just because you have not trusted anyone since you were fifteen years old –" His voice cracked with anger, and I felt the half-truth of it strike me.

"I have trusted no one since *you* betrayed me! You sold me to Uriens –"

"I saved both of our lives with that marriage. You should be *grateful* –"

"You will regret, Arthur," I snarled, "that you did not believe me."

And I faded from the room.

Chapter Fifty-Seven

I watched Arthur and Guinevere for the next few days, hidden away as the servant girl, but I saw nothing changed. He was kind and affectionate towards her as always, and she was reserved and aloof as she always was. She was near Lancelot often, but tense and cold to him. I would have to force it all out into the open.

There was a tournament being prepared for Lancelot's return, and the final end of the quest for the Grail. I knew that Guinevere could be jealous, and the thought struck me that the best thing to force their love-affair out into the open would be if I could make Guinevere angry enough with Lancelot that it would be so obvious that even Arthur could not ignore it. I was surprised, too, that though he had been away for more than five years, they had not rushed together in secret yet. Truly, though Mordred and I had watched them carefully, they had never been alone. What I had shown Arthur had been from long ago, before the men had left looking for the

Grail. I needed something he could see now, without my magic, and perhaps a raging argument would be just as good.

I waited until I saw Kay go into his bedroom one night, and took his shape, slipping into Lancelot's room beside his. Lancelot, when he heard me come through the door, looked up. He sighed when he saw me.

"Kay, what is it?" He sounded weary and annoyed, but I knew he would listen to me. But his sad look made me curious, and I knew he would tell Kay the truth.

"What is wrong, Lancelot?" I asked, hearing Kay's bright voice.

Lancelot sighed and rubbed his forehead with the heel of his hand.

"Kay," he said, "you don't want to know. You've already told me you don't want to hear."

"I'll listen," I said. So, it was about Guinevere.

"I just can't make her understand." He sighed again, shaking his head. "We are in danger. I can't – I thought I could be near her, and we could just – without – but all I think about is her, I remember what it was like to –" He sighed again. He was shy, and the words to describe what he meant escaped him. "I came back resolved to live as a good man, but I do not know how much longer I can stand it, to be close to her, to touch her hand, to smell the scent of her hair, to hear her voice, without being able to –" He groaned low in frustration. "And we are in danger. Mordred is watching everything I do. And Aggravain. Aggravain knows. So these two problems, one cannot be solved without ruining everything for the other. She thinks – I don't know what she thinks. It is killing me to be near her, and not *with* her, but it would be worse to be apart. Kay," he turned to me in desperation, "what should I do?"

This was a gift. I gave him a sympathetic smile. "If you want my advice, Lancelot, I would suggest that you create a public distraction. New gossip wipes out old gossip."

Lancelot looked confused, and surprised that Kay for once seemed to be on his side about this, but he was too relieved to question it.

"How?" he asked.

"Wear another woman's token in the tournament tomorrow," I told him. "Someone young, marriageable. Someone men could believe you were serious about taking as a wife."

"I couldn't."

I shrugged. "Then live like this forever."

348

"Kay, she would not understand," he said, but I could see the thought was going to work in his mind.

"Surely, she would be pleased that you had thought of something to protect you both so that you might... enjoy your love in secrecy," I suggested. I knew that I did not sound like Kay, but Lancelot was too relieved to notice, or too distracted to care.

The day of the tournament, I sat with the common folk, in my plain serving woman's shape, to watch the jousting. It was smelly, and cramped and uncomfortable down there. From where I sat, I could see the high platform above us, with its chairs and cushions, Arthur and Guinevere sat side by side at the front, dressed in their fine clothes, the light canopy of silk over them. Here, everyone crushed onto the thin wooden benches, straining to see. The gossip was better here, though, than on the platform. If I twisted around in my seat, I could see Arthur talking to Guinevere, and she was nodding, smiling very slightly. I expected he was boring her talking about the men and who had won before, and who had not. Gawain was with them, not down among the jousting, and Marie, and a few others. Kay was not up there, which meant that he must have been taking part. Down on the benches, everyone was talking about Lancelot. Looking out for Guinevere's cloth-of-gold token on a knight's helmet and seeing none, people were whispering that he was dead, or that Arthur had found out about his affair with the Queen and sent him from court. I heard someone say that he had become a monk.

Mordred rode out onto the field, deliberately without his helm. He wanted everyone to see his face, his golden hair, his striking resemblance to Arthur, before he slid his helm onto his head and squared up for the first bout of jousting. No one sitting on the low benches bothered to call him Arthur's nephew. The advantage of being far from the political centre of Camelot was the ability to speak the truth.

I recognised Kay from his black armour, riding against Mordred first. I was a little disappointed to see him knocked down so easily, but while Mordred was a strong fighter on foot, he was even better in the joust. His natural brutal recklessness served him well, and he threw all his weight behind every blow. He knocked down Aggravain, too, who must have weighed half what he did again in vast, muscular bulk. He was doing well. There were more knights, whom I did not recognise, but I knew that none of them could be Lancelot, for Mordred knocked them down easily. I glanced up at Guinevere. She was peering across the field as though looking intently for something that she could not find. She was looking for her token. She turned and said something to Arthur, who shrugged.

Then, far at the edge of the field, came the last knight to ride against Mordred. This knight, too, had knocked down all those that Mordred had. The sleeve tied on his helmet was red and white. The colours of the castle town Astolat. It was not far from here, and every report said that the lord of the castle's virginal daughter was the greatest of beauties. A fine choice, I thought, to distract attention from the rumours of him and Guinevere.

At last Mordred's violent strength had met its match, for where he threw himself against Lancelot, Lancelot was quick and deft enough to lean out of the way, and Mordred's own weight and power unbalanced him in his seat, making him pitch forwards. Lancelot struck him from the side, knocking him down from his horse with a soft, swift blow. Lancelot would have been capable of a blow as strong as Mordred's, but his skill allowed him to be almost gentle as he pushed Mordred from his saddle. Mordred hit the floor with a heavy thump, and his helmet rolled away.

All around me the crowd rose to its feet, cheering, and I with it. Lancelot, still hidden under his helm, with the colours of Astolat disguising him, rode once around the field to the sound of cheers, and then stopped before the high platform. Suddenly, all the cheering around me turned to silence in my ears, and I could hear my heart beating over it, loud and hard. This was the moment. Lancelot pulled his helm off, and when the crowd saw who it was, their cheers became wilder. I turned to look over my shoulder. Arthur was laughing and cheering with the crowd. Beside him, Guinevere's hands had stopped as though half way to coming together to clap with the rest of the crowd, and fell down by her side. When I looked back at Lancelot, he was looking at her, his expression one of desperate disbelief. In his longing for things to come right, he had put all his trust in what I had said to him in Kay's shape. He had truly believed that she would not be angry with him, fool that he was.

Now it would begin.

Chapter Fifty-Eight

I was woken very early by Mordred hammering on the door of my room as though he was trying to break it down. When I opened it, he seized hold of me by the shoulders, lifting me almost off my feet.

"She sent him away."

"What?"

"Guinevere. She has banished Lancelot from court."

I went to her, in the shape of her Breton maid, Marie, but I did not get much from her. "It's a coward who fights in disguise, Marie," she shouted, and then there was a string of Breton words which I guessed, from their resemblance to some of the French and Latin I knew, were obscenities. "I hear, Marie, that the girl is fourteen years old. *Fourteen years old.*"

It seemed that my sister Morgawse was the only woman in Britain that did not feel the threat of younger women.

Arthur was angry when he realised that Lancelot had gone without taking leave of him. Some weak excuse had been made about business to attend to at Joyous Guard. Mordred was quiet and frustrated. I grew increasingly afraid that he would act suddenly, violently and alone.

Spring turned to autumn and autumn to winter. Tired of waiting and watching, tired of Mordred watching for me, and always watching Guinevere, I went to Lothian to spend Christmas with Morgawse. I was glad of the distraction. Camelot was stifling. The whole city was pressed over with Guinevere's frustrated longing for Lancelot, for her anger had changed quickly to wistfulness. I had thought she would be angry for longer.

All the news that came to Lothian was of Lancelot fighting in some tournament or other, and in all the news that came the messenger made sure to mention that he had fought under Guinevere's cloth-of-gold token. I was surprised that she did not call him back herself, but perhaps she was too proud.

I enjoyed the respite from Camelot deeply, but it was strange; when I was not thinking of bringing Arthur down, I did not know what to do with myself. I left when the snows thawed. I needed Camelot, I needed my revenge.

It was early spring when I got back to Camelot. It did not seem, at least, that Mordred had done anything ill-advised. I saw him take notice of me when I first appeared again in my disguise. I did not want to wait again for him to come to me. I came to him early on a morning at the beginning of spring. It was quiet enough around that I came in my own shape. I did not want him to forget what power and secret knowledge I had. I knocked, hard and sharp on his door.

Mordred obviously knew it was me, and called me in by name. So, he had been expecting me. Hoping for me, probably. I stepped through the door. He stood before me in his breeches, his chest bare, looking disgustingly pleased with himself. I saw that there was a woman in his bed. It took me a moment to recognise her, naked with the sheet held against her, and with her golden hair loose around her shoulders, but then I realised from her resemblance to Lynesse, Gareth's wife, that she must have been the sister, whom Gaheris had married. Mordred grinned at me when he noticed that I had recognised her.

"Good morning, Morgan," Mordred greeted me cheerily.

"I can come back when you are finished with your brother's wife," I said, sharply.

Mordred shrugged. "Gaheris does not miss her."

"No," the woman, Lynet, added irritably from the bed, pulling up her knees and wrapping her arms around them. "No he does not. He is probably with his Breton whore."

She was mean-faced where her sister was kind. She was beautiful, yes, but her features were pinched with sulking.

Mordred laughed and climbed back on the bed with her, but he was not fond, or kind. He leaned over and grasped her face by the chin, turning her roughly to look at him. "You think I will take your side in this because I have fucked you? No, no, sweet Lynet." He laughed again, and I saw her try to pull back from him, wincing at his harsh language. He grabbed her by the hair, and she gave a murmur of pain, but it hardly had the strength of a protest. He had done this before, then. "Gaheris' little Breton peasant is no whore. She does no more than is right for her to do. My brother is a prince of Lothian, and he may have any woman he wishes. It is only what he deserves. You, sweet lady," he shook her by the hair a little, and she raised one hand to try to pull his away, but he did not move, "you are the whore, coming to offer yourself to your husband's brother – and why? Because you are jealous, or bored, or full of lust, or whatever it is that was your excuse this time." He pulled her face right up close to his. I could see he was enjoying himself, enjoying humiliating her. "Gaheris tells me his Breton girl takes him in her mouth. You fine ladies don't do that, do you? And how much better than her are you, really? All you have of your own is a small castle in the middle of a forest. You're practically a peasant yourself. You ought to be grateful that I or my brother would ever deign to fuck you."

She looked as though she was holding back her tears, and though my shock and disgust had held me back before, I could not let him continue.

"Mordred," I snapped, crossing my arms over my chest. "If you are going to continue like this I am going to leave. Don't talk to her like that."

"I'll talk to her however I please," Mordred retorted, but he let go of her hair and got off the bed, picking up some crumpled item of clothing from the floor and throwing it at her.

"Put your clothes on," he ordered her. She picked up the underdress from where it had fallen on the bed before her and pulled it over her head, casting him, and me, a dark, unfriendly look. He picked up her dress from the floor and threw that at her as well. She was prepared this time and caught it. She pulled that on, too, but the lacing was at the back. She would have to find someone to lace her up, and I was not going to offer.

Angry and sulky, she went to push past Mordred to leave, but he caught her as she went, wrapping an arm around her waist and pulling her against him. To my surprise, she relaxed willingly into his arms, and when he kissed her, took his face tenderly in her hands. She should have slapped him. He pushed her round roughly and yanked the laces tight on her dress. When he was finished, he pulled her back against him, leaning down to whisper in her ear.

"Come back tonight," he told her. She didn't say anything, but I was sure that she would obey him. It was disgusting. He pushed her roughly out of the door, and slammed it behind her. He was still grinning.

"What was that repulsive little display in aid of, Mordred?"

He shrugged, picking up his shirt and pulling it over his head.

"I got bored of waiting for your return. It has been to my annoyance to find my father's wife so unfriendly. Far less friendly than almost every other wife in Camelot."

I supposed it was some sort of game to him.

"What have you come for, Morgan?" he demanded, turning to me. I gave no ground. I had regained my strength a little with my sister in Lothian and I did not intend to be caught off guard by Mordred. He took a step towards me, and I met his gaze evenly. I was glad of my height around Mordred. "Just to scold me? My bitter old aunt. I am not sure I need you here."

I let my shape slip into Guinevere's and I saw the vulnerability that Mordred's greed gave him flicker across his face.

"Only *I* can give you what you want," I said, softly, my borrowed voice rich with Breton. He put a hand around my throat, and I felt him squeeze. I could feel my pulse against his hand, but I was not afraid. I knew what made him feel weak.

"No more of your tricks, Morgan," he hissed. I could see that I had made my point, and I took my own shape again.

"You need my tricks, Mordred."

He drew his hand away, turning away from me to pace around his room. The room was small and plain. Hardly the room befitting a king's son, even a bastard child. It was less than his brothers, I was sure. More like Kay's room, and Kay's was, I was sure, plain by his own choice.

Mordred was getting desperate. He had all the impatience Arthur had had as a young man. He did not want to wait for what he had seen happen. I had learned patience the hard way, and I did not have any sympathy for his haste.

"What do we do, then?" he demanded.

I gave him a sly smile. "I will bring Lancelot back from Joyous Guard, and we will not have to wait for long." Mordred made a gruff noise of agreement. He did not have a better suggestion. "But you *wait* now. I will bring Lancelot back, and we shall arrange it so Arthur sees the truth. Then, war between them shall begin, and I shall take the sword as payment, and you can do what you like with all the rest."

"*All* the rest?" Mordred insisted. I felt sick at the thought of it, but I knew I had to agree to get his obedience. I nodded.

Chapter Fifty-Nine

I had not been to Joyous Guard before, so I had to ride there. It was not far, a little more than a day's ride, and it passed quickly. Soon I saw before me its tall, thin shape rising on the horizon. It was not a welcoming place, despite its name, but a siege fortress made of dark grey stone. It was not even a castle like Rheged or Lothian Castle; it was a warrior's stronghold.

I was not sure that he would be there, but he was. I could see lights within as the day began to fade. There was no way in that I could find apart from the barbican gate. There were no men I could see in the courtyard, but I took the shape of a rangy-looking cat I had seen in Lothian Castle and slipped between its bars. It was almost entirely empty. I could only see a single light, high up. There was no one to stop me, so I followed towards it, up a tight set of spiral stairs, up, up to what must have been a bedroom. I could hear someone moving around inside – Lancelot, I was sure – and out in the corridor, I took Guinevere's shape. I could feel my heart racing. I was not sure yet how far I intended to go to convince Lancelot that he was forgiven. I was not sure how guilty I ought to feel about what had happened between us – how I had deceived him – since I suspected I had been deceived by Nimue all along. But there was no time for doubt now.

I pushed the door open and strode in. I had wanted him to believe it was really Guinevere, so I had changed into her form dressed in the rich gold and green dress I had seen her in, her hair plaited back and dressed with the little gold circlet. He looked up as I came in, and I saw the breath rush out of him at the sight of me. It did for me as well. Out here, far from Camelot, he had not bothered to shave every day, and a light handsome stubble of dark hair shaded his chin. I stepped further into the room, pushing the door shut behind me. He took a step towards me, too. His eyes, dark blue, dizzyingly intense on me, were wide with surprise.

"Guinevere..." he breathed.

I stepped forward, rushing across the space to place my fingers lightly against his lips. I did not want to hear her name. He closed his eyes against my touch and sighed, putting his arms around me. I felt his hands at the small of my back, pulling my body against his, and I slid my hand into his hair as we came together in a kiss that was as light and sensual as it was deep and passionate.

Slowly, reluctantly, he held me away from him, gazing into my eyes.

"Guinevere," he whispered, "I am sorry. Truly, I am."

I hushed him, leaning up and gently brushing my lips against his. He gave a low groan of yearning and pulled me hard against him again. I could feel the heat of his body through my dress, and the hunger in his touch as he ran his hands down my back. I had lost all the thoughts I had of what I had come planning to say, how I could convince him to return. In that moment I did not care about that. I wanted his hands all over my body, and his mouth. I wanted him more intensely than I thought I ever had before.

He moved his lips to my neck, and I sighed against him, closing my eyes, feeling my own heat rise in response to his, and to my long-sleeping desire.

"Truly, you forgive me?" Lancelot whispered by my ear, his hands winding through my hair, pulling it loose. I felt a flash of annoyance that his words were distracting me. Why was he talking so much?

"Truly," I replied.

He seemed to pause then, only for a moment, and then he began kissing down my neck again, and I felt his lips across my collarbone.

"How did you get here? How did you come in secret?" he murmured between his kisses. I wanted him to be quiet. I didn't like speaking, didn't like hearing her voice coming from my mouth, reminding me that it was she not I that he wanted.

"I found a way. I was desperate to see you," I replied.

Suddenly, he drew away, holding me by the shoulders, peering down at me. He looked at me thoughtfully for a moment and then sighed deeply.

"Morgan," he sighed. To my surprise, his tone was weary, annoyed, rather than furious or hurt.

I had missed my chance to lie. I let my own shape return and Lancelot sighed again and shook his head.

"Morgan, that isn't fair," he said, his eyes on mine a little sad, a little hopeless.

"She does want you to come back," I told him, gently. "She has forgiven you. Come back to Camelot. Please, come back."

He ran his hands through his hair, closing his eyes, then rubbed his face, hard.

"Morgan..." he groaned, and he looked down at me again, his face slowly growing suspicious. "What do you have to gain from this?"

I shrugged, crossing my arms over my chest.

"I suppose you wouldn't believe that I have reformed my character and I am trying to be kind?"

Lancelot said nothing.

"Fine. Come back because Mordred is going to hurt her if you don't. Arthur doesn't see anything that happens, including you with his wife day and night right in front of him." Lancelot gave me a sharp look, but it was the truth. I continued, "And he certainly doesn't see what Mordred is trying to do."

Lancelot, to my surprise, nodded. So he knew.

"I was afraid that my leaving would give him an opportunity. But she is safe at the moment?"

"*For* the moment," I insisted. Lancelot sighed once again, pressing his fingers into the middle of his forehead in despair. Slowly, he nodded.

"Arthur has sent to me, inviting me for his Mayday hunt. I will come back then. You think she will be safe until then?"

I had not realised until I said it that I had not needed to lie about my reason for wanting him back there. He would check Mordred, and he would keep Guinevere safe. He would be upset when he learned that I was trying to use him to punish Arthur, but he might well end getting what he wanted.

"I will make sure of it," I assured him. He nodded, thoughtful.

What was it about her? What made all these men risk anything to have her?

"What does she have," I asked him, and I could not hide the plaintive sadness in my voice, "that I did not?"

Lancelot gave me a sad and gentle smile, putting his hands in comfort on my shoulders. It was unbearably little, and I knew what he was going to say.

"Nothing, Morgan. There is nothing *wrong* with you. I just... love her."

And you don't love me, I thought. Lancelot sighed and shook his head, his gaze growing far away again, getting lost in his thoughts of her. I wished that I had not begun it.

"I tried, Morgan. I tried so hard to forget. I wanted to live a good man's life, but," he paused, closing his eyes for a moment, "I could not forget her. Even when I went to seek the Grail, and I was supposed to fix my thoughts on God, all I thought about was her. I used to dream, again and again and again, that I was walking through Camelot, through the courtyard, up the stairs of her tower. I knew she was in her bedroom, just behind the door, but when I opened the door, I would wake, without seeing her. But she was always there. I knew she was there. No thoughts of God, or sin, or hell could erase the memory of her, of her hands against my skin, of her –" His words caught in him, and I could see he was remembering even now, and he knew that I saw it, and he blushed. "We are bound together, she and I. I will love her until the world ceases to exist. Until heaven and hell fall away into nothingness. I wish it were not so, but also I am not sure I could bear this world without her love. She is..." a slight smile flickered across his face, "undeniable. Like a force of nature. Wild, yes, passionate – cruel, too. She is cruel, sometimes."

"How did you know, then?" I asked him. "How did you know it was me this time?"

Lancelot laughed softly. "Morgan, it was a long time ago that I was so easily fooled. I was little more than a boy then, and I have long been a man now. I have loved my Lady nearly fifteen years. I know her as well as I know myself." He laughed again, looking down at his feet, a strange, secret smile on his face. "She would never have told me she had been *desperate* to see me. No, she would have come to me demanding to know why I had not come to her. Besides, I know her kiss, her touch, the sounds she makes when I have her in my arms. I remember it all, though, in truth, it has been six years since I have even kissed her."

I was shocked. I remembered what he had said to me, when he thought I was Kay, that he was trying to be near her without giving into what he knew was wrong. I could see that he regretted that now. He had not held me away from him when I had come in her shape.

"She is angry with you for that, too," I replied, and he nodded, pacing away from me.

"It is all such an awful mess, Morgan," he said, quietly facing away from me, out into the darkness. The window was open, and the cool spring breeze wafted in, lifting the loose curls of his hair lightly. I could hold him in my arms for a moment, but he would never be mine. He had been hers from the moment he laid eyes on her. I did not know why I had never seen it before. I felt suddenly cruel with my jealousy.

"Because of Arthur?" I demanded. All this talk of Guinevere, of *his Lady*, and he seemed to have forgotten that she was someone else's wife. Lancelot groaned and rubbed his face.

"Arthur," he sighed. "Yes, because of Arthur. If only it were any other man. The only other man in this world who could possibly be worthy of her love, and he is her husband." He half-turned back to me. He was desperate to excuse himself, but I was not convinced. "And she does love him, Morgan. I've taken nothing from him. She does not love him less on my account. What we have is outside of that, beyond this world, beyond time, beyond control." He shook his head again, suddenly angry and suspicious again, pacing back towards me. Perhaps it should have been him, not Mordred, whose help I should have sought. I could not have been totally honest with him, but he was destroying Arthur's perfect world from its secret centre far more effectively than Mordred could ever have done with violence. "But why are you really here, Morgan? What do you *want*? Kay told me that you tried to have Arthur killed. How do I know you're telling me the truth? After all, you came here trying to deceive me again. You are not trying to harm Arthur again, are you?"

I gave him a harsh laugh. It was rich of him to lecture me about doing Arthur harm. I felt cold, and angry and vengeful suddenly again. I was ready for cruelty, for Mordred's savagery. I wanted to hurt them all. Stupid, selfish Lancelot with his talk of his love beyond everyone else – he was not beyond everyone else; the rules that had held me back and tied me to Uriens, and had forced me to suffer and live the life that everyone else wanted me to live – he was not really

358

outside of those, and neither was his *Lady*. He would not live beyond them forever. He thought he could have Guinevere and somehow some great god of love would protect them? He was wrong. I would make him suffer, too. If he wanted to have her, he would have to kill Arthur for her. If these men wanted us to live in a world where they possessed us, then they would have to fight each other to the death for us. I would set them at each other, and watch them tear themselves to pieces. They would feel it; they would feel how I had felt when the door had closed behind me on my wedding night, how I had felt when Arthur had sent my sister, pregnant, from Camelot, how I had felt when Lot held me against his table, my face pressed against the wood. How I had felt standing naked on the shores of Avalon.

I did not answer Lancelot, but let myself fade away, back to Camelot. He would come. I was sure.

Chapter Sixty

I did not have to go to Mordred again. He was already working on a plan of his own, his mean little mind busying away while I was gone. He sought me out as soon as he saw me back, in my borrowed shape.

"You did not bring him back with you, then," Mordred demanded, standing in the doorway to my bedroom, his arms crossed over his chest.

"He will come soon," I told Mordred, dismissively.

"We need better than soon. We need *now*."

I could tell that Mordred felt time running short. He would be nineteen years old when Mayday came. He was acutely aware of how much Arthur had achieved at that age. By that age, too, Arthur had had a son. I wondered if this was what Mordred's suddenly rampant interest in any and every woman was about.

I shrugged. "It will be for the Mayday hunt."

Mordred nodded, but he did not seem satisfied. "You can make sure he comes here, but I have heard something that concerns me greatly, Morgan. I have heard it said that since his return from the quest for the Grail he has kept himself from her bed, from being alone with her, even, out of concern for his immortal soul, or some such nonsense."

I nodded.

"Ah, *Morgan*," he stepped towards me, his eyes wild, "this is our problem! We bring him back, and what if he still consigns himself to this life of virtue?"

I didn't think he would, but Mordred did not look in the mood to be taking chances.

"What is to be done, then?" I asked him.

He did not answer, but took my hand, leading me from the room, down the stairs, across the courtyard, back to his room. He had planned something already, then.

In Mordred's room, sitting as though he were waiting for us to arrive, was a shortish man whom I knew by sight from around Camelot, dressed in a faded surcoat of dark purplish red. It looked strangely dusty, and I suspected that if I came closer to him he would smell damp and musty. He had the look about him of a man who was trying to appear much finer than he was. All of his clothes looked old, and though he had a neat straw-coloured beard, he had an unpleasant slightly feminine softness to his features. I did not like the look of him. I noticed that his hands, folded in his lap, had longish, greyish fingernails. I had heard Gaheris call him Mad Meleagaunt. He was a joke well known among the sons of Lot; a poor, weak-minded knight who entertained himself with dreams of grandeur. He had challenged Gawain to a joust once, and Gawain had laughed about it for more than a week. What on earth did Mordred want with this pathetic creature?

"Who is this?" Meleagaunt asked. His voice did not match his features, it was rough and assertive.

Mordred turned to me with a cruel grin. "This?" he answered. "Oh, this is just my whore."

If I had not been eager to find out what Mordred wanted with this fool, I would have slapped him.

"Now –" Mordred turned back to Meleagaunt, business-like, pulled up a chair and sat facing him. I hung back, leaning against the wall. Meleagaunt seemed to have forgotten already that I was there. "How can we help one another?"

"I have spoken to you before of my dear, true love of the Queen, which I have held for many years now," the man began, his face showing no sign that he did not utterly believe in his own words, though I had heard nothing, nor ever seen her even look at him. I doubted that she knew he existed. Mordred, however, nodded earnestly in response. "And yet, Sir Mordred, all my efforts are lost. Lancelot is ever by her side, and there is no way that I may..." He paused, as though looking for the right word. He glanced at me again, as though he were embarrassed, but he continued, "Be alone with my lady to... persuade her of my affections."

Mordred furrowed his brow into a frown. "But you know, Meleagaunt, Lancelot is far from Camelot, and no one knows where he has gone, or if he will return, or if he even lives, still."

Meleagaunt nodded thoughtfully. "But ever her husband is with her."

"Yes, yes," Mordred agreed, nodding, as though he were thinking it out with this repulsive little man, when I was sure he would have plotted it all out long ago. "Ah, but Meleagaunt, there will be a Mayday hunt, and she will ride out for that. She will be with my Lord King Arthur, of course, but she is a woman and rides slow. If you are wise, you will be able to spot your opportunity to speak with her alone." Mordred leant forward, placing his hands on Meleagaunt's shoulders, staring into his eyes. "Just remember, my friend, that a woman will not love a man she does not respect. Sometimes a little... force is necessary, if you want to convince her of the seriousness of your affections."

I felt suddenly sick. I opened my mouth to object, but I knew I could not without giving myself away. Besides, Meleagaunt was already speaking, jumping from his seat in excitement.

"I will take her back to my castle – yes. When she sees what a fine castle it is, and what a fine lord I myself am, then – yes. And besides, I have a small retinue of knights there. They will ensure that she is... attentive to what I have to say."

I tried to catch Mordred's eye, but he was deliberately avoiding mine, standing to clap the madman on the back and direct him from the room. As soon as Mordred shut the door behind him, grinning to himself, I switched back into my own shape and stepped towards him. I could feel the anger twisting through me. I did not like the way Meleagaunt had talked about *persuasion*, about Guinevere being *attentive*. That had hardly sounded like *love* to me. I resented Mordred for throwing a woman into danger so callously. I did not see, either, how it helped him. I could feel my breath catching in my chest, and I was unable to keep the memory from playing over and over again in my head of Uriens with his hand over my mouth. This was not part of any agreement I had made with Mordred. I could not stop him trying to take her for himself, but this was disgusting, and I would not allow it.

"Mordred," I hissed, "what are you *doing?*"

I was trying to be angry, and strong, but I could feel the tears pricking at the back of my eyes, and I could not stop my heart racing, my mind running over and over again how it had felt to have Uriens on top of me, squashing the breath from me.

Mordred shrugged.

"Mordred, I thought *you* wanted to have the Queen for yourself." I tried a different approach. I thought an appeal to Mordred's pride might be more persuasive. "How does it help you to offer her to another man for – what? To convince Lancelot to save her? What if he's too late?"

Mordred shrugged again. "Lancelot may well be too late. But that is no difference to me. Besides, it might do her good to learn a little humility."

I slapped him then, hard. I felt the rage pounding in my veins, and I felt my eyes burn from holding back the tears. I would not let Mordred see that. Mordred grabbed me by the shoulders and shook me, hard.

"Morgan, get a hold of yourself." He shook me again, then held me still, staring into me with his black, black eyes. "Do not let this get inside your head," he said, softly. "It is you, and it is I. That is what matters. It does not matter what happens to anyone else. You and I. It must be done. How else will Lancelot learn that if he does not make love to his lady, someone else will? He will not leave her side, after this, and I do not see how he could be long at her side without us having our opportunity. This must be done, Morgan."

I only wanted to leave then, to be alone, but when I was alone all I could picture in my mind was Uriens. *He is dead*, I told myself. Long dead. He could not harm me now, but I could not get him out of my mind.

I lay awake a long time, afraid that I would dream of Uriens. When I did sleep at last, I did dream, but thankfully it was not of Uriens. No, it was a sweet dream, a dream of Accolon. A dream thick with pleasant memories; the heat of his bare skin, the feel of his hands running through my hair. But it was fleeting, and just as I felt the remembered pleasure begin to gather through me, the dream slipped away, and I woke in darkness with the feel of a man still on top of me, but one who clamped his hand over my mouth and pushed me down, hard and rough, upon the bed. He leaned down close, and awfully, the voice I heard at my ear was Mordred's.

"Don't let me get inside your head, Morgan," he whispered.

I screamed then, and woke myself properly, sitting up in bed with my heart pounding. I could still feel his hand over my mouth, and where I had been briefly, blissfully, warm from my dream of Accolon,

362

I felt now a cold sweat prickling against my skin. I rushed from the bed to light a candle, and checked all through the room that I was alone. In the depths of the night I was suddenly, deeply afraid of Mordred. I did not know what dark powers I had given him with my black magic drink. I supposed I should not have burned all of Merlin's books, but at the time it had seemed so much better for those secrets to be lost.

Chapter Sixty-One

With the memory of Uriens fresh in my mind, I was sure that I could not go through with it. I could not submit another woman to that, not for the sword, not to be revenged on Arthur, not for anything. I knew it would be useless trying to talk Mordred out of it, and I would have to act alone to stop it. Besides, I did not want to see him. Not until I felt stronger, and I had some distance between now and my dream.

I decided that the only thing I could do was go to Arthur, and convince him to leave Guinevere behind when he went for the hunt. I toyed with the idea of going in my own shape; though I knew Arthur had reasons to suspect me, I thought being the trusting fool he was he might not. But I thought it safer, more effective, if I went to him as Kay. He would believe some excuse about Mayday preparations around the castle, and might even be relieved at the thought of an excuse to leave his wife at home while he went hunting.

I went across the courtyard in the shape of the plain maid, wary that I might run into Kay in his own form. There was a festive air about the castle, and the courtyard was decorated around with garlands of flowers. Camelot liked its celebrations, and I was sure that Mayday this year would be no different, though I was also sure that Arthur would remember that this was the day that Mordred had been born.

I rushed up to Arthur's bedroom, but it was empty. I walked around the room, letting my fingers trail across the tabletop, the windowsill, the edge of the bed. It was truly a long time since I had been here, and yet I could not see that anything had changed. The last time I had been here, I had come to steal my scabbard back. Of course, the whole world had changed. Lancelot and Guinevere had fallen in love, Arthur had killed Accolon, Merlin was gone. But I had not changed, and Arthur had not changed. Arthur was still naïve and selfish, and I was still bitter and angry, and we would be locked together like this, Arthur not caring, me yearning for reparation, until he was made to understand.

Well, if Arthur was not there, I would have to seek him out elsewhere.

As I walked down the stairs, I heard Arthur's voice coming from the room where he kept the Round Table. I closed my eyes and let my shape change to Kay's. The door was hanging slightly open. Wary that it might be Kay he was speaking with, I crept closer, peering in.

It was not Arthur I could see, it was Guinevere, standing at the table, a book open before her, her fingertips resting lightly against the page, as though she were following the words. I could see her soft, red lips moving with the words, but she was speaking too softly for me to hear what she was reading. Arthur was saying something to her, and I saw a slight smile flicker across her face, though she did not look up, or stop reading. I could see from her attitude that she was ignoring him on purpose, teasing him. He did not seem to mind. I wished that I had found him alone.

I was about to stride through the door and interrupt them, for I was sure that this was the sort of thing that Kay would do, when it became clear that Arthur did not intend to simply listen to his wife read. He came up behind her, resting his hands possessively on her hips, pulling her back gently from the book she was reading. He kissed lightly against her ear.

"Arthur," she sighed, sounding annoyed, though I could see her smiling, "I'm reading."

And stubbornly she continued to read as he kissed her neck until he reached around and spread his hand flat against the page, and she stopped. I saw him press himself tighter against her and she leaned back against him, closing her eyes.

"Guinevere, your book will still be there at vespers, but I don't intend for *this* to be." He pushed a little harder against her and they both bumped against the table.

"Arthur..." Guinevere laughed softly, and shook her head, but her tone was indulgent. I supposed she must have been used to his demanding behaviour by now.

Arthur pushed the book off the table, and when she went to pick it up, pulled her back against him, his hands winding into her hair, pulling it loose, turning her face around to his in a passionate kiss. She relaxed back into him for a moment, until his other hand ran softly down her throat, and then down across her breasts, his fingers tucking down, into the neckline of her dress.

"Arthur, shut the door," she mumbled, not drawing properly away from the kiss. Either he didn't hear her, or he wasn't listening. He pulled hard at the front of her dress, and I heard the fabric tear. That must have been an expensive dress of fine, thin silk, but I supposed Arthur did not care. Guinevere gasped, but it was not a gasp of surprise. It was one of excitement. I could not imagine Lancelot ripping a woman's clothes. Arthur slid his hand into her dress at the opening he had torn at its neck, and I heard her sigh softly for a moment, before she pulled away from him to speak again.

"Arthur, *the door*," she insisted.

With a low laugh, Arthur lifted his hand from her dress and without moving away from her leaned over to slam the door shut. Just before it shut, I saw him turn her around in his arms and push her up on to the table.

I could see, then, why Arthur believed so strongly that his wife did not love another man. I was surprised, though, that her response seemed to match his desire. I did not believe that she had given up on Lancelot.

I did not want to burst in now, nor stand outside waiting. I would just have to try again later. I went back to my room and let Kay's shape slip away from me, curling myself into the window seat that I had sat in so many years ago when Morgawse had burst through my door, flushed and giggling. We had not had any idea, then, what she had begun. Without that one mistake, there would have been no war with Lot, no marriage for me. Arthur might not have married Guinevere. Lancelot might never have met her, and then perhaps he might have wanted to marry me. Mordred would never have been born.

I slid down from the window seat, trying to think of what I could do, what I remembered from the books of magic I had burned, that I could use to control Mordred, to protect myself from him.

"Morgan."

I turned around. I had not heard the door. I was not prepared. I was in my own shape, and it was too late, for it was Kay. He pushed the door shut behind him, and slid the bolt. His thick, fine dark hair stood up on his forehead as though he had just run his hand through it. His face which I had last seen up close, still charmingly boyish, now was the face of a sensitive grown man, his brown eyes still bright and mischievous, though now they held me with an even stare.

"Kay," I replied softly. "How did you know I was here?"

Kay shrugged. He looked desperately lost all of a sudden. "I have known all along. And then, from across the courtyard, I saw myself walking up here."

I nodded. Of course he had. I had not been thinking, I had not been careful.

Kay walked a few paces towards me, and I did not back away.

"What do you want, Kay?"

"I want to know what you're plotting here, in secret," he said, soft and threatening, stepping towards me. I turned my face up towards his. He was close enough that I could smell his skin, and I was surprised at how familiar it seemed. I felt myself, against all my resolve, leaning towards him. He was my enemy now. It was not wise.

"Nothing, Kay," I whispered.

I ought to have told him the truth, I thought, suddenly. Told him I was in too deep with Mordred, that I needed his help. He would do it. He would keep Guinevere from going out with the hunt on Mayday. I was about to open my mouth, to confess it all when he reached out and grabbed hold of my hair by the plait, suddenly sharp and rough, pulling me up against him, his eyes flashing angry.

"Do not lie to me, Morgan," he hissed.

I slapped him across the face, and he stepped back, letting go of my hair, cursing under his breath. No, he had not expected that. He looked at me and still saw the shy girl raised by the nuns. He pretended that he saw a wicked witch, but he did not.

"Morgan," he sighed, and his eyes fixed on me, slightly sad. "Just tell me if I need to be watching Arthur's back. Or anyone else's. I'm not going to tell anyone you're here. Far be it from me to get in the way of your mad little quest for revenge. I'm sure you get as much satisfaction from hiding here plotting than you would from actually doing anything."

I lost all the thoughts I had of warning him, of asking for his help. I stepped forward to slap him again, and he jumped lightly away. He was still nimble on his feet.

"How little you men know. No one here cares how my sister Morgawse suffers, alone in Lothian. No, no one; not you, not Arthur, not anyone else who has fucked her." Kay flinched, but I did not care. "You all forgot me in Gore. Not one of you cares about anyone but yourself."

"Oh, Morgan, you think you are the only one who has suffered, don't you?" he sneered, a smile spreading cruel across his face. "No one has suffered as much as poor little Morgan." I lunged towards him, moving as if to slap him again, and he caught me by the wrist, yanking me towards him, pulling me against him. When he had me close, he leaned down to say, softly in my ear. "You are every bit as self-obsessed as the rest of us, Morgan."

As I opened my mouth to retort he kissed me, hard. But it was an act of aggression rather than desire and it only served to remind me of how much we had lost, and I pushed him away. I didn't want to be fogged with desire, like the rest of them. Everything was already a sickening tangle of Mordred and Guinevere and Arthur and Lancelot. Unbidden, I remembered the awful dream, the ghost of a hand over my mouth. I needed my focus. I was here to save my enemy.

"What is it, Morgan, that you want?" Kay demanded. Folded in on himself, his arms wrapped around his chest, he was like an animal; wary, suspicious.

"I need you to do something for me."

"I'm not playing this game with you again, Morgan," Kay snapped, turning towards the door. I rushed into his way, backing up against the door so that he could not get past.

"Kay, please. I can't explain why. Not now. It's Guinevere. She's in danger."

Kay looked suddenly as though he was no longer interesting in leaving. He had a strange look in his eye, fear, and worry, and something darker and more complex. Well, now I had his attention.

"Morgan, what do you know?" His voice was low and tense with suspicion.

Where did I start? With Mordred? Kay had already seen that. I could not explain what I knew without revealing myself to be in league with him.

"Kay, I can't explain, but please – make sure she does not go on the hunt."

Kay gave me a long, wary look.

"How can I be sure that *you* are not trying to harm her?" he said.

I lifted my hand and put it over his eyes. Before us we saw the Breton queen sitting in the bath in Rheged Castle, me sitting, heavily pregnant, at the foot of her bath, then kneeling down beside her to wrap a strip of linen around her wounded arm. Then, again, me watching her buckle on her armour while she talked about her daughter until Arthur and Uriens came, to lead her away to her death.

When I drew my hand away, I could see that Kay was convinced enough. Convinced by the woman's likeness to Guinevere – even stronger, now that Guinevere was almost the age that her mother had been then – and my own clear memory of it. Kay nodded, and I knew I could be sure of him.

"But Morgan," he said, softly, "truly you cannot tell me the whole truth of this?"

I shook my head.

Chapter Sixty-Two

Mayday came, and I watched the hunt leave nervously. I was only calmed when I was sure that Guinevere and Kay were not with it. It would be easy enough for him to keep her in the castle. But I began to feel concerned again when I could not see them in her garden, or anywhere around the castle. In the shape of the plain maid, I asked Marie where the Queen was.

"She has gone out Maying with Kay the Seneschal," she told me, dismissively.

I felt cold with anxiety. How could Kay have been so stupid? I had meant for him to keep her *in the castle*. I felt an increasing sense of dread when, wandering down to the armoury, I found his black armour and his shield, marked with the great grey keys of the Seneschal, still lying down there. I had no idea if any of the swords were his, though I hoped even Kay would not go out without his sword. I should have told him the whole truth. They would have been safer with the hunt, surrounded by armed men, than out Maying alone. What if Lancelot did not come?

But he did. I ran out to meet him as I saw him riding up to the gates in his armour. He stopped when he saw it was me. I did not care anymore if anyone saw I was there. I did not wait for him to get off his horse, but as soon as he had lifted the helm from his head, I told him that the Queen was in danger, and pointed off in the direction she must have gone with Kay. I was about to explain, to explain that it was not Mordred, that it was not what I had told him of before, but he was already gone, riding off. He had let his helm drop to the floor in his haste and I picked it up, cradling it against my chest, wrapping my arms around it, but it gave me no comfort.

I stood in the courtyard as dusk began to fall, wearing the shape of the serving girl no one ever seemed to notice, and I watched Arthur ride in through the gates of Camelot. He was smiling and laughing. Gawain was at his side, and Mordred just behind them. Mordred caught my eye as he rode in, and his smile deepened. I felt sick. If he was not angry that Guinevere had not gone with the hunt, and she was not yet back with Kay, I dreaded to know what he was pleased with himself about. And what about Kay? Did this mean that Kay was dead, or a prisoner, too, somewhere?

Arthur was jumping down from his horse, pulling off the game birds and rabbits he had caught and tied to his saddle, and handing them to a squire, but he was not looking at what he was doing. He was looking for Guinevere. He did not seem troubled, yet. Gawain jumped down beside him and, smiling at each other, and Arthur clapping Gawain on the back, they walked off past me, to clean the sweat and dirt of the hunt off them. As they passed me, I heard Arthur say to Gawain, "It is a shame that Lancelot did not come back for the hunt," and Gawain gave a low grunt of assent.

Arthur would expect to find his wife waiting for him in his room. How long would it be before he realised that she was missing? Would he check in her room for her? When would he raise the alarm?

I did not know what to do, so I wandered back to my room to wait. I did not know where Meleagaunt's castle was. I did not know how Lancelot would find Kay and Guinevere without knowing the way. I had set his helm on my table and I stood there, staring at it, as though it would give me some kind of answer.

Suddenly the door of my room flew open, and Mordred stood there. He was furious. I stepped back from him, but he was fast across the room, throwing the door shut behind him, grabbing me by the throat and slamming me hard against the wall. I wrapped my hands around his wrist, pulling his hand back enough for me to breathe. He let me have that, but he did not move back. He leaned down, his face threateningly close to mine. I heard his voice again in my head, as I had in my dream: *Don't let me get inside your head.* I was afraid that he was already there.

"I know what you did, little Morgan," he hissed. I was shocked to hear him use the name my mother had called me. Had Morgawse said it to him? How much did he know that he ought not to know? Did he know about Accolon? No, surely he could not know about that. He pressed his hand harder against my throat. "If you act against me again, I will kill you."

I closed my eyes, and let my shape change to Arthur's. I had guessed well enough that Mordred was still not quite as strong as his father, trained from years on the battlefield, and I pushed him off me. He stumbled back, but at the sight of whose form I had taken, he looked amused, his anger suddenly fading.

"Morgan, I am not afraid of my father."

I slipped back into my own shape, shrugging. "And I am not afraid of you. I need be afraid of no one when I can take any man's

369

form. Don't come here and threaten me. You got what you wanted anyway. Lancelot has come, and ridden off after the Queen. We are to have our success soon, unless you want me to have killed *you* before you get what you desire." I stepped towards him, and he did look wary, though he did not back away. "I have killed men before, Mordred," I told him softly. "Have you? Do you know you have the heart for it?"

To my surprise, Mordred baulked at this. He was young, I supposed, and had grown up under Arthur's peace. What cause would he have had to kill a man? I was suddenly, painfully, aware of how young he was.

"I have the heart for it," he insisted, but he knew that I had seen his inexperience. I did not doubt that if the moment came, then Mordred would be ready to kill his father, but I was not sure he was strong or skilled enough. We were into this too deep. How was this man both a child and a monster? How could I be afraid of him one moment and embarrassed by him the next?

I did not have to work out where I would go from there with Mordred, because I could hear shouting out in the courtyard. Mordred rushed out before me, and I followed as the plain servant. Arthur had noticed that his wife was missing when he had sent for his Seneschal to ask where she was, and found them both gone.

Though it was late into the night, the courtyard was full of people, torches lit, running around. I could hear Gawain shouting, and Gaheris. I could hear Arthur shouting too, far away.

Quietly, beside me, I heard Aggravain lean close to say to Mordred, "If my wife were missing overnight along with the most notorious lover of anyone and everyone in Camelot, I would be searching for her with my sword in my hand, foster-brother or no."

Mordred, beside him, shrugged.

Chapter Sixty-Three

I heard the search die down just a few hours before dawn. I slept badly, stirring and waking often. I would not feel right until Lancelot returned with Guinevere and Kay. If they came back safe, I did not have to feel guilty, and I could continue with my plan, my plan to teach the truth to Arthur. To have what was mine returned to me.

It was a tense day. I could feel it all around me. Arthur strode through the castle, his face dark with anger, and when the daylight brought no more news, and their search through the forest no sign of

Guinevere or Kay, he stood with Gawain in the middle of the courtyard, even as the sun was beginning to sink down in the sky, and they began to arm themselves as though they were about to ride out far into the falling night to look for them. Ector stood with them, and though I could not hear what he was saying, I could hear the gentle concern in his voice. He did not want Arthur lured away from Camelot to be harmed. He suspected some kind of trap. He had no success, and when Arthur waved him away, he left.

But, as their horses were brought from the stables, someone gave a shout and I turned with everyone else to see a single horse ride through the gates. On it were Guinevere, Kay and Lancelot. As soon as they were through the gates, Arthur rushed forward and Guinevere slipped from the horse into his arms. He wrapped his arms around her, and right in front of everyone, he kissed her passionately. She gently took his face in her hands. Even from where I was, I could see she was trembling. She was dressed, too, in men's clothes. I tried to push the thoughts from my mind. The sleeves of the shirt fell back from her wrists, and I saw there familiar bruises that made my stomach turn.

Lancelot and Kay were on the horse still, and I could see that Kay was badly injured. He slumped back against Lancelot, his face pale, his eyes falling closed. His father and Gareth stepped forward to lift him down gently from the horse. Lancelot jumped down then, and went over to Arthur and Guinevere. I could not hear what they said over the sounds of my heart pounding in my ears, but Arthur was thanking him, or congratulating him. He would not have done so, surely, if Guinevere had been hurt.

I waited in my room for Mordred, pacing back and forth. Though we no longer trusted one another, we still knew that we could not cut the other loose. I was sick with it, sorry for it, but it was too late.

Mordred came late in the night. Meleagaunt was dead. Killed by Lancelot. I was glad to hear it, glad to hear from Mordred that Guinevere was returned without harm. He could see I was relieved.

"It is of no matter," he told me, evenly. "Lancelot is returned now, and he will not leave her alone after this. Now, we wait. It is only a matter of time."

I had to see Guinevere. To reassure myself that she had indeed come to no harm. The next morning, I slipped up to her room in the form of Marie, whom I was sure had, wild with relief that her mistress had come safely back, rushed into Gaheris' comforting arms, and would not be there.

As I climbed the stairs, I passed Arthur coming down. He gave me a friendly smile as I passed him, and stopped me with a casual, friendly hand on my arm to tell me Guinevere wanted her bath. I watched him go, and wondered if he, too, had known the strange practices of the Breton maid. I never saw him with other women, and he had only been friendly, but I knew how he had been when we were young, and knowing what I did of men, I could not imagine Arthur being satisfied with only his wife.

I stopped some other girls going past to help me, and they were quick and obedient. I supposed Marie had been in charge here a long time. I looked around for the older woman, Christine, until I heard one of the other girls mention that she had died. I felt a sudden spark of pity for Guinevere, losing her women until there was just one left. The other women at Camelot were servants, or the wives of knights who came and went. It must have been a lonely life, without a child.

When the other women had set down the bath and left, and I had filled it with water, Guinevere slipped out from under the bedcovers and into the bath. She was silent, which I had not expected, and when she sank into the water, it was absently, as though she did not feel it on her skin. She sank slowly beneath the water, closing her eyes and slipping down in the bath until the water covered her face and hair. I stared down at her as she stayed there for a moment, her eyes closed. Through the water a bubble rose from her mouth and broke on the surface. Through the clear, rippling water I could see the startling colours of her, white and red.

Slowly, she sat up in the bath, pushing her hair back from her face, and it was as though she suddenly became herself again, noticing I was there.

"Marie," she said, with a smile, reaching out a wet hand towards me. I took it, not knowing what else to do. Between us, the water dripped off her skin onto the wooden floor.

"What happened to you?" I whispered, hearing Marie's chirping Breton accent come from my mouth, and being surprised by it. It was always hearing another's voice that was the most surprising.

She sighed deeply, drawing her hand away and flicking her fingertips through the bathwater absently.

"Marie –" She shook her head. "Someone else will tell you the story. I –"

I nodded. I understood this better than Marie would have done. She saw my nodding and gave a gentle smile in return.

"But, Lancelot came for you?" I asked, kneeling beside the bath.

"He is a faithful champion," she replied, distant again. She could not have been more different than she had been when I had heard her cursing him in Breton. All that anger had melted off her, and her eyes half-closed in sweet remembering, she sank down a little in the bath as the vapour from the hot water rose around her.

I said nothing, but she did not seem to be expecting me to say anything, nor did she seem interested in talking. She sat up and looked at me expectantly, until I remembered that I had seen Marie combing through her hair before. I sat behind her, drawing the comb through her thick curls while she winced and complained, until I had wound it into a bun. The whole time, all I could think about was Lancelot's hands on her long white thighs as I saw them rising from the bathwater, his mouth against her neck as I brushed it with my fingers. I wished that I could not picture it so clearly; I wished I could forget Lancelot, or at least not feel anything like the raw jealousy that I felt when I remembered how it had felt to be with him, and know that she had that, that she would always have that from him, whenever she desired it.

When I was finished, she stood, patting the back of her hair with her hand to check it was in place, while the water ran down her naked body. I passed her a sheet to dry herself with. She wrapped it around herself, looking at me with a suddenly intense gaze.

"How is Kay?" she asked. I had forgotten Kay. If she were worrying at another's injury then surely she must have been well enough herself. I did not know how Kay was, but I made some kind of comforting non-committal response and left.

I was sure that Kay would be well now that he was back in Camelot. If he had survived the night and the ride back. Just to be sure, I made the potion for blood, and went to his room, and pressed it into his hands. When, bleary-eyed with sleep, he saw it was me, he said nothing, but drank it all in a huge gulp. When I turned to leave, he took my hand, just for a moment. He did not say anything, and neither did I.

It was then that a summons came from Morgawse, calling us up to Lothian. I did not want it, for things were just beginning to come together in Camelot, but to my surprise, Mordred wanted to go. I think he missed his mother. I supposed a little time would not hurt. I would be pleased to spend the summer with my sister, and a short absence would make Lancelot and Guinevere feel safer, and more daring.

In the end, it was a small party of knights that rode for Lothian. When Gawain and Gaheris heard that Mordred was going, they wanted to go too, and Lamerocke made some excuse to go with them. Mordred regarded him with a hostile eye, but did not stop him. Kay was healing, Lancelot and Guinevere were getting themselves more deeply tangled in the net that Mordred and I would draw around Arthur, and everything would take care of itself while I was gone. Besides, I had missed Morgawse.

I went ahead of the men riding, since I had no need of it. When Morgawse saw me appear before her in her bedchamber, she burst forth in bright giggles, and drew me into a tight embrace. I held her to me and kissed her cheek. It was only when I held her back to look at her that I realised that she was beginning to look old to me. She was forty six. She had lines at the corner of her eyes now, from smiling and laughing, despite everything, and her hair now was a pale golden colour where it had once been a glorious golden-red. Still, she had the same wicked glint in her eye, which only got brighter when I told her that Lamerocke would be among the knights coming to Lothian Castle.

Before their arrival I had my sister to myself. I listened to all her talk of how Lothian had been in our absence, how she had missed us. She asked for the gossip at court, and I gave her a little of what I knew. That night, we slept side by side like children, and I felt the same homely comfort I always did from Morgawse's presence. It was only when I woke the next day that I realised that I was dreading Mordred's coming.

For the arrival of her sons, and of her secret lover, she dressed in one of her finest dresses, one of the few she had for summer, made of light blue and dark blue silk brocaded into a pattern like rose vines, and a necklace of gold set with a huge pendant pearl. She brushed her long pale gold hair until it shone and pulled it back in a clasp of pearl and gold.

She rushed out into the courtyard to meet them. Gawain was first to jump from his horse, and he picked his mother up in his huge arms into a fierce embrace. She kicked up her feet behind her in the air, laughing. When he had set her on the ground again, she took his face in her hands and kissed him on both cheeks. She was intensely proud of Gawain, I could see that. She asked where Aggravain was, and no one was quite sure why he had stayed behind. Either that, or they would not say.

She kissed Gaheris next, who had come to stand beside Gawain, and asked him where his wife was. He made some feeble excuse, but I was sure that Gaheris had come to Camelot to get away from the wife that he had almost entirely ignored since he had married her. I had asked Mordred if he were not worried about Lynet producing a child when Gaheris had not been near her in months. Mordred had told me then that she had had one miscarriage after another until he had discarded her. He told me that he thought her womb was not strong enough to grow a child of his black magic blood. If anyone else had said that, I would have laughed. Since it was Mordred, I had felt a chill dread settle on me. Mordred did want a son. Of course he did. He seemed to believe only more strongly after that that Arthur's wife was the woman he ought to have, since he had heard the talk of her ancient Otherworld blood. When I told him she was barren, he had laughed. He seemed to think himself above the processes of nature. Perhaps he was. He was, after all, conceived against it.

It was to Mordred that Morgawse came next, and he wrapped his arms around her tight, burying his face in her hair. I could see his chest rising and falling with emotion, and I was shocked. I had forgotten how deeply Mordred loved his mother, and I had forgotten that everyone – even Mordred – was capable of such deep love. Such vulnerability. Morgawse held him back, smiling with tears in her eyes to see Mordred back, brushing his cheek with her thumbs. When she told him she had missed him, he pressed a tender kiss against her lips. I thought it was too close, too intimate, but when I glanced at Gaheris and Gawain, they did not seem to have seen it. Still, I caught Lamerocke's eye, and he looked away too fast not to betray his discomfort.

Chapter Sixty-Four

That night, Morgawse had arranged a great feast to welcome her sons back to their castle. She was a little put out that Gareth had not come with his wife and her granddaughter, but Lynesse was delicate and shy, and the little girl small for her age. Morgawse did not seem to be concerned by the excuse, telling the story again of how Gawain and Aggravain had been born tiny as baby birds, and had grown into giants of men.

Morgawse spent all night smiling and laughing, and it made me feel happy to see her. She grew lightly flushed with the wine, and began to lean her head back lightly against Mordred's chest, since he sat behind her with his arm around her shoulders. After the sweet cakes were taken away, Morgawse sighed and settled back further against Mordred, and he kissed the top of her head, then ran his hand slowly, softly down her arm and twined his fingers with hers. It was then that I saw Gaheris watching the pair of them, wary. Lamerocke was watching, too. Gawain had not noticed. He was singing, loud and raucous and drunk as always.

I stayed at the feast as late as I could. I did not like the watchful looks, nor the tense atmosphere that descended once Gawain and most of the other knights had retired to bed, but it seemed as though my concern was for nothing, for both Mordred and Lamerocke left when Morgawse yawned and declared herself ready to retire. I walked back with her to her room, and kissed her goodnight on the cheek. She did not ask me to come inside, so I was sure that she was expecting Lamerocke, and was wise enough to ask him to come later, in secret, when her sons would not see.

I could not get to sleep in my bed for a long time. Something had unsettled me, and I was not quite sure what it was. It was only in the depths of the night when I was just beginning to drift away into sleep that I heard, deep in the distance of the castle, a shout. Filled with an instinctive dread, I jumped out of bed, threw my cloak around my shoulders and rushed down the stairs and out into the courtyard. As I ran, I heard more shouting, and louder.

I followed the sound of shouts, and as I came across the courtyard I saw Lamerocke, in his shirt and breeches, running, as if for his life. I felt my heart quicken. I began running then, wishing as I had wished so many times that I had Excalibur by my side.

I felt no comfort as I followed the shouting up towards Morgawse's bedroom. *No*, I thought. If Lamerocke had escaped alive and there were still men shouting, then that only meant that my sister was in danger.

When I reached the top of the stairs, the first person I saw was Gawain, his face twisted with anger. But it was not Gawain who caught my eye. Gaheris stood a few paces past him, right beside Morgawse's bedroom door, which was opened onto a crack of darkness, and I could not see within. Gaheris was bloodied from the fingertips to the elbow, still clutching his sword in both hands before him, holding it out towards Mordred who stood the other side of the doorway, in his shirt and breeches, his feet bare, blood splattered down his shirt. Gaheris' face, too, was spattered with blood, and his chest was rising and falling as though he were half way through a fight. His and Mordred's gazes were locked together, both hostile. Neither of them seemed injured, and Lamerocke had not been. Where had the blood come from?

"What is happening here?" I demanded.

No one spoke. Gaheris and Mordred were staring at one another, and Gawain was staring at Gaheris.

"*What has happened?*" I shouted. That seemed to shake Gaheris' gaze away from Mordred, and he turned to me with his mouth hanging open, as though he had something he desperately wanted to say, but that was beyond him. Behind him, in the half-dark of the corridor, I heard Mordred's voice, cold and flat with anger, and it chilled me to the bone.

"Gaheris has killed our mother."

My sister. My dear sister. We had been the only one the other could rely on, and I had not stopped this and − *her own son.*

"Gaheris..." I breathed in disbelief. He looked at me, wide-eyed and speechless, shaking his head. Why had he killed her? I had just seen her, and she had been alive and wonderful and beautiful as always. No one had a stronger, brighter sense of life about them than Morgawse. I wanted to scream.

Mordred's bare feet caught my eye again, and my stomach churned. Lamerocke running across the courtyard. What had Gaheris seen that he could not force into words? What had been so awful that he had acted so terribly? Lamerocke had not been bare-footed when I had seen him run. He had not, even, appeared to come from this direction.

I turned to Gawain. "What happened?" I demanded.

Gawain glanced between his brothers, as though looking for help, or information. I could smell blood. Acrid, iron. I was no longer in any doubt about whose it was. When I got no answer, I strode towards the bedroom door, hanging awfully a quarter open, and Gawain caught hold of me and pulled me back, wrapping his arms around me and holding me against him, as though for his own comfort as well as mine. He rested his head against mine, and suddenly I was aware that I was this huge warrior's aunt, and that as well as trying to protect me from what I might see in the room, he expected some kind of strength and comfort from me. I put my arms around his, where they wrapped around me at the shoulders.

"Gawain," I said softly. "Please, what has happened?"

It was not Gawain, but Mordred who answered, and he did not look at me, but stared, hard at Gaheris. I felt Gawain press his forehead against my shoulder, in grief and distress. I rested a comforting hand on the back of his head. His hair, thick and soft, felt like Morgawse's. I could have cried then, but I did not.

"Gaheris came upon our mother with the knight Sir Lamerocke, and in his anger at the *shame* this brought to all our family –" He gave Gaheris a meaningful look, slightly threatening. "In his anger, he drew his sword, and struck at our mother, and the blow cut off her head."

I felt sick. It was an awful death. An *awful* death. How could Gaheris have done this? Of course I ought to have trusted in my instinct about him from the start. He had Lot's impulsive, cruel anger. I leaned back against Gawain, and felt him hold me tighter against him. He was as bereft as I was at the loss of Morgawse. I heard him hold back a sob.

Gaheris did not seem capable of saying anything. He looked between me and his brothers, and turned and left. There was blood on his boots, and it smeared across the floor.

I should have stopped him. If I had had Excalibur in my hands, I would have killed him. *Morgawse.* I had spent too much of my time parted from her, and now she was gone for ever.

I moved gently from Gawain's arms, stepping towards the door. I had to see. But, as I stepped towards it, Mordred stepped into my path, putting his hand on the door frame, barring my way with his arm.

"Morgan, you do not want to see," he told me, his voice cracking. I heard Gawain leave behind me. Clearly, he did not want to linger with Mordred.

"Mordred..." I did not know what to say. I wanted to see my sister.

Mordred grabbed me by both hands, pulling me towards him. He had blood spattered across his face. He had blood on his white shirt, which was not tucked into his breeches. His hair was ruffled through. What had Gaheris seen? Why had he let Mordred speak for him? Gawain, too, had had nothing to say. But whatever Gaheris had seen, he had struck the blow.

"Morgan," Mordred said, his eyes locked on mine, "curse him. Curse Gaheris. He must pay for this."

I shook my head. I had to see Morgawse, I had to know it was truly so.

378

"That is not how it works, Mordred," I told him, bitterly, wishing that it was. For all his strange, Otherworld gifts he still did not understand. I could not just curse a man to his death.

"Yes it is," Mordred insisted, and he closed his eyes, gripping my hands tighter. I could smell the blood that was spattered across his face. I could see it drying already in his hair. I felt sick, and I held back my desire to retch. He began to speak, his voice grim and cold. I felt his anger, his curse, run through my blood, feeding off the magic in his blood and mine, and the blood we shared, and the blood on his face. "I curse Gaheris, son of Lot. I curse him on our mother's blood. May his death be without honour. May his line be without sons." He paused for a moment, opening his eyes. I could see right into their black centres, black on black, blood mixing with blood. I could not look away. I could not say no. Morgawse was dead. I repeated his words back to him, feeling the magic rush in my blood, and the strength of it coming off him. It was as if all around us was filled with our black desire for revenge.

And then I saw it before me. Gaheris, standing in a crowd, unarmed. The day was dark, overcast. The vision was so strong that I was sure I felt slight, spitting raindrops against my skin. He stood in his surcoat, no sword at his side. As the vision expanded I saw that he was holding someone, his hand gripped hard around their bare arm. It was Guinevere, in her underclothes, her hair loose. Her lip was swollen and split, a small line of dark dry blood threading down it. They were not looking at one another. When was this? Before or after I had seen her side-by-side with me? I knew what he was doing. He was taking her to be burned for treason. It couldn't be anything else. There was no other way Arthur would let one of his knights drag his Queen through a crowd in her underclothes. I had not thought he would have her killed. Was this what I was leading us to? Certainly, it would be the end of Arthur. I had not wanted to cause her death in the process, but I was too deep in to turn back. The sounds were coming now, too. I could hear the crowd shouting around them, and I could see that at the other side of Guinevere, his grip much lighter than that of his brother, stood Gareth. He looked lost, and sad, unable to understand what had brought him to that moment. He looked reluctant. Gaheris on the other hand looked bored, and Guinevere's arm under his grip was already turning red.

I heard screaming, but I could not see where it was coming from. Not until the crowd split in two before them and a black horse reared over them. I looked up. It was Lancelot. His head was bare, but he was wearing his mail, and he had a sword in his hand. His eyes were wild as though he did not see anything before him apart from Guinevere. Gareth saw him before his brother did, and shouting his brother's name, he stepped forward to push Gaheris from the path of Lancelot's sword, which was crashing down towards him. Gareth was not fast enough, and the blow sliced through both brothers at once, spattering Guinevere with blood. I saw her mouth open in a scream, but I did not hear it, because the vision, that had been so painfully vivid, suddenly passed away.

I stared at Mordred, feeling the dread spread through me. I felt cold and heavy, and awful. How many innocents were going to die before Mordred and I got what we wanted? *Gareth*. It was Gareth whose blood I had taken to give myself my black magic powers, whose blood had made Mordred strong with them, too. It was his innocence that had bought me this strength, and it was going to kill him. No. I was not going to do it. There had been enough death. I had already lost enough.

"Undo it, Mordred," I demanded.

"Why?" He was defiant, aggressive. He stepped towards me, pulling his hands from mine, threatening.

"Gareth," I said, firmly. "You will kill one brother for revenge on the other? No, Mordred."

Mordred shrugged. "It is too late to be undone."

"Don't you care?" I shouted. "Don't you care if an innocent man dies?"

Mordred grabbed me hard by the front of my nightdress, pulling me up towards him. I could feel the terrifying strength in his hands, but I knew that well enough. No, it was the mania in his eyes that frightened me now, the hollow conviction that he was right, and that everything he did was without error if it got him what he longed for.

"There are no innocent men," he hissed, holding me there for a moment, then throwing me back. I felt shaken and bruised. I had, truly, lost control of him. Worse. I had lost control of myself. I had said his black words back to him. He had made me complicit in it all, in all of the darkness of it, and the horror. I was suddenly aware of how long I had been staring into the void, without even knowing it.

I knew that he would not turn back, he would not relent until he had got every last thing he intended to get, but I had lost too much. Morgawse, for whom I had done anything and everything without question, was gone, and I had no one left. I was not going to plunge innocents into the blackness I could feel yawning up around me. I had been willing when it was only Arthur who was to be harmed, but Mordred had no compassion, no mercy. I would not be a part of it any longer. He would kill them all until there was no one to stop him. He would turn on me, too, if I stood against him. I had created something beyond my power to control. I had not expected him to be so strong, or so ruthless. I had seen a child. I had not understood.

I had no choice now. There was only one person who might have the power to stop him. Nimue.

Chapter Sixty-Five

I went right then. I thought if I did not, I would not have the strength to climb down from my pride.

Though I had not been there since I was fifteen years old, I remembered every detail of Avalon's great chapel. I knew Nimue would sense my coming, and I knew that she would be there, though it was the middle of the night. When the great chapel with its gaping windows, its roof open to the sky – which tonight was filled with the bright, sharp points of stars – came into focus around me, Nimue was sat already in the great stone seat of the Lady of Avalon, her long white-blonde hair loose around her shoulders down to her waist. She had looked like a child for so long, I was shocked to see how terrifying and powerful she looked right there. Her sharp-featured face was set with wrath, her ice-blue eyes fixing me through with a stare that went right to the core of me. She was wearing a dress like the one she had made for me, sewn with gems from the neck to the waist, but hers was a pale blue, and swirled through with green like the blue-green patterns of woad that traced across her white skin. She had a circlet of white gold on her head, set with diamonds in the form of the five-pointed star that was the insignia of Avalon. But more than all of this, I felt the strength of her magic coming off her, like a mountain breeze, cold and strong. I had only made it to Avalon alive because she wished it so.

One of Arthur's knights stood behind her in full armour. From the shield he bore, I knew the man as one named Pelleas. He was famed for his strength, but I had not seen him at Camelot in a long time. He must have been in Avalon, in Nimue's service.

"Morgan." Nimue's voice was stern, and cold, and in the night-time in the hollowed chapel, it rang. I gathered my old woollen cloak more tightly around myself. My feet were bare; I had run from my bed without getting dressed.

Nimue stood to her feet, and I fell to my knees before her. I was not sure if it was her power, her magical strength, or my own body collapsing under the loss of Morgawse, under the realisation of what I had done when I had made my devil's pact with Mordred. I had given my soul to a demon, and he had consumed it, and it had not satisfied him.

"How *dare* you come before me, Morgan," she snarled, walking slowly down the steps before her stone seat towards me. "You disobeyed my order not to plot Arthur's harm. You burned Merlin's books. You scorned my favour and my friendship for – for what? To make Arthur's son into your creature of revenge? And now you have lost control of him, and you come to me begging me to save you?"

She stopped before me. She placed a cold, papery hand under my chin and turned my face up to hers. Her eyes were cold with anger, and I felt it sink into me, like a knife. I had no words for her, nothing to say. I closed my eyes, shaking my head, feeling the tears prick the back of my eyes. All I could think of, over and over again, were the words *my sister is dead*.

Roughly, Nimue turned my face back up to hers.

"*Answer me*, Morgan," she demanded.

I opened my mouth, but no sound came out.

Nimue turned over her shoulder to the knight behind her. "Pelleas," she commanded. I heard him draw his sword. I could hear the plates of his armour scrape against one another as he moved towards us. I closed my eyes. I could feel myself trembling, I could feel my own awful weakness, I could feel the low, dark creature I had become, and I did not care if he killed me. I did not care if Nimue killed me. I just wanted it all to be undone. All of it. I wanted to wake in the Abbey, and hear Kay shouting in the garden, and run out to see him and Arthur, just two brothers from the farm nearby again. I wanted to hear Ector scolding them like children. I wanted to run with them through the woodlands, and swim in the lake. It was becoming a king that had made Arthur give me away in marriage, changing to a woman that had made me a thing to be bought and sold. He had saved my sister's life with that marriage. He had saved the lives of hundreds of innocent people in Logrys. I had suffered, but I had suffered as much from my own bitterness as from my marriage. Kay had been right, long, long ago. I had lost the girl who had grown up in the Abbey. Slowly, pieces of her had been taken from me. By Merlin. By Uriens. By Lot. I had blamed it on Arthur and Kay, because they had been there back when I had been sweet and innocent, and life had been good. I had blamed it on Arthur because he had never suffered. I was jealous of him. I was jealous of him, not wronged by him. It had taken me so many painful years to understand it.

I did not realise that I had been crying until suddenly the brush of Nimue's fingertips against my cheek, wiping the tears away, brought me back to Avalon, to the open stone of the great chapel, and the vastness of the night sky behind. At Nimue's back, a crescent moon cut sharp into the sky.

"There is nothing left of me to save," I choked through my tears. Nimue, suddenly gentle, leaned down and kissed my forehead. "It is too late. It cannot be undone."

"Morgan," she sighed, kneeling down before me, brushing my tears away lightly and taking my face in her hands. "It is never too late."

She did not say *anything can be undone*, for she knew that that was not true. Morgawse would not come back to life. The knight at her side, his visor still down, his helm still on, slid his sword back into its sheath. Nimue stood, and offered me her hand. I followed her dumbly from the great chapel down to the rooms where I had learned my Black Arts as a girl, and to a room beside her own, where she left me with a drink she told me that she had prepared for me. She had known this time would come. She kissed me on the cheek and left, with the knight Pelleas following behind her.

I drank the drink down in one long gulp and lay back on the bed closing my eyes, without even throwing off my cloak. I did not care if it brought my death. Morgawse was gone, and I was not sure I could stand the pain of her loss, and what I had let myself become.

It did not, though it did bring me dreams, the fierce bright dreams of Avalon. But they were not dreams of the future. They were dreams of the past. Things I had not known. I saw again the argument we had had when Arthur demanded that I be married. I saw myself leave, and Kay leave right after me, slamming the door, and Arthur sink into his chair, running his hands through his hair. Then I saw Arthur standing in a small, dusty church, Uther's old rusted sword in his hands. There were men around cheering, but Arthur's face was pale and slack with shock and apprehension. Ector fell to his knees before him and pulled Kay down beside him, and Arthur stared at both of them. He had tears in his eyes. The image before me shifted again, and I watched Arthur gather Guinevere up in his arms, blood running down her legs from whatever Merlin had done to her to get the King's blood he wanted. Last of all I saw him and Guinevere standing together, she leaning back against him, his arm protectively around her, her hands holding onto his arm as though to steady herself. In the distance, I could see a huge party of knights riding away from Camelot. The quest for the Grail. Arthur had lost more than half of his knights – of his friends – in the search for the Grail. Nimue had demanded sacrifices of him as well. Merlin, too. Arthur, like I, had only wanted to survive.

When I woke in the morning, I had Kay's words in my head: *you think you are the only one who has suffered.*

When Nimue came to me in the morning, she smiled and kissed me on the cheek as though she were pleased to see me.

"Did you see what you needed to see?" she asked me, gently.

I nodded. "But I already knew it," I told her. She put her hands gently on top of mine.

"We always do." She lifted a hand to rub my shoulder in gentle comfort. I was suddenly aware of how motherly her manner had become, although she had no children of her own. "All is not lost, Morgan. It can be mended."

I looked up at her, and she gave an enigmatic smile, and kissing me on the cheek again, left. I was not sure how. All I knew was that I had to get back to Camelot before Mordred. I had to stop him. I had been no match for him; with me gone, Arthur would be all the more vulnerable. I had turned my hate on the wrong man for too long. Because of Mordred my sister was dead.

Chapter Sixty-Six

When I got back to Camelot, Mordred was waiting for me. He was in my bedroom when I appeared there, and he grabbed hold of me roughly by the neck of my dress – one Nimue had given me for my return, made with lace and covered in gems like my other gift from her, only this one was a dark, glossy blue – and I felt the delicate fabric tear a little under his grip.

"Where have you been?" he demanded in a whisper.

I shook him off lightly. I had to pretend I still wanted what he wanted, if I was going to have any hope of saving anyone from him. Including myself.

"In Avalon," I told him. I could not get from my mind the image of him spattered in blood.

There are no innocent men.

He seemed pleased by that. I supposed that he thought I was gathering magical strength in Avalon, to help him. I had helped him to curse Gaheris, after all.

"I hope you are ready for this," he told me, coldly.

I was ready, now. More ready that I had ever been, for now I knew that I had to stop him.

It was high summer, and stiflingly hot. Everyone was uncomfortable, sweating in the heat. I moved about the castle in the secret form I had. I was not yet ready to reveal myself to Arthur, because there was too much to explain. I had taken too many wrong steps, there was too much for me to apologise for. I was not ready. Besides, he did not trust me.

One hot day, the knights were gathered in the courtyard, training with one another. No one's heart was really in it, for it was too hot, and most of the men lounged in the shade of the stone buildings. It was just Mordred and Gawain fighting, and neither of them were really trying, but there was nothing else to do when it was so hot. Arthur stood with Kay, leaning against the wall, and I moved closer to them to overhear their conversation. I was pleased to see that Kay showed no signs of his injuries. I could see, on the other side of the courtyard, Lancelot standing with Guinevere. They were side by side, leaning into the shadow of the tower that housed Arthur's chambers, she with her back against the wall, he turned slightly towards her, leaning down slightly, speaking softly in her ear. She turned her face towards his, the hint of a smile passing across her face. They did not touch each other, nor did anyone seem to think it was unusual, and yet as I stood there, looking across at them, it felt unbearably raw, exposed. I did not know how Arthur did not see it. He was looking right at them.

Kay, however, had noticed it.

"Arthur," I heard him say, softly. "Don't you think it might be time for Lancelot to go out to tourney again? We cannot let the border kingdoms think our knights have forgotten how to fight."

"Oh no, Kay," Arthur complained. "Not yet. He's just been away a long time. It's good to have him here. Good for the men – they follow his example. Besides, Guinevere likes having him here."

Kay made a noise of reluctant agreement.

"You don't understand, Kay, because you never married," Arthur said, gently, and I thought I heard something a little like sadness in his voice. "I am with her as much as I can be, but I have many duties, and she gets lonely. I can feel it; I could while he was gone. With

Christine dead and Margery gone, she was lonely without him, and it made her quiet, a little bit... lost from me. But since he has come back, she has been more like she used to be. She has been happy. I do not think we can understand how lonely it is to be a woman, sometimes."

"I have been a friend to her," Kay objected, indignantly. Arthur put a hand on his shoulder and gave him a kind smile.

"I know, Kay, but look at her now." Arthur smiled more deeply, watching Guinevere laugh at something Lancelot had said to her, looking down at her feet shyly. "You cannot say she has not been lonely without Christine and Margery. And she does not make friends easily."

"No. That is because she is bossy and demanding. And rude," Kay replied. But he was grinning, as though he was fond of her *because* of those qualities. Arthur laughed softly.

"Kay, if you were not my brother, I would have to punish you for saying such things about my wife." But Arthur was grinning, too.

On the other side of the courtyard, Guinevere was moving away from Lancelot and disappearing through the stone archway that led to her walled garden. After a moment, Lancelot went, too. Arthur did not seem to notice, but I watched Mordred's eyes, and Kay's, follow Lancelot as he left.

"Still," Kay persisted, absently, watching Lancelot disappear after Guinevere, "it might be for the best, to send him away."

Arthur did not answer. He seemed tired of the discussion, and I had heard enough. I slipped away, to the walled garden. I could feel Mordred watching me, too.

I stepped through the archway and let myself melt into the shape of one of the rose vines climbing the side of the wall. In the summer, the grass in the garden was yellowing a little, and the smell of the roses was sweet and overpowering. Guinevere was picking up a petal from the ground where it had fallen and was about to tuck it into her plaited hair when Lancelot took it lightly from her fingers and reached around to tuck it himself, their eyes locked together. I could see it all in the way they looked at one another. It had begun again. He brushed his fingertips down her cheek, and she closed her eyes, sighing as they brushed across her lips.

"Lancelot..." she whispered. He looked up and around them for a moment. When he was satisfied that no one could see them, he slowly, softly, pressed his lips against hers. For a moment, she sank into it, running her hands into his hair, but almost as soon as she weakened, she pushed him back. I could see she was flushed already. One hand brushed down the front of his surcoat as though she longed, but did not dare, to touch. He reached for her hand. She stepped back, shaking her head, but as he stepped towards her again she took his face in her hands and gave him one brief, tantalising kiss before she slipped away. Lancelot groaned and rubbed his face. The pair of them were drunk with it, reckless, unable to resist. Kay was right. Lancelot ought to leave.

When I came back out into the courtyard, Guinevere was standing with Arthur, and Kay was fighting with Gawain. Arthur had his arm possessively around her waist, holding her against him, and she rested her head on his shoulder, but I could see her eyes gaze, unfocussed, into the distance. In her mind she was in another man's arms. She only seemed to come back to herself when she saw Lancelot walk from the little garden, through the courtyard, and off up to his room.

I wrote to Nimue, too, telling her she should come to Camelot, because whatever danger there would be would be soon. I wanted her close. Nimue was the only person I knew who had no need to be afraid of Mordred.

Mordred came late in the night, and put my hand over his eyes without speaking. He watched that one secret kiss that I had seen with rapt attention, and seemed disappointed when they moved apart, throwing my hand back to me and pacing before me.

"They are cautious now," he murmured as he paced, more to himself than to me. "We need to give them an opportunity to be alone."

I gave a nod of agreement. I hoped to delay him until Nimue came. It was easier than I thought. He was engrossed with watching Guinevere. His eyes followed her everywhere she went. Every moment he saw her with Lancelot gave him hope that she would accept him, too, once he had killed his father.

Summer was beginning to draw to an end when Nimue arrived. The time was right. I went with her to Arthur, in my own shape. Nimue warned me to say nothing of what I knew. She did not want Arthur finding out about Lancelot and his wife. I had suspected that she would want to reveal it to him, for I knew how she felt about Arthur, but she seemed to be long past that, and when we met with him in the room with the Round Table, her manner with him was entirely different. Calm and authoritative rather than shy. Then I heard Arthur refer to the knight Pelleas as her husband, and I was glad for her. I was pleased, too, that she had brought Pelleas and there would be one more knight in Camelot that we could rely on.

Arthur greeted me warmly when he saw me, as though he had forgotten what I had shown him before and how we had argued. He kissed me on both cheeks and told me that he had missed me. He asked after my son. I realised that I did not know how Ywain was. There was someone else I needed to forgive. He could not help what a man his father had been.

"Do you come with news?" Arthur asked Nimue, his tone friendly.

"There is none," Nimue replied with a smile. "Happily, peace brings little news."

"I have news," I interrupted. Nimue glanced at me warily, but I was not thinking of betraying her. I drew in a deep breath, steeling myself to say the words I knew would hurt me more than they hurt Arthur. "Morgawse is dead."

Arthur nodded slowly, taking it in. He sat back against the table, and I could see him thinking it over. He had loved her once.

To my surprise, he put his head in his hands, and said thickly, "God will punish me, too, for my unkindness to her."

I stepped forward and put a hand on his shoulder, and he looked up at me.

"She did not blame you," I told him, gently. It was a lie, but it was better for him to never know the truth. He stood and wrapped his arms around me in a tight embrace. For him, things had never changed between us. We had argued, but I was his sister. He had always loved me as a sister, always the same. In the face of Arthur's simple, enduring brotherly love, I felt myself crack a little more, I felt how cold my bitterness had made me, and I felt the tears come again, for Morgawse, and for myself.

Chapter Sixty-Seven

Mordred was suspicious of Nimue's arrival, and of me moving about the castle in my own shape, but I assured him that it made no difference, that I too was trying to win Arthur's trust as he was. He seemed satisfied, but not entirely. He was pushing, now, for some definitive action.

Late one afternoon at the very end of summer when the sun was still bright, but the air beginning to turn chill, I was with Nimue in

Arthur's council chamber. We sat on the edge of the great Table, talking over our times at Avalon. When I remembered with her, I found myself laughing, and the sound of it surprised me, for I had not laughed in a long time. Not with happiness.

But we were interrupted by the arrival of Aggravain and Gawain, and following them, Mordred, and then Kay. Aggravain and Gawain were arguing, but when Aggravain saw us, he stopped in the doorway.

"Arthur is not in here?" he demanded. Nimue shook her head.

"Well, that is for the best," Gawain declared, gruffly, turning to his brother.

"It is *not* for the best," Aggravain insisted, pacing before the rest of them. Mordred hung at the back, watching carefully. Kay crossed his arms over his chest, leaning against the wall. When he caught my eye, he gave me a strange look of resignation. "Arthur has to face the truth. He has to *deal* with the truth. It is dishonour to us all that Lancelot has been with his wife, not just once but many times, and he must deal with it."

"Be quiet, Aggravain," Gawain hissed. "He might be nearby, and he might hear you."

"I *want* him to hear me," Aggravain shouted.

"You will dishonour us all if you insist on bringing such things to light," Gawain said, stubbornly, squaring up to his brother. "It is not worth destroying both Lancelot and Arthur's honour for the sake of one woman. As you said once, just an *ordinary* woman. These matters are better kept private. If Arthur does not mind then I think we should leave the matter."

"Arthur does not *know*," Aggravain shouted. He was red-faced with his anger, and I thought he looked ready to strike Gawain.

Gawain shrugged. "This is a man's business with his wife. I will not get involved. It is you who dishonour Arthur with your gossiping."

Before Aggravain could answer, Gawain left, pushing past Mordred. It was only moments later that Arthur stepped through the door, pushing it shut behind him. His brow was creased in confusion. He must have seen Gawain on the way down, storming out.

"What is going on here?" Arthur demanded, his voice low. Aggravain looked between Mordred and Kay for a moment, to see if either of them would try to stop him. He did not look to Nimue, or me. As women, witches though we were, we were beneath his interest.

"Arthur..." he began, tentatively. Arthur seemed to know what it was already and shook his head, raising a hand to quiet Aggravain.

"No, Aggravain." Arthur was fired with anger already. I saw Mordred glance towards him, unable to keep a sly, unpleasant smile from his face to see his father so disturbed. "Not more of your malicious rumours."

"Arthur," Aggravain tried more forcefully, "you have to take this seriously. Lancelot has had your wife. You must *do* something about it."

Arthur lunged forward as though he was going to strike Aggravain, and Kay stepped into the way to hold him back. He stumbled a step under Arthur's force, but held him steady before he struck Aggravain, who stepped back, but continued speaking, undeterred.

"It's plain to see, Arthur, and it's no good. I don't know how you can stand the shame of it. You have to do something about it. Everyone is talking about it, saying they are lovers, and it's dangerous for you." He was calm now, and he fixed Arthur with an even stare.

Arthur drew back under it, straightening his red and gold surcoat. "Aggravain, I can't give out justice based on rumour. There are tales all around that are not true. Her and Kay, at Meleagaunt's castle. Isolde and Palomides. You don't see me rushing to have Kay's head, for the sake of a bit of gossip. If you stop talking, others will stop talking." Arthur sounded annoyed, tired.

Kay was watching Aggravain, waiting to see if he would give up. I was not. I was watching Mordred. After a moment of tense silence, Mordred stepped forward, behind his father, to speak softly in his ear.

"Yet, my Lord, the rumours about Isolde and Tristan *were* true. And, Lancelot harboured them at Joyous Guard. He's obviously not a man who has a problem with adultery. Don't you think it is suspicious that she goes missing overnight and he brings her back without any of her clothes?"

"You're being ridiculous," Kay said to Mordred, sharply. He turned to Arthur, his look deeply serious and said, "There are always rumours, Arthur. The best thing to do is ignore them." And over Arthur's shoulder, he stared back at Mordred.

"My Lord, they are *always together*. Always talking together and walking together. It's plain to see from the way he looks at her that he has had her," Aggravain persisted.

"*Enough*," Arthur's voice boomed, so loud that I felt the vibrations of it through the wood of the table. "I won't tolerate any more accusations based on gossip. I don't want to hear any more about it, nor do I want to hear that any of you have spoken of it. Do you understand?"

There was a long silence. Aggravain was not going to back down.

"We cannot ignore this, Arthur," Aggravain said, very softly. "Some action must be taken. Against Lancelot. Against his kin."

That meant Kay. And Ector as well. I saw the thought pass across Kay's face, and I felt the danger thicken in the room.

"I cannot be fighting everyone over every little rumour. What good is a king who cannot keep the peace?" Arthur said.

"What good is a king who cannot keep his *wife*?" Aggravain replied.

"*I can keep my wife* —" Arthur roared again, and once more Kay stepped between him and Aggravain. We were moments away from an open brawl between Arthur and Aggravain in Arthur's own council-room. Nimue looked up at me. I wondered if she would step in. I did not think I could. Not in front of Mordred, not after what I had shown Arthur.

"What if... proof could be obtained?" Mordred's voice came, quiet and sly, from behind Arthur. Arthur turned around, and Kay stepped back from him, watching Mordred.

"It cannot, because it is *not happening*," Arthur answered.

"If you are so sure," Mordred continued, "then surely there is no harm in... arranging an opportunity to catch Lancelot in the act... as it were."

"*No*," Arthur insisted, and before Mordred and Aggravain could speak again, he stormed out, slamming the door. Kay, throwing a dirty look at Aggravain, went after him. Aggravain groaned.

"How can we make him understand?" he complained.

Mordred shook his head. "Now we wait. We have put the idea into his mind. We wait."

Aggravain seemed reluctant, but without speaking to either of us, they left. When they left, Nimue assured me that she would keep watch over it. She said there was nothing else to be done.

That night, Arthur ate with his men and Nimue in the room with the Round Table. I hid among the servants, making an excuse to Arthur, still trying to convince Mordred I was on his side. All seemed well, until the food had been cleared and Arthur moved from Guinevere's side to talk with Gawain. She turned to Lancelot beside her, and I watched them talking, becoming more and more engrossed in one another. He was saying something to her, she was staring down at the table before her, leaning towards him. Lightly, he brushed his hand against hers where it rested on the table, and I saw a flush rise in her cheeks. I was not the only one who saw. Arthur, the other side of the room, had frozen mid-conversation with Gawain and was staring right at his wife. Lancelot noticed before she did, drawing back suddenly, pretending he had not noticed Arthur and he was merely continuing the conversation, but Guinevere looked up, across the room, right back at him, her eyes wide and empty with the blankness of panic. She had given herself away. Arthur looked away, pretending not to have noticed, but I looked to Nimue, and I could see from her face that she was afraid that it had begun.

It was soon after that when Arthur called us – Nimue, myself, Kay, Aggravain and Mordred – to his council chamber. He paced in front of us before he spoke, and I could see his jaw clenched in anger, the tension of it running through his whole body. He turned to Aggravain.

"How is it to be done?" he demanded.

Aggravain took a moment to understand what Arthur meant. He opened his mouth to respond, but Mordred was there first.

"Arrange a hunt. Say that we will travel out and stay overnight. Lancelot will not come. When she thinks you are gone for the night, she will send for Lancelot. Aggravain and I will surprise them, and bring them to you, who will have been waiting here all along, and you may deal with them as you please."

"Arthur –" Nimue stood, stepping towards him. "This is not wise, this is not honourable –"

He raised his hand for silence, and to my surprise, she stepped back. He was staring at Aggravain and Mordred still.

"I must know the truth. And if you find nothing, you will never, *never* speak of this again."

Mordred grinned. "Never."

Arthur nodded. "See that it is done," he ordered, and turned from the room, slamming the door hard as he left. I felt cold and sick with dread. When I looked at Nimue she only looked back with cold resignation. When the others had left, I asked her if we ought not to warn Lancelot. She sighed.

"Dissuade him, if you can."

I went to him, in my own shape. He was not surprised to see me. The hunt had been called, but he had declined it, as Mordred had predicted that he would, in the hope of seeing Guinevere alone. The other knights had already ridden out, with the exception of Mordred, Aggravain and Arthur, and those men that Aggravain had gathered to him in case he had to fight with Lancelot. He was in his shirt and breeches as though getting ready for bed, but he was pacing his room uneasily when he called me in.

"Morgan," he sighed. "I was expecting someone else."

Marie, I thought, *calling you to your Lady.*

"Do you not want to join the hunt?" I suggested.

Lancelot shook his head. "I have to speak with Guinevere. I need to go from here." He sighed and ran a hand through his hair, pushing it back from his forehead. "I think Arthur suspects something, and Aggravain and Mordred are watching. I only want to say goodbye, and I will go to Joyous Guard for a while. Until things die down."

I nodded. As long as he could say his goodbye before Aggravain and Mordred came. As long as he could be content with only *saying* goodbye.

"Just, Lancelot, be careful. Do not linger too long. There are still others in this castle watching you." He nodded, and there was a knock at the door. Marie was there, and she gave a little bobbing curtsey to see him. Lancelot only half-opened the door, so she did not see me there. I thought that was uncharacteristically sensible of him, since I knew the Breton women did not trust my woaded face.

"Sir, my Lady wants to speak with you. Tonight," she told him. I could not tell from the tone of her voice how much she knew, or suspected. Lancelot nodded and shut the door. He drew in a deep breath, and when he looked at me, his eyes were wide with sorrow.

"This will be hard," he said.

"Could you not write from Joyous Guard?" I asked, hoping he would relent.

He shook his head. "I have learned too well how she would feel about that. It must be now."

He turned to go, and I caught him by the arm, holding him back.

"Be careful, Lancelot. Don't linger there. Don't – there are still some in the castle tonight that would wish to catch you in some guilty act." I sighed, seeing he was not really listening to me. "Just – be careful," I insisted. He nodded, putting a comforting hand on top of mine. I felt no comfort at all.

"I will," he promised, and he left.

Chapter Sixty-Eight

Kay came soon after that to Lancelot's room, and when he saw me there, where I had decided I would wait until he returned, he groaned with resignation, running his hands through his hair.

393

"He has gone?" he asked me, his face wild with apprehension. I nodded and he covered his face with his hands, leaning back against the door frame. Through his hands he groaned again. "I thought it was over, a long time ago. She told me it was. When he left for the Grail. But it's not true, is it?" I shook my head. He sighed, hard, then stood up, taken with a sudden thought. "I will go and stop him."

He made to stride away and I jumped up to catch him by the arm.

"Kay, don't," I said gently. "If you try, Mordred will kill you."

He turned back to me, and I could see the distress in his usually laughing brown eyes, and I could see the way the years of lying and hiding for Lancelot had made him tired, and hopeless.

He was filled with an idea again and grabbed me by the shoulders. "Take his shape, Morgan, and we will go to Arthur, and he will –"

I shook my head, and Kay fell quiet. "Mordred will know, and he will try again."

"What can be done, then?" Kay asked.

In a small voice, I answered, "I don't know."

We sat together, side by side on Lancelot's bed, waiting for a while, but the tense silence was worse than being alone. I wondered where Nimue was, what she was doing. I thought perhaps she was with Arthur, trying to talk him out of it. I strained to hear in the darkness, any sounds of shouting, or fighting, or the sound of Lancelot's boots walking up the stairs, coming safely back to his room.

In the end, I left. Kay could stay there and wait for Lancelot. I wanted to be alone with my anxious thoughts in my own room. I listened, but all I heard was empty darkness.

It was deep into the night when Mordred burst through my bedroom door. His chest was heaving, and blood was smeared across his face, his armour. I stood from my window seat to face him, forcing myself to have an air of steely calm. Without speaking, he unbuckled and pulled off his breastplate. Underneath, he had a wound to his stomach, gaping open with his movements, and oozing dark blood. When he pulled the greaves from his legs, I could see that he was wounded deep into his left thigh, as well. What I wanted to know was if Lancelot had escaped alive, but I dared not ask.

"Heal me," Mordred demanded. I gestured to the chair, and he sat heavily in it. I thought about killing him then.

But I gave him some of the potion to strengthen his blood, and bound the wounds he had with strips of linen. I did not put my hands against them. I would not give him the benefit of my healing touch, and he did not ask for it.

"What happened?" I asked him.

He reached down and put his hand over my eyes. I could see, as if through a dream, or underwater, Mordred at the head of a line of men, twelve or more of them, and Aggravain just behind him standing in the corridor outside Guinevere's bedroom. He was shouting, and banging against the door with his fist, but I could not hear what he was saying. Lancelot burst out then, dressed in armour that was not his own, and already smeared with blood. He had another man's sword, too, in his hand. The fighting was wild, and desperate, and I could not see who was striking whom, but I saw Aggravain fall, a wave of dark red spreading down across his breastplate where Lancelot's sword had sliced across his throat. Mordred was already covered in blood, but when Lancelot struck him the second time, his sword cutting through Mordred's thigh, Mordred fell back and lay still. From where we stood in his memory, I could see him lying back as the sounds of fighting continued further and further away, his eyes so wide open that I could see white all the way around his dark irises. When they died down, he slowly stood back up, wincing against the pain, and glanced around. All the other men lay dead, but nowhere did I see Lancelot's body. He had escaped alive. I thought Mordred was about to leave, and hobble here with his wounds, but he turned back towards the bedroom door. I went with him as he walked back up towards it, and pressed his ear against the door. Suddenly, awfully, I could hear what he heard the other side – the sound of Guinevere's terrified breathing, and her hands fumbling at the bolt. *No*, I thought, *do not open the door.*

But she did. A small crack at first, as if to peer out, but Mordred saw it open and slammed himself against it, throwing it open. She jumped back. Her hair was loose; she was dressed in her nightgown.

She and Mordred stood for a second, staring at one another; then she made to run past him, and he seized hold of a handful of her hair, and her arm, and began dragging her down the stairs while she struggled against him.

The vision before me shifted, and I was watching him drag her before Arthur, who sat at the Round Table, with Ector and Gawain either side of him. He was just in his shirt and breeches, as though he had been dragged from his bed. So was Ector. I could not hear their words, but Mordred was grinning as Arthur spoke, pulling Guinevere's head back by her hair. I could see Gawain shouting, too, and Arthur shook his head in resignation, and waved to Mordred to take her away. He had both expected and not expected it to be true. He had hoped that everything he heard had been wrong.

What had Arthur said? What had been decided? I supposed I already knew. I had seen her being led away to be burned.

Mordred dragged her up to Arthur's bedroom and pushed her inside. He stared at her for a moment, then hit her hard across the face with the back of his hand. I flinched as she fell hard against the floor from it. He was already on top of her, holding her down. I realised with a chill that I had seen this before. She was trying to push him off her, to kick him away, but he was too strong. All of a sudden, he stopped still, drawing his hand out from where he had shoved it up her nightdress, and holding it in front of her face. I could see that she was shaking, her eyes wide with terror. In the low firelight, I could see what he was showing her; his fingers glistened, and I was disgusted. I heard his voice coming sharp through his memory, as he leaned close to her and hissed, *Liar*. I saw him shove her hard against the floor again, and stand to leave, wiping his hand against her nightdress. It faded around me then, and I stepped back from him.

"Proof, beyond doubt," said Mordred. "Though Arthur did not need it. Did you see his face?"

I could feel myself trembling, too. Mordred stepped forward and grabbed me by the shoulders, trying to steady me, but I did not want his help, I wanted to get away from him.

"Morgan," he asked, gently, "what's wrong?"

I shook my head, unable to speak. I hated him, I was disgusted by him. He pulled me against him into an embrace, thinking I needed his comfort. I could smell his blood. It smelled like the blood of a normal man, of iron and mortality, but it was not.

I gently pushed him back from me, as though I were gathering myself. In truth, it was all I could do to be in the room with him without retching. He stank of blood, and death.

As though suddenly satisfied that I was well, Mordred sighed in annoyance.

"Arthur puts her to the fire tomorrow, at midday. I did not get what your magic visions promised me, Morgan." It took me a moment to remember what he was talking about, and when I realised I could not believe that he was still lusting for Guinevere after all of this.

I shrugged. "A man can change his fate."

I was relieved when he left. I went to Nimue and was unsurprised to find her awake, though it was not yet dawn, and I told her everything I knew, putting my hand over her eyes to show her everything that Mordred had shown me. She looked worried, more worried than I had ever seen her. And where was Lancelot? Long gone, it seemed. When I walked past his room, it was empty, and Kay, too, was nowhere to be found.

When dawn came, Nimue and I went to wait for Arthur in his council room. I felt dirty and clammy from being awake all night and in my dress, but there was no time to wash or to change. Or to sleep. I heard men moving up and down the stairs in the corridor outside, but it was already past prime when Arthur came into the room. He closed the door gently behind himself and stepped into the room.

"I suppose you know," he said to us, evenly.

Nimue nodded.

"You will put her to the fire?" Nimue asked him, sharply. He nodded, pacing past her.

"Arthur, you will come to regret this," she told him, fiercely. He did not turn around, but stared out of the window, down at the courtyard. Someone down there was building the pyre.

"It is done, Nimue. I cannot turn back from the truth, nor from my own laws," he answered, after a long silence.

"You do not know for sure," I pointed out.

"It was *you*, who showed me with your black magic –" he began, wheeling back around and stepping towards me.

"That was not true, Arthur," I snapped. It was a lie, but perhaps it would be enough to save her. "That was fabricated from rumours. And all the rest you know is only Mordred's words. Consider, Arthur," I dropped my voice, still wary of Mordred, "consider what he stands to gain from this."

Arthur paced away from me, grasping hold of the back of one of the chairs, as though he needed to steady himself.

"No, no. He is the only one of them who told me the truth. I have trusted all of the wrong men. *My son*, he has been the only one brave enough to protect me from this."

"Arthur." I tried again, feeling more and more desperate. "*Reconsider.*"

I glanced at Nimue, and the look she gave to me in return was one of resignation.

"*No*," Arthur shouted. I saw his knuckles go white where he gripped the back of the chair, and he leaned down against it, closing his eyes.

"Arthur." Nimue stepped towards him, placing one of her hands gently over his. "A king shows his honour in the giving of mercy. You can put her away, send her to an abbey, to Avalon, wherever you prefer, but show mercy. Men will remember your grace, your kindness, not this. You will come to regret this."

Arthur shook his head, standing up straight suddenly. "No, Nimue. No. There will be no mercy. Not for her, not for him." Nimue opened her mouth to speak again, and I could see that she too was angry, now, but Arthur continued, stepping towards her, gesturing in violent appeal towards us for understanding of the rage that consumed him. I had felt it. The poison of betrayal. It would only harm him the worse if he could not give it up. "*You don't understand.* I keep playing over and over again in my head, everything she ever said to me about him, trying to work out *when did it begin?* Five years ago? *Ten?* Trying not to picture them together. Trying not to ask myself over and over again, was she with him the way she was with me? Did she kiss him the same? Did she say the same things to him when they were alone? Did she –" He choked on whatever he had to say, sinking back for a moment, before he began again. "And I can't stop thinking, how many times when we – how many of those times was she thinking of him instead?" He looked between us in desperation. "So, no," he continued, and the air seemed to rush out of him, and the anger with it, and instead he was awfully, hollowly sad. "No, there can be no mercy." He shook his head, staring down at the floor again.

"Arthur –" I stepped forward and put a hand against his shoulder; to my surprise he put a hand on top of mine, and rested his head against mine.

"I saw him kiss her," Arthur said, very quietly. "I saw the way they smiled at one another. But it all seemed so innocent. I was *glad* to see it. I only thought that... I don't know what I thought. I was glad that she had a companion, and that she kept him at court. What a fool this makes me. And still, *still,* I know that if she does not die, I will take her back, and I will have to spend the rest of my life with Lancelot at the back of my mind every time we are alone together. Besides," he added very softly, and absently, as though he were repeating someone else's words, "that is the law of this land, and even a queen must live and die by the law. It cannot be changed."

I did not say anything, but I did not move. I leaned against him and closed my eyes. I heard Nimue move beside him as well, and we stood there in silence until I felt Arthur stop shaking. It was getting towards midday, and they were taking Guinevere out to the pyre.

Chapter Sixty-Nine

I stood with Nimue in the crowd gathered to watch the Queen burn. Someone had set up a small platform of wood at Camelot's gates, and out in the field a pile of tarred logs stood, waiting for the men beside them to touch them with their torches. It was an overcast day, the clouds low in the sky, and a very fine drizzle falling.

There was a loud shout from the crowd, and I saw Guinevere step up onto the platform. There was a man behind her pushing her forward, and when I saw the glint of golden hair, I thought it was Arthur, but when he stepped around, though he wore Arthur's coat of red and gold, it was clear to me from the way he moved that it was Mordred. *Arthur has not come,* I thought, *and everyone will think Mordred is him.* In the end, Arthur had not been brave enough to carry out the sentence himself. Gareth and Gaheris stood either side of them on the platform, neither of them armed. With a sudden flash of panic, I realised that this was the moment I had seen. I should have thought. I should have realised this was coming. *I did not warn Gareth.* I had been distracted. I should have warned him. It was too late now. Much too late.

Guinevere stood up tall and straight, staring out expressionless over the crowd. Her face was proud, and set. She was dressed in a fine dress of dark green silk embroidered in gold with the sign of the cross, and on her head she wore the circlet of gold I had seen her wear many times before. If her hands were not bound behind her, no one would have thought her a prisoner. She had come to her death as a queen, cold and defiant.

Mordred was shouting over the roar of the crowd, "People of Camelot, we have before you a traitor queen, brought to the fire for her crimes."

The crowd responded with shouts and jeers. A few people threw things, little stones, whatever they had in their hands. Guinevere closed her eyes, lifting her face as though to feel the breeze. I glanced at Nimue beside me. She was watching the platform intently.

Mordred began to shout again, gesturing with his hands for the crowd to move apart. Instantly obedient, they parted, making a way between the platform and the fire. The men holding the torches gripped them harder in readiness to set them against the tarred logs. Guinevere stared across the space that led to her death. I wondered then if she thought Lancelot was dead. I wondered, too, if Arthur had said goodbye to her with any last vestige of tenderness.

Just as Gareth and Gaheris took one of her arms each and made to step down from the platform, Mordred stepped down before them, his back to the crowd. A murmur of unease went through it. The crowd had come for blood, and they would be unhappy if they were denied. But then we watched as Mordred grasped hold of the front of her dress with both hands and violently tugged it apart. With a loud ripping sound, it tore from the neck to the hem. He tore through the rest, throwing the dress to the crowd, bit by bit. They screamed with delight.

Then Mordred grabbed hold of the front of her underdress in his fist, hard enough that he pulled her up towards him. Her face was blank still, and she stared past him, towards the pyre. I saw Gareth lean over to say something softly to Mordred, and he let her go. I felt another stab of guilt for forgetting to warn Gareth. She hardly seemed to notice any of it at all. I had expected a little fight from her, a little screaming, a little protest.

Mordred pulled her hair loose, and it fell around her shoulders. It was lighter now than it once had been, not quite the deep red of the years gone by. It was growing more coppery. More like how I had seen her when I stood with her on the shores of Avalon. I was catching up with my destiny, but those things would not come to pass for sure. What if I had blackened what I had seen, warped it out of shape by bringing Mordred into it?

Mordred stood for one moment longer before her. I think he was longing for her to break, to cry, to beg for her life, but it seemed as though she did not see him at all.

When he stepped aside, Gareth and Gaheris led her down and through the gap in the crowd.

The crowd pressed close around them, and I could hear them shouting *traitor*, and *whore*, and also *witch*.

Then it happened, as I had seen it happen. I heard the shouts first. I did not see Lancelot riding towards us until he was upon us, tangling with the crowd. I saw the flash of his sword. I heard Guinevere scream. Then it was over. He was riding away, her clutched before him on his horse, and the crowd was drawing back in horror from the two bloodied bodies lying on the ground. They were screaming still, but the screaming had changed from the sound of baying for blood to the sound of panic. As they backed away, as though drawn irresistibly towards the bodies of my dead nephews, I walked forwards. The crowd was scattering fast, and by the time I reached them, had mostly gone. I could see Gareth, fallen half on top of his brother where he had stepped forward to try to save him from the path of Lancelot's sword. He was still, his surcoat of dark blue soaked black with blood spreading down from the neck.

I heard a noise, like a soft gurgling, a gentle choking, and I glanced at Gaheris. His eyes were wide, wide open, so wide that I could see white all the way around his bright blue irises. His mouth was open as though he were trying to speak, trying to call my name, but beneath his mouth, at the side of his neck, a dark gash gaped open. I could have leaned down, and placed my hand over the gaping hole that was still leaking blood, though slow now, and dark, the blood of his heart and his bones; I could have leaned down and given him my healing touch, and it might have been enough. He might have survived long enough for me to take him into the castle and give him my healing potion for his blood, but something in me refused. I could see, over and over again, him covered in blood from the fingertips to the elbow. He had not shown his mother mercy. I watched until slowly, Gaheris sank down, and his eyes sagged closed, and he fell still. He had not deserved his life.

I felt a hand on my shoulder, and turned to see Nimue. I followed her as she walked through the great open gates into the castle. The castle was filled with shouts and screams already. The scent of blood was in the air, and worse, war. In the courtyard we passed Gareth's young wife Lynesse, running out towards the now-abandoned pyre, screaming her husband's name and choking on her sobs. Just before Nimue and I turned to climb the stairs to Arthur's tower, I saw Mordred step into her path and catch her in his arms.

Arthur stood at the window, staring out. He must have seen from where he stood. The window gazed out across the fields before Camelot's great gates. In his hand, he was holding something, some piece of clothing. Something of Guinevere's.

He did not turn around as he heard us come in. He looked calm, detached, even, but he was breathing deep to hold himself under control.

"Arthur?" Nimue called, softly.

Arthur turned around.

"They are dead," he said, as though in a trance, as though he was seeing it over and over again.

Nimue nodded gently, and stepped forward, resting a comforting hand on Arthur's arm. Absently, he put his hand on top of hers. He did not look at her.

"Are they coming up here now?" Arthur asked.

Nimue glanced back at me. I did not know what he was talking about.

"Arthur, they will take them to be buried," I said, gently.

Arthur shook his head. "No, Lancelot. And Guinevere. Where are they? I want them brought here."

Arthur still looked lost, gazing blankly between me and Nimue.

"Arthur," I answered, "he has gone. He is not returning to Camelot. I can only imagine that he has taken her..." I glanced at Nimue, looking for her lead, but she was as blank with it as I was. "He will have taken her to Joyous Guard."

"*What?*" Arthur shouted, suddenly coming to himself, and it was worse. Worse than him absent and distant, reeling from the deaths of Gareth and Gaheris. He took a violent stride towards me and unconsciously I jumped back. Nimue, too, stepped away from him as he pulled his arm away from her.

"Arthur –" Nimue began, but Arthur cut her off. He was shaking, his face flushed dark with rage.

"*No.* This is an act of war. She is *my wife*. He has taken *my wife*. If he had come to question the accusation, then why did he not return her? He has *stolen* my wife from me. After all of this. After all of the accusations, and the gossip and – What kind of King am I if I cannot stop another man from *taking my wife*?" he shouted.

"Arthur," Nimue tried once more, "simply send to Joyous Guard requesting her return. Let Lancelot speak for himself. Hold a proper trial."

"No." Arthur shook his head. "*No.* A man is no more than his honour, and if I want mine back from Lancelot then there must be war. Send to the vassal kings of Britain for their armies and –"

"Arthur." The voice I heard from behind me in the doorway was Gawain, and Nimue and I turned together. There he stood, this huge grizzled warrior, and his eyes were red, and bright with tears. He had seen, too, then. Arthur stared back at him, his anger draining away, and turning to grief. Gawain strode past us as if we were not there, and into Arthur's embrace.

Thickly, I heard Gawain say to Arthur, "As you love me, you will make no peace with that man."

And Arthur, his arms tight around his nephew, his forehead pressed against Gawain's massive shoulder, nodded.

Chapter Seventy

I left Camelot then, and its preparations for war. The time had come for me to return to Rheged Castle, and to see my son, and to know what part he was going to take in all of this.

When I appeared in my old bedroom, the serving woman scrubbing at the window screamed and ran out. I was irritated, for it meant that Rheged Castle had forgotten that its mistress was a witch. I picked up my crown from where it sat on the table in my bedroom, and set it on my head. I dressed then, too, in one of my mother's old dresses of dark red samite, and wrapped a rich cloak of furs around myself. If I was to command Rheged as the Queen of Gore, then I had to look the part.

I found Ywain in Rheged's council chamber, with four other men who from their dress appeared to be knights, though I recognised not one of them. As soon as he saw me, he waved them away with a swift hand of dismissal. It was late on an early autumn day, and the sun came low, orange-red and slanting through the windows, throwing long gaping shapes of burning light against the wooden floor and the old wood table that stretched between us.

Ywain was grown to a man now. I was shocked by how much he had grown to be like me. Tall, skinny and – I did not know how I had not noticed before – with thoughtful grey eyes. Like my mother's. Like Arthur's. Like mine. And he had learned to rule. He commanded his men like a prince. I had heard that from the corridor as I approached. I felt an awful guilt, a sinking sorrow that I had had no part in making such a man of my own son.

"Ywain..." I began, stepping into the room.

"Mother." He nodded curtly, fixing me with a business-like look.

"I see you are preparing Rheged for war," I said.

He nodded.

"Have you chosen for whom Gore will fight?" I asked.

Ywain looked shocked. "For my Uncle Arthur, of course."

I nodded, glancing down. "Of course."

So, he had a fierce sense of honour rather than one of self-preservation. What was it my mother had said to me? *We are all either wise or brave. Your sister is brave. You and I are wise.* I had given birth to a brave son.

"Do you not think that best?" he asked me.

I shook my head. "It is well, Ywain, that you fight with your uncle. Have you sent word to Camelot?"

He nodded. "Just now, before you arrived."

I nodded along with him again. He could do it all on his own. He had had to. He had done everything without me. I wondered who had taught him to read, to speak, to walk. I wondered if anyone had taught him Latin. I could have taught him to read in Latin. It was too late now, and I had eaten up all my life and my youth with bitterness and regret.

"Ywain," I said, quietly, afraid that if I spoke the words too loud, I would not bear them, "I am sorry, that I was no good mother to you."

Ywain stared back at me for a moment, before he spoke. "No," he replied evenly, "you were simply no mother at all."

I was surprised, then, when the next day as I stood on the battlements of Rheged, staring out at the land beyond, back south to Camelot, that Ywain came to stand beside me. It was a windy day, overcast still, and I could not see far into the distance because the heavy sky leaned down to touch the hills, leaking down grey into the low valleys that stretched away from Rheged Castle. From here, the world could have been at peace, and nothing changed, and yet it had all changed, and Rheged and Gore would feel it sooner or later.

Ywain came to stand beside me as I stared out. He was quiet for a moment, following my gaze out into the murky autumn sky.

"I am sorry, Mother," he said, softly, "for what I said yesterday. I did not mean —" He sighed, unable to find the right words. But I did not need him to apologise. It was, after all, the truth. "My father told me, when I was very young, that you were a woman of Avalon, and it was to Avalon that you belonged, not to Gore. That you had responsibilities – duties – outside of our home, and you had to attend to those. I always understood. And the nurse you chose for me, she was kind. She died, a few winters ago, but I did not want for anything, Mother. I understood."

Even though he had hated me, Uriens had lied to our son, to make me seem a kinder mother. He had not done it for my sake, of course, but repellent though he had been, and cruel, and brutish, he had loved our son.

"Did you marry?" I asked him.

He shook his head. "It does not seem to mean much in Britain, anymore," he said, still gazing far away. "It did not make you or my father happy, that is what everyone says. And that bastard cousin of mine, Mordred, his mother was married to someone else, when my Uncle Arthur made him. And now this war with Lancelot. No." He shook his head again, more emphatically. "There have been offers, but I – I don't see the need for it. I still remember," he turned to me, then, "the half-brother I had. Born a few years after my father died. Where is he?"

I had not thought about Galahad in a long time. Somehow, it all seemed to have happened very, very long ago, almost in a different life.

"He is dead," I replied, softly. Ywain nodded, taking it in.

After a long pause, he spoke again, leaning down, staring at his feet, bracing his hands against the edge of the battlements.

"I have never been to war before," he said.

I did not know what to say to him. I had seen it all. The blood, the fear. I had heard the screaming. But worse than that, all my life had been a war. I couldn't say all the things I wanted to say to him. I couldn't tell him not to let war into his heart, or not to go at all, just to shut the gates of Rheged and hole up for a siege. I could not tell him it was better never to begin. I couldn't say those things without giving myself away, and I did not want to do that. I wanted my son to live a life untouched by mine.

The days passed quickly, and it was almost winter by the time the armies of Rheged were ready to ride out to join Arthur. The other kingdoms of North Wales, supposedly vassal to Rheged and Gore, seemed to have already emptied their armies, and though Ywain and I demanded to know to where in our various ways, none were forthcoming. Either they had left, afraid of war, or they were fighting with Lancelot. Ywain was discouraged and upset, thinking his vassal lords had abandoned him because of his youth. I tried to explain about Lancelot. No man would stand against him in battle if they could stand with him. He did not understand. He had never seen him fight.

So, in the end it was a small army, with Ywain and myself riding side by side at the head of it, that came to Arthur's camp, where it spread around the foot of Joyous Guard. Ywain and I would never be as other mothers and sons were, but we had found between us at least a tentative sympathy.

I was disappointed to see nothing with Avalon's mark at Arthur's camp. I had the sense that Nimue was more angry with Arthur than she would care to show. He had not listened to her. He had not relented or shown any mercy. She would not lend her magical strength to Arthur's war. I was the only one left. Little did he know how I had once longed for his death.

The Arthur who strode from his pavilion to greet us looked nothing like the boy I had seen in London's great cathedral holding Uther's rusted sword in his hand, his eyes wide. He was nothing like the boy who had married a foreign princess and hardly seemed to notice how angry she was. He was a man now, a man in his middle years, a man marked with everything that had passed him by. His face was grim and set, and his grey eyes dark and fierce. Mordred stood at his side, bearing the shield that had once been Kay's, the shield that carried the insignia of the keys of the Seneschal. So, Arthur had given Kay's office to his son. That meant that Kay had never returned to Camelot, and he was in Joyous Guard, with Lancelot. At Arthur's other side, Gawain stood in his armour, his heavily scarred face a knot of rage.

Ywain dismounted before me, moving to kneel before Arthur, who was dressed in his armour for battle, his crown on his head, Excalibur at his side.

"My Lord, King Arthur," Ywain greeted him. Arthur put a hand on his shoulder, and Ywain looked up at him.

"You are welcome here, Ywain. You do not have to bow to me. I am grateful to have all of my nephews fighting at my side."

Ywain stood, clearly in awe of Arthur, whom I supposed he had never met before. All he had heard were stories of Arthur's conquering, the sack of Rome, the victories in Britain. And, at last, the tales of Arthur's wife. Arthur must have seemed a giant to my son, a man from legend, beyond reality.

This was becoming a war of bloods. Arthur, Gawain and Ywain on one side, Lancelot and Kay on the other. Ector, too, I noticed was not with Arthur's party. I hoped that the kind old man still lived. If he did, he would be inside Joyous Guard, not at its feet.

Gawain stood forward to greet Ywain with a clap on the shoulder that made my son – who had not expected it, and who was slighter than his cousin – stumble a little.

I slipped from my horse and got down to greet Arthur, and to my surprise he pulled me into an embrace, and kissed me on both cheeks. I felt his armour, hard and cold, scrape against the gemstones on my black jewelled dress. It had been rare, before, that I had seen Arthur dressed for war. I noticed, too, that I saw no other women around. There must have been some, at the edges, in the villages, but I could not see them. Perhaps they were few, or perhaps they were hiding, afraid.

I felt Mordred's eyes light on me, and flicker across my son, who was already being led away by Gawain, back to his army, so that they could be told where to pitch their camp.

I followed Arthur back to his pavilion. Once we were inside, he pulled off his armour to sit heavily down in a small wooden chair that creaked slightly under his bulk. He was strong still, muscular like a bull, but it did not matter. He was weary. I could see it in all of his movements. He put his head in his hands.

Before I could speak, Gawain and Ywain stepped in behind us. Arthur did not look up, but gestured to a table set with fruits, and cured meats, and cheese and wine, as though inviting them to eat. Ywain, young enough not to put awkwardness before hunger, and ignorant enough of the tangled web of emotions that Lancelot's betrayal had drawn tight over us all, stepped forward and began to eat hungrily. Gawain had always had a hearty appetite, but he hung back, moving slightly to my side. The last time I had been close to Gawain, he had been clinging to me for comfort, and I knew it was comfort he wanted from me now, too. I was this huge man's aunt, and though he was not so very much younger than I was, that did not matter. I had to fill the void his mother's death had left.

I was pleased that Mordred was not there, although I was unsettled that I did not know where he was, what he was doing. I did not know if he knew that I no longer intended to help him, and that I was with Nimue now, working against him. Arthur shrugged, leaning back in his chair, fixing me with an empty look. He was lost. I did not think I had seen him so lost ever before.

"How are you?" I asked, quietly.

"At war," he said, simply, and I understood. He picked up a single sheet of parchment in his hand from the table beside him, scrunching it in his fist as he drew it towards him. He knew what was on it. He wasn't planning to read it. He held it out towards me. "Nimue writes to me urging me to take my wife back. To sue for peace, to have her back, and to return to Camelot as though nothing has happened."

"But there will be no peace," Gawain said, tersely, staring hard at Arthur. Arthur nodded. "There will be no peace with Lancelot until one of us is dead."

Arthur was too weary to argue. He nodded slowly again.

"Arthur, could you not take her back, and settle with Lancelot alone, you and Gawain? Does there need to be a *war*?" I took a deep breath. "I did not want to tell you this, but most of North Wales has not stood with you. Or with us. Your kingdom is breaking into pieces, and each is turning on the other. Call an end to this war."

"*Don't you think I know that, Morgan?*" Arthur bellowed, suddenly jumping from his chair and striding towards me across the tent. I stood my ground, and he turned back before he reached me, pacing away. "She is in there with him. In his castle. He ought to have brought her back to me. She is there of her own desiring." Arthur stopped, and I saw his shoulders sink, but he did not turn back around to face me. "I stand down here, staring up at the towers of Joyous Guard, and I wonder, is she sleeping in his bed? And I can't stop thinking about it. Can't stop picturing him in my place."

He was lost in himself now, lost in his thoughts, talking to himself. I was sure he had forgotten that we were there. Ywain had finally stopped eating, and was staring at his uncle. He had expected a great king, and before him all he saw was a miserable man approaching middle age crippled by sorrow for his stolen wife. The wife that he himself had sent to her death.

Chapter Seventy-One

When I got back to my pavilion, which Ywain's men and mine had set up for me while we ate with Arthur – or Ywain ate and Gawain, Arthur and I stood around too tense to eat – Mordred was waiting for me, lounging in my chair, an apple in his hand. He had taken a bite, and when he gave me his smug grin as I came in, I could see he had a lump of it in his cheek. When he relaxed his grin, he bit down on it hard, and it crunched. Casually, he took another bite.

"What do you want, Mordred?" I asked, annoyed. I had wanted to be alone.

"I thought you were a virgin," he said, flatly, fixing me with his hollow stare.

"Why would you think that?" I snapped, pulling off my cloak and turning away from him to fold it and set it on the little table set up for me. Unlike Arthur's table of food, mine was set with candles, and writing material. I hoped that if I ignored him he would get bored and go away.

I had not heard him stand, but suddenly he grabbed me from behind, pulling me against him, his hands against my hips, gripping hard.

"You were always so uptight," he whispered by my ear.

"Let go of me, Mordred," I hissed. I did not want to be *grabbed*. I hated the way it felt, the weakness of my body in a man's hands when

I knew the power of my magical strength. I hated the way they always tried to make me afraid. Mordred did not let go.

"And besides that, your life with the nuns. And you blushed when you saw me in the bath. But you have a son. Perhaps you were not blushing because you had never seen a naked man before." Mordred slid one of his hands around my waist, to press against my stomach and pulled me back more firmly against him. I turned around and slapped him hard across the face.

"What is *wrong* with you?" I demanded, forcing myself to keep my voice below a shout. I did not want Ywain to come in. I did not want there to be any chance that Mordred might get his hands on my son. Not now we were just beginning, tentatively, to find one another. Mordred did not move away from me. He leant over me. I had changed to his own shape before, to Arthur's, and both had briefly dissuaded him, but I was as yet holding back, until I needed to frighten him away.

"I did not get what you promised me, Morgan, with your little visions of the future." He leaned further towards me, and I found myself leaning back against the table, in a position of weakness that made the anger thrum harder in my veins. "I am beginning to suspect that you made it up, to use me as your puppet. I don't like that, Morgan. I expect you to provide me with some kind of suitable... substitute."

Just as I was prepared to take his shape and push him off me, he darted out his hand and laid it against my face, and I felt my own body twist under his will. I heard my heart thud in my ears for an awful moment, and I was pushed back, under, somewhere dark. I was afraid for a moment that I had become someone lost or dead, and that this was the oblivion that Macrobius had warned of, but it was not. Mordred had pushed me under the power of the dark Otherworld powers I had given him in the womb, and when I came back to myself, blinking against the light, dark spots before my eyes, I could see that he had changed me. I could see thick wild curls of red hair falling before my face, and I knew what he had made me become – who he had made me become. I tried to take my own shape again, but with his hand on my face, I could not. *Where had he learned this?*

He pressed up against me, grabbing my wrist with his other hand as I raised it to slap him across the face again. "I need a son, Morgan. But no ordinary woman can sustain it, the magic in my blood. I need *her*, Morgan. Or," he leaned closer, pressing his forehead against mine, "you."

I felt the bile rise up in my throat. I tried to take my own form again, his, but I was locked in. He was wrong, too. There were many children of only one parent with Otherworld blood. It had been the father Morgawse and I shared who had had it, and who had given it only to me. Kay's father had had not a drop of it in him. It was Mordred's own particular blackness that left him without a child, but I doubted he would believe me if I protested.

Mordred pushed his lips against mine, hard and unkind and forceful. My mind flashed back through Lot, holding me down against the table, and Uriens. He had a handful of my hair in his hand, tight and painful.

He pushed me up onto the table, and he grasped the skirts of my dress — which had changed with me into the thin nightdress I had worn in Guinevere's shape before — and began pushing it up. I pushed him back hard, but he did not seem to feel it. Nor even did he when I bit down hard on his lip. In fact, he seemed, to my disgust, to like it. I could feel my throat closing in panic, the nausea sweeping through me. I beat my fists against him, but I could feel his hands running up my thighs, pushing the skirts of the nightdress back. I could feel my skin, cold and sickeningly clammy all over, prickling with resistance.

Suddenly, rushing with panic, I felt my magical strength return to me. It had not fled me, then, at the moment of my most need. I thought for a moment about taking his own shape, but that had not been enough to frighten him off me before. I remembered his face when Kay had threatened to prove his rumours true, and before I realised what I was doing, I was becoming Kay in his hands. He did not realise for a moment, lost, I supposed, in his lust, as the woman's body before him changed to a man's, and beneath his hands it was men's breeches rather than the smooth, pale thighs of the stolen Queen, but when he did, he leapt back from me.

He stared at me in Kay's form with open disgust. I had been stronger than him in the end, had wrenched the power back from him. I was sure he was disgusted with that too.

"You're a pervert," he said, accusingly. If I had not still been so shaken, so angry, I would have laughed. All I could manage then was a derisive shrug. He left.

My immediate panic carried me from my tent to Arthur's. I think I was half-filled with the idea that I would tell him that Mordred was mad, and out of control. I was not sure what I expected him to do. Arthur's tent was lit from within by a low, orange light from a fading brazier. As I stepped in, I could see him sat beside it, his forearms resting on his knees, his head hung down low. Excalibur lay at his feet, in the scabbard that did not belong to it.

Arthur looked up when I came in. He looked haggard and weary, but he made the effort to smile when he saw me. I felt the twinge of guilt within me. He had continued to think of me as a dear sister all the while I had hated him.

"Morgan," he said, gently, "is everything well?"

I did not know what to say.

When I did not speak, he sat up in the chair. He looked as though he was about to speak again, but I could not take my eyes from Excalibur, and I stepped forward towards it unconsciously. It was as though the sword was calling me home, but perhaps its destiny was lost, since I did not know how I would see myself side by side with Guinevere on the banks of Avalon's lake anymore.

Arthur followed my gaze.

"Oh, you want my sword?" he said, casually, leaning back against the chair, shrugging. "I suppose the camp doesn't seem too safe to a woman alone. Take it. It won't do me any good."

I froze where I stood. So easy? Did Arthur care so little for it? *It won't do me any good.* Did some part of him know that the sword was not made for his blood? I could hear nothing but my own breathing, see nothing but the glinting pommel of the sword. I leaned down, slowly, and wrapped my hand around the hilt. I felt it then, the rush and surge of the Otherworld, a presence that reminded me distinctly of Nimue, and Avalon, and then of Merlin, standing behind me, pressing his lips against my neck, telling me how much I had to learn. I pushed the thought away, drawing Excalibur from the scabbard slowly, listening to it whistle against it, soft and low. I could feel my body filled with a bright Otherworld strength that came neither from me nor the sword alone, but from our being together. This sword was *made* for me. I ran my hand down the flat of it. As I did, I saw before me as though I were back there, me standing with Accolon, the sword drawn and raised between us, and then him stepping through my bed curtains and throwing down the duplicate he had made to take me in his arms, hard and rough with victory. I had sacrificed him to my desire for revenge. I pulled my hand away, suddenly sick with guilt, and the vision faded away.

"No, Arthur," I said softly, laying the sword gently back down against the grass at our feet, between us, the blade still naked and shining in the firelight. As I released my grip around it, I felt its wonderful power ebb away. I could not bear it. "Excalibur should stay with you."

He nodded.

"Arthur," I began again, and he looked up, hearing my voice catch, as I felt the strength of the remorse clutch hard at me. "I'm sorry."

"Morgan –" He stood to his feet, his face a picture of surprise and disbelief. "For what?"

I shook my head, feeling the tears prick at the back of my eyes.

"I did this," I choked out. "All of this."

"Morgan," Arthur sighed, pulling me into a brotherly embrace. I let my head rest against his chest, and closed my eyes. He smelled like the days of my youth. Like fresh straw, like Ector's farm. I could not believe how familiar, how homely, the smell still was to me. "None of this is your fault." I could not speak to protest. My words choked me in my throat.

"You are not to blame for... Guinevere," he said distantly, softly. "You know, Morgan, I dream over and over again that I am running through Camelot throwing open the door to every room, shouting her name, and every room is empty. I can hear her, in the distance, laughing. I don't suppose you have ever heard her laugh. It is like the sound of spring rain falling, or like a little bell singing. Well, she is laughing, and I can't find her anywhere. Then, I open the door to my bedroom, and when I open the door, I see myself just standing there, staring back."

I did not know what to say to him. That sounded to me like the dream of a man who was going slowly, quietly mad.

Chapter Seventy-Two

The days passed and nothing happened. Ywain was quiet and troubled. I wondered if he was anxious that he had picked the wrong side. Winter set in around us, and our men gathered. Mordred stayed away from me, but I did not yet feel safe.

The siege went on without any respite. Every so often a party of knights, led by Ector's brother Bors, made a sally out, but never for long. On one of those days, Gawain at the head of the armies of Lothian met them, and Gawain killed Lamerocke. I saw him carrying Lamerocke's head through the camp, his rough hand tangled in its matted hair. Gawain did not look as though he got any satisfaction from it.

Christmas came, and Arthur and Gawain made an attempt at festivity. Arthur called all of the leaders of his men into his pavilion where there was a feast of sorts laid out. There was plenty of food – I was sure that Christmas in Joyous Guard could not have been so plentiful – but it was all cured meats and cheeses, dried fruits and anything that could be scavenged. The men had left their ploughs to come and plant their tents around Joyous Guard, so there were precious little fresh vegetables, or fresh meat, and no fresh bread.

Still, there was wine. I sat beside Ywain, and he drank too much, and talked too loud, and laughed too hard at Gawain's jokes, which had changed in quality from the last Christmas that I had shared with him from bawdy to grim. Still, I did not mind. I liked to have him by my side. Mordred sat the other side of Arthur, in the place that had for a long time been occupied by Lancelot. Arthur did not show him any more kindness than before, but he talked about his son, not his nephew, and he had honoured Mordred with the office of Seneschal. I thought of Kay, in Joyous Guard. He would be playing no games this Christmas.

Arthur was quiet and serious all evening, but he did drink. He drained cup after cup until he slumped back in his chair and closed his eyes.

Nimue had not come. I had hoped that she would. Perhaps she had withdrawn her favour from Arthur because he had not listened to her. Or perhaps she was in Avalon biding her time. Perhaps it was not even that complex. It was just that she was there with Pelleas, her husband, living a simple life of happiness, and she was forgetting the rest of the world. If it were so, I would be jealous.

We left early, Ywain and I. Many of the men went with the women who followed the camp. They had wives somewhere at home, but they were drunk, and had been long at siege alone. As we left, I saw one slide into Arthur's lap, and he pushed her roughly away. He might have felt better if he had not, I thought. It might have made him less angry to think that he, too, could be weak.

It was the next day that the gates of Joyous Guard opened and the armies within poured out, with Lancelot and Kay in his black Otherworld armour at their head. Arthur was ready to meet them. I stood back at the camp, and watched from far away. I knew what would happen. I had seen it. Arthur thrown from his horse, Lancelot standing over him with his sword drawn.

I waited for the news to come, of the end. I hoped that Lancelot would have killed Mordred, too.

But back they came, Arthur, Mordred and Gawain, riding at the head of the men who were left. When I asked Arthur what had happened, he shook his head and strode into his pavilion without a word. I did not linger to ask Mordred. I sought out Ywain, who told me that Lancelot had had his chance to kill Arthur, and had spared him.

It was after that, when spring was beginning to waken in the air, the grass beginning its shoots, the camp beginning to smell of new flowers and new life, that Arthur called his council. I was sorry to see that Mordred was there, but I was pleased that Arthur had taken my son as well as me into his confidence. Ywain had proved himself a natural warrior, accomplished and level-headed on the battlefield. I supposed I had his father to grudgingly thank for that.

Arthur had another letter in his hand. When we were all gathered, he slammed it down on the table flat. I could not read the words from where I stood, but I could see that it was Nimue's hand.

"The Lady of Avalon writes once more, instructing me to take my wife again," Arthur declared tersely. Gawain and Mordred exchanged a glance.

"Have you sent for her before?" Ywain asked. I was surprised to hear him speak, but in his time at Arthur's side, he had grown bolder.

Arthur shook his head.

"So," Ywain continued, "we do not yet know if Sir Lancelot is keeping her against what he imagines to be your wishes, or her own."

"He *knows* it is against my wishes," Arthur growled.

"Arthur, you put her to the fire for the sake of accusations against him. If they are untrue, then he is acting in your interests protecting her until he can prove his innocence. You charged here to besiege him, without a trial. It would be a disservice to you to let your wife be burned for his sake, on a false charge," I interjected. Gawain glared at me resentfully, but I was not suggesting reconciliation with Lancelot. I only wanted Arthur to draw away from this war.

"What do you suggest I do, then?" he asked, hopelessly.

"Send to Joyous Guard, requesting that he return the Queen," I answered.

"There will be *no peace* with Lancelot," Gawain protested. He had in him the burning need for vengeance. Perhaps we had it both of us in our blood.

Arthur sighed under Gawain's powerful rage, nodding, sinking into it. He did not want this. I could see that.

414

"No," he said wearily, staring down at the table. "But I will have her back."

"Are you sure?" Mordred interjected coldly.

Arthur nodded. Mordred left with Gawain, but they seemed to accept it. When they had gone, Ywain and I discussed the terms that Arthur would send. I wrote the letter.

Ywain went back to his tent, but I stayed with Arthur. He lay down on his bed, and I sat at the foot of it, waiting with him.

I did not realise that I had fallen asleep until Ywain came back with the reply, and I woke to find that I had slept side by side with Arthur on top of his bed. It reminded me painfully of Morgawse and all of the nights I had spent with her, us comforting one another.

Ywain stepped through the pavilion door, and Arthur and I sat up.

"He will bring her back," was all he said.

That night, I saw them in my dreams. It was not really a dream of the future, but it was clear like one, and sharp, and strangely cold. They were together – of course they were, not even Arthur was fooled anymore – and alone. It must have been in his chambers at Joyous Guard. There was a fire, and the room was filled with its warm light, but the sense I got from looking in there was one of foreboding. She stepped towards him, and I heard her say his name, soft, sad and desperate, already a goodbye.

Then I saw them, deep late into that same night, lying side by side, neither of them sleeping, she on her front with her hair spilling down her bare back, her arms stretched out before her, as though reaching for something, but there was nothing there. He lay beside her on his back, staring up at the ceiling above them in the dark. His eyes were blank and empty. It was over for them, this little escape they must have dreamed of so many times before. But the reality was harsh, and cruel and destructive, and everything that they had dreamed had turned the real world around them to darkness, and ash.

Then I saw them in the morning, the morning coming for all of us, when she would go back to Arthur, and he would go far away to France, and Gawain's war – which I knew he would not leave – would begin in earnest. She held her hair up out of the way while Lancelot pulled tight the laces of a dress that could not have belonged to her. She looked thin, and it gaped at the neck. It was, too, a summer dress, made of light, pale silk. She would feel the new spring chill through it, though I was not sure, as things were now, that she would notice, or care. He left her, with a soft kiss against her neck,

415

and she stared out, into nothing, into me, though she did not know I was there before her in my dreams, and into her future where she would be returned to Arthur, like something borrowed. I was not sure that when my morning came, I could bear to watch.

I did not go. I lay alone in my pavilion, listening to the far off sounds of Gawain shouting, and Arthur, and even Lancelot. I had not expected that. I had expected Lancelot to come as a supplicant to Arthur, but he was angry, too. He was angry that Guinevere had been put to the fire, angry that he was being treated like a traitor.

But where the shouts and anger had come quick and fast, they fell away quickly, too. I still did not go out. I could not bear to watch Lancelot give her away. In the end, though they both talked of their great love for her, she was a thing to them, to be given back and forth. That was why Mordred wanted her so badly, for she was his father's most prized possession.

I came to the door of my pavilion when I heard it go quiet. I stood and watched as Arthur came back to his pavilion with Guinevere. I saw his hand, tight around her upper arm. She came willingly beside him, but it looked still almost as though he was dragging her. She did not see me. I was sure that her thoughts were of Joyous Guard. She looked, too, thinner and more tired than I had seen her in my dream, and worse than that, absent from herself and from Arthur beside her. This would only go better for Mordred, only feed his grim obsession. I was sick with it, sick with the thought of it. Sick, too, with the thought that Arthur would take her now into his tent and – what? – I could not pretend I did not know Arthur. Nor could I pretend I did not know what a husband did to his wife once he has found out that she has loved another.

Chapter Seventy-Three

As I stood at the mouth of my own tent, staring at Arthur's, listening to the violent shouting – from both of them – within, and trying not to picture what might be going on inside, Mordred strode up beside me.

"So," he said, low and dark, "my father has his wife again."

It fell suddenly, awfully quiet in the tent. I did not say anything to Mordred. I did not turn to look at him. It was dark overhead, the clouds low, the night growing bitterly cold as the sun sank away.

Perhaps it would even snow. There was an awful, grim atmosphere around the camp, and it was not just the ominous weather. No one knew what the next move would be. It all depended, I supposed, on what happened tonight, in that tent. I did not know if war would ever end if Guinevere confessed the truth to Arthur, or worse, gloated of it, to punish him for wanting her killed. That did not seem beyond her. Would Arthur rest until Lancelot was dead? Or would it only hollow him out from his heart, that the one man he could not bear to kill had done this crime against him?

Mordred reached for my hand. He wanted to know what was going on inside. I snatched it away. He reached for it again, and I jumped back.

"You will not benefit from my magic arts again, Mordred," I told him, cold and aloof, drawing myself back from him, crossing my arms over my chest.

"Why not?" he demanded.

"*Why not?*" I snarled. "Mordred, you tried to force yourself on me. Our agreement is over. Do you understand?" I took a threatening step towards him. I did not know how much black magic I was capable of, but I knew what Nimue had done, and I knew if I summoned her to lock Mordred beneath the earth until he was crushed to death by his own self-love then she would come, and she would see it done. I had an ally stronger than he was now, and I would not forget it.

"So, it will be war between you and me, then?" he asked. His empty black eyes bored into me, but I did not feel them. Not anymore. Somehow it was a relief to be openly his enemy.

"Mordred, it has always been war between you, and everyone else."

He turned around and left.

The next day we rode back to Camelot. Arthur must have been satisfied with what was returned to him. They rode side by side, Arthur and Guinevere, as though they were the same King and Queen they had been long ago, only now they did not look at each other, or speak to each other at all. I hung back with Ywain in the column of men leaving the camp. As we went, I turned over my shoulder and looked at Joyous Guard disappearing into nothingness over the horizon. Kay was there still, and Lancelot. If I could have done without breaking Arthur's heart even more, I would have closed my eyes and opened them there.

"Is it over, then?" Ywain asked quietly, beside me.

Without turning to look at my son, I shook my head. "No, Ywain. It is not over."

I did not want to go to Camelot. When the two paths opened up before us, I turned my horse towards Rheged, and Ywain and his men followed. I was pleased at that. So, my son was with me. Perhaps Arthur would be angry that I had absented myself from his and Gawain's war, but I did not care. I wanted to absent myself from the whole thing.

Nimue was in Rheged when we arrived, waiting in my room. I walked in with Ywain, who was still wanting to talk strategy. I could tell he was considering whether to put the might of Rheged behind Arthur once more, but the war had moved from Britain. Even now it would be moving across the sea, Lancelot retreating to his father's castle at Benwick and gathering all the men who owed him allegiance or who had heard of his strength on the battlefield. That was where it would be decided, far from here, and Rheged would retreat into its peace. Perhaps I would have to punish the lords of the other lands who had not put their strength behind Arthur, but that would come later. Besides, it did not seem worth it to me to punish our own people, when we too, Ywain and I, might have been swayed to pledge our allegiance to a different leader.

Nimue smiled when she saw Ywain and me together, and I felt the pain run through me again. I did not want her pity, I did not want her painful sympathy. It only made me think of all that wasted time.

I stepped forward into the embrace she offered me. She did not look like a child anymore, but she still felt small as one in my arms.

"Nimue," I said, lost in my confusion, in all I needed to know, "where have you been?"

"In Avalon," she replied simply. "There was no right cause to stand behind in Arthur's war. Avalon will not move against Lancelot. He was fostered there, and the island is his home. It was the same reason, Morgan," she added, delicately, "that Avalon never moved against you, even after you tried to kill Arthur. Avalon does not abandon its own. I can take no part in their war."

I nodded. I understood.

Ywain was uncomfortable around Nimue. I think something deep in his blood, some vestige of my magic, sensed the strength of her power, and it made him uneasy. He made a polite excuse to leave.

I sat with Nimue in my window seat, us both facing each other with our knees drawn up. I knew I did not have much time.

"Nimue…" I felt uneasy, unsure how to begin. I had asked for death before, but that had been in the heat of my anger. I drew in a sharp breath. "Now is the time. You must take Mordred, and you must do whatever you did to Merlin to him. Shut him beneath the earth. Kill him. I know he is Arthur's only child, his heir, but there is no other way."

Nimue took my hands in hers. "Morgan, I cannot. Merlin put himself into my hands. He loved me. He came to me of his own free will and I – I had to. To protect Arthur, to protect Britain. To protect you. Perhaps if we had acted earlier – perhaps I could have done something while Mordred was still a child, but now –" She shook her head. There were tears shining in her eyes, and her voice was beginning to crack. For the first time I felt truly, deeply and completely afraid. "Even if I could lay my hands on him, I do not know if I have the strength in me to do it. There is something. I –" She shook her head again. "There is a blackness around him. I cannot see where he is, who he is with, what he is doing. I do not understand it – perhaps if we still had Merlin's books. No, no, Morgan I know why you did it, and perhaps you were right. But Morgan," her look grew steely again, and she leaned towards me, the tears in her eyes still unfallen, "I will do everything in my power, I will give all my strength, to stop him, and to save Arthur. I have sacrificed so much, Morgan, to keep him safe."

She did not say *Avalon will do everything in its power*. She did not say *I have defended my King*.

"Was there ever anything between you?" I asked, softly.

"What?"

"Between you and Arthur."

Nimue shook her head, but she did not meet my eye.

"Arthur loves his wife," she said tersely, leaning back away from me, letting her hands trail out of mine.

"And you are happy with Pelleas."

She nodded. "The ones you want so much you think you will die without them, they are not the ones who make you happy."

I thought of Lancelot, and then of Accolon and Kay.

"You are right, Nimue." Now I had begun I could not stop thinking about Kay, and the way that we had been. I should have held tighter to that. I should not have let it go. "You know, I wished over and over again that Ywain would be Kay's," I told her.

To my surprise she sat up suddenly beside me. "Is he not?" she asked.

419

"Isn't it plain? He looks just like Uriens – he did, more so, anyway, when he was a boy."

I felt my heart flutter for a moment, the old wish gathering around me, but then she shrugged in agreement. "I suppose he does. But I have always thought that he looked just like you."

I let it pass away. Worse, far worse, it would have been for her to say he must have been Kay's, and for me to have been cold to him for Uriens' sake for all these eighteen years.

Chapter Seventy-Four

With the start of summer came the news that Arthur was taking his armies south across the water to France. War was coming to Lancelot's castle. I was surprised at how well I remembered Benwick Castle from my time there. It had been so long ago. Ywain had been an infant, still. But I remembered.

I was tired of war. I had watched three wars already. I had waited pregnant in Rheged while Arthur fought with Lot, I had ridden with the armies to Rome and stood back in the camp while the men sacked the city and sang their songs of victory, and I had waited in the camp outside Joyous Guard, not wanting to know what was going on. Not wanting to guess. Another war. I did not want to go.

Ywain wanted to. He was a young man, and all he had ever been told was that the measure of a man was his victories in battle. All the great men he had ever heard of were fine warriors. His Uncle Arthur, the great warrior king who conquered all of Europe. Sir Lancelot, the man that no one could defeat on the battlefield. Sir Gawain, the brave Prince of Lothian from whom entire armies fled. This was the size the men I had known as boys came to my son as. Big, and bright and bold as heroes. Like gold statues. But I had seen Gawain cry, and seen Arthur twelve years old in his nightshirt, pouting because his brother had a boy in his bedroom, and seen Lancelot lying beside me, wounded.

I sat with Ywain in the council room that had been his father's and, I supposed, his father's father's before that. I realised that I knew nothing about the ancestors of my son on his father's side. They were kings too. Perhaps once they had been kings of all of Wales, although now Rheged was still powerful enough to have the other kingdoms nearby under its vassalage. I sat in the window, gazing out across Rheged's courtyard. The knights below were gathering and preparing for war. I had seen the same sight, almost, long, long ago when I had been pregnant with Ywain. I felt the same things then that I did now. How pointless it was. And once again it was for the sake of Arthur and a woman.

I gazed at Ywain, sitting at the table, leaning over a map. His lips were moving with his thoughts as he traced his finger down across the spine of France to Benwick. I thought perhaps he was counting the miles, or working out the men he could take there. He was quick and sharp. I wondered again who had taught him.

"You should think, again, about marriage," I told my son, gently.

He looked up from the map. "Marriage?" he asked, unsure of where my words had come from. If there was to be war, then my son might be killed. He should try to leave a child behind him, if he could, before it was too late.

"Yes."

He shook his head. "To whom? There are no princesses in Britain, and we are at war with France."

"There are girls in Avalon. No, they are not princesses, but it is an honour for a man to have a wife who has had her woad in Avalon. An honour your father always failed to appreciate."

To my surprise, Ywain seemed a little more interested. He turned in his seat to face me, looking away from the map.

"A witch?" he asked.

I nodded. "You have magic in your blood, from me. I am known in Avalon. You could choose a girl with whom you could be happy. You wouldn't have to worry about allegiances, or politics. Besides, it would give you Avalon's protection, once I was gone."

He turned back away from me, after I had said that. I supposed he had not realised that Avalon only protected its own. Perhaps he had thought that half my blood in his veins made him one of Avalon's own as well, but that was not how Avalon worked.

"Do I need it?" he asked, quietly.

"We all do."

But as it turned out, there was not enough time. Arthur called us before the end of spring came, to go to France. It would be hot down there in the south, and perhaps Arthur wanted an end to it, before the heat that came with the full ripeness of summer would make warring unbearable.

So Ywain prepared for war, not marriage, and I prepared myself for the fact that I might never take my son to Avalon. Somehow I had felt that this might be a kind of redemption for us. Well, I would have to put all of my strength and skill, then, into keeping my son alive.

Nimue left as the last preparations were being made. She kissed me on the cheek, and told me to come to Avalon when it was over. I hoped I would live to see it. I did not know, truly, if war between Arthur and Lancelot would ever reach an end. Arthur would not win, and Lancelot would not kill him.

It was the day she left, as though her presence, her power had been keeping him away, that I returned to my room, and found Mordred there. When I saw him I could feel the fear pumping in my heart, but I pushed it away. I would not be afraid of him. I was in my castle. I was Queen here. He was just a nasty, greedy boy.

"Leave, Mordred," I told him from the doorway.

"I need a potion of yours," he told me, ignoring me.

"I already told you, Mordred, you will get no more magical help from me."

He darted forwards towards me and I rushed out of the way. I changed into his own shape. He would not intimidate me. Besides, I calculated that Mordred loved himself enough to be put off striking someone who looked exactly like himself. I noticed that he wore Arthur's surcoat, the coat of red and gold emblazoned with Uther's dragon, and as I had taken his shape so, too, did I.

"Morgan." His tone was low and threatening and he stepped towards me, but I felt safe. I was prepared this time. "Give it to me of your own will, or I will take it."

"Take what?" I sneered. "The books are burned, and you have no magic skill of your own. Sure enough you have power in your blood, but you have no knowledge. Take anything you like from here. In your hands, it will be no good."

I did not even know what he could possibly want. Perhaps it was just the potion for his blood. Perhaps even Mordred was afraid of death, though I could not see what joy life held for such a bitter creature as him. He turned from me and began searching through the cupboards in my room. I leaned back against the doorframe, watching him. Eventually he found something, something about which I had forgotten, but I was not worried. It was the remnants of the potion I had given Uriens the night I had killed him. It would be old, weak. It would hardly have any power left in it. Still, Mordred had a cruel look of victory on his face, and he held the neck of the leather skin of it tightly in his hand, and shook it before me.

"You have forgotten something, sweet Aunt!" he cried in delight.

I shrugged. "You wish to put a man to sleep? That drink is fifteen years old." I shrugged again. "Take it."

He seemed pleased by that, though I could not see why. As he went to walk past me, I put out my hand to stop him.

"Mordred, what did you come here for? Surely not just to see if I had any potions?"

"I came on my father's orders. To make sure Rheged was emptied, for war."

The next day, we departed. Mordred lingered behind to make sure that everyone left. The men were all afraid of him, I could see that. Ywain tried to show that he was not afraid, but he did a poor job of it, and his men sensed that Mordred was someone to be feared.

I rode side by side with my son at the head of the armies of Gore. It was a long ride, and tedious. The horses did not like the journey across the sea, and there were not enough boats so we were packed on tight. Mordred did not follow close behind. There must have been men to collect back at Camelot, or some other task he had to perform for his father. I was grateful for it. I did not like having him around.

Even on the boats, men were getting ill, and injured. There were rats, and men were bitten and grew infected. I gave my healing touch to everyone that I could, but without the herbs I needed, without the time to prepare, there was little more than that that I could give. When we landed in Calais, we had already lost almost fifty men.

The journey down was perilous, too. No one had warned us in Rheged that Carhais, the city of Guinevere's ancestors, was not with Arthur. No, the Breton folk had decided that they owed their allegiance not to their princess Guinevere's husband, but to her protector Lancelot, and they were unwilling for us to pass and go to his aid.

Carhais closed its gates to us. It was not a fortress city like Rheged or Lothian Castle, nor even like Camelot. It was a low, flat town, its wall made of wood and earth. Still, with its great wooden gates shut, and its armies pressed against them, we would get no food or shelter there.

A boy who I thought was no older than my son Ywain came to the battlements beside the gates, calling himself the Prince of Carhais. He had the same dark red hair as Guinevere, the same fierce angry expression. It was ugly on a man, and his forcefulness ill-suited his youth. He looked slight and untested in war, and he appeared slightly hysterical in his shouts to us that we could fight the armies of Carhais and its allies in Brittany, or go home.

Ywain moved forward on his horse to reply, and I put my hand out to stop him, moving forward myself. From what I had experienced of the Breton women in Camelot, this "Prince" would be at least afraid of my woad, and understand what it meant.

"I am the one they call Morgan le Fay," I shouted up to him. He tried to hide it, but I could see it strike him, and he hesitated. "True, we are King Arthur's allies, but we are not the enemies of the Breton people. Not the Breton Queen, Arthur's wife, and not you. Let us pass by your city in peace, and I, and the witches of Avalon will not turn their anger against you."

The Prince of Carhais hesitated, but I knew he would agree.

"You cannot enter," he shouted back. His tone was sulky, ill-befitting a prince.

So, we turned our army aside, and continued hungry and unrested down into France. We lost men from that, but not as many as if Carhais had poured out its army on us. That boy had not really wanted to fight. He only wanted to hide in his castle until it was all over. Perhaps that was the wisest choice. He was too young to have even known Guinevere when she was there as a girl, so I doubted that there was any real moral sentiment in Carhais' decision not to honour its allegiance to Arthur. He did not want to fight with Lancelot. I did not blame him for that.

Chapter Seventy-Five

So we arrived at Arthur's camp mid-summer. It was late in the day, but it was still stifling hot. The grass had dried and crackled under the horses hooves. The horses were panting and sweating, and it had been too long since we had stopped for water. Mercifully, Arthur's camp was by a stream, and I could see all the horses straining for it.

Arthur came out to meet us, and as Ywain and I dismounted, he embraced each of us.

"Morgan, Ywain," he said, "I am pleased to see you."

We left the men to set up our tents and to tend to the horses. Arthur did not notice that our army was small, and looked ill-equipped and under-prepared. There were other things on his mind.

When Ywain and I followed him into his tent, I saw what it was. Gawain lay on his bed, in the dirty shirt and leggings he must have been wearing under his armour. Around his head wrapped a strip of linen, bright red with blood at the centre, darkening as it moved out. The strip was dirty, too, and wrapped without skill. I realised that Arthur must have done it himself. I sent Ywain to fetch my things.

Arthur pulled me aside, and spoke quietly, but I thought it unlikely that Gawain could hear me.

"He fought with Lancelot," Arthur told me, softly, "and he insists he will fight again, until one of them is dead. Can you save him? He is... badly hurt."

I sighed deeply. "I *can* save him. But, Arthur –" I hesitated. I was not sure it was right, to say what I was about to say. I loved my nephew dearly, but I was tired of war. Tired of war and anger and revenge. "I do not *have* to. Arthur, he will never have done with this. Don't you want to go home? Once he is gone, you can reconcile with Lancelot, and *go home*."

Arthur shook his head, his expression tight and tense. He had not brought Guinevere with him. Going home meant going back to her, and I did not know what that meant for him, truly.

"Do you not want to return to your wife?"

Arthur sighed deeply, and I saw his shoulders sink. "My wife. I have her back, and I do not have her back."

I was not sure what he meant, but I did not ask again.

"But Morgan, please, save him." He nodded his head towards Gawain.

I agreed.

When Ywain returned, I climbed onto the bed beside Gawain. I looked down at him. He looked, in his sleep, unbearably like the boy who had shouted at his mother all those years ago for coming back from Camelot pregnant. He looked so much like my sister. His hair the same copper colour, the same broad, proud face – though his face now was lined and marked with scars.

Gently, I unwound the strip of linen Arthur had set roughly around his head. The wound was deep, into his skull above his ear, but he would live from it, with my help. It smelled unpleasantly sweet, until I put my hand gently against it, and felt the healing power within me rush into Gawain. I had Ywain hand me the herbs I needed, and made a poultice for the wound. I wrapped it again, carefully, in a clean strip of linen. We could only wait now.

The days passed, and Gawain woke from his deep, wounded sleep. At first when he woke he tried to jump from the bed, and Arthur, Ywain and I had to hold him down between us, or he would have rushed out on the battlefield then, right up to the gates of Benwick Castle to shout to Lancelot to come out.

From the camp, Benwick loomed dark on the horizon, tall, closed off. I did not see lights from within. If Arthur had not told me that Lancelot and his army were in there, I would not have believed it. But where were the rest of the armies of France? If Lancelot had called his allies, then they could have chased Arthur, who had only Logrys, Lothian and Gore with him, back to Britain. But he had not. It seemed that some decision had been made that he would settle with Gawain in single combat. That was better, I supposed, though it would have been kinder of him to finish with Gawain properly, than leave him wounded and dying.

Summer was coming to an end when Gawain was recovered from his wound. I was not sure how I felt about healing him, since he insisted that he would go out and fight again. What was the good of my saving his life, if he would only throw it away? He paced around the camp, deep in his anger. Not even his wound could make him forget the death of Gareth, and the dishonour to Arthur, wrought by Lancelot. Worse, he talked about it day and night to Arthur and Ywain. I could see it making Arthur sad and weary, but to my alarm it was beginning to bring a kind of fanatic light to Ywain's eyes, as though he were becoming convinced by Gawain's hunger for revenge.

Eventually, we could keep Gawain in the camp no longer. He insisted that he would fight. I sent Ywain back to the men on some task as Arthur and I helped Gawain arm himself for battle. I did not want him listening to Gawain's increasingly violent ramblings about revenge. I wanted the war to be over once Gawain had been killed by Lancelot.

"Gawain," I said, gently, handing him his gauntlets. "You do not have to do this."

Gawain shook his head. "It must be done, Morgan. I have nothing left now, except my honour. I have nothing left to give my lost family, except revenge."

I glanced at Arthur. His face was set, unreadable. It was an unpleasant day. The end of summer, a thunderstorm gathering, tense and uncomfortable. But Gawain would not wait until after the storm.

Arthur showed nothing. Gave nothing. They talked of the practicalities of battle, the equipment. No one mentioned Lancelot. No one said Guinevere's name. Gawain did not bid us goodbye when he went with his huge shield and his sword, dressed in his armour, out onto the field outside Benwick, to beg once more for death.

I stood with Arthur, side by side in the opening of his pavilion. The late summer rain fell heavily around us, smelling of the tired dry grass brought back to life by the rain, and of the last fruits of summer, rotting in the ground, and, obliquely, of regret. Why had it taken me so long to come to this point? Why had I not realised for so long that my hate for Arthur was destroying me faster than it was destroying him? And Lancelot. And Guinevere. And Kay. How had the five of us been tied so tight that we had come to such a place as this? And I could not tell who was responsible for it; I only knew it was either her or me. The men had followed us blindly, first one then the other, as we had rushed, blindly, too, at our own desires. They had been weak, and blind and foolish. They should have been stronger. So, too, should we. But then there were others – Nimue, Gawain, Morgawse – who had made it so these were the only paths we could take.

Arthur was staring out through the rain, his eyes fixed on Lancelot and Gawain crashing together on the field before us. Gawain had driven Lancelot back hard all morning, and Lancelot had seemed to buckle under his powerful blows, his shield shattering until all he held was the iron boss of it, with shards of broken wood sticking out from it like some ugly misshapen star. But Gawain was a powerful fighter who relied on his strength, and Lancelot was quick and had evaded him until, as noon passed, Gawain began to grow tired, wearying under the weight of his own rage, the crushing power of his blows, and his strength had waned, and now, as night was falling, Lancelot was driving him back easily towards our camp. Arthur's eyes followed his nephew with a wild intent. Though Lancelot's shield was shattered to pieces in his hand, he did not have a mark on his body. Gawain was injured, dragging his left leg with him as he moved back from Lancelot's blows, which were fast and stinging now they had the chance to fall. And yet Lancelot held back from striking a fatal blow. He could have done, long ago, once Gawain's strength had begun to tire, but he did not want to kill Gawain. It was obvious even from as far away as Arthur and I stood that Lancelot was desperate for a reconciliation. So was Arthur. Lancelot was hoping that if Gawain were too injured to fight, he would accept terms for peace, but I knew my nephew well enough to know that the only terms for peace he would accept were his death, or Lancelot's.

Arthur was tired of war. I could see it on his face. I was aware, suddenly, of how much we had all aged. Arthur's boyish looks had faded, and he looked weary now, grizzled as Uther before him had done. That had come to him fast. Only a few years ago, he had been a man in his prime. He had had all the looks of a mighty king about him. He had been happy. He had been strong, and famous and brave. Now he was the king everyone knew as one whose wife had loved another man. This had torn the heart from him, his betrayal by Guinevere.

I had got what I wanted. He had suffered. It was in every line of his face. I was not sure, anymore, if I had truly wanted it. Even Lancelot, whose face had once been smooth and fair as a lovely young girl's, wore the marks of age. His face was lined with his troubles, and at his temples, thin lines of grey threaded through his hair. Only Gawain, carried through by his rage, had any stomach for it anymore.

"What did he have," Arthur said, suddenly, thoughtfully, catching me by surprise as I watched the fighting, "that I lacked?"

I shrugged.

"He is not bigger than me," Arthur continued, resentfully. "I have seen him."

I was shocked that Arthur's understanding of this was still so simple. Had he known his wife at all?

"Arthur," I replied gently, "I am sure you lacked nothing as a husband. You are just... different men. You forget — you chose her, she did not choose you."

He turned to look at me. I could not read his expression. This war with Lancelot had robbed him of that open look, perhaps of his generous heart as well. He had, after all, put Guinevere to the fire.

"Not every husband was like your husband, and your sister's husband," he answered, sharply. "I was kind. I was a good husband." Turning away from me, he glanced back to the fighting. I could see Lancelot hold back from a blow that would have sliced under Gawain's breastplate. Very softly, he added, "I loved her."

It was awful, the way he said it, as though she were dead.

"You will not forgive her?" I asked.

Arthur shook his head and rubbed his face. "No, no. Of course. Of course I will. I love her, it is just... Something is lost, Morgan. I thought that I was everything to her, and I was not. She was, in a way, everything to me."

I thought he was lying to himself, just a little, in that. He had been as concerned with jousts and games with his men, with his own power, with the glory of his knights, as her. He had never learned her language. He had never told her the truth about her mother. He had never gone with her back to Carhais. He had sent her home from war, for his own sake, not for hers. He had loved her, as well as he could, but she had not been everything to him. She had been his wife.

There was a huge crash as Lancelot's sword struck Gawain's helm, and Gawain sank to his knees. Lancelot stood over him, still. Once more, he did not strike the death-blow. I could hear Gawain shouting, desperate for an end, but I saw Lancelot shake his head. The rain ran down his face, plastered his hair to his head. He had fought without his helm all day, as though daring Gawain to strike a blow that he knew Gawain could not. Or perhaps he hoped that Gawain would, and it would all be over for him. Lancelot threw down his broken shield between them in the mud, churned up from the rain and their fighting, and he turned away. Arthur gave the shout, and men rushed out to bring Gawain inside the tent.

With a chill, I realised suddenly that Mordred had never come. How had I not noticed before? I had assumed he would go to France, and wait for his chance with Arthur. I had thought to catch him at his plotting here. No. He was in Britain. He had my potion.

"Arthur," I asked, with dread gathering around me, "where is your son?"

"Oh," he replied absently, his eyes still on his nephew, and the men trying to lift the wounded bulk of him on to a stretcher to bring him back to the camp. In the distance, Benwick Castle lifted its portcullis for Lancelot to enter, and he was swallowed up by it. "I left him at Camelot, to take care of Britain, and to guard Guinevere."

"You did what?" I cried, in utter disbelief that Arthur could still have been so naïve, so stupid. Mordred must have laughed with glee when Arthur told him all his ambitions were to be granted in one, foolish bequest.

Arthur turned back to me, angry and defensive. "He proved himself loyal. Someone had to guard my kingdom, and my wife."

"Arthur –"

"What, Morgan?" he demanded, irritably. "What have you known about this, too, that you have neglected to tell me until it is too late?"

I could not speak, I was too frustrated, too desperately angry with him. But, it was with myself, too. I had unleashed Mordred on Camelot in my own desire to do Arthur harm.

Turning from Arthur, I closed my eyes and pictured the courtyard in Camelot. It was raining there, too, the fat, heavy raindrops of late summer, and I felt them on my skin before I saw it come into place around me. It was late in the night, and no one was around. I wondered if I still had time.

Chapter Seventy-Six

I rushed up her tower, to her room. The door hung open on its hinges, and I saw within the wreckage of some awful fight. One of the bed curtains was torn down from the bed and lay in a heap on the floor, stained with blood, and there was blood, old and dried, soaked into the bare floorboards.

Well, she was not there now. But she had to be in Camelot. Mordred would not have left. He would want to stay at the heart centre of Arthur's kingdom until he could take it for his own. He would not be happy if he was not sitting in Arthur's throne, and sleeping in Arthur's bed.

As I turned to leave, I almost bumped into Gareth's wife. She must have seen me appear, and followed me up here. I would have rushed past her, but she had a desperate look in her eye. She thought I had come to save her. She looked as though she needed it. A little bruised, very frightened. I knew what Mordred was like.

"Tell me where the Queen is," I said urgently, taking her by the shoulders. She shook her head.

"Tell me, Lynesse," I insisted.

She began to cry, shaking with her tears.

"Promise me you'll take me away with you, and I'll tell you," she said thickly, through her tears.

I did not think that I could. I promised, anyway.

"He keeps her in Arthur's rooms," she mumbled.

Without replying, I rushed away. I could save them both, take them away from Camelot, but then what? I still had to stop Mordred.

I raced up the stairs, past the room with the Round Table, and up to Arthur's bedroom. I pulled at the door. It was bolted from the inside. I put my ear to the door. Silence. I pulled harder at the door, but it only rattled against the metal bolt. I had not even seen any evidence of Mordred in Camelot, apart from Lynesse's distress. Perhaps he was not there.

As I stepped back from the door, someone inside wrenched it open and I jumped back. Mordred strode out into the corridor, his face dark with anger, but when he saw it was me, he grinned, pushing the door gently shut behind him. I noticed then, in the darkness of the night, and the low light of the torches burning, that he was naked except for his breeches, which had clearly been pulled on in haste, the laces pulled closed, but hanging down untied.

"I thought you were a servant. I was going to scold you. You might have woken my Lady." His grin deepened as he stepped towards me, and I felt suddenly, strongly repulsed by him.

"Mordred...?" I murmured. Surely, he could not have won Guinevere over, after she had refused him so many times. She had been here waiting for Arthur's return. The drink he wanted, I thought. And his own words came back to me: *In the dark, I don't need your black magic to take my father's shape.* I felt sick.

"Ah yes, Morgan, you arrive too late." He shrugged, as though it was nothing. "She will complain when she realises that it was I, and not my father, but she did not seem to find me unpleasant." He grinned deeper, leaning towards me. I had grudgingly enjoyed his mother's confessional nature, but this was making me sick, making me wish I had the strength to kill him. "I had wondered what it was about this woman that made all the men mad, and now I have known it, I must confess that it was no exaggeration. I have had my hands all over her body, and I know that she loved it. My father never loved her like that, I am sure. And, Morgan – Morgan, what I have known, *you cannot imagine.*" He laughed, soft and cruel. The worst of it all was that he had gone to it imagining his own father, too, in comparison.

I stepped back from him, and he grabbed my wrist, pulling me up close to him.

"I have it all, Morgan. I have had letters-patent made declaring that Arthur is dead, killed by Lancelot in France. Soon they will crown me King. After this, Guinevere will have no choice but to consent to be my wife, and then I will have everything of my father's in my possession, as it should be. All except my father's sword." I tried to wrench my hand away, but he did not let go. "That could have been yours, if you had not betrayed me. I will have that sword."

"Arthur has the sword. You will have to fight him like a man on the battlefield if you want it. You won't have any of my help."

Mordred struck me hard across the face, and I tasted blood in my mouth as my teeth bit into the inside of my cheek. I didn't care.

"You will bring my father to me," he hissed, grabbing me by the chin with his other hand, turning my face up so that I could not look away from him. I looked back, impassive.

"I will bring him to you, Mordred, and he will kill you. I have seen it." It was a lie, but he did not know that.

"A man can change his fate. You changed Gaheris' fate with me, or don't you remember? It was not long ago. I have changed my fate. I have taken my father's destiny –"

"Wearing your father's surcoat and raping his wife hardly counts as that, Mordred," I told him.

Mordred laughed, low and unpleasant, leaning down to whisper at my ear. "There was no *force*, Morgan. Only willingness. Enthusiasm, even. Look."

I could feel my skin creep, and before I realised what his last word meant, he clamped his hand over my eyes, and for the moment before I managed to tear it away, I saw as I had in my dream, long ago, Mordred with the Queen, lying on top of her. She was splayed out beneath him, her limbs trailing as though she were drunk, or not entirely conscious. He kissed her, and I was surprised how tenderly he did so, though I supposed that he was trying to imitate someone else. His hands ran lightly down her body, over her nightdress, and when she sighed against him, her closed eyes fluttering but not falling open, he pulled the lacing open and slid a hand inside. Just before I wrenched his hand away, though I could not hear her, nor anything that I saw, I saw her open her mouth to say something, and her lips form the word *Arthur*.

I pushed Mordred back, stepping away. He was pleased with himself now he had upset me. I remembered how Arthur had been, cold and distant. Troubled. He had not forgiven her before he left. How desperate she must have been for even the smallest token of forgiveness. How unbearably ready to believe that Arthur had come back to her.

"I do *not* want to look."

Mordred shrugged. "I have heard that you have done the same. I heard that you wore another woman's shape to lie with Lancelot. *I* have committed no such magical trickery."

I felt my face burn. *Who had told him about Lancelot?* What could I say to him? That I regretted my sins? That would only give him what he wanted. He wanted to see me weak, and repentant.

"You men have your strength, I have mine. There's no honour for a man in deceiving a woman."

He made a lunge towards me and I jumped back.

"Believe me, Morgan, she is deceived now, but before long she will *beg* me for more."

"You are disgusting," I told him, and he shrugged once more.

"I am no different from you," he said.

When I came back to my room, following my feet and my instincts and memory, I found Lynesse waiting for me. She had her daughter with her, too. A small girl of, I supposed now, nine years old. Lynesse sat in my window seat, her arms around her daughter who sat against her. The girl had her mother's sweet looks, and big, wide, innocent blue eyes, that – despite their innocence – reminded me painfully of Morgawse. The girl had her father's red-gold hair, too. She looked up at me without fear, but worse with a desperate wide-eyed belief that I had come to save them.

I shut the door sharply as I stepped in.

"What is it, Lynesse?" I demanded, more briskly than I meant to.

"Aren't you going to take us away, now?" she asked, her eyes shining with tears.

I shook my head. Perhaps I should have been gentler.

"Not tonight, Lynesse. I will make sure that you and your daughter are safe."

Lynesse kissed the side of her daughter's head. The girl was pretty, would grow to be beautiful. I felt a flash of grim relief that Mordred's taste seemed to be exclusively for women older than himself. I wondered where the sharp-tongued Lynet was. Vanished, disposed of – it didn't matter. She was gone.

Chapter Seventy-Seven

The next morning I waited, watching out of my window until I saw Mordred come down, out into the courtyard. His men were preparing for war, preparing to depart.

When I closed my eyes and pictured myself back in Arthur's bedroom, it was nothing like it was when I opened them. The bed, which was where I appeared, had its covers thrown back, and on the floor, an empty cup lay on its side, and some white, crumpled garment that must have been Guinevere's nightdress. At first, I could not see her in the room, and I hoped this meant she had managed to escape. But then, with an awful jerk of panic, I realised that I could not see her because I could not see her red hair. She was leaning out of the window, looking awfully as though she were about to throw herself out.

"Guinevere!" I cried. She jumped around, her face slack with shock, her red lips parting. Her hair was loose around her shoulders, still red, just, but fading. Soon it would be as I had seen it when we stood together on the shores of Avalon. We were coming towards the end. She was dressed in a plain dress of dark violet. I was sure she would have preferred her armoured dress. I could see that she was trembling. I realised, suddenly, that it was what I had seen her wearing when Mordred had brushed against me in her shape, and seen her kissing him. It gave me an idea.

She moved back from me, instinctively. She did not trust me. She thought I was someone else come to harm her. Unlike Lynesse, she did not have the marks of his hands upon her, but I had never seen her show anything that she felt before, and now I could see her open distress on her face. She had lost all of her protectors. I knew that Kay had watched over her, and was now gone, and now her husband and her lover were in France trying to kill one another. They had forgotten about her.

"I've come to help you," I told her. She did not move. She drew more into herself. I had caught her off guard, and she was already resistant to showing me any weakness.

"Why?" she demanded.

"*Why?*" I asked in disbelief. I had thought she would be grateful.

"You hate me," she said.

"*Hate* you?" I repeated. The last time that she had seen me, the realisation dawned on me, I was wearing her shape, and trying to take Lancelot from her. She was as much of a child at heart as her husband if she thought *that* was hate. "Guinevere..." I slipped from the bed, and went over to her, taking her hands. She did not move back from me, though her look was still wary. Her hands were strong, competent hands – not really the hands of a princess, or a queen – but I could feel them trembling slightly in mine. She met my look steadily, evenly. What a creature she was. Even now she was holding it all tight inside her, drawing back, drawing in, so that I would not see her pain. "We were rivals for a man's love, once," I explained, "and we both did everything we could to win him. I never hated you." I gave a shrug of confession; I knew I had been unfair. "I know I... play a little rough. True, I have had no love for Arthur. His father raped my mother, and he got that monster on my sister, and married me to that disgusting old man against my wishes –" I stopped myself. I did not want to let myself run away with my anger at Arthur. Not now. Not now there was peace between us. "But," I continued, "you? No." I shook my head. "You're an innocent really in all this, aren't you?"

It wasn't until I had said it that I realised it was true. She closed her eyes, and I saw her lips tense, as though she were forcing herself not to cry.

"Oh," I sighed, "Mordred was cruel to you."

It had not been fair of Arthur to leave her open to this, for them all to treat her like a possession. Mordred had taken her like one, because Arthur had left her like one.

I could feel the power of the Otherworld from her, an unfamiliar kind, and more subdued than what I felt from Mordred, or even Kay, but it was there, in her blood. At once I was met with a blur of disorientating images; her holding out her gold token for Lancelot and him taking his hands in hers instead, her eyes closing, leaning in. Then Arthur, sleeping, and she with her eyes wide open, staring up at nothing in the darkness. Lancelot in his armour, turning away from her. Blood, her hands smeared with it, blood tangling in her hair, Lancelot pulling her into his arms as she rushed towards him, and the pair of them falling into a wild kiss. Only then did I see the body of the man Mordred had offered her to lying on the floor beside them. She and Lancelot lying wound together, he with his lips pressed softly against her brow in a moment of tender intimacy, and then them sitting up, panicked, at a sound I could not hear, but which I knew was Mordred banging at the door. Mordred whose fist I then saw closing over the front of her dress, ready to tear. Lancelot putting her hand in Arthur's. And then I saw Arthur, young again, wrap his arms around her from behind and press his lips against her neck as she leaned back against him. A flash of more and more moments like that of casual, marital intimacy. And among them, images of Lancelot in moments of blinding passion. And then suddenly Mordred's grinning face, a handful of her fading hair in his fist. It was here, in Arthur's bed. Cold panic on her face. Mordred, laughing. I stepped back from her. We would, she and I, destroy Mordred.

"We are women together and I have come to protect you from Mordred," I told her, briskly. I could not believe how she gave none of it away. Though I had just seen the whole knot of it for her, she showed none of it on her face. I supposed that was how Arthur had never guessed. Well, it would give her the strength to escape Mordred. I knew she had the strength to do it. "Agree to be his wife. Agree to be his wife until you can get to somewhere safe, and I will come to you again. Just pretend to give in. He will show his weakness when he thinks he has won." I took her hands up again and squeezed them hard. She did not trust me, but it was me or Mordred, and I knew I would win with her.

"I will come to you again," I told her.

I closed my eyes and let myself melt away, down to the courtyard. When Mordred saw me appear before him he gave his smug grin.

"Where have you been, Morgan le Fay?" he sneered, "Playing at spells with the other witches? Come to try and stop me?"

I shrugged. "Why would I stop you rushing towards your death?"

He didn't look pleased. Perhaps he was more worried about it than I had thought he was. He was putting on his armour, buckling it on to himself. It was his own, battered already though he was young.

A girl came rushing out towards us across the courtyard.

"Sir Mordred, Sir," she called.

He turned.

"What is it?" he snapped. "I'm about to leave."

"Sir," the girl was shaking, "the Queen wants you. Wants to see you."

Mordred flashed me a smug smile. He turned to me. "I told you, did I not, Morgan? I told you she would *beg*." He turned back to the girl. "Not now. You can tell her I will come back for her. We have invaders from France at our shores. I must ride to war."

"Sir." The girl tried again, and I was surprised. "Sir, she is very insistent."

Mordred sighed with annoyance, and strode off. I felt the little jump of victory within me.

The next part of it would be Kay. I knew where I hoped to find him. I closed my eyes and pictured Joyous Guard.

Chapter Seventy-Eight

When I appeared outside the gates, they opened for me. Someone in the watch-tower must have known the sight of me from far away.

When I walked into the courtyard, Kay stood there, in his black armour, his helm under his arm, and Ector by his side. Ector stepped forward to hug me into a tight, fatherly embrace.

He held me away, gently, his kind eyes large with worry.

"What news, Morgan?" he asked me.

I shook my head. "None good. Mordred has forged letters saying that Arthur is dead, and is having himself made King."

Ector nodded. I could feel Kay's eyes on me. He must have been sorry, truly, that he had left the brother of his childhood to come to fight with Lancelot. I realised, then, that I had not heard Arthur speak of him.

"News came here of that, too," Ector told me.

I nodded. Mordred would not have stinted to have his victory announced anywhere it could be.

"You should stay here, stay safe. I will go to Ywain, see how things are with Arthur's army. Check that Arthur is... well," I told him.

"Ywain?" Kay asked, confused, stepping forward.

"My son," I replied sharply, annoyed.

"No, I know, but is he old enough for that?" Kay asked, more to himself than to me. He shook his head thoughtfully. "You know, Morgan –" He looked up at me, his gaze suddenly intimate and intense. I wanted to draw away from it, to back away. "I have never seen him," he said, softly.

I did not reply. I did not want to speak intimately with Kay with Ector there. Besides, I knew what Kay wanted to see, and he would not see it.

"I hope you will live to, Kay," was all I said, before I closed my eyes and pictured myself back in Arthur's camp. I hoped that they would still be there, and I would not open my eyes onto empty barren earth, but I also hoped that they were gone, riding for Britain already.

When I opened my eyes, it was to an empty field, but Nimue was there. She held out her hand to me.

"Avalon could not protect Arthur over Lancelot, but it will throw every power it has behind protecting him from Mordred."

I nodded, and took her hand, but I wondered as we drifted away from wherever we were to where Nimue knew Arthur was, if it would not have been better for us to go inside Benwick Castle and beg Lancelot to come with us. Though he could not. Not with Gawain still raging against him. While Gawain lived, there would be no allegiance between them.

When Nimue and I appeared in Arthur's tent, he did not look surprised. They were already back in Britain. He did not say anything. He was sitting in a chair beside Gawain, who was lying on Arthur's bed, a strip of linen around his head in the same place. His face was grey-white, pale with coming death, and though I could see his lips moving, I could not hear what he said. Arthur leaned close to hear it, and I could see him writing down the words in his still-clumsy hand.

I waited until Gawain's breathing had stopped, and Arthur had stopped weeping silently beside him and fallen asleep, to take it in my hands and unfold it. It was a letter to Lancelot, from Gawain. A letter of forgiveness, begging him to return. I handed it to Nimue, and she disappeared before me.

Ywain was at the camp, and I was glad to see him. He looked well, older again already. I supposed that was war. I got a letter from Kay, telling me he had gone to London, to the old Roman tower. He told me Guinevere had called him there, and was there with him. They were barricaded in, with the knights left in Joyous Guard and I supposed whoever she had taken with her when she had fled from Camelot, for a siege. It was some safety. They would be safe enough until they ran out of food.

I had been at war so many times before. This was the worst of them, for Arthur was grim and set and seemed to go each day in his armour with a fatal set to his face, as though he longed for his death.

We were losing. Every time I saw Ywain and Arthur ride back from the battlefield I felt a desperate clutch of relief. Mordred had more men. Lothian was with him now, as its only surviving heir, and those who had favoured Lancelot before had mostly gone to him. Arthur had only his own men, and Ywain's.

It came to the point where we had to offer Mordred a truce, a deal. Just until Lancelot came with his armies from France. I was confident enough that when Lancelot's old allies saw he was once again with Arthur, they would come back to us. Nimue had not returned, which either meant that Lancelot was reluctant or preparations were taking longer than they should. She wrote to me, assuring me that if we got three months of truce with Mordred that would be more than enough time, and we would, with Lancelot's help, crush him. Arthur was quiet, and dark, and thoughtful. I wondered if he wanted to see Lancelot again, if they would shout at each other. If they would talk about Guinevere. Arthur and I did not speak much, nor did I say much to Ywain. By this point, when we could all feel the awful end of it around us, there was not much to say.

Mordred sent a letter, agreeing to meet to discuss terms of the truce. With dread, we went.

It was a dark day for the start of summer; the clouds, low and heavy in the sky with rain, felt as though they were pressing uncomfortably down on us. In Mordred's pavilion, it was stiflingly hot, humid. Mordred was stripped to his shirt and breeches, and Arthur's red and gold surcoat hung casually over the back of a chair as he paced before us, reading over Arthur's terms for peace, his lips moving with the words but his voice, whispering, lost to us. I glanced at Arthur beside me. He was tense, uneasy. His hand rested on the hilt of Excalibur and in his armour he was sweating. I could see a bead of it rolling down from his temple, where at last his gold hair was beginning to pale to grey. Mordred had Arthur's crown, too. I saw it set on a table at the back of the pavilion.

Many of the men who stood armed behind Mordred were men who had fought with Lancelot at Joyous Guard. I supposed it made sense to them to keep the same enemy. Arthur, on the other hand, was flanked by young men. I was aware, suddenly, of how all of his friends were gone. Gawain and his brothers dead, Lancelot in France, Lamerocke, Percival and Tristan dead, Ector and Kay in the Tower hiding from Mordred. The only one of the knights who had sat with him around his Round Table and pledged to make Britain great who stood with him now was Dinadan, and he was much changed. His laughing face was scarred and thick with greying stubble now, and if I had not known his shield, I would not have recognised him. Besides, it was not he who stood at Arthur's side, but Ywain.

Arthur watched Mordred pace back and forth and back and forth until he finished reading the terms. At last, Mordred sighed and set the paper down on the table, regarding Arthur lazily across it, an unpleasant smile flickering across his lips.

"These terms seem... reasonable," he admitted, with a shrug.

Arthur stepped forward, and I saw one of the knights behind Mordred put his hand to the hilt of his own sword.

"There is one more thing, Mordred," Arthur said. "I left Guinevere in your keeping."

"Ah, yes." Mordred leaned forward over the table, grinning at his father. I closed my eyes for a second and prayed that Arthur would keep his temper. We only had to appease Mordred until Lancelot came. "I have had her, in Camelot, in your very own chamber."

"Keeping her as your prisoner is not part of the agreement," Arthur insisted, oblivious as always to what was really being said to him. "You will return her to me."

Mordred gave a cruel laugh, looking down and shaking his head for a moment.

"Father, you misunderstand me," he said, looking back up at Arthur with his cold black eyes. "I mean to say that I have *enjoyed* her."

Arthur lunged forward towards him, and I heard Ywain shout "*Arthur!*" as I did, and we both jumped forward to catch him and hold him back. I could not have held him on my own, and I was glad Ywain was there.

"Arthur," Ywain said, quietly, "he is lying. He is only trying to make you angry."

Mordred was laughing, and I could hear some of the knights behind him laughing along with him.

Arthur relaxed back just a little, though he did not look convinced by Ywain's words. Mordred shrugged at them both, still grinning.

"You can wait at your leisure to see whether or not I am lying. She rides to meet me, and she has consented to be my wife. Once you are dead. She will be glad to be free of you. She longs for me, Father. I have heard it from her own lips, how she *wants* me. How the love she had from you – even the love she had from that French idiot Lancelot – was *nothing* to what she had from me."

Arthur lunged forward once more, though this time Ywain was ready for it, and held him back fast. It only made Mordred laugh harder to see his father struggle against his anger. I felt an unbearable stab of pity for Arthur, then. He had not seen any of this coming. *Any* of it. I had wanted to make him see how fragile his perfect world was, and now I had done it, I wished deeply, painfully that I had not. The truth was ugly, and hostile, and the world had been a better place when lovers had met in secret, and Arthur had lived in his blissful ignorance.

Mordred suddenly slammed both of his palms down flat on the table top, leaning forward and staring hard at Arthur, who stared hard back, past Ywain, who was warily moving back from him.

When Mordred spoke it was soft, and low, and as though he and Arthur were the only two in the room. "Father, we would not have come to this if you had acknowledged me as your heir. But now I possess everything that was once yours – everything except the kingdoms of Britain, and the sword. I have your castle, your home, I wear your crown, I have Uther's coat, I have the loyalty of the men who were once yours. I have known the secrets of your marriage bed." Arthur did not move, but I saw Ywain close his gloved hand around the greave on Arthur's arm, just in case. Mordred leaned forward, his grin leering now. I myself longed to strike him across the face. "And *what secrets they are*, Father."

He was daring Arthur to strike him. To break the truce. He was hungry for war. He wanted the truce because it was so well in his favour to have Cornwall and North Wales – for we had promised him almost everything we had to give – but he would rather have come to blows with Arthur then and there.

"But," Mordred continued, suddenly casual, striding around the table, towards Arthur, until he stood face to face with him, "can something truly be called a secret if it is something that *many* men have known?"

Arthur stared back at him.

Mordred gave a sigh of false defeat, as though Arthur's angry stare had convinced him of something. "Very well, Father. Give me the sword, and I will return her to you, *if* she is willing. Though, be prepared that she might not wish to return to you, now she has felt what it is like to be loved by a man who is neither a coward who cannot kill his enemies in battle like Lancelot, nor a fool, like you."

He must have known by now that Guinevere had no intention of joining him, or marrying him, and yet he bore the illusion well. His natural arrogance helped him.

Arthur grasped hold of Excalibur by the hilt, and I put my hand over his, desperate that he should neither give the sword away, nor strike Mordred with it, as satisfying as that would have been. We had to wait for Lancelot to come.

"Do not," I hissed, "give him the sword."

In Mordred's hands, I had no idea what Excalibur would do. Mordred took a threatening step towards me, but I did not take my hand from over Arthur's, over Excalibur's hilt.

"And you, my dear Aunt Morgan." He leaned down towards me. "What treachery are you plotting now? To wait until my father and I have killed each other, and take the sword for yourself? How *easy* it is for a woman like you to change her sides. There was a time not so long ago when I thought I could have been sure of your allegiance to me, but no. A creature like you has no allegiance. Only to herself." He turned back to Arthur, holding out his hand for the sword. "This is the last time I will make the offer. The sword, and I will tell Guinevere when she comes to me – which she will – that she is free to go to you. If she wishes."

Arthur's hand moved on the hilt of the sword, and I put my other hand over his as well.

"Arthur, *no*," I insisted.

Without waiting for Arthur's response, Mordred gave a curt nod, walking back around to the other side of the table.

"Nonetheless, the truce stands," Mordred said, his tone business-like. He began flicking through the sheets of terms again, as though giving it final consideration. A movement in the grass caught my eye, and I watched as an adder slithered across the grass at our feet. I saw Ywain notice it, too, and watch it come towards him. Mordred, on the other side of the tent, was giving quiet orders to his men. I was not sure if it was time for us to leave.

Suddenly, the adder rose from the grass as though it were about to strike Ywain, and carried through by instinct, he drew his sword and struck down at it, slicing through it. I shouted out *No*, but it was too late. Mordred's men had already seen the flash of naked steel, and heard the threatening hiss of a sword draw from its sheath and suddenly all around us was shouting and men drawing their swords. I reached out and grasped Ywain by the hand, and closed my eyes. He, Arthur and I swam in the in-between for a moment, caught by surprise, but the memory of Arthur's pavilion came back to me, sharp with panic, and we were there. I hoped that the others who had come with us would make it out alive. We could not afford to lose more men.

The truce was over.

Chapter Seventy-Nine

Arthur strode away from us into the tent, unbuckling his breastplate and throwing it off. I glanced at Ywain and motioned for him to leave. He went, silently. It would be he that gathered Arthur's troops for the battle that was about to begin.

I stepped into the tent.

"Morgan, *leave*," he growled.

I stepped forward again and took hold of him by the shoulders, hard. He needed to calm down if any of us were going to survive this, to survive Mordred.

"Arthur, he is lying." Arthur stilled a little under my grip, but I could feel his muscles tensed under my hands still. "He does not have Guinevere. I have her."

"*You* have her?" Arthur cried. "Where?"

"She is safe. She has gone to the Tower. Kay and Ector are with her, and some of the knights from Camelot. But she will only remain safe if you can kill Mordred. She *pretended* that she was willing to be his wife, and escaped to the Tower and barricaded herself in. He is furious that she deceived him. She cannot last in there forever, and if Mordred gets inside, there will be no mercy for her, or those who hid her there. So, you *have* to pull yourself together." I shook him hard, but it seemed to be working. I could see a steely determination settle over him. We only had to survive and keep Mordred and his army engaged until Lancelot arrived. It would be soon. It *had* to be soon.

"And, Arthur." I felt the breath rush out of me, and the strength, and all of the anger I had held tight to for so many years, and instead I felt nothing but hollowness and regret. "Arthur, I am sorry."

Arthur took my face in his hands and hushed me gently. How had I forgotten for so many years that he was gentle, and kind? That he was naïve and forgiving? Oh, those fine qualities of his had made him weak, weak to me, to his wife's deception, to Mordred's. Truly, we did not live in a world where it was safe for a man to be gentle or trusting.

"Morgan, you did not do any of this. You tried to tell me the truth, and I wouldn't listen. You didn't make my wife fall in love with another man. You didn't make Mordred hate me. I did those things. I never noticed her. I was happy, so I just thought she must have been happy as well. I never asked her. I just thought that she loved me as I loved her. I suppose I was arrogant enough to believe that no one could want anyone else when they had me. Mordred – well, if I could have been a father to him, all might have been well. The rest –" Arthur shook his head. "It's destiny, it's chance, it's whatever you call it. Either way, I know my death is coming. It's alright, Morgan," he reassured me, when I opened my mouth to speak. "I'm ready for it. There's nothing left for me now. Besides, I saw it, long ago, in Nimue's enchanted woods. I saw the moment. If it will not be now, it will be soon."

"What about Guinevere?" I asked him, softly.

He sighed then, and nodded, sadly. "I am sorry that I will never say goodbye to her." Arthur gave a weary smile. "Though, if I saw her now, she would only be angry with me, wouldn't she? For leaving her alone with Mordred. For not writing to her when I was in France. Still, I would have liked to, one last time, have held her in my arms." Arthur shrugged again. "We can't un-love those who hurt us, I suppose. It will be her I'm thinking of, when the time comes."

I nodded. I did not know what to say. I put my head on his shoulder, and he wrapped his arms around me. *Why did you have to give me away to Uriens?* I thought. *Why?* But he had been so young when he had done that, and desperate. He had felt his enemies closing in around him, and panicked. He had not had the years to understand me, nor I him.

Ywain returned, and Arthur buckled his armour back on, and they both kissed me on the cheek, and put on their helms and rode out to war.

Each day they came back alive, I was relieved, but I also knew, and Arthur knew, each day *he* returned alive was only prolonging the coming of what must. One day, deep into summer when it was uncomfortably hot and dry, Arthur stepped from his tent to go to battle in the morning and gazed up at the sky, thoughtfully.

Just quiet enough that only I beside him would hear, he said, "It will be today."

Too soon, too soon. I had had letters from Nimue saying that Lancelot's armies had reached Carhais. They were just a few days' journey from here. *No, Arthur,* I thought. But it would not be changed. Perhaps Arthur was wrong, but I understood fate, and I did not think he was. I wanted to tell Ywain not to ride out today, for he was always at Arthur's side, but the hope that Ywain might protect him outweighed my anxiety for his safety. He was a grown man. I could not hold him back. He would *want* to go.

So I mounted my horse and rode to battle with them, in my dress of black gems and with the crown of Gore on my head. Men stayed away from me, from my glinting dress of black, my woaded face, from the name *Morgan le Fay* that hung around me now like a mantle, protecting me.

I watched as at last, after so many weeks of waiting and trying, Mordred finally found his way to Arthur on the battlefield. Ywain moved between them, his sword drawn. I wanted to cry out, to step forward, but I held back. Mordred lunged forward with his spear, which pierced the chest of Ywain's horse. Ywain climbed clumsily from the screaming beast as it fell, dragging his foot out from beneath it just before it would have fallen hard enough there to break his leg.

"Get out of the way," Mordred growled at him. Weighing his sword in his hand, my son stepped forward, even as Mordred's horse reared over him. He struck up, fast, sinking his sword into the horse's chest as Mordred's sword swung down at him. I saw it catch, hard, against his shoulder, and Ywain stumbled back as Mordred's horse crashed down underneath him. Ywain was scrambling back as Mordred, seemingly unharmed, stepped from the body of his horse, swinging his sword. *Run, Ywain,* I thought. I almost shouted it, but I did not need to.

"Mordred," Arthur called out, jumping from his own horse, his spear in his hand. Mordred froze where he stood at the sound of his father's voice. I could not see his face through his helm, but I was sure he wore his cruel grin.

Mordred turned back to Ywain.

"Step aside, boy." Ywain stood his ground.

"*Ywain*," I shouted. He half-turned over his shoulder to me, but did not move.

"Run back to your mother, Ywain," Mordred sneered, stepping towards him.

Ywain shouted something back at him that I did not hear, for he was turned away from me, and his helm swallowed the noise. Mordred lunged at him again, and Ywain met his blow with his sword. I saw Ywain crumple under Mordred's force. He was already hurt in the shoulder from where Mordred had struck him before, but still he did not move out of the way. Not until Arthur lowered his spear and called out to Mordred again, and Mordred, having struck Ywain again, knocking him to his knees, turned aside from him and stepped towards his father.

"It's time, Mordred," I heard Arthur say.

Mordred did not say anything, but stepped forward, and as he did, Arthur stepped forward as well, thrusting hard with his spear. The strength of the blow knocked Mordred back, and the helm fell from his head, rolling away on the grass. I rode softly to Ywain's side and offered my hand. Silently, he took it and climbed heavily onto the horse behind me. He leaned against me, and I could hear him breathing ragged with his wounds.

Arthur struck again, fast, and Mordred, still unbalanced, reeling back, having foolishly miscalculated his father's strength – or perhaps the strength of his father's anger – exposed the small gap in his armour beneath his breastplate. Arthur struck fast once more, and I heard Mordred choke with pain as the spear went through him. I felt the relief wash over me. I couldn't quite believe it. Arthur wasn't going to die. Mordred was. It was over.

I was just about to turn my horse around and leave, when I saw Mordred grasp hold of the shaft of Arthur's spear, and begin to drag himself up, pushing himself further on to it. His teeth, already dark with the blood that was seeping up into his lungs from the wound, were set together in an awful grimace against the pain, and behind him on the wooden shaft he left a trail of his blood. He had dropped his sword to drag himself up it with both hands. Arthur stared, frozen, at Mordred pulling the fatal spear deeper onto himself. When he was right up by his father, whose hands, too, were both still around the shaft of the spear, he snatched Excalibur from the scabbard Arthur wore it in at his side, and in a swift, ringing blow, holding it in a single hand, he brought it crashing against Arthur's head. I saw the sword slice easily through the metal of the helm, and

445

grow dark with blood. With that, Mordred let Excalibur fall from his hands and collapsed as Arthur's hands slackened on the spear and Mordred fell with it. Arthur fell heavily to his knees.

I wanted to cry out, wanted to jump down, to put my healing hands around Arthur's wound, but I was with my son. It was Arthur or Ywain. I was frozen, could not move. But then around Arthur appeared Nimue, and three more women whom I knew from their woad to be women of Avalon. They would heal him. All would be well. But then I thought, with awful dread, if Excalibur struck the blow, how could it ever be healed?

I called out to Nimue, and she turned to me. I could see the open distress on her face.

She left the other women with Arthur, trying to lift him to his feet, and walked over to me.

"I saw it, Morgan," she said, absent with grief. "And still I came too late. I must have seen it... only as it happened."

"Can he be saved?"

Nimue shook her head. "We must take him to Avalon."

I nodded, though I was not sure what good Avalon would do him.

I turned to Ywain over my shoulder. He had pulled off his helm. His face was pale, greyish, covered in a light film of clammy sweat.

"Can you ride?" I asked him.

He nodded. Nimue handed up a skin of something. I supposed it was the potion for healing the blood. If she was handing it to Ywain that meant that it would be no good to Arthur now.

"Ywain, ride to London, to the Tower. The Queen is there. Tell her that Mordred is defeated. That," I glanced at Nimue, "... Arthur is wounded, and it is the end of him, and we are taking him to Avalon. I will follow."

Ywain nodded, and drinking deep from what Nimue had given him, he turned on his horse as he did and rode away.

Beside me, quietly, Nimue said, "We should bring her to him." I nodded, and she took my hand.

Either Ywain had ridden fast, or we had come slow through the middle-lands of magical travel, because we arrived to see him, his back to us, framed in the great doorway of the Tower, its doors thrown back and open. Beyond him, I could see Guinevere, dressed in her armoured dress, the crown of the Queen of Logrys on her head, and Kay beside her, his arm around her as though he were prepared to catch her for a fall. Her eyes were wide, and glassy, her look distant. Kay was saying something to her. I could see his lips moving, but she did not seem to hear him.

"Lancelot, then, did not come?" I heard her say. Her voice was still thick with her Breton accent, as though all her years in Logrys had not taken any part of her away. She had not changed. Her face gave nothing away. So strange, even now, to not show how she was feeling.

"He did not come, my Lady," Ywain answered her softly. Nimue and I came closer, but she did not seem to see us. She did not seem to see anything before her at all. "They say he has gathered his armies to ride to Arthur's aid, but he has not come. Not in time."

Her eyes fluttered closed; for a moment it was as though she were blinking, or holding back tears, but then she collapsed and Kay jumped to catch her, scooping her up easily in his arms. It was then that he saw me, and as our eyes met I could see everything that he was feeling. Regret for the choices he had made, going with Lancelot and leaving his brother behind, sorrow for Arthur's death, fear for Guinevere now that Britain would be thrown into confusion. Truly, Kay did not know how many were dead. I did not know. There was no heir to Lothian anymore, not now that Mordred was dead. Two great kingdoms without a king, and Britain without a single ruler, the single ruler who had given it peace. My son was Arthur's closest living heir now, and I would not give him up to the throne, not now that it had proved itself to be a seat of death.

Nimue and I rushed after Kay and Ector, following them upstairs to a bedroom where Kay set Guinevere gently on the bed. I sent him for water. I didn't want him there, raw and open, with his sorrow pouring out of him. I didn't want to think about it. What I had done to Arthur, how awful it had been to feel relief and then have it snatched from me, as coming death had not abated Mordred's desire for revenge. Nimue put her hand gently on Ector's shoulder, and he put his hand on hers in comfort. I realised, suddenly, that she was wearing black. Dressed for mourning. She had known, really, that this would happen. How awful for her, then, that even she who knew could not have prevented it.

When Kay came back with the water, I took it from him and sat beside Guinevere where she lay on the bed. Kay leaned back against the wall, crossing his arms over his chest, watching. She had held it all in too much, and at last it had all overwhelmed her. I took the linen cloth Nimue handed me and dipped it in the water, then wrung it out and held it against Guinevere's brow. There was no magic in it, but Guinevere did not need magic. No magic would help her now. Her chest rose and fell slowly, as though she were deep in sleep, but the shock of the cold seemed to wake her from it. She opened her eyes slowly, and I saw them widen with surprise as they saw me. She still did not trust me.

"Do you want us to take you to him?" I asked her, softly.

From the corner of my eye, I saw Kay step forward as though to protest, but Ector put a fatherly hand against his chest and Kay fell back. Ector understood. He had lost his wife, and he understood the need to say goodbye.

Guinevere nodded, and I took her hand. Nimue reached out and took the other, and I opened my eyes to see us standing on the shores of Avalon. This truly was the end. Arthur dead, Guinevere in her armoured dress. Soon the sword would come, and we would stand side by side and I would know, at last, that it was over. I had lived out the days of my destiny.

Guinevere saw Arthur before I did, slumped against a tree at the shore, the three women we had left him with kneeling before him in mourning. She slipped her hand from mine, and ran bare-footed across the grass. As they saw her coming, the other women stepped back and Guinevere fell to her knees before Arthur, taking his face in her hands. She kissed him. He did not move. I could see her lips moving, and I knew she was calling his name.

"What kind of woman is she," Nimue asked softly, "that she has it in her to love *two* men like that?"

I did not answer. I knew, surely enough, that I was the same. I had loved Kay, and Lancelot, and Accolon, at one point all at once, and I was sure that Nimue still loved Arthur, in a way, though she was happily married now with Pelleas. It was easy to see in someone else the tangled knots of love, but not in oneself.

We walked forward slowly. As we approached, Nimue's women gently lifted her away, and she slumped in their arms. Nimue and I knelt before him and began unbuckling his armour. I placed my hand over the cut in the side of his skull, but under my hand I felt a raw, hostile burning. It was the work of Excalibur, and had its own magic, that wound. It would not be healed by me. Not by any of us.

Excalibur was still at his side. Someone, one of the women, must have recognised it and slipped it back into its scabbard. I paused for a moment, but only a moment. The time had come. In the end, Arthur had not needed it, or even wanted it. I reached down, unbuckled the belt and pulled it away, buckling it around myself. My sword had come home, but it was bittersweet. I leaned down to Arthur.

"My dear brother," I whispered in his ear, kissing him on the cheek. It was all I had it in me to say. There was too much, and I would not cry. He murmured, as though he heard something, but the end was upon him, and he would never speak to any of us again.

Nimue had somehow got his surcoat of red and gold, and we dressed him in it, and with the women who let go of Guinevere – who seemed to have steadied herself enough to stand – we lifted him into a little barge moored at the end of the lake. When he passed through into the mist, he would go into the between-lands before the Otherworld, and Nimue would ease his passing, and then he would be gone. I hoped he would be remembered as the great king he had once been, and not the broken man he had been at the end.

Nimue stepped into the barge with him, but I did not go. Too many times I had broken the oath I had not really made to the Breton queen, and now I would remain to keep it.

As Nimue pushed the barge away, Guinevere ran forward again, shouting after Arthur one last time, but as she reached the edge of the lake, the barge moved just beyond her reach, and she fell to her knees. I could not hear her, but I could see her shoulders shudder, as though she were crying.

I stood beside her to watch the barge move out of sight, watch Arthur move from life to death through the middle-lands of Avalon. The grief for me, I knew, would be slow, and long. It would come gently, and I would miss Arthur, and then it would wear at me, heavy, for I would know what a wicked part I had had in it all.

Guinevere stood slowly beside me, staring out until Arthur was gone. She turned to me suddenly, and made a grab for the sword. She was angry. I could see *that* clearly on her face. Though the clean lines of tears were visible through the dirt and the blood caked on her face from the siege, her eyes were dry now, and shining with the anger that – I was sure, for her – was far easier than grief. I stepped back and drew it between us, instinctively. Then I saw it, as I had seen it before. She and I, and the sword between us, and I felt my heart race.

"Do you know for whom Excalibur was forged?" I asked her.

She stepped forward as though she was going to try and take it again, but I moved back, lifting it a little away.

"For Arthur," she said, stubbornly.

"You know that isn't true. Arthur can barely lift it without both hands. Excalibur was forged for me, but Merlin tricked me, and took it from me. Said it was Arthur's destiny. Like you, I suppose."

Both had brought his death. She and I and the sword, we had tangled together and each played a vital part. Her – what was it about

449

her that he could not have lived without her, and knowing how she had loved another could not have just sent her away? And the sword – he had kept the sword though it meant little to him because Merlin had given it to him. And me? What about me and the sword? I was never going to fight. No. No, it was worse. It was a wicked thing that had put greed and death in my heart. Nimue had made it to keep me safe, and my greed for it had brought me only suffering.

I threw it out, hard, into the centre of the lake. With my Otherworld strength behind it, it went far, so I did not see it fall as it plunged into the mist, but I heard it sink into the water.

Chapter Eighty

I heard hooves behind me, and turned around to see Kay and Ector riding up towards us. I felt suddenly resentful, not of them in particular, but of the whole lot of them. Knights. Kings. Men.

"You are too late," I told them.

Kay strode past me as though he did not see me and pulled Guinevere into his arms. I felt a stab of jealousy that only made my resentment worse. I saw the way she grasped hold of his arms as he held her, how she buried her face against his shoulder, and his hand, on the back of her head, tangled with her loosening hair. I did not think I could have been blamed for thinking that there had been more than friendship between them. Kay had held me tight like that, too, long ago.

"Say your goodbyes. I am taking her to Amesbury," I said sharply, fixing Kay with a harsh look. I was suddenly unbearably tired of them all, passing her around between them as the sword had been passed between us. To my surprise, she did not protest. Kay did not release his grip on her, but buried his face in her hair. I wondered if he was crying.

"Are you sure, Morgan, that this is best?" Ector said to me, gentle and kind.

I nodded, still watching Kay and Guinevere.

"I am, Ector. Soon enough there will be greedy kings wanting to make her their wife if she doesn't go to an abbey. She is the Kingdom now. Someone will try. Probably Mark."

Beside me, Ector nodded. "But what about Lancelot? What happens when he comes?"

"I don't know," I said.

"You'll take care of her, Morgan?" he asked me, earnestly.

I took his weathered old hand in mine. "I promise, Ector."

"Guinevere," I called out to her, "it's time."

She moved away from Kay, taking his hands in hers. She was saying something quietly to him. I could only see the back of him, but he nodded gently. She leaned up and kissed him on the cheek.

"I never did know," Ector said, soft and solemn beside me, "how close they truly were."

She walked past Kay, who did not turn around to watch her go, and came to take my hands, and I closed my eyes and pictured the Abbey where I had spent my years as a girl, and we were there.

She did not say much, but she seemed to like it there. She walked around the cloister garden slowly, looking everything over with those bright, fierce, unreadable eyes of hers. She said nothing when I led her to the room where she would stay. I did not tell her it had once been my room, as a girl. She sank down to sit on the bed with a sigh that went right through her. She had lost none of her charming abandon, though there was something dark to the recklessness now, as though she somewhat hoped some careless move or other would bring her death. She did not say anything to me as I left her there, but she did give me a strange half-smile, something like gratitude.

It was strange, the way the time went on passing after that, as though the world were the same. But it was not the same. Not once Arthur was dead. We had all forgotten to appreciate the peace that his rule had given Britain, and now the greedy lords, with no one to be afraid of anymore, turned on one another. The Lords of Wales, unhappy with Ywain's youth and his English mother, the witch, turned their allegiance away from him, eager to grab the land from one another. He stayed in Rheged, and held Gore – no one would take that from him – but could not make the other men leave off their fighting, or swear themselves to him.

I could not bear to go back to Lothian, since I was sure I would feel Morgawse's ghost beside me. Perhaps she blamed me, wherever she had gone, for not being able to save her. Perhaps she blamed me, too, for Gareth's and Gaheris' deaths. Well, now they were all gone. And Nimue and I, and Guinevere, and Kay and Ywain, were the only ones of any of us left. The war with Mordred had seen the end of Dinadan, and not just of everyone else I knew, but anyone else I recognised. Britain was a country of young men, young and angry and ambitious. Mark still ruled in Cornwall, and turned his greedy eye on the rest of Britain. Having put his wife Isolde to death for her adultery, he was looking for a way to marry himself into more power. There was a princess in Carhais again, an infant daughter of the boasting Prince who had not let us inside, but the Breton people were more reluctant now than ever to give their girls away in marriage, and refused to send even a cousin of the Prince to be Mark's bride. The Lord of Orkney ruled Lothian now, and his own kingdom. He, too, was looking for a wife to secure his lands. They both wanted Gareth's daughter, Anna, but the girl was lost, disappeared. She had disappeared from Camelot with her mother at the beginning of Mordred's war, and no one knew where the little Princess of Lothian had gone. I knew that she was with Kay, wherever he was, but I would not say that she was with him, nor would I have told them where Kay was living, even if I knew.

I went to Avalon, to Nimue. I spent a long time with her there. I was pleased to be away from the world outside, past the sickly fragrant mists and close to the Otherworld. I went between there and Rheged, and sometimes back to Amesbury, to Guinevere, who sometimes would even give me her sudden smile when she saw me now, though it was less somehow. More muted. Nimue called me back to Avalon when it was time to set Arthur in his tomb. After she had set him there, I went to the Abbey to take Guinevere to see it. She stood before it as though she could not see it, and reached out her hand to touch it, and ran her fingers over the stone surface of it, the Latin letters Nimue had inscribed on the stone, but she did not seem to take it in. She did not cry as she had when the barge had sailed away from her. She must have been thinking of him, and how he had been when they were alive together.

She looked strange in the nuns' clothes, the plain black that I had worn when I lived there. She looked like a different woman entirely, until she moved with the same wild briskness. Her bright hair was hidden beneath its black veil, and she looked as though she could have been a nun all her life. She had the same impassive face I had seen on many of the nuns growing up.

So the months passed, and turned into years, and the world around me was grim again with greed and war. War until one of the minor kings of Britain had killed all the others. Avalon was drawing back from the outside world, no longer giving its favour or power to any one king. I did not think Nimue could bear to find another king to favour. Instead, she sat in her great stone hall with Pelleas, and carefully oversaw the training of the women of Avalon. But there were fewer, I thought, than there had been when I was young. The Otherworld blood was dwindling away. I did not know of any marriages of two Otherworld parents, and certainly my Otherworld father had only passed his gifts to me, and I had not managed to give them to my surviving son. Magic was draining out of the world. Merlin's books were burned – I was not so sorry for that – and there were fewer and fewer of us who had it in our blood.

It was some years – two, perhaps three years after Arthur's death – that I found Kay again, quite by chance. I had been with Guinevere in the Abbey. She was ever quiet, never as forthcoming with me as she had been with her maids, though I was not sure if that was because of who I was, or because now it must have seemed to her unbearable to joke about such things as she had with them, now Arthur was dead, and Lancelot lost. For Lancelot had not come, or not to any of us. Some said he had never left France, some said he had died on the journey, but others said that he wandered Britain alone searching for his lost love. I could not believe anything but the last of those to be true.

"You know," I told her gently, one evening as the summer sun was dipping into the horizon, its orange light slanting through the stone window, lighting bright against her pale profile as she stared out, "Lancelot will come for you."

She nodded, without replying. In the late evening light, her white skin lit with red along its edge, she could have been the girl I had seen scowling at her own wedding, the young, conquered princess brought to Britain as a prize. But she was not. Twenty five years had passed since then, or thereabouts. With the veil over her hair, I could not see how it had faded from deep red to pale gold, and her face, though marked with loss and weariness, was still beautiful. If she had not come to the Abbey, ageing and barren though she was, there would have been kings fighting to marry her, not just for the right to call themselves King of Britain. I was sure that this was a relief for her.

"Will you go with him?" I asked her, softly. There was nothing stopping her. I did not see why they should not be together, why they could not escape into some kind of reckless happiness. It ought to come to someone, I thought.

She turned to me then with a sad smile, and shook her head. "And, what, Morgan?" she sighed. "Go back to France with him and live as his wife? So, we grow old, and talk of Arthur, and how between us we killed him? And at night, when we make love, we both pretend that Arthur is not there beside us, every time? No." She shook her head, gazing away again, out across the land beyond the window where the dark shadows were growing sharp, and long. "There is not room in this world for our love anymore. And besides," she sighed again, heavily, "I am old, and will give him no children. He should find a young girl, and marry her, and have children of his own. If he had not loved me, he would have had children. I know –" She paused, glancing down at her hands, folded in her lap. "I know he wanted that."

I came and sat beside her, but I had no words to say. She had been selfish. We had all been selfish. Still, I was not sure that if the time came and Lancelot found her that she would not go with him.

It was then that one of the novice nuns knocked on the door.

"My Lady," she peeped her head in, and tried to hide her alarm at the sight of my woaded face, "Sir Kay has come to see you."

Guinevere nodded and, giving me an unsteady smile, stood to leave.

It surprised me that I had not known before. Kay was nearby, and he still came to see her.

She told me later that he lived now in his father's house, and he had married. I had not expected that, but I was pleased. I told myself that I would not go to him, not back to the house where we had loved in innocence as children, but somehow I found myself there, and when he saw me from where he stood in the doorway of his father's house, he ran out as he had run across the cloister garden all those years ago. Only this time he did not throw his arms around me in an embrace. He stopped short, wary, but his smile was there, still warm.

"Morgan..." he greeted me. He looked at me thoughtfully for a moment, then gestured with his head for me to follow him. "Come. You should meet my wife. And my daughter. I have a daughter now." He paused, looking at me. "It's been too long, Morgan."

I followed him round the back of the house, where I used to watch him fighting Arthur with sticks. There was a woman there, golden-haired and slender, and a little girl. A little way away, half-hidden in the shade of the house, I thought for a moment I saw Morgawse's ghost in the shape of a pretty girl with coppery hair disappearing into the kitchen with a pail of milk, but it was only Gareth's daughter, Anna, who now – somehow – was almost grown.

Kay leaned back against the wall of the house, gazing out at his wife and little girl playing in the long grass. She was young, perhaps twenty years old, and pretty. She had a sweet face, and an easy smile.

The easy smile of innocence, of youth. The little girl had the same fair hair as the mother, shining golden in the midsummer sun, but Kay's bright, mischievous brown eyes. She was perhaps a couple of years old, and had a loud, infectious laugh like her father's already. I wondered why, after the great and complex loves he had had in his life, Kay had chosen the sweet, simple girl before us, full of rural innocence, as his wife. She must, too, have been more than twenty years younger than him. But Kay was a man; he could have another chance at life, at simple happiness. For Guinevere, and for me, that chance was past.

"Why her, Kay?" I asked softly, gently.

Kay shrugged, still watching his wife as she lifted the little girl in her arms, and the girl kicked her little feet in the air with delight.

"She doesn't know any of it, I suppose. She doesn't know who I am. I mean, she knows that this is my father's land, she knows who Anna is – well, sort of. She knows why we have to hide her here. She knows that I fought in two wars with Arthur, but she doesn't know that we grew up as brothers. She knows that he was the King for a long time, but she doesn't really know what happened, or how he was killed. She doesn't know that I fought beside the great hero Sir Lancelot, or lay beside him. She doesn't know that I have loved queens, and witches, and men. None of it really touched her. Life in the little villages here stays the same. Everyone has heard of King Arthur, and Queen Guinevere and Sir Lancelot. They have *all* heard of Morgan le Fay. They have even heard of Sir Gawain, but no one has heard of Kay the Seneschal. Well, that's a mercy. When I go to visit Guinevere at Amesbury, I tell my wife I am going to pray for my mother. It's half true. When I talk about her, I call her Queen Guinevere, as though I never knew her. She wants to see the child. Guinevere, I mean. She wants to see her, but I can't bring myself to do it. I think it would break her heart." Kay's voice was low and soft, wistful. He was the only one of us who had escaped, but he had only seemed to escape. He still thought of it, I could see that. I wondered what he dreamed about at night, with his innocent young wife at his side. He turned to me, a look on his face of sadness that was only half-wry. "I was... with her. Once."

I was not quite sure what he meant.

"What... Guinevere?" I asked in disbelief.

He nodded, looking back away, back towards his wife, but this time his eyes were fixed into the distance.

"At Joyous Guard. Just once."

"With Lancelot there?" I had meant in the castle, but evidently Kay understood something different.

"Oh yes. He was there. The way I remember it, it was somewhat his idea." Kay sighed deeply once more, as though the memory of it all weighed him down, and he could not shake it off. "But neither of them saw anything apart from one another, did they? I'm not sure they really saw each other, either. Not really. Maybe people like you and me can't understand that kind of love; I don't know, but it seemed a lot like madness to me. But I loved her. As much as either of them did. As much as I loved Lancelot when I was a boy. And you."

He turned to me with a tight, sad smile. I had to tell him, and I felt the tightness grow within my throat, the tears that I would not cry, I could not. We had lost so much, Kay and I. And we had even lost each other. Ector's voice came to me, across the huge chasm of the years: *You can't always have the life you want. You have to learn to be happy with the life you have.* None of us had been happy. We had all wanted more, and now here we were, all broken and alone. I sighed, tensing myself for the blow that I knew I had to deliver before I left Kay.

"Kay, she is dying," I told him, as gently as I could. I had felt it, sitting beside her. I thought it must have been what Merlin had done to her all those years ago. I could feel the dark, heavy lump of it when I came too close. It would not be long. I had not said so to her. I had not said so to anyone but Kay before, and now I had said it, it seemed unbearably real. I felt as though I had missed something with her, and that we could have been close, if things had been different.

Kay nodded.

"Does she know?" he asked.

I shook my head. "I don't know. I think she senses it. I will take her to Avalon soon, when the time is right." *When Lancelot has come,* I thought, but I did not say it.

Kay nodded again. "To be with Arthur?" he asked.

"Kay," I said, gentle but firm, "Arthur is dead. Nimue has set him in his tomb. Being in Avalon eased his passing, and it will hers, but death is death. Arthur is not coming back."

I could not believe that Kay of all people had trusted in the peasant rumours that Arthur would return. Kay knew the Otherworld better than that. Perhaps it was easier for him to think that the brother he had not seen since he left him in the middle of the night to join Lancelot might come back, and they might be reconciled.

"I know," Kay said, quietly, gazing down at the ground before him.

Kay's wife and little girl were walking back towards us, and Kay crouched to the ground and held out his arms for his little daughter to run into. He scooped her up, laughing with her, his smile breaking bright across his face. It was as though he had not been sad moments before, had not been wistful, and regretful. Perhaps he *could* forget, when he was with them. Kay kissed his daughter on the cheek, and she giggled, grabbing on to his shirt with her little fists and Kay wrapped his arms around her. His wife came up beside him and kissed him on the cheek, and he turned his bright smile to her.

"My love, this is —" He hesitated for a moment. "This is Morgan. She grew up in the Abbey. We were childhood friends."

His wife smiled and stepped forward to kiss me on the cheek. She had not connected me, despite my woaded face, with Morgan le Fay. Of course not; she thought Kay far from any of that, and besides, Morgan le Fay was to her not a real woman, but a creature of myth.

"It is lovely to meet you," she said. Her voice was sweet and low, and light with youth. There was no suspicion in her. I felt suddenly warm with gladness that Kay, at least, had this second chance at happiness with a sweet girl who would ask nothing of him that it would hurt him to give. We had all asked too much of Kay, Lancelot, Guinevere and I. Even Arthur. Too much of one another.

"Where did you two meet?" I asked.

That was when Kay grinned, at her, and then at me, and I saw he had his spark of wicked brightness still strong within him. Kay had survived.

"Actually, we met on the shores of Avalon," he said, and I felt the smile creep onto my face as well.

To discover more great books like
Morgan by Lavinia Collins visit :
thebookfolks.com

Made in the USA
Charleston, SC
30 September 2016